SelectEditions

SELECTED AND EDITED

SelectEditions

BY READER'S DIGEST

THE READER'S DIGEST ASSOCIATION, INC.
MONTREAL • PLEASANTVILLE, NEW YORK

READER'S DIGEST SELECT EDITIONS

Vice President, Books & Home Entertainment: Deirdre Gilbert

The condensations in this volume have been created by The Reader's Digest Association, Inc., by special arrangement with the publishers, authors, or holders of copyrights.

With the exception of actual personages identified as such, the characters and incidents in the selections in this volume are entirely the products of the authors' imaginations and have no relation to any person or event in real life.

FIRST EDITION

ISBN 0-88850-496-9
Printed in the U.S.A.

246-263-0300

CONTENTS

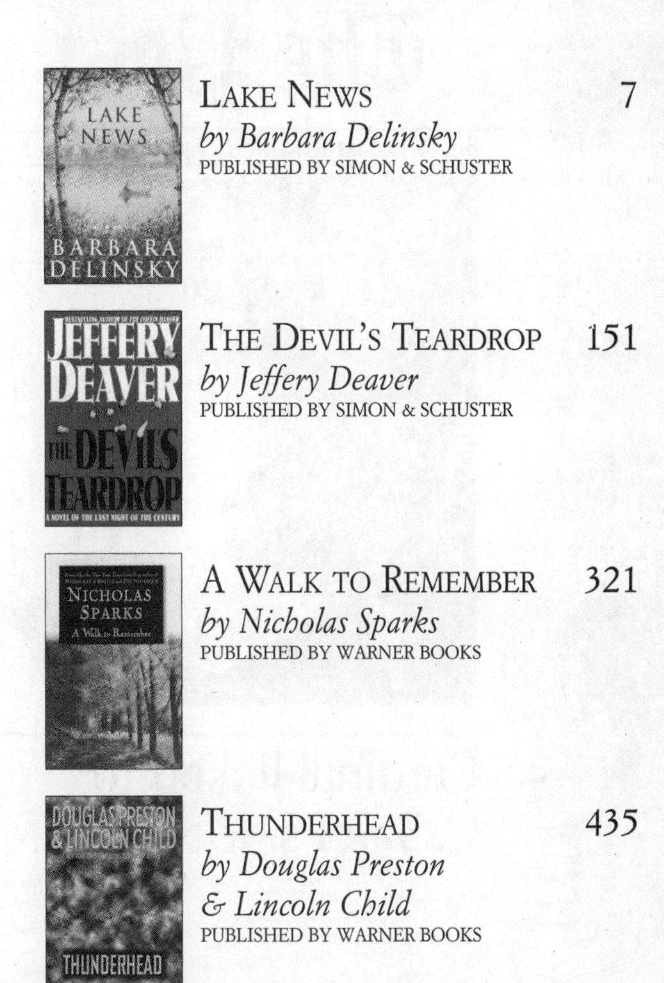
LAKE NEWS
BARBARA DELINSKY
JEFFERY DEAVER
THE DEVILS TEARDROP
A NOVEL OF THE LAST NIGHT OF THE CENTURY
NICHOLAS SPARKS
A Walk to Remember
DOUGLAS PRESTON & LINCOLN CHILD
THUNDERHEAD

The Post
Boston Massachusetts September 10,199
Cardinal linked to
Cabaret singer

Lake News

by Barbara Delinsky

Lily Blake was
tired of reporters
and cameramen.
She was tired of
being a spectacle.

Chapter 1

Lake Henry, New Hampshire

LIKE everything else at the lake, dawn arrived in its own good time. The flat black of night slowly deepened to a midnight blue that lightened in lazy steps, gradually giving form to the spike of a tree, the eave of a cottage—and that was on a clear day. On this day, fog reduced the lake to a pool of milky glass and the shoreline to a hazy wash of orange, gold, and green where, normally, vibrant fall colors would be. Details were lost in the mist. The effect, with the air quiet and still, was of a protective cocoon.

It was a special moment. The only thing John Kipling would change was the cold. He wasn't ready for summer to end. The sun set sooner and rose later than two months before, and the chill of the night lingered. He felt it. His loons felt it. The foursome he watched—two adults and their young—were growing restless with migratory thoughts.

They floated now not twenty feet from John's canoe, not ten feet again from the tiny fir-covered island in whose sheltered cove they had summered. The island was one of many that dotted Lake Henry. Between the clarity of the water, the quiet of the lake, and the abundance of fish, those islands lured the loons back year after year.

They were a sight to behold. Since the chicks' birth in July, John had watched their plumage go from baby black to toddler brown to a juvenile gray, but they had their parents' tapered beaks and sleek necks and a promise of future brilliance. And those parents—ahhhh, they were brilliant indeed. Their backs were crisp checkerboards of white on black. A white-stripe necklace encircled each black neck, and they had solid black heads, distinctive pointed beaks, and round red eyes that didn't miss much.

The birds lay low in the water, swimming gently around the cove, alternately rolling and contorting to groom themselves and diving deep for fish. Later that morning the adults would leave their young, run laboriously across the surface of the lake, and lumber into the air. After circling until they gained enough altitude, they would fly to a neighboring lake to visit other loons. Breeding was a solitary time, and with two fledglings to show for months of vigilance and work, this pair had done well. Now they had to refresh their social skills in preparation for wintering on the warmer Atlantic coast.

For eons, loons had repeated this ritual. They knew that September was half over, October would bring colder days, and November would bring ice. They had to leave the lake before it froze. And they would. In all his years growing up on the lake, then returning as an adult to watch again, John hadn't seen many icebound loons. They rarely erred.

John, however, erred—and often. Hadn't he done it again this morning, setting out in a T-shirt and shorts, wanting it to be summer still and finding himself butt-cold now? He wasn't twenty anymore. He was well into forty, still six three and fit, but his body didn't work the way it once did.

But cold or not, he wasn't leaving. He hadn't yet had his fill of the loons. He sat rock-still in the canoe with his hands in his armpits for warmth. These loons were used to his presence, but he took nothing for granted. As long as he kept his distance, they would reward him with preening and singing. When the world was eerily quiet—at night, at dawn, on mornings like this, when the fog muffled other noise—the loons' song shimmered and rose. And it came now—breathtaking—a primitive tremolo, so beautiful, so mysterious.

Goose bumps rose on John's skin. This was why he had returned to the lake, why, after swearing off New Hampshire at fifteen, he had reversed himself at forty. Some said he'd done it for the job, others for his father, but the truth had to do with these birds.

A loon's life consisted of eating, grooming, and procreating. Its life was honest, devoid of pretense, ambition, and cruelty. A loon harmed others only when its existence was threatened. John found that totally refreshing.

So he stayed longer, though he knew he should leave. It was Monday. *Lake News* had to be at the printer by noon on Wednesday. He already had material from his staff correspondents, one per town, but he was still expecting articles promised by local movers and shakers, which meant he would have a wad of reading and editing, keystroking, cutting and pasting. If those articles weren't in, he'd call around Lake Henry and the neighboring towns, get information, and write what he could himself. And if he still ended up with dead space, he would run more Henry David Thoreau.

There wasn't a book in any of that, he told himself. A book had to be original. He had notebooks filled with ideas, but nothing sparked an urge to hustle to write a book. He *did* hustle when it came to *Lake News,* but only between noon Tuesdays and noon Wednesdays. He wrote better under the threat of a deadline closing in, liked keeping the managing editor on edge.

Of course, he was the managing editor now. And the production editor. And the photography editor and society editor. *Lake News* wasn't the Boston *Post,* not by a long shot. At times that bothered him. This, however, wasn't one of those times.

His paddle remained stowed, and the loons continued to call. By the time patches of blue showed through the mist, John guessed it was nearly nine. Turning his face to the sun, he closed his eyes and listened to silence, water, and loon. Then reluctantly he picked up his paddle and headed home.

THE beauty of a beard was that it eliminated the need to shave. John kept his cropped close, which meant only occasional touch-ups. No need for a necktie here either. Or for a pressed shirt.

He still felt the novelty of showering, dressing, and hitting the road in ten minutes flat, and what a road. Framed by trees, cracked by years of frost heaves, it wove in and out in a rough tracing of the lake. Most other roads in town were the same. They imposed speed limits all on their own, and Lake Henry's residents liked it that way. The town didn't cater to tourists. Its population was 1721. Eleven babies were due, which would raise the count. Twelve citizens were terminally old or terminally ill, which would lower it. There were twenty-eight kids in college. Whether they would return was a toss-up.

John made what he intended to be a brief stop at the general store, but got to talking national politics with Charlie Owens, who owned the store, and Charlie's wife, Annette.

Then he continued on past the post office to the yellow Victorian building that stood near the lake. Climbing from his Chevy Tahoe, he reached in for his briefcase, shouldered its strap, and scooped up the day's editions of four different newspapers, a bag of doughnuts, and his thermos. With the bag clutched in his teeth, he sifted through his key ring as he opened the screen door.

The door behind it was mahogany, carved by a local artist. Between swirls on its bottom half were a dozen mail slots identified by brass plaques. The first row was devoted to the neighboring towns—ASHCROFT, HEDGETON, COTTER COVE, and CENTER SAYFIELD. The lower rows were Lake Henry–specific, with slots assigned to POLICE AND FIRE, CONGREGATIONAL CHURCH, GARDEN CLUB. High on the door, with no slot attached, was the largest plaque: LAKE NEWS.

The door moved even before John inserted his key. As he elbowed it open, the phone rang. "Jenny?" he called.

"In the bathroom!" came the muted yell.

Nothing new, he thought. But at least she had come in to work.

He took the stairs two at a time, past the second floor and on up to the attic room, which had been his office since he had returned to town three years before. There were no dividing walls here, which made it the largest room in the house. A slew of windows and skylights also made it the brightest.

The phone continued to ring. Letting the papers slip to the editorial desk, he dropped the doughnut bag and thermos nearby and picked up the phone. "Morning, Armand."

"Took you long enough," his publisher said. "Where you been?"

"Oh, out and around."

" 'Oh, out and around.' You give me that every time—you know I can't argue with it. Damn lake has so many bends, I can't see what goes on around yours. But the paper's my bottom line, and you're doing that okay. Did you get my piece? Liddie put it in the slot."

"It's there," John said without checking, because Armand Bayne's wife was totally reliable and totally devoted to her husband.

"What else you got?" the old man asked.

John pulled a handful of papers from the briefcase. He had dummied the week's pages at home the night before. Now he spread out the sheets. "The lead is a report on the education bill that's up before the state legislature. I'm following it with opinion pieces."

"What's your editorial say about it?"

"You know what it says. We either put money into schools today or into welfare tomorrow." The source of that money was the problem. Not wanting to argue it again with Armand, a wealthy landowner who would be soaked if property taxes doubled, he went on. "Page three leads with a report on Chris Diehl's trial."

John uncapped the thermos, filled his mug with coffee. "There's also police news, fire news, school news, library news. There's the Week in Review from papers in Boston, New York, and Washington. And ads. Lots of ads this week."

"Praised be," said Armand. "Want some breaking news?"

Breaking news was one of the things John missed most.

Armand said, "They read Noah Thacken's will yesterday, and the family's in a stew. He left the house to daughter number two, so daughter number one is threatening to sue. Look into it, John."

But John said, "That's private stuff."

"Private? The whole town'll know by the end of the day."

"Right, so why put it in the paper? Besides, we print facts."

"This is facts. That will is a matter of public record."

"The will is. Not the personal trauma. I thought we agreed—"

"Well, there isn't a hell of a lot of other excitement up here," the old man remarked, and hung up.

No, John thought, there isn't. Even Christopher Diehl's bank-fraud trial was a far cry from the murder trials he used to cover.

His eye went to the wall of photos at the far end of the room. There was one of him interviewing someone on Boston's City Hall Plaza. There were photos of him shaking hands with politicians and of him laughing it up with colleagues in Boston bars. There was one of a Christmas party—he and a crowd of friends in the newsroom.

The photos were trappings of an earlier life, like the deactivated police scanner that sat on a file cabinet. He had started his tenure at *Lake News* by setting one up, but static without voices for hours on end had grown old fast. Besides, he knew everyone who would be involved in breaking news. If anything happened, they called him. In three years he hadn't missed a local emergency. How many had there been? Three? Four?

Nope, no big best seller would ever come from covering emergencies in Lake Henry. With a sigh he pulled a doughnut from the bag and tipped back his chair. A moment later Jenny Blodgett appeared at the door. She was nineteen, pale and blond, and so thin that the big bulge of the baby in her belly looked wrong. Knowing she probably hadn't eaten breakfast, he offered her a doughnut.

"It isn't meat or milk, but it's better than nothing," he said, gesturing her back down the stairs. Her office was on the first floor, in what had once been a parlor. He followed her there, eyed the papers on the desk. "How's it going?"

Her voice was soft and childlike. "Okay." She pointed to the papers. "This year's Letters to the Editor. What do I do now?"

He had told her twice. But she hadn't been in since the week before. So gently he said, "Put them in alphabetical order and file them in the cabinet. Did you type out file labels?"

Her eyes went wide. "I forgot," she whispered.

"No problem. You can do it now. Eat first," he reminded her on his way out the door.

Up in his office again, he ate his doughnut at the window overlooking the lake. A small breeze ruffled the water in shifting patches.

The phone rang. *"Lake News,"* he answered.

"John, Allison Quimby," said a bold voice. "My place is falling apart. I need a handyman. Is it too late to put in an ad?"

"No. You want the sales desk." He put her on hold, jogged across the room, and picked up the phone at the sales desk. "Okay." He slipped into the chair at the computer. "Do you have something written?" He suspected she did. Allison owned the local realty company and was the quintessential professional.

She read. He typed. He took her credit card number. As soon as he hung up the phone, he made a call of his own.

A tired voice answered, "Yeah."

"It's me. Allison Quimby needs a handyman. Call her." He heard swearing. He said, "You're sober, Buck, and you need work."

"Who are you? My guardian angel?"

John kept his voice low and tight. "I'm your older cousin, the one who's worried about the girl you knocked up, the one thinking you may not be worth the effort but that girl and her baby are. Come on, Buck. Allison pays well. Call her," he said, and hung up.

Seconds later he was back at the window. All it took was a look at the lake to give him a grip on his patience. People like Buck and Jenny didn't have that. They had the Ridge, where houses were too small and dirty to uplift anyone, much less someone battling alcoholism, physical abuse, or chronic unemployment. John knew. He had the Ridge in his blood as well.

The phone rang. He picked it up. *"Lake News."*

"Hi, Kip. It's Poppy."

John grinned. How not to? Poppy Blake was a smiling pixie, always bright and upbeat. She was his answering service. She was the answering service for half the town. "Hi, sweetheart. How's it going?"

"Busy," she said. "I have someone named Terry Sullivan on the line to your house. Want me to patch him through?"

John's eye flew to the wall of photographs, to one of the prints in which he was partying with other Boston reporters. Terry Sullivan was the tall, lean, dark one, the one with the mustache that hid a sneer. He was competitive to the extreme, self-centered to a fault, and wouldn't know loyalty if it hit him in the face. He had personally betrayed John, and more than once.

John wondered where he found the gall to call. Curious, he told Poppy to make the connection. "Kipling here," he said.

"Hey, Kip, it's Terry Sullivan. How goes it, bro?"

Bro? John took his time answering. "Fine. And you?"

"Aaah, same old rat race. Must be pretty quiet up there. There are times when I think I'll retire to the sticks."

"People here are honest. You'd stick out like a sore thumb."

There was a pause, then a snort. "That was blunt."

"People here are blunt, too. So what do you want, Terry?"

"Okay. I'm calling journalist to journalist. There's a woman named Lily Blake, born there, living here. Tell me all you know."

Lily was Poppy's sister, the elder but barely, which would make her thirty-fourish. She had left Lake Henry to go to college and had stayed in the city for a graduate degree. In music, he thought.

Folks around town still talked about her voice. She had been singing in church since she was five. She had been back several times since John had returned—once for her father's funeral, other times for Thanksgiving or Christmas. From what he heard, she and her mother didn't get along. John might not know Lily, but he did know her mother, Maida, who was one tough lady.

"Lily Blake?" he asked Terry, sounding vague.

"Come on, Kip. The place is tiny. Don't go dumb on me. Tell me about her family. What do they do?"

"Why do you want to know?"

"I met her. I'm thinking of dating her."

Fat chance. Lily Blake was a stutterer—much improved from childhood, John understood, but Terry didn't date women with problems. They demanded more than he wanted to give.

"Is this part of some story?" John asked.

"Nah. Purely personal."

"And you're calling *me?* Tell me why you *really* want to know."

"Okay. My friend wants to date her."

John knew a lie when he heard one. He hung up the phone. Then he snatched back the receiver and called Poppy.

"Kip," she said. "That was fast. What can I do for you now?"

"Two things," John said. "First, don't let that man speak to anyone in town. Cut him off, drop the line. He's not a good person. Second, tell me about your sister."

"Rose?"

"No, Lily. What's she been doing with her life?"

Chapter 2

Boston, Massachusetts

IN THE weeks to come, when Lily Blake was trying to understand why she had been singled out for scandal, she would remember the soggy mess she had made of the Boston *Post* that rainy Monday afternoon and wonder if an angry newspaper deity had put a curse on her. At the time, she simply wanted to stay dry.

She waited as long as she could at the foot of Beacon Hill, under the high stone arch of the small private school where she taught, thinking that the rain would let up. But it fell steadily. She was due to play at the club and had to get home and change.

Pulling the *Post* from her briefcase, she opened it over her head and ran out into the rain. She hurried along the narrow cobblestone streets. Hugging the briefcase to her chest, she made herself as small as possible under the newspaper. She was small to begin with, but the *Post* was quickly soggy around her ears, and the tank top and short skirt that had been perfect in the morning's heat left far too much skin exposed to the cool rain.

She pushed on. By the time she'd gone the five blocks to her apartment building, her hair was as wet as everything else. Entering the lobby, she fished in her briefcase for keys. Seconds later she was inside, where she dropped the sodden *Post* in the paper bin. She hadn't read it yet but doubted there was much to miss. Other than Archbishop Rossetti's elevation to cardinal, which had been covered in depth the weekend before, the city scene was quiet.

She slipped the mail from her box, then took the elevator to the fourth floor. She got off just as one of her neighbors was about to board it. Elizabeth Davis owned a hot public relations agency and had the breathless lifestyle to prove it. As always, she was dressed to the hilt. Her suit was red and short, her lipstick high gloss.

"Lily, good timing." Head tipped, she was fastening an earring. "I'm doing a bash for the Kagan for Governor Committee and need a pianist. It would be background music, not much singing. You'd be perfect. Understated elegance, which is what we want. The fund-raiser is two weeks from tomorrow night. What do you say?"

Lily was flattered to be asked. Elizabeth ran top-notch functions, and Lily liked playing at them. "I'll do it," she said.

Elizabeth smiled broadly and stepped into the elevator. "Mark your calendar. It's a go." The elevator door closed.

Hurrying down the hall, Lily let herself into her own apartment, a small one-bedroom rental. The living room was dominated by an upright piano against one wall and a bookcase against another. The kitchen was one wall of the living room, and the bedroom was just big enough for a double bed.

She headed for the shower and was ready in record time. She applied makeup and dried her chin-length dark hair. She ate a quick sandwich, then slipped into a plum-colored dress, stepped into black heels, and clipped on silver earrings. Grabbing a purse and an umbrella, she set off.

The Essex Club thrived in a large brownstone on Commonwealth Avenue, an easy three-block walk from her apartment. It was a private dinner club, elegantly decorated and skillfully run. She checked in at the office, where Daniel Curry, the club's owner, was taking a last-minute reservation.

A square-built man of forty-five, he acknowledged her arrival with a hitch of his chin and finished up on the phone.

She glanced at the reservation book. "Good crowd

"Very, for a Monday. We'll be full in another hour

"Any special requests?" she asked.

"One thirtieth wedding anniversary—Tom and
They'll be arriving at eight, table six. He's arranged
roses and asked if you'd play 'The Twelfth of N
champagne is uncorked."

Lily loved doing that kind of thing. "Sure," she said.

She left the office and climbed the winding staircase to the main dining room. It was decorated in the club's trademark dark wood, with nineteenth-century oils on the walls. The color scheme was hunter green and burgundy. The effect was rich and old-world.

She greeted the maître d' and smiled at patrons as she crossed to the piano, a beautiful Steinway baby grand. At times she felt sinful being paid for playing it, but she wasn't about to tell her boss that. What she earned at the Winchester School teaching music appreciation and giving piano lessons barely paid for rent and food. Without her work here and at private parties, she wouldn't have money for much else. Besides, this job was what had brought her to Boston.

Settling comfortably on the bench, she slipped into variations on popular songs. The piano stood on a platform in the corner, allowing her to look out over the room as she played. The crowd was mellow. She segued into a set of smooth oldies. She kept going until seven thirty, when Dan brought her a glass of water. "Any questions?" he asked while she took a drink.

"The foursome at table twelve," she said. "They look familiar."

"The men are the governors of New Hampshire and Connecticut, in town for a conference."

Lily definitely recognized the man at table nineteen. There was no mistaking that dark mustache. He was a reporter with the *Post.* "Is Terry Sullivan here watching the governors?"

Dan smirked. "Not to my knowledge, or I wouldn't have let him in." The club protected its members. Journalists were welcome when they were guests of a member, as Terry Sullivan was. "This is his third time in as many weeks. He likes you."

said. "It's business. He's doi a series of profiles of
ners and wants to do one "
" Dan glanced at th grinned. "Ah. There

Lily broke her own at the sight of
Archbi named Cardinal Ros-
ld y and the cardinal went
back a ways. on as was Dan, who was
married to his niece.

Dotty Frische.
for a dozen red
Never,' when the

Lily wasn't Catholic. She anything, but for several minutes, sipping her water, sh at the man's charisma. He was tall, stood straight, and wo black clerical suit, pewter pectoral cross, and thick silver style.

Lily was a frequent pianist at ar iocesan events and had played at a lawn party at his residence last night. Without conscious thought she began playing the theme from *Chariots of Fire*.

He heard it, looked over, and winked.

Pleased, she finished the song and moved on to others. Promptly at eight a couple was seated at the table with the red roses. Soon after, when the wine steward uncorked a bottle of champagne, Lily played "The Twelfth of Never," singing in a rich alto.

The woman glanced at Lily, then beamed at her husband.

Lily did other Johnny Mathis hits, then returned to Broadway. By the time she was done, it was time for a break.

"Fifteen minutes," she told her audience.

Dan was talking with the maître d' at the dining room's entrance. He gave her a thumbs-up when she approached. "You did good."

"You didn't tell me your uncle was coming," she scolded.

Dan glanced behind her. "Here he comes now."

She turned with a wide smile. When the cardinal gave her a hug, she hugged him back. Though a church icon, he came from a large family with an earthy style.

"Thank you for playing my song," he said.

"How's your table?" Dan asked.

"Great. Great food. Not what Mama used to make," he hedged,

"but close." He squeezed Lily's arm and returned to the dining room.

Lily climbed the staircase to the third-floor ladies' room. She came out just as the *Post* reporter was leaving the men's room. He was tall, slim, and pleasant-looking, but the mustache remained his most compelling feature.

"You have a wonderful voice," he said.

He had told her that on his earlier visits to the club. She gave him a smile and a quiet thanks and headed for the stairs.

He kept pace. "You're good. You never disappoint. By the way, you didn't seem nervous playing for the cardinal."

She laughed. "He's heard me play many times."

"That's right. I did hear he likes music."

"He doesn't just like it. He's good at it."

"Sings? Plays instruments? A Renaissance man?"

Wondering if he was being sarcastic, Lily stopped at the bottom of the stairs to search his face. "Actually, yes."

He smiled and held up his hands. "No offense meant. I'm a fan. He fascinates me." Terry narrowed an eye. "Half the women I know are in love with him. He's a virile guy."

Lily was embarrassed even thinking about Fran that way.

"Don't tell me you haven't noticed?" he asked.

"In fact, I haven't. He's a priest."

"And you're not even a little bit in love with him?"

"I love him as a person. He's insightful and supportive."

"Sounds like you know him well."

She was proud to admit it. "We have a history. I met him when he was Father Fran, about to be appointed bishop of Albany."

"No kidding?"

Something about his nonchalance reminded her that he was a reporter. She checked her watch. "I have to get back to work."

"Can I buy you a snack when you get off?"

She smiled, shook her head, and said, "Thanks anyway."

Back at the piano, she began playing again. Tuning out the audience, she let her heart take over. Singing had always been her salvation, the only time when she was naturally free of a stutter. Though time and training had freed her to speak, singing remained special. She might not have been able to make it on Broadway, but when she was lost in a song this way, she could just as well have been there. The feeling of pleasure, of success, of escape was the same.

Halfway through the second set, a patron sat beside her on the piano bench and sang harmony. When he returned to his table, the cardinal took his place. She was playing "I Dreamed a Dream" from *Les Miz.* He played along in the lower registers. When it was done, he gave her hand a squeeze and rejoined his guests.

LILY was tired but satisfied when she finally closed the piano lid. A handful of guests lingered over coffee, but the rest of the tables had been cleaned and reset.

Outside, she found Terry Sullivan leaning against the wide stone stoop. He looked innocent enough in the gaslight's glow, but a part of her was starting to feel harassed. She had refused him before. She went quickly down the steps and hit the sidewalk at a trot.

"Hey, hey." He fell into step. "Where're you running to?"

"Home."

"Mind if I walk along?"

"That depends," she said. "I haven't changed my mind about your interview."

"The publicity would be great for you."

Lily might have agreed several years before, but she had been struggling then. Now, between teaching and the club, she received two monthly paychecks. Add what she earned playing at private functions, and she was content. She didn't need more work, hence didn't need publicity.

"Is it me?" Terry asked. "Does something about me offend you?"

"Of course not," she said. "I'm just private."

"It's the public you I'm interested in, the one who rubs hips, so to speak, with people like Cardinal Rossetti." He took a long breath. "Would you talk to one of my colleagues?"

"No."

"Ah. You hate the press. But I'm a good guy, Lily. I'm Catholic, and you're Cardinal Rossetti's pal. Would I dare do anything bad knowing I might risk eternal damnation?"

Lily slowed down a notch.

"I feel like I should know everything about the guy," Terry said conversationally. "What's so fascinating is the way he is so normal. I mean, there he was, sitting beside you playing the piano. I half expected him to start belting out the words."

Lily smiled. "He's done that in private, in small groups."

"So you met him in Albany. What was he like?" He sounded genuinely intrigued, and Lily was a sucker for fans of her friend.

"Warm," she said. "Vibrant. But I actually met him in Manhattan at a reception at the mayor's house. I was playing."

"You played at the mayor's house? I'm impressed."

She laughed. "I was a Broadway wannabe and taught piano to pay the bills. The mayor's kids took lessons. That's how he knew me."

"So you met the cardinal in the city and followed him to Albany?"

"I followed the *mayor* there. Oops. That came out wrong." She felt a tightness at the back of her tongue and focused on relaxing it. "My relationship was with his kids. They'd been shaken by their parents' divorce. When the mayor was elected governor, he had to move to Albany and the kids went with him. He figured that if I kept teaching them, it would be one thing that didn't change in their lives. When a position opened up in a private school there, the timing seemed right."

"You gave up on Broadway?"

"It gave up on me." She slid him a wary look. "You're smooth—getting me to talk after I said I wouldn't."

"This is what's called a social conversation." He held up his hands. "No pen, no paper. Off the cuff. Like I say, the cardinal intrigues me. Did you ever dream he'd be a cardinal one day?"

"No. But I'm not surprised. Father Fran understands people."

They had reached the corner and were waiting to cross. Traffic sped by. "He understood me," she added. "I've been grappling with things. He's been—" How to describe Fran Rossetti? Friend? Adviser? Therapist? "He's been a comfort."

"So you followed him to Boston?"

Here was the reporter again, more prodding than casual. "Not that way. I followed him to Boston only in that I moved here soon after he did. He told me about the Essex Club. It was a step up from the club I played at in Albany. When I found a teaching position here, it was like it was meant to be."

Terry looked thoughtful. "Isn't the Essex pricey for a cardinal?"

"Not when his nephew owns the place," she said. "And the people he's with get the tab. Big donors to the church."

"Is that kosher? Bribery. Favor seeking."

"From a cardinal? What does he have to sell?"

"Political clout." He wiggled his brows. "Maybe a kiss."

She leveled him a look. "I don't think so."

"I'm kidding," he chided.

She wasn't sure she liked the joke, but then, she tended to take things too literally. "A kiss?" she kidded back. "Why not a weekend? Auctioned off for charity."

Terry laughed. "Dozens of women would bid."

She smiled. "Can you imagine some woman telling a friend, 'The cardinal and I are having an affair'?"

"A *passionate* affair?" Terry asked.

Lily played along. "What other kind is there? Forget the auction. We've been doing it for years."

He put back his head and laughed.

She laughed, too. "Cute. But not Father Fran. This is it," she said, coming to a stop in front of her building.

"You're an interesting person." He grinned. "Think you could fit me in between dates with the cardinal?"

She grinned back. "I don't know. He takes a lot of my time. I could probably fit you in next week. I'll have to check." She went into the building without looking back.

SINCE Lily rarely had class before eleven, she usually took her time waking up. This morning the phone jolted her out of bed at eight.

"Lily Blake?" said a man she didn't know. "This is George Fox.

I'm with the *Cape Sentinel.* Would you comment on your relationship with Cardinal Rossetti?"

"Excuse me?"

"Are you having an affair with Cardinal Rossetti?"

"A *what?* Good Lord, no!" It was a prank call but not a blind one, since she did know the cardinal. Cautious, she said, "This number is unlisted. How did you get it?"

"Were you having an affair with him in Albany?" the reporter asked just as her call waiting beeped. She was unsettled enough by his question to switch right to the second call. "Yes?"

"Lily Blake?"

"Who is this?"

"Paul Rizzo, *Cityside.*" *Cityside* was a renegade daily. "I'm looking for a comment on the *Post* story that you and the cardinal are sexually involved."

She hung up on both calls. She didn't believe there was any story in the *Post,* but after two calls she had to see for herself. Slipping a coat on over her nightshirt, she took the elevator to the first floor and had barely started for the lobby when she saw a man with a tape recorder and a microphone. At the sight of her he came to life.

She slipped back into the elevator seconds before the door closed and quickly pressed her floor. As soon as she was in her apartment again, she linked her laptop to the phone line and accessed the *Post* on-line. She didn't have to go past the home page. It was right there in big, bold letters—the lead story: CARDINAL LINKED TO CABARET SINGER. Beside it was a picture, taken the night before, of the two of them hip to hip on the piano bench, smiling at each other.

Horrified, Lily began to read.

> Less than a week ago Archbishop Francis P. Rossetti was elevated to cardinal amid an outpouring of praise for his humanitarian achievements and religious devotion. The *Post* has learned that Cardinal Rossetti has led a double life. An exclusive story reveals a long-term relationship between the cardinal and Lily Blake, 34, a cabaret singer at the posh Essex Club.

> Blake and the cardinal met eight years ago in New York City. They were introduced by then Mayor William Dean, who had first seen Blake on the Broadway stage. When the mayor and his wife separated, Blake became a regular guest at Gracie Mansion.

Incredulous, Lily read on with a morbid fascination.

> Two years later, when the mayor was elected governor of New York and moved to Albany, Blake went with him. Between twice-weekly visits to the Governor's Mansion, she sang at a nightclub. In addition, the governor set her up entertaining at private parties.

"No, he didn't," she cried. "Those bookings came from my work!"

> Francis Rossetti, then bishop of Albany, often attended those parties. He began inviting Blake to play at events at the bishop's residence. Within months she became a frequent visitor and was often seen leaving the residence in the early morning hours.

"With other people," she said to the screen in outrage.

> Three years ago, when the bishop was named to lead the Archdiocese of Boston, he secured a job for Blake at the Essex Club, owned and managed by his nephew Daniel Curry.

Scrolling farther, she cried out in disbelief when two pictures appeared. One was of the cardinal hugging her in the Essex Club lobby. The other, taken through a window at his residence, showed the cardinal with an arm around her shoulder.

She was sick to her stomach, but she couldn't stop reading.

> Blake teaches part-time at the Winchester School on Beacon Hill. A native of Lake Henry, New Hampshire, she studied at N.Y.U. and the Juilliard School. Though she auditioned for leading roles on Broadway and occasionally served as an understudy, she never made it out of the chorus line. She was twenty-eight when she left Broadway and moved to Albany.

> Blake's relationship with the cardinal has been a well-kept secret. When contacted by the *Post,* a spokesman for Cardinal Rossetti denied the allegations.
>
> Blake was more forthcoming. "The cardinal and I are having an affair," she confirmed. "I love him. We have a history." She described the cardinal as a warm, vibrant man.

The article closed by saying, "Governor Dean of New York has denied having a sexual relationship with Blake." Furious, Lily returned to the start of the piece and read the byline. The article had been written by Terrence Sullivan.

She felt betrayed. Disconnecting the laptop, she grabbed the phone book, found the number of the *Post,* and called the newsroom. Terry Sullivan wasn't in.

Frustrated, Lily pressed the disconnect button. Scrabbling through the phone book again, she located the Boston Archdiocese and called the cardinal's secretary, Father McDonough, with whom she had dealt when she played at church events. His line was busy.

Feeling stymied, she went to the window. There was a van parked out front with the markings of a local television station on its side.

It was insane. *Insane.* Surely a mistake. And easily corrected once she reached the right people. In the meantime she had lessons to give and classes to teach.

She showered and dressed, then took the elevator down to the garage and slipped out the back door unnoticed. Hurrying down the street, she cut through the Public Garden and reached school in record time. The teachers lounge was empty when she arrived, but she had barely poured a cup of coffee when a bell rang to mark the end of the first period. Within minutes several faculty members wandered in. Since they weren't ones she knew well, she ignored their glances and murmurings.

Peter Oliver was something else. A history teacher, tall and blond, he walked in as she was stirring powdered cream into her coffee. "Whoa. The lady of the hour."

Lily felt a sinking in her stomach. Her tongue tightened up.

"The *Post* story?" he prompted. "Is it true?"

She shook her head.

A different voice said a low "Lily."

Her eyes flew to the door. Michael Eddy, the headmaster of the school, motioned her to follow. Leaving her coffee, she walked to his office.

Michael closed the door. "Is it true?" he asked.

She shook her head, shook it fast and hard.

"Did you say those things?"

She swallowed and forced her throat to relax. "Not like that. And not on the record." When Michael closed his eyes in defeat, Lily's anger reared up. "I've tried calling the man who wrote this. He'll have to retract this. It isn't true."

He sighed. "Well, as long as you've denied it, I can answer the parents. Several have called. I wish you hadn't given the paper the name of the school."

"I didn't!"

"Then how did they get it?"

"I guess the same way they learned that I went to N.Y.U. and Juilliard. They didn't s-s-s-say that the only reason I went to the governor's mansion twice a week was to give piano lessons to his kids." The reality she had been trying to ignore was finally taking root. "This is all over Boston. All over the state." The horror of it was in her eyes. "Oh, Lord. This could ruin the cardinal. What do I do?"

"Hire a lawyer. You need a spokesperson. Someone to issue a denial. Someone to challenge the *Post*."

She took a breath and tried to remain calm. "But this is a mistake. Governor Dean denied it. So did the cardinal."

Michael held up his hands. "My concern is this school."

"This is unreal," she said. "But it's all right. The cardinal will clear everything up." She glanced at the clock. "I have a class."

IF ANY of the fifteen students taking music appreciation were aware of the *Post* article, none mentioned it. By the time fifty minutes had passed and the period ended, Lily had convinced herself that the cardinal would raise Cain and get a retraction printed, that the whole matter would be forgotten.

With five minutes to spare before a piano lesson, she went to the cafeteria for a cold drink. The first lunch period was under way. One step into the large, high-ceilinged room, and she heard the sudden drop of conversation, felt dozens of pairs of eyes.

It isn't true, she wanted to say, but her tongue was tight. So she simply shook her head, got her drink, and left. By the time her student arrived at the practice room, she had recomposed herself.

Afterward she tried calling the cardinal. She got through to his secretary. After identifying herself, she said to Father McDonough, "Thank goodness. Your line's been tied up. What's going on?"

"I take it you saw the story. It's made a mess."

"But it's all false. Has the cardinal demanded a retraction?"

"Our lawyers have," came the cool reply.

"Oh. Sh-sh-sh-should I hire a lawyer?" She wanted him to say that there was no need, that the cardinal's team would resolve it.

Instead he sounded distant. "Our concern is protecting the church. We're trying our best to do that. But it might be better if you didn't call here again until everything is straightened out."

Things went downhill from there. After one more private lesson she packed her briefcase. She had no sooner breathed a sigh of relief on the front steps of the school when a woman with a microphone appeared. "Ms. Blake, a comment on the *Post* story?"

Lily shook her head and hurried on.

A male voice said, "Paul Rizzo, *Cityside.* You were seen leaving the cardinal's residence Sunday night. Why were you there?"

I was hired to play the piano, she wanted to tell him, but her tongue was tight. So she lowered her head and kept moving.

"Can you explain the late-night phone calls?"

"Is it true you were in the cardinal's arms at the Essex Club?"

When Lily looked up to say an angry "No," a cameraman snapped her picture. She hurried on, but the questions got worse.

"Where did you do it?"

"What kind of sex?"

"What does your family think of this?"

Lily shuddered to think that her family *knew,* period. But they did. She learned it soon after she reached home and listened to her messages. Between calls from newspapers and television stations was the voice of her sister Poppy. "What's going on, Lily? The calls are coming in hot and heavy. Mom is furious! Phone me, will you?"

Lily's stomach turned over. Her relationship with her mother was precarious enough. This wouldn't help.

She sank into the chair by the phone and punched in Poppy's number. Poppy was barely two years her junior and the sweetest, most upbeat person Lily knew, despite circumstances that might have caused her to be anything but. Poppy Blake was a paraplegic, confined to a wheelchair since a snowmobile accident a dozen years before. If anyone had a right to self-pity, she did, but she refused to waste energy on it. After the accident she had moved into her own place on the lake and started an answering service.

"Lily," Poppy said, "thank goodness. What's happening?"

"Nightmare. Total nightmare. When did you hear?"

"Early today. Calls started coming in from reporters. And then there's the tube. Pictures of you and the cardinal."

"Mom saw?" Lily asked in alarm.

"Mom saw. Kip called yesterday to warn me about the *Post* guy, but he didn't say why. I wish you'd told us."

"How could I? It's a bogus story."

"I know that, but Mom doesn't," Poppy said.

Lily fought tears. "I thought this reporter was a friend. He came on to me, asked if I'd go out with him. What kind of person does that? How can he do this to the cardinal? Or is it just that the papers are starved for sleaze? What did Mom say?"

"Doesn't matter," Poppy said. "What should I tell her?"

"Tell her not to look at the paper. There's no basis to this. It'll wear itself out."

"You need a lawyer. This is libel. You have a job—two jobs—to protect and a reputation. They've all but labeled you a whore."

Lily paused, alert. "What was that click?"

"What click?"

She listened, heard nothing. "I must be paranoid."

"What do you want me to tell the reporters?"

"That the story isn't true. That I'm suing." Lily paused and asked, "What about Rose?"

Rose was the last of the three Blake girls. She was a year younger than Poppy, which made her thirty-one. More relevant, she had been barely pubescent when Lily's problems had peaked, too young to question what her mother said. Rose had been her mother's mouthpiece from the start.

She was married, with three children. She and her husband lived on land that had been her wedding gift from the senior Blakes. Always close, Rose and Maida had grown even closer in the three years since Maida's husband, the girls' father, had died.

Experience told Lily not to expect support from Rose.

Poppy said an uncharacteristically cross "Rose is an old poop. She doesn't have an independent thought in her head. As for the rest of town, I'll tell them what to say if anyone calls. They don't take kindly to having one of their own maligned."

Chapter 3

LILY refused to turn on the television. She didn't want to see whether she was in the news, preferring to think the story was already old. But when she reached the lobby dressed for work, the crowd of journalists outside was larger than ever. Dismayed, she went to the garage, but the reporters were there, too.

Resigned, she lowered her eyes and walked quickly, ignoring the questions shot at her. But the media phalanx grew, jostling so closely that she found it hard to walk. She was close to tears when she finally reached the club.

Mercifully, Dan was at the door, letting her in, shutting the press out. She went straight to his office and sank into a chair.

"Rough day?" he asked kindly.

Not trusting her voice, she nodded.

He smiled sadly. "No need to wonder. I know you, and I know the cardinal. There's nothing between you but the kind of friendship he has with people all over the city, all over the country."

She took a breath. "What happens now? They got their splashy headlines. There's no more story, so it dies. Right?"

"I hope so," he said, but without conviction. He seemed tired.

She had the awful thought he wasn't saying everything he knew. "How does tonight look here?" she asked with caution.

"Booked solid."

She brightened. "That's good, isn't it?"

The answer was relative. Yes, the dining room soon filled with paying guests, but most were new faces, guests of members, and they spent an inordinate amount of time watching the pianist.

Lily tried to tune them out. And she succeeded, losing herself in the fantasy of a song until the flash of a camera broke her concentration. Dan spoke with the offending party, but two other flashes went off during the evening, and by the end of the last set she couldn't try to pretend things were normal.

That night Lily slept in fits and starts. She woke up to a dreary day, but she refused to let her mood match it, refused to even look out the window to see whether television vans were still there. She showered, dressed in dark slacks and a sedate blouse, and forced down breakfast, all the while telling herself things had to get better. Either there would be a retraction in today's paper or nothing at all.

When someone knocked on her door after eight, she tensed. She crept to the peephole. Relieved, she opened the door.

"I knew you hadn't left," her neighbor Elizabeth Davis said. She wore a T-shirt over biking shorts and had her blond hair bunched in a clip. "How're you doing?"

"Horrible," Lily said with a glance at the newspapers under Elizabeth's arm. "Are those today's?"

"Two Boston, one New York. Want to see?"

"You tell me. I'm hoping for a retraction."

"You didn't get one," Elizabeth warned. She tossed the papers on the table. "The *Post* reports that you drive a BMW and bought a slew of expensive furniture when you moved here. *Cityside* reports that you're big into Victoria's Secret shopping. And New York reports that you spent a week last winter at a posh resort in Aruba that you couldn't have afforded on your own."

Lily was stunned. "How do they know all that?"

"Any computer buff can get it in five minutes flat."

"But that's personal stuff! *My* life. My private information. Where I shop is no one's business!" Her mind began to spin. "I bought the BMW used, I paid off the furniture over two years' time, I mail-order more from L.L. Bean than Victoria's Secret, and I booked the place in Aruba through a travel clearinghouse. This isn't fair."

But Elizabeth wasn't done. She crossed to the small radio on the counter by the stove. The arrogant tenor of Justin Barr, a right-wing talk-show host, filled the room. ". . . an insult to Catholics everywhere! Why, this woman is an insult to people of every faith. Is there any act of disrespect more offensive than smearing the good name of a beloved leader?"

"*Me* smearing a n-n-n-name?" Lily cried.

"No, my friends," Justin Barr ranted, "the question is how Lily Blake was able to get close enough to a man of the stature of Cardinal Rossetti to spread the stain, even indirectly, and now, Lord help us, she teaches our children."

Elizabeth turned the radio off.

Lily was stricken. "I don't believe this. Why? Why me?"

"Because they smell weakness," Elizabeth said. "Wolves after a wounded deer. You have to take a stand, Lily. Let me give it a try. I'll get dressed, the two of us will go down there, and I'll be your spokesperson. What do you say?"

LILY'S statement was simple. Elizabeth had advised her to tackle only the major allegations and leave minor misrepresentations alone for now. An experienced image shaper, Elizabeth coaxed and cajoled the media crowd into moving back and showing a little respect. Then, while Lily stood silently, Elizabeth read Lily's statement, which denied a romantic involvement with either Governor Dean of New York or Cardinal Rossetti of Boston.

Thanks to Elizabeth, Lily was able to walk to school unmolested, thinking that maybe, just maybe the scandal had begun its retreat.

Michael Eddy didn't think so. He knew how much the school paid her and wanted to know how, even allowing for her work at the club, she could afford Aruba and a BMW. She told him how, as she had told Elizabeth. When people stared at her in the halls, she simply walked on. When faculty members left her sitting alone in the cafeteria, she read a book. Midafternoon, as soon as she finished work, she left school, genuinely happy to be done for the day.

She took heart when the press contingent remained lighter than it had been the day before, and dared turn on the evening news. It was a mistake. The story was covered on every channel, taking parts of the morning's stories and giving them lurid twists.

She didn't know what to do and told Dan Curry as much when she arrived at the club. He gave her the name of a lawyer. More comforting, he had word from the cardinal. "He's sick about this, Lily. His lawyers have told him not to be in direct touch with you, but he's thinking of you. As far as he's concerned, you don't deserve it. He knows you have the strength to weather this."

Lily clung to those words through a difficult night of playing before an audience that crowded in on her. She went to bed praying that this was the worst, and woke up feeling tense.

She was listening to a CD of a ponderous Tchaikovsky piece that reflected her mood when Elizabeth appeared at the door with the morning *Post.* The headline read DETAILS EMERGE ON CARDINAL'S WOMAN.

> Blake comes from a well-to-do family in the small north-central town of Lake Henry, New Hampshire. Her father was a major landowner until his death three years ago. Her mother

lives in the family's large stone farmhouse and oversees the family's apple-cider business.

The *Post*'s Headline Team has learned that Blake grew up with a severe stutter that kept her apart from other children. She turned to singing as a means of communication. Experts on speech defects confirm that this is common. Susan Block, a Boston speech therapist, also confirmed that severe speech defects may create emotional problems.

In Blake's case these took the form of rebellion. At sixteen she was involved in the commission of a felony. Charged along with a twenty-year-old accomplice, who spent six months in prison for the crime, Blake was put on probation. She completed that sentence shortly before graduating from high school and left town soon after.

Devastated, Lily looked at Elizabeth. "That file was sealed! The judge told us no one would ever see it!"

Elizabeth couldn't hide her curiosity. "What did you do?"

What did she do? She'd been dumb was what she did. Dumb and young and dying to be popular.

"The boy I was with stole a car. There I was, smiling and laughing, having the time of my life because Donny Kipling was so tough he was cool. I went out with him in that car, and he just kept saying, 'Don't worry, this is fun,' but he told the police I planned it."

Numb, she picked up the paper again.

Blake rarely returned to Lake Henry after that. Anonymous sources have told the *Post* that she is estranged from her mother and her sister Rose. Another sister, Poppy, refused to comment on a recent conversation she held with Blake.

"How did they know I talked to Poppy?" she asked, then remembered. "Someone listened in on my phone. I heard a click."

"Wouldn't surprise me," Elizabeth said. "They'll do what they have to for a story."

"That's not *fair.*"

Elizabeth was suddenly apologetic. "Neither is this. I have to cancel you out for the Kagan fund-raiser."

Lily stared at her, stunned.

"Campaign manager's orders." Elizabeth gestured toward the newspaper. "This is too inflammatory. It's distracting from the candidate. Don't take it personally. It's politics. I'm sorry, Lily."

LILY packed up for school, went down the back way, and ran off through the waiting crowd, wearing sunglasses so no one would see if she cried—and if she did, it wouldn't be from fear or sadness. She was absolutely furious.

Michael Eddy was waiting for her at the school door. He let her in and held up a hand to the press, but the warning shifted her way when he said, "My office." She followed him there.

He didn't offer her a seat. "I'm getting calls from parents and trustees," he said. "They want to know how we could hire someone with a criminal record to teach their children. I told them we didn't know. I want you to tell me why we didn't."

Lily's heart was pounding. She said, "I don't have a criminal record. The case was dismissed. The file was sealed. I was told by the judge that that protected me."

"Didn't you think the parents here would care?"

As she thought about how to answer, she grew angry. "I've told the truth. I was never convicted of anything."

"Then why the probation? Why the sealed file? You're teaching *children* here, Lily. You should have said something."

She disagreed. But Michael wasn't in her shoes, and she wasn't in his.

He sighed. "I won't fire you," he said. "You've done too good a job. But I'm asking you to take a voluntary leave of absence."

Her eyes went wide. She loved her work here; she needed the money. "For how long?" she asked. "Until this blows over?"

"An indefinite leave. Until you find a job somewhere else."

She stared, angry at him now and not caring that he knew it. He could play with words all he wanted, but he *was* firing her.

When Lily arrived back at her apartment, the phone was ringing. Dropping her briefcase, she gripped the back of the chair until the ringing stopped. She heard her own voice, then remembered that she had turned the machine off that morning. Ten consecutive rings would have turned it on again, which meant she'd had at least one persistent caller.

"I'm calling for Lily Blake," said a hungover-sounding male voice. "If you, uh, want someone to write your story, we should talk. I, uh, called my publisher. They like the idea of sex and religion. They can get something out fast. So if you want, call me." He left a number.

Lily erased the message, then listened to those preceding it. Justin Barr must have been the persistent one, because his call came first. "Lily? Are you there, Lily? This is Justin Barr, and we're on the air. My listeners want to hear your side of the story—"

He called three more times, at twenty-minute intervals. There were also calls from reporters in Chicago and Los Angeles—all leaving names and numbers. Two friends had called to express concern, and two clients had called to cancel appointments.

There was also a message from Dan Curry, asking her to call. His voice held an odd edge. Nervous, she punched out his number. "Tell me," she said, steeling herself.

"You know how I feel, Lily. I believe in both of you. I love both of you, so this tears me apart, but here's my problem. The phone has been ringing off the hook with complaints. Regulars can't get reservations. Others complained about having to wade through reporters last night. These people are the backbone of the club."

Lily gripped the phone. She knew what was coming.

"I've always run the club a certain way," Dan said. "It's a quiet, classy place. That's why we loved having you play. Because you *are* classy. But this whole business is sordid. It's creating a notoriety we just don't need."

Lily remained silent, her head bowed.

"This kills me," Dan went on, "because we all love you here." He sighed. "But I think you should take some time off."

"Are you firing me?" Two firings in one hour. A record.

"No. I'm just telling you to stay home for a couple of days, until this thing dies down."

But she was discouraged. "Will it?"

"Definitely. It's like a car. No fuel, no go."

"There's never been fuel, but the car went! If they don't find it one place, they'll find it another."

"Is there anything else they can find?"

"Yesterday I wouldn't have said there was anything, period." She sank into a chair. "There was my one and only brush with the law. There's been nothing since. What's left for them to write?"

THEY wrote about Lily's suspension from the Winchester School, front-page news on Friday morning. Terry Sullivan interviewed Michael Eddy, whose statements had enough force and indignation to restore his luster in the eyes of parents and trustees. Reporter Paul Rizzo focused on members of the board, with a string of quotes expressing dismay at Lily's deceit and her immorality. Justin Barr, the radio talk-show host, went wild about what he called the Lily Blake problem, inciting irate parents to call in discussing the teacher as a role model.

The papers reported that Lily was taking time off from the Essex Club, but they did not elaborate. Lily suspected that Dan had refused to talk and that the print media, at least, was backing off from anything to do with the cardinal.

The focus was on Lily, and Lily alone. She had become the story.

She was so angry that she put aside her distaste for lawyers and called the one Dan had recommended. Maxwell Funder was articulate, experienced, and among the most visible attorneys in the state. She had seen him on the news many times and wondered if his promise to be at her apartment within the hour had to do with the publicity attached to the case. But beggars couldn't be choosers. She could only afford to pay him for a consultation.

In person he wasn't nearly as impressive as the television cameras made him out to be. He was older, shorter, broader. But he was pleasant and patient. Sitting on the sofa, he listened while she vented. He frowned in dismay, widened his eyes in disbelief, shook his head from time to time. The sympathy felt good.

"How can this happen?" she finally asked. "How can so many lies be printed? How do I make it stop?"

The lawyer sat straighter. "For starters we can go to court, file papers, and initiate a suit. Tell me, who's the worst?"

"The *Post,*" she said. Terry Sullivan had used her and lied.

"The *Post* it is," Funder said. "Our suit will expose the falsehoods. We'll get affidavits from the cardinal and the governor corroborating your side of the issue. I'll call a press conference and lay it all out"—his passion rose—"calling this the most reckless example of bad press. I'll demand an investigation of the *Post* for printing this slander and demand a retraction."

"A retraction. That's what I want. Will I get it?"

"Now?" The rhetoric cooled. "No. They'll fight to defend their basic integrity. Maybe years down the road . . ."

Years? "How many years?"

"From now to the time a jury hears the case? Three years. The thing is, in order for you to be vindicated, you need a big verdict. So we'll sue for, say, four million. But I have to warn you, the *Post* will fight dirty. They have some of the toughest First Amendment lawyers in the country. They'll put your life under a microscope, take depositions from your family, friends, teachers, neighbors, boyfriends, ex-boyfriends. Their private investigators will get phone records, school records, medical records. They'll be looking for even the tiniest hint of something that can help their client show you're a disreputable person. If there's anything there, they'll find it. They'll try to prove that your reputation is so bad that even if they made a mistake and libeled you, it doesn't matter, because no damage has been done. They'll try to prove that your life has been filled with lies."

Lily was beginning to panic. "What about my rights? The media has no right to do this."

"That's why we sue."

"All I want is a retraction. I don't want money."

"Well, you ought to. This kind of case can cost upwards of a million, between legal fees, court costs, experts, private investigators."

She felt weak. "I don't have that kind of money."

"Few people do." He studied her, laced his fingers. "Look, I don't normally take cases unless the client has the full ability to pay—I mean, I have to live, too—but what's happening to you is a disgrace. So I'll handle the case for two fifty, plus fifty for expenses, plus twenty-five percent of what you recover."

"Two hundred and fifty thousand dollars." She gulped in a breath. "I don't have that kind of m-m-money."

"Your family does. I read there was a family business."

"It's a working business. There isn't cash lying around."

"There's land. That would be good collateral for a loan."

"I can't ask that," Lily said. Cash, a loan—it didn't matter. She couldn't ask her mother for money. Nor could she imagine Maida giving it. Lily was the greatest disappointment of Maida's life—the daughter who went bad. Lily hadn't taken a cent from her family since she was eighteen.

"I did read that you don't get along with your family, but if they have money to get you out of this mess, my advice is to take it. Good lawyers don't come cheap."

But Lily couldn't ask her mother for money. And even if she had the money herself, she couldn't conceive of spending it all on this. Quietly she stood. "I need to think. Thank you for coming."

He followed her to the door. "No need to make a decision now. My offer stands for another day or two."

After he left, Lily went to the window to see if he would talk to the press on his way out. But suddenly faces and cameras were all looking up. Jolted, she stepped back and stood frozen, gazing blankly out, until she realized that a telephoto lens in a window of a building across the street could see her anywhere in her apartment.

She quickly closed the blinds in the living room and in the bedroom. That left her in a small dark apartment, with no job, no freedom, and no prospects for a speedy return of either. Not knowing what to do with herself, she spent the rest of the day wandering around the tiny apartment, letting strains of a strident Wagner drown out the ringing of the phone, feeling alternately caged, terrified, and very angry. Angry at Terry Sullivan and Justin Barr for playing with her life. Angry at the media. Angry even at the cardinal for freeing himself from the mess but leaving her in it up to her ears.

She couldn't stay in Boston. That much was clear. Even if the story died the next day, she would be stared at for months. She couldn't bear that—couldn't bear knowing that millions of strangers knew private details of her life, couldn't bear the humiliation or the injustice. And then there was the issue of a job. Who would hire a woman with the morals of a snake?

She could cut her hair short, dye it blond, and go somewhere new. She could waitress. But without knowing a soul? Having to use a phony name and lie to every person she met? That was no life.

What she wanted most was justice. Second to that, she wanted to dig a hole and climb in. She was tired of reporters and cameramen, tired of being a spectacle. But human beings didn't dig holes and climb in. They went to places where they could hide, places like Lake Henry.

Not Lake Henry, she protested, but the idea stuck in her mind like a burr. She had a place to live there. She owned it free and clear. It had been a bequest from her grandmother, a small place on the lake separated from the world by acres of trees. It was as close to a hole in the ground as she was apt to find.

WHEN darkness fell, Lily packed up the car, locked the doors, and left the garage. She fully expected a few diehards left outside, even one or two following in a car, but she figured she would lose them once she hit the Mass Pike. Indeed, figures emerged from dark shadows, hoisting equipment, shouting questions, and yes, a pair of headlights fell in behind her. A large satellite van parked at the corner joined the chase.

She sped up in an attempt to bury herself in traffic, but her chasers easily kept pace. By the time a red light stopped her, not only was the big van on her bumper but a motorcyclist with a press pass around his neck started knocking on her window.

Shaken, she revised her plan. Driving carefully, she went around the block until she reached the opposite end of the alley from the one she had left minutes before. She inched her way down the narrow stretch and turned in at her building. When she lowered her window to key-open the garage door, the motorcyclist came up close. Lily was incensed. "Th-th-th-this garage"—she fought the stutter—"is private property. If you come in while this door's open, I'm c-c-calling the police." She turned the key, and as soon as the garage door was high enough, she rolled forward.

No one followed as the door closed behind her. She drove on to her parking space, got out of the car, loaded her arms with as much as she could carry, and took the elevator to the fourth floor. Rather than going to her own apartment, though, she went to Elizabeth's.

"I need your help," she said after she explained what had happened. "I can't stay here, and the problem isn't just a small dark apartment. It's the whole thing. The media won't let this die. The problem is how to get out without their following me."

Elizabeth tipped up her chin. "I know how."

ELIZABETH'S plan involved smuggling Lily out in the nondescript Ford station wagon that Elizabeth's brother, Doug, had left sitting in his Cambridge garage while he was teaching in Brussels for the year.

It went off without a hitch. Lily and her belongings successfully hid under piles of KAGAN FOR GOVERNOR banners in the back of Elizabeth's Lexus. Elizabeth drove down the alley and around the block, heading toward Cambridge free and clear. At Doug's house, she pulled up to the garage and killed the lights.

"It's battered but trusty," she said as they stowed Lily's things in the wagon. "Step on the gas twice, pause, then turn the key. Works every time."

Lily couldn't afford to be fussy. Sliding behind the wheel, she took a minute to see where everything was, then rolled down the window, pumped the gas twice, paused, and turned the key. The engine started up in the next breath.

"You're the best," she told Elizabeth by way of thanks.

"Want me to get your mail or anything?" Elizabeth asked.

"Actually, I would." Lily handed over her mailbox key.

"Where should I send it?"

"Just hold it."

"Where'll you be?"

Lily wasn't sure she should say, which was another thing she despised Terry Sullivan for. He had taught her that unless she knew someone well, she had to be on her guard. So she simply smiled. "I'll let you know." Backing out, she put on the headlights and set off.

The trip took two hours. Lily spent the first hour watching her rearview mirror to see if she was being followed. She even left the highway once, reversed direction, went back an exit, reversed direction again, and continued north. But no car followed.

She had escaped—a small victory. The pleasure of it carried her into the second hour, across the Massachusetts border into New Hampshire and steadily north.

She checked her rearview mirror when she left the highway and again when she drove through the center of Lake Henry. But everything was dark, closed up tight for the night, and no car followed, not then or when she turned off Main Street onto the road that circled the lake. Bumping around familiar curves, she felt a mellowness that the lake always brought.

She turned onto a narrower road that led to the shore at Thissen Cove. Several hundred feet from the water she turned again, onto a rutted dirt path. At its end she killed the engine, then the lights.

At first glance the lake was pitch-black. Gradually her eyes adjusted. The small cottage of wood and stone was on her left. On her right, tall trees were silhouettes against a dark sky.

Slipping silently from the car, she stood and inhaled. The woods smelled of pine, of dried leaves, of logs burning in a neighbor's woodstove. They were smells common to Lake Henry in the fall, but in Lily they conjured up childhood images. She crossed the small clearing between cottage and lake. Down a short stairway of railroad ties, and she reached the water's edge.

She listened to the soft slap of water against shore. She made out clouds in the sky, but as she watched, they broke open to patches of stars and, minutes later, a crescent moon. And then—and then came the hauntingly melodic tremolo of a loon.

She was being welcomed home. Suddenly the contrast between the hell she had left and the beauty of this cottage, this lake, this town was so stark and heartfelt, she knew she'd been right to come here.

Feeling stronger than she had in days, she returned to the car, got the key to the cottage from her purse, climbed the steps to the porch, and let herself in.

JOHN Kipling sat utterly still in his canoe. He had been drawn here in the wee hours, to the shadow of Elbow Island, opposite Thissen Cove. Call it instinct, a hunch. If her life in the city had become as awful as he imagined, where else could she go?

Still, he didn't know for sure until the light went on in the house. He whispered a satisfied "Yesssss."

He had read the *Post* story and knew firsthand how deceitful Terry Sullivan could be. He had talked with Poppy, who was dismayed at what her sister was enduring, and he had talked with townsfolk, who had differing opinions on the matter. He wondered what the truth was. It was the journalist in his blood. Now that Lily Blake was back in town, right here on his turf, he could pursue it.

Smiling, he drew his paddle through the water and headed home.

Chapter 4

LILY slept deeply and awoke disoriented. It was a full minute before she realized where she was and seconds more before she realized why. Then everything came back in a rush—the lies, the embarrassment, the anger, the loss. She squeezed her eyes shut and willed the images away, but they were part of her now.

Thinking that the images wouldn't be as vivid if she were upright and active, she slipped from bed and went to the top of the spiral stairs that led down from the sleeping loft. Comfort was instantaneous. The magic, of course, was in these four walls. For Lily this cottage was filled with warm memories of Celia, her grandmother, whom she had visited here practically from birth.

Celia St. Marie had spent her first fifty years in a remote Maine town some seventy miles to the northeast. Widowed early, she had supported herself and Maida by doing bookkeeping for a paper mill. When she wasn't working, she was bailing out her brothers, an irresponsible lot. But Maida married well. Not only did George Blake run a successful family business, he had a good heart. Soon after his marriage to Maida he bought this piece of land for Celia and built her this cottage.

It wasn't a large cottage. Celia hadn't wanted anything large. It was enough to have her own home. With a beautiful lakefront she enjoyed open space outside and was snug and cozy inside.

Coziness was definitely what Lily associated with the cottage, with its dark wood, exposed beams, and built-in bookshelves. The ground level was a single large room. The living area was marked by an upholstered sofa, a pair of overstuffed chairs, two floor lamps, and a square pine coffee table. The dining area contained a wood trestle table.

The kitchen was small and modern. Celia St. Marie might have been parochial, but she was smart. She had arrived in Lake Henry with a small savings account that grew considerably over the years, allowing her to upgrade and add conveniences.

But her savings account wasn't all that grew. Celia herself grew. She made friends, joined the garden club and the historical society, and played bingo on Monday nights at the church. In her seventies she came into her own. How else to explain the wide-mouthed bass she had caught in a contest on the lake, then had stuffed and hung on the kitchen wall? Or the exquisite macramé piece of hers that hung on a living-room wall?

In her golden years Celia blossomed, and that included standing up to Maida about Lily. What little self-confidence Lily took from childhood had come from her grandmother's ever open arms. Celia had been dead for six years, but Lily felt those arms around her as she sat at the top of the stairs. It helped that she wore one of Celia's old nightgowns. It was long and soft and smelled faintly of the jasmine bath oil that Celia had used.

It was nine in the morning. Pale dapples of sunshine broke through the trees and spilled through the window onto the braided rug. Barefoot, Lily went down the stairs, wrapped herself in a crocheted shawl, and stood where a beam of sun hit the floor. The warmth of it satisfied briefly before fading.

Outside, a loon called from the lake. Pleased at the familiar sound, Lily opened the door to a world that glowed. With the morning sun behind her, the lake reflected the deep blue of the western sky. Trees that had already turned color burned a fiery red and gold against dark evergreens.

The loon called again, but she couldn't see it. Risking cold feet, she darted down the railroad-tie steps to the shore. She tucked herself into one of the small cubbies of exposed pine roots that were characteristic of Thissen Cove, and watched and waited.

When the loon called again, she sorted through the water's reflection of trees at the edge of Elbow Island until she saw it. Them, actually—two birds, easily identified by their pointed beaks and the graceful sweep of their heads and necks. Energized, Lily ran back to the house for Celia's binoculars, and returned. That's when she saw the small motorboat at the dock.

She froze. The man in the boat was looking at her. That windblown head of brown hair, a jaw so square a close-cropped beard couldn't hide its shape, an alertness so like that of the vultures she'd left behind—she knew who he was, oh, did she ever. She also knew that he knew *her.*

Appalled, heartsick, furious to have been found out so soon and by a man she had reason to hate, she raced back to the house, pulled a kitchen chair to the front door, climbed up, and snatched Celia's gun from the hooks above the door. Then she stormed back outside. By then John Kipling was halfway across the lawn.

"That's far enough," she shouted from the porch in a voice that shook with fury. "This is my land. You're trespassing."

He stopped walking. With measured movements he set a large brown paper bag on the ground. Slowly, not quite leisurely, he turned and started back toward the boat.

He was barefoot and wore a gray sweatshirt and denim cutoffs. In other circumstances she might have admired his legs.

"Stop!" she ordered. "What's in the bag?"

He stopped and slowly turned. "Fresh stuff—eggs, milk, veggies, fruit. You have nothing inside but canned goods."

"How do you know that?"

"I know the woman who keeps up this place. She's my assistant's aunt."

"And she *told* you?" Another betrayal. "Who else d-i-i-id she tell?"

"Only me," he said, "and only because I asked. I was trying to think where I'd go if I were you. I figured you'd come here."

"How did you know that I had?"

"Your lights were on at one in the morning. Hard to miss."

"But you can't see this place from the road."

"No. I live on the lake, at Wheaton Point."

"You can't see Thissen Cove from there," she said, not about to let him play her for a fool. "So you were out at one in the morning?"

"I couldn't sleep."

"And now you come bearing gifts."

"Put the gun down, and we'll talk."

She lowered the muzzle. "What do you want?"

He slipped his hands into his back pockets. "To help."

She barked out a disbelieving laugh. "You? You're media. On top of *that,* you're D-D-Donny's big brother."

"I was gone when all that happened between you and him."

"And if you'd been here? You'd have stood up for your brother, just like your dad did, just like your uncles and cousins did."

"He was a troubled kid. He already had a rap sheet. He'd have gotten twice as much time if he hadn't said you'd egged him on.

That was the story he gave them. They thought it was the truth."

"It wasn't."

He inhaled deeply. "I know that. He told me. I saw him in the hospital the day before he died."

Donny Kipling had done time for his alleged theft with Lily. Two years later he did time for breaking and entering. Three years after that he crashed his car during a police chase and died a week later, at the age of twenty-eight. That was ten years ago.

"I'm sorry," Lily said now.

But John seemed lost in thought. "I don't know what went wrong. He was fine, perfect up to the age of ten. I was the bad one. So I was sent away, and Donny stayed and took my place." His eyes met hers. "For what it's worth, my father hasn't been the same since Donny died. He's a tormented man."

I'm glad, Lily wanted to say. Only she'd had a glimpse of Gus Kipling in town several years back. He had looked broken and old. She would have had to have a hard heart to wish him worse.

She glanced at the food. "Then this is for guilt?"

He made a sputtering sound, a sigh. "That's direct."

"I don't have time to play around. I came here to hide. You've found me out. Now I have to leave."

"You do not. I'm not telling anyone. It's between you and me."

"You, me, and who else? The *Post?* The *Lake News?*"

John stood his ground and shook his head. "No."

She didn't believe him and told him as much with a stare. The shotgun remained in the crook of her arm.

"Good Lord," he said, exhaling loudly. "You're hard."

Dropping her guard for a minute, she cried, "Do you know what I've been through in the past week?"

"Yes. Yes, I do." His eyes were dark and troubled. "I've seen what journalists do, Lily. I've done it myself."

"So I heard."

"Good. Then let's put it all on the table. What you probably know is that I ruined a family. I did a story on a politician who entered the presidential primary and failed to reveal that he'd been involved with a married woman. The affair had ended years before, but there was the stink of adultery and the lure of lascivious details that were sure to sell papers. The man had enemies, and I loved talking with them. So the story broke, and his political career ended, right along with his marriage and his relationship with his kids." A tic pulsed under his eye. "Did I get it all?"

"You missed the part about his blond aide," she prompted.

"Didn't miss it. Repressed it. Turns out it wasn't true. There was no affair with a blond aide. That fact came out later."

"You left out the part about the guy's suicide," she added.

"Yeah, well, that's haunted me since the day it happened. Afterward I couldn't do the hard stuff the paper wanted. So I left. That suicide is the single greatest influence in the work I do now." His eyes held hers. "More than anyone, I do know what you went through."

Lily let her guard fall again. "I didn't want to come back here. If I'd had anywhere else to go, I would have."

"I figured that. But people will find out you're here without my saying a word. They'll see a light, like I did. Or see smoke from the chimney. You won't stay a secret for long."

"That's fine. I won't be staying for long. Once the story dies, I'm going back to Boston. Or somewhere else."

"Today's *Post* isn't as bad as it's been."

"What does it say?"

"That you're holed up in your apartment. Then the story shifts to Maxwell Funder. He's quoted ad nauseam on First Amendment rights, the difference between a public person and a private person. Speculation on possible legal action. Did you retain Funder?"

She shook her head. "I can't afford him. Besides, me against the *Post?*"

"How about you against Terry Sullivan?"

Lily stilled. She hadn't mentioned him to John Kipling.

"I know Terry Sullivan," he said. "We went to college together, then worked together at the *Post.* He shafted me good."

"How?"

"The blond aide? She was Terry's connection. He knew all along she lied. That means he deliberately set me up. So I hold a grudge against him. We share that, you and me." He turned to leave.

"I don't hold a grudge," Lily told him. "Worse than that. If this gun had been loaded and you'd been him, I'd have shot you."

With his back to her John hung his head. When he turned, she saw a crooked smile. "I have ammo. Call if you want it." Then he walked off.

JOHN started up the motor and glided away, but the emotions churning inside him belied the lazy pace. Three years ago, returning to Lake Henry, he'd had a plan—to write a book that would bring him fame and justify his having left Boston. And he had tried. He had written the beginnings of a dozen books. Only none interested him enough to keep on. This book had the potential to be big. Lily's situation was the microcosm of an increasingly frightening phenomenon. The media was out of control, and individual rights were being trampled. John knew the media mind. Guilty of doing trampling in his day, he was the perfect one to write this book.

There was Lily's story, and there was Terry Sullivan's story. Terry was a great writer, and he knew it. He was arrogant and ambitious, but ambition alone couldn't explain the kind of meanness that ruined innocent people. Reporters who were driven usually had cause that went beyond the purely professional.

John was a perfect example. His driving force was a need to stand out. When he was young, it had manifested itself in minor run-ins with the law. When he left Lake Henry, his drive took the more positive path of competitiveness in school, in work. The latter culminated in the debacle at the *Post,* however, after which his need to make a name for himself had been muted. But with the prospect of writing this book, the drive was back. If he could help Lily Blake exact revenge at the same time he redeemed himself—both as a writer and a human being—what could be better?

He guided the boat back to shore and tied it up beside his canoe at the ratty patch of wood he called his dock. Then he slid in behind the wheel of his Tahoe and set off for town. The air was brisk, but he kept his window rolled down. It was another stellar fall day, brilliant with foliage. He drove on around the lake.

Lake Henry center was buzzing. If people weren't fetching mail at the post office, they were buying supplies at Charlie's general store or pulling in at the end of the parking area behind it. There sat the police station, the church, and the library. All three were of white wood, with black shutters. Each played multiple roles. The police station, a long single-story frame structure, also housed the town clerk and town registrar. The library, a square Federal-style building, rented out its generous third floor to the Lake Henry Committee. The historical society worked out of the basement of the church, which stood tall, venerable, and proud.

Today the historical society was having a plant-and-shrub sale. Plant-and-shrub sales in Lake Henry—or bake sales, or art sales, or garage sales—were as much for socializing as anything else. There were as many people standing and chatting as there were buying.

John scanned the cars and trucks, picking out an unfamiliar one or two. Tourists passing through? The media in disguise? He skimmed the crowd for cameras, but didn't see a one. Not yet.

POPPY Blake's home, like Lily's, was small, surrounded by trees, and on its own little patch of the lake, but that was where the similarities ended. Poppy's land was on the west shore rather than the east, a wedge of her parents' property given as a gift to her after her accident. The cottage itself comprised three connected wings on a single level. The left wing housed the bedroom; the right wing housed the kitchen and a weight room. But Poppy spent most of her time in the center wing. It held an arc of desks facing windows on the lake. In the middle, with a picture-perfect view, were the multiple banks of buttons connected to the telephone that was Poppy's stock-in-trade.

"Boudreau residence," she said into her headset in response to a blinking light.

"Poppy, it's Vivie." Vivian Abbott, the town clerk. "Where *are* the Boudreaus?"

"On their way to see you," Poppy told her.

"I'm leaving in two minutes. If they don't get here before then—Oh, wait! Here they are! Thanks, Poppy!" As fast as that she was gone, and another light blinked.

It was on the main telephone unit, Poppy's private line. "Hello?"

"Is this Poppy Blake?"

She recognized the voice. "That depends."

Terry Sullivan made a sound that might have been a chuckle. "Is your sister around?" he asked nonchalantly.

"Is she?" Poppy asked right back. "Far's *I* know, she's in Boston." The words were barely out when she saw the slight figure of Lily standing on her deck in a baseball cap, a plaid hunting jacket, and baggy shorts.

Poppy sat higher and vigorously waved Lily inside.

"She tried to leave last night," Terry said. "Didn't make it. Or let us think that. I'm trying to imagine what I'd do if I were her."

"And you imagined she'd come here? Why would she do that?"

"By default. Where else would she go?"

"Manhattan? Albany? I don't know," Poppy said. She mouthed his name to Lily, whose eyes registered instant horror.

"Would you tell me if she was there?" Terry asked.

"Not on your life," Poppy vowed, and with the sweep of a finger disconnected the call. She reached out to Lily, grinning broadly. "I had a hunch," Poppy said. Hugging Lily, she felt how much thinner Lily was than when they had seen each other five months before, at Easter.

"You don't look so good," she said. "Beautiful but tired."

Lily's eyes filled with tears.

Poppy held her, thinking that "beautiful" was an understatement. Poppy and Lily looked very much alike—same dark hair, same oval face, same slender build. But Poppy was the best buddy, Lily the siren. Lily was more endowed on top, but she was also quieter, more dignified, more mysterious, which added to her allure.

Poppy had spent a childhood following Lily around, suffering when Lily stuttered, taking pride when she sang. She knew that Lily hadn't asked for a stutter or for the impossible standards Maida had set for her.

"How'd you get away?" Poppy asked.

"A borrowed car. Does Terry Sullivan think I'm here?"

"Not yet."

"They'll come," Lily said, looking haunted. "Sooner or later."

"A few reporters have already. But no one's talking."

"They will. Sooner or later. Someone'll offer money. Someone'll take it." She clasped her hands. "John Kipling saw my lights last night. He pulled up at the dock this morning. He says he won't tell anyone. Can I believe him?"

Poppy liked John. She knew about the ruthless journalist he'd been, but she had seen nothing but decency in him since his return.

"I'd believe him. Besides, what's your choice?"

"I don't have one. They'll follow me wherever I go." Lily looked down. "John told me about today's paper. They're still at it, Poppy."

"You need to talk with a lawyer."

"I did."

"And? Don't you have a case for libel?"

"Yes, but it'll drag the whole thing out. And it'll cost a fortune. He told me to borrow money from Mom."

Poppy might have shared Lily's wry expression if she hadn't been flooded with guilt. Maida had given *her* so much—land, the house, a van equipped with everything she needed to get in and out and to drive herself around. Poppy's problems were physical. Maida could deal with physical things. Emotions were something else.

Lily pulled off the baseball cap. "Is she s-s-still angry?"

Poppy's heart broke at the stutter. It only came out now at times of stress, but she remembered when it was virtually a constant thing. She couldn't begin to imagine the pain Lily must have felt in front of friends, schoolmates, boys. Maida might have helped, but she had always seemed paralyzed where Lily was concerned.

"Be grateful it's harvesttime," Poppy said now. "She's preoccupied with work. Are you going over there?"

Lily looked at the lake. "Think I should?"

"Only if you're a glutton for punishment."

Lily's eyes found hers, beseeching now. "Maybe if I explain it to her—tell her my side of the story."

Poppy wished it was that simple. Maida was a complex woman.

"But what if she hears it from someone else? She'll be hurt."

"I won't tell," Poppy promised.

Lily let out a breath, looking close to tears again. "I thought I could come here and be invisible for a while."

"Is there *anything* I can do?"

Lily's expression was suddenly pointed. "More of what you did just now when Terry called."

LILY left Poppy's feeling marginally better. Wearing the baseball cap and sunglasses, she drove the station wagon back to Celia's the same way she had come—around the opposite end of the lake from the center of town. The less she tempted people with a familiar nose and chin, the better.

She held her breath when she turned onto the road to Thissen Cove, half expecting to find a strange car parked at the cottage. But there were no cars. She drew in beside the cottage and looked carefully around. Then she climbed out and ran to the door.

No one was around. She went from window to window, peering out. When she was certain no one lurked on land, she opened the door to the lake. No threat there. And no sign of John Kipling.

Everything in sight was crystal-clear and serene. She let herself relax, and once she did that, exhaustion hit.

Within minutes she was asleep on the big iron bed.

WHILE Lily slept, John was busy at the plant-and-shrub sale picking up gossip for the *Lake News.* He heard talk about the play that the Lake Henry Players had chosen for their winter drama, talk about the library cat's new litter of six kittens, born behind the biography shelves. Near a large wooden cart filled with pumpkins, he caught talk of the season's bumper crop. But he had little time to jot down any notes before people turned the questions on him.

"Paper says she's hiring that lawyer," remarked Alf Buzzell, director of the winter drama and treasurer of the historical society. "Think there'll be a big TV trial?"

"Beats me," John said.

"How'd they find out about the stutter?" asked the librarian, Leila Higgins. She had been a year ahead of Lily in school.

"They must have seen medical records," John answered.

"But how? Who would have let them see those?"

"There was probably mention of the stutter in the court file."

"But who would have let the public see *those?*" Leila insisted.

John didn't know. He planned to look into it.

From the pumpkin-cart owner came, "I keep wondering if she'll come here." Like the others, he felt no need to identify the "she."

Since there wasn't a question, there was no need of an answer. Grateful to be spared evasiveness, John ran his hand over a rounded pumpkin. He took an appreciative breath. Between the smell of sweet junipers, rich loam, and ripe pumpkin, fall was definitely in the air. It was worth lingering over, but not now. Tucking his notebook into the breast pocket of his flannel shirt, he mingled with the crowd and kept an eye out for media. John knew how they worked. Everyone assumed that strangers passing through town on a Saturday would stop, particularly during foliage season. In the absence of a camera there was no instant way of differentiating a leaf peeper from a reporter. But as John listened to ongoing conversations between unfamiliar faces and locals, he heard nothing untoward.

So he walked across to the police station, where the chief was sitting on the front-porch bench, watching the goings-on with a leg up on the rail and a toothpick sticking out of his mouth.

Willie Jake was nearly seventy. He'd been police chief for twenty-five years, second-in-command for another twenty before that. No one complained that he had slowed down. He still walked straight and still kept his uniform crisp enough to make an impression.

"See anything interesting?" John asked.

"Some," the chief said. "There's a few no-names mixing in out there. They show up elsewhere in town, I'll remembuh."

John didn't doubt it for a minute.

"Think she was involved with the cahdnal?" The chief spared him a quick glance.

"No. I used to know the guy who broke the case. He makes things up. What about you?" John asked, because he had his own agenda. "Do you think she was?"

Willie Jake was looking out at the town again. "Hahd to say. Hahd to know the woman she's become since she left."

"Do you remember the business with my brother?"

Another glance his way. "I put the case togethah."

"Donny said she wasn't at fault. Deathbed confession."

"He wasn't sayin' that at the time. And when they were drivin' around in that cah, she looked to be havin' a grand old time."

"She hadn't done anything wrong before that."

"Dud'n' mean a thing. She was ripe to act up."

"Why?"

"Maida. She was a stiff one. Kids rebel against stiff ones."

"You don't like Maida, do you?"

Willie Jake shrugged. "I like her just fine now. Did'n' like her much then. Not many in town did." He darted John a look. "Did'n' tell that to the reportuh from Rhode Island who came by this morning, though. Did'n' tell him a thing. I don't like outsiduhs snooping around. Don't know what's wrong with you guys. Think you can write whatever you want. Dud'n' matter if it's true."

"Hey," John said, "I'm not the bad guy here. If I were you, I'd be trying to find out who leaked the business about the arrest."

Willie Jake yanked the toothpick from his mouth. "Emma did it." Emma was his wife. She often answered the office phone. "Said someone called from the State House in Concahd tryin' to straighten out files. I called the State House. They did'n' call us. They wasn't straightenin' out any files, but they did get a call on Lily Blake. The clerk who took it bought the line about the calluh bein' a shrink needin' background infuhmation on his patient. Guess is good it was the press."

Guess is good it was Terry Sullivan, John thought.

Lily slept until four in the afternoon. She awoke famished and made an omelette and a salad, which she ate on the porch looking out on the lake. She might not trust John Kipling, but she was surely grateful for his food. Fresh things were better than canned any day.

She sated her hunger but not her mind. She kept thinking about John having ammo and wondering what he meant by that. There was no sign of his boat, which brought her some relief. A second visit would be a dead giveaway she was here.

So did Maida know she had come? Suspect it? John was right. It was only a matter of time before someone else on the lake saw signs of life at Celia's. Then word would spread, and Maida would know. Lily didn't want her learning it from someone else. She would be badly hurt, and that wouldn't help Lily in the least.

Fast, before she chickened out, Lily went into the house, changed clothes, and drove the station wagon out around the lake. It was dark now. Moonbeams slanted through the trees from time to time.

Her heart began to race when she neared the stone wall that marked the Blake Orchards entrance. She turned in and started up the gravel road that cut between acres of stubby apple trees. After half a mile the house loomed in the dark. Only one side of the first floor was lit, but Lily knew the place by heart: its two stories, field-stone front, shingled overhangs, and eaved windows.

Pulling in under the porte cochere, she left the station wagon, climbed the stone steps, opened the door, and slipped into the front hall. Classical music came from the library, a sure sign that Maida was there. Taking a steadying breath, Lily raised her eyes up the winding staircase to the mahogany-railed balcony. The elegance of the hall was impressive.

On her left was the large dining room, with its Chippendale table and chairs. Turning in the opposite direction, she entered the living room. A single lamp was lit there, casting a glow on upholstered sofas and chairs, mahogany tables, an Oriental carpet.

Maida had good taste. Lily couldn't fault her on that. If some in Lake Henry felt that she had decorated the stone farmhouse with more elegance than was appropriate, she had done it well. The best garden, the best apple pie, the best children—Lily had learned at a tender age that the best mattered to Maida.

When Lily's eye fell on the baby grand in the corner, she felt an ache. She had learned to play here. She had felt strong and competent sitting at those ivory keys. She had discovered her voice here.

"I thought I heard a car," Maida said quietly.

Lily's eyes flew to the far end of the room. Her mother was backlit in the library doorway, hands at her sides. "I figured you'd be back," Maida went on. "Poppy was evasive when I asked."

"Poppy didn't know m-m-my plans," Lily said, hating even the small hesitation. She folded her arms on her chest and tried to think of something to say, but all she could think was that Maida looked remarkably good. At fifty-seven, she was slim and stood as tall as her five-five height allowed. Her hair was dark, short, and stylishly cut. She wore jeans and a sweater.

"You look good, Mom."

Maida grunted and withdrew into the library. Lily watched her settle into her chair at the desk. She was shutting Lily out.

Lily debated leaving, her only recourse in the past. Then, though, she'd had things to do and places to go. She had neither now. What she did have was a need to talk to her mother.

Slowly she walked the length of the living room and stood in the doorway to the library, with its shelves of leather-bound classics, part of Maida's fairy-tale show of aristocracy. At the desk Maida looked at the computer screen, then riffled some papers. "Bills," she murmured, sounding resigned. "I'm getting good at juggling, paying a little here, a little there. I thought things'd be better with the season being good and production up, but greater production puts a strain on equipment—it's showing its age." She leveled an accusing stare at Lily. "Your father left me with a mess that keeps me busy dawn to dusk. And then there's the telephone. Calls are pouring in from people wanting to know about you. I don't need those calls."

"I'm sorry," was all Lily could say.

"Poppy takes most of them, but a few sneak by. Do you know what they ask? Do you know what they *know?* The business about the stutter, the business about that no-good Donald Kipling. Do you know how embarrassing this is for me?"

Lily felt a stab of anger. "It's worse for me."

"Welllll," her mother said with a dry laugh, "that's what you get when you play with fire. What was in your mind, Lily? Late-night tête-à-têtes with the cardinal, hugs and kisses. Didn't it occur to you that people might get the wrong idea?"

"Nothing happened."

"Then why did you say you loved him?"

"Father Fran is a close friend. That's what I told the reporter. He took my words out of context. Mom, I didn't ask for this."

"You set yourself up for it," Maida declared. "You let it happen."

Lily was astonished. "What could I do? I denied every allegation. I demanded a retraction. I talked with a lawyer."

"And? What's he doing?"

"I couldn't hire him. He wanted a quarter of a million dollars."

That silenced Maida. Her eyes went to her papers.

Lily was about to say that she wouldn't take the money from Maida even if she had it, when she heard a noise behind her. She turned to see Rose's oldest child, Hannah, coming toward her on bare feet. A huge T-shirt hid her chubbiness. Long brown hair framed her round and serious ten-year-old face.

Lily broke into a smile. "Hi, Hannah!"

Hannah stopped. "Hi, Aunt Lily."

Lily gave her a hug. "What're you doing here so late?"

"She's sleeping over," Maida said in a businesslike voice. "What happened to the movie, Hannah?"

"It was boring. And I heard voices."

"Your aunt and I have to talk. Go on back up."

Hannah shot Lily a quick look before pulling away.

Lily watched her until she had disappeared into the hall. Then she turned back to Maida. "Does she sleep over often?"

"Saturday nights, when Rose and Art go out."

"Where are Emma and Ruth?" They were Hannah's younger sisters, ages seven and six, respectively.

"A baby-sitter. It's easier if Hannah is here." In a lower voice she asked, "Why did the newspaper imply you were hiring that lawyer?"

Lily spoke softly. "The lawyer implied it. But it wasn't only the money that bothered me. He said a lawsuit would take years and that they'd pick at my life even more than they already have."

Maida sat back. "Is there an alternative?"

"The story is a lie. Everyone will know it once the cardinal gets a retraction."

"Smears linger even after the facts come clear. You put yourself in a vulnerable position. A single woman having a close friendship with the cardinal? If you'd been married, this wouldn't have happened. A husband would have given you stability."

"And that would have made a difference?" Lily shot back. "If I was married, they'd have called me an adulteress."

"You should have been married," Maida insisted flatly, done with the argument. "I take it you're staying at Mother's?"

Lily didn't bother to say that the cottage was legally hers. Tired, she simply nodded.

"You'll lead them here, you know."

"Not if you don't let it out. Will Hannah?"

"No."

"She'll tell Rose," Lily said. "Rose will tell Art. Art will tell his mother, and she'll spread it around the mill."

But Maida insisted, "Hannah won't tell Rose. She doesn't tell Rose anything. But other people will notice you're at Mother's."

"Where else can I go?"

Maida threw up a hand. "I don't know. All I know is that I don't want the media nosing around here. Why are you doing this to me? What do you want from me?"

Lily lost it then. Tears sprang to her eyes. "Support," she cried. "Sympathy. Compassion. You're my mother. Why can't you give me those things? What did I ever do to offend you so much?"

Maida looked taken aback, but Lily couldn't stop. "My stutter embarrassed you. It said that one of your children wasn't perfect, but did I ask to s-s-stutter? Do you think I like doing it? I made one m-m-mistake—*one* mistake, with Donny Kipling. Have I burdened you since then? Have I asked anything of you? No. But now I'm asking for understanding. Is that so much?" She was shaking with fury now. "I worked so hard to build a good l-l-life, and they've taken it away, and I don't know why! I don't know wh-wh-why Terry Sullivan did this to me, and I don't know why my own mother can't f-f-feel for me for a change!"

Whirling around, she stormed from the house.

Chapter 5

LILY spent much of Sunday detesting the helplessness she felt. She even reconsidered taking legal action. But reality returned the minute she thought of the emotional price of taking the case to court. She wasn't ready to sign on for that.

What else to do? She wondered again what John Kipling had meant when he said he had ammo. And she wondered whether she could trust him to share it. Still, she knew that he saw the papers each morning. So first thing Monday morning she phoned him.

"You're my link to the outside world," she said in an attempt at levity. "What's out there today?"

"Nothing on the front page," he replied. "The story is on page five. The Vatican cleared the cardinal of suspicion and condemned the irresponsibility of the paper. The *Post* countered by issuing a formal apology to the cardinal. That's it. It was a small piece."

"That's all? No apology to me?"

"No."

She was dumbfounded, then irate. "But I'm the one who's suffered most. I'm the one who's out of work. I deserve an apology, too. What about exonerating m-m-m-me?" she cried. She was as angry as she had ever been. "What about the other papers?"

"Same thing. Small piece. That's it."

Through her fury Lily managed a quick "Thank you" before disconnecting. Then she called Cassie Byrnes.

LIKE many of its neighbors, Lake Henry had a town-meeting form of government. For two nights every March, residents gathered to vote on issues pertinent to town life in the coming year. Every other year they elected a moderator. Since he determined the meeting's agenda, he should have been the most powerful person in town. But it wasn't so. The everyday details of town life were handled by the police chief, the postmaster, and the town clerk. The more weighty matters, like preserving the beauty of the lake and its land, were handled by the Lake Henry Committee.

Cassie Byrnes was in her fourth year as committee chairman. She was the first woman to hold that position, but her selection had been unanimous. Now thirty-five and a lifelong resident of Lake Henry, she had left town to attend college and law school, then returned to hang out a shingle. In the ten years since, she had become something of a local activist.

Lily was waiting on the cottage porch when Cassie pulled up in a compact car that was every bit as worn as Lily's station wagon. Crammed into the back, along with heavy jackets, a hockey stick, and fast-food wrappers, were two child seats.

Cassie was a working mother, but the only frazzle about her was her curly blond hair. As she climbed from the car, she looked fully composed. She wore jeans, a white silk shirt, a blazer, and boots.

"Thanks for coming," Lily said.

Cassie smiled. "We were wondering if you'd come back. Speculation is second nature to Lake Henryites. No one knows I'm here, though." She extended a hand. "It's been a long time."

Cassie had been a year ahead of her in school and light-years more popular. Her handshake now was confident and firm.

Lily led her into the cottage and offered her coffee. They sat in the living room—Lily in the armchair, Cassie on the sofa.

"Have you seen today's papers?" Lily began.

"I have. The Vatican cleared the cardinal, and the *Post* apologized to him but not to you." Her quickness was encouraging.

"But how could I not have been included in an apology? If I was half party to an alleged affair and the other half has been exonerated, how can I be ignored? How can charges be made on the front page and apologies issued somewhere in back?"

"That's how it works," Cassie said in disgust.

Lily swallowed, trying to organize her thoughts. "What's been done to me is morally wrong. But laws have been broken, too. That's what I need to talk with you about."

"You're not working with Maxwell Funder?"

"No." She told Cassie the figure Funder had tossed out.

Cassie rolled her eyes. "He may be giving you a cut rate on his hourly fees, but they're still out of sight." She added, "Court costs aren't much in a case like this. At least not up here."

That was a new thought. "Can I sue in New Hampshire?"

"Why not? The papers in question are all sold here. You've been libeled in New Hampshire as much as in Massachusetts."

Lily took heart. "Libel *is* what it is. They've said things that are lies, and what they didn't say, they implied."

Cassie cautioned, "What they implied will be harder to prove." She took out paper and pen. "Let's start with what they said."

"That I was having an affair with the cardinal, which is not true. And that I was having an affair with the governor of New York."

"Said or implied?"

"Implied, but strongly."

"That's a maybe. Any other direct accusations?"

"That I said I was in love with the cardinal and followed him to Boston."

"Didn't you say those things?"

"Not the way he implied," Lily said. "We were talking about a hypothetical situation. I said I loved the cardinal like so many other people love him. It was generic. And I did follow him to Boston, but only chronologically."

Frowning, Cassie made notes. "Those are all maybes. You said those words. He took them out of context. Happens all the time. The case won't make it to court unless we can prove malice. Do you know Terry Sullivan?"

"No," Lily answered. "He'd been approaching me for a piece he was doing on performers, but I kept turning him down. The first time we did any real talking was at the club the night before he broke the story. But then there's the rest of what they printed," she raced on. "I didn't tell them where I shop or go on vacation. I didn't tell them about the incident here when I was sixteen. Those charges were dropped. The file was sealed."

Cassie made a note on the pad. "Someone leaked it. The problem with the rest—where you shop and vacation—that kind of information is available on the Internet. It shouldn't be, but it is."

Lily was discouraged. "But they broke laws, too. Someone tapped my phone. I heard a click when I was talking to my sister, and that conversation appeared in the paper the next morning."

"For that we lodge a complaint with the state attorney general."

"I don't have much money," Lily said. "I'll give you what I have."

"Hold your money. We'll discuss it as I incur costs." Cassie turned to a fresh sheet of paper. "I want to know everything about your relationship with the cardinal, everything about your talk with Terry Sullivan, everything since the story broke."

Lily talked for an hour. It was cathartic. Her voice rose and fell with emotion. Though Cassie injected an occasional question, she mainly listened and made notes. Finally Lily finished.

Cassie quietly reviewed her notes, then said, "I think you have a case for libel. But there are several issues. A major one is whether, by any stretch of the imagination, you can be considered a public figure. If legal precedent says that you are, a libel case becomes harder to prove. That's when malice becomes the major issue. In any event, the first step is to demand a retraction. It's required by law before we file a suit. We have to give the *Post* an opportunity to respond."

"How long do we give them?"

"A week. They don't need more. Want me to go ahead?"

Lily felt strong with Cassie there, felt empowered. As Poppy had pointed out, it was her life, her work, her name. If she didn't fight for it, no one else would. "Yes," she said. "I want to go ahead."

WHILE Lily and Cassie talked at the cottage, John sat at his desk in his office, his eyes on the foggy lake and his mind on why the *Post* had ignored Lily. It was no sweat off his back; his book would work either way. But the more he thought, the more annoyed he grew. On impulse he picked up the phone and punched out a number.

"Brian Wallace," mumbled a distracted voice. Brian had been John's editor at the *Post.* He continued to be Terry's editor.

"Hey, Brian. It's Kip. How are you doing?"

The voice picked up. "Busy. It never lets up. And you're up there in the sticks. Who'da known a big story would break right in front of your nose."

"It's in front of *your* nose. It happened in Boston."

"But she's from your town. Terry says you're clamming up."

"Terry wanted information I didn't have. And even if I'd known something, I wouldn't have given it to him." John knew Brian would understand. Terry made enemies right and left.

"She isn't up there?" Brian asked.

"If she is, she's hiding out good." The statement wasn't a lie, just misleading. "We're just following the story. Today's was interesting. It isn't often the paper issues an apology. Everyone up here is wondering why Lily didn't get an apology, too."

Brian swore. "Lily Blake should apologize to us. If she hadn't said those things, we wouldn't be embarrassed now."

Not wanting to tip his hand about talking with Lily, John began treading with greater care. "Do you really think Lily Blake said those things? Or did Terry manufacture them?"

"I wouldn't have run it if he had."

"Come off it, Brian. I worked with Terry. It wouldn't be the first time he's fabricated a story."

"Careful. Statements like that can be libelous."

"And what he's written about Lily Blake isn't? The story's false."

"Come on, John," Brian shot back, "do you think we'd have run a story like that without good cause? I watch Terry closely. He'd been telling me about that relationship for weeks, right from the first rumors that Rossetti might be elevated. I told him I wouldn't touch it unless he got more than circumstantial evidence. He got it. I have a tape, John. Lily Blake said those things. I heard it myself."

John hadn't expected that. His mind shifted gears. "Did she know she was being taped?"

"We were told she did. But, hey, we're being cautious. That's why we're not going public with it. But listening to the tape, we had cause to believe the story. No malice was involved. The lady's nuts."

After John hung up, he couldn't stop thinking about the tape. Its existence added a whole new twist to the story. But it was Monday, which meant that the week's *Lake News* was priority one. He had dummied the pages and scanned in photos. Now he had to add meat. But rather than writing the feature he had planned, he found himself in cyberspace, accessing the *Post*'s archives. There had always been grumbling when Terry Sullivan fabricated stories. John quickly located and printed out four such questionables that had appeared during his own final years with the paper. Then he called Steve Baker, an old pal who was still a reporter there.

"Hey, you!" Steve said with pleasure when he heard John's voice. "Your ears must be burning. You're the talk of the newsroom. We're all wondering what you know about Lily Blake."

"Not much," John said. "She left here when she was eighteen, and I left ten years before that. Me, I'm wondering what you all know about Terry Sullivan. Is this another one of Terry's cherries? Did he make it up?"

"That depends on who you ask," Steve said without missing a beat. "The official story is that Lily misled Terry."

"That's the official story. What's yours?"

There was a pause, then a lower "He's been building this story for months. When Rossetti was named archbishop of Boston, everyone knew he was in line to be elevated to cardinal. Terry got busy. It was a fishing expedition. He was looking for anything he could find. Nothing panned out."

"Does he have something against the cardinal?"

"Terry doesn't need something to savage a subject. He's vicious when he smells a good story."

"Okay. But the paper says Terry's work was on the up-and-up. What's the newsroom buzz?"

"Geez, Kip, I'm not exactly unbiased. Terry has stolen good assignments from me."

"The buzz?" John coaxed.

Steve kept his voice low, but it was vehement. "He decided there was a story, only he couldn't find anything incriminating. He was out of time and everything else had fallen through, so he wrote a piece that was half speculation, half imagination. Most of us have met Rossetti. He's a decent, honest, upstanding guy."

"But Lily Blake is quoted as saying it was true."

"Oh, yeah, we know how that works. Ask a leading question, you get a malleable answer."

"Do you know about the tape?"

Steve's voice remained low. "What tape? If there was a tape, you'd have read about it on page one. Did you?"

"What about if he made a tape without her knowing?"

"That's a crime. If the paper knew about it and didn't do anything, they're guilty of aiding and abetting. So the *Post* is in deep. And," Steve hurried on, talking under his breath, "if the *Post* ran a potentially libelous story on the say-so of an illegally gotten tape, I'd say that gives Terry Sullivan the kind of protection he likes."

John agreed. So did two other old media friends he called. Then he called Jack Mabbet, a former FBI agent.

Ten years earlier Jack had been involved in the investigation of a notorious mobster. Terry Sullivan had written a series of scathing articles critical of the investigation and of Jack Mabbet. Jack had been forty-five at the time, with a wife and four children, all of whom had suffered through a public tarring. The mobster was subsequently tried and convicted, with no further mention of Jack Mabbet as a potential G-man on the take.

Jack resigned from the FBI soon after that. It didn't matter that his superiors had total confidence in him; he felt the doubt of his fellow agents. Worse, his family had become known for being related to "that man" and "that case." So they had moved to Virginia, where he became a private investigator.

John had come to know Jack Mabbet in the course of covering cases and had the utmost respect for the man. John had argued with Terry when the incriminating articles were printed, had even argued with the editors, but the situation was like many media ones. Terry hadn't made any libelous accusations. He had simply made suggestions. He had done to Jack what he was currently doing to Lily. John figured Jack would sympathize with her.

"Damn right I'll help," the man said before John had done much more than say that he was looking into the Rossetti-Blake case. "You want information on that jackass, I'll get it. No charge."

They were the magic words. But John wanted to be involved. This was his story, his revenge as much as Lily's. So he and Jack divided up the search. What was he looking for? Anything and everything. He knew surprisingly little about Terry, given that they'd been friends—a relative term, there—for nearly twenty-five years. He wanted little mistakes and big mistakes. He wanted things that didn't add up. Ideally, he wanted a reason why Terry had gone after Francis Rossetti with a vengeance.

Hanging up the phone, John opened a drawer and pulled out notes he'd been writing on Lily, along with a file he had made earlier on her father, George Blake. George was newly deceased when John first returned to town, three years ago. At the time, John had seen him as exemplifying the old-time town families that had made their living off local land. There was a potential book there, hence the file, but the idea had gone stale. Now the file had potential from a different angle.

By all accounts George Blake had been a gentle man, more easygoing than his wife. And then there was Lily, who had overcome a debilitating stutter and made a successful life. So was she easygoing like George? Driven like Maida?

His book would focus on the big picture—the power of the

media to destroy—but he needed detail and depth to make the point. Terry was the way he was for a reason. Same with Lily. The past explained things.

Psyched, he put in a call to Richard Jacobi, a book editor he knew in New York. Richard was at a meeting, but his assistant put John through to his voice mail. John left a short greeting, followed by his number and a request for a callback.

LILY spent the rest of Monday alternately curled in a chair by the woodstove and bundled in a chair on the porch. She remained angry, but for the first time her anger was overlaid by calm. She had a lawyer now, which meant she wasn't quite so alone. Within an hour of their meeting, Cassie had called and read the proposed retraction demand. She faxed it to the *Post* shortly thereafter.

Lily imagined the *Post* editors discussing it, the unfeeling newsroom forced to consider that she was a human being, not a doormat. She liked the idea of Terry Sullivan looking like a fool.

So when would she return to Boston? It occurred to her that she wouldn't rush back. Better to wait a few days, maybe even a week or two. The more distance she put between herself and the scandal, the better. Besides, it was nice being in Lake Henry. There was comfort in the quiet of Celia's cottage, comfort in the lake's serenity. It gave her strength. And hope.

TUESDAY morning, feeling energized, she called John for the news.

"The Yanks won again," he said.

Either he had a weird sense of humor or the news wasn't good. Instinct suggested the latter. "No retraction?"

"No. They got the story wrong from the start, so now they're trying to cover their tails."

"You're being evasive. Wh-wh-what does it say?"

"There isn't an article per se." He paused, sighed, said, "It's an op-ed piece by a columnist, who attributes the scandal to your infatuation with the cardinal."

She was horrified. "They're blaming *me?*"

"I told you. They need a scapegoat."

The energy high Lily had woken with was gone.

"Lily?" he asked gently. "Just so you know, Justin Barr is taking the *Post*'s angle, blaming the scandal on your being unbalanced. But there were many calls in disagreement with that."

That was small solace. Lily hung up, feeling defeated.

By midafternoon she was restless and bored. She needed something to do. So she changed into jeans and a plaid flannel shirt, tucked her hair under a Red Sox cap, wrapped a loose scarf around her neck, and drove into town.

The fog hung heavy on the road as she neared the center of town. With the air raw, few people lingered outside. That gave her extra cover as she drove in broad daylight for the first time since her return. She turned in at the post office, pulled up to the yellow Victorian housing the newspaper office, and parked.

After ringing the bell, she let herself into the kitchen and followed the sound of a voice to the front of the house. A young woman sat at a desk holding the phone to her ear, frowning as she studied something on the desk. It wasn't until she turned to look at Lily that Lily realized this was more girl than woman, and very pregnant.

Seconds later Lily heard footsteps on the stairs, and John appeared at the opposite door. He shot her an uneasy glance, then bent over the girl's desk to see what she was trying to do. Taking the phone from her, he finished getting information for a classified ad.

"There," he told the girl when he hung up. "You did just fine, Jenny. You had most everything we need."

"I have to leave," she said. "Buck's coming at three."

John sighed. "Fine. I'll take it from here."

With surprising agility given the bulk of her belly, the girl slipped past Lily and was gone. Lily looked at the dismay on John's face.

His was a handsome face, she realized—tanned skin, close-cropped beard. She was drawn to his eyes in particular. They were a deep brown, gentle even in frustration.

"I'm trying," he said in a controlled voice. "That girl's gonna need a skill after that baby's born."

Lily hadn't been so long gone from Lake Henry that she didn't remember the cast of characters. "Buck, your cousin?"

John nodded. "Total jerk."

"Is the baby his?"

Another nod. "Poor thing." He glanced at his watch.

"Is this a bad time?"

"No. The paper's supposed to be at the printer at noon tomorrow. If it's a little later, no one'll die."

The kitchen door sounded, then footsteps. When Lily turned fast, fearing that rather than Jenny it would be someone more apt to recognize her, John touched her arm. "Go on up the front stairs," he whispered. "To the top. I'll be up in a sec."

She moved quickly and quietly, turning on the second-floor landing, continuing on to the third. The openness of the place struck her first, then the brightness. There were three desks, each with a computer. More interesting were the walls. One held timeworn maps of the lake and aged photos of the town. Another held newer photos, richer in color, taken on the lake itself, shots largely of loons.

A third wall was black and white, and busy. She approached that one and felt a chill. Here were newspapermen at work, photos taken during John's time in Boston, if the banner on the wall was any indication. There were faces with the very same ardor she had seen in her nightmares. Terry Sullivan's face jumped out at her from one print. But mostly she saw John. He was like the others—tightly wound, frightening, definitely a man to avoid.

"Scary, isn't it?" John said from the door. If he'd known she was coming, he might have rethought the decor.

She glanced at the manila envelope in his hand.

He tossed it on his desk. "Essays and poems from the kids at Lake Henry Academy. I always try to print a few."

She looked at the loon pictures. "Did you take these?"

"Every one," he said with pride.

Lily went from print to print. There were nearly a dozen in all, taken at various times—an adult grooming itself, a pair leaving a smooth liquid trail, a family of adults and their young.

"Are they the same pair of loons?" she asked.

"I think so." He pointed at the short white lines ringing the neck of one bird in each of two shots. "Two different years but the same little break in the line right here. I imagine he has a scar that prevents feathers from growing."

"He?"

"I think. He's bigger. Hard to tell otherwise." He pointed to one of the other pictures. "Also, this was taken last April, my first sighting of the year. See that break in the neck marking? Males typically return before females—to scout for nesting sights. I'm not sure if the female is the same one both years, though. Loons are monogamous through a breeding season, but we don't know whether they mate for life."

He looked down at the top of Lily's cap. It didn't quite reach his chin. Wisps of dark hair—shiny hair—escaped at the neck and at the hole in the back. The bill prevented him from seeing her eyes.

"When I was growing up," she said softly, "there was concern about a decline in the loon population."

When John was growing up, he hadn't given a hoot about loons. He had been gone from Lake Henry by the time the concern had been voiced, but he had read about it since.

"The decline continued," she said. "Eventually people realized that big boats and Jet Skis were taking a toll. Too much noise for loons, too much sediment stirred up—loons rely on clear water to fish. And too much wake—eggs were being washed right out of nests. So Jet Skis were outlawed and boat speed was limited. The loon population rebounded."

Lily looked up, and something inside him flip-flopped. Her eyes were as soft as her voice. He hadn't expected that. He swallowed. "Life's solutions should always be so easy." He couldn't look away. Her face was exquisite.

"They're magnificent creatures. And wonderful pictures."

His heart was beating faster. "Thanks."

Her eyes grew vulnerable. "You said you had ammo. What did you mean?"

For an absurd minute John felt disappointment that business

could intrude. But he said, "Terry Sullivan has a history of rigging stories. It's never been proved, but a lot of people know exactly what he does."

"Do they know why?"

"Ambition. Ruthlessness. Greed. I'm working on malice. The obvious thing is that he concocted the scandal as a personal vendetta. You didn't know him from Adam, so it wasn't against you. Rossetti's personal secretary says *they* didn't know each other. So I'll have to come at it from a different angle."

"I'd have to prove malice in court. I could go through years of agony and still lose."

"Possibly." He sighed. "Do you know there's a tape?"

Her startled look said she didn't.

"He taped your conversation without telling you. That's illegal. It's something to add to the arsenal."

Lily looked crushed. "A tape will show that I did s-s-say those things, only not the way he printed them."

John was thinking that he believed her one hundred percent, when she said, "I met with Cassie Byrnes. We demanded a retraction yesterday. To-d-d-day"—he saw her blink with the stutter, a split second's bid for control—"there's no retraction. Cassie says not to panic, but I'm tired of doing n-n-n-nothing."

Lily was looking at him. Again something turned inside him. He kept thinking about Lily showing up at his office, asking about his ammo, kept thinking that if he helped her out, he could be shooting himself in the foot if the point was to save things for his book. But those soft eyes of hers felt good touching his. So he said, "There's another way to fight Terry. You could turn his own methods back on him. Fight fire with fire."

Her brows arched. "How?"

"Discredit him. Go public with allegations about him."

"I don't know what those allegations are."

"I do."

"And you'd share them?"

Here it was. "I might."

"In exchange for what?"

He thought for a minute. He didn't see why it couldn't work for them both. "Your side of the story."

He was immediately sorry he'd said it. There was the faintest widening of her eyes. "You said you wouldn't."

"I won't without your say-so."

She started for the door

"Lily?"

"I'd rather prove malice," she said, and left.

POPPY'S Tuesday was quiet, thanks in part to the weather. When days were cold, wet, or snowy, many of her clients stayed at home. Dense fog at the end of September had much the same effect.

The quiet also had to do with a slowdown in media calls, which didn't surprise Poppy one bit. Blaming the scandal on Lily had been a ridiculous move. Everyone in town knew that. Lily Blake unbalanced? It was the final straw, a major blow to what little credibility the case had. Poppy guessed that the press knew it, too.

Oh, there was still the occasional halfhearted media call requesting reaction to the story's latest twist. But no such requests came from major outlets, and by late afternoon the only calls that possibly could be related came from Lake Henry's librarian, Leila Higgins, who had seen a station wagon with Massachusetts plates parked outside the *Lake News* office.

Poppy knew whose it was, but she had no idea why her sister was there. So she called Kip. "You had a visitor."

Kip sounded cross. "How'd you know?"

"I got a call about the car. Why was she there?"

"She wanted to say hi," he muttered.

"To you? Try again."

"She was bored."

"And she figured that was the liveliest place to be?"

"Ask *her,* Poppy."

"I will," she said. She ended the call wondering what was stuck in his craw.

LILY SAT CROSS-LEGGED ON HER dock. She had the scarf on, plus a wool cap, a down parka, hiking boots, and mittens. The fog had lifted to allow a near peak sunset to be seen over the lake. The air was dry and cold, but it was a glorious night. The surface of the lake was mirror-smooth, reflecting the moon, the North Star, and even the yellow of autumn birch on the edge of Elbow Island. With the loon silent, the tiniest sough of water against shore could be heard.

A movement westward on the water drew her eye, and at first she thought it was the bird. She held her breath and listened, but it was paddle and canoe, more distinct with each rhythmic stroke. She hugged her knees, watching the canoe cut through the water, a dark sliver in a wedge of moonlight. When it was thirty feet out, the paddle ceased its movement, and the boat glided alongside the dock.

"That's ESP for you," John said. "Hop in."

ESP? Not quite. Lily hadn't been thinking about John.

She unfolded her legs and slid to the edge of the dock. Lowering her feet to the floorboard of the canoe, she shifted her weight. She was barely seated in front of John when he pushed away from the dock and turned the canoe back the way he'd come.

"Where are we going?" she asked.

"To see my loons. They'll be leaving soon. My visits are numbered." His voice turned teasing. "Warm enough?"

She glanced back. He wore jeans and a sweatshirt, with a fleece vest—unzipped. His head and hands were bare.

"I'm not sharing my mittens," she announced.

John hit stride with his paddle, propelling the boat forward with a minimum of sound and effort. Lily raised her head, breathed in the night, and smiled. Much as she loved Boston, it didn't have this. Her visits here over the last sixteen years had been brief and preoccupied. It struck her that she had missed this leisure on the lake.

It also struck her that John knew that and was buttering her up for another bid for her story. If so, he was in for a grand disappointment, particularly if he ruined the night with his voice. But he didn't say a word. Other than the slip of his paddle through the water, they moved in silence.

They had passed a handful of small islands before John stopped paddling and let the canoe glide toward another. It was covered with hemlock and pine. John brought the canoe to a standstill.

Here the lake moved against low-growing brush. John put his mouth to her ear. "The nest was over there." He pointed to a wad of grass in the dark. "The big guy scouted out the spot in late April. His mate was here by the middle of May. By the middle of June there was one egg, the next day a second."

"How did you get pictures of the eggs without scaring the loons off the nest?" she whispered back.

"Caution and a very long lens. I sat here once for three hours waiting for one parent to relieve the other."

There was movement from the island. One bird, then a second glided into a stream of moonlight. Then came a third, a fourth.

She caught her breath.

"The front two are the parents, the rear two the kids."

"The kids are nearly as big as the parents."

"They grow fast," he said.

The loons were swimming down the edge of the island, floating in and out of moonbeams. One of the loons released a long, arching wail.

Lily gasped.

"Wait," John whispered.

Sure enough, an answering call came from the east. The voice was crystal-clear. "One lake over," John whispered.

The Lake Henry loon repeated its call, and the distant bird answered again. The sound of it had barely died when a third call came from even farther east. For nearly ten minutes the three birds called back and forth. Lily had heard night chorusing before but never when she was on the lake. It was totally eerie, totally beautiful.

When the stillness returned, she let out a breath. John remained as quiet as she until the loons swam out of sight.

Still without a word he lifted his paddle and, with a deft combination of strokes, turned the canoe. When he set them moving again, Lily grew melancholy. What they had just seen and heard had pleased her so, but that was it. The beauty of the night, the lake, and the loons was a lush, tight-woven tapestry. By contrast, her life—the life John propelled her back to now—was a lone thread. She felt small and insignificant. Lost. Alone.

When they reached her dock, he was out of the canoe before she could get herself up. He tied the boat to a cleat on the dock and held out a hand. She couldn't feel that hand through her mittens, but she took it and held on tightly as he helped her out of the canoe. She was about to thank him for taking her out, when he put a gentle hand at the back of her waist and began walking her up toward the house—and she felt that hand. Oh, she did. Right through her parka, right through her flannel shirt and the T-shirt under that.

It felt good. It was gentle and supportive. Companionable.

At the bottom of the porch steps she turned. "Th-th-thanks," she said, despising the nervousness, but she didn't know what to expect or whether to trust him, whether he was truly friend or foe.

"Thank you," he said. "I'm usually out alone. That was nice."

He touched her cheek, then turned to go. But in the aftermath of that touch she felt something—a connection, perhaps a germ of trust. It could be real. Or deception. Even wishful thinking.

Not knowing which made it absolutely terrifying.

Chapter 6

JOHN was out on the lake again early Wednesday morning, his mind more filled than it had been in three years. With a dawn mist rising, lake life was muted. He tried to let the stillness of it seep in. But his thoughts hung on Lily the whole way out and back—the feel of her skin when he had touched her cheek. He was attracted to her. That complicated things. He wanted to write a book about her, but she wanted privacy. That put them on opposite sides.

He drove into town for the newspapers. Back home, her call came. "There's nothing today," he said in response to the inevitable question. "Nothing in *any* of the papers."

Cautiously hopeful, she said, "That's okay, isn't it?"

John told her that it probably was, that the story had run out of steam, and that yes, indeed, if the *Post* was going to issue a retraction, it would do so as unobtrusively as possible. But John knew how newspapers worked. Mistakes were rarely admitted.

John had mixed feelings. Lily wanted her retraction, and he wanted it for her, but it was to his own advantage to see the story die. The longer it lingered, the deeper an odd reporter might dig. John wanted the diggings for himself.

THERE were no diggings that day. *Lake News* consumed him from the minute he arrived at the office until two in the afternoon, when he transmitted the last page to the printer.

With six hours free before the finished paper would be ready for pickup, John stopped at Charlie's store for supplies and drove out to see his father. He felt the same heaviness in the pit of his stomach that he always felt approaching the Ridge—a long, broad ledge etched into the hills several hundred feet above the lake. Even now, at foliage time, the place looked bleak. And he felt the same tugging of his heart when he entered his father's house.

The table in front of the sofa was pushed crooked, and a lampshade was askew. The sofa itself was covered with remains of the morning paper. What might have been breakfast—a plate with pieces of egg and torn-up toast—was on the floor.

"Dad?" he called. Scooping up the plate, he went on through to the kitchen. Gus was there, hunched at the table, pressing against a fork with hands that were gnarled and chapped.

"What are you doing?" John asked kindly.

Gus didn't look up. "Straightenin' it out."

John put the plate in the sink, which was otherwise clean. Disconcertingly so. "Have you had any lunch?"

"Wasn't hungry."

John suspected he hadn't had the strength to make anything, and felt a tug inside. He put milk, cream, eggs, and a rotisserie chicken, cut into quarters, into the fridge. He took out half a loaf of bread, opened a can of tuna, and mixed it with mayonnaise. When three sandwiches were made, he refrigerated one for a later meal for Gus. After putting the other two on plates, he poured two glasses of milk and sat down to eat.

"The paper just went to the printer," he said conversationally. "It's a good issue, I think." He took a bite of his sandwich, suggesting Gus should eat, too. "The lead is about new families in town."

"We don't need 'em."

"They need us. That's the point. It's about quality of life."

Gus snorted. "Up hee-uh?"

John knew not to pursue the matter. "Have you followed the story of Lily Blake and the cardinal in Boston?"

"Am I s'posed ta cay-uh?"

"Lots of people do, since Lily's a native."

Gus raised his eyes slowly, insolently.

John weathered his father's state of mind for a minute. Then, because his father wasn't biting at gentle bait, he sharpened it. This was his own need, he knew, but it was a big one. "She was innocent in that business with Donny. You know that, don't you?"

Gus dropped his eyes. It was the only sign that, yes, he did know and, yes, he wasn't proud of it.

"I've often wondered whether things wouldn't have been different if I'd been here," John said. "I might have saved Donny from whatever it was that he felt he needed to do. He was okay before I left. When I was the bad boy, he was the good. Maybe if I'd stayed, he'd have been all right."

"But you'da gone to hell. So I saved one."

"Why me? Why not Donny?"

"She had to have one."

She, John's mother, was happily remarried and living in North Carolina. "But why me?" he asked.

"Ask her."

"I did. A million times." Back then his relationship with his mother had been precarious. He had always suspected she would have preferred to take her youngest, had often suspected that Gus had ruled it the other way around precisely because he knew that. "She always said to ask you. I'm doing that now."

Gus shot him a level gaze. "She wanted outta the marriage. I said fine, go ahead. Jus' leave me the good one, an' she did."

The good one. John was hurt enough to lash back. "Looks like you didn't have much insight." He bit into his sandwich with force. He realized he was getting no further than he ever did. So he changed the subject. "You knew George Blake well, didn't you?"

"I did not. I only weuked f'him once."

John knew that it had been far more than that. Gus had done stonework in both the big house and Celia's, and his stonework was more artistic than stonework had a right to be. John had firsthand knowledge of it. He had watched, albeit from a distance. "What do you think of him?"

"Geawge? Didn't know him. Maida's the one I was dealin' with. Prissy little thing. Cold as a bass outta the lake in Mahch. Somethin' wasn't right about her from the minute she came to town. Too uppity. Always expectin' somethin'. No wunduh the daughtuh's in trouble." His eyes narrowed on John. "She'll be back."

"Lily? You think?"

Gus mimicked him. " 'Y'think?' Whadda *you* think, smaht man? You think she'll be back?"

John wanted to share the secret of Lily's return. But the trust wasn't there. Gus might turn right around and tell the first person he saw. Three years of regular visits, and John still didn't know what made his eighty-one-year-old father tick. He didn't know how a man could send away a son and not care what happened to him, but Gus hadn't called or written once—not on a birthday, not on Christmas.

John didn't know how a man could be as angry and unfeeling as Gus seemed to be. He figured perhaps it had something to do with Gus's being illegitimate, a fact that John had discovered when he was twelve. Angry with his father, John had called him a bastard. Gus had gone all quiet and hard and stalked out of the house. Only then did John learn the truth from his mother.

Illegitimacy, a failed marriage, a lifetime of laying stone and the silence of that lonesome work—these must have taken their toll on Gus. Yet John figured there had to be something softer inside the man, figured that if they saw each other enough, it would come out. So when word came that Gus's heart was failing, John had returned to Lake Henry. He imagined their talking about Donny, about his mother, about stories he had written that made him the most proud. He had imagined finding a father. What he found was a man as hard and unyielding as those long, beautiful stone walls he built.

JOHN had returned to the office and was rereading files, making notes, when Richard Jacobi called from New York. He was interested in the book idea. Several questions later the editor was very interested. He offered John a huge amount of money to settle the deal there and then. No need for an agent, he said. The issue is speed and surprise. "I can get your book out in six months. I can publish it well. You *know* the reputation of this house."

What John knew was that the house was small but hungry. When it aimed at the best-seller lists, it often hit its mark, and the advance being offered John was large enough to suggest that his book might be another big one.

He hung up the phone feeling breathless. Richard wanted an outline and introductory chapters as soon as possible. That meant organizing his thoughts fast.

LILY left the cottage and drove around the quiet end of the lake. She took the wide road that led up the hill toward Maida's. But she soon turned off onto another road. Rose lived there with her husband, Art Winslow, and their three daughters.

The house was a dozen years old, built as a wedding gift from the senior Winslows to complement the gift of the land given by the senior Blakes. It was a smaller version of Maida's—the same fieldstone, the same porch, the same eaves. Lily thought it a beautiful house. It was particularly so now, with gaslights framing the drive and lighting the porch.

Lily had timed her visit so that she would arrive after the children were in bed. It wasn't a visit she wanted to make, but there was danger in Rose's finding out from someone else. Coming in person seemed the decent thing for Lily to do.

She knocked softly. A minute later the heavy oak door was drawn open by her brother-in-law.

That Art Winslow was far gentler than Rose might have been a problem if he had been anything but a Winslow, but his family owned the mill, which gave him a vehicle for authority. That meant he could take a back seat to Rose at home, which was the only reason Lily could figure why the marriage worked.

Art was clearly surprised to see her, which meant neither Hannah nor Maida had told Rose that she was back.

"Come on in. *Rosie?*" he yelled, then explained to Lily, "She's with the girls."

"I thought they'd be asleep. M-m-maybe I should come back another time. I'm lying low. I hate to ask them to keep a secret."

"They *love* keeping secrets," Art insisted.

The foyer light suddenly came on. In that instant Rose spotted Lily. Both of them stopped short. Same dark hair, same pale skin, same ample figure—to Lily, looking at Rose was like looking at herself in the mirror.

"Well, hello," Rose said, coming to stand beside her husband. "The prodigal daughter returns. When did you get back?"

Lily considered lying, but said, "Saturday."

"And you're only now coming here? This is Wednesday."

"I'm in hiding."

"Does Mom know? Poppy?"

"Yes."

Rose let out a breath and said a hurt "Thanks a lot."

Three faces were at the door.

"Come say hi to your aunt Lily," Rose said.

The girls straightened and ran forward—six-year-old Ruth first, with seven-year-old Emma on her heels. They were adorable little girls, with dark curly hair and sweet little flowered nightgowns. Hannah, in the same kind of oversized T-shirt she had worn at Maida's, looked chubby and plain beside them. Lily held out an arm to her. "It's good to see you, Hannah. I like your T-shirt." She studied the cat on the front. "You don't have one, do you?"

"Forget a cat," Rose said. "I have enough trouble keeping *her* groomed."

"A cat grooms itself," Hannah said.

"Cats shed. Do you want cat hair all over you?"

Lily was sorry she had mentioned it.

Art said to the little ones, "Show Aunt Lily your teeth."

They opened their mouths wide to show gaps.

"Impressive," Lily said. She squeezed Hannah's hand. "Boring for you. You've been through this."

"Speaking of teeth"—Rose looked at the younger two—"go brush. Daddy'll watch. I need to talk with Aunt Lily."

"What about Hannah?" cried Ruth.

"Hannah doesn't need watching," her mother replied. "She's ten. I can't yell at her for everything. Her teeth are her responsibility."

Art corralled the two little ones. Hannah stayed beside Lily.

"Did you finish your homework?" Rose asked Hannah, and, when she nodded, said, "Go on up, then, and read."

Lily hugged her. "I'll see you another time." She watched the girl plod up the stairs, sensing an ache there.

Rose leaned against the wall. "I should have realized you were back. Mom's been in a foul mood. She's been in a foul mood since this whole thing began. Newspaper headlines, pictures, phone calls. She's convinced everyone is talking and watching. It makes her nervous. And when she's nervous, she takes it out on me. Who else? I'm the one who's here all the time, taking care of her."

"She's self-sufficient."

Rose sputtered out a laugh. "Not as much as she thinks. Fine, she runs the business, but she's not getting any younger. She should be relaxing. Traveling." The phone rang. "Enjoying her grandchildren."

"Wasn't Hannah over the other night?"

Rose shot her a look. "Hannah is not a child one enjoys."

"How so?"

"She's ornery." The phone rang again. "Headstrong. Fat."

"She isn't fat."

"She's on her way."

"She'll slim out. She has a beautiful face."

The phone rang again. *"Get that, Art?"* Rose yelled, then, "What if the press follows you here? Mom will flip out." She looked around when her husband trotted down the stairs.

"That was Maida," he told her. "Two of the Quebecois were doing night work in the meadow when the backhoe bucked and overturned. She called an ambulance. I'd better go up."

"I want to go, too," Rose said.

"I'll stay with the girls," Lily offered.

"They're in bed," Art said, handing Rose her sweater. "They won't even know we're gone."

"We'll be fine," Lily said, and softly shut the door after them.

AS ACCIDENTS went, this one was not too bad. Neither worker was seriously injured, though both suffered enough broken bones to count them out for the rest of the harvest. That was why Lily rose at dawn the next morning, put on jeans and her warmest layers, and drove around the lake again. She went up Maida's road, turned right after the big house, and followed the road around a bend to the cider house, a squat stone building covered with ivy. The insides had been gutted and rebuilt twenty years before to shore up the structure and allow the addition of new equipment.

The instant Lily slipped into the house, she was enveloped in the sweet smell of apple. She had come here often as a child, intrigued by the cider press. By the time she was sixteen and big enough to help, she was too busy with music and school. Besides, her father believed that the orchard was man's work.

She pictured him now, larger than life in a long rubber apron and high rubber boots, scooping apples through the water in the wash bin toward the lift that took them up to the chopper.

"Oh, my," came a voice from behind, and Lily turned to the startled face of Oralee Moore. Oralee was Maida's foreman. Tall and sturdy, with wiry gray hair, she had to be nearing seventy.

Lily liked Oralee, who had always had a kind smile for her, as she did now. But Lily's gaze moved to the young man on her heels.

In that instant Lily realized what she'd done. Oralee wasn't a concern; she was loyal and discreet. But the young worker behind her was only one of many who would see Lily in the course of a day here. Her secret would be out.

After an initial moment of panic she suddenly relaxed, surprised to realize she wasn't sorry. She was in Lake Henry. She had been born and raised here. She was tired of hiding. Besides, it was done.

Oralee waved the young man into the cider house. "This is Bub. He's from the Ridge."

Bub was tall, solid, and not a day over eighteen. He made such a point of not looking at Lily that she knew that he knew just who she was. Leaving them, Lily went outside to wait for Maida.

It was the coolest morning yet. A fine sheen of frost lay on the grass. Each breath Lily exhaled was wispy and white.

Maida came into sight then, rounding the bend, walking up from the main house with her head bowed. She was nearly upon Lily before she looked up, startled.

"You're shorthanded," Lily said. "I can help."

Maida paused, said nothing, and Lily feared she might refuse her help. The verdict remained in doubt until Maida stepped forward and held the door open for her.

The machines were already warming up—the whirlpool bath, the conveyor belt, the grind, the press chugging away. Maida wore the rubber apron now and seemed fully in control.

Lily traded her jacket for a hooded oilcloth slicker, put on boots and long rubber gloves, and climbed up to stand opposite Bub on the platform beside the press. She went right to work. She had never done this before, but she had watched the process hundreds of times as a child. Bub picked up a latticework rack three feet square and set it in place between them. A nylon cloth was draped over it, with the corners left hanging down. When the first apples came through the grind into the large funnel above, Bub shifted a lever, and mash fell to the cloth. Lily folded the left corner of the cloth up over the mash, waited while Bub folded over his left corner; then she folded her right corner over and Bub folded his. While he smoothed the cloth, she picked up the next rack and placed it on top of the folded parcel. Bub spread a second cloth there, then pulled the lever. More mash splattered down. They alternately folded over the four corners of cloth, straightened the packet, added another rack and cloth, and let more mash fall.

The pile of racks and cloths grew. When there were eleven in all, they capped the whole stack with a spare rack, then pushed the pile onto runners until it was centered under the large iron press. Bub tightened the stacks, and Maida shifted a lever to start the stacks rising. In no time, juice was seeping from the cloth, spilling down the sides of the racks to the reservoir below.

Lily lost count of the number of stacks they built, pressed, and broke down. At one point Maida started the pump that moved the cider from the reservoir to the large refrigeration unit at the far end of the room. At another she used a walkie-talkie to call for more apples. At yet another she hosed down the concrete floor.

No amount of washing, though, could erase the heady smell of fresh apple and sweet juice. The memories Lily had carried with her since leaving Lake Henry were mostly negative. But now she was remembering things like sitting with Poppy and Rose in this room, scrunched up in a corner, chomping on apples.

By the time Maida called a midmorning break, Lily was too pumped up to be tired. She washed off her oilskins and went down to the main house.

The morning paper was on the large wood table in Maida's kitchen. Feeling the beginnings of a knot in her stomach, Lily skimmed through it. There was nothing there.

She went to the phone and called Cassie. "We give them a week,"

Cassie said before Lily could ask. "Then we file suit for defamation of character."

Filing suit meant a trial, which would take forever. From the start Lily hadn't liked that idea. For the first time now, with her name absent from the Boston papers for two days in a row, she wondered if it might be better to just let the whole thing die.

Then again, if she was destined to be stared at each time she left the apartment, or followed each time she went to work, she couldn't return to Boston. Her choice would be filing suit, starting a new life incognito somewhere else, or staying here.

So it was good that orchard workers would see her and spread the word that she was back. She needed to know where she stood.

JOHN was in the office after lunch when Armand called. Excitement livened his raspy voice. "Lily Blake's back in town. You ought to get yourself over there and do an exclusive."

John was startled. He hadn't heard about a leak. "The paper's just come out. There won't be another one for a week."

"Yes, well, we'll do a special supplement. I'll pay for it."

"What's to put in a supplement? A rehash of what everyone else has been printing? What's new in the story?"

"She's back," Armand bellowed. "That's news. People in town will want to know why, for how long, where she's staying."

"Everyone in town will know that before the day is out."

"If you don't interview her, someone else will. Come on, John. What's your *prob*-lem? She's *our* girl. This is *our* story."

"Bingo. She's our girl, and we protect our own. Our story should be that there is no story."

John hung up feeling duplicitous on two counts. The first involved Armand and what might indeed have made a good story for *Lake News*. The second involved Lily. John liked and admired her. And the more he admired her, the worse he felt about exploiting her for his book.

So he took the fighting mood and focused on Terry Sullivan. On one side of his computer he put the list of tips that he'd gotten from

Jack Mabbet, the P.I. On the other side he put his growing file. Logging on to a database, he used Terry's current address to call up his Social Security number, two bank account numbers, four credit card numbers, and ten other places of residence in four states over a period of twenty-three years.

John studied the ten. The three most recent were in the Boston area—a total of four moves in twelve years. That didn't raise any flags. Seven in the previous eleven was a little stranger.

The first two were college apartments. The next two were in Connecticut—one in Hartford, one in a nearby suburb. They covered the four years immediately following college, when Terry had freelanced for several local papers. He moved to Rhode Island when he was offered his first staff position. During the five years he was there, he lived at three different addresses within commuting distance of Providence.

John tried to think of all the reasons a man would move so often. He knew that Terry hadn't been able to get along with landlords, neighbors, roommates. Psychotic? Schizophrenic? Possibly. It was also possible he was mentally fit but simply driven by private demons. John was wondering what those might be, when the phone rang. "*Lake News.* Kipling here."

"Kip!" It was Poppy. "Terry Sullivan's calling for you. Do you want to take it?"

For a second John felt guilty, as if Terry knew exactly what he'd been doing and thinking. Then he realized it couldn't possibly be so. "I'll take it," he told Poppy. Seconds later, more coolly, he said, "What's up, Terry?"

"I hear she's back."

John chose his words with care. "I haven't heard that."

"Can you confirm it, yes or no?"

"I can't confirm it," John said. "Why are you asking? The story's done. You've been proved wrong."

"No. I stand by my story. Did you know Lily was married?"

John was silent a second too long.

"You didn't know," Terry gloated. "It was a quickie, the summer after her freshman year in college. The guy was a senior. They were both studying in Mexico. A month after they got back, she had it annulled. I have proof, John."

"And what are you going to do with it?" John asked in disgust. "Because a quickie marriage years ago has no relevance to anything or anyone now."

"That remains to be seen," Terry said.

John felt a sudden sharp loathing. "Don't even try," he warned. "You've done her harm enough. It was wrong the first time, arguably libelous. Do it this time, and I'll go after you myself."

JOHN spent the night thinking about Lily. By dawn he felt a need to see her. Knowing how early she would be leaving the cottage if she were working with Maida again, he threw on the nearest clothes, grabbed a down vest, and drove down the road to Thissen Cove. The station wagon was still parked beside the cottage.

He crossed over the pine needles to the porch and knocked.

When Lily opened the door, she looked frightened—and disheveled enough to suggest that he had woken her up. She was in her nightgown."Has something happened?" she asked.

"Uh, no. I mean, I don't know. I haven't seen the paper." He swallowed. "Can I come in for a minute?"

She ducked out of sight and returned wrapped in a shawl. When he was inside, she closed the door and crossed to the kitchen. She put an old-fashioned coffee percolator under the faucet.

Feeling oddly inept, John stood with his hands on the back of one of the kitchen chairs. "I'm sorry. I didn't mean to wake you. I figured you might be going to the cider house again."

She scooped coffee. "Oralee has to go to the dentist, so we're not starting till nine." She put the percolator on the stove, then turned. "What's happened?" Her eyes held his.

"Terry Sullivan called. He said you were married once. It's really none of my business—" he began.

She didn't blink. "It's true." She slipped into the nearest chair. "I was studying art in Mexico the summer after my freshman year.

Brad was a senior. I thought I was in love. I'd been so lonely that first year at college that it seemed the perfect thing. We had fun those six weeks. Getting married was part of it. The fun ended the day we got back. He said he loved someone else."

John saw hurt, embarrassment. "So you had it annulled."

"I paid a lawyer to do that, but there was no need. The ceremony wasn't legal. Brad knew it all along. I felt like a fool."

"Does anyone here know?"

She shook her head. "We did it two days before the summer semester ended. He said we should keep it a secret for a while. That was fine with me. I was afraid of what my parents would say about the rush. Then it didn't matter."

She stopped, waiting. It didn't take a genius to hear the question she wasn't asking.

"I won't tell," he vowed.

She didn't look assured. "What about Terry? Will he tell?"

"Not so soon after the apology. He'll lie low for a while."

"Then what?"

"That depends. If we have dirt on him, he'll be neutralized. No one will listen to what he says."

The coffee began to perk, and Lily lowered the flame. The smell of coffee began filling the room. When it was ready, she poured him a cup. Five minutes later he had a refill. By the time he left the cottage to head into town, he was feeling wide-awake but mellow.

It wasn't until he was in the Tahoe again that guilt set in. Lily's early marriage spoke of a craving for love and affection. It helped flesh out the picture of who she was. But if he included it in a book about the invasion of privacy, he would be invading Lily's privacy even more.

LILY didn't trust John. She liked him, but she wasn't taking chances. When she called him thirty minutes after he left the cottage, it was just for the news.

"Nothing," he said with frustration. "No retraction, no apology."

"They're just dropping the story, leaving me the bad guy?"

"They're trying."

Lily considered calling Cassie, but she knew Cassie couldn't do anything yet. Besides, Lily had to get to work.

So she drove to the cider house and let herself get lost in the smell of fresh apple mash and the rhythm of the machines. She did love the work. Though rote, it demanded attention, and the remaining morning hours passed quickly. Come lunchtime, Lily headed for town. She didn't bother with a disguise this time. The town knew she was back. Indeed, she turned heads as she drove down Main Street. Angry enough, defiant enough, she smiled and waved.

She turned in at the *Lake News* office. She had barely set the brake when John came out of the yellow Victorian. Head down, he was sifting through keys. He looked up, startled to see her.

She rolled down her window. "I need help," she said when he came closer. "Can we talk?"

He rounded the wagon, slid into the passenger's seat, then faced her. "I'm all yours."

She might have smiled if she hadn't felt so driven. "I want to fight. How do I do it?"

"Fight Terry? Dirty?"

"Well, Cassie's doing it clean, but I'm tired of sitting and waiting. What are my options?"

"That depends. Are you talking about revenge?"

"Let's call it justice."

He smiled crookedly. "Whether you call it justice or revenge, there's a right and a wrong way to do it. Want instant gratification? I'll give you a list of questionable articles Terry's written. You call a press conference and lay them out. Bingo, public embarrassment."

"Is that what you'd do?"

He shook his head. "I think fabricating stories is the tip of the iceberg. There were four separate instances of alleged plagiarism in college. My source has copies of reports stating that. Other sources may produce other instances. Clearly, the more we dig up, the stronger our case. But digging takes time. You have to decide how instant the gratification has to be."

"Not instant. But not long. This is humiliating. Terry conned me into trusting him. I can't be the only one who fell for that."

"No. I'd lay money on there being others. I'd also lay money on there being something wrong with his personal life."

"I want to know why he went after me."

"I want to know why he went after the cardinal," John added, and Lily knew then that they were thinking alike. Was she making a deal with the devil for this?

If so, he was a handsome one—square jaw, trim mustache and beard, hair that fell over his brow and looked great even with receding temples. His eyes were a warm cocoa. They invited trust.

"Is the price the same?"

He met her gaze. "Yes."

So much for warm eyes. "My story."

He nodded. "An exclusive."

"For the paper?"

"No. I want to do a book on the media versus an individual's right to privacy. What's happened to you is an example of things run amok. Your case would be the focus. Media dysfunction is a hot topic right now. I could have a book published by summer."

"If I cooperate, I'll need honesty. And veto power," she added.

"You don't want the marriage coming out?"

"No."

"Anything else?" he asked.

She said, "I don't know. I'll tell you as I go. It's the best I can do. How bad do you want that best seller?"

The look in his eye suggested a whole other story behind the question. "You can't talk with anyone else."

"I wasn't about to. I'm not a talker."

He smiled. "You do fine when you want to make a deal."

LILY was reinvigorated. Upon returning to work, hidden again under rubber coverings, she worked deftly, positioning racks and folding cloths. Her heart pulsed in time with the gears of the press, steady and rhythmic, purposeful now.

Maida directed the work through the midafternoon break, but when it came time to transfer cider from the refrigerator unit to the bottling station, she left Oralee in charge. When two hundred gallons of fresh cider had been bottled and sent off to the warehouse, Lily went down to the main house. She found Maida in a rocker on the porch, looking pale.

"Are you all right?" she asked.

"Tired. Accidents take a toll."

"How are the men?"

"Fine. The backhoe isn't. I'll need a new one."

Lily leaned against a post and looked out over the orchards. The apple trees were a muddy green, drab in comparison to the vibrant foliage down by the lake, but there remained a lushness. They were squat and full. "How is the yield this year?" she asked.

"Oh, it's good. But costs are rising more than profit. I worry sometimes, not that any of you girls want the business. There are times when I wonder why I work myself to the bone. I'll die, and the business will be sold. I should have had a son."

Lily had heard that before. It had always made her feel doubly guilty for who and what she was. But, Lord, she was tired of feeling that way. Sharply she asked, "Why didn't you?"

"I put in an order, but it came through wrong." There was actually humor in Maida's voice, in her eyes.

"You could have tried again," Lily said more gently.

Maida smiled, shook her head. "I'd had trouble carrying Rose. They suggested I leave it at that. So I had my girls."

Lily felt a whisper of warmth. It wasn't the words but the way Maida said them. There was satisfaction, even peace. It was uncharacteristic and welcome.

A clamor came from around the corner of the house, footsteps on the gravel, breathless little laughs. Rose's youngest daughters appeared, kicking up their heels as they ran. Rose and Hannah came at a more sensible pace in their wake. Looking at Rose, Lily marveled at the strength of certain genes. She and her sisters looked just like Maida.

Rose climbed the porch steps and set a large pot on the rail. She turned to Maida. "I made a chicken stew. It should last you several days. How do you feel?"

"I'm fine."

"Were you sick?" Lily asked.

"She gets headaches," Rose answered. "From tension."

"No," Maida said. "From eyestrain. I need new glasses."

"There's a good optometrist in Concord," Rose said. "We thought Hannah needed glasses. The teacher said she was squinting. Thank goodness it was a false alarm."

"I wouldn't have minded," said Hannah, who sat quietly on the stairs while her sisters ran on the grass.

"You'd look awful with glasses," said Rose.

"Movie stars wear glasses. They look cool."

"You wouldn't have," Rose told her, then turned in dismay to Maida. "She argues with everything I say."

Lily thought it might be the other way around. "Actually," she said to Hannah, "you'd look good in a pair of those wire-thin ones."

Rose waved a hand. "Her eyes are fine, thank the Lord. She's only ten."

"Almost eleven," Hannah said. "My birthday's in a week."

Lily smiled. "Are you celebrating?"

Rose said, "That's a whole other bone of contention. She wants a party. I wouldn't even know who to invite."

"I would," said Hannah.

"Who? Melissa and Heather?" To Maida she said, "These are the only names I hear. This is not a girl with a large circle of friends. I don't see the point of throwing a party for three girls."

"I do," Lily said. Her heart was breaking for Hannah. It was bad enough that Rose was thinking those things, worse that she was saying them in front of the child.

Rose turned to her. "Fine. You throw the party."

Lily was good for the challenge. "I'd like that." She held out a hand to Hannah. "Walk me to my car. I need to know what kind of party you want."

It struck Lily that she might be worsening the situation between Hannah and Rose, but someone had to give the child a boost. She closed her hand around Hannah's. Passing Maida, she said, "I'll be here Monday morning."

Maida seemed startled, but not by Lily. Her eyes were on Rose.

THAT night Lily sat in a pine-root cubby at the edge of the lake thinking about the upheaval in her life. Maybe it was working at the cider house. Or planning a birthday party with Hannah. Or hiring Cassie. Or dealing with John. Maybe it was simply the passage of time. But the shock was over. She didn't feel as lost as she had.

It was a beautiful night. A robust moon hung over the center of town, making an elegant white wand of the church steeple before shimmering gently out over the lake and its islands. Softly the lake brushed the shore. The air smelled of woodsmoke.

She waited, listening intently, but didn't hear a loon. So she began humming her own song, a Celtic chant that captured the haunting quality of the lake at night. She hugged her knees and rocked gently, feeling a deep reverence as she sang. She felt connected to this place. She felt peaceful here. Content.

Chapter 7

JOHN spent a good part of Saturday at the office, working on next week's paper. Mostly, though, he researched Terry Sullivan.

With the windows open, the office smelled of the candied apples that the garden club was making in a huge pot hung over a wood fire, part of the crafts fair set up in the town center. The weather was perfect—cold enough to set the candy coating, warm enough for people to linger. He might have gone down there himself if he hadn't been intrigued by the information coming up on his screen.

He moved from one link to the next and made phone calls in between. Quitting at seven, he drove home. As the sun set over the woods, he was drawn to the lake. Pulling on an old sweater, he unbeached his canoe, picked up the paddle, and shoved off.

He had barely reached the island where his loons swam, when they emerged from the shadows. The two juveniles were there, but only one parent. He guessed that the other was out visiting and would be back. The adult that remained was duller in color than it or its mate had been even two days before. The more vibrant the leaves, the less vibrant the loons. It was one of nature's sad quirks. Soon the leaves would wither and the loons would be gone.

John wasn't looking forward to winter. He loved skiing, snowshoeing, ice fishing. Still, winter was a lonely time of year.

Moving his paddle through glassy water, he backed away, turned the canoe, and set off for Thissen Cove. By the time he reached it, the sun had dropped behind the west hills, and the shadows along the shore were more purple than blue. Thirty feet out from shore, he let the canoe drift, then waited for a sign. He got three.

First came a light in Lily's window. Second came the call of a loon. Third came a song.

LILY had never been much of a cook. As a child, she had stayed out of the kitchen to avoid Maida. As an adult, she hadn't cared enough about eating to prepare more than perfunctory meals. Now Lily had the kitchen, the time, and the desire to cook.

Celia had left a notebook filled with recipes, and Lily made two of her grandmother's favorites, both appropriate to the season. One was sweet-corn chowder. The other was corn bread made with newly picked corn plus cornmeal, eggs, butter, maple syrup, and walnuts.

Between the chowder and the bread the smell of the cottage was heavenly. And when the call of a loon came through the open window, it struck Lily that she could do a lot worse on a Saturday night.

She sang while she stirred the soup and while she took the corn bread from the oven. Humming, she set the table with a pretty woven mat, picked the soup bowl and a plate that she liked best from

Celia's collection, gathered three candles from other parts of the cottage, and lit them. Singing softly again, she opened a bottle of wine. She was filling a wineglass when she heard a knock on the door.

Her singing stopped abruptly, and she held her breath.

Then came a voice through the open window, a familiar face peering at her through the screen. "It's just me," John said.

Relieved, she pulled open the door.

"Sorry. I didn't mean to scare you."

Her heart kept pounding, but she figured that was a side effect of facing someone this tall and good-looking. She tucked her hands into her jeans. "What's up?" she asked, but he was looking past her to the table.

"Uh-oh. I've come at a bad time."

She laughed. "Not really. It's just a party for one."

"Some party." He inhaled loud and long. "Whatever you've cooked smells incredible."

"Have you eaten?"

"No. But I don't crash parties."

With a chiding look she waved him in. She set a second place at the table, then cut the corn bread into squares and dished out the chowder while John stood in her living room and looked around. She filled another wineglass, pleased with herself.

"Are you taking notes?" she asked.

"Not for my book," he promised, approaching the table. His eyes were wide. "Do you always eat this way?"

"No. I'm not a cook. Eat at your own risk."

"Anything that smells this good can't possibly be bad." He pointed to the place setting nearest him. "Want me here?"

She had barely nodded, when he ran around the table and pulled out the chair for her. She was impressed. Given his excitement, she wondered when he'd eaten his last square meal.

He circled to his own chair, settled in, and put the napkin on his lap. Then he looked at the stove. "I didn't ask if you had enough."

She smiled. "I have enough for ten other people."

He grinned, then grew serious and touchingly sincere. "Thank you. I didn't expect this when I headed over here. I was just out on the lake checking up on my loons, and before I knew it, I was hearing you sing. You have a beautiful voice." He lifted his wineglass. "To your voice."

"Thank you." She let the wine warm its way down her throat. "I've missed singing. It struck me tonight how long it's been."

"You've had other things on your mind."

For several minutes they ate in silence. Since the loons had stopped singing, Lily slipped away from the table and put on a CD. It was a Liszt kind of night—a major-key mood for a change. She was marveling at that as she returned to the table.

"The cottage is great," John said.

She looked around. "It could use a piano. I have one in Boston. I miss it." She held his gaze. "So when can I have it back?" The answer, of course, had to do with restoring her name.

"Are we talking business here?"

"I guess. Have you found anything?"

"Yes. I just don't know what it means." He took a bite of corn bread. "I now know that Terry drives an eight-year-old Honda and has a spotty registration record. He has a problem with parking tickets and speeding tickets. He's also been married three times."

"How old is he?"

"My age. Forty-three. I know what you're thinking—plenty of guys my age have been married three times."

No. Lily was thinking—wondering—whether John had been married at all.

"The odd thing here," he went on, his eyes a deeper brown, "is that no one knew he was married. I mean, no one. The first happened when he was in college. Terry and I were classmates, but I didn't know about a wife. I called two other people, and neither of them knew. He was married the second time while he was in Providence. The third time was in Boston. Blowing three marriages is one thing. The fact of no one knowing about any of the three is another thing. I'd say that's bizarre."

"Do you have the names of the women?"

John nodded. "My next step is contacting them."

By the time John had gone through seconds of chowder and corn bread, Lily was tired of speculation about Terry Sullivan and curious about John. She heated apple cider, then filled mugs and led him out to the porch. They sat on the steps, looking at the lake, sipping cider, and she was aware of him, of his hands holding the mug.

"Tell me about you," she said.

"What do you want to know?"

She wanted to know if he was honest, if he would put his own interests before hers, if she could trust him. But if she wasn't sure about trust, the answers would be meaningless. So she asked, "Terry's been married three times. What about you?"

"I was in a long-term relationship once. Marley and I were together for eight years. She would say we came close to getting married. I wouldn't."

"Why not?"

"She didn't like my hours."

"Didn't she work?"

"She was an ad executive. Her hours were worse than mine. Plus Marley wouldn't have appreciated Saturday mornings in the center of town. She wouldn't have appreciated loons. She wasn't a person who liked to relax. I do."

Lily asked, "Did you come back here because of your father?"

"Yeah." His voice was quiet. "We have unfinished business, Gus and me."

"Are you getting it finished?"

"Not yet. He's a tough nut."

Lily knew about those. Maida was another. She shivered, then felt the weight of John's sweater settle on her shoulders. The warmth felt good. She looked up and smiled. "Was that because you're a nice person or because you want to get on my better side?"

"Both. I haven't had a dinner like that in years."

"Soup and bread? It was barely dinner."

"Thick chowder, sweet-corn bread, mellow wine, and a beautiful woman—it was, too, dinner."

Lily turned her head sideways. His features were barely lit, but he saw a smile. It warmed her deep inside. She looked down. His knees were inches from hers.

As she was wondering what he might do next, he said, "I'd better go." Before she could object, he was off the porch and heading for the lake with purposeful strides.

She thought to call out, *Here's your sweater* or *Don't leave yet.* But she didn't move, didn't speak. She sat there embraced by his scent, and watched the canoe leave her dock.

HOW to sleep, thinking about that? How to sleep with a whole new realm of possibility suddenly opened up?

Lying in bed that night, Lily felt lonely. The sweater didn't help. It lay on a chair, smelling of John. She fell asleep frustrated, and the next morning awoke confused. She didn't know whether to trust him. She didn't know whether to mix business with pleasure. She didn't know whether to add a complication to her life at a time when there were so many others.

So seeking a measure of peace, she decided to go to church.

A measure of peace—it sounded simple. But showing up at Lake Henry's First Congregational Church on Sunday morning meant being seen. But it was time to break the ice.

Nervous but determined, she drove to church, parked, and went in. The foyer was empty of people but not of sound. There were organ chords, then the choir singing "Faith of Our Fathers," and suddenly a world of memory opened up, images of Sundays, when she had sung in the choir herself. She had loved doing that.

Taking a shaky breath, she passed through the foyer and stood at the meeting-hall door. Row after row in the large room was filled, but she spotted a small space on the aisle in the next-to-last pew. She slipped in and sat with her fingers laced in her lap and her head down. She didn't need to look to know that her mother would be with Rose and the Winslows in the fourth pew on the right or that other Lake Henry families would be glancing her way.

So she concentrated on the sounds of the organ, the hymns, the choir, the responsive readings. She didn't participate, but she listened to every word. From the pulpit came talk of charity, forgiveness, and love. She focused on the minister's voice, wiping frustration and confusion from her mind for this little while at least.

She slipped out of the church before the benediction. The sense of calm was joined by something else, something unexpected—the sense that for those few moments, sitting quietly with the rest of Lake Henry, she had belonged to a community.

ON MONDAY morning, before leaving for the cider house, Lily called Cassie. There was no retraction in the day's paper, and the week was up. Cassie promised that she would have a suit filed by the end of the day, but Lily was deeply disappointed. She had been praying for a faster resolution. She needed to move on.

The rhythm of the cider press was more welcome than ever. Lily lifted, pushed, pulled, and folded, even took over hosing down the floors when Maida left to get more apples. When the others stopped for coffee, she drove the loader herself, maneuvering large crates of fruit and feeling no small amount of satisfaction at having done so. As soon as the others returned, she was back on the platform beside the press, layering racks of mash.

By lunchtime she knew what she needed. She cleaned herself up and ran down to the main house. In the living room she sat at the baby grand and opened the lid.

She felt relief before she touched a single key. Here were old, loving friends. She brushed them with her fingers and began to play. She didn't think about songs, just let her fingers move on their own, and they knew her heart. They created sounds that were sweet and melancholy. She was pleased, so pleased to be here.

Closing her eyes, she let the beauty of the chords take her away. The tension in her stomach began to dissolve. Her thoughts calmed. When she felt strength return, her hands fell still, and she opened her eyes.

Maida stood in the middle of the living room. Her head tipped, she seemed as taken as Lily. "No one else can bring quite that sound from those keys," she said in a wistful voice. Then she said a more neutral "Would you like lunch?"

Lily was warmed by the compliment and, yes, suddenly hungry. She started to get up.

"Stay here and play. I'll bring it in."

A second compliment? Maida waiting on her?

So Lily played. She did songs that her mother liked, in part to thank her, in part because entertaining people was what she did best. She continued to play when Maida returned carrying a large silver tray with ham-and-cheese sandwiches and fragrant tea.

They sat on the sofa, and Maida squeezed lemon into her tea. "You've been good in the cider house."

"I don't mind helping. What else would I do?"

Maida took a bite of her sandwich, then put it down. "I miss Celia," she surprised Lily by saying.

"Me, too."

"She was a good person. Had a big heart."

"Had big *ears.* I could talk to her about most anything."

Maida sat straighter. "Your generation is different that way. Mine was never given permission to talk about certain things."

"You don't need permission. Just speak your thoughts."

She looked at Lily. "What would you have me say?"

Lily felt the old tightness at the back of her tongue. She focused on easing it, then said, "What your childhood was like."

"Why does it matter? My life began when I married your father. And you're a fine one to say I should talk. You told your thoughts to Celia but never to me."

Lily refused to look away. "I was afraid of stuttering."

"I don't hear you stuttering now."

No. She was thinking clearly. She was in control of herself.

From the other end of the house came Rose's voice. *"Mom?"*

"In here," Maida called back.

Rose appeared and gave a startled look at the silver tray, the sandwiches. "This is nice. Elegance in the middle of a workday."

"We had to eat," Maida explained. "Like some?"

Rose shook her head. "No time. School got out early. I have the girls in the car."

"Only Emma and Ruthie," said Hannah, slipping past her. "Hi, Gram. Hi, Aunt Lily."

"I asked you to wait in the car," Rose said.

"They were pinching me." She leaned against the sofa arm nearest Lily and gave her a glowing smile. "They can come to my party. All three of them."

"Super!" Lily said.

The party was a movie and supper. Hannah had asked if she could invite three friends. When Lily readily agreed, they had written invitations on pretty stationery, then mailed them on Friday.

"She's driving me crazy about this party," Rose said now.

"I'm not," Hannah told her, but her glow had faded. She murmured to Lily, "I don't know what to wear."

"She has a closet full of clothes," Rose put in. "It's not my fault if they don't fit."

"You bought them too small."

"You outgrew them too fast."

Lily remembered too many such arguments from her own childhood to bear listening. "Hannah can come shopping with me. We'll both get something. My treat."

They went the following afternoon. Lily had barely finished at the cider house and cleaned up when Hannah ran up the road. Her big T-shirt and baggy jeans were as unflattering as ever, and her ponytail exaggerated the roundness of her cheeks, but those cheeks were rosy, and her eyes were alive. Lily was pleased.

They drove south to Concord. At the very first store Hannah fell in love with a Black Watch plaid dress cut in an Empire style. She couldn't take her eyes off her reflection in the mirror, and Lily knew why. The dress made her look remarkably slim.

They bought a matching hair ribbon, a pair of tights to match the green in the plaid, and a pair of shoes with a small heel.

Setting those things aside, they moved to the part of the store that had clothes for Lily, and again Hannah fell in love. Moments after she touched it, Lily was trying on a long skirt, vest, and blouse. The skirt and blouse were a soft heather-blue rayon; the vest was woven of a dozen compatible colors. Lily couldn't have chosen better.

JOHN felt pressured Wednesday morning. He was scrambling to put the week's *Lake News* to bed, but Jenny was home with a cold, and the phone kept ringing. The calls from outside media were handled fast; he said he didn't know where Lily was, which at any given time was true. The call from Richard Jacobi was more demanding.

Richard had heard Lily was back in town, and was worried that if John didn't get something together fast, someone else would beat him to it. John pointed out that there were no other insiders on the scene. Richard reminded him that the deal was for an exclusive book in time for summer reading. John said he understood, but countered that he knew publishers could execute a one-month turnaround from manuscript to bound book if they chose. He also reminded Richard that he didn't have a contract yet. Richard said it was in the works.

They ended on an amiable note, but John hung up the phone feeling a churning in his stomach. Part of the problem was that he liked Lily too much to push for information she wasn't ready to give. Part of the problem, though, was *Lake News.* This was still his real job, his responsibility.

So he wiped all the rest from his mind and focused on inserting postdeadline community-service ads, rereading his major stories one last time, and finalizing the placement of photos. He sent the last page off to the printer just before one, then sat back in his chair. He was thinking that maybe he wasn't cut out to be writing books after all, when Terry Sullivan called.

Terry said a smug "Your girl was seen in a store in Concord yesterday. Are you still playing dumb about where she is?"

Irritated, John sat forward. "Why are you still thinking about Lily Blake? The story was a lot of hot air. It's done."

"My story stands."

"Because of that tape?" John charged. "She didn't know about any tape. That's illegal."

"So you did talk with her. That means she's back."

"Illegal, Terry. I'd be worrying about that, not about whether she's here. What is it to you anyway?"

"I'm doing a follow-up story."

John was incredulous. "What in the hell would you do a follow-up on? Journalists who create bogus scandals?"

"Try nightclub singers who get carried away and confuse the lines between fantasy and reality."

"Yeah, right. You gonna prove that with an illegal tape?" He had a sudden thought. "How about a tape that's been edited?"

There was a pause, then, "You have nerve."

"Not me, pal," John said. "It takes nerve to pursue something that's already been discredited. But here you are, calling me again. I'm just letting you know there's another side to this story. For starters I know who called the wife of the chief of police here under false pretenses and tricked an innocent old lady into mentioning a case whose file was sealed eighteen years ago. Know how I know? There's a tape. What goes around comes around, pal. Only this tape's legit, because it's an official police line, and it has your voice on it. I also have a growing collection of articles you plagiarized during college."

"You're investigating *me?*"

"And then"—John was on a roll—"there's the weird personal stuff, like three wives. I thought we were friends back then, Terry, but I never knew you were married once, let alone three times. Why the big secret? What did you do to them, Terry? Keep them tied up and gagged? And then there's the cardinal. What is Rossetti to you? Do you have a personal grudge against him? Or against the church? There has to be a reason you battered an innocent woman in an attempt to bring down the cardinal."

"What's she to you, Kipling?" Terry threw back. "Trying to make me look bad to make you look good?"

John rose from his chair. "I don't make anyone out to be something he isn't, but I'm warning you. You look into her life, she'll look into yours."

"She will, or you will?"

"Same difference." He slammed down the phone.

Seconds later he called Brian Wallace at the *Post.* "Quick question. That tape Terry made of his conversation with Lily Blake—have you checked its authenticity? Whether it's been cut and spliced? You know, words shifted or removed."

"Why do you think that?"

"Because the lady in question denies saying the things he quotes her in the paper as saying. Did you hear the whole thing?"

"I heard the incriminating parts."

"But how do you know he didn't take those parts out of context? You could have the tape checked."

"Why would I want to?"

"To cover your butt," John said.

TYPICALLY, on a Wednesday afternoon John visited Gus, but he didn't today. His exchange with Sullivan had fired him up. He spent the afternoon making phone calls. Following a trail of rental applications, he located Terry's first wife, Rebecca Hooper, who sounded like a quiet and simple sort. She recognized John's name.

"He said you'd call," she said in a timid voice. "He said you'd try to blackmail me into telling things about us. But there's nothing to tell. Honest."

"I won't hurt you. I'm only trying to understand Terry."

"Good luck," she said.

John chuckled. "Yup. He's an enigma. He only lets you get so close. I figure something happened to make him that way."

"Do you know where he grew up?"

"No. Do you?" he asked Rebecca.

"Meadville, Pennsylvania. And you're right."

"About what?"

"Something happening in Meadville."

"Any idea what?"

"No. I have to go."

She hung up the phone then, but that was fine. John turned to his computer and began to browse. In no time he had the phone number of the assistant principal at the high school in Meadville. The man seemed delighted that John had called and was more than happy to talk. "Terry left here well before I arrived, but you can be sure all of us newcomers know about him now. Our current principal taught him sophomore English. Al was the one who tipped us off that Terry had broken that story."

"Was he that memorable?" John asked.

"To an English teacher he was. He was an anomaly among sixteen-year-olds. He could write. His brother couldn't. That one was a total loss in the literary department, but he was smart peoplewise, the nicest guy in the world."

John hadn't known there was a brother, as he hadn't known there were wives. "How many years between them?"

"Oh, a good four or five. Like I say, I wasn't here then. Someone mentioned it the other day, but mostly they're talking about Terry. Are you doing a story on him?"

"I am," John admitted.

"Well, he did some wonderful pieces for the school magazine. One that he wrote as a sophomore won all sorts of awards, was even reprinted in the *Tribune.*"

"The Meadville *Tribune?*"

"The same. I have a copy of it sitting right here on my desk. We circulated it when we learned of Terry's role in exposing the Rossetti-Blake affair. I'd be happy to fax it to you if you'd like."

Five minutes later John had a copy of the article. It was about life in an Italian neighborhood in Pittsburgh in the aftermath of World War II. Reading it, John saw germs of Terry's current style. Even back then Terry described local personalities in ways that made them come alive. Not that John wanted to cross paths with any of them; the piece wasn't flattering. Its villain was the local Catholic church. The view was surprisingly dark for a sixteen-year-old. But it wasn't surprising at all if that sixteen-year-old had a gripe.

John was on the right track. He could feel it in his gut. He needed to know what that gripe was.

Satisfied to put the matter on hold at such an optimistic point, he drove up to the printer in Elkland, where *Lake News* was ready for pickup. He loaded three thousand copies of the paper into his Chevy Tahoe, then delivered them to the area's post offices and general stores. It was well into evening by the time he finished. Through it all, there had been enough to distract him that he didn't think about Terry again until he was heading home.

Then it hit him.

LILY was at the cottage, sitting on the porch listening to a CD of Harry Connick, Jr., singing "Where or When," when she heard tires on gravel. A car engine stopped. A door opened and shut.

"Lily?" John called as he came around the side of the cottage.

"Good news," he said, taking the first two steps in a single stride. His face was nearly level with hers, lit by the lamp behind her. It gave his eyes an excited glow.

Sounding triumphant, he said, "Terry Sullivan grew up in Meadville, Pennsylvania. The family moved before his junior year, but up until then he wrote for his high school magazine. His most renowned piece was about life in an Italian neighborhood in Pittsburgh in the late '40s." He paused, waiting for her to react. "Sound familiar?"

Bemused, she shook her head.

He beamed. "Cardinal Rossetti grew up in an Italian neighborhood in Pittsburgh. It was buried in all the material written about him after his elevation to cardinal. How many Italian neighborhoods were there in Pittsburgh back then?" He held up a lone finger in answer. "So is this a coincidence?"

Lily could see his excitement. "You don't think so?"

He shook his head. "The same Terry Sullivan who tried to skewer Francis Rossetti wrote—at the tender age of sixteen—a vividly detailed essay about the cardinal's hometown. It wasn't Terry's hometown. So how did he know the details?"

"Maybe he visited there? Maybe someone he knew came from there? Someone who knew Father Fran?"

"I don't know. The essay didn't mention him."

"He'd have told me if he knew Terry."

"They don't have to know each other personally for there to be a connection," John said, and Lily bought it. She burst into a grin. If they could prove a personal connection between Terry and the cardinal, there would be a solid case against him for malice.

She couldn't stop grinning. She locked her hands around John's neck. "This is good."

He was grinning right back. "Yup." Before she knew what he was up to, he slipped his arms around her waist, swept her off the porch, and whirled her around in a jubilant circle, then pulled her into a hug.

Lily loved it. She couldn't remember the last time anything had felt so good. And it wasn't done. When Harry Connick started in with "It Had to Be You," John began to sway with her. With the air fresh and his body firm and supportive, she was entranced.

Letting go was easy because he led well. Lily felt the soft brush of his beard when he hummed at her ear. Then he kissed her. It was delicious. She welcomed seconds and thirds. And when he began dancing again, it was different. She was aware of his body in more intimate ways. And her own? On fire with a sudden wanting.

He felt it, too. The kiss he gave her when the song was done was deeper and hungrier. Wrapping her arms around his neck, she let it carry her away.

Then something intruded. It was a minute before she realized that it was a car. Seconds later headlights swept past them.

She gasped and tried to leave John, but he held her immobile.

"Wait," he whispered.

The car stopped. A familiar voice called, *"Lily?"*

"Poppy," Lily whispered, and, suddenly frightened, looked up at John. "Something's wrong."

She pulled away, but John was right beside her as she ran to the car. Poppy had her door open, so that light filled the van. Lily's thoughts were on Maida, but Poppy's eyes were on John.

"I played a hunch when you didn't answer your phone," she told him. "So here I am. It's Gus. He had a heart attack."

Chapter 8

THE hospital was in North Hedgeton, a thirty-minute drive from Lake Henry. John drove faster than was safe, but he had visions of Gus dying before he got there. He couldn't let that happen. He and Gus had to talk.

Pulling up at the hospital, John left the Tahoe at the emergency entrance, took Lily's hand, and hurried inside. A nurse directed him to the second floor, where he made a beeline for the trio of doctors conferring at the door to one of the rooms. Gus was in that room.

"How is he?" John asked the doctors.

"Not good," Harold Webber answered. Gus had been under his care since an initial attack three years earlier, shortly before John had returned to town.

"Is he conscious?" John asked.

"In and out."

John's fingers tightened around Lily's. "Can we go in?"

Harold said, "He's ornery by nature. You won't upset him more than he'd be anyway."

Gus was outnumbered by machines. One delivered oxygen, another medication; one monitored his heart, another his oxygen level. Gus himself was positively ashen. He was long, thin, and utterly still under the sheets. John approached the bed. "Gus?" he said quietly.

Gus didn't respond.

"Dad? It's John. Can you hear me?" When there remained no sign of awareness, he said to Lily, "I always see him on Wednesdays. I skipped today. I shoulda gone." He snorted. "My relationship with Gus in a nutshell—forty-three years of shoulda dones."

Lily, who stood a bit behind him, rubbed his arm, and it settled him. He studied his father's face. It seemed frozen in anger.

"I haven't a clue," John said quietly.

"About what?" Lily asked.

"The anger that makes him scowl. I used to think it was me. Do you know, I can only remember one time in my life when I saw him smile at something I did. I went to bed with a stone he'd carved. He'd chisel out little faces—eyes and noses and mouths. He gave me one when I was six."

"For your birthday?"

"No. He didn't believe in birthdays. Just gave it because he felt like it, I guess. I never knew why."

An hour passed. Gus didn't move, didn't blink, didn't make a sound.

At one point Lily said, "All families have those never-knew-why things."

"You and Maida?"

"Especially."

"You're lucky she's in good health. There's still time." But time was running out for Gus. John felt it keenly.

By the time Wednesday became Thursday, John was feeling a sense of futility. Lily was curled in the chair beside his. Her eyes closed from time to time, but as soon as he suspected she had fallen asleep, she opened them and gave him an encouraging smile.

He touched her hand. "You don't have to stay," he whispered.

"Would you rather be alone?" she asked gently.

He shook his head.

She smiled. Tucking up her legs, she settled into the chair.

Watching her, John felt an incredible fullness swell his heart. That was the moment when he guessed he was in love.

LILY dozed off. John might have, too. It was the middle of the night, the room was dim, and the beep of the heart monitor was hypnotic. But John refused to sleep. When an angel in scrubs brought hot coffee, he drank every drop.

Gus slept on. When John thought he saw the flicker of an eyelid, he came out of his chair and leaned over the bedrail. He reached for his father's hand but drew back just shy of a touch. His voice held raw urgency. "Gus? Talk to me, Gus."

Lily appeared at his side. "Maybe you should talk to him."

John opened his mouth but found no words. "I can't."

"Why not?"

It was like touching. "We just don't."

"Then talk to me. What do you love about him?"

He could more readily have said what he hated. Or what he didn't understand. "He builds beautiful stone walls," John said at last. "Probably built hundreds of them. I was always in awe of them."

"He's an artist," Lily said.

John nodded. "He never did anything else. Mom told me he dropped out of school when he was fourteen. For months no one knew where he went during the day. Then they found him helping an old stonemason. He was keeping out of trouble and learning a trade, so no one dragged him back to school. I missed a *day* of school, and he hit the roof!"

"He wanted better for you."

"I could have been perfectly happy working with him, but he wouldn't hear of it. Not for me or for Donny. Said we'd mess things up. He was a perfectionist. Took pride in what he built."

"Don't you take pride in what you write?"

"I suppose."

"Then you're like him in that."

John wanted to think so.

SHORTLY before dawn Gus's eyelids flickered and opened. John was quickly up and leaning over the bed. "Dad?"

Gus focused on nothing at all, then on John, but if there was awareness, he didn't let on. When his eyes shut, John looked at the heart monitor. The beat took an erratic turn, then steadied.

John stepped back when a nurse arrived. She checked Gus, checked the monitors, and withdrew. John didn't know whether to try to get Gus to wake up again or not. Waking up was a good sign, and John allowed himself to hope. He envisioned the two of them having a few months more and Gus being mellowed by having a near brush with death.

As morning became afternoon, Gus woke up occasionally. Each time, he pulled himself from disorientation to focus on John—and he did recognize him. Then, come midafternoon, the beat of the heart monitor shifted. Doctors and nurses came on the run, and after a medication change Gus's heart steadied. But there was talk of a secondary attack, fluid in his lungs.

John waited in the hall with Lily while the doctors worked, but as soon as the bedside was clear, he was back again. He took his father's hand. It felt awkward in his, limp and cold.

"Come on, Gus," he murmured. "Come on. Don't leave me hanging here." When Gus didn't respond, he said, "You can hear me. I know you can. You always could, just turned away and made like what I had to say wasn't worth your while. I let you down. I'm sorry I did that. I let you down, and I let Donny down. But I'm here now, and I want a chance."

Defeated, he studied those old, scarred fingers. They seemed vulnerable in ways Gus himself never had. John murmured, "How to ask forgiveness from a man who won't listen?"

Those fingers moved then, and Gus was looking straight at him. "You gut it backwuds," he said. " 'T's me let you down. . . . 'T's me failed. . . . 'T's me was . . . nevuh good 'nough."

"That's not true," John said, but by then Gus had closed his eyes, and something was different this time. It wasn't until Lily was touching his arm and the room was filled with doctors and nurses that John realized the monitor had gone flat.

They tried resuscitation. They shocked Gus once, twice, a third time. There was a moment's pause, then a reluctant exchange of glances.

"He said what he needed to say," Lily whispered. Then she left, and John didn't try to stop her. For a final few minutes he needed to be alone with his father. He stood there holding Gus's hand, studying the face that he had hated and loved. He bent and kissed his father's cheek. When he was sure that Gus's soul had passed to wherever it was headed, he left the room.

JOHN left Lily at her cottage. He felt the loss immediately, but the need to go to Gus's place was great. Gus's place? It was his place, too. He had grown up there. No amount of repainting, relandscaping, or refurnishing could change that fact. Driving down Ridge Road now, with Gus dead and gone, he had to acknowledge the connection.

John parked beside the tiny house and walked inside, as he had thousands of times as a kid. The small living room was the bedroom that he and Donny had shared. Dropping onto the sofa, he heard the sounds of those years—yelling, but laughter, too. Gus wasn't happy by nature, but John's mother was. And Donny.

John put his head back and closed his eyes. He felt weary in ways that went beyond the physical, weary in ways that had to do with being the only surviving male in this house. The weight of it was too much after a night without sleep. John dozed off, sitting right there on the sofa, as Gus had done so often of late. A muffled cry brought him awake with a start.

Dulcey Hewitt, who lived next door and who came in to clean, stood just inside the front door with a hand pressed to her chest. "You scared me," she breathed. "Here I'd just heard about Gus, and I was comin' over to straighten up so's you wouldn't find a mess, and there you are, sitting just the way he was."

For a minute John was groggy enough to be confused. "What time is it?"

"Eight. I'm sorry about Gus. Were you with him?"

He nodded, then looked around. "Nothing much is messed. He didn't have the strength at the end. Go home, Dulcey. Be with your kids."

John watched her go, feeling confused about things he couldn't put his finger on.

Dulcey had no sooner left when a neighbor from across the street came to offer condolences. She didn't come inside. Nor did any of the others who came by. They just stood at the door, told John they were sorry about Gus's death, and left. He was touched. Gus hadn't been any warmer to his neighbors than he had been to his family, yet these people found it in themselves to come by. They made John feel guilty for every negative thought he'd had about the Ridge.

Knowing he had a funeral to plan, John found a couple of shirts and a suit. He pulled the suit out of the closet and brushed at a place where the jacket bulged. Feeling something there, he pulled back the lapel. Suspended from the hanger on a string was a plastic bag. John laid the suit on the bed, removed the bag, and opened it. Inside was a collection of clippings. Some were old and yellow, some more recent, arranged chronologically and neatly. John looked at them, until the heartache was too great. Here was his work, preserved by a father who had never once told him he loved him.

Moaning, John straightened, went out the back door, and paced the yard in the dark, trying to sort through his thoughts.

It was me who let you down. Me who failed. Me who was never good enough.

Understanding then, feeling a gut-wrenching sorrow for a man who had suffered—an illegitimate child born at a time when illegitimate children were marked, a man John had loved for no other reason but that he was his father—John sank to his knees on the grass. He cried softly for everything that he hadn't known, hadn't done.

The tears flowed until they ran out. Then John dried his eyes and went inside. He returned the packet of clippings to the bag where Gus had kept them, and rehooked the bag on the hanger, to be buried along with the suit and Gus. He collected a clean shirt, tie, underwear, socks, and shoes, then drove home.

After hanging Gus's clothes in his closet, he set off in the canoe. When he reached his loons, he stowed the paddle. All four birds were here, swimming slowly, diving occasionally, raising their voices in the night.

There was timelessness here, a sense that death was no more than a progression of life. There was history, a returning from season to season, and survival—two young successfully raised to perpetuate the species. Yes, the years had seen losses. But there was reason, order, and meaning.

Breathing that in, feeling both loss and gain, John put his paddle in the water and set off. The call of his loons followed, carrying across the water to Thissen Cove.

Lily was sitting on her dock. She stood when he neared, as though she had been expecting him. When the canoe glided alongside, she took the line from John and tied it to a cleat.

Seconds later he was on the dock, taking her in his arms, and it was the most natural, most right thing he had ever done. He kissed her once, then again—sweet, then deeper.

At Lily's urging they went up to the house, up the stairs to the bed in the loft, and again it was the most natural, most right thing. He found her more beautiful than he imagined. He felt the comfort she gave, the consolation, the hope, and his body came alive as never before.

Eventually exhaustion caught up. Safe in Lily's bed, warmed by the heat of their bodies, he sank into a deep sleep.

GUS'S funeral was held two days later. The service was a simple send-off for a complicated man, but the church was full. Most of the Ridge was there to bury one of its own, but there were enough others to suggest that they had come out of respect for John.

As she had the Sunday before, Lily sat in a back pew, her head bowed. She would have stayed out of sight at the graveyard, too, if John hadn't caught her hand and drawn her into step with him behind the casket on his way out of church. He held her hand as though she were a mooring, the only thing keeping him steady.

Unsure about how that would play in Lake Henry, Lily kept her eyes low. After a few prayers the casket was lowered into the ground. She could feel the tension in John but wouldn't have dreamed of stepping away. Mourners passed John with a brief word, the shake of a hand, and always their eyes caught hers. Lily nodded awkwardly and thanked her lucky stars she didn't need to speak.

She didn't leave until John did, which was only after the grave was filled with dirt. By then the townsfolk had left, and there was no one to express curiosity or disapproval.

That was small solace for Lily. She couldn't help but fear that she and John had opened a whole new can of worms.

John didn't think so. If the respect the townsfolk felt for him spread to her, it would help. The more they warmed, the more welcome she would feel; the more welcome she felt in Lake Henry, the more she might consider staying.

He wasn't thinking of his book. He felt uncomfortable when he did that, felt as though it cheapened what they had shared. His wanting her to stay was totally independent of the book.

But she wouldn't stay unless things were resolved. Lily had pride. She wouldn't stay in Lake Henry by default, wouldn't stay because she had nowhere else to go. She had to actively want to stay, and she wouldn't do that if she couldn't make peace with Maida. He wanted to help her do that. But with his relationship with Lily still so new, digging into Maida's secrets felt intrusive.

Terry was something else. He was fair game where Lily was concerned. John liked the idea of helping her prove malice.

He hit the office early Monday and picked up where he had left off before Gus had taken ill. He contacted a church in the Italian section of Pittsburgh and eventually found a priest old enough to have known Terry Sullivan. Indeed, the priest knew the name, but only from the recent scandal. He informed John that Terry Sullivan had never spent time in his parish.

So he hadn't been a practicing Catholic in Pittsburgh, not in the neighborhood he'd written about.

Backing up a step, John returned to Meadville, but the church there was a dead end. No one in the rectory remembered the family, and though he might have worked his way through lay leaders in the parish, John returned to the same assistant principal he had talked with before. Still eager to help, the man put John in touch with a middle school teacher, who put him in touch with an elementary school teacher. The two corroborated each other's stories. Both marveled at Terry's success given the difficulty of his childhood.

"Difficulty?" John asked them.

"He was a puny little boy," one confided. "Skinny. Defensive. Poor thing, following in the footsteps of a brother like that."

"Like what?"

"Neil—he was a good-looking child. Sweet, personable, friendly. He was a natural leader. Terry was a better student, but children that age don't care about brains. He didn't have an easy time at home, either. His father was a difficult man."

The other teacher mentioned that, too. "When we see children like Terry now, we report them as victims of abuse."

"What did you see?" John asked.

"Bruises. Terry's father had a temper and a belt."

"Did he hit the brother, too?"

"Lord, no. He didn't dare. His wife would have left him for sure if he'd laid a hand on the boy. She worshipped Neil. She had him earmarked for priesthood right from the start."

John's pulse skipped. "Did he become one?"

"He certainly did. We were all proud of him for that."

Was it enough of a connection? Could playing second fiddle to a priestly older brother cause enough hatred for the church to warrant Terry's malice toward Cardinal Rossetti?

"Couldn't the brother stop the father from beating Terry?"

"No one could stop that man. He was large and strong and angry."

"What about Terry's mother?"

"Oh, she's dead. Died in a car crash years ago."

John knew that, and that Terry's father was gone, too. "But where was she when her husband was swinging his belt?"

"In the way, I gather. She got it first."

"What was the problem? Did he drink?"

Neither teacher knew for sure, but one gave him the name of the woman who had lived next door to the Sullivans in Meadville. She still lived there and had no qualms about speaking her mind. "Did James Sullivan drink? Yes, he drank," the woman said. "He was insanely jealous. Jean could barely raise her eyes in public without him accusing her of looking at one man or another."

"Was there a man in her past?"

"Oh, yes. A longtime sweetheart through high school and college. The love of her life, if the look on her face meant anything."

"What happened? Why did they break up?"

"I don't know. I asked once, but she seemed sorry she'd said as much as she had."

"Where did she grow up?"

"I don't know. She never said. I suppose she was afraid."

"Because of the other guy?"

"It's a fair guess."

John's imagination was running wild. He needed more. "Do you know her maiden name?"

"Bocce. Like the game."

Bocce. Like the game played in Italian neighborhoods. Italian neighborhoods like the one where Francis Rossetti had lived.

Sitting forward, playing a hunch now, John finished the call and turned to his computer, but he had barely reached the Internet when Richard Jacobi called with news that Terry Sullivan was trying to sell the Rossetti-Blake story to *People* magazine. John said he doubted they would buy, since Terry was about to be thoroughly discredited. Richard pointed out that that wouldn't necessarily hurt magazine sales. He said that if John put his nose to the grindstone, they could have something on bookshelves by March and that discrediting Terry would make the book all the more timely.

John didn't like the word grindstone. He didn't like the sound of March.

Fast, thorough, and exclusive, Richard reminded him. John asked where his contract was. Richard said it was in the works. John reminded him that he'd said the same thing a week before and that nothing was final until a contract was signed.

He hung up the phone. He needed to think.

While he thought, he worked. In several clicks of the computer mouse, he had the name of the high school the cardinal had attended and a phone number.

He said a bright "Hi" to the woman who answered the phone.

"I'm trying to track down an old friend. Her name is Jean Bocce. If my information is correct, she was there with Fran Rossetti."

The woman chuckled. "What a coincidence. We have his yearbook right here."

"Had a few calls lately?" John teased.

"You could say that. Bocce?"

He spelled it.

" 'Alexander. Azziza. Buford,' " she read. "Sorry. No Bocce."

"She may have been a year behind or in a club with Fran. Music? Debating? They had to know each other somehow."

"You may be right." There was the sound of turning pages. "Ah, here we are. It was the select chorus. There she is, second row up. Very pretty. Actually, familiar. Hold on. . . . Here she is again. It looks like she may have been Fran Rossetti's senior-prom date. Let me see if I have current information on her."

On his feet now, John practically danced while he waited, and had to pretend disappointment when the school had no current address. If he was a bit fast thanking the woman and ending the call, he figured it was better than giving a whoop. He did that the second he hung up the phone.

Seconds after that he was surfing the Internet for information on celibacy and priestly vows. It didn't take long to find what he wanted. Then he called Brian Wallace at the *Post.* "I just learned something that you ought to know," he said.

Brian sighed. "Why do I get the feeling I don't want to hear this?"

"Because your instincts are good, but you were taken in, pal. Terry Sullivan had good cause for wanting to smear Rossetti. Did you know he was an abused kid? Terry's father beat him, usually at the same time he beat Terry's mother. The guy was insanely jealous of the real love of her life, someone the mother was with for years before she married. Three guesses who that was."

There was a long silence.

"There's a picture of them together at Rossetti's senior prom," John said. "It's in his high school yearbook."

"That's no proof he was the love of her life."

"A neighbor who knew her said she was with the same guy through high school and college."

Brian sounded skeptical. "Rossetti's a priest."

"Priests don't have to be virgins. Once they are ordained, they have to be celibate. There's a difference. Brian, the pieces fit. Terry is repeatedly beaten, probably defending his mother, who is beaten because she's in love with Fran Rossetti. So Terry grows up despising Rossetti, writing essays condemning the church in that Italian neighborhood where his mother grew up, which just happens to be the same one where Rossetti grew up. Rossetti is elevated to cardinal. Terry stews. He looks for dirt, finds none, so he produces it himself."

"It's all speculation. I still have that tape."

"Test it."

JOHN could have left it at that. But he hadn't even mentioned the brother—Neil Sullivan, the priest. If that brother had been favored over Terry—if he had been loved more than Terry, beaten less than Terry, and held up ad nauseam to Terry as an example of everything Terry wasn't—Terry's resentment would be understandable. All things considered, John had a good case. But the journalist in him wanted the best case. And that meant locating the brother.

Chapter 9

HANNAH'S birthday was Tuesday. Lily had arranged to leave the cider house early to help her dress. They were picking her friends up at four, heading to a movie and dinner.

Lily was startled to find Hannah alone. It seemed that Rose had dropped her home after school and taken off with the younger girls. "I told her to go," Hannah said. "Emma and Ruthie had gymnastics." She was newly showered and draped in a huge towel, her hair dripping down her back in unkempt twists. But her face was full of excitement.

Lily pushed aside her qualms about Rose. Playing the beautician, she sat Hannah on a stool in the bathroom and dried her hair until it was glossy and smooth. She helped Hannah pull on the green tights, then helped her into the Black Watch plaid dress. After she put the ribbon in her hair, she turned her to the mirror. Her cheeks were a soft pink on flawless ivory skin. Hannah was Rose's daughter indeed.

"You look absolutely beautiful," Lily told her.

It was an auspicious start for an auspicious event, the most surprising part of which, for Lily, was Hannah's friends. They were delightful. Listening as she drove, Lily heard their comments on Hannah's awesome dress, awesome hair, awesome shoes. Hannah was lovely and poised. More than once Lily wished Rose, Art, and Maida could see her.

Since Hannah had a wonderful time, Lily did, too. She suspected she was predisposed to it. What John had learned about Terry changed the picture. The newspaper hadn't yet agreed to test the tape, but it hadn't refused. Cassie thought that was a good sign. If the tape was found to be suspect, a settlement would surely follow. But Lily didn't want money. She wanted a public apology, and she wanted it with as much fanfare as when the story first broke.

The outing went perfectly. After the last of Hannah's friends was dropped off at home, Hannah scrambled into the front seat and wrapped an arm around Lily's neck. "Wasn't my party wonderful?" she cried with glee.

Lily smiled as she drove. "It was."

Hannah went on for a while about the movie. Then she said, "I liked dinner even better, and not because of the food. Because my dress was pretty and I was with my friends."

"It was pretty, but the girl in it was beautiful."

"They kept saying that, didn't they?" she said, beaming. "Oh, Aunt Lily, you missed the turn to my house."

"Want to stop at Gram's? Tell her about the party?"

"Yeah!"

But Maida wasn't alone. Rose was there with Emma and Ruth, both of whom were in pajamas and ready for bed. Hannah thought this was the greatest thing—her mother being there. She needed Rose to tell her how pretty she looked, to see that she wasn't all bad.

But Maida was the one to come forward first. "Look at you," she said with genuine enthusiasm. "You're gorgeous. But where's the little girl? This one's so grown up!"

"It's me." Hannah's eyes went to her mother.

"How was the party?" Rose asked. For a minute the night's silence was broken only by the chirp of a cricket.

Maida glanced at Rose.

"It was neat," Hannah told her mother.

Fearing she would say something ugly to Rose, Lily went into the living room. She settled in behind the baby grand and stroked the keys. It didn't take long for her anger to fizzle. Drawn into the music, absorbed by it, she didn't hear Maida arrive. She only realized her mother was there when she stretched and her eyes happened to pass the doorway. She stopped. "Have they left?"

Maida nodded. She seemed tense. "Is history repeating itself?" she blurted out. "Rose. Just now. Is that what I did to you?"

Lily's heart began to pound. "Different circumstances—"

"But the same effect."

Lily paused, then nodded.

Maida folded her arms. Her eyes were lined with tears. "I'm sorry," she said.

"It's okay," Lily rushed out. "You had other things on your m-m-m-mind. Daddy and us kids."

"It was wrong of me." There was a challenge in it, a demand, and just enough edge in her voice to catapult Lily back in time.

"Then why did you do it? Was I so hard to love?"

Maida's eyes went wide. "I loved you. I do."

"You never said it, showed it. You were glad when I left."

"It seemed the right thing to do after . . . that incident."

"I didn't steal any car."

"I know."

"But you wanted me gone. Why?"

Maida shook her head.

Lily wanted to ask what that meant, but she suddenly wanted something more. All Maida had to do was cross the room and take Lily in her arms. And Lily might have forgiven her anything.

But Maida didn't. She stood at the door wearing a tormented look. After a bit she averted her eyes, bowed her head, and left.

"I MAY skip work tomorrow," Lily told John that night. They were lying in her bed, face to face in the reflected light of a full moon. A pair of loons chorused on the lake. It should have calmed her, but a thread of fury deep inside wouldn't go away.

"How come?" he asked.

"My mother takes me for granted."

"Did you have a fight?"

"No. She apologized."

"For what?"

"The past."

John raised his head. "Well, that's something, isn't it?"

"It's not enough."

He stroked her hair. "You're very demanding."

"Yes." A month ago an apology would have been fine. But a month ago Lily had no interest in a life in Lake Henry. Now here—suddenly—she needed more. "She was awful to me. She made me f-f-f-feel unloved and ugly. Like there was something wrong with me. Know who finally got me feeling better about myself?"

"The cardinal."

"He taught me that we all make mistakes. Well, the whole world knows mine. I want to know hers. I want her to *talk* about what she felt for me and why. I need her to say it wasn't me."

LILY did go to work on Wednesday. Having vented her feelings to John, she had slept well and felt rested by morning.

Maida wasn't. She looked tired. For the first time Lily thought about widowhood and what it meant. There was no one to turn to at night, no one to give the kind of comfort John had given Lily.

But Maida did have a business, and she was running it well. Lily had to admire her for that and to feel compassion when Maida took a break from culling apples to rub her lower back. When they broke for lunch, Lily walked to the house with her.

"Is your back bothering you?" she asked.

"A little. It's a muscle. Nothing important."

"You pull too much weight getting the crates on the lift."

"Someone has to do it."

"I could."

Maida said a tentative "You could."

They changed places that afternoon. Maida layered racks and cloths. Lily got crates on the lift, dumped apples in the bath, adjusted pulleys, and raised and lowered the press. She drove the loader when it was time to bring more apples in from the yard. She loved it all, because she could do it all. She hadn't felt such a sense of accomplishment since . . . since she couldn't remember when. And contentment. That, too. There was something about putting in a full day's work at a place with her family name on the sign.

FATHER Neil Sullivan, Terry's brother, lived in Burlington, Vermont. When he wasn't at his church, Christ the King, he was counseling college students at a guidance center in town. John might have saved himself the trip and simply called on the phone, but he didn't think the man would talk. So, having arranged for one of his correspondents to distribute *Lake News,* he left Lake Henry as soon as he finished wiring the paper to the printer.

John reached Burlington after a five-hour drive. He knew and liked the city—liked the way it rose on a hill overlooking Lake Champlain, liked the aura of energy and excitement that came from the area's six colleges and sixteen thousand students.

At Christ the King, John learned that Father Sullivan was at the guidance center, which he drove to in no time. It was located on the second floor of one of the Federal-style buildings that overlooked the waterfront. He was greeted in the reception area by a woman with long center-parted hair and wire-rimmed glasses. He asked for Father Sullivan.

"Father Neil will be done shortly," she informed him. "Do you have an appointment?"

"No. I thought I might catch him at the end of the day."

"For . . ."

"To talk." Evasion seemed pointless. "About his brother."

The change in her expression was subtle. "Why?" she asked. "Are you with a newspaper?"

"A small one in New Hampshire. I used to work with Terry in Boston." He extended a hand. "John Kipling."

Her hand met his. "Anita Monroe. I'm the director here."

Just then a door opened behind her. A young man came out first. His age and worn backpack said he was a student. He slipped past them and hurried out.

John looked at the man in the clerical collar who was watching from the office door. There was a family resemblance, though Neil was clearly older than Terry, with graying hair and creases in his forehead and cheeks. But Neil looked far more friendly and warm than Terry ever had.

The woman cut to the chase. "Father Neil, meet John Kipling. He wants to talk with you about Terry."

Father Neil inhaled sharply and tipped his head back as if to say, *I'm found out.* But the handshake he offered was warm. "Lots of Sullivans in the world. I was wondering when someone would make the connection. How'd you do it?"

"An old neighbor in Meadville said you were in Vermont. The local diocese did the rest. I've known Terry for years."

"I'm afraid you know him better than I do, then. There were seven years between us growing up. We were never close."

"Aren't you in touch with him at all now?"

"No. So I'm not sure what you're looking for."

John explained his quest, telling of his friendship with Lily and of the losses she had suffered since being implicated in the scandal.

"She's trying to fight her way back. I want to help her. We're trying to understand why Terry hated Fran Rossetti enough to go after him and ruin an innocent woman in the process. I know that your mother and Rossetti were sweethearts, that your father was jealous of that, and that Terry was physically abused."

"If you know all that," the priest said, "why do you need me?"

"You're the only one who can pull it all together."

"I'm sorry. I can't do that. He's my brother."

"Doesn't it bother you that Terry has caused so much harm?"

"It isn't my job to judge. God does that."

John sought Anita's help. "Can't you see this from Lily's point of view?"

Anita surprised him by saying, "I can. If I were her, I'd want to learn everything I could. But I'm not the one whose brother it is."

John knew when to quit. "Okay," he told the priest. "Tell you what. I'll be spending the night at the Inn on Maple. If you change your mind, will you call me there?" He took a business card from his wallet and wrote down the number.

The priest tucked the card in his pocket without a glance.

JOHN was discouraged. Convinced that the priest wouldn't call, he stayed out late walking after dinner and returned to the inn tired enough to fall quickly asleep. When he awoke in the morning, there was neither a call nor a message.

As he entered the inn's dining room for breakfast, he spotted Anita Monroe sitting with a cup of coffee at one of the small tables. He helped himself to coffee from an urn on the sideboard, filled a small plate with pastries, and joined her.

"You're not the one whose brother it is," he reminded her.

Her voice was softer than yesterday. "No. I'm the one who has watched the one whose brother it is suffer the guilt and regret."

"He sent you?"

"Not explicitly. But he knew I would come." She smiled. "You pushed the right button. If this can help Lily, then he needs to do it. The thing is, I need a guarantee of confidentiality."

"It's yours. I need my conclusions supported, that's all. Was Rossetti the problem in the Sullivan marriage?"

"Yes. Jean—Neil's mother—knew that Rossetti planned to enter the seminary, but she thought she could change his mind. Obviously, she couldn't. They were together for more than eight years, and then he was gone. She turned around and married the first guy who came along."

"On the rebound."

"Apparently. There was little love there. James had a drinking problem, a jealousy problem. Worse, he was a devout Catholic."

"Why worse? Wouldn't that have helped?"

Anita shook her head. "It made him more conflicted. James hated Rossetti, but he couldn't lift a hand against Neil. Neil was going to be a priest. That made him untouchable. But every time James looked at Neil, he thought of Rossetti."

"Because of the priest thing?"

"And the timing. Neil was born nine months into the marriage. James was convinced he was Rossetti's son."

Whoa, John thought. An interesting twist. "Is he?"

"No. Absolutely not. Rossetti was out of her life two months before Jean married Neil's father. But she would alternately admit it and deny it."

"Admit it? Why would she do that?"

"Wishful thinking. Part of her wanted to think Neil was Rossetti's son, wanted to believe she had a little bit of him with her forever. So there you have Neil, whose presence aggravated his father, and you have the father, who took it out on Jean."

"And on Terry."

"And on Terry," Anita admitted. "Neil coped by focusing on life outside the home. He was forever doing things at school or spending time with friends. When he left for college, he left for good."

That sounded familiar. John left for good, too—or so he had thought. "Didn't he try to help Terry? Or his mother?"

"He was a kid," she said. "He wasn't God or a saint, much as Jean wanted to think it. She fawned over him, made him the substitute for a lost love. There wasn't anything sexual in it, but it was oppressive, smothering. And what could he do? She was his mother, and he loved her. So he tried to please her. Tried to be perfect. Tried to emulate Rossetti." She took a breath and straightened. "If you don't think he resents Rossetti even a little himself, think again."

"Then it didn't bother him when Terry broke the scandal?"

"Not at first. He could easily buy into the idea of Rossetti having a woman. So here's a priest doubting a cardinal, and he felt guilty for that. Then came the official apology, and gradually Neil felt sorrow, then shame."

"Not enough to speak up when the papers kept after Lily."

But Anita was suddenly fired up. "Wait a minute. What about the cardinal? Did he speak up? No, he didn't. He didn't want to open himself up to speculation about lovers and illegitimate children. Can you imagine the field day the press would have had with that? And Neil would have been right in the middle." She grew beseeching. "Neil's a good man. He may not have been there for Terry, and he'll carry the guilt of that to his grave, but he's helped countless other kids who've gone through nightmares of their own." She sat back and lifted her coffee cup.

"Why have you told me all this?" he asked.

She took a deep breath. "Because I've watched him suffer. I've watched the secret swell up in his throat until he comes close to choking on it. I like him. I want him happy. If this gives Lily Blake a better understanding of why Terry did what he did, some of the burden will be lifted from Neil's shoulders."

LILY'S muscles had ached the night before, but after a hot bath she was ready to go again the next morning. Maida was amenable. The apple pickers coming from the orchards gave Lily their tallies, since she was the one in the yard. And when Maida drove off that afternoon to bid at auction for a backhoe, Lily was in charge.

All in all, it was a grand day. No matter that the foliage color had crested and was starting to fade. She drove home with the radio blaring and a sense of satisfaction. Her pleasure doubled when she saw

John's Tahoe parked at the cottage. She had missed him. He was sitting on the tailgate and jumped off when she pulled up.

"You're late," he said, but he was smiling.

"Lots to do at the old homestead. So? How'd it go?"

"It went . . . great." As they walked toward the porch, he told her about Father Neil Sullivan, Anita Monroe, and more than she had ever thought to know about Francis Rossetti.

"They thought Neil was his son?" she asked.

"Terry's father did. No one else seriously believed it. But there'd have been hell to pay if the press had gotten wind of it. So even if he wasn't being fair to you, I can almost understand why Rossetti stayed in the background once the *Post* issued its apology."

Lily looked out at the lake, trying to digest it all. "At least there's a reason why he's been so silent. John?"

"Hmm?"

"We can't put this in print."

"I know. But it doesn't mean we can't use the rest, the part that has to do with Terry. He won't be pleased."

JOHN went to the office Friday morning with a sense of resolve. He hadn't been there five minutes when Brian Wallace called. "We got the report," he said. "The Blake tape was spliced. Terry's been fired."

"And?" John prompted. "What about Lily? Is the paper doing a story?"

"Nah. Terry's firing is a postscript. Irrelevant."

"Excuse me?" John was incredulous. "An innocent woman was skewered by your paper based on a tape that you didn't authenticate, and you don't owe her anything?"

"What would you have us do?" Brian asked.

"Her lawyer demanded a retraction."

"Gimme a break. We acted in good faith. We believed the story to be legitimate. Apologizing to the cardinal was bad enough. Listen to me. The thing is done. We're not groveling."

John was livid when he hung up the phone. But he knew a dead end when he heard one.

Lily needed a public apology. She needed justice. Terry being quietly fired wasn't justice. John would bet that Terry would get another job and start right in again with barely a blip in his career.

So John could threaten to make the firing the lead story in *Lake News* if the *Post* didn't issue an apology. Reverberations in the media would be assured. But front-page vindication wasn't in John's best interest. Any revival of the story, especially one focusing on Terry, introduced the risk that another curious reporter would discover what John had. If that happened, John could kiss his book deal good-bye.

But would that be so terrible? He had to decide—and soon.

Chapter 10

JOHN took Lily to church Sunday morning. He took her to brunch at Charlie's afterward and for a ride in the hills. Then he took her to the *Lake News* office and let her pick the week's articles from the Lake Henry Academy and do the dozen small payment checks that went to town correspondents.

She was delighted to help, which pleased him immensely. Being hooked on the paper was akin to being hooked on him, not to mention that her help was badly needed. He was getting little of his own work done.

Forget writing a book. *Lake News* had to be done. But he was having trouble drumming up enthusiasm. His heart wasn't in it.

After a while, pleading the need to air out his mind, he left Lily at the computer, walked up to the graveyard beside the church, and stood at Gus's grave. Leaves had drifted over the dirt, a dusting of pale yellows, curled reds, muted browns.

It was quiet here—peaceful, as eternity was—because John did believe that his father was in heaven. Gus deserved that.

It was me who let you down. Me who failed. Me who was never good enough.

Sad that that should be his father's dying thought. Sad that worthiness had been so important to him. A man without a conscience had it easy, John decided. A man without a conscience didn't have a worry in the world.

Gus had a conscience. So did John.

Gus wanted to be worthy. So did John.

Gus built beautiful stone walls. John wrote beautiful articles. But neither was enough to guarantee worthiness. It was very simple, really. The essence of worthiness had to do with people.

NO, LILY did not want to think about what she felt for John, but those feelings weren't going away. Her heart insisted on squeezing and tugging whenever he came to mind.

This Sunday she felt his distraction. She helped out at the office as best she could, then made dinner back at the cottage, trying to please him. He ate every last bite and thanked her. But she turned back from the sink when the dishes were done to find him outside on the dock. Pulling on a jacket, she followed him out.

A wind was up, rippling over the water. October was in full gear. November would bring snow.

Her sneakers made noise on the planks. John looked up and smiled. Taking her hand, he drew her down and settled her between his legs, facing the lake, holding her close.

"Listen to the water," she whispered, content.

"Mmm-hmm. Lapping up a storm." His mouth touched her temple, the gentle brush of his beard. "I love you, you know."

Her heart bumped and beeped.

"Is it mutual?" he asked, endearingly unsure.

"Very."

"I want what's best for you."

She believed him. More, she believed what she heard in his sudden somberness. The cause of his distraction wasn't her. It was the other mess. She was relieved, frightened. "What are my choices?"

He breathed in a sigh. "You have three," he said, still warm and close. "First, you can take the legal course. Hunker down, let Cassie pursue the case, get what remedy you can."

"Hunker down" was the operable phrase. That choice would take time.

"Second," he said, "you can say it all in my book. Jacobi wants to put it out in March. That would bring quicker results."

You can say it all in my book. Not, *I can say it all.*

"Third," he concluded, "I can devote this week's *Lake News* to the scandal. Blow the whole thing wide open. The mainstream press will pick it up. You'd have your forum."

She swallowed. She would have exposure, which she hated. But this time there would be vindication, the final revenge.

"If I do, you won't have your book."

"It may be that you need this more than I need my book."

She was touched. "But you wanted that book."

"I can still have the book. But right now you need headlines, you need flash."

"I hate flash."

"You may hate it, but it works. Flash took your jobs, your home, your reputation. Do you want those back? Do you want to punish the people who did this to you?"

Did she ever.

JOHN spent the night at Lily's. In the morning he went straight to the office. He had plenty to write, and the words came in an effortless flow from his brain through his fingers to the screen. He wanted this issue of *Lake News* to be the best thing he'd ever done. Journalistically speaking, it was John's dream. He had followed a hunch, done his homework, and found new information to recast an old story. He had uncovered the truth and was making it known.

TUESDAY morning, when Liddie Bayne arrived with Armand's column, John was at the door. "For your better half," he said, handing her a large envelope as he took her smaller one. "How's the boss?"

"Crotchety," Liddie said, but with affection.

John grinned and gestured toward the envelope he had given her. "That should cheer him up."

It took Liddie five minutes to drive home and Armand another five to see enough of what John had sent to react.

"What is this?" Armand barked into the phone. "Why wasn't I told? I'm the publisher. Do you know the implications here?"

"It was a last-minute decision. So what do you think?"

"What do you *think* I think? I'm psyched! I want to run it. The question is, what do we do with it once it's run?"

John grinned. "I have ideas. But I'll need your help."

TIMING was everything. The key was to get people curious without allowing them to look into the story themselves. It was tricky.

John and Armand spent Tuesday evening making calls to reporters. It was something of a game for John, calling old friends in the media, then confiding that Lily Blake was indeed home, that *Lake News* had a scoop, that yes, there would probably be a news conference at press time, and that if it did materialize, it would take place in the church in the center of Lake Henry Wednesday at five.

That was the earliest John could get *Lake News* back from the printer. The story would also break in time for the evening news.

JOHN stayed at the office Tuesday night, making calls until midnight and working on the paper. He was on the phone again by eight in the morning, making the last of his calls by eleven. Then he put the finishing touches on the paper and sent it to the printer.

That was when Richard Jacobi called. The grapevine was active. He had heard the word scoop. He wasn't happy. "Listen, John, I have your contract here on my desk ready to be mailed, but if you're telling everything now, what's to tell later? Our deal was for an exclusive. I imagined prepub hype that would have bookstores and readers champing at the bit. Marketing is already on it. So's publicity and art. The package was going to be great, and *then* we'd launch with a press conference. You do that now, and the deal is off."

"Then maybe it's off," John said. He didn't feel disappointed in the least.

LILY spent Wednesday morning feeling as jittery as she had those last few days in Boston. Seeking relief in routine, she devoted herself to the cider making, but the sense of anticipation never left her for long. Thinking about the press arriving that afternoon, about the renewal of media attention on her made her queasy. "Something's on your mind," Maida remarked as they walked down to the house for lunch. "Does it have to do with John Kipling?" she asked.

Lily followed her into the kitchen, frantically wondering how much she knew about the press gathering. "Why do you ask?"

Maida sent her a disbelieving look. "I'm not stupid, Lily. Nor am I deaf. Even if I managed not to hear the calls you make, even if you hadn't told me yourself that you were with him the whole time Gus was dying, then again at the funeral, I'd have heard it from friends."

Maida took a pot of soup from the refrigerator. She put it on the stove and lit the gas. "Are you serious about John?"

"I'm not sure."

"He's a Kipling."

"He didn't have anything to do with the car business. And Donny and Gus are both gone."

Maida stirred the soup with undue force. "Did you have to go to the funeral?"

There it was—disapproval. But at least it wasn't outright condemnation of John. Lily said a quiet "Yes, I did." As she went to the cupboard for dishes, the phone started ringing.

Maida picked it up. "Yes," she snapped into the receiver.

Lily heard threads of an excited voice at the other end of the line. Maida looked sharply back at her, her shoulders stiffening.

Lily had a sinking feeling.

Maida hung up and turned. "That was Alice," she said. Alice Bayburn, her best friend. "She says phones are ringing all over town. Something about a press conference. Something about reporters coming today."

What could Lily say? "Yes. We have information on Terry Sullivan that proves—"

"I don't care about Terry Sullivan," Maida cried, looking betrayed. "I care about us. Everything had quieted down. The press lost interest. It was over and done." She grew pleading. "We were doing just fine, you and I. Weren't we?"

Softly Lily said, "This isn't about you and me."

"It is," Maida argued. "It's about respect, which you have never once shown me. Singing at church wasn't good enough. You had to sing and dance on Broadway. You knew I'd hate it, but you did it anyway."

"It was what I did well."

"And then the business in Boston. Couldn't you have let it rest?"

"No, I couldn't. Terry Sullivan has taken s-s-something from me. I need to try to get it back."

"What did he take? An apartment that was too expensive to begin with? A nightclub?"

"My name."

"Your name is perfectly good here. Why do you always need more?"

"Not more, Mom. Different."

"But you're not different," Maida shouted. "You let people take advantage of you, just like I did. Let people use you, just like I did. Donald Kipling . . . Terry Sullivan . . . John Kipling now. He's not doing this for you," she cried in disdain. "He's doing it for him. So don't you stand up there on your high horse and say we're different. You're not any better than me. If there's any difference at all, it's that I had the sense to put it behind me once and for all."

With a cry of dismay she stalked out of the house.

LILY didn't eat lunch. She turned off the flame under the soup pot, then walked up to the cider house and went to work. But she was distracted, wondering where Maida was, whether they could patch things up. She didn't want things with her mother to be up in the air. She wanted to try again.

With three hours to go until the press conference, Lily returned to the house. The kitchen was empty. Likewise the office. Lily guessed that Maida might be upstairs, but going up there would be an invasion of her privacy. Instead she sat at the piano and began to play. She was halfway through "Amazing Grace" when Maida appeared at the door. She looked tired, older than her years. Lily stopped playing.

Maida said in a reed-thin voice, "You don't understand why I like living my quiet life here and why this business with the cardinal is so upsetting to me, but there are things you don't know. Things I did before I met your father."

Lily's heart pounded as she waited for Maida to go on.

"Did you never wonder why I never talked about my childhood?" Maida asked.

"All the time. I asked you about it. You would never say."

"If they come here and see us and start digging again . . ."

Lily started to get up, then stopped herself and stayed put.

"My father died early," Maida said. "There was other family in Linsworth. Celia had four brothers."

Lily had thought there were three—and that, only from pictures she had found in a drawer after Celia passed away.

Maida spoke softly. "The brothers were all younger than Celia, the last one by twenty years. He was more my generation than hers. He was a friend, a baby-sitter, a brother, a lover."

Lily could barely breathe.

Maida's eyes filled with tears. "He used to sneak in at night when everyone was asleep. He was handsome and sweet and smart. When I was sixteen, they found out about us and sent him away."

Sixteen was the age Lily had been when she had been caught joyriding with Donny Kipling in a stolen car. She could only imagine the sense of déjà vu Maida must have felt.

"They said it was all his fault, that I was too young to understand," Maida went on. "But I understood. I wanted what happened. To this day it's my only bright memory from those years. Call me immoral or depraved, but you don't know what it was like. We all lived together in a small place. My father worked with Celia's brothers, and Celia had always been a mother to them. We were poor. We pooled our resources. I was the only girl, so I had my own room. It was cold and dark. Phillip was my warmth and my light." Her chin trembled. "I loved him. He was the only luxury I had."

"Wasn't Celia a luxury?" Lily cried, offended.

"You didn't know her then," Maida scoffed. "She was busy all the time, and she was hard. After my father died, she took care of her brothers and me. She ran the house and earned the money."

"Didn't the brothers work?"

"They didn't earn much, and most went for drink. Phillip stashed away enough for me to have when I needed to leave. There was a note saying where it was. It was in his hand when he died."

Lily caught her breath.

"He killed himself. Two months after he left. He had been wandering around the whole time, not knowing what to do with himself. His body was found in the woods less than a mile from us."

She pressed a hand to her middle, seeming in pain. Lily was up from the piano bench in a flash, but Maida held up a hand. "There's more. You wanted to know. You can hear it all."

Lily felt pain and sorrow enough to bring tears to her eyes.

"We buried Phillip in the family plot. Celia wouldn't have him anywhere else. She had loved him, too. She blamed herself for what happened. She and I grew closer, because we shared the grieving and I wanted to help her. So I dropped out of school and went to work in the logging office where she worked."

Her eyes and voice grew distant. "It wasn't easy. Everyone in town knew what had happened. Except for Celia and me, the logging operation was all men. They touched me whenever they could, like it was a game to see how much they could get. They asked me out, and I refused every time, but that made it worse."

She wilted a little. "It became clear to us that I couldn't stay there. We were trying to decide where to go and what to do when George showed up one day wanting to buy equipment from my boss. He spent long enough talking with me for us to know that he wasn't married, but we figured if he stayed around long, he'd learn enough to decide he didn't want me. So Celia and I went out and bought me some nice clothes with the money Phillip had left, and Celia managed to get me sent to Lake Henry with the deliveries. I went back to hand-deliver a bill and back again to deliver a receipt."

The memory lifted her some, pride showing its face. "I acted a part then. My life depended on it. I created a woman who was intelligent and poised, a woman with a clean past. She did things right. Your father fell in love with that woman."

Jaws tight, she fixed her eyes on Lily. "How do you think I felt when the newspapers started digging up dirty little things from your past? How do you think I felt wondering when they'd dig a little deeper and find out about me? No one here knows. I have a good life here. I have friends and a business."

"No one will find out," Lily vowed.

"How do you know?"

"Because this isn't about me anymore. It's about Terry Sullivan."

But a look of horror had appeared on Maida's face. Because her daughter now knew.

"It's all right," Lily whispered, starting forward. "It doesn't change my feelings—"

But Maida stepped back with a frantic shake of her head, then turned and hurried upstairs.

Lily knew that Maida's look of horror marked the moment when parent and child changed places in the approval game, the moment when they became equal.

Aching for Maida, she drove back to the cottage to get ready for the press conference. She was frightened of what was coming. She rushed in and out of the shower, hurried with her makeup and hair, pulled on a pantsuit, then drove to town.

There were cars and vans there—vans with satellite dishes on top, the names of local stations and national affiliates on the sides.

She turned in at the post office, but she had to pull up on the grass beside the yellow Victorian because there were cars there, too—and reporters. She was barely out of the station wagon when they spotted her. As she ran toward the door, they fell into step.

"Have you talked with the cardinal?"

"Would you comment on the lawsuit?"

John opened the door and closed it the instant she was inside. She was shaking badly as he held her.

"It's starting again," she said, panicky.

"Are you ready for this?" he asked softly.

She was not. She wanted to go home and hide. More, though, she wanted vindication. She nodded.

John straightened, took a deep breath, and opened the door.

THE meeting hall was full. Every pew was taken. Floodlights glared down on television reporters who stood in the aisles adjusting earpieces and feeding preliminaries to their stations. Townsfolk filled the back of the hall and the small balcony.

A long table had been set up at the front. A gaggle of microphones, held together with duct tape, was already mounted there, with a snake pit of wires spilling out across the floor.

Lily took the seat John indicated. He had barely taken the one on her right when Cassie slipped into the one on her left and whispered, "Just in case someone tries to trip you up."

Lily spotted faces reminiscent of the pack that had followed her in Boston. She saw friendly familiar faces, too, including Poppy at the end of a row. When their eyes met, she gave Lily a thumbs-up and a grin. It helped.

John leaned in, his voice soft but filled with barely bridled excitement. "Check the guy at two o'clock, way over on the end."

There was no mistaking that mustache. Lily felt revulsion, then glee. She whispered, "What's he doing here?"

"Must think he's getting stuff for his piece."

"Doesn't he know?"

John smiled. "I didn't say." The smile faded. "Ready?"

JOHN couldn't have been happier with the turnout. He had expected the New England contingent, plus a handful of other stalwarts, but the hall was packed. The fact that Sullivan was there was a treat.

John leaned toward the microphones and began by thanking everyone for coming. He gave a short history of *Lake News* and credited Armand, seated in the front row, with its success. Then he drew up the paper's new issue. "Last month I followed the story about the alleged relationship between Cardinal Rossetti and Lily Blake with interest, in part because Ms. Blake was from Lake Henry, in part because I used to work with the reporter who broke the story, Terry Sullivan. I had doubts about the story's validity from the start, so I wasn't surprised when the Vatican cleared Cardinal Rossetti, and the Boston *Post* had to issue him an apology. But then I had to stand by, as did Ms. Blake, and watch the papers blame her for the scandal."

He heard the hum of video cameras, the snap of cameras.

"Everyone who knew her here vouched for Ms. Blake's reasonableness, her competence, and her stability. Not a single person voiced anything remotely consistent with the kind of unbalanced condition the papers reported. To us it sounded suspiciously like the *Post* trying to justify publishing a bad story. The question is why a bad story was written in the first place."

He held up *Lake News.* "This issue addresses that question. You'll all get copies, but I'd like to summarize. From the start this story was Terry Sullivan's. He lobbied for it even when his editors at the *Post* were wary. They resisted printing it until he produced a tape in which Ms. Blake's own voice confirmed an affair with Cardinal Rossetti. That tape was illegal. Ms. Blake didn't know it was being made. Last week that tape was also proved to be bogus." A murmur slipped through the crowd.

John saw Terry's features tighten. He went on. "Those of us who know how Mr. Sullivan works urged the *Post* to examine the tape for authenticity, but they refused. It was only after evidence emerged pointing to malice on his part that they acted. The tape had been cut and spliced, which is consistent with Ms. Blake's story."

Terry was slowly shaking his head.

"Last Friday," John said, "the *Post* fired Mr. Sullivan. It was done quietly, with Ms. Blake left as the villain. The real villain is what this week's *Lake News* is about. Mr. Sullivan was the force behind this scandal. He falsified evidence to make it happen. Common sense said he had a reason for doing that. *Lake News* discloses that reason."

Lily watched and waited. Terry had gone very still. But something drew her eye farther back in the hall. Maida was there. Lily tried to catch her eye, but it was riveted on John as he went on.

"Mr. Sullivan grew up in Meadville, Pennsylvania. An essay of his that was published in the local paper when he was a teenager suggests that even then he held a grudge against the Catholic Church, and no wonder. Sources in Meadville confirm that his father used to beat him and his mother. Why? Jealousy. His mother came to that marriage loving someone else, someone she had been with through high school and college but who had left her to enter the seminary. That man was Fran Rossetti."

A murmur rose. Terry slid from his pew and snaked toward the rear, but the townsfolk wouldn't let him through. The audience turned, searching him out as he tried to escape. Cameras flashed.

An eye for an eye, Lily thought in a moment's perverse rage. People in glass houses. Do unto others.

Unable to get through, Terry turned and drew himself up. Looking straight at Lily, he said in a loud voice, "This is a classic case of shooting the messenger when you don't like the message."

John's voice boomed. "Wrong. It's a case of the misuse of power."

"Exactly," Terry shouted back. "You're trying to turn this story around for the sake of a book. Let's talk about your hefty contract."

"There's no contract," John said. "There's no book. Anything that might have been in it is here in this paper."

"That paper is filled with slander," Terry charged. "I hope you're prepared for a lawsuit." Indignant, he swung his arms and forced an opening in the crowd.

Lily remembered doing much the same thing in Boston when she'd had to fight her way through the streets. She hoped Terry was feeling even a tad of the same humiliation. She wanted him to think twice before inflicting it on others again. She wanted his colleagues to learn from his example.

Two photographers, one reporter, and a cameraman followed Terry out, but the rest of the audience turned back to John.

Maida was sitting straighter. Lily prayed that her mother was understanding more about the situation now, even feeling an iota of satisfaction on her behalf.

"That's all I have," John said. "If there are questions, we'd be glad to answer them."

Hands shot up, voices rang out.

"Was the cardinal involved in this investigation?"

"No."

"Do you have proof of a connection between Mr. Sullivan's mother and the cardinal?"

"Yes. There's a senior-prom picture in the cardinal's high school yearbook and numerous people able to verify it." He wasn't mentioning Terry's brother. It wasn't his intent to sic the press on the priest. John said only what he had to to vindicate Lily.

"Does the cardinal know about the connection to Mr. Sullivan?"

"I don't know."

"Has the *Post* issued an apology to Ms. Blake?"

"No," John answered.

"Will you demand one?" a reporter asked Lily.

Cassie leaned toward the microphones. "A lawsuit is pending. Ms. Blake has no comment at this time."

Another question came to John. "You've tried and convicted Mr. Sullivan. Isn't that an abuse of power?"

"This isn't a trial. It's investigative journalism."

"How does that differ from what he did to Ms. Blake?"

"He fabricated. He falsified. What's in *Lake News* is fact."

"You didn't have to call a press conference for that."

"Yes, I did. Ms. Blake was smeared on the front page. She deserves to be exonerated the same way."

Another raised hand. "Ms. Blake, you're an entertainer. Do you anticipate that this notoriety will give your career a boost?"

Lily was feeling surprisingly strong when she leaned toward the mike. "I'm a teacher. I lost my job because of the charges in the *Post.* I'm also a pianist. I lost that job, too, because the . . . notoriety was bringing the wrong kinds of people." She paused. "This has been a very negative experience. I don't know that I'll ever want to be in that kind of limelight again."

Then from somewhere came a defensive "We're not all bad."

John stood. "I know. That's why I'm counting on you to cover this story the way you covered the original scandal. Reporters who make up facts dirty the rest of us who don't. Now, if there are no more questions, thank you for coming."

He turned to Lily, bent over, and said, "I'd give you a hug, except I don't trust that that won't be what they report. So consider yourself hugged."

Lily felt overwhelmed—with relief, triumph, satisfaction, love.

"Are you returning to Boston?"

"Will you try to get your job at the Essex Club back?"

"Has the cardinal called?"

"That's all," Cassie told the crowd, and drew Lily away.

Lily asked, "What do you think?"

"John did good," Cassie said. "They'll report what he said. If you don't get front page, you'll come close."

"Will this affect our suit?"

Cassie grinned. "My guess is that once the *Post*'s lawyers look at their own case vis-à-vis that tape, they'll want to settle fast."

"It's not about the money," Lily said. She wanted no part of it.

"If it comes, you'll donate it somewhere. But if there isn't a penalty for libel, what's the incentive not to do it again?"

Lily barely heard the question. In the crowd she saw Maida moving to the front of the hall. "Excuse me," Lily said to Cassie, then started toward her mother, stopping when she was less than an arm's length away.

Maida took a deep, shuddering breath. She raised a tentative hand to Lily's cheek. It was light, awkward, testing. "Forgive me?" she whispered.

Lily went into Maida's arms with a sense of relief so great that she was suddenly sobbing. She wasn't alone now. She had friends here now. She even had someone she loved. But Maida was her mother, which made what she offered very special.

THE celebration was spontaneous, a gathering of friends in the back room of Charlie's general store. When reporters tried to join in, Charlie turned them away. "Sorry. Private party," he said.

Lily talked and laughed and was part of something she hadn't known to miss but wouldn't have given up for the world. John rarely left her side. Maida smiled each time she caught Lily's eye. Lake Henry had come through for her when she needed it most. Lily couldn't remember a day when she had felt so strongly that every element in her life meshed so well.

Then the cardinal called. She and John had just returned to the cottage when the phone rang. She assumed it was Poppy.

"Hey," she said, a bit breathless. "Was that fun?"

"Hey, yourself," the cardinal said, playfully sober.

She caught her breath. "Father Fran!"

"Your sister gave me this number. I'm off to Rome tomorrow, but I wanted to talk with you first. I owe you an apology, Lily. I knew who Terry Sullivan was. I didn't know him personally, but I knew the name. When he broke that story, I guessed that he knew about his mother and was getting back at me for hurting her. I didn't know about the beatings until tonight, when the first call came after your press conference."

"They called you?" Of course they would. "I'm so sorry—"

"Don't be," he scolded gently. "It's easily handled. I have no problem confirming that relationship. Jean and I were sweethearts, but I never hid from her the fact that I wanted to be a priest. My conscience is clear on that score, but not on the matter of what Terry suffered because of it and not on the matter of you. If I had acknowledged the connection, the whole thing might have stopped sooner and you wouldn't have lost so much. I'm sorry, Lily. That was wrong of me. You deserve better."

Yes, she did. Another person in her situation might have said that the cardinal's apology came too late. But Lily wasn't another person. She was gentle, and she was forgiving.

"For what it's worth," he said, "of all the doubts I've had about my worthiness since I was elevated to cardinal, a great many of them relate to this mess. There's no place for pride in my work. Or for dishonesty by virtue of omission."

"But the world needs leaders like you."

"It isn't my job to cause suffering."

"But I'm home," Lily insisted. How to resent anyone when her life was this full? "So maybe the suffering had a purpose."

He paused then. The tide of the conversation seemed to turn. "Are things working out for you there?"

"Very much. I think I've found me."

"Ahhh," he said. "That does my heart good. It doesn't forgive my selfishness—God will have to forgive that—but it does make me happy. Not surprised, mind you. I always said you were strong."

She was smiling now. "You did."

"You finally believe it, then?"

"I'm . . . getting there."

THEY had to be crazy coming out on the lake. There was no moon. The night was stark and, in the third week of October, the air too cold for canoeing, but Lily wouldn't have been anywhere else. The past hours had been chock-full of so many different emotions that she was on overload. Here, now—even in a chilling breeze—things were simpler.

"Winter's coming," John said. "You can smell it."

Lily smelled woodsmoke from a chimney onshore, and the piny clean scent of John, against whom she was nestled, but the predominant aura on the lake was of something else. "Snow?" she asked.

"Soon. Then comes ice. When it happens, it happens fast."

The canoe rose and fell. They were thirty feet out from the island in whose shallows John's loons lived.

Lily searched the darkness for the birds. "I can't see them."

Gently he cupped her head and turned it left. "There."

Then she saw, but only two. They floated close together, finding solace in each other.

"Mom and Dad have left," John said.

"Will these two ever see them again?"

"Not for three years at least. That's when they return here to mate. Whether they'll recognize their parents is anyone's guess."

"Sad," Lily said. She was thinking about Maida, about how rich she felt now that they had breached a gap.

"Let's be honest," John chided. "These guys may be whizzes at survival. But sensitive? Sentimental? I don't think so."

"No? Aren't you the one who said they come out to see you all the time?"

He chuckled. "I like to think that, but the truth is if you wait here long enough, they just float into range."

She tipped her head back. Even in the dark his face was handsome. Taking care not to tip the canoe, she shifted sideways so that she was cradled in the crook of his arm. "I like the other explanation better. I think you do, too. You're sensitive. You're sentimental." Then, because she had been wondering for hours, she asked, "Did you mean what you said about not writing a book?"

"I meant it."

"What about Terry's story? What about money and fame?"

John looked at her as she lay so trustingly in his arms. "Funny thing about money and fame. They can't go canoeing with you in the freezing cold or warm up in bed with you afterward. They can't talk. They can't sing. They can't have kids."

Her eyes went a little wider. "I can have kids," she said.

"You wouldn't want them if you were still hoping to go back to Boston. At least you wouldn't want to have them with me, because I really don't think I want to leave here. So. Do you?"

"Do I what?"

"Still want to go back to Boston?"

Lily hadn't made a conscious decision, but that didn't mean the decision wasn't made. It was made. It was easy. "What in the world is back there for me?" she asked, unable to think of a single thing that mattered more than what she had right here.

"Your car. Your piano. Your clothes."

"Funny thing about that," she said. "A car can't go canoeing with you in the freezing cold. A piano can't warm up in bed with you afterward. Clothes can't talk or sing or have kids. Besides, how can I be with you in Boston if you won't leave here?"

"But I shouldn't be the reason you stay here."

"Why not?"

She had him there. He grinned. "If you stay, what'll you do?"

"I could work for *Lake News* so that the editor in chief has more free time. I could see if there's a chamber music group in Concord in need of a pianist." There were choices. "Did I tell you how good you were today?"

John didn't mind hearing it. "I think I got my point across."

"Totally." She touched a mittened hand to his cheek. "Thank you for doing that for me."

"I did it for me, too."

"Gus would have been proud."

John wanted to think it. "Hard to tell with him."

She was looking at the sky. "Here come the stars. He's up there. He knows. He agrees."

"God?"

"Gus."

John wanted to laugh away the possibility, only the laugh didn't come. Looking at Lily, feeling her goodness and her love, he suspected she might well be right.

BARBARA DELINSKY

© SIGRID ESTRADA

What prompts a writer to start a new book? With *Lake News* it was Barbara Delinsky's concerns about privacy and press abuses. "I've been appalled by how much personal information is available to complete strangers," she says. Starting from there, this best-selling novelist proceeded to do what she does so well: "imagining the possibilities."

The book's setting, however, sprang from Delinsky's own life. She and her lawyer husband happened to be shopping for a New Hampshire lake house at the time she was researching the book. The two projects dovetailed perfectly. "I succeeded on both counts," says the author, who now divides her time between the lake house and her home base in suburban Boston.

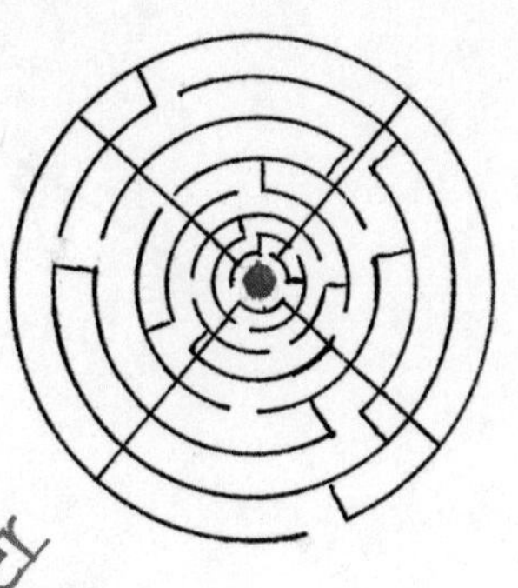

By Jeffery Deaver

The Devil's Teardrop

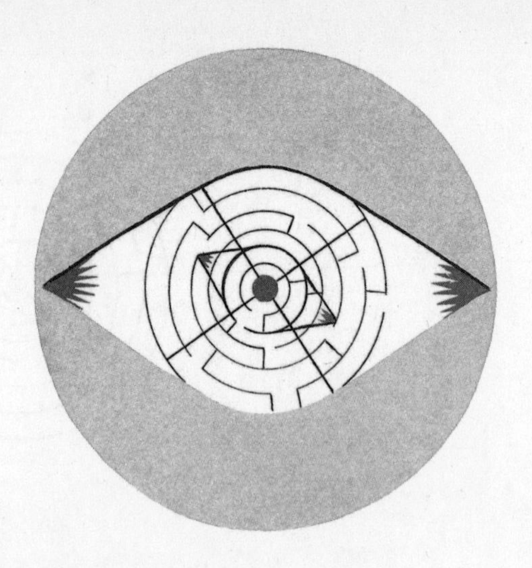

It's the last night of the century, and the clock is set for disaster.

One man can stop it. But first he must penetrate the puzzle of . . .

The Devil's Teardrop.

"Deaver is the master of ticking-bomb suspense."
—*People*

Chapter One

9:00 a.m.

THE Digger's in town.

The Digger looks like you; the Digger looks like me. He walks down the wintry streets the way anybody would, shoulders drawn together against the damp December air.

He's not tall and not short; he's not heavy and not thin. If you glanced at his eyes, you wouldn't notice the shape or the color but only that they don't seem quite human, and if the Digger glanced at *you* while you were looking at him, his eyes might be the very last thing you ever saw.

He wears a long black coat or a dark blue one, and not a soul notices him pass by, though there are many witnesses here. The streets of Washington, D.C., are crowded because it's morning rush hour. The Digger's in town, and tonight is New Year's Eve.

Carrying a Fresh Fields shopping bag, the Digger dodges around couples and singles and families and keeps on walking. Ahead, he sees the Metro station. He was told to be there exactly at nine a.m., and he will be. The Digger is never late.

A man bumps into him and smiles and says, "Sorry," but the Digger doesn't glance at him.

"Don't let . . ." *Click.* "Let anybody see your face."

This is Dupont Circle, home of money, art, the young and the chic. Nobody notices the Digger, and that's one of the reasons he's so very good at what he does.

"You're the best," says the man who tells him things.

The Digger arrives at the mouth of the subway tunnel. He thinks of a picture he saw once. He and his wife, Pamela, were at a museum. They saw an old etching of the entrance to hell.

The Metro escalator disappears sixty feet underground—passengers rising, passengers descending. It looks just like that picture.

At 8:59 the Digger walks to the top of the down escalator, which is filled with people disappearing into the pit. He reaches into the bag and curls his finger around the grip of the gun, which may be an Uzi or a Mac-10 but is definitely loaded with a hundred-round clip of bullets. His other hand—clutching the shopping bag to his chest—is curled around what somebody might think is a loaf of Fresh Fields bread but is in fact a heavy sound suppressor, packed with mineral cotton and rubber baffles.

The Digger's hungry for soup, but he ignores the sensation.

Because he's the . . . *click* . . . the best.

His watch beeps. Nine a.m.

He pulls the trigger.

There is a hissing sound as the stream of bullets begins working its way down the passengers on the escalator, and they pitch forward under the fire. The *hush-hush-hush* of the gun is suddenly obscured by the screams and all the terrible clangs of the misses—the bullets striking the metal and the tile. The sounds of the hits are much softer.

Everyone looks around, not knowing what's going on.

The Digger looks around, too. Everyone frowns. He frowns.

Nobody thinks that he or she is being shot. They believe that someone has fallen and started a chain reaction of people tumbling down the escalator. The hundred rounds are gone in seconds.

The Digger lowers the shopping bag, which has one small hole where the bullets left. The bag holds all the hot brass shells.

"Shut off the escalator! Look, they're being crushed."

The Digger looks. Below is just a mass of bodies growing higher, writhing. Some are alive, some dead, some struggling to get out from underneath the crush that's piling up at the base of the escalator.

The Digger is easing backward into the crowd, moving along the sidewalks filled with people. Nobody notices the Digger.

As he walks—slowly, don't run, never run—he thinks about his motel, where he'll reload his gun and repack his silencer with bristly mineral cotton and sit in his comfy chair with a bottle of water and a bowl of soup beside him. He'll sit and relax until this afternoon, and then—if the man who tells him things doesn't leave a message to tell him not to—he'll pull on his long black or dark blue coat once more and go outside. And do this all over again.

It's New Year's Eve. And the Digger's in town.

WHILE ambulances were speeding to Dupont Circle and rescue workers were digging through the ghastly mine of bodies in the Metro station, Gilbert Havel walked toward city hall, two miles away. He paused and opened the envelope he carried and read the note one last time.

> Mayor Kennedy—
>
> The end is night. The Digger is loose and their is no way to stop him. He will kill again—at four, 8 and Midnight if you don't pay.
>
> I am wanting $20 million dollars in cash, which you will put into a bag and leave it two miles south of Rt 66 on the West Side of the Beltway. In the middle of the Field. Pay to me the Money by 1200 hours. Only I am knowing how to stop The Digger. If you ~~[illegible]~~ apprehend me, he will keep killing. If you kill me, he will keep killing.
>
> If you don't think I'm real, some of the Diggers bullets were painted black. Only I know that.

This was, Havel decided, about as perfect an idea as anybody could've come up with. Months of planning. Every possible response by the police and FBI anticipated. A chess game.

Buoyed by that thought, he replaced the note in the envelope, closed but didn't seal it, and continued along the street.

The security at city hall was ridiculous. Havel walked past the entrance and paused at a newspaper vending machine. He slipped the envelope under the newsstand and walked away. At the corner he stopped at a pay phone and dialed a number.

A voice answered, "City hall. Security."

Havel held a tape recorder next to the phone and pressed PLAY. A computer-generated voice said, "Envelope in front of the building. Under the *Post* vending machine. Read it now. It's about the Metro shooting." He hung up and crossed the street, dropping the tape recorder into a wastebasket.

Havel stepped into a coffee shop and sat in a window booth, where he had a good view of the vending machine and the side entrance to city hall. He wanted to make sure the envelope was picked up—and it was, before Havel even had his jacket off.

The waitress stopped by his booth, and he ordered coffee and, though it was still early, a steak sandwich—the most expensive thing on the menu. Why not? He was about to become a very wealthy man.

"DADDY, tell me about the Boatman."

Parker Kincaid set down the cast-iron skillet he was washing. He'd learned never to seem alarmed by anything the children asked. He smiled down at the boy as he dried his hands.

"The Boatman?" he asked the nine-year-old boy. "You bet. What do you want to know?"

The kitchen of Parker's house in Fairfax, Virginia, was fragrant with the smells of a holiday meal in the works.

Robby was blond and had his mother's blue eyes. His floppy cowlick leaned to the starboard this morning. "I mean," the boy began, "I know he's dead and everything. . . ."

"That's right," Parker said. He said nothing more. ("Never tell the children more than they asked for." This was one of the rules from Parker Kincaid's *Handbook for the Single Parent*—a guide that existed solely in his mind, yet one he referred to every day.)

"It's just that outside . . . sometimes it looks like him. I mean, I looked outside, and it's like I could see him."

"What do we do when you feel like that?"

"I get my shield and helmet, and if it's dark, I put the lights on."

Parker remained standing. Usually, when he had serious conversations with his children, he subscribed to the eye-level approach. But when the subject of the Boatman arose, the therapist had recommended that Parker stand—make the boy feel safe in the presence of a strong, protective adult. And there was something about Parker Kincaid that induced a sense of security. Just forty, he was a little over six feet and in nearly as good shape now as he'd been in college. Thanks not to aerobics or health clubs, but to his two children's soccer scrimmages, Frisbee tourneys, and the family's regular Sunday morning runs. (Well, Parker's run—he usually brought up the rear behind their bicycles.)

"Let's take a look. You have your helmet and your shield?"

"Right here." The boy patted his head and then held up his left arm like a knight's.

"I've got mine, too." Parker mimicked the boy's gestures.

They walked to the back porch. "See those bushes," Robby said.

Parker looked out over his half-acre in an old development twenty miles west of Washington, D.C. At the back of the property was a tangle of forsythia and kudzu and ivy he'd been meaning to cut back for a year. Sure enough, if you squinted, some of the vegetation *did* resemble a human form.

"That looks spooky," Parker conceded. "Sure does. But you know the Boatman was a long time ago. How long ago was it?"

"Four years," Robby answered. "But . . ."

"Isn't that a *long* time?"

"Pretty long, I guess."

"Show me." He stretched his arms out. "This long?"

"Maybe."

"I think it's longer." Parker stretched his arms out farther. "As long as that fish we caught at Braddock Lake?"

"That was *this* long," the boy said, starting to smile. He ran the length of the kitchen, lifting one arm, then ran back and lifted the other. "*This* long!"

"That's how long a shark is," Parker cried. "No, a whale. No, I know—a Tufted Mazurka!" A creature from *If I Ran the Zoo.* Robby and Stephie loved Dr. Seuss. Parker's nickname for the children was the Whos, after the creatures in *Horton Hears a Who,* which was their absolutely favorite story of all time.

"How 'bout tomorrow we cut down all those bushes?"

"Can *I* use the saw?" the boy asked quickly.

"We'll see," Parker said.

"All right!" Robby ran upstairs, memories of the Boatman lost for now. Parker soon heard some gentle bickering between Robby and his sister, Stephanie, about which Nintendo game to play.

Parker's eyes lingered on the brush in the backyard. The Boatman . . . He shook his head.

The doorbell rang. He walked to the door and swung it open.

The attractive woman offered a smile. Her earrings dangled below her sharp-edged blond hair. Her tan was scrupulous.

"Well, hello," Parker said tentatively.

He glanced past her and was relieved to see that the engine of the beige Cadillac parked in the driveway was still running. Richard was behind the wheel, reading *The Wall Street Journal.*

"Hi, Parker. We just got in to Dulles. St. Croix was wonderful." She hugged him. "I just stopped by a minute."

"You look good, Joan. The kids're upstairs—" He turned to call them.

"No, that's all right," Joan started to say.

"Robby, Stephie! Your mommy's here."

Thuds on the stairs. The Whos turned the corner fast and ran up to Joan, who smiled, though Parker could see that she was miffed he'd called them.

"Mommy, you're all tan!" said Stephie. She had a long, serious face, which, Parker hoped, would start to look intimidatingly intellectual to boys by the time she turned twelve or thirteen.

"Where were you, Mommy?" Robby said, frowning.

"The Caribbean. Didn't Daddy tell you?" A glance at Parker. Yes, he'd told them. Joan didn't understand that what the children were upset about wasn't miscommunication, but the fact that she hadn't been in Virginia for Christmas.

"Did you have a nice holiday?" she asked.

Stephie said, "I got a soccer ball and the new Mario Brothers and the whole set of Wallace and Gromit—"

"That's nice. Did you get my presents?" Joan asked.

"Uh-huh," Stephie said. "Thank you." The girl was impeccably polite, but Barbie dolls in pageant dresses no longer held any interest for her. Eight-year-olds now were not the eight-year-olds of Joan's childhood.

"Daddy took back my shirt," Robby said, "and got one the right size."

"I told him to do that if it didn't fit," Joan said quickly.

"We didn't get to talk to you on Christmas," Stephie said.

"Oh," Joan replied to her daughter, "it was so hard to call from where we were staying. It was like *Gilligan's Island.* The phones were never working." She tousled Robby's hair. "Richard and I have to go now. We have to pick up Elmo and Saint at the kennel. The poor puppies have been in cages all week."

Robby said, "We're having a party tonight, and we're going to watch the fireworks on TV."

"Oh, that'll be fun," Joan said. "Richard and I are going to the opera."

"Wait," Stephie blurted, then pounded up the stairs.

"Honey, I don't have much time. We—"

The girl returned a moment later with her new soccer outfit.

"My," said her mother, "that's pretty." Not knowing what to do exactly, Joan held the clothes awkwardly.

Parker Kincaid was thinking, First the Boatman, now Joan . . . How the past was intruding today. Well, why not? After all it was New Year's Eve. A time to look back.

Joan said, "I just stopped by now to say hi and to talk to your father for a minute. I'll bring gifts from the trip tomorrow when

I come to visit." She was relieved when the children ran back to Stephie's bedroom, buoyed by the promise of more presents.

As Joan turned to Parker, her smile was gone. "Parker, I didn't have to do this." She reached in her purse.

Oh, no, he thought, she got me a Christmas present, and I didn't get her one. But then he saw her hand emerge with a wad of papers.

"I could've let the process server take care of it on Monday."

Process server?

"But I wanted to talk to you before you went off half-cocked."

The top of the document read "Motion to Modify Child Custody Order." He felt the blow deep in his stomach.

"Joan," he said, despairing, "you're not . . ."

"I want them, Parker, and I'm going to get them. Let's not fight about it. We can work something out."

"No," he whispered, feeling the panic sweep through him.

"Four days with you, Fridays and weekends with me. Maybe Mondays, depending on what Richard and I have planned. Look, it'll give you more time to yourself."

"Absolutely not."

"They're my children . . ." she began.

"Technically." Parker had had sole custody for four years.

"Parker," she said reasonably, "my life is stable. I'm doing fine. I'm working out again. I'm married." To a civil servant in county government, who, according to the Washington *Post,* just missed getting indicted for accepting bribes last year. Richard was also the man Joan'd been sleeping with for the last year of her marriage to Parker.

Concerned that the children would hear, he now whispered fiercely, "You've been a stranger to Robby and Stephie from the day they were born." He slapped the papers. "Are you thinking about them at all? About what this'll do to them?"

"They need a mother."

No, Parker thought, Joan needs another collectible. Several years ago it had been horses. Then championship weimaraners. Antiques. Houses in increasingly fancy neighborhoods.

"Why on earth do you want to do this?"

"I want a family."

"Have children with Richard. You're young."

But she wouldn't want *that,* Parker knew. As much as she'd loved being pregnant—she was never more beautiful—she had fallen apart at the work involved with infants. You can hardly have children when emotionally you're one yourself.

"You're completely unfit," Parker said.

"My, you *have* learned how to take the gloves off, haven't you? Well, maybe I *was* unfit. That's in the past."

"I'll fight it, Joan," he said matter-of-factly. "You know that."

She snapped, "I'll be by tomorrow at ten, and I'm bringing a social worker to talk to the kids."

"Joan . . . On a *holiday?*" Richard would have pulled strings for this. "Wait until next week. Some stranger talking to them on the holiday? It's ridiculous. They want to see *you.*"

"Parker," Joan said, exasperated, "she's a professional. She's not going to upset them. Look, I have to run. The kennel's closing soon because of the holiday. Those poor puppies . . . Oh, come on, Parker. It's not the end of the world."

But yes, he thought, that's exactly what it is.

MAYOR Gerald Kennedy looked at the piece of paper on his desk.

Mayor Kennedy—
The end is night. The Digger is loose and their is no way to stop him.

Attached to the sheet was an FBI memo, which was headed "Annexed document is a copy. METSHOOT case, 12/31."

METSHOOT, Kennedy thought. Metro shooting. The Bureau loved their acronyms, he recalled. Sitting hunched like a bear over the ornate desk in his Georgian office in the very un-Georgian Washington, D.C., city hall, Kennedy read the note once more, then looked up at the two people seated across from him—an attractive blond woman and a tall, lean gray-haired man. Balding, Kennedy often thought of people in terms of their hair.

"You're sure he's the one behind the shooting?"

"What he said about the bullets being painted," the woman said. "That checked out. We're sure the note's from the perp."

Gerry Kennedy, a bulky man comfortable with his bulk, pushed the note around on his desk with his huge hands.

The door opened, and a young black man in a double-breasted Italian suit and oval glasses walked in.

Kennedy gestured him to the desk. "This is Wendell Jefferies," he said. "My chief aide-de-camp."

The woman agent nodded. "Margaret Lukas."

The other agent gave what seemed to be a shrug. "Cage."

They all shook hands. "They're FBI," Kennedy added.

Jefferies's nod said, Obviously.

Kennedy pushed the copy of the note toward the aide. Jefferies looked at it. "He's gonna do it again?"

"So it seems," the woman agent said.

Kennedy looked over the agents. Cage was from Ninth Street—FBI headquarters—and Lukas was the acting special agent in charge of the Washington, D.C., field office. Her boss was out of town, so she was the person running the Metro shooting case. Cage was older and seemed well connected in the Bureau; Lukas was younger and appeared more cynical and energetic. Kennedy had been mayor of the District of Columbia for three years now, and he had kept the city afloat not on experience and connections, but on cynicism and energy. He was glad Lukas was in charge.

"Bastard can't even spell," Jefferies muttered, reading the note again; then he checked his watch.

Kennedy looked at the brass clock on his desk. It was just after ten a.m. "Twelve hundred hours . . . noon," he mused, wondering why the extortionist used twenty-four-hour European or military time. "We have two hours till we have to pay the ransom."

Jefferies said, "You'll have to make a statement, Gerry. Soon."

"I know." Kennedy stood. He glanced at Jefferies—the man was young but, Kennedy knew, had a promising political career ahead of him. Jefferies's face twisted into a sour expression, and Kennedy understood that he was thinking the same thing that the mayor was: Why did this have to happen now? Why here?

Kennedy glanced at a memo about the special reviewing stand at the New Year's Eve fireworks tonight on the Mall. He and Claire, his wife, would be sitting with Representative Paul Lanier and the other key congressional zookeepers of the District. Or they would have been if this hadn't happened.

He asked the two agents, "What're you doing to catch him?"

Lukas answered immediately. "We're checking CIs—confidential informants—and handlers who've got any contact with domestic or foreign terrorist cells. So far, nothing, and my assessment is this isn't a classic terrorist profile. We're also running license plates from every car parked around city hall after we learned about the note. And we're running the tags from cars around Dupont Circle this morning. We're checking out the drop area by the Beltway and all the hotels, apartments, and houses around it."

"You don't sound optimistic."

"I'm not optimistic. There're no witnesses. No reliable ones anyway. A case like this—we need witnesses."

Kennedy examined the note once again. It seemed odd that a madman should have such nice handwriting. "Should I pay?"

Lukas looked at Cage, then said, "We feel that unless you pay the ransom or an informer comes forward with solid information about the Digger's whereabouts, we won't be able to stop him by four p.m. We just don't have enough leads." She added, "I'm not recommending you pay. This's just my assessment of what'll happen if you don't."

"Twenty million," Kennedy mused.

Without a knock the office door opened, and a tall man of about sixty stepped inside. Representative Paul Lanier shook the mayor's hand and then introduced himself to the FBI agents.

"Paul," Kennedy told them, "is head of the District Governance Committee." Though the District of Columbia had some autonomy, Congress had recently taken over the power of the purse and doled out money like a parent giving a reckless child an allowance.

For Lanier's benefit Lukas ran through her assessment again.

"Are you sure you want to pay?" Lanier asked Kennedy. "It's going to send the wrong signals. Kowtowing to terrorists."

Kennedy glanced at Lukas, who said, "It *is* something to think about. The floodgates theory. You give in to one extortionist, there'll be others."

Kennedy asked her, "What can you do to find him if we *do* pay?"

Lukas responded, "Our tech people'll rig the drop bag with a transmitter. We'll try to track the perp to his hideout. If we're lucky, get both him and the shooter—this Digger."

"Lucky," Kennedy said skeptically. Margaret Lukas was a pretty woman, he thought, though her face hadn't once softened since she'd walked into his office. No smile, no sympathy. Her voice was flinty now as she said, "We can't give you percentages."

"No, of course you can't." Kennedy rose and stepped to a window, looked out on the trees speckled with brown leaves. Tonight the forecasters were predicting the first big snow of the year, but at the moment the air was warm.

Kennedy glanced at Wendell Jefferies, who took the cue and joined him. The mayor whispered, "So Wendy, the pressure's on, huh?"

The aide, never known for his restraint, responded, "You got the ball, boss. Drop it, and you and me both—we're gone."

Twenty-three people were dead. And so far all they knew was that this psychopath was going to try to kill more people at four o'clock and more after that and more after that.

Mayor Kennedy turned back to his desk and looked at the brass clock. The time was 10:25. The desk lamp shone on the note. To Kennedy it seemed that the piece of paper glowed like white fire.

Representative Lanier said, "I say we don't pay. We're taking a hard line. We're standing tough on terrorism. We're—"

"I'm paying," said Kennedy.

"Hold on," the Congressman said. "Not so fast."

"It's not fast at all," Kennedy snapped. "I've been considering it since I got this thing." He gestured at the fiery note.

"You don't have the right to make that decision," Lanier said. "Congress has jurisdiction."

Agent Cage said to Lanier, "No, it doesn't. It's exclusively the District's call. I asked the Attorney General on my way over."

"But we've got control of the money," Lanier snapped, "and I'm not going to authorize it."

Kennedy glanced at Jefferies, who said, "Twenty million? We can draw on our line of credit for discretionary spending."

"Gerry, this is ridiculous," Lanier said. "Never deal with terrorists. Don't you read Department of State advices?"

"No, I don't," Kennedy said. "Nobody sends 'em to me. Now, Agent Lukas, go stop him."

THE sandwich was okay. Not great. Gilbert Havel decided that after he got the money, he was going to have a real steak. He finished his coffee and kept his eye on city hall.

The chief of police of the District had come and gone quickly. A few reporters and camera crews had been turned away. Then a couple of what were clearly FBI agents had disappeared inside some time ago—a man and a woman. It was definitely a Bureau operation. Well, he'd known it would be. So far no surprises.

Havel looked at his watch. Time to go to the safe house, call the helicopter charterer. There was a lot to get ready for. The plans for picking up the twenty million were elaborate—and the plans for getting away afterward were even more elaborate.

Havel paid his check and pulled his coat and cap on. He left the coffee shop, turned, and walked through an alley, headed for Pennsylvania Avenue, where he'd get a bus down to Southeast D.C.

Gilbert Havel emerged from the alley and turned onto a side street. The light changed to green. Havel stepped into the intersection. Suddenly a flash of dark motion from his left. He turned his head, thinking, Damn, he doesn't see me! He doesn't— "Hey!" he cried.

The driver of the large delivery truck had been looking at an invoice and had sped through the red light. He glanced up, horrified. With a squeal of brakes the truck slammed into Havel.

The truck caught Havel between its front fender and a parked car, crushing him like a cricket. The driver leaped out and stared in shock. "You weren't looking! It wasn't my fault!" Then he saw two people running toward him from the corner. "Oh, God." He debated for a moment, but panic took over and he leaped into his truck. He gunned the engine and backed up—Havel dropped to the ground—then the driver sped away.

Two men in their thirties ran up to Havel. One bent down to check for a pulse.

"Is he dead?" the standing one asked his friend.

"Oh, yeah," the other man said. "Oh, yeah, he's dead."

WHERE?

Margaret Lukas lay on her lean belly on a rise overlooking the Beltway. Traffic sped past, an endless stream.

She looked at her watch again and thought, Where *are* you?

There'd been no way to get a mobile command post near the ransom drop zone and not be seen by the extortionist. So here she was, in jeans, down jacket, and cap turned backward, lying on the rock-hard ground. Where they'd been for an hour.

"Sounds like water," Cage said.

"What?"

"The traffic."

He lay on his belly too, next to her. They were on Gallows Road—yes, "Gallows," an irony so rich that not one of the agents had bothered to comment on it. They studied the field a hundred yards away. Where was the unsub? There's twenty million bucks there for the taking, and he's not taking it.

"Where is he? Why's he late?" muttered another voice. It belonged to a somber man of about thirty, with a military hairstyle and bearing. Leonard Hardy was with the District police and was part of the team because it would look bad not to have a District cop on board. Lukas would normally have protested having non-Bureau personnel on her team, but she knew Hardy casually from his assignments at the Bureau's D.C. field office and didn't mind his presence—as long as he kept doing what he'd done so far: sitting quietly and not bothering the grown-ups. His immaculate hands, with their perfectly trimmed nails, jotted notes for his report to the District chief of police and the mayor.

"Anything?" She turned her head, calling in a whisper to Tobe Geller, a curly-haired young agent in jeans and windbreaker.

Geller, in his thirties too, had the intensely cheerful face of a boy who finds complete contentment in any product filled with microchips. "Zip," he responded. He scanned one of three portable video monitors in front of him. If there was any living thing larger than a raccoon for one hundred yards around the ransom, Geller's surveillance equipment would find it.

When the mayor had given the go-ahead to pay the extortion money, the cash had made a detour en route to the drop. At a small unmarked garage near FBI headquarters, Geller had repacked the ransom into two Burgess Security Systems KL-19 knapsacks. The canvas looked like regular cloth but was in fact impregnated with strands of oxidized copper—a high-efficiency antenna. The bag transmitted a Global Positioning System beacon.

Geller had also rewrapped forty bundles of hundred-dollar bills with wrappers of his own design. There were ultrathin transmitting wafers laminated inside them. Even if the unsub transferred the cash from the canvas bag, Geller could still track down the money—up to a range of sixty miles.

The bag had been placed in the field just where the unsub had instructed in his extortion note. The agents had backed off, and the waiting began.

"Where are you?" Lukas muttered. "Where?" She compulsively scanned the field once more, though Geller's sensors would have picked up the unsub long before her blue-gray eyes could spot him.

"Hmm." C. P. Ardell, a heavyset agent, squeezed his earphone, then nodded his bald, glossy pale head and glanced at Lukas. "That was Charlie position. Nobody's gone off the road in the woods."

Lukas grunted. She was wrong. She'd thought the unsub would come at the money from the west—through a row of trees a half mile away from the expressway. "Bravo position?" she asked.

C.P., who worked undercover a lot, seemed to be the most patient of all the agents on the stakeout. He hadn't moved his two-hundred-and-fifty-pound frame an inch since they'd been here. He made the call to the southernmost surveillance post.

"Nothing. Kids on a four-wheeler is all."

More time passed. Detective Hardy jotted notes. Geller typed on his keyboard. Cage fidgeted, and C.P. did not.

Lukas asked Cage, "Your wife mad you working the holiday?"

Cage shrugged. It was his favorite gesture. A senior agent at FBI HQ, he and Lukas worked together often. Usually with Lukas's boss, too, the special agent in charge of the Washington, D.C., field office. This week, though, the S.A.C. happened to be in a Brazilian rain forest on vacation, and Lukas had stepped up to the case.

She felt bad for Cage and Geller and C.P., working today. They had dates for tonight or wives. As for Len Hardy, she was happy he was here; he had some pretty good reasons to keep himself busy on holidays.

Lukas herself had a comfortable home in Georgetown, a place filled with antique furniture, embroideries and quilts of her own design, an erratic wine collection, nearly five hundred books, and more than one thousand CDs. And her mix-breed Labrador, Jean Luc. It was a nice place to spend a holiday evening, though in the three years she'd lived there, Lukas had never once done so.

She now scanned the field again. No sign of the perp. She glanced at her watch. A little over three hours until the next shooting. A voice crackled in her earphone, speaking her name.

"Go ahead," she said into her mike, recognizing the voice of the deputy director of the Bureau.

"We've got a problem," he said. "There was a hit-and-run near city hall a little while ago. White male. Killed. No ID on him. Just an apartment key and some money. The cop who responded heard about the extortion thing and, since it was near city hall, thought there might be a connection."

She understood immediately. "They compared prints?" she asked. "His and the ones on the extortion note?"

"Right. The dead guy's the one who wrote the note."

Lukas remembered part of the note. It went something like: "If you kill me, he will keep killing. Nothing can stop The Digger."

"You've got to find the shooter, Margaret," the deputy director said. "You've got to find him in three hours."

Chapter Two

1:15 p.m.

IS IT real? Parker Kincaid wondered.

Bending over the rectangle of paper, peering through his heavy, ten-power hand glass. Joan had been gone for several hours, but the effect of her visit—the dismay—still lingered, trying though he was to lose himself in his work. The letter he was examining—on yellowed paper—was encased in a thin poly sleeve. It *appeared* to be real. But in his profession Parker Kincaid never put great stock in appearances.

He wanted badly to touch the document, to feel the rag paper, the faint ridge of the iron gallide ink. But he didn't dare take the paper from the sleeve; even the slightest oil from his hands would start eroding the thin sheet. Which would be a disaster, since it was worth perhaps fifty thousand dollars. *If* it was real.

Upstairs, Stephie was playing Nintendo. Robby was at Parker's feet, accompanied by his *Star Wars* figures—Han Solo and Chewbacca. The basement study was a cozy place, wood paneled, forest-green carpet. On the walls were hundreds of framed documents—the less valuable items in Parker's collection. Letters from Woodrow Wilson, FDR, Bobby Kennedy, the Old West artist Charles Russell. Hundreds of others. On one wall was a rogues' gallery—forgeries Parker had come across in his work. His favorite wall, though, was the one opposite the stool he sat on. This wall contained the Whos' drawings and poems.

The room was silent. Usually Parker would have the radio on, but there'd been a shooting in the District and Parker didn't want Robby to hear the special reports, not after the flashback to the Boatman.

He hunched over the letter eagerly, the way a jeweler appraises a beautiful yellow stone, ready to declare it false if that's how he saw it, but secretly hoping it will turn out to be rare topaz.

"What's that?" Robby asked, standing and looking at the letter.

"You know Thomas Jefferson?"

"Third President of the United States."

"Good. This's a letter that somebody thinks he wrote. They want me to check it and make sure."

One of the more difficult conversations he'd had with Robby and Stephie was explaining what he did for a living. Not the technical part of being a document examiner. But that people would fake letters and documents and try to claim they were real.

"What's it say?" the boy asked.

Parker didn't answer right away. Oh, answers were important to him. He was, after all, a puzzle master. His lifelong hobby was riddles and word games and puzzles. But the content of the letter made him hedge. "It's a letter Jefferson wrote to his oldest daughter." He didn't tell the boy that the subject of the letter was Jefferson's second daughter, Mary—whom he called Polly. She had died of complications from childbirth, as had Jefferson's wife some years before.

"Back here in Washington I live under an extreme pall, haunted as I am by visions of Polly on horseback. . . ." Parker, certified document examiner, struggled to ignore the sadness he felt reading Jefferson's words and to remain analytical. Concentrate, he told himself, though the thoughts of a father being deprived of one of his children kept intruding.

He was about to slip the letter under one of his Bausch & Lomb compound microscopes when the doorbell rang again.

Oh, no. It was Joan. He knew it. She'd picked up her dogs and had come to complicate his life further.

Parker slid off the stool, climbed the stairs, mad now. He was determined that the Whos would have a fun New Year despite their mother. He flung the door open.

"Hello, Parker."

It took him a second to remember the name of the tall, gray-haired man. He hadn't seen the FBI agent for several years. Then he recalled. "Cage." He didn't recognize the woman beside him.

"How you doin'?" Cage said. "Never expected to see me, did you?" The agent had changed very little. A bit grayer. A little more gaunt.

From the corner of his eye Parker saw Robby appear in the hallway with his co-conspirator, Stephie. They edged closer to the door, gazing out at Cage and the woman.

Parker turned and bent down. "Don't you two have something to do up in your rooms? Something *very* important?"

"No," Stephie said.

"Well, I think you do. Upstairs now. Let Daddy talk to his friends."

As the children started up the stairs, Parker closed the door behind him and turned back, appraising the woman. She was in her thirties, with a narrow, smooth face. Pale, nothing like Joan's relentless tan. She reached out a strong hand with long fingers. "I'm Margaret Lukas, A.S.A.C. at the Washington field office."

Parker recalled that within the Bureau, assistant special agents in charge were referred to by the acronym ASAC—Aye-sack—while the heads of the offices were never called "Sacks." Yet another aspect of his former life he hadn't recalled for years.

She continued. "Could we come inside for a minute?"

He responded, "You mind if we stay out here? The children . . ."

"Fine with us," Cage said for both of them. He nodded after the kids. "They're growing."

"They do that," Parker answered. "What exactly is it, Cage?"

The agent gave a shrug toward Lukas. "We need your help, Mr. Kincaid," she said quickly.

"You watch the news, Parker?" Cage asked.

"The guy in the subway—that's what you're here about."

"METSHOOT," Lukas said. "That's what we've acronymed it. He killed twenty-three people. Wounded thirty-seven. Six children were badly injured."

"What on earth could you possibly want from me? I'm retired."

"You still do document examination," Lukas said. "You're in the yellow pages, and you've got a Web site."

Parker said firmly, "I'm a *civilian* document examiner. I don't do any criminal forensics."

Lukas said, "Cage tells me you were head of the document division for six years. He says you're the best in the country."

What weary eyes she has, Parker thought. She's probably only thirty-six or thirty-seven. Great figure, trim, athletic, beautiful face, but eyes like blue-gray stones. Parker knew about eyes like that.

Daddy, tell me about the Boatman.

"Parker was also a candidate for S.A.C. Eastern District," Cage said. "Except he turned it down."

Lukas lifted her pale eyebrows.

"And that was years ago," Parker responded.

"Yes, it was," Cage said. "But you're not rusty, are you?"

"Cage, get to the point."

"I'm trying to wear you down," the graying agent said.

"Can't be done."

"Ah, I'm the miracle worker. Remember?" To Lukas, Cage said, "See, he didn't just catch forgeries. Parker used to track people down because of what they wrote, where they buy writing paper, pens, things like that. Best in the business."

Parker thought of the Whos, of their party tonight. Thought of his ex-wife. He opened his mouth to tell lanky Cage and deadeye Lukas to get the hell out of his life, but she was there first. Bluntly she said, "Just listen. The unsub—"

Parker recalled: unknown subject. An unidentified perp.

"And his partner—the shooter—have this extortion scheme. The shooter lights up a crowd with an automatic weapon every four hours unless the city pays. Mayor's willing to, and we drop the money. But the unsub never shows up. Why? He's dead."

"You believe the luck?" Cage said. "On his way to collect twenty million, and he gets nailed by a delivery truck."

Parker asked, "Why didn't the *shooter* pick up the money?"

Lukas said, " 'Cause the shooter's only instructions are to kill. He doesn't have anything to do with the money. The unsub turns the shooter loose with instructions to keep going if he doesn't get a call to stop. That way if we collar the unsub, he's got leverage to work out a plea bargain in exchange for stopping the shooter."

"So," Cage said, "we've gotta find him. The shooter."

The door behind him started to open.

Parker quickly said to Lukas, "Button your jacket."

"What?" She frowned.

As Robby stepped outside, Parker reached forward and tugged her jacket closed, hiding the large pistol on her belt. He whispered, "I don't want him to see your weapon."

He put his arm around his son's shoulders. "Hey, Who. How you doing?"

"I was winning, but then Stephie hid the controller."

Parker turned and called, "Stephie-effie, is that controller going to appear in five seconds? Four, three, two . . ."

"I found it!" she called down.

"My turn!" Robby cried, and charged up the stairs again.

Parker noticed Lukas's eyes follow Robby as he climbed to the second floor. "What's his name?" she asked.

"Robby."

"But what did you call him?"

"Oh. 'Who.' It's my nickname for the kids. It's from a Dr. Seuss book." Parker turned to Cage. "Look, I'm sorry. But I really can't help you."

"You understand the problem here?" Cage said. "The only link we've got—the *only* clue at all—is the extortion note."

"Run it by PERT." The Bureau's physical evidence response team.

Lukas's thin lips grew slightly thinner. "If we have to, we will. And we'll get a psycholinguistic from Quantico. And agents out to every paper-and-pen company in the country. But—"

"That's what we're hopin' you'd take over on," Cage filled in. "You can look at it, tell us what's what. Stuff nobody else can.

Maybe where he lived, where the shooter's going to hit next."

Parker was imagining what would happen if Joan found out he was working on an active investigation.

"We have nothing," Lukas said angrily. "No leads. We have until four o'clock before this crazy shoots up another crowd of people. There were children shot down—"

Parker said, "I'll have to ask you to leave now. Good luck."

Cage shrugged, looked at Lukas. She handed Parker her card. "Cell phone's on the bottom. . . . Look, if we have any questions, do you at least mind if we call?"

Parker hesitated. "No, I don't." He stepped back inside, said "Good-bye," and closed the door. Robby stood on the stairs.

"Who were they, Daddy?"

Parker said, "That was a man I used to work with."

"Did she have a gun?" Robby asked. "That lady."

"Did you *see* a gun?" Parker asked him.

"Yeah."

"Then I guess she had one."

"Did you work with her?" the boy asked.

"No. Just the man."

"Oh. She was pretty, Daddy."

Parker started to say, For a lady cop. But he didn't.

"THE weapon," Margaret Lukas called abruptly. "I want the details on the shooter's weapon."

"Any minute now," C. P. Ardell called back.

They were in the Bureau's new strategic information and operations center on the fifth floor of headquarters.

Cage walked past Lukas and whispered, "You're doing fine."

Lukas didn't respond. She caught sight of her reflection in one of the huge video screens on the wall, on which was displayed the extortion note. Thinking, Am I doing fine? She hoped so. She'd sent the dead unsub's prints to every major friction-ridge database in the world. She had two dozen agents tracking down witnesses. Hundreds of tag numbers were being checked out. Handlers were milking informants all over the country. Phone records in and out of city hall for the past two weeks were being checked.

A call came in. Len Hardy started to pick up the phone, but Cage got to it first. Detective Hardy had shed his trench coat, revealing a white shirt with thin brown stripes and razor-crease slacks and a brown tie. Despite lying in a northern Virginia field, his hair was still perfectly in place, and there was not a bit of dirt on him. He looked less like a detective than a clean-cut Jehovah's Witness about to offer you some brochures on salvation.

"You okay, Detective?" Lukas asked him, seeing his disgruntled expression as the agent swept the phone out from under his nose.

"Right as rain," Hardy muttered, not too sardonically.

She gave a faint laugh at the expression, which she hadn't heard for years. "You from the Midwest?"

"Can'tcha tell from the accent? Outside of Chicago."

He sat down. Her smile faded. *Right as rain . . .*

Cage hung up. "Got your details. That was firearms. Gun was an Uzi. Mineral cotton in the silencer. Hand packed. Not commercial. The shooter knows what he's doing."

She called to C. P. Ardell, "Have somebody check out Web sites that give instructions for homemade silencers. See if they'll give up any E-mail addresses of recent hits."

The agent made his call, then reported, "Tech services is on it."

To Cage, Lukas said, "Hey, got an idea. We can get that guy from human resources, the one who examines applicants' handwriting and writes up their personalities."

"Don't bother," a voice from behind them said.

Lukas turned and saw a man in a leather bomber jacket. He walked into the lab. He wore a visitor's badge around his neck and was carrying a large attaché case.

"Artie let me up," Parker Kincaid said. The employee-entrance night guard. "He still remembers me after all these years."

This was a different side of Kincaid, Lukas thought. At his house he'd been wearing a frumpy sweater and baggy slacks. The black shirt and jeans he wore now seemed much more *him.*

"Hello, Mr. Kincaid," she said. "Don't bother with what?"

"You can't analyze personality from handwriting."

She was put off by his peremptory tone. "I thought a lot of people do it."

"People read tarot cards, too. Waste of time. We'll concentrate on other things."

"Well. All right." Lukas pledged that she'd try not to dislike him too much.

Cage said, "Hey, Parker, you know Tobe Geller? Doubling as our computer-and-communications man tonight. We tracked him down on his way to a ski trip in New Hampshire."

The trim agent with a ready grin said, "For holiday pay I'll do anything." He shook hands with Parker.

Cage nodded to another desk. "This's C. P. Ardell. Nobody knows what C.P. stands for. I don't think even he knows."

"Did a while ago," C.P. said laconically.

"And this is Len Hardy. He's our District PD liaison."

"Nice to meet you, sir," the detective said.

"Don't really need the 'sir.' You forensic? Investigative?"

Hardy hesitated. "Actually, I'm research and statistical."

"So where's the note?" Kincaid asked Lukas. "The original."

"In identification. I wanted to see if we could raise a few more prints."

Kincaid frowned, but before he could say anything, Lukas added, "I told them to use the laser only. No ninhydrin."

His eyebrows lifted. "You've worked in forensics?"

"I remember from the academy," she told him.

"What's that?" Hardy asked. "Nin . . ."

Lukas said, "Ninhydrin's what you usually use to image fingerprints on paper."

"But," Kincaid finished her thought, "it ruins indented writing. Never use it on suspect documents."

Lukas phoned ID. The tech told her that there were no other prints on the document and that a runner would bring the note up to the crisis center. She relayed this to the team. Parker nodded.

"Why'd you change your mind?" Cage asked him. "About coming here."

He was silent for a moment. "You know those children you mentioned? The ones injured in the subway? One of them died."

With equal solemnity Lukas said, "I heard."

"I'm here on one condition," Kincaid continued. "Nobody except the immediate task force knows I'm involved. If my name gets out, whatever stage the investigation's in, I walk."

Lukas said, "If that's what you want, Mr. Kincaid, but—"

"Parker."

Cage said, "You got it. Can we ask why?"

"My children," Kincaid said. "I've had custody since my wife and I got divorced four years ago. And one of the reasons that it's me who has custody is that I work at home and I don't do anything that'd endanger them or me. That's why I only do commercial document work. Now it looks like my wife's reopening the custody case. She can't find out about this."

"Not a problem," Cage reassured him. "You'll be somebody else. Who d'you want to be?"

"I don't care if you make me John Doe or Thomas Jefferson, as long as I'm not me. Joan's coming by tomorrow morning at ten with presents for the kids. She's going to cross-examine them, and if she finds out I went off on New Year's Eve to work on a case . . ."

"What'd you tell them?" Lukas asked.

"That a friend of mine was sick in the hospital. I *hated* lying."

Recalling his beautiful boy, Lukas said, "We'll do our best."

"It's not a question of best," Kincaid said to her, holding her eye. "It's either keep me out of the picture, or I'm gone."

"Then we'll do it," she said. C.P., Geller, and Hardy all nodded.

"All right." Parker took his jacket off. "Now, what's the plan?"

Lukas ran through the status of the investigation. She tried to read Kincaid's face, see if he approved of what she was doing. Then she said, "The mayor's going on the air soon to make a plea to the shooter. He's going to suggest that we'll pay the money to *him*. We're hoping the shooter will contact us."

Cage took over. "Then Tobe here'll track him from the drop back to his hidey-hole. Jerry Baker's tactical team is on call."

Kincaid looked around the crisis center, taking in the banks of phones, computers, desks. His eyes ended up on the video monitor displaying the extortion note.

"Can we set up the ready room someplace else?" he asked.

Lukas considered this. "Where do you want to be?"

"Upstairs," he said absently, staring at the glowing note.

PARKER walked through the sci-crime document lab, looking over the equipment and supplies he knew so well. Two Leitz binocular stereo microscopes with a fiber-optic light source, the latest Foster + Freeman video spectral comparator, the VSC 2000, equipped with a Rofin PoliLight. Also, an electrostatic-detection apparatus and a thin-layer gas chromatograph for ink-and-trace analysis.

Parker turned on several of the machines and tried not to think about his talk with the children an hour before. When he'd told them that he had to visit a friend in the hospital and asked them who they wanted to baby-sit.

"Mrs. Cavanaugh!" they'd said in unison. Mrs. Cavanaugh, everyone's grandmother, baby-sat on Tuesdays when Parker sat in on a neighborhood poker game, usually winning, while Mrs. Cavanaugh played Monopoly with the Whos, graciously losing.

"You'll be back before midnight, won't you?" asked Robby.

"I'm going to try as hard as I can," Parker said.

"Daddy?" Stephie asked. "Would your friend like me to make him a get-well card?"

Parker had felt his betrayal as a physical blow. "That's okay, honey. I think he'd like it better if you just had fun tonight."

Now, intruding on these difficult thoughts, the door to the document lab swung open. A lean, handsome agent with swept-back blond hair walked in. "Jerry Baker," he announced, walking up to Parker. "You're Parker Kincaid." They shook hands.

"You're the tactical expert?" Parker asked him.

"Right."

Lukas said, "Jerry's got some S&S people lined up."

Search and surveillance, Parker recalled. "How many good guys do we have?" he asked.

"Thirty-six of ours, four dozen District PD," Baker said.

Parker frowned. "We'll need more than that."

"That's a problem," Cage said. "Because of the holiday, there're a couple hundred thousand people in town. And a lot of Treasury and Justice agents are on security detail, what with all the diplomatic and government parties."

Len Hardy muttered, "Too bad this happened tonight."

Parker gave a short laugh. "The unsub *picked* tonight because he knew we'd be shorthanded." And he added, "Because of the crowds, the shooter's got himself a firing range."

Parker opened his attaché case—a portable document examination kit. It was filled with the essential tools of his trade. Also, it seemed, a Darth Vader action figure.

"The Force be with you," Cage said.

Parker found his hand glass, a Leitz lens, twelve power, which was wrapped in black velvet. Joan had bought it for him for their second anniversary at an antiques store in London.

Hardy noticed a book in Parker's attaché case. Parker saw the cop looking at it and handed it to him. *Mind Twisters Volume 5.* Hardy handed it off to Lukas.

"Hobby," Parker explained as she scanned the pages.

Cage said, "Oh, this man loved his puzzles. That was his nickname—the Puzzle Master."

"They're lateral-thinking exercises," Parker said. He looked over Lukas's shoulder and read, " 'A man has three coins that total seventy-six cents. The coins were minted in the United States within the last twenty years, are in general circulation, and one of them is *not* a penny. What are the denominations of the coins?' "

"Wait, one of them *has* to be a penny," Cage said.

Hardy looked at the ceiling. Parker wondered if his mind were as orderly as his personal style. He reflected for a moment. "Are they commemorative coins?"

"No. Remember, they're in circulation."

Lukas's eyes scanned the floor. Her mind seemed to be elsewhere.

"What's the answer?" Cage asked.

"He has a fifty-cent piece, a quarter, and a penny."

"Wait," Hardy protested, "you said he didn't have a penny."

"No, I didn't. I said *one* of the coins wasn't a penny. The half-dollar and the quarter aren't, but one of them is."

"That's cheating," Cage grumbled.

"It sounds so easy," Hardy said.

"Puzzles are always easy when you know the answer," Parker said. "Just like life, right?"

Lukas turned the page. She read, " 'Three hawks have been killing a farmer's chickens. One day he sees all three sitting on the roof of his chicken coop. The farmer has just one bullet in his gun and the hawks are so far apart that he can hit only one. He aims at the hawk on the left and shoots and kills it. The bullet doesn't ricochet. How many hawks are left on the roof?' "

"It's too obvious," C.P. observed.

"Maybe *that's* the trick," Cage said. "You think it should be complicated, but the answer really *is* the obvious one. You shoot one, and there're two left. End of puzzle."

Lukas flipped to the back of the book. "Where are the answers?"

"There aren't any. An answer you don't get on your own isn't an answer." Parker glanced at his watch. Where was the note?

Lukas turned back to the puzzle, studied it. Her face was pretty. Joan was drop-dead beautiful, with her serpentine cheekbones and ample hips. Margaret Lukas was trimmer. She had thin, muscular thighs, revealed by tight jeans.

She was pretty, Daddy. For a lady cop . . .

A young clerk in a too tight gray suit walked into the lab.

"Timothy, what have you got for us?" Cage asked.

"I'm looking for Agent Jefferson," he said.

Parker was saved from asking, "Who?" by Cage.

"Tom Jefferson?" Cage asked.

"Yes, sir."

Cage pointed to Parker. "This's him."

Parker hesitated only for a moment, then took the envelope and signed for it, carefully writing, "Th. Jefferson," the same way the statesman had done.

Timothy left, and Parker cocked an eyebrow at Cage, who said, "You wanna be anonymous. *Poof.* You're anonymous."

"But how—"

"I'm the miracle worker. I keep telling you."

THE Digger is standing in the shadows outside his motel—$39.99 a day, kitchenette and free cable, and we have vacancies.

This is a lousy part of town. Reminds the Digger of where . . . *click* . . . where?

Boston, no. White Plains . . . *click* . . . which is near New . . . New York.

He's standing beside a smelly Dumpster watching people coming and going, the way the man who tells him things told him to do. Watching his front door. People walk past on the sidewalk. Nobody sees the Digger.

"If somebody looks at your face, kill them," said the man who tells him things. "Nobody can see your face. Remember that."

"I'll remember that," the Digger had answered.

He checks his watch. He's waited for fifteen minutes. Now it's okay to go inside.

Have some soup, reload his gun, repack the silencer. Which he learned how to do on a fall day last year—was it last year? They sat on logs, and the man told him how to reload his gun and repack the silencer, and all around them were pretty-colored leaves. Then he would practice shooting the Uzi, spinning around like a whirligig, leaves and branches falling. He remembers the smell of hot, dead leaves.

Opening the door, walking inside. He calls his voice mail. There are no messages from the man who tells him things. He thinks he's a little sad that he hasn't heard from the man since this morning. He *thinks* he's sad, but he isn't sure what sad is.

No messages. Which means he should repack the silencer and reload his clips and get ready to go out again.

But first he'll have some nice hot soup and put on the TV.

DOCUMENTS have personalities. The extortion note sitting in front of Parker was choppy and stark. Still, Parker was examining it the way he approached any puzzle: with no preconceptions. He'd resist drawing conclusions until he'd analyzed it completely.

> *Mayor Kennedy—*
> *The end is night. The Digger is loose and their is no way to stop him. He will kill again—at four, 8 and Midnight if you don't pay.*
> *I am wanting $20 million dollars in cash, which you will put into a bag and leave it two miles south of Rt 66 on the West Side of the Beltway. In the middle of the Field. Pay to me the Money by 1200 hours. Only I am knowing how to stop The Digger. If you apprehend me, he will keep killing. If you kill me, he will keep killing.*
> *If you don't think I'm real, some of the Diggers bullets were painted black. Only I know that.*

Parker looked at the envelope that had contained the note. It had been placed in an acetate sleeve. On the front of the envelope was the same handwriting: *To The Mayor—Life and Death.*

He donned rubber gloves—not worried about fingerprints, but rather about contaminating any trace materials that might be on the paper. He unwrapped his Leitz hand glass and examined the glue flap on the envelope. The faint ridges left by the glue-application machine at the factory were untouched.

"No spit on the glue," he noted. "He didn't seal it."

Lukas shook her head. "But we don't need saliva. We got blood from the corpse and ran it through the DNA database. Nothing."

"I figured you'd run the unsub's blood," Parker said evenly. "But I was hoping the Digger'd licked the envelope."

"Good point," she conceded. "I hadn't thought about that."

Not too full of herself to apologize, Parker noted. He looked at the note again and asked, "What exactly *is* this 'Digger' stuff?"

Cage offered, "Maybe he's another Son of Sam?"

"Let's see if behavioral has anything on the name Digger."

Lukas agreed, and Cage made the call down to Quantico.

"Any description of the shooter?" Parker asked.

"Nope," Cage said. "It was spooky. Nobody saw a gun or saw a muzzle flash."

"At rush hour?" Parker asked. "Nobody saw anything?"

"He was there, and then he was gone," C.P. said.

Hardy added, "Like a ghost." Parker glanced at the detective. He was clean-cut, trim, handsome. Wore a wedding ring. Had all the indicia of a contented life, but there was a melancholy about him.

Bending over the letter again, studying the cold paper and the black type, Parker read it several times. *The end is night . . .* He moved the powerful examining light closer. Talk to me, he silently asked the piece of paper. Tell me your secrets.

He wondered if the unsub had tried to doctor his handwriting. Many criminals try to disguise their writing, but it's very difficult to suppress one's natural hand. Document examiners can usually detect "tremble"—a shakiness in the strokes when someone's trying to disguise his writing. But there was no tremble here. This was the unsub's genuine writing.

Normally the next step in an anonymous writing case would be to compare the suspect document with knowns by sending agents to public records offices with a copy of the extortion note and have them plough through files to find a match. Unfortunately, most writing in public records are in block or manuscript style—"Please Print," the directions always admonish—and the extortion note had been written in cursive. Even a document examiner with Parker's skill couldn't compare printing with cursive writing.

But there was one thing that might let them search public files. A person's handwriting includes both general and personal characteristics. General are the elements of penmanship that come from the method of handwriting learned in school. Years ago there were a number of different methods of teaching writing, and a document examiner could narrow down a suspect's location to a region of the country. But those systems of writing—the flowery Ladies Hand, for instance—are gone now, and only a few methods of writing remain, notably the Zaner-Bloser System and the Palmer Method. But they're too general to identify the writer.

Personal characteristics, though, are different. These are those little pen strokes that are unique to us—curlicues, mixing printing and cursive writing, adding gratuitous strokes—like a small dash through the diagonal stroke in the letter Z or the numeral 7.

Parker continued to scan the extortion note with his hand glass, looking to see if the unsub had any distinctive personal characteristics in his handwriting. Finally he noticed something.

The dot above the lowercase letter *i*.

Most dots above *i*'s and *j*'s are formed by either tapping the pen directly into the paper or, if someone is writing quickly, making a dash with a dot of ink to the left and a tail to the right. But the METSHOOT unsub had made an unusual mark above the lowercase *i*'s—the tail of the dot went straight upward, so that it resembled a falling drop of water. Parker had seen a similar dot years before—in a series of threat letters to a woman by a stalker who eventually murdered her. The letters had been written in the killer's own blood. Parker had christened the unusual mark "the devil's teardrop" and included a description of it in one of his textbooks.

"Got something here," he said.

"What?" Cage asked.

Parker explained about the dot.

"Devil's teardrop?" Lukas asked. She leaned in, her short silver-blond hair falling forward. "Any connection with your perp?"

"No, no," Parker said. "He was executed years ago. But this could be the key to finding out where our boy lived. If we can narrow down the area to a county, then we'll search public records."

Hardy gave a short laugh. "A little thing like that? You can find somebody that way?"

"You bet," Parker said. "It's usually the little things"

He placed the note under the scanner of the VSC. This device uses different light sources—from ultraviolet to infrared—to let examiners see through obliterations. Parker was curious about the cross-out in front of the word "apprehend."

"What do you see?"

"Tell you in a minute. Don't breathe down my neck, Cage."

"It's two twenty," the agent reminded.

"I can tell time, thanks. My kids taught me."

Parker walked to the electrostatic-detection apparatus. The ESDA is used to check documents for indented writing—markings pressed into the paper by someone writing on pages on top of the subject document. In TV shows the detective rubs a pencil over the sheet to visualize the indented writing. In real life it would probably destroy any indented writing. The ESDA machine, which works like a photocopier, reveals lettering that was written as many as ten sheets above the document being tested.

Parker ran the unsub's note through the machine. He lifted a plastic sheet off the top and examined it. Nothing.

He tried the envelope. He felt a bang in his gut when he saw the delicate gray lines of writing. "Yes!" he said. "We've got something."

Lukas leaned forward, and Parker smelled a faint flowery scent. Perfume? No, she wasn't the perfume sort. Probably scented soap.

"We've got a couple of indentations," Parker said. "The unsub wrote something on a piece of paper on top of the envelope."

Parker held the electrostatic sheet in both hands and moved it around to make the writing more visible. "Okay, somebody write this down. First word. Lowercase *c l e,* then a space. Uppercase *M,* lowercase *e.* Nothing after that."

Cage wrote the letters on a yellow pad. "What's it mean?"

Parker knew immediately. "It's the first crime scene."

"Sure," Lukas said. "Dupont C-i-r-c-l-e, capital *M* Metro."

"Of course!" Hardy exclaimed.

Puzzles are always easy when you know the answer.

"There's something below it," Parker said. "Can you read it?"

Lukas leaned forward. "Just three letters. Lowercase *t e l.*"

"Telephone company, telecommunications?" Cage asked.

"No, no," Parker said. "Look at the position of the letters in relation to the '*c l e Me.*' If he's writing in fairly consistent columns, then the '*t e l*' comes at the end of the word. It's a—"

Lukas blurted, "Hotel. The second target's a hotel."

"That's right."

"Or motel," Hardy suggested.

"I don't think so," Parker said. "He's going for crowds. All the events tonight will be in hotel banquet rooms."

"And," Lukas added, "he's probably sticking to foot or public transportation. Motels are in outlying areas. Traffic's pretty bad tonight to rely on wheels."

"Great," Cage said, then pointed out, "but there must be two hundred hotels in town. How do we narrow it down?"

"I'd say go for the bigger hotels." Parker nodded toward Lukas. "You're right—probably near public transportation."

Jerry Baker dropped a yellow pages on the table. "D.C. only?"

Parker considered the question. "It's the District he's extorting, not Virginia. I'd stick to D.C."

"Agreed," Lukas said. "Also, we should eliminate anyplace with hotel first in the name, like Hotel New York, because of the placement of the letters. And no inns or lodges."

Cage and Hardy joined C. P. Ardell and Baker. They all bent over the phone book, circling possibilities. After ten minutes they had a list of twenty-two hotels.

Parker suggested, "Before you send anybody there, call and find out if any of the functions tonight are for diplomats or politicians. We can eliminate those."

Lukas responded, "Armed bodyguards, right?"

Parker nodded. "And Secret Service."

But even eliminating those, how many locations would remain?

A lot. Too many. Too many possible solutions.

Three hawks have been killing a farmer's chickens. . . .

Chapter Three

2:45 p.m.

THEY powdered his forehead; they stuck a plug in his ear; they turned on the blinding lights.

Through the glare Mayor Gerry Kennedy could just make out a few faces in the blackness of the WPLT newsroom, located just off Dupont Circle. There was his wife, Claire. There was his press secretary. There was Wendell Jefferies.

"Three minutes," the producer called.

Kennedy waved aside the makeup artist and motioned Jefferies over to him. "You heard anything from the FBI? *Anything?*"

"Nothing. Not a word."

Kennedy couldn't believe it. Hours into the operation, his only contact with the feds had been a fast phone call from some D.C. detective named Hardy, who was calling for that agent, Margaret Lukas, to ask Kennedy to make this appeal to the killer over the air. Lukas, Kennedy reflected angrily, hadn't even bothered to make the call herself. Hardy, a District cop who sounded nearly intimidated by the feds, hadn't known any details of the investigation—or, more likely, didn't have permission to give out any. The mayor had tried to call Lukas, but she'd been too busy to take his call.

Kennedy was furious. "Dammit, I want to do something. I mean, other than this." He waved his hand at the camera. "It's like the city doesn't exist, like I'm sitting on my hands."

"You hear the commentary on WTGN?" Jefferies whispered.

He had. The popular station had just aired a comment about how Kennedy and his administration had pledged to take back the streets from criminals and yet had been willing to pay the terrorists a multimillion-dollar ransom.

"I've got to pull in some favors, Gerry. We've no choice."

As usual, the aide was right. "Do what you have to," Kennedy said.

Jefferies bent close to the mayor's ear. "Remember," he whispered, waving his hand around the TV studio, "if the killer's listening, this might be the end of it. Maybe he'll go for the money, and they'll get him. It'll all be over with. You'll be the star."

Before Kennedy could respond, the voice from on high called out, "One minute."

THE Digger's got a new shopping bag.

All glossy red and Christmassy, covered with pictures of puppies wearing ribbons round their necks. It's the sort of bag he might be proud of, though he isn't sure what proud is. He hasn't been sure of a lot of things since the bullet careened through his skull last year.

Funny how that works. Funny how . . .

The Digger's sitting in a comfy chair in his motel, with a glass of water and the empty bowl of soup at his side. He's watching TV. A commercial. Something flickers on the TV screen. Brings back a funny memory.

He had been watching a commercial—puppies eating puppy food, like the puppies on the shopping bag—when the man who tells him things took the Digger's hand and they went for a long walk. He told him that when Ruth was alone, the Digger should break a mirror and find a piece of glass and put the glass in her neck.

"You mean—" The Digger stopped talking.

"I mean, you should break the mirror and find a long piece of glass, and you should put the glass in Ruth's neck."

And the Digger did what he was told.

Now the Digger is sitting with the puppy bag on his lap in his room, looking at his empty bowl of soup.

Another program comes on the TV. He reads the words out loud, " 'Special Report.' Hmm. This is . . ."

Click. This is familiar.

A man the Digger's seen pictures of comes on the air. "Washington, D.C., Mayor Gerald D. Kennedy"—that's what it says on the screen. He's talking, and the Digger listens.

"My fellow citizens, good evening. As you all know by now, a terrible crime was committed this morning in the Dupont Circle Metro station. At this time the killer or killers are still at large. But I want to reassure you that our police force and the federal authorities are doing everything in their power to make sure there will be no recurrence of this incident.

"To the persons responsible for this carnage, I am asking you from my heart, please, please, contact me. We need to reestablish contact so that we can continue our dialogue. On this last night of the year let's put the violence behind us and work together so that there'll be no more deaths or injuries. We can—"

Boring . . . The Digger shuts the TV off. He likes commercials for dog food with cute puppies much better. Car commercials, too.

The Digger calls his voice mail and punches in the code. The woman's voice says that he has no new messages. Which means it's time for him to do what the man who tells him things told him.

He finds his gloves with ribs on the backs of the fingers. The smell makes him think of something in his past, though he can't remember what. He wears latex gloves when he loads the bullets into the clips of his Uzi. He wears his leather gloves when he opens doors and shoots the gun and watches people fall like leaves in a forest.

The Digger buttons his dark coat. He puts the gun into the puppy bag and puts more bullets in the bag, too.

Walking out the door of his motel room, the Digger locks it carefully, the way you're supposed to do. The Digger knows all about doing things you're supposed to do. Eat your soup. Lock the door. Find a bright new shiny shopping bag. One with puppies on it.

"Why puppies?" the Digger asked.

"Just because," said the man who tells him things.

Oh. And that was the one he bought.

PARKER Kincaid, sitting in the same gray swivel chair he himself had requisitioned many years ago, did a test that too few document examiners performed.

He read the document a half-dozen times.

He took careful note of the unsub's syntax—the order of the sentences, his grammar, the general constructions he'd used in composition. An image began to emerge of the soul of the man who'd written it—the man lying in the FBI morgue.

Tobe Geller called, "Here we go." He leaned forward. "It's the psycholinguistic profile from Quantico."

Parker often used this type of computer analysis. The text of a threatening document—sentences, fragments, punctuation—is fed into a computer, which then analyzes the message. An expert compares the letter to others in the database and decides if they were written by the same person. Some characteristics of the writer can also be determined this way.

Geller read, " 'Data suggest that unknown subject is foreign-born but has been in this country for two to three years. He is poorly educated. Probable IQ is one hundred, plus or minus eleven points. Threats contained in subject document do not match any known threats in current databases. However, the language is consistent with threats made in both profit and terrorist crimes, and it is recommended that this subject be considered extremely dangerous.' "

He printed out a copy and handed it to Parker.

"Foreign," Lukas said. "I knew it." She held up a crime-scene photo of the unsub's body. "Looks Middle European to me."

But Parker crumpled up the psycholinguistic profile sheet and tossed it into a wastebasket.

"What—" Lukas began.

Parker said, "The only thing they got right is the extremely dangerous part. He wasn't foreign, and I'd put his IQ at over one sixty."

"Where do you get that?" Cage asked, waving at the extortion note. "My grandkid writes better than that."

"I wish he had been stupid," Parker said. "It'd be a lot less scary." He tapped the picture of the unsub. "Sure, European *descent* but probably fourth generation. He was extremely smart, well educated in a private school, and I think he spent a lot of time on a computer. Oh, and he was a classic sociopath."

Lukas's laugh was nearly a scoff. "Where do you get *that?*"

"It told me," Parker said simply, tapping the note.

Parker was a forensic linguist, too. He'd been analyzing documents without the benefit of software for years—based on the words people chose and the sentences they construct.

"But that's how foreigners talk," Cage pointed out. " 'I am knowing.' 'Pay to me.' "

"Well, let's go through it," Parker said, and put the note on an old-fashioned overhead projector. It flashed onto a large screen mounted to one wall of the lab.

Parker pointed to parts of the note. " 'I am knowing' and 'pay to me' *sound* foreign, sure. The form of the verb 'to be' with a present participle is typical in a Middle European or Germanic-Indo-European-root language. German or Czech or Polish, say. But the use of the preposition 'to' with 'me' is not something you'd find in those languages. They'd say it the way we do. 'Pay me.' That construction is more common in an Asian language. So he's throwing in random foreign-sounding phrases, trying to fool us."

"I don't know," Cage began.

Parker persisted. "Look at how he tried to do it. Those expressions are close together, as if he'd gotten the fake clues out of the way, then moved on. If a foreign language was really his first, he'd be more consistent. And look at the last sentence of the letter. He falls back to typical English construction: 'Only I know that.' Not 'Only *I am knowing* that.' "

"But what about the twenty-four-hour clock?" Hardy asked. "He demanded the ransom by 1200 hours. That's European."

"Another red herring. He doesn't refer to it that way earlier—when he writes about when the Digger's going to attack again. There, he says, 'Four, eight, and midnight.' "

"Well," C.P. said, "if he's not foreign, he's *got* to be stupid. Look at all the mistakes."

Parker responded, "All fake."

"But," Lukas protested, "the very first line: '*The end is night.*' He means 'The end is *nigh.*' He—"

"Oh, but that's not a mistake you'd logically make. People say, 'Once *and* a while,' even though the correct expression is 'once *in* a while,' because there's a certain logic to it. But 'The end is night' makes no sense, whatever his level of education."

"What about the misspellings?" Hardy asked. "And the capitalization and punctuation mistakes?"

Parker said, "The misspellings? Look at the sentence 'Their is no way to stop him.' 'Their' is a homonym—words that are spelled differently but are pronounced the same. It should be T-H-E-R-E. But most people only make those homonymic mistakes when they write quickly—usually when they're on a computer or typing. Their mind sends them the spelling phonetically not visually. But with handwriting they're rare.

"As for the capitalizations, you only find erroneous uppercasing when there's some logical basis for it—concepts like art or love or hate. Sometimes with occupations or job titles. No, he's just trying to make us *think* he's stupid, but he isn't."

Hardy said, "It looks like he tried to spell 'apprehend' and couldn't get it right. What do you make of that?"

"Looks like it," Parker said. "But you know what he wrote first? I scanned it with an infrared viewer."

"What?"

"Squiggles," Parker said. "He didn't write anything. He just wanted us to *think* he was having trouble spelling the word."

"But why'd he go to all this trouble to make us think he's stupid?" asked Lukas.

"To trick us into looking for either a stupid American or a slightly less stupid foreigner. And to keep us underestimating him. Of *course* he's smart. Just look at the money drop."

"The drop?" Lukas asked.

C.P. asked, "You mean at Gallows Road? Why's that smart?"

"Well . . ." Parker glanced up at the agents. "The helicopters."

"What helicopters?" Hardy asked.

Parker frowned. "Aren't you checking out helicopter charters?"

"No," Lukas said. "Why should we?"

"The field for the money drop was next to a hospital, right?"

Geller was nodding. "Fairfax Hospital."

Lukas cursed, angry with herself. "It has a helipad. The unsub picked the place so a surveillance team would get used to incoming choppers. He'd chartered one and was going to set down, pick up the money, and take off again."

"I never thought about that," Hardy said bitterly.

"None of us did," C.P. said.

Cage added, "I've got a buddy at the FAA. I'll have him make some calls."

Parker glanced at the clock. "No response from Kennedy's news conference?"

Lukas made a call. She spoke to someone, then hung up. "Six calls. All cranks. None of them knew anything about the painted bullets."

The door swung open. It was Timothy, the runner who'd brought the note. "I've got the results from the coroner."

Lukas took the report, then handed it to Hardy to read aloud.

The detective cleared his throat. " 'White male approximately forty-five years old. Six foot two. One hundred eighty-seven pounds. No distinguishing marks. No jewelry except a Casio watch—with multiple alarms.' " Hardy looked at them. "Get this. Set to go off at four, eight, and midnight." Back to the report: " 'Wearing unbranded blue jeans. Polyester windbreaker. JC Penney work shirt. Jockey underwear. Cotton socks. Wal-Mart running shoes. A hundred twelve dollars in cash, some change. Minor trace elements. Brick dust in hair, clay dust under nails. Stomach contents reveal coffee and beef—probably inexpensive grade of steak—consumed within the past eight hours.' That's it."

Hardy read another METSHOOT memo, attached to the coroner's report. " 'No leads with the delivery truck—the one that hit him.' " Hardy glanced at Parker. "It's so frustrating. We've got the perp downstairs, and he can't tell us anything."

"*He* can't," Parker responded, "but the note can." He shut off the projector, put the note back on the examining table.

Cage looked at his watch. He pulled on his coat. "We've got forty-five minutes. We better get out there." He nodded toward the door. "To help check out hotels."

Parker was shaking his head. "I think we should keep going here. With the note. We can find more."

"They need everybody they can get," Cage persisted.

There was silence for a moment. Parker stood with his head down, opposite Lukas, across the brightly lit examining table, the stark-white extortion note between them. He looked up, said evenly, "I don't think we'll be able to find him in time. Not in forty-five minutes. I hate to say it, but the best use of our resources is to stay here. Keep going with the note."

C.P. said, "You mean you're going to write off the victims?"

He paused, then said, "I guess that's what I mean. Yes."

Cage asked Lukas, "Whatta you think?"

She glanced at Parker. Their eyes met. She said to Cage, "I agree with Parker. We stay here. We keep going."

Len Hardy walked over to Lukas. "Let me go at least," he said to her. "To help with the hotels."

She looked at his earnest young face. "Len, I can't. I'm sorry."

"Agent Cage is right. They'll need everybody they can get."

Lukas gestured Hardy into the corner of the document lab. "Talk to me," she said to him.

"I want to *do* something," the detective replied. "I know I'm second-string here. Only from the District, only research and stats."

"You're here as liaison only. That's all you're authorized for."

He gave a sour laugh. "Liaison? I'm here as a *stenographer.*"

After a moment she said, "You volunteered, didn't you? That's why you're here."

"Yeah, I did."

"Because of your wife, right?"

"Emma?" He sighed, and his eyes fell to the floor. "It's. . . hard."

"Being home?"

He nodded.

"I know it is," Lukas answered sincerely.

In fact, if it had been anybody but Len Hardy who'd shown up earlier in the afternoon as the District police liaison, she would have kicked him right back to police headquarters. She had no patience for interagency turf wars. This was a Bureau operation. But Lukas knew a secret of Hardy's life—that his wife was in a coma, after her Jeep had skidded off the road and hit a tree. Hardy had been to the D.C. field office several times to compile statistical data on crime in the District and had gotten to know Lukas's assistant. Lukas had overheard him talk sadly about his wife and her terrible injury.

He didn't have many friends, it seemed, just like Lukas herself. She had stepped out of character and asked some personal questions—about Emma. Several times they'd had coffee in the park next to the field office. He'd opened up slightly, but like Lukas, he kept his emotions tightly packed away.

"I want to *do* something. I want a piece of this guy."

Lukas knew that what he wanted was a piece of God or Fate. "Len, I can't have somebody in the field who's"—she looked for a benign word—"distracted." Suicidal was what she meant.

Hardy was angry, but he nodded and returned to a desk.

Poor man, she thought. But seeing his intelligence, his sense of propriety and perfection, she knew he'd come through this terrible time. Changed. Yes, he'd be changed.

The way Lukas herself had been changed.

If you looked at Jacqueline Margaret Lukas's birth certificate, the document would reveal that she'd been born on the last day of November, 1963. But in her heart she knew she'd been born five years ago, on the day she graduated from the academy. Assigned to the Washington field office, she was walking to work one morning, her Colt Python snug on her hip, a case file under her arm, when she realized, I am a changeling, switched at birth, as in some children's story. Jackie Lukas had been a part-time librarian for the Bureau's Quantico research facility, an amateur clothing designer, a quilter, needlepointer, wine collector, a consistent top finisher in local five-K races. But that woman was long gone, replaced by Special Agent Margaret J. Lukas, a woman who excelled in criminalistics, investigative techniques, the care and handling of confidential informants. And now, with her boss away, she was running the biggest case to hit Washington, D.C., in years.

"Hey," a man's voice intruded on her thoughts. Parker Kincaid was speaking to her. "We've done the linguistics. I want to do the physical analysis of the note now. Unless you've got something else in mind."

"This is your inning, Parker," she said, and sat down beside him.

FIRST he examined the paper the note was written on. It measured six by nine inches, and the envelope matched. The size was too common. Size alone would tell Parker nothing about the paper's source. Its composition was common, too.

"The paper won't help us," he announced finally. "It's generic. Nonrecycled, high-acid, coarse pulp, with minimal optical brighteners and low luminescence. There's no watermark, and no way to trace it back to a particular manufacturer. Let's look at the ink."

He lifted the note carefully and placed it under one of the lab's compound microscopes. From the indentation made in the paper by the tip of the pen, the occasional skipping and the uneven color, Parker could tell that the pen had been a cheap ballpoint. "Probably an AWI—American Writing Instruments. The bargain-basement thirty-nine center."

"And?" Lukas asked.

"Impossible to trace. They're sold in just about every discount and convenience store in America." He started to pull the note out from under the microscope. He stopped, noticing something curious. Part of the paper was faded. This was interesting. He studied it again.

"See how the corner's faded? I think it's because the paper—and part of the envelope too—were bleached by the sun."

"Where, at his house or the store?" Hardy asked.

"Could be either," Parker answered. "But given the cohesion of the pulp, I'd guess the paper was sealed until fairly recently. That would suggest the store."

Lukas said, "It'd have to be a place with a southern exposure."

Yes, Parker thought. Good. He hadn't thought of that.

"Why?" Hardy asked.

"Because it's winter," Parker pointed out. "There's not enough sunlight to bleach paper from any other direction."

Parker walked to a cabinet and pulled out an examining board and some sheets of collecting paper. Holding the note by its corner, he ran a camel-hair brush over the surface to dislodge trace elements. There was virtually nothing. He wasn't surprised. Paper is one of the most absorbent of materials; it retains a lot of substances from the places it's been, but generally, they remain firmly bound into the fibers.

Parker took a large hypodermic syringe from his attaché case and punched several small disks of ink and paper out of the note and the envelope. "You know how it works?" he asked Geller, nodding at the gas chromatagraph/mass spectrometer.

"Oh, sure," he said. "I took one apart once for the fun of it."

"Separate runs—for the note and the envelope," Parker said, handing him the samples.

The GC/MS separated chemicals found at crime scenes into their component parts and then identified them. The machine, in effect, burned the samples and analyzed the resulting vapors.

Parker brushed more trace off the note and envelope and mounted the slides on two different Leitz compound scopes. He peered into one, then the other, turned the focusing knobs. To Geller he said, "I need to digitize images of the trace in here. How do we do that?"

"Ah, piece of proverbial cake." The young agent plugged optical cables into the base of the microscopes. The cables ran to a large gray box, with cables of its own. These Geller plugged into one of the dozen computers in the lab. He clicked it on. A moment later an image of the trace particles came on the screen.

He called up a menu and said to Parker, "Just hit this button. They're stored as JPEG files."

"And I can transfer them on E-mail?"

"Just tell me who they're going to."

"In a minute. First I want to do different magnifications."

Lukas said, "I've got a couple of examiners standing by in materials and elemental."

"Send 'em home," Parker said. "There's somebody else I want to use. He's in New York."

"NYPD?" Cage asked.

"Was. Civilian now. The best criminalist in the country."

"But," Hardy said, "it's New Year's Eve. He's probably out."

"No," Parker said. "He hardly ever goes out."

"Not even on holidays?"

"Not even on holidays."

"PARKER Kincaid," said the voice of Lincoln Rhyme on the speakerphone, "I wondered if you might be calling in."

"You heard about our problem, did you?" Parker asked.

"Ah, I hear everything. I thought you were retired, Parker."

"I was. Until about two hours ago."

"Funny, isn't it? They never let us rest in peace."

Parker had met Rhyme once. He was a handsome man, about Parker's age, dark hair. He was also paralyzed from the neck down. He consulted out of his town house on Central Park West.

"I enjoyed your course, Parker," Rhyme said. "Last year."

Parker remembered Rhyme sitting in a fancy candy-apple-red wheelchair in the front row of the lecture hall at John Jay School of Criminal Justice in New York. The subject was forensic linguistics.

"Now let me guess," Rhyme said. "You've got this unsub shooting people in the subway, and your only clue to him is the— What? A threat letter? An extortion note?"

"How's he know that?" Lukas asked.

"Because it's the only logical reason for Parker *Kincaid* to be calling *me,*" Rhyme replied. "Whom did I just answer?"

"Special Agent Margaret Lukas," she said. "You're right. It's an extortion scheme. We tried to pay, but the primary unsub was killed. Now we're pretty sure his partner—the shooter—may keep going."

"And my belated Christmas present is a piece of the case."

"I GC'd a bit of the envelope and letter," Parker said. "I want to send you the data and some pictures of the trace. Can I E-mail it to you?"

"Yes, yes, of course. When's the deadline?"

"Every four hours, starting at four, going to midnight."

"Four p.m.? Today?"

"That's right," Lukas said. "We think he's going after a hotel then, but we don't know anything more specific than that."

"All right. Send me your goodies. I'll get back to you as soon as I can."

Parker took down Rhyme's E-mail address and handed it to Geller. A moment later the agent had uploaded the images.

"*He's* the best criminalist in the country?" Cage asked.

But Parker didn't respond. He was gazing at the clock. He hadn't realized it was so late. Somewhere in the District of Columbia those people that he and Margaret Lukas were willing to sacrifice had only thirty minutes left to live.

Chapter Four

3:30 p.m.

THIS hotel is beautiful; this hotel is nice.

The Digger walks inside, with puppies on his shopping bag, and no one notices him. In the lobby the crowds are milling. There're functions here. Office parties. Lots of decorations. Fat babies in New Year's banners. Old Man Time looking like the grim reaper.

He and Pamela . . . *click* . . . and Pamela, his wife, went to some parties in places like this.

The Digger buys a *USA Today.* He sits in the lobby and reads it.

He looks at his watch. Twenty minutes to four. He takes the cell phone out of his pocket and places a call to his voice mail. He listens. "You have no new messages." He shuts the phone off.

He lifts the puppy bag onto his lap and looks out over the crowd. No one notices him.

THE phone in the document lab began ringing.

As always, when a telephone chirped and he was someplace without the Whos, Parker felt an instant of low-voltage panic. He glanced at the caller ID box and saw a New York number. He snagged the receiver. "Lincoln. It's Parker. Any clues?"

The criminalist's voice was troubled. "Not much, Parker."

Parker turned on the speakerphone.

"I'll tell you what I've got," Rhyme said. "The most prominent trace embedded in the letter is granite dust."

"Granite," Cage echoed.

"There's evidence of shaving and chiseling on the stone. And some polishing, too."

"What do you think it's from?" Parker asked.

Rhyme rattled off, "New construction, renovation or demolition, bathroom, kitchen and threshold manufacturers, tombstone makers, sculptors' studios, landscapers . . . The list's endless. There're also traces of red clay and dust from old brick, sulfur, and a lot of carbon—ash and soot, consistent with cooking meat or burning trash that has meat in it. Now the *envelope* showed a little of the trace substances I found on the letter, but also significant amounts of salt water, kerosene, refined oil, crude oil, butter—"

"Butter?" Lukas asked.

"That's what I said. And there's some organic material not inconsistent with mollusks. So all the evidence points to Baltimore."

"Baltimore?" Hardy asked.

From Lukas, "How do you figure that?"

"The sea water, kerosene, fuel oil, and crude oil mean it's a port. Well, the nearest port to D.C. that does major crude oil transfer is Baltimore. And there are tons of seafood restaurants on the harbor."

"Baltimore," Lukas muttered. "So he wrote the note at home, had dinner on the waterfront the night before. He came to D.C. to drop it off at city hall. Then—"

"No, no, no," Rhyme said.

Parker, the puzzle master, said, "He staged it, didn't he?"

"Just like *Hamlet,*" Rhyme said. "All that trace . . . There's too *much* of those elements. The unsub got his hands on some trace and impregnated the envelope. Just to send us off track."

"And the trace on the letter?" Hardy asked.

"Oh, no, that's legit. The amount of material in the fibers was consistent with ambient substances. No, no, the letter'll tell us where he lived, but the envelope tells us something else."

Parker said, "That there was more to him than meets the eye."

"Exactly," the criminalist confirmed.

"So where he lived, there's the granite, clay dust, brick dust, sulfur, soot, and ash from cooking or burning trash."

"All that dust—might be a demolition site," Cage said.

"That seems the most likely," Hardy said.

"Likely?" Rhyme said. "It's a *possibility.* But then isn't *everything* a possibility until one alternative's proven true?"

"Mr. Rhyme," Lukas said, "this is all good, and we appreciate it. But we've got ten minutes until the shooter's next attack. You have any thoughts about which hotel the unsub might've picked?"

"I'm afraid I don't," Rhyme said. "You're on your own there."

"All right."

Parker said, "Thank you, Lincoln."

"Good luck to all of you." With a click the criminalist disconnected the phone.

Parker glanced at the note, feeling it was mocking him.

Then Lukas's phone rang. She listened, and her mouth blossomed into the first genuine smile Parker had seen on her.

"Got him!" she announced. "Two rounds of the black-painted shells were found under a chair at the Four Seasons Hotel in Georgetown. Every available agent and cop're on their way there."

Cage was on his cell phone now, too. "Our man says the lobby bar's full—some kind of reception," he reported. "In the banquet rooms downstairs, there're four New Year's Eve parties going on."

Parker thought of what an automatic weapon could do there.

Tobe Geller had patched the operation radio frequency through speakers. The team could now hear Jerry Baker's voice. "This is New Year's Leader Two to all units. Code Twelve at the Four Seasons on M Street. Unsub is on premises, no description. Believed armed with a fully auto Uzi and suppressor. You are green-lighted."

Meaning they were free to shoot rather than arrest the Digger.

"The first cars are just getting there," Cage called out, listening to his cell phone. Then announced, "He's not getting out."

Parker bent over the extortion note again.

> Mayor Kennedy—
> The end is night. The Digger is loose and their is no way to stop him.

Then he glanced at the envelope. *The envelope tells us something else. . . . That there was more to him than meets the eye.*

Parker's head shot up. He looked at Lukas. "We've got it wrong. He's not going to hit the Four Seasons."

The others in the room froze, stared at him.

"Stop the response. The police, agents—stop them. The note—it's lying to us. It's leading us away from the real site."

C. P. Ardell looked at Lukas. "What does he mean?"

Parker ignored him and cried, "Stop them! The response teams have to stay mobile. We can't tie them up at the hotel."

Hardy said, "Parker, he's *there.* They found the rounds. That can't be a coincidence."

"Of course it's not a coincidence. The Digger *left* them there. Then he went someplace else—to the real target. The unsub's too smart to leave a reference to the hotel accidentally. He tried to fool us with the trace on the envelope. He *had* to make the evidence subtle. Otherwise we wouldn't believe it. No. We have to stop the tactical teams and wait until we can figure out where the real target is."

"Wait?" Hardy said, exasperated, lifting his hands.

C.P. whispered, "It's five minutes to four!"

Parker saw Lukas lift her stony eyes to the clock on the wall. The minute hand advanced one more notch.

THE HOTEL WAS NICER than *this* place.

The Digger looks around him, and there's something about this theater he doesn't like.

This is . . . *click* . . . the Mason Theater, just east of Georgetown. The Digger is in the lobby, and he's looking at the wood carvings. He sees flowers that aren't yellow or red but are wood, dark like dark blood. Oh, and snakes. Snakes carved in the wood.

He'd walked into the theater without anybody stopping him. You can walk into most theaters toward the end of a show, said the man who tells him things. They think you're there to pick up somebody. All the ushers here ignore him. It's nearly four.

The Digger hasn't been to a concert or a play for years. Pamela and he went . . . *click* . . . went someplace to hear music. Someplace where people were dancing, listening to music . . . People in cowboy hats. The Digger remembers a song. He hums it.

When I try to love you less,
I just love you all the more.

But nobody's singing today. This show is a ballet. A matinee.

They rhyme, he thinks. Funny. Ballet . . . matinee . . .

He walks through the lobby, eases to the lobby bar—which is now closed—and finds the service door, steps through, and makes his way up the stairs to a door that says BALCONY. The Digger steps into the corridor and walks slowly along the thick carpet.

"Go into box number fifty-eight," said the man who tells him things. "I bought all the seats in the box, so it'll be empty."

Now, nearly four p.m., the Digger walks slowly toward the box. A young woman in a white blouse walks up to him. She holds a flashlight. "Hello," she says. "Lost?" She looks at his face.

The Digger nuzzles the puppy bag against her breast.

"What—" she starts to ask.

Phut, phut . . . He shoots her twice, and when she drops to the carpet, he drags her inside the empty box. He stops just on the other side of the curtain and looks out over the theater.

My, this *is* . . . *click* . . . this *is* nice. The Digger decides that he likes this place after all. Dark wood, flowers, plaster, gold, and a huge chandelier in the middle of the ceiling.

He watches people dancing on the stage. Listens to the music. He reaches into the puppy bag and wraps his fingers around the grip of the gun, takes the suppressor in his left hand.

He looks down over the crowd. At the girls in pink satin, boys in blue blazers, women with skin showing in V's at their necks.

Four o'clock. His watch beeps. He steps forward, grips the suppressor through the crinkly bag, and starts to pull the trigger.

Then he hears the voice.

It's behind him in the corridor. "We got him!" the man whispers. And the man pulls the curtain aside as he lifts his pistol.

But the Digger heard him just in time. He throws himself against the wall, and when the agent fires, the shot misses. The Digger cuts him nearly in half with a one-second burst from the Uzi. Another agent is behind the first. He kills that agent, too.

The Digger doesn't panic. He never panics. Fear isn't even a piece of dust to him. But he wants to shoot into the crowd, and he can't. There are more agents rushing onto the balcony floor. The agents have bulletproof vests; some have helmets; some have machine guns that probably shoot as fast as his Uzi.

The Digger sticks the bag out through the curtain into the corridor and holds the trigger down. Glass breaks, mirrors shatter. He should . . . *click* . . . should shoot into the audience. That's what he's supposed to . . . He . . . For a moment his mind goes blank.

More police. Shouting. There's so much confusion.

The Digger unscrews the suppressor and aims the gun at the chandelier. He pulls the trigger. A roar like a buzz saw. The bullets cut the stem, and the huge tangle of glass and metal tumbles to the floor, trapping people underneath. A hundred screams.

The gun is empty, but he has no time to reload. He eases over the balcony and drops onto the shoulders of a large man, fifteen feet below. They tumble to the floor, and the Digger is up on his feet, being rushed through the fire door with the rest of the crowd. He still clutches the shopping bag.

Outside, he's blinded by the spotlights and flashing lights from the fifty or sixty police cars and vans, but there aren't many police outside. They're mostly in the theater, he guesses.

He jogs through an alley away from the theater and in five minutes is walking along a residential street, the bag tucked neatly under the arm of his black or dark blue coat.

"MAN, Parker," Len Hardy said. "Good job. You nailed it."

Margaret Lukas, listening to her phone, said nothing to Parker. But she glanced at him and nodded. It was her form of thanks.

Yet Parker Kincaid didn't want gratitude. He wanted facts.

Lukas cocked her head as she listened to her phone. She looked up and said to the agents and Parker, "Two agents dead, two wounded. An usher killed, and one man in the audience was killed by the chandelier. A dozen injured, some serious. Some kids were hurt bad in the panic. Got trampled. But they'll live."

But their lives will never be the same, Parker thought grimly.

Daddy, tell me about the Boatman.

Parker asked, "And he got away?"

"He did, yes," Lukas said, sighing. "Nobody got a look at him."

Parker closed his eyes. "Forensics?"

"PERT's going over the place with a microscope," Cage said. "But—I don't get it—he's firing an automatic weapon, and there're no shell casings."

Parker said, "He's got the gun in a bag or something. Catches the casings."

It'd been a photo finish. Lukas had finally agreed to go along with Parker, saying icily, "All right, we'll stop the response to the hotel. But God help you if you're wrong, Kincaid."

Then they had spent a frantic few minutes trying to guess where the Digger might've gone. Parker had reasoned that he'd leave the bullets at the hotel not long before four—so he'd have ten minutes tops to get to the real target. The killer couldn't rely on getting a cab. He'd have to walk. That meant about a five-block radius.

Parker and the team had pored over a map of Georgetown.

Suddenly he'd looked at the clock and said, "Are there matinees today in the theaters?"

Lukas had grabbed his arm. "Yes."

Tobe Geller mentioned the Mason Theater, a five-minute walk from the Four Seasons. Parker ripped open a copy of the Washington *Post* and found that there was a performance of *The Nutcracker.* He asked Lukas to send all the troops there.

God help you if you're wrong, Kincaid.

But he hadn't been wrong. Still, what a risk he'd taken. And though many lives had been saved, some had been lost. And the killer had escaped.

Cage's phone rang again. He spoke for a few minutes, then hung up. "That was a shrink. Teaches at Georgetown. He's done some work for behavioral. Says he's got some info about the name."

"The Digger?" Parker asked.

"Yeah. He's on his way over."

"Good," Lukas said. She asked Parker, "What's next?"

He thought for a moment. "Well, I'd find out if the box in the theater where he shot from was empty, and if it was, did the unsub buy out the whole box. If so, did he use a credit card?"

Lukas nodded at C.P., who called Jerry Baker and posed the question to him. When C.P. disconnected, he said, "Nice try."

Parker said, "He bought them two weeks ago. Paid cash."

"Three weeks ago," the agent muttered.

"Hell," Parker snapped in frustration. He turned to the notes he'd taken of Lincoln Rhyme's observations. "We'll need some maps. Good ones. I want to figure out where the trace in the letter came from. Maybe we can narrow down a part of town."

Lukas nodded at Hardy. "If we can do that, we'll get Jerry's team and some of your people from District PD and do a canvass." She handed Geller a copy of the crime-scene photo of the unsub in the morgue. "Tobe, make a hundred prints of this. We'll flash his pic and see if anybody's seen him."

Parker looked over Rhyme's list of trace. Granite, clay, brick dust, sulfur, organic ash—where were they from?

The young clerk who'd brought them the note earlier appeared in the doorway. "Agent Lukas, security wanted me to tell you there's a guy downstairs. A walk-in. Says he knows something about the Metro shooter."

"Credentials?" Lukas asked.

"Claims he's a journalist, writing about a series of unsolved murders. License and Social Security check out. No warrants."

"What's he say about the Digger?"

"All he said is that this guy's done it before—in other cities."

Lukas looked at Parker, who said, "We better talk to him."

"SO HE'S in D.C. now, is he?" the man asked.

They were downstairs in reception area B. Within the Bureau, however, it was called Interrogation Room Blue, after the shade of the pastel decor inside.

Parker, Lukas, and Cage sat across the table from him—a large man with wild, gray hair.

"Who would that be?" Lukas asked.

"I call him the Butcher," said the man. "What do *you* call him?"

Henry Czisman was in clean but well-worn clothes. A white shirt straining against his large belly, a striped tie. His jacket wasn't a sport coat, but the jacket from a gray pin-striped suit. A battered briefcase sat on the table. He cupped a mug of ice water, which sat in front of him.

"You're saying the man involved in the subway and theater shootings is called the Butcher?"

"The one who actually did the shootings, yes. I don't know his accomplice's name."

Lukas and Cage were silent for a moment. She was wondering exactly how Czisman knew about the Digger and his crime and, particularly, his partner. The news about the dead unsub had not been released to the press.

"What's your interest in all this?" Parker asked.

From the briefcase Czisman took out several old copies of the Hartford *News-Times,* dated last year. He pointed out articles with his byline. "I'm on a leave of absence, writing a book about the Butcher. That was his nickname in Boston earlier in the year."

Parker asked, "What happened in Boston?"

Czisman glanced at Parker's visitor's pass. It had no name on it. Cage had introduced him as a consultant, Mr. Jefferson.

"There was a shooting at a fast-food restaurant, Lucy's Tacos."

Lukas had heard of it. "Four killed, seven injured. Perp drove up to the restaurant and fired a shotgun through the window. No motive. If I recall, there was no description of that perp either."

"Oh, he's the same. You bet he is. And no, there was no description. Just guesses. He's probably white. How old? Thirties or forties. Height? Medium. Build? Medium. He could be anybody."

Lukas was about to ask a question, but Czisman interrupted her. "You said there was no motive in the restaurant shooting?"

"Not according to the report I read."

"Well, did you know that ten minutes after the Butcher finished lobbing rounds through the plate-glass window, killing women and children, a jewelry store was robbed four miles away?"

"No. That wasn't in the report."

Czisman asked, "And did you know that every tactical officer for two miles around was at the restaurant? So even though the owner of the jewelry store hit the silent alarms, the police couldn't get to the store in time. The thief killed him and a customer."

"He was the Butcher's accomplice?"

Czisman said, "Who else would it be?"

Lukas sighed. "We need any information you have. But I don't sense you're here out of civic duty. What exactly do you want?"

"Access," he said quickly. "Just access."

"To information."

"That's right."

"Wait here," she said, getting up. She gestured Parker and Cage after her.

JUST off Room Blue, Tobe Geller was sitting in a small darkened room in front of an elaborate control panel.

He had watched the entire interview with Henry Czisman on six different monitors. The Bureau didn't use two-way mirrors in its interrogation rooms. Rather, on the walls of the room were three prints of paintings by the Impressionist Georges Seurat. Six of the tiny dots in each of the three paintings were in fact miniature video camera lenses.

Lukas had instructed Geller to perform data analysis. Czisman would mention a fact, and Geller would instantly relay the information to Susan Nance, a young agent standing by upstairs in communications. She would then contact the field office and seek to verify the information.

Czisman had never drunk from the mug of water Cage had placed in front of him, but he did clutch it nervously. The mug had a pressure-sensitive surface and a microchip transmitter in the handle. It digitized Czisman's fingerprints and transmitted them to Geller's computer. He in turn sent them to the Automated Fingerprint Identification System database for matching.

One of the video cameras was locked onto Czisman's eyes and was performing retinal scans for "veracity probability analysis"—that is, lie detection. Geller was also doing voice-stress analysis.

Cage, Lukas, and Parker hurried into the observation room.

"Anything yet?" Lukas asked Geller.

"It's prioritized," he said, typing madly.

A moment later his phone rang. Lukas switched on the speaker.

"Tobe," a woman's voice said, "I've got some info on that guy."

"Susan, it's Margaret," Lukas said. "What've you got?"

"Okay, prints came back negative on warrants, arrests, convictions. Name Henry Czisman is legit, address in Hartford, Connecticut. The image you beamed up matches his Connecticut driver's license photo. Employment record through Social Security Administration and IRS shows him working as a journalist since 1971, but some years he had virtually no income. Listed his job those years as freelance writer. A year ago he quit a fifty-one-thousand-dollar-a-year job at the Hartford paper and is apparently living off savings."

"Quit, fired, or took a leave of absence?" Parker asked.

"Not sure," Susan Nance responded. "We couldn't get as many credit card records as we wanted, because of the holiday, but he's staying at the Renaissance. And he checked in after a noon flight from Hartford. Made the reservation at ten a.m. this morning."

"So he left just after the first shooting," Lukas mused. "What do we think?"

"Damned journalist is all, I'd say," Cage offered.

"And you, Kincaid?" She glanced at him.

"What do I think? I say we deal with him."

Lukas said skeptically, "He seems like a crank to me. Are we that desperate?"

"Yes," Kincaid said, glancing at the digital clock above Tobe Geller's computer monitor, "I think we are."

IN THE stuffy interrogation room again Lukas said to Czisman, "If we can talk off the record now and if we can bring this to a successful resolution, we'll give you access to materials and witnesses for your book. I'm not sure how much yet, but everything we tell you now will be completely confidential."

"Agreed," Czisman said.

Parker asked, "Does the name Digger mean anything to you?"

"Digger?" Czisman shook his head. "No. As in gravedigger?"

"We don't know. It's the name of the shooter—the one you call the Butcher."

"I only call him the Butcher because the Boston papers did. The New York *Post* called him the Devil. In Philadelphia he was the Widow Maker."

"New York? Phillie, too?" Lukas asked, troubled by this news.

Czisman said, "They've been working their way down the coast. Headed where? To Florida for retirement?"

"What happened in the other cities?" Parker asked.

"The International Beverage case in White Plains, New York?" Czisman responded. "Ever hear of it?"

Lukas again was up on her recent criminal history. "The president of the company, right? He was kidnapped."

Czisman continued. "Yes. The police had to piece it together, but it looks like the Butcher took the president's family hostage. His wife called and told him to get some money together. The president tells the kidnapper he'd pay, then calls the police. They surround the house while the president goes to his bank to get the ransom. But as soon as they open up the vault, a customer pulls out a gun and begins shooting. Killed everyone in the bank, including the International Beverage president. The video camera shows another man, with him, walking into the vault and walking out with a bag of money."

"So there was nobody in the house?" Lukas asked, understanding the scheme.

"Nobody alive. The Butcher had already killed the man's family."

"Can the bank's security video help us?" Cage asked.

"You mean, what color were their ski masks?"

"What about Phillie?" Lukas asked.

Czisman said cynically, "Oh, this was very good. The Butcher'd get on a bus, sit next to someone, and fire one silenced shot through his pocket. He killed three people; then his accomplice made the ransom demand. The city agreed to pay, then set up surveillance to nail him. But the Butcher and his accomplice figured out which bank the city was getting the money from. As soon as the rookies escorting the cash stepped outside the bank, the Butcher shot them in the back of the head and escaped."

Parker said, "Massachusetts, New York, Pennsylvania, Washington. You're right. He was on his way south."

Czisman frowned. *"Was?"*

Parker glanced at Lukas. She told Czisman, "He's dead."

"What?" Czisman seemed truly shocked.

"The partner—not the Butcher. Hit-and-run after he dropped the extortion note off. And before he could collect his money."

Czisman's face grew still for a long moment. "What was his scheme this time?"

Lukas was reluctant to say, but Czisman guessed. "The Butcher shoots people until the city pays the ransom. . . . But now there's nobody to pay the money to and so the Butcher's going to keep right on shooting. Sounds just like their MO. You have any leads?"

Parker asked, "How did you follow him here?"

"I read everything I can find about crimes where somebody has no qualms about killing. When I'd hear about that happening, I'd go to the city where it had happened and interview people. Would it be all right if I took a look at the body?"

Lukas said, "Sorry. It's against procedure."

"A picture maybe," Czisman persisted. "Please?"

Lukas opened the file and took out the photo of the unsub.

Czisman took it and stared for a long moment. He nodded. "Can I keep this?"

"After the investigation."

"Sure." He handed it back and rose. He shook their hands and said, "I'm staying at the Renaissance downtown. I'll be interviewing witnesses. If I find something helpful, I'll let you know."

Lukas thanked him and walked him back to the guard station.

THEY huddled once more in the surveillance room, a circle around Tobe Geller. Geller looked at his control panels. "Voice stress and ret scans—normal readings. Stress is low, especially for somebody being cross-examined by three FBI agents. But I'd give him a clean bill of health. Nothing consistent with deception."

Lukas's phone rang. She listened, then said into her phone, "No detention for subject." She hung up, glanced at her watch. "The shrink from Georgetown?"

"He's on his way," Cage said.

Parker asked, "What're we doing about that map? We've got to analyze the trace."

Geller said, "The best map is in the Topographic Archives."

"The archives?" Parker could only imagine the difficulty of finding civil servants willing to open up a government facility on a holiday night.

Lukas flipped open her phone.

Cage said, "No way."

"Ah," she said, "you don't have the corner on miracles."

THE BRASS CLOCK MEANT SO much to Mayor Gerry Kennedy.

The gift was from students at Thurgood Marshall High, in the war zone of Southeast D.C. Kennedy had been touched by the gesture. He'd spoken to them about honor and working hard and staying off drugs. Platitudes, sure. But a few in the auditorium had gazed up at him with the look of sweet admiration on their faces. Then they'd given him the clock in appreciation of his talk.

Kennedy touched it now, looked at the face: 4:55.

So the FBI had come close to stopping the madman, but they hadn't. Some deaths, some injuries. And more panic around the city. Press reports were berating Kennedy and the District police for being soft on crime and hiding out. The reviews of his TV appearance were not good either. One commentator had actually echoed Congressman Lanier's phrase "kowtowing to terrorists."

The phone rang. Wendell Jefferies, sitting across from the mayor, grabbed the receiver first. "Uh-huh. Okay . . ." He shook his head, then hung up. "They've scoured the entire theater and can't find an iota of evidence. And no reliable witnesses."

"What is this guy, invisible?" Kennedy sighed. "Why doesn't he contact us? He could have twenty *million* dollars. He must not have heard the TV broadcast."

Kennedy looked out his window at the domed wedding cake of the Capitol building. When Pierre L'Enfant came up with the plan of the city of Washington in 1792, he had a surveyor draw a meridional line north and south and then another perpendicular to it, dividing the city into the four quadrants that remain today. The Capitol building was at the intersection of these lines.

"The center of the crosshairs," some gun-control advocate had once said at a congressional hearing. But the figurative telescopic sight might very well be aimed directly at Kennedy's chest. The city was foundering, and the mayor, a native Washingtonian, was passionately determined not to let it go under.

An odd hybrid of body politic, the city had had self-rule only since the 1970s. For most of the two hundred years since it had become the nation's capital, the District had been ruled by Congress.

But twenty-five years ago the legislature had turned the reins over to the city itself. And since then, a mayor and the thirteen-member city council had struggled to keep crime under control (at times the worst murder rate in America), schools functioning, finances in check (forever in the red), and racial tensions defused.

There was some possibility that Congress would step in once more and take over the city; the legislature had already removed the mayor's blanket spending power. But for Kennedy, governance wasn't ultimately the issue. He didn't care if the city became part of Virginia or Maryland, as long as his administration lasted long enough to help the city and its citizens.

He *knew* how to save Washington's sixty-nine square miles, which he'd grown to love. The answer was education. If you could get the children to stay in school, then self-esteem and the realization that they could make choices about their lives would follow. Knowledge had saved him, pulling him out of poverty, boosting him into William and Mary School of Law.

No one disagreed with the basic premise that education could save people. But *how* to solve the puzzle was a different matter. Kennedy had a vision of how to make sure kids in the District continued their education, and his plan could pretty much be summarized by one word: bribery. He and Wendell Jefferies called it by another name—Project 2000.

For the past year Kennedy had been negotiating with members of the Congressional District Committee to impose yet another tax on companies doing business in Washington. The money would go into a fund from which students would be paid cash to complete high school—provided they remained drug free and weren't convicted of any crimes.

In one swoop Kennedy managed to incur the political hatred of the entire political spectrum. The liberals had problems with the mandatory drug testing as a civil libertarian issue. The conservatives simply laughed. The corporations to be taxed had their own opinion, of course—some threatening to pull out of the District altogether. Still, in Kennedy's months of horse trading with Congress, it appeared that the measure might actually pass, thanks largely to popular support.

But now he worried that that support might dry up. If he stumbled today, if the Digger sent more of his citizens to their deaths, if he appeared ineffectual, there'd be no hope for Project 2000.

He looked up and saw Jefferies on the phone again.

The aide put his hand over the receiver and said, "He's here."

Kennedy nodded. "All right. Go talk to him."

Jefferies nodded. "We'll get through this, Gerry. We will."

IN THE hallway outside the mayor's office a handsome man leaned against the wall. Wendell Jefferies walked up to him.

"Hey, Wendy."

"Slade." This was the man's real first name, believe it or not, and—with the surname Phillips—you'd think his parents had foreseen that their handsome infant would one day be a handsome anchorman for a local TV station. Which, in fact, he was.

"Got in on the scanner," said the anchorman. "Dude lit up two agents, did a Phantom of the Opera on a dozen poor bastards in the bleachers. Capped one, I think."

Because Jefferies was black, Slade wanted him to think he talked the talk. Jefferies didn't tell him that in gangsta slang the verb "cap" meant "shoot to death" not "chandelier to death." Today Jefferies had no patience for men like Slade Phillips. He waved him quiet. "We need some help." He lowered his voice to a pitch that resonated with the sound of money changing hands. "We can go twenty-five on this one."

"That's a lot. What do you want me to do?"

"I want Kennedy to get through this like he's a hero. I mean, people are dead, and more people are probably gonna die. Get the focus on him for visiting vics and standing up to terrorists. Get the focus *off* him for any glitches. He's not running the case."

Phillips said, "It's a Feebie operation, right?"

"That's true, but we don't want to blame the Bureau for anything either. Find someone else to point the finger at."

"Okay . . . So"—Phillips began writing copy in his head—"Kennedy's taking a tough line. He's marshaling cops. He went to the hospitals . . . But wait." He nodded toward the pressroom. "The guy from the *Post* said Kennedy *didn't* visit anybody."

"No, no. He went to the families who wanted to remain anonymous. He's been doing it all day."

"Oh, he has? That was good of him. Real good."

It was amazing what twenty-five thousand dollars could buy you, Jefferies thought.

OUTSIDE, in the cool air, Parker, Cage, and Lukas walked to the Topographical Archives.

At dusk in the winter Washington, D.C., becomes a murky place. As they walked, Parker Kincaid glanced up at the overcast sky. He remembered that snow was predicted and that the Whos would want to go sledding tomorrow.

Lukas interrupted these thoughts by asking him, "How'd you get into this business?"

"Thomas Jefferson," Parker answered. "I was going to be a historian. I wanted to specialize in Jeffersonian history. That's why I went to the University of Virginia."

"He designed the school, didn't he?"

"The original campus he did. Anyway, one day I was in the library, looking over this letter Jefferson had written to his daughter Martha. It was about slavery. Jefferson had slaves, but he didn't believe in slavery. Fundamentally, he wanted to abolish it. But this letter, written just before he died, was adamantly proslavery and recanted his earlier opinions. He said that slavery was one of the economic cornerstones of the country. The more I read it, the more I began to think the handwriting didn't look quite right. I compared the writing with a known handwriting specimen."

"And it was a fake?"

"Right. Caused quite a stir—somebody slipping a forgery like that into the Jefferson archives. Anyway, from then on I was hooked."

Parker gave Lukas his curriculum vitae. He had an M.S. in forensics from George Washington University, and he was certified by the American Board of Forensic Document Examiners.

"I did freelance work for a while, but then I heard that the Bureau was looking for agent-examiners. Went to Quantico, and the rest is history."

Lukas asked, "What appealed to you about Jefferson?"

"His character, I think. His wife died in childbirth. Just about destroyed him. But he rose above it. Nothing was too much of a challenge for him."

Lukas paused, looking at a window display of some chic designer clothes. Parker was surprised something like this would distract her. But Cage said, "Margaret here's one amazing seamstress."

"Cage," Lukas said absently. She turned away from the window, and they continued walking.

Lukas asked Parker, "And you really turned down an S.A.C.?"

"Yep."

Parker remembered the day that Cage and the then deputy director came into the office to ask him if he'd leave the department and take a field office, but he'd had to turn them down. A special agent in charge works long hours, and at that time in his life he needed to be home—for the children's sake.

But none of *this* he wanted to share with Lukas.

He wondered if she'd ask more, but she didn't. She pulled out her cell phone and made a call.

"Keep walking," she whispered, "and don't turn around."

He realized she wasn't talking on the phone, just pretending.

Cage asked, "You got him, too? I put him twenty yards back."

"No visible weapons. And he's skittish. Erratic movement."

Parker realized that that had been why Lukas had stopped and gazed at the dresses in the window—she'd suspected somebody had been following them. He, too, glanced into a window they passed and saw a man trotting across the street—to the same sidewalk the agents were on. About fifty feet behind them.

Parker now noticed that both Cage and Lukas were holding their pistols. He hadn't seen them draw the weapons. They were black automatics. His service pistol had been a clunky revolver, and he remembered hating the regulation that required him to be armed at all times. The thought of having a loaded gun anywhere near the Whos disturbed him terribly.

"You think it's the Digger?" he asked.

"Could be," she said.

The Digger behind them! He must have been staking out headquarters and somehow learned they were on the case.

"You take the street," Lukas said to Cage. "Kincaid, you cover the alley. In case there's backup. On three. One . . . two . . . ."

"But I—" Parker began.

"Three."

They separated fast. Cage stepped into the street, scanning cars. Lukas turned and sprinted in the direction they'd just come from. "Federal agent!" she shouted. "You there! Freeze."

Parker glanced into the alley and wondered what he was supposed to do if he saw somebody there. He looked behind him, at Lukas. Beyond her, the man stopped abruptly, but then he turned and took off in a dead run down the middle of the street.

"Hold it!" Lukas tried to follow, but a car turned the corner quickly and nearly slammed into her. Lukas flung herself back onto the sidewalk, inches from the fender.

When she started after him again, the man was gone. Parker saw her pull her phone out and speak into it. A moment later three unmarked cars with red lights flashing skidded into the intersection. She conferred with one of the drivers, and the cars sped off.

At a slow jog she returned to Parker. Cage joined them.

"You get a look at him?" Cage asked.

"Nope," Parker answered.

"I didn't either," Lukas muttered. Then she glanced at Parker's hands. "Where's your weapon?"

"I don't have one."

Lukas gave him a disdainful look. She bent down and tugged up her jeans cuff, pulled a small automatic out of an ankle holster. She handed it to Parker.

He shook his head. "No, thanks."

"Take it," she insisted, and pushed the gun toward him.

He decided the battle wasn't worth it. He reached out, took it, and slipped it into his pocket.

As they walked up the street, Parker felt the weight of the pistol in his pocket. It gave him no comfort. A moment later he realized why. Not because the weapon reminded him that the Digger might have been behind them a moment ago or even because it reminded him of the Boatman from four years ago.

No. It was because the gun seemed to have some kind of dark power that was pulling him further and further away from his children with every passing minute.

THE Digger is standing in an alley, looking around him. He's worried that the man who tells him things will be unhappy, because he didn't kill as many people at the theater as he was supposed to.

The Digger hears sirens in the distance. Many sirens.

Ahead of him, in the alley, he sees some motion. There's a young boy. He's black and skinny. About ten years old. The boy is listening to someone talk to him. Someone the Digger can't see.

Suddenly the Digger hears Pamela's voice: "Have . . . have . . . children with you? Have . . . have . . . your baby?"

> *If we had us a child or three or four,*
> *you know I'd love you all the more.*

Then the memory of the song goes away, because there's a tearing sound and the gun and the suppressor fall through the bottom of his shopping bag. He bends down to pick them up, and as he does, he looks up. Hmm.

The young boy and an older man, dressed in dirty clothes—the man who was talking to the boy—are walking up the alley. The man is bending the boy's arm upward. The boy's nose is bloody.

They are both looking at the Digger. The boy seems to be relieved. He pulls away from the man and rubs his shoulder. The man grabs the boy's arm again, then stops. He looks down at the Uzi. He gives the Digger a crooked smile. Says, "Whatever you doing, ain't my business. I'ma just go on my way."

"Leggo my arm," the boy whines.

"Shuddup." The man draws back his fist. The boy cowers.

The Digger shoots the man in the chest. He falls backward.

If somebody sees your face . . .

The Digger aims the gun at the boy, who is staring at the body of the man who was beating him.

The Digger lowers the gun. The boy whispers, "Yo, you cap him! Man, just like nothin'." The boy is now staring right at the Digger's face.

Words rattling around. Kill him he's seen your face kill him.

The Digger stoops and picks up the spent shells, and then the suppressor, and wraps it and the gun in the torn puppy bag and walks out of the alley, leaving the boy standing there.

Go back to the motel . . . *click* . . . to the motel and wait. See if the man who tells him things has called to tell him to stop shooting.

> *When I hear you coming through the door,*
> *I know I love you all the more.*

Some soup would be nice now. He made soup for Pamela. He was making soup for Pamela the night she . . . *click.* It was Christmas night. A night like this. Cold. Colored lights.

Here's a gold cross for you. And this box is for me? . . . A present? Oh, it's a coat! Thank you thank you thank you.

The Digger is standing at the stoplight, waiting for the green.

Suddenly he feels something touch his hand. He grips the gun in the torn puppy bag. He turns slowly.

The boy stands there, holding the Digger's left hand. He's looking straight ahead.

> *Love you love you love you . . .*

The light changes. The Digger doesn't move. "Yo, we can walk," says the boy.

Holding hands, the two of them walk across the street.

Chapter Five

5:15 p.m.

THE District of Columbia Topographic and Geologic Archives is housed in a musty old building near Seventh and E streets. There's no reference to it in any tourist literature, and visitors are politely turned away by three guards at the front desk.

Cage, Parker, and Lukas—on her ever present cell phone—waited in the lobby. She shut off the unit. "Nothing. He just disappeared. A couple of drivers saw a man in dark clothes running. They think he was white, medium build. But nobody'd swear to it."

They were joined by Tobe Geller, who entered the facility at a slow trot. He nodded a greeting to the other members of the team. Then their fingerprints were checked by an Identi-Scanner and their weapons secured in a lockbox. They were directed through to an elevator. Lukas hit the button marked B7, and the car descended for what seemed like forever.

They stepped out into the archives proper. It turned out not to be stacks of musty old books and maps—which Parker had been looking forward to checking out—but a huge room filled with banks of twenty-four-inch NEC computer screens. Even tonight, New Year's Eve, two dozen men and women sat in front of these screens, on which glowed elaborate maps.

"What *is* this?" Parker asked Geller.

He replied, "Topographic and cartographic database of a hundred square miles around the District. Ground zero's the White House, though they don't like it when you say that. In case of natural disaster, terrorist attack, nuclear threat—whatever—this is where they figure out if it's best for the government to sit tight or get out of town, and if so, how they ought to do it."

"What're *we* doing here?"

"You wanted maps," Geller said, looking excitedly at all the equipment, "and this is the most comprehensive physical database of any area in the world." He nodded affectionately toward a long row of six-foot-high computer towers.

Lukas said, "They're letting us use the place, under protest, provided we don't take any printouts or downloads with us. Now, what're the materials Rhyme found?"

Parker read his notes. " 'Granite, sulfur, soot, ash, clay, and brick.' "

Geller sat down at a monitor, turned it on, clicked buttons. An image of the Washington, D.C., area came on the screen. The resolution was astonishing. It looked three-dimensional.

Lukas said to Parker, "Where do we start?"

"One clue at a time," he responded. "First granite, brick dust, and clay. They point to demolition sites, construction . . ." He turned to Geller. "Would they be on this database?"

"No," the young agent responded, "but we can wake up somebody at building permits."

"Do it," Parker ordered. "What next? Sulfur and soot . . . That's industrial. Tobe, can you highlight areas based on air pollutants?"

"Sure. There's an EPA file." He hit more buttons. On the screen portions of the city began to be highlighted—in, appropriately, pollution-tinted yellow. The majority were in Southeast.

"Let's add another clue—the organic ash," Parker said. "Basically burned animal flesh."

Lukas asked, "Meat-processing plants?"

Geller responded, "None listed."

"Restaurants?" Cage suggested.

"Too many of them," Parker said.

"Where else would there be burned meat?" Lukas asked.

"Veterinarians?" Parker wondered out loud. "Do they dispose of the remains of animals?"

Geller typed, then read the screen. "There are dozens."

Then Lukas looked up at Parker, and he saw that the anger and chill from earlier was gone, and in her blue-gray eyes the dullness had been replaced by something else. It might have been excitement. She said, "How about *human* remains?"

"A crematorium!" Parker said. "Yes! And the polished granite—that could be from tombstones. Let's look for a cemetery."

Cage gazed at the map. "Arlington?"

But Parker pointed out, "It's not near any industrial sites. Nothing with significant pollution."

Then Lukas saw it. "There!" She pointed. "Gravesend."

Tobe Geller highlighted the area on the map, enlarged it.

Gravesend—a neighborhood in the District's Southeast quadrant. Parker had a vague knowledge of the place. It was a decrepit crescent of tenements, factories, and vacant lots around Memorial Cemetery, which had been a slave graveyard dating back to the early 1800s. Parker pointed to another part of the map. "Metro stop right here. The unsub could've taken the Metro to Judiciary Square—City Hall. There's a bus route nearby, too."

Lukas considered it. "I've collared perps there. There's a lot of demolition and construction going on. It's pretty anonymous, too. Nobody asks any questions about anybody else. And a lot of people pay cash for rent. Perfect place for a safe house."

A young technician nearby took a phone call and handed the receiver to Geller. As the agent listened, he broke into an enthusiastic smile. "Good," he said. "Get it to the document lab ASAP." He hung up. "Somebody got a videotape of the Mason Theater shooting."

"A tape of the Digger?" Cage asked enthusiastically.

"They don't know what it's of exactly. Quality's pretty bad. Tech services'll get it to me stat. Are you going to Gravesend?"

"Yep," Parker said. Looked at his watch. Two and a half hours until the next attack.

"MCP?" Geller asked Lukas.

"Yeah. Order one."

Parker recalled: a mobile command post. A camper outfitted with high-tech communications and surveillance equipment.

"I'll have a video data analyzer installed," Geller said, "and get started on the tape. Where will you be?"

Lukas and Parker said simultaneously, "There." They were pointing at the same vacant lot near the cemetery.

Lukas said, "Tobe, pick up C.P. and Hardy, and bring 'em with you in the MCP."

The agent hesitated. "Hardy? We really need him?"

Lukas said, "If it's not him, the District'll put somebody else on board. At least we can control Hardy."

Geller pulled on his jacket and ran for the elevator.

Lukas stared at the map of Gravesend. "It's so big."

"I've got another thought," Parker said. He was thinking back to what they knew about the unsub. "He probably spent time on a computer. Let's get a list of everybody in Gravesend who subscribes to an on-line service."

Cage protested, "There could be thousands of 'em."

Lukas said, "I doubt it. It's one of the poorest parts of the city. Computers'd be the last thing people'd spend money on."

Cage said, "True. Okay, I'll have tech services get us a list."

MAYOR Kennedy paced in a slow circle around his office. He gestured toward the radio. "They're making it sound like I've been sitting on my butt while the city's getting the hell shot out of it."

Kennedy had been to three hospitals to visit the people wounded in the Digger's attacks. No one cared. All anyone asked him was why wasn't he doing more to catch the killer.

"Slade'll come up with something," Jefferies said.

"Too little, too late." The mayor sat down in his chair. If it weren't for the Digger, he and Claire would have been attending four parties tonight. With that madman out there it would be impossible for him to attend any parties, do any celebrating. A wave of anger passed through him, and he grabbed the phone. He began dialing a number from a card on his Rolodex.

The call to FBI headquarters was patched through several locations. A man's voice answered.

"This's Mayor Gerry Kennedy. Who'm I speaking to?"

"Special Agent C. P. Ardell. What can I do for you?"

"That Agent Lukas—she's still in charge of the METSHOOT operation?"

"That's right."

"Can I speak to her?"

"She's not here. I can patch you through to her cell phone."

"That's all right. I really want to talk to the District liaison officer."

"That'd be Detective Hardy. He's right here."

A distressingly young-sounding voice said tentatively, "Hello?"

"Hardy, this's your mayor."

"Oh. Well, how are you, sir?"

"Can you update me on the case? I haven't heard a word from Agents Lukas or Cage. Where's the Digger going to hit next?"

A pause. "They aren't exactly keeping me in the loop, sir. My orders are just to write a report on the operation."

"A report? That's bull, son. How close are they to stopping him?"

Hardy sounded uneasy. "They have a few leads. They think they know where the unsub's safe house is—the guy who was killed by the truck."

"Where?"

"I'm not supposed to give out tactical information, sir."

"It's my city that's under attack. I want answers."

Silence. Kennedy forced his anger down. He said, "Let me tell you what I have in mind. If I can just have a chance to talk to the killer, I think I can convince him to give up. I'll negotiate with him."

Kennedy did believe this, because one of the aspects of his persona was his charm. He'd sweet-talked two dozen of the toughest presidents and CEOs in the District into accepting the tax that would fund Project 2000. Twenty minutes with this killer would be enough. He'd work out some kind of plea arrangement.

"Now come on, son. Where's that safe house?"

Kennedy watched Jefferies cross his fingers. Please . . . It would be perfect. I show up there with truckloads of reporters. I try to talk the man into coming out with his hands up. He surrenders, or they kill him. Either way, my credibility survives.

Kennedy heard voices from the other end of the line. Then Hardy was back. "I'm sorry, Mayor. I have to go. There're people here."

The line went blank.

GRAVESEND. The car carrying Parker and Cage bounded over gaping potholes and eased to a stop at a curb where trash and rubble spilled into the street. They climbed out.

Lukas had driven in her own car, a red Ford Explorer, and was already at the vacant lot that was the rendezvous point. She was standing with her hands on her trim hips, looking around her.

Two black teenagers who'd been leaning against a wall covered with graffiti looked at the men and women arriving—obviously law enforcers—and walked away slowly, uneasiness and defiance on their faces. Parker was troubled—though not by the danger, by the hugeness of the place. It was three or four square miles of slums and row houses and small factories. How could they possibly find the unsub's safe house in this much urban wilderness?

There were some riddles that Parker had never figured out.

Three hawks have been killing a farmer's chickens. . . .

Smoke wafted past Parker. It was from fires in the oil drums where the homeless men and women burned wood and trash for warmth. He saw hulks of stripped cars. Just past the Metro stop, over a tall, decaying brick wall, the chimney of the crematorium rose into the night sky. The sky above rippled in the heat. Parker shivered. The sight reminded him of old-time pictures of—

"Hell," Lukas muttered. "It looks like hell."

A car arrived. It was Jerry Baker, wearing a bulky windbreaker over body armor. Cage handed him the stack of computerized pictures of the unsub. "We'll use these to canvass the area."

More unmarked cars and vans began to pull up. White-and-teal District police cars too, their light bars revolving. There were about twenty-five men and women in total, half of them federal agents, half uniformed cops. Baker motioned to them, and they congregated around Lukas's vehicle. He distributed the printouts.

Lukas called, "If you could listen to Mr. Jefferson here."

It took a second before Parker recognized the reference to his stage name. He said, "The man in the picture you've got there is the perp responsible for the Metro and Mason Theater shootings. We think he was working out of a safe house somewhere here in Gravesend. Now he's dead, but his accomplice—the shooter—is still at large, so we need to find the safe house fast."

"You have a name?" one of the District cops called.

"The unsub—the dead one—is a John Doe," Parker said. "The shooter's got a nickname: the Digger. That's all. His description's on the bottom of the handout."

Parker continued. "You can narrow down the canvassing area some. The safe house is probably near a demolition or construction site and probably closer to the cemetery than farther away. He also recently bought some paper like this—" Parker held up the clear sleeves holding the extortion note and the envelope. "Now, the paper was sun-bleached, so it's possible that he bought it in a store that displays its office supplies in or near a south-facing window. So hit every convenience store, drugstore, grocery store, and newsstand that sells paper. Oh, and look for the type of pen he used, too. It was an AWI black ballpoint. Probably cost thirty-nine or forty-nine cents."

That was all he could think of. With a nod he handed off to Lukas. She stepped in front. "Now listen up. We don't know if the shooter's in Gravesend, and we don't know if he's living in the safe house. But I want you to assume he's ten feet behind you and has a clean path to target. So as you go through the neighborhood, I want everyone to be looking for ambush positions. I want weapon hands free; I want jackets and coats unbuttoned."

She paused, looked over the officers in front of her. "At eight o'clock—that's just over two hours—he's going to find someplace that's filled with people, and he's going to empty his weapon at them again. Now I do *not* want to work that crime scene and have to look into the eyes of someone who's just lost a parent or a child. I don't want to have to say, I'm sorry but we couldn't find this beast before he killed again. That is not going to happen. I'm not going to let it. And you're not. Any questions?"

"Anything more on his armament?" one agent asked.

"He's been armed with a full-auto Uzi loaded with long clips and a suppressor. You are *totally* green-lighted. Anything else?" No one raised a hand. "Okay. Now go find me that safe house."

Half of the agents started off on foot; some climbed into their cars and sped away. That left Cage, Lukas, and Parker standing on the curb. Cage made a call. He spoke for a moment. Hung up.

"Tobe's got an MCP. They're on their way. He's analyzing the tape from the theater. Oh, and that psychologist from Georgetown is on his way, too."

Most of the streetlights here were out. Pale green illumination lit the street from the fluorescent lights of the few stores that were open. Two agents were canvassing across the street. Cage looked around and saw two men rubbing their hands over an oil drum in which a fire burned. Cage said, "I'll talk to them."

Lukas nodded toward a pizza parlor half a block away. "I'll take that," she said to Parker. "You want to wait here for Tobe?"

"Sure."

Lukas started up the street, leaving Parker alone.

The temperature was continuing to fall. There was now a sharp edge to the air. He stuffed his hands in his pockets and happened to glance across the street.

He saw a thrift store. It was closed, and at first he didn't pay much attention to the place. But then he noticed boxed sets of cheap stationery on shelves near the cash register. Could this be where the unsub had bought the paper and envelope for the note?

He crossed over to the window of the thrift store and gazed through the greasy window, trying to see the packages of paper. His hands shook in the chill, and beside him a rat nosed through a pile of trash. He thought, This is crazy. I have no business being here. But still, he lifted his sleeve and wiped the grimy glass in front as carefully as a diligent window cleaner so that he'd have a better view.

"MAYBE I seen him. Yeah, maybe."

Margaret Lukas felt her heart pump faster as the counterman at the Gravesend pizza place—a chubby Latino—continued to study the picture of the unsub. "Take your time," she said. Please, she thought, let's have a break here.

"Maybe. I no so sure. We get tons of people in here. You know?"

She'd remembered that the coroner had found steak in the belly of the unsub. There was no steak on the menu here. Still, it was the only twenty-four-hour restaurant on the street near the Metro stop, and she figured that the unsub might have stopped in.

The clerk's brown eyes lifted, and he shook his head. "No, I no think so. Sorry. Hey, you want a slice? It's fresh. I just made it."

She shook her head. "Anybody else working here?"

"No, just me tonight. I got the holiday. You did too, looks like."

Lukas said, "Thanks," and walked to the front door. She paused, looked outside. Had she been right? she wondered. You can read all the books on investigative techniques, but the bottom line is improvisation. It was just like solving one of Kincaid's puzzles. You had to look beyond the formulas and rules.

She wanted Tobe Geller here; she wanted the Georgetown psychologist; she wanted the list of on-line subscribers. . . . Everything was taking too long! And there were far too few leads!

"Miss?" came the voice behind her. "Miss Agent?" She turned. The counterman stood offering her a Styrofoam cup of coffee. He said simply, "It's getting colder out."

Touched, she took the cup and poured in a packet of sugar.

"Hope you get some celebrating in tonight," he said.

"You, too," she said, and pushed out the door.

Walking down the cold streets of Gravesend, she scanned the area. The two agents from the field office were out of sight, probably on an adjacent block. Cage, too, had vanished, and Kincaid was gazing into a store window near the staging area.

Kincaid . . . What exactly was *his* story? Turning down a special-agent-in-charge slot? Lukas couldn't understand that—an S.A.C. was the next destination on *her* road map to the dep director spot. And beyond. Still, she respected him more for saying no than if he'd taken the job without wanting it.

What *did* explain the walls he'd put up around his life? She couldn't guess, but she saw them clearly. Margaret Lukas knew walls. He reminded her of herself—or rather of her *selves,* plural. Jackie and Margaret both. The changeling.

Lukas's eyes happened to fall on a young Latino couple walking down the sidewalk toward the staging area. The wife in a black scarf, the husband in a thin jacket. He pushed a baby carriage, inside of which Lukas caught sight of a swaddled infant. She thought instinctively about what kind of flannel she'd buy to sew the child a pair of Dr. Dentons. Then the couple moved on.

Oh, Kincaid, you like puzzles, do you? Well, here's one for you. The riddle of the wife and the mother. How can you be a wife without a husband? How can you be a mother without a child? It's a tricky one, but you can figure it out, Parker.

Lukas, alone on the nearly deserted street, leaned against a lamppost, curled her right arm around it. She gripped the metal hard; she gripped it desperately. Struggled to keep from sobbing.

A wife without a husband, a mother without a child . . .

Give up, Parker? *I'm* the answer to the riddle. Because I'm the wife of a man lying in Alexandria Cemetery. Because I'm the mother of a child lying beside him.

Here's another riddle: How can ice burn?

When an airplane drops from the sky into a field on a dark November morning, two days before Thanksgiving, and explodes into a million pieces. That's how ice can burn.

And that's how I became a changeling.

Oh, puzzles *are* easy when you know the answer, Parker.

Hold on, she thought, letting go of the lamppost. Taking a deep breath. Locking away the urge to cry. Enough of that.

"Focus," Special Agent Lukas ordered herself.

Another breath. She looked around, saw some motion in a vacant lot—a young kid wearing gang colors. She tossed out the remains of the coffee and walked toward him to see if he knew anything.

PARKER stepped away from the thrift store, disappointed.

The stationery he'd seen inside wasn't the same as the extortion note or the envelope. He looked around the deserted streets. No Lukas, no Cage. He watched a young couple wheeling a baby carriage toward him. They were about thirty feet away. He thought about the times just after Robby was born when he and Joan would take after-dinner strolls like that.

His eye caught someone in a dark coat huddling in the alcove of a check-cashing store. He decided to be useful and fished in his pocket for a picture of the unsub. He'd do some canvassing himself. But something odd was happening. . . . The man looked up and seemed to be studying him. Then he reached into his coat and pulled out something black, shiny.

Parker froze. It was the man who'd followed them near the archives. It was the Digger!

Parker reached into his pocket, but the gun wasn't there. He remembered the pistol pressing into his hip as he sat in Cage's car. It must have fallen out into the front seat.

The man glanced at the couple, who were between him and Parker, and lifted whatever it was he held.

"Get down!" Parker cried to the couple, who stared at him.

"Down!" he shouted again, and tried to leap into the shadows of an alley. But he tripped over a pile of trash and fell heavily to the ground. His breath was knocked out of him, and he lay on his side, gasping. Where was Cage or Lukas or the other agents?

The man turned toward the couple, now only ten feet from him. Parker tried to climb to his feet, waving desperately to the couple to get down. The Digger moved forward, his face an emotionless mask. He lifted the gun.

"Get . . . down," Parker rasped, and huddled on the ground.

Then a woman's brash voice was shouting, "Freeze! Federal agents! Drop the weapon, or we'll shoot!"

The man turned, gave a choked cry as Lukas screamed, "Drop it, drop it!" her gun extended in front of her.

The man dropped what he held, and his hands shot into the air.

Cage was running across the street, his weapon in his hand.

"On your face," Lukas shouted, her voice raw. "On your face!"

The man dropped like a log.

Cage was on his phone as Parker climbed unsteadily to his feet.

Lukas crouched on the ground, her gun pressed into the killer's ear. She cuffed him, using only her left hand.

"What the—" the man choked.

"Shut up!" Lukas snapped, holstering her weapon. She walked to the couple and spoke to them for a few moments. Wrote their names in her notebook and sent them on their way.

Cage frisked the man, then picked up his weapon.

"Not a gun. It's a video camera." He flipped through the man's wallet. "Andrew Sloan. Lives in Rockville."

Another agent pulled out his radio and called in a warrants request—federal, Maryland, and Virginia.

"You can't—" Sloan began to protest.

Lukas took a step forward. "You keep your mouth shut."

Cage pulled a business card from Sloan's wallet. Showed it to Lukas and Parker. It read NORTHEAST SECURITY CONSULTANTS. Cage added, "He's a private eye."

"No warrants," said the agent who'd called in the request.

"Who's your client?" Cage asked.

"I don't gotta answer."

"Yeah, Andy, you do gotta answer," Cage said, pulling him roughly into a sitting position.

Sloan swore at Cage. "I got a law degree. I know my rights. I'm on a public street here and—"

Parker leaned in for a better look. "Wait. I know him. I saw him at the Starbucks near me. And I think someplace else, too."

Cage kicked the man gently in the leg. "You been following my friend here? Huh? You been doing that?"

Oh, no, Parker thought, finally understanding. He said, "His client's Joan Marel. My ex-wife."

Parker was in despair. He closed his eyes. Until tonight, every foot of tape the private eye might've shot would have shown Parker to be a diligent father, going to PTO meetings, chauffeuring the kids to school. But tonight Sloan was an eyewitness to Parker's being right smack in the middle of one of the city's most dangerous police actions. In harm's way, his children lied to and entrusted to a baby-sitter on a holiday.

"That right?" Cage asked Sloan ominously.

"Yeah, yeah, yeah. She hired me."

Cage saw Parker's expression and asked, "The custody thing?"

"Yeah." What was he going to do? Parker stared at the ground.

Lukas said, "Get Sloan outa here. Give him back his camera."

"It's broke," Sloan snapped. "You're going to pay for it." Cage undid the cuffs, and Sloan stood unsteadily. "I think I sprained my thumb. I'm going to file a complaint."

"Andy," Cage asked, "were you the one following us on Ninth Street tonight? An hour ago?"

"Maybe. But I wasn't breaking any laws there either."

Parker said, "Is there any way we could talk about this?"

"Talk? What talk? I give my client the tape; I tell her what I saw. That's all there is to it. I may sue you, too."

"Andy, here's your wallet." Cage motioned Sloan aside and handed it back. Then the tall agent lowered his head and whispered into Sloan's ear. Sloan started to speak, but Cage held up a finger. Sloan continued to listen. Two minutes later Cage stopped talking. Sloan asked one question. Cage shook his head, smiling.

The agent walked back to Lukas and Parker, Sloan right behind. Cage said, "Now, Andy, tell Mr. Kincaid, have you seen anything that Mrs. Marel could use to her advantage in the custody battle?"

"No, I haven't. In fact, Mr. Kincaid seems to me to be a—"

Cage prompted, "Flawless."

"Flawless father. I've never witnessed him doing *anything* that would jeopardize his children or their happiness."

"And you didn't videotape him doing anything dangerous?"

"No, sir. I didn't take any tape at all. I didn't see anything that might be helpful to my client by way of evidence."

"What are you going to go back and tell your client?"

"That Mr. Kincaid went to visit a friend in the hospital."

"Okay," said Cage. "Now get out of here."

Sloan ejected the tape from what was left of the video camera. He handed it to Cage, who tossed it into a burning oil drum.

"How'd you do that?" Parked asked when Sloan was gone.

Cage offered a shrug. Parker took it to mean, Don't ask. Cage the miracle worker . . .

"Kincaid, where the hell was your weapon?" Lukas demanded.

He turned to her. "I thought I had it. It must be in the car. I—"

But Lukas's face was contracted with cold fury. "Look, Kincaid, you've been living life on Sesame Street for the last five years. You can go back to that world right now and thanks for the help. But if you're staying on board, you'll carry your weapon and you'll pull your share of the load. Now, you going or staying?"

Cage was motionless. Not even the faintest shrug.

"I'm staying."

"Okay," Lukas said. "Now let's get back to work. We don't have much time."

A WINNEBAGO camper eased up to the curb. It was the mobile command post, and it was plastered with bumper stickers.

> NORTH CAROLINA AKC DOG SHOW.
> WARNING: I BRAKE FOR BLUE RIBBONS.
> BRIARDS ARE OUR BUSINESS.

Parker wondered whether the stickers were intentional or if the Bureau had bought the van secondhand from a real breeder.

Lukas motioned Cage and Parker inside. One whiff of the air told him it *had* belonged to dog owners. Still, it was nice and warm, and Parker was glad to be out of the chill.

Sitting at a computer console was Tobe Geller. Detective Len Hardy sat nearby, and C. P. Ardell was wedged into a booth against the wall. The psychologist from Georgetown hadn't yet arrived.

"This is the video from the Mason Theater shooting," Geller said, not looking away from the computer screen. The image on it, a dim view of the interior of the theater, was very blurry. The camera bobbed as people ran for cover.

"When the Digger started shooting," C.P. explained, "some tourist in the audience turned on his camcorder."

Geller typed more, and the image grew slightly clearer. Then he froze the tape.

"There?" Cage asked, touching the screen. "That's him?"

"Yep," Geller said. He ran the tape again, in slow motion.

Parker could see nothing distinct. The scene was dark. As the frames flipped past in slow motion, faint light from the gun blossomed in the middle of the smudge that was the Digger.

Geller continued. "Now, this one's about the clearest." The frame froze. The image zoomed in, but as the pixel squares grew larger, they lost all definition. "I've been trying to enhance it to see his face. I'm ninety percent sure he's white."

"Back out again," Parker said. "Slowly."

As Geller pushed buttons, the squares grew smaller, began to coalesce into the image of the Digger from the chest up.

"Stop," Parker ordered. "Look at that." He tapped the screen. In the center of the Digger's chest were some bright pixels, surrounded by darker ones.

"It's just a reflection," Lukas muttered, impatient.

Parker persisted. "But what's the light reflecting *off* of?"

They stared for a moment. Then, "Ha, think I've got it," Geller said. "Our boy's wearing a gold crucifix."

"Add that to our description of the shooter, send it out," Lukas ordered. "And tell them we've confirmed he's white."

Cage radioed Jerry Baker with the information. Then his phone rang. He listened. Hung up. "My contact at the FAA. Man fitting the description of the unsub contracted to charter a helicopter from a company in Clinton, Maryland. Gave his name as Gilbert Jones. Paid cash. The pilot was supposed to pick up some cargo in Fairfax; then there'd be another hour leg of the flight, but Jones didn't tell him where. Was supposed to call instructions in to the pilot at ten thirty this morning, but he never did. The pilot checks out okay."

"Did Jones give him an address or phone number?"

Cage's shrug said he did, but they were both fake.

The camper door opened, and a young agent said, "Agent Lukas, I've got Dr. Evans here." He ushered in the psychologist.

"Evening," said Dr. John Evans. His dark hair was shot with gray, and he had a trim beard. He wore an easy smile and carried a backpack instead of a briefcase. Parker liked him immediately.

"Appreciate your coming down," Lukas said to him. "These are Agents Cage and Geller. Agent Ardell's over there. Detective Hardy. My name's Lukas. And this's Parker Kincaid—he's a document expert, used to work for the Bureau." She added, "He's here confidentially, and we'd appreciate your not mentioning his involvement."

"I understand," Evans said. "What's going on?"

He sat down as Cage ran through a summary of the shootings, the death of the unsub, the extortion note, and the killer.

Evans looked at the death-mask picture of the unsub. "So you're trying to figure out where his partner's going to hit next."

"Exactly." Lukas said. "We've got to get a leg up here."

Parker asked, "You've heard the name before—the Digger?"

"I did a little research. There was a man in California in the '50s called the Gravedigger. He was killed in prison. Then there was a motorcycle gang in Scottsdale called the Gravediggers. But they disbanded in the mid-'70s. Now, the only reference to quote *The Digger* is a man in England in the 1930s. John Barnstall. He was a nobleman—a viscount or something like that. Killed his wife and children and two or three local farmers. He'd dug a series of tunnels under his house and kept the bodies down there. The press called him the Digger because of the tunnels."

"Any chance," Lukas asked, "that either the unsub or the Digger had heard about Barnstall? Used him as sort of a role model."

"I can't really tell at this point. I need more information. We'd have to identify patterns in their behavior."

Lukas said, "A freelance writer contacted us. He's convinced the shootings are part of a pattern of similar crimes in Boston, the New York suburb of White Plains, and Philadelphia. Always the same—larceny or extortion, with tactical murders to support them."

Evans said, "Then it doesn't sound like there's any connection with Barnstall. His diagnosis was paranoid schizophrenia, not generalized antisocial behavior—like your perpetrator here."

Lukas shook her head, disappointed. "I was hoping the name 'Digger' meant something. I thought it might be the key."

Evans said, "Oh, it still might. I'd be happy to hang around, see if you get any more information. I've never profiled a corpse before."

"We could use the help," Lukas said.

He opened his backpack and took out a large metal thermos. He opened the lid and poured black coffee into the lid cup. "I'm addicted," he said, then smiled. "Something a psychologist shouldn't admit, I suppose. Anybody else?"

They all declined, and Evans put the thermos away. He pulled out his cell phone and called his wife to say he'd be staying late.

This reminded Parker of the Whos, and he took out his own phone and called home.

"Hello?" Mrs. Cavanaugh's grandmotherly voice answered.

"It's me," Parker said. "How's the fort?"

"They're driving me into bankruptcy. And all this *Star Wars* money. I can't figure it out. They're keeping me confused on purpose." Her laugh included the children, who would be nearby.

"How's Robby doing?" Parker asked. "Is he still upset?"

Her voice lowered. "He got moody a few times, but we pulled him out of it. He'd love for you to be home by midnight."

"I'm trying," he told her, then hung up.

Cage had overheard. He asked, "Your boy? He okay?"

Parker sighed. "He's fine. Just having some bad memories from, you know, a few years ago."

Dr. Evans lifted an eyebrow, and Parker said to him, "When I was working for the Bureau, a suspect broke into our house." He noticed Lukas was listening, too. "You ever hear of the Boatman?"

Evans said, "I remember something from the papers."

"He was a serial killer. He'd kidnap a woman, rape and murder her, and leave the body in a dinghy or rowboat. We had leads to a guy, but we couldn't make a case. Finally I was able to connect him to one of the murders through a handwriting sample. SWAT arrested him. He was convicted, but he escaped on the way to federal detention. At that time the kids and I were living in a house in Falls Church. One night, around midnight, Robby starts screaming. I go to his room. There's the Boatman, trying to break in."

Even now, years later, Parker's heart trembled at the memory—not only at the image of the face looking through the window but at his son's distilled terror. And the five minutes—they seemed like hours—of absolute horror: shepherding his children into the housekeeper's room, guarding the door while listening to the Boatman stalk through the house. Finally he had stepped into the hallway, his service revolver in hand.

He realized that Evans was looking at him closely, studying him. The therapist asked, "And you shot him?"

"Yes, I did."

The gun is too loud! Parker had thought manically as he fired, knowing how the explosions were adding to his children's terror.

Parker had worried about post-traumatic stress disorder and had taken Robby to a specialist. The doctor, though, had reassured him that because the boy had been very young and hadn't actually been injured by the Boatman, he probably wasn't suffering from PTSD.

Parker told them this and added, "The incident happened just before Christmas. So this time of year he has more memories than otherwise. I mean, he's come through it fine. But . . ."

"I've got kids, too," Evans said. He looked at Lukas, "You?"

"No," she said. "I'm not married."

Evans said to her, "It's as if you lose a part of your mind when you have children. They steal it, and you never get it back. You're always worried that they're upset, they're lost, they're sad."

"Is that right?" she asked, distracted, her eyes stony.

Then the case began to move. A sheet of paper flowed out of the fax machine. Hardy read it. "It's from building permits. Demolition and construction sites in Gravesend."

Geller called up a map of the area on his monitor and highlighted the sites as Hardy called them out. There were a dozen.

Lukas called Jerry Baker and had him disperse the teams there.

Ten minutes later Baker's voice crackled through the speaker in the command post. "New Year's Leader Two to New Year's Leader One. One of my teams found a convenience store selling paper and pens like the kind you were describing. The display faced the window. Some of the packs of paper are sun-bleached."

"Yes!" Parker whispered.

Then another call came in. Lukas took it. Listened. She hung up and said, "That was com-tech." This was the Bureau's crack computer-and-communications tech group. "They're sending the list of Internet subscribers for Gravesend."

The fax phone rang, and another sheet fed out. Parker glanced at it, discouraged. There were more on-line subscribers in Gravesend than he'd anticipated—about fifty of them.

"Call out the addresses," Geller told Hardy. "I'll type them in." Hardy did, and in two minutes all the addresses were highlighted. Parker saw that his concern had been unfounded. There were only four subscribers within a quarter-mile radius of the convenience store and the demolition site.

Lukas called Jerry Baker and gave him the addresses. "We'll meet you at the convenience store. That'll be our staging area. Let's go," Lukas called to the driver of the MCP.

"Wait," Geller called. "Go through the vacant lot there." He tapped the screen. "On foot. You'll get there faster than in cars. We'll drive over and meet you."

Hardy pulled his jacket on, but Lukas shook her head. "Sorry, Len, I'd rather you stayed. This could be a tactical situation. We need negotiators and shooters."

The young officer lifted his hands. "So I'm just sitting here, twiddling my thumbs. Is that it?"

"I'm sorry. That's the way it's got to be."

HENRY Czisman took a tiny sip of beer. He wanted to be as sober as possible. But a man in a bar in Gravesend on New Year's Eve had better be drinking or else incur the suspicion of everybody in the place.

The door opened, and Czisman saw several agents walk inside. He'd been expecting someone to come in here for the canvass, and he'd been very concerned that it might be Lukas or Cage or the fake Jefferson who would recognize him and wonder why he was dogging them. But these men he'd never seen before.

The wiry old man beside Czisman continued. "So then I go, 'The block's cracked. Tell me what'm I gonna do with a cracked block?' And he ain' have no answer for that."

"No answer, hmm?" Czisman asked, eyes on the agents.

They were showing a piece of paper—probably the picture of the Digger's dead accomplice—to a table of three local crones.

Czisman looked past them to the Winnebago parked across the street. He had been staking out FBI headquarters on Ninth Street when he'd seen the three agents hurry outside, along with a dozen others. Well, they wouldn't let him go for a ride-along—so he'd just followed the motorcade of ten or so cars. They'd parked in a cluster near the bar and, after a briefing, had fanned out to canvass for information. Czisman had parked up the street and had slipped into the bar. Then there was nothing to do but sit back and wait.

"Hey," said the old guy, noticing the agents. "Who they? Cops?"

"We're about to find out."

A moment later one of the feds came up to the bar. "Evening. We're federal agents." The ID was properly flashed. "I wonder if either of you've seen this man around here?"

Czisman looked at the photo of the dead man. He said, "No."

The old guy said, "He looks dead. He dead?"

The agent asked, "You haven't seen him?"

"No, sir."

"There's somebody else we're looking for, too. White male, thirties or forties. Wearing a dark coat."

Ah, the Digger, thought Henry Czisman. Odd to hear somebody he'd come to know so well described from such a distant perspective. He said, "That could be a lot of people around here."

"Yes, sir. The only identifying characteristic we know about him is that he wears a gold crucifix. And that he's probably armed. He might have been talking about guns, bragging about them."

"Sorry." Czisman shook his head.

"Sorry," echoed the old guy.

"If you see him, could you please call this number?" The agent handed them both cards.

When the agents left, Czisman's drinking buddy said, "What's that all about? Bet it's drugs. Something's always going down round here. Anyway, so I gotta truck with a busted block—"

Just then Czisman caught a glimpse of the Winnebago door opening and Jefferson and Cage hurrying outside. That woman—Agent Lukas—stepped out a moment later. They were running.

Czisman tossed money down on the bar and stood.

"Hey, you don' wanna hear 'bout my truck?"

Without a word Czisman stepped quickly to the door, pushed outside, and started after the agents.

Chapter Six

6:25 p.m.

BY THE time the team met up with tactical expert Jerry Baker, two of his agents had found the unsub's safe house. It turned out to be a shabby duplex two doors from an old building that was being torn down. Clay and brick dust were everywhere.

Baker said, "Showed a couple across the street the unsub's picture. They've seen him three or four times over the past week. Always looked down, walked fast. Never spoke to anybody."

Two dozen agents and officers were deployed around the building. "Which apartment was his?" Lukas asked.

"Bottom one. Management company says the tenant is Gilbert Jones. The Social Security number was issued to somebody who died five years ago. The unsub signed up for the on-line service—

name of Gilbert Jones again—with a credit card in that name. It's one of those credit-risk cards. You put money in a bank to cover it, and it's only good as long as there's money there."

Baker asked, "Entry now?"

Cage looked at Lukas. "Be my guest."

Lukas said, "Remember—this guy packs his own silencers, so he knows what he's doing."

Baker nodded, then pulled on his flak jacket and helmet and called five other agents over. "Dynamic entry. We'll cut the lights and move in through the front door and the rear-bedroom window simultaneously."

The agents moved quickly into position, machine guns ready. Then the lights went out in the duplex, and there was a loud bang as the agents blew in the front door.

Parker expected to hear shouting. *Freeze, get down, federal agents . . .* But there was only silence. A few minutes later Jerry Baker walked outside, pulling his helmet off. "Clean."

The lights went back on.

Parker prayed, Please let us find *something*—some trace evidence, a fingerprint, a note describing the site of the next attack. Let us finish this and get back home to our families.

Cage went in first, followed by Parker and Lukas.

The apartment was cold. The lights were glaring. It was a depressing place, the four rooms mostly empty. In the living room Parker could see a computer on a stand, a desk, a musty armchair shedding its stuffing, several tables. But to his dismay he could see no notes, scraps of paper, or other documents.

Parker glanced at the living-room window and wondered about the unsub's dietary habits. Cooling in the half-open window were four or five large bottles of Mott's apple juice and a battered cast-iron skillet filled with apples and oranges.

Lukas phoned Tobe Geller and asked him to come check out the computer and any files and E-mail the unsub had stored inside.

Geller arrived a few minutes later. He examined the computer carefully, then looked up. "Place stinks," he said. "What is that?"

Parker smelled it, too. Something sweet and chemical. The cheap paint on the hot radiators, he guessed.

The young agent clicked on the computer's POWER switch.

"Won't it take forever to figure out the password?" Lukas asked.

"No. It'll take . . ." Geller pulled the housing off the computer and reached inside. Suddenly the screen reported, "Loading Windows 95." Geller said, "About *that* much time."

Lukas's phone rang. She answered, listened, then hung up, not pleased. "All he's called from the phone line here is the connection for the on-line service. Nothing else coming in or going out."

The man had been smart, Parker reflected. A puzzle master in his own right.

"Found something in the bedroom," a voice called. An agent walked into the living room, holding a yellow pad with writing on it. Parker's heart sped up a few beats when he saw this.

He opened his attaché case and pulled on his latex gloves. He set the pad on the table next to Geller, bent the desk lamp over it. With his Leitz hand glass he studied the first page and noticed immediately the devil's teardrop over the lowercase *i*.

Parker scanned the sheet. Much of it was doodlings of mazes. So the unsub *was* a puzzle master. Parker tried one or two of the mazes. Most were very complicated.

He lifted the top sheet and found a dense page of notes. Toward the bottom he saw a column. The first two entries were:

> Dupont Circle Metro, top of the escalator, 9 a.m.
> George Mason Theater, box No. 58, 4 p.m.

My God, he thought, this's got the *real* targets on it.

Just then Lukas stepped into the doorway from the bedroom and shouted, "I smell gasoline! Where's it coming from?"

Gas? Parker realized *that* was the smell they'd detected earlier. He looked at the bottles of apple juice. It was a trap—in case the agents got into the safe house.

Parker leaped to his feet. "Everybody out! The bottles!"

But Geller said, "They're okay. There's no detonator. You—"

And then the stream of bullets exploded through the window, shattering the bottles and spraying gasoline over the walls and floor.

Parker now huddled on the floor, the precious yellow pad still on the desk. He tried once to grab it, but a cluster of slugs pummeled the floor in front of him and he fell back.

Lukas and Cage crawled out the front door into the hallway, weapons drawn, looking for a target. Tobe Geller pushed back from the desk, but the chair legs caught on the uneven floor and he tumbled backward. The computer monitor imploded as a dozen slugs struck it.

There was a pause in the fusillade. Then the Digger, somewhere outside, on a rooftop maybe, lowered his aim and fired toward the metal pan that the fruit rested in. That, too, had been placed there for a purpose. The bullets clanged off it, and sparks shot into the gasoline, which ignited with a huge roar.

Parker was blown into the hallway by the explosion.

"No, Tobe!" Parker cried, trying to get back inside. But a wave of flame forced him back, and the Digger kept firing.

They crouched in the windowless corridor. Lukas on one phone, Cage on another. "Call DCFD. . . . One agent down. Make that two. He's still out there. Where is he?"

"Tobe!" Parker shouted again.

"Somebody!" Geller called. "Help me."

Parker caught a glimpse of the young man curled on the floor on the other side of the raging flames. The Digger kept shooting into the flaming living room. Soon Geller was lost to sight. It seemed that the table where the yellow pad rested was consumed in flames. No, no! The clues to the last sites were burning to ash!

"Tobe!" Cage shouted, and tried to climb back into the apartment. He, too, was driven back by the astonishing heat—and by yet more shooting.

Through the noise they could just make out poor Tobe Geller's voice. "Help me! Please! Help me. . . ." Growing softer.

Lukas made one last attempt to get inside but got only a few feet before a ceiling beam came down. She gave a scream and fell back.

Parker, choking on smoke, helped her toward the front door as a tornado of orange and black flames poured into the corridor.

A moment later they and the other agents were tumbling down the front stairs into the cold air. Despite their racking coughs and blurry vision, Cage and Lukas instinctively dropped into defensive positions, scanning building tops, searching for targets.

C. P. Ardell held an M-16 close to his thick cheek, and Len Hardy brandished his small revolver, head moving back and forth, fear and confusion, mixed, in his eyes. They could find no targets.

Baker was speaking into his cell phone. "Subject was east of us, shooting downward at a slight angle. Okay . . . Where? . . . Okay. Just be careful." He said nothing for a long moment. Then he cocked his head as somebody came back on the line. Baker listened. He said, "They're dead? Oh, man. . . . He's gone?"

He stood up and walked over to Cage. "He got into the building behind us. Killed the couple who lived upstairs. He disappeared down the alley. Nobody got a look at him."

Parker looked back at the building, which was now engulfed in flames. Oh, Tobe . . .

Sirens cut through the night. He could see flashing lights reflected along both ends of the street. All the evidence gone, too. Why hadn't he glanced at the yellow pad earlier? Why had he wasted precious seconds looking at the mazes? Parker sensed that the document itself was the enemy and had intentionally distracted him to give the Digger time to attack them.

"Hey," somebody shouted. "Hey, over here! Need some help!"

Parker, Lukas, and Cage turned toward an agent in an FBI windbreaker running to an alley beside the burning duplex. "There's somebody here," he called.

A figure lay on the ground, on his side, surrounded by an aura of blue smoke. Parker assumed the man was dead. But suddenly he lifted his head and cried, "Put it out!" in a gruff whisper.

"Tobe!" Lukas ran toward him. Parker was beside her.

The young agent must have jumped through the flames and out the window. A medic sprinted up to him. "Where're you hurt?"

But all Geller would offer was a crazed shout. "Put it out. The pad of paper! Put the fire out!" He was gesturing toward a small fire near his leg.

Parker glanced at it. It was the yellow pad. In a split-second decision Tobe Geller had forgone the computer disks and grabbed the unsub's notes. But they were now on fire. Parker tore his jacket off and carefully laid it over the pad to extinguish the flames.

"Look out!" somebody called. Parker looked up, just as a huge piece of burning siding crashed to the ground three feet from him. A cloud of sparks swarmed. Parker ignored them and carefully lifted his jacket off the pad, surveying the damage to the paper.

The medic said, "We gotta get out of here." He waved to his partner, who ran up with a gurney. They eased Geller onto the stretcher and trotted off with him, dodging falling debris.

"We gotta pull back," a man in a black fireman's coat shouted. "We're going to lose the wall."

"In a minute," Parker answered. He glanced at Lukas. "Get out of here!"

"You can't stay here, Parker." She retreated a bit, then paused.

"The ash is too fragile! I can't move it." Lifting the pad would crumble the ash into powder, and they'd lose any chance to reconstruct the sheets. A gutter fell from the roof and stabbed the ground, end first, eighteen inches away.

"Parker," Lukas called again. "Come on!"

Parker had an idea. He ran to the basement windows of the duplex next door and kicked out the glass. He picked up four large pieces. He returned to the pad and dropped to his knees. He carefully sandwiched the two sheets of scorched paper—the only ones with writing on them—between pieces of glass. Then as timbers, bricks, and fiery siding fell, Parker slowly rose and, holding the glass sheets in front of him, walked carefully away, perfectly upright and taking tiny steps, like a servant carrying a tray of wine at an elegant cocktail party.

ANOTHER picture. *Snap.*

Henry Czisman stood in an alleyway across the street from the burning building. Sparks were flying leisurely into the sky like fireworks seen from miles away.

How important this was. Recording the event. Tragedy is so quick, so fleeting. But sorrow isn't. Sorrow is forever. *Snap.* He took another picture with his camera.

Picture: a trooper with blood cascading down her face.

Picture: the flames reflected in the chrome of the fire trucks.

By the time Czisman got to the duplex, the fire had already started and the agents and cops were stumbling out. All he could do was take his pictures. *Snap, snap, snap . . .* He couldn't take enough shots. He was driven to record every detail of the sorrow.

He glanced up the street and saw the man who called himself Jefferson. He was resting something on the hood of a car, bent forward to read it. A magazine? No, it glistened like a sheet of glass. The man was all rigid attention as he stripped off his leather jacket and wrapped it around the glass the way a father might bundle up his infant for a trip outside in the cold night air. *Snap.*

EXCEPT for Tobe Geller, who was in the hospital, the team reassembled inside the document lab at headquarters.

Margaret Lukas was on the phone. Parker glanced at her. Her cryptic return look brought to mind something Cage had said in the car on the way back to the document lab.

"Whatta you think about Lukas?" the agent had asked.

"What do I think? She's good. She'll go places."

"That's not what I'm asking. What about her as a woman?"

"You trying to set us up, Lukas and me?"

"Of course not. It's just I wish Margaret had more friends. She's not married. No boyfriends. And I don't know if you noticed, but she's good-looking, don't you think?"

Of course Parker was attracted to her—and by more than just her appearance. But what he told Cage was, "She can't wait till this case is over, and she doesn't have to see me again."

"You think?" the agent asked, but cynically this time.

"I've been stepping on her toes, and she doesn't like it. But I've got news for her. I'm going to keep on stepping if I think I'm right."

"Hey, that's just what *she'd* say. Aren't you two the pair . . ."

"Cage, take a break. Why do *you* think she's on my case?"

After a moment the agent answered, "Maybe she envies you."

"Envies me? What do you mean?"

"That's not for me to say. Think of it like one of your puzzles. Either you figure it out, or she'll give you the answer. That's up to her. But I'm not giving you any clues."

Now, as Lukas looked down at the notes she was scribbling, Parker observed her handwriting. The Palmer Method. Precise and economical. No nonsense.

Parker set the glass sheets on the examination table. He took a bottle of diluted ammonia and began to clean the glass protecting the ash.

Lukas shut off her phone. She looked at Cage and the others. "The safe house's completely gone. PERT's going through it, but there's nothing left. The computer and the disks were totaled."

Cage asked, "How 'bout the building the Digger shot from?"

"Clean. They got shell casings this time, but he wore—"

"Latex gloves," Parker said, sighing.

"Not a bit of trace."

Parker finished cleaning the glass and turned his attention to the evidence. He studied what was left of the two pages. To his dismay much of the ash had disintegrated. Still, it would be possible to read some of the unsub's writings on the larger pieces of ash. This is done by shining infrared light on the surface. Burned ink or pencil marks reflect a different wavelength from that of the paper, and you usually can make out much of the writing.

Parker carefully set the glass panes holding the yellow sheets side by side in the infrared viewer. He picked up a hand glass he found on the table, thinking angrily, The Digger just destroyed my five-hundred-dollar antique Leitz.

Hardy glanced at the sheet on the left. "He drew mazes."

Parker examined the pieces of ash one at a time, focusing on the sheet that had the reference to the Mason Theater on it. He shook his head. "The targets the Digger's already hit are perfectly legible. But the next two . . . I can't make them out. The last one . . . Write this down," he said to Hardy.

The young detective grabbed a pen and paper. "Go ahead."

"It looks like, 'Place where I . . .' Let's see. 'Place where I took you.' Then a dash. Then the word 'black.' No, '*the* black.' Then there's a hole in the sheet. It's gone completely."

Hardy read back, " 'Place where I took you, dash, the black.' "

Parker looked up. "Where the hell is he talking about?"

But no one had any idea.

Cage asked, "What about the eight-o'clock hit? That's what we oughta be concentrating on. We have less than an hour."

Parker scanned the third line of the writing, right below the Mason Theater reference. He studied it for a full minute, crouching. He dictated, " '. . . two miles south. The R . . .' That's an uppercase *R*. But after that the ash is fragmented."

Parker took the transcription and walked to a chalkboard mounted on the wall of the lab. He copied the words for everyone to read:

> . . . two miles south. The R . . .
> . . . place where I took you—the black . . .

"What's it mean?" Cage asked, but Parker didn't have a clue.

The door opened, and Parker did a double take. "Tobe!"

Tobe Geller walked unsteadily into the room. The young man had changed clothes and seemed to have showered, but he smelled smoky and was coughing sporadically.

"Hey, boy, you got no business being here," Cage said.

Lukas said, "Are you crazy? Go home."

"To my pathetic bachelor quarters? Having broken my last date with what is undoubtedly my *former* girlfriend tonight? I don't think so." He started to laugh; then the sound dissolved into a cough. He controlled it and breathed deeply. "They don't even make a degree for my burns," Geller explained. "It's like I got a South Carolina tan. I'm fine." He coughed again. "Well, aside from the lungs. Now, where are we?"

"That yellow pad?" Parker said ruefully. "Hate to say it, but we can't make out very much."

"Ouch," the young agent said.

Lukas walked to the examination table and stood next to Parker. "Hmm," she said, pointing to the hundreds of tiny fragments of ash. "Some of these little pieces might fit after the letter *R*, right?"

"They might."

"Well, what's that remind you of?"

Parker looked down at the pad. "A jigsaw puzzle," he whispered. "Tobe? There're computer programs that do anagrams."

"Anagrams, anagrams? What're those again?"

It was C. P. Ardell who answered. "Assembling different words out of a set of letters. Like n-o-w, o-w-n, w-o-n."

Geller said, "Oh, sure." He laughed. "It's brilliant. We'll scan a handwriting sample from the note. That'll give us standards of construction for all of his letters. Then I'll shoot the pieces of ash on the digital camera with an infrared filter, drop out the tonal value of the burned paper. That'll leave us with fragments of letters. The computer can assemble them."

"Will it work?" Hardy asked.

"Oh, it'll work. I just don't know how long it'll take."

Geller took several pictures of the ash and one of the extortion note with a digital camera. He plugged the camera into a serial port on a computer and began to upload the image.

Everybody remained silent. Which made the sound of Parker's phone a moment later particularly startling. He opened his cell phone, noted the caller ID was his home number. "Hello?"

His heart froze as Mrs. Cavanaugh said in a taut voice, "Parker." In the background he heard Robby sobbing.

"What is it?" he asked, trying not to panic.

"Everybody's okay. Robby's just got scared. He thought he saw that man in the backyard. The Boatman."

Oh, no . . .

"There was nobody there. I turned the outdoor lights on. Mr. Johnson's dog got loose again, that was all. But he's scared."

"Put him on."

"Daddy? Daddy!" His voice was limp with fear.

"Hey, Robby!" Parker said brightly. "What happened?"

"I thought I saw him. The Boatman. In the garage."

Parker was angry with himself. He'd lazily left the door up, and there was plenty of junk inside that could resemble an intruder.

Parker said to his son, "Remember what we do, Robby-O?"

A pause, then, "I've got my shield."

"Good for you. How 'bout the helmet?" Parker glanced up and saw Lukas staring at him raptly. "You have your helmet?"

"Yes," the boy answered.

Oh, it was so hard, hearing his son's voice and knowing what he had to do now. He looked around the lab and thought, You can—with luck and strength—pry yourself loose from wives or lovers or colleagues, but not from your children. Never from your children. They have your heart netted forever. Into the phone he said, "I'll be right home. Don't worry."

"Really?" the boy asked.

"As fast as I can drive."

He hung up. Everyone was looking at him, motionless.

"I have to go," he said. "I'll be back."

"Hey, Parker," Cage began, "I'm sorry he's scared, but—"

Margaret Lukas lifted her hand and silenced the older agent. She said, "There's no way the Digger could know about you, but I'll send a couple of agents to stay outside your house."

He thought this was a preface to talking him into staying. But then she added quietly, "Your little boy? Go home. Make him happy."

Parker held her eyes for a moment, wondering, Had he found a clue to the maze of Special Agent Lukas?

He started to thank her, but he sensed suddenly that any show of gratitude, any response at all, would throw this tenuous balance between them off. So he simply nodded and hurried out the door.

PIXEL by pixel. Watching the images fall into place on Tobe Geller's screen. Still a jumble.

Margaret Lukas turned to Dr. Evans, watched him examining the extortion note. The psychologist sipped more coffee, poured from his thermos, then announced, "I've got some thoughts about the unsub."

"Go ahead."

"I think, from what we've seen, the Digger's just a machine. We'd call him 'profile-proof.' It's pointless to analyze him. It'd be like doing a profile of a gun. But the perp, the man in the morgue—that's a different story. He was a highly organized offender. He planned everything out perfectly. Had backup plans upon backup plans. And he found the perfect weapon—a functioning human being who does nothing but kill."

"Kincaid said he was highly educated," Lukas said. "He tried to disguise it in the note, but Parker saw right through it."

Evans thought for a moment. "What was he wearing?"

C.P. found the list and read it to the doctor.

Evans summarized. "So, cheap clothes. Not exactly what you'd expect from somebody with the intelligence to set this whole thing up and who was asking for twenty million dollars."

"Which means what?" Lukas asked.

"I see a class issue here," Evans explained. "I think he'd rather kill rich people than poor people."

Hardy pointed out, "But in the first attack he had the Digger gun down everybody, not just the wealthy."

Evans said, "But consider where—Dupont Circle. It's yuppieville there. And the Mason Theater? Tickets for the show must've been selling for sixty bucks each. I think he was angry at the rich."

"Why?" Cage asked.

"I don't know yet, but he did hate them. We should remember that when we're trying to figure out what his next target will be."

Lukas pulled the morgue shot of the unsub closer, stared at him. What *had been* on his mind? What *were* his motives?

"Hold on, folks," Geller said. "We're getting something." Everyone leaned toward the screen on which they could see the words ". . . two miles south. The R . . ." Behind that phrase the computer was inserting combinations of the letters from the fragments of ash. It had now added a letter *i* behind the *R*. Another one was forming behind that.

"It's that funny *i* with a dot Parker mentioned," Geller said.

"The devil's teardrop," Lukas whispered.

"Right," Geller said. "Then after that . . . a letter *t*."

"What's that next letter?" Hardy asked in a whisper.

"It's too fuzzy," Lukas muttered. "A short letter." She leaned over the tech's shoulders. "Looks like a zigzag. An *x* maybe?"

Cage's head shot up. "Zigzag? Could it be a *z*?"

"Ritz," Hardy said. "Maybe the Ritz-Carlton?"

"Got to be!" Lukas said. "He's going after more rich people."

In the office chair Geller rolled to a different computer. In five seconds he had a yellow pages telephone directory on the screen. "Two Ritz's. One at Tysons Corner and one in Pentagon City."

Lukas said, "But they're both outside the District. Parker said he'd stick to D.C."

Evans said, "Maybe at first he would, but he'd know we'd start to catch on and he'd want to change the rules."

"But which hotel?" Cage asked.

"We're not taking any chances," Lukas said. "We'll cover both."

She called Jerry Baker and told him about the latest target. "I want every tactical agent in the District and northern Virginia mobilized." She added, "You're not going to like it, but no hoods and helmets." Shorthand in the Bureau for going plainclothes.

"You sure?" Baker asked uncertainly.

"Has to be, Jerry. We've almost nailed this guy once, and he's gonna be skittish as a deer. He sees anything out of the ordinary, he's going to bolt. I'll take responsibility." She hung up.

She found Len Hardy staring at her. "You're going plainclothes? Does that mean you're not going to evacuate the hotels?"

"That's right," she answered. "He can't suspect a thing."

"For God's sake," Hardy said. "At least get the kids out."

She looked into his eyes. "No. If we tried to evacuate anybody at all, word would spread and there'd be panic."

"So you're just going to go in and hope for the best?"

"No," she said. "We're going to go in, and we're going to stop him." A glance at Evans, "Doctor, if you could stay here." Then a glance at Hardy. "You handle communications."

Hardy sighed. He spun around to the control panel.

"Let's go," Lukas said to Cage. "I've got to stop by my office for some party clothes. We've got to blend."

"HE'S got something good for us," said Wendell Jefferies.

By "he" Mayor Kennedy knew the aide meant Slade Phillips.

The two men were in the city hall office. The mayor had just given another embarrassing press conference. All he could report on was the morale of some of the victims he'd visited at hospitals.

"He's going on the air at ten," Jefferies now told the mayor.

"With what?"

"He won't tell me," Jefferies said.

The phone rang. Jefferies answered it. "Hello?" A pause. "Sure. Hold on." He handed it to Kennedy. "This is interesting."

Kennedy took the receiver. "Yes?"

"Mayor Kennedy? This is Detective Len Hardy. I've been thinking. . . . About what we were talking about."

Kennedy sat up straight. "Go ahead, son."

"I think she's making a mistake. I had to do something."

"Lukas?"

"They found out the shooter's going to hit the Ritz-Carlton."

"Pentagon City?"

"They're not sure. Probably that one. Maybe Tysons. But Lukas isn't evacuating the hotels. She's—"

"Wait," Kennedy said. "They know where he's going to hit, and they're not telling anyone?"

"No. She's going to use them for bait, I guess. I mean, that's the only way to say it."

"That's at eight?"

"Eight, yes. I can't talk any longer, Mayor. I thought about what you said, and I just had to tell you."

"You did the right thing, Officer."

"I hope so. I really hope that."

Kennedy hung up and rose to his feet. "He's going to hit the Ritz," he told Jefferies. "Probably at Pentagon City. I want my car now. And a police escort."

As he strode to the door, Jefferies asked, "How 'bout a news crew? I can get a cameraman who works with Phillips."

Kennedy nodded. "Call him."

THEY'RE both standing awkwardly, side by side, arms crossed, in the Digger's motel room, watching TV. The pictures on the TV look familiar. They are from the theater. The place where the Digger was supposed to spin around and send bullets flying. Where he wanted to spin, but he couldn't. The theater where . . . *click* . . . where the police came to kill him.

He looks at the boy as the boy looks at the TV. The boy's name is Tye. He is thin and frail. The area around his right eye is slightly darker than his dark skin, and the Digger knows that the man he killed had hit the boy a lot. He's happy he shot the man. Whatever happy is.

The Digger wonders what the man who tells him things would think about the boy. The boy *has* gotten a look at his face, but it doesn't seem . . . *click* . . . seem right to kill him.

Why, it seems to me that every day,
I love you all the more.

He goes into the kitchenette and opens a can of soup. He spoons some into a bowl. Looks at the boy's skinny arms and spoons some more in. He heats it in the microwave, then sets the bowl in front of the boy. Hands him a spoon.

The boy takes one bite, then another. Then he stops eating. He's looking at the TV screen. His small head lolls to one side, his eyes droop, and the Digger realizes he's tired. The Digger motions to the couch, and the boy goes and lies down. The Digger gets a blanket and drapes it over the boy.

He says to him, "I'm going . . . *click* . . . I'm going out."

"You comin' back?" the boy mutters.

The Digger nods his head, his head with the tiny indentation above the temple. "I'm coming back."

The boy closes his eyes. The Digger pulls the blanket up higher.

He goes to the closet and takes out one of the boxes of ammunition. He reloads the Uzi, then repacks the silencer.

The Digger looks at the torn puppy bag. He is about to crumple it up and throw it out, but he remembers that Tye looked at the bag and seemed to like it. The Digger smooths it and puts it beside the boy so that if he wakes up while the Digger is gone, he'll see the puppies and won't be afraid.

The Digger puts the Uzi into a new bag—a brown paper bag—pulls his dark coat and gloves on, and leaves the room.

Downstairs, he gets into his car, a nice Toyota Corolla. He opens the glove compartment. There are several pistols inside. He takes one and puts it into his pocket. "After the theater," warned the man who tells him things, "there'll be more police looking for you. Be careful. If anybody sees your face . . ."

UPSTAIRS, in Robby's room, Parker sat with his son. The boy was sitting in bed. Parker, in the bentwood rocker, was reading to him from *The Hobbit.*

Robby was lost in the story, even though he'd heard his father read it to him a number of times. They gravitated to this book whenever Robby was frightened because of the scene of slaying Smeagol the dragon. That part of the book always gave him courage.

When Parker had walked into his house not long ago, the boy's face had lit up. Parker had taken his son's hand and walked to the back porch, showed him once again that there was nothing in the backyard or the garage.

Stephie had hugged her father and asked how his sick friend was.

"He's fine," Parker had said, looking for but not finding a bit of truth to hang the statement on. Oh, the guilt of parents . . .

Stephie had watched sympathetically as Robby and Parker walked upstairs to read a story. She might have joined them, but instead she vanished into the kitchen, saying, "I'm making a surprise for Robby."

As Parker read, he would glance occasionally at his son's face. The boy's eyes were closed, and he looked completely content.

"You want me to keep reading?" he whispered.

The boy didn't respond.

Parker left the book on his lap and remained in the rocking chair, easing back and forth. Watching his son, worrying as he often did, if he was raising the children right. After all, he'd separated them from their mother. That it was the only sane thing to do made little difference. Was it truly for the children that he'd done this, or was it to escape from his own unhappiness? Joan had seemed so sweet before they were married. But much of it, he'd realized, was an act. After the Whos were born, when married life demanded responsibility, hard work, and sacrifice, Joan gave rein to her dissatisfactions and moods.

Parker tried everything he could think of. He went with her to therapy, took over more than his share of the children's care, tried joking her out of it, planned parties, took her on trips.

But among the secrets Joan had kept from him was a family history of alcoholism, and he was surprised to find that she'd been drinking much more than he'd believed. She'd do a Twelve Step program from time to time, but she always relapsed. She withdrew further and further from him and the children. And then there was the Incident. June, four years ago.

Parker returned home from work at the Bureau's document lab and found Joan away from home, a baby-sitter looking after the Whos. This wasn't unusual or troublesome in itself. But when he went upstairs to play with the children, he saw immediately that something was wrong. Stephie and Robby, then four and five, were assembling Tinkertoys, but Stephanie was groggy. Her eyes were unfocused and her face slick with sweat. And both she and her brother seemed very evasive.

The boy's eyes kept going to their toy chest. Parker started toward it, and Robby began to cry, begging him not to open the lid. But of course, he did. And stood frozen, looking down at the bottles of vodka Joan had hidden there.

Stephanie was drunk. She'd tried imitating Mommy, drinking from her Winnie the Pooh mug.

"Mommy said not to say anything about her secret," she told him, crying. "She said you'd be mad; you'd yell at us."

Two days later he started divorce proceedings. He hired a savvy lawyer and got child protective services involved.

Joan fought, and fought hard—but it was the way someone fights to keep a stamp collection or sports car, not something you love more than life itself. And in the end, after several agonizing months and tens of thousands of dollars, they were his.

He'd thought that he could concentrate on putting his life back together and giving the children a normal life. And he had—for the past four years. But now Joan was at it again.

"Daddy," Robby said suddenly, "you stopped reading."

"I thought you were asleep." He laughed.

"My eyelids were just resting. They got tired, but *I'm* not."

Parker glanced at the clock. Quarter to eight. Fifteen minutes until— No, don't think about that now.

He picked up the book and began to read once more.

Chapter Seven

7:45 p.m.

MARGARET Lukas looked over the families at the Ritz-Carlton Hotel connected to the Pentagon City Mall. She and Cage stood in the main lobby, where hundreds of people were gathering for the final dinner seating before midnight. Lukas was wearing a navy-blue worsted suit she'd made herself. It was cut close to her body and had a long, pleated skirt. She had cut a special dart in the jacket to make certain that the Glock 10 on her hip did not ruin the outfit's stylish lines.

Lukas and Cage scanned the guests, the bellhops, the clerks.

Nobody came close to their fragile description of the Digger: probably white, average build, wearing a gold crucifix. She realized they were standing with their arms crossed, looking just like well-dressed feds on stakeout. "Say something amusing. Pretend we're talking."

"Okay," Cage said, smiling. "So whatta you think of Kincaid?"

The question threw her. "Kincaid? I don't know."

"Sure you do." Cage persisted. "Well?"

"He's perp smart, not street smart."

Cage shrugged. "That's good. I like that."

They studied a dozen possible suspects. She dismissed them for reasons she knew instinctively but couldn't explain.

A moment later Cage said, "He's a good man."

"I know. He's been very helpful."

Cage said, "He lost his parents just after college. Then there was that custody battle a few years ago. Wife was psycho."

"That's hard," she said. "What happened? With his folks?"

"Car accident. One of those crazy things. His mother'd just been diagnosed with cancer. They got nailed by a truck on the way to Johns Hopkins for chemo. Dad was a history professor. Met him a couple times. Nice guy."

"Was he?" she muttered, distracted.

"Kincaid's a stand-up guy," Cage offered. "And he's smart. You should see him with those puzzles of his."

"Yeah. I'm sure he's great. Look, Cage, I just need some phony conversation, not matchmaking."

"I'm only saying you don't meet a lot of people like Kincaid."

"Uh-huh. We've got to stay focused here, Cage."

But she *wasn't* focusing. She was thinking about Kincaid.

So he had his own Incidents—deaths and divorce. And a struggle to raise the children by himself. Thinking about him, she thought again about the postcard. Joey's postcard.

On the trip from which they'd never returned, Tom and Joey had been visiting her in-laws in Ohio. Her six-year-old son had mailed her a postcard from the airport as they were leaving. Probably not a half hour before the 737 had crashed into the icy field.

The boy hadn't known you needed a stamp to mail postcards. He must have slipped it into the mailbox before his father knew what he was doing. It arrived a week after the funeral. Postage due.

> Were having fun mommy. Granma and I made cookys
> I miss you. I love you, mommy . . .

A card from the ghost of her son. It was in her purse right now. Her wedding ring was stored in her jewelry box, but this card she kept with her and would until she died.

It's as if you lose a part of your mind when you have children. They steal it, and you never get it back. . . .

Dr. Evans had said that, and she knew it was completely true.

And here was Cage trying to set her up with Kincaid. Yet the same instincts that made her a good cop told her that there was no future between them. She had returned to a "normal" life as much as she ever could. She had her dog, Jean Luc. She had some friends, her CDs, her runners club. But Margaret Lukas was emotionally plateaued, to use the Bureau term for an agent no longer destined for advancement. No, she knew she'd never see Parker Kincaid after tonight. And that was perfectly all right—

Her earphone crackled. It was C. P. Ardell, stationed downstairs at the garage entrance. "Margaret, we've got a problem. The mayor's here with a dozen cops and a camera crew, too. The shooter sees this, he'll take off."

"I'll be right there."

"YOUR Honor, this is a federal operation. I'll have to ask you to leave right now."

They were in the parking garage. Lukas noted immediately that to get in, you needed a ticket. That meant license plates were recorded and that in turn meant the Digger would probably not come in this way. But Mayor Kennedy and his entourage were headed for the main entrance to the mall, where they could be spotted in a minute.

Kennedy looked down at Lukas. He was eight inches taller. "You have to get these people out of here. And at Tysons Corner, too.

Evacuate them. When the killer shows up, let me talk to him."

"We can't do that," she said. "He'll know something's wrong."

"Well, tell them to go to their rooms at least."

"Most of them aren't guests. They're just here for dinner and parties." Lukas looked around the entrance to the mall and whispered fiercely, "He could be here at any minute. I don't have time to argue with you. I want you and your people out of here now."

Kennedy looked at his aide. A reporter was nearby, filming. "I'm not going to let the FBI risk people's lives. I'm going to—"

"Agent Ardell," she said, "put the mayor in custody."

"You can't arrest him," Jefferies snapped.

"Yes, she can," Cage said with the most minute of shrugs.

"Get him out of here now," Lukas snapped.

"Lockup?"

"No. Just stay with him and keep him until the operation's over."

The mayor said, "I'm calling my lawyer and—"

A flash of anger burst inside her. "Mayor, this is my operation. You're interfering with it. I'll let you go on your way with Agent Ardell, or I'll have you detained downtown. It's up to you."

There was a pause. Kennedy said, "All right." He nodded toward the hotel. "But if there's any bloodshed, it'll be on your hands."

"Goes with the territory," she muttered. "Go on, C.P."

Together she and Cage walked back toward the hotel.

"Damn," Cage said. "If Kennedy found out we were here, that means we've got a leak. Where do you think it is?"

"Oh, I *know*." She opened her cell phone and made a call.

"Detective," she said when Len Hardy answered, "give me a reason why I shouldn't refer you to the U.S. attorney."

She expected him to deny or at least offer some slippery excuse, but he surprised her by saying briskly, "Kennedy wanted a chance to negotiate with the shooter. I gave it to him."

"Why?"

"Because you were willing to let, what, a dozen people die? Kennedy said he could talk him into taking the money. He—"

"You know he showed up with a TV crew?"

Hardy's voice was no longer so certain. "He what?"

"He was playing it for the media. If the Digger'd seen the lights, he'd take off and find another target."

Silence for a moment. "I'm sorry, Margaret." He sighed. "I just didn't want any more people to die. I'm sorry."

Lukas gripped her phone. She knew she should kick him off the team, and yet she had an image of the young man returning to his house, a house as silent as the one she returned to in the year after Tom and Joey had died. He'd spend the holiday alone, mourning for a wife not alive and not dead.

He seemed to sense her weakening and said, "It won't happen again. I still want to help."

"Okay, we'll talk later. We've got to get back on stakeout."

She clicked off the phone abruptly and headed for the lobby of the Ritz-Carlton. It was a few minutes to eight.

THEY looked over the yacht's railing at the dark water and ate the shrimp and talked about wine and about interest rates and about upcoming elections and about congressional scandals. Most of the men were in tuxedos or dinner jackets, most of the women in dark dresses whose hems hovered an inch above the lacquered deck.

The hundreds of partiers had stationed themselves all over the lengthy yacht. There were three decks and four bars, and everyone at the New Year's Eve bash was feeling great.

Pretty people, handsome people. Everyone was happy. Everyone was thankful. Thankful for the view they'd have of the fireworks at midnight, thankful for the chance to celebrate, thankful for the creature comforts on board the luxury yacht, *The Ritzy Lady,* which floated regally at her dock on the Potomac, exactly two miles south of the Fourteenth Street Bridge.

BY A little after eight o'clock Robby had moved from *The Hobbit* to Nintendo. He wasn't upset anymore, and Parker could stand it no longer. He had to find out about the Digger, about what had happened with the most recent attack.

He walked downstairs, where Stephie was in the kitchen with Mrs. Cavanaugh, scrubbing a pot. She'd made a caramel corn Christmas tree. It sat, charmingly lopsided, on a plate on the counter.

"Beautiful, Who," he told her. "Robby'll love it."

He started for the phone but saw her face. He stopped, put his arm around her. "I'm sorry tonight's gone all kerflooey. But honey, you know my friend? I may have to go back and see him."

"Oh, I know," she said. "I could tell. Sometimes you're all the way here, and sometimes you're partway here. And tonight, when you came back, you were only partway here."

"Tomorrow I'll be all the way here. It's supposed to snow. You want to go sledding?"

"Yeah! Can I make the hot chocolate?"

"I was hoping you would." He hugged her, then rose and walked into the den to make the call, but he stopped. Through the curtained window he saw someone in a dark coat. He slipped his hand into his pocket and kneaded the cold metal of Lukas's gun.

Oh, not again . . . Thinking of the Boatman, remembering that terrible night. *The gun is too loud. . . .*

The doorbell rang.

"I'll get it," he called. Hand in his pocket, he looked through the window in the door and saw an FBI agent he recognized from earlier in the evening. He relaxed, breathed deeply to calm himself, then opened the door. A second agent walked up the steps.

"Agent Kincaid? S.A.C. Lukas sent us to keep an eye on your family."

He nodded, then looked over his shoulder to make sure Stephie was out of earshot. "Thanks. Just park out of sight if you would."

"Sure thing, sir."

He glanced at his watch. He was relieved. If the Digger had struck again, Cage or Lukas would have called. "The shooter in the Metro killing?" he asked. "The Digger. They got him?"

The look that passed between the two men chilled Parker.

"Well, sir, the shooter, he got on board a party yacht on the Potomac. Killed eleven, wounded twenty. Thought you knew."

Oh, God. Here I was reading children's books while people died.

Inside the house the phone started to ring.

He asked, "Is Agent Lukas all right? And Agent Cage?"

"Yes, sir. They weren't anywhere near the boat. They found some clue that said 'Ritz,' so they thought the Digger was going to hit one of the Ritz hotels, but that wasn't it. The name of the boat was *The Ritzy Lady.* Bad luck, huh?"

The other agent said, "Security guard got off a couple shots. That scared the shooter off, so it wasn't as bad as it might've been."

Bad luck, huh? No, not luck at all. When you don't solve the puzzle, it's not because of luck. *Three hawks . . .*

Mrs. Cavanaugh called, "Mr. Kincaid? Phone for you."

Parker walked into the kitchen. He picked up the phone, expecting to hear Lukas or Cage. But it was a smooth-sounding baritone he didn't recognize.

"Mr. Kincaid? My name's Slade Phillips, WPLT news. We're doing a special report on the New Year's Eve shootings. And we have an unnamed source reporting that you've been instrumental in the investigation and may be responsible for the mix-up in sending the FBI to the Ritz-Carlton Hotel when, in fact, the killer had targeted another location. We're going on the air with that story at nine, but we want to give you the chance to tell your side."

Parker inhaled sharply. This was it. Joan would find out.

"Mr. Kincaid?"

"I have no comment." He hung up.

THE Digger returns to his motel room.

The boat—where he spun around like . . . *click* . . . like a whirligig and fired his Uzi and watched the people fall and fall—wasn't like the theater. No, no. He got a lot of them this time.

The Digger locks the motel door, and the first thing he does is walk to the couch and look at Tye. The boy is still asleep.

The Digger turns the TV on and sees pictures of *The Ritzy Lady* boat. He sees a man he recognizes—the . . . *click* . . . the mayor. He's wearing a nice suit, speaking into a microphone, but the Digger can't hear what he's saying, because he doesn't have the sound up, because he doesn't want to wake up Tye.

He watches for a while, but no commercials come on, so he shuts off the TV, thinking, Good night, Mayor.

He begins to pack his belongings, taking his time.

Motels are nice; motels are fun. They come and clean up the room every day and take away your empty soup bowls and bring you clean ones. Even Pamela didn't do that. She was good with flowers and good in bed. He remembers Christmas Day when he made soup for Pamela and then gave her her present.

He looks at Tye. He'll take the boy out . . . *click* . . . out west with him. The man who tells him things told him he'd call after they finished in Washington and tell him where they'd go next.

"Where will that be?" the Digger asked.

"I don't know. Maybe the West. California. Maybe Oregon."

"Oh," responded the Digger, who had no idea where those places were. Sometimes, late at night, he thinks about going out west. He'll take the boy with him.

Yes, that would be good. That would be fun. They could eat soup and watch TV. He could tell the boy about TV commercials.

Pamela, the Digger's wife, used to watch commercials with him. But they never had a child like Tye to watch with.

"Me? Have a baby with *you?* Are you mad crazy nuts? Why don't you take your lousy present and go *away?* Do you need me to spell it out for you? I've been seeing William for a year. Everybody in town knows except you. If I were going to have a baby, I'd have *his* baby."

But I love you all the more.

"What are you doing?" *Click.* "Put it down!"

The memories are running like lemmings through his cranium.

"No, don't!" she screamed, staring at the knife in his hand.

But he did.

He put the knife into her chest again, just below the gold cross he'd given her that morning, Christmas morning.

And bleeding, Pamela ran for the closet. Bleeding and screaming.

Lifting a gun, pointing it at his head, her hand blossoming into a beautiful yellow flower as he felt a thud on his temple.

The Digger woke up sometime later. The first thing he saw was the kind eyes of the man who would tell him things. *Click.*

He now calls his voice mail. No messages. *Where* did he go, the man who tells him things?

But there's no time to think about it, about being happy or sad, whatever they are. There's only time to get ready.

Two guns this time. And lots and lots of bullets. The man who tells him things told him that this time he has to shoot more people than he's ever shot before.

Because this will be the last minute of the last hour of the last night of the year.

PARKER Kincaid ran into the FBI document division lab.

Lukas walked up to him. "I got your message," she said. "That reporter—Phillips—he got to one of the mailroom people. Somehow he found out your real name."

"You *promised,*" he raged.

"I'm sorry, Parker. I don't know what happened."

Dr. Evans and Tobe were quiet. Cage was not in the room.

Parker had called them on his cell phone as he sped from Fairfax to downtown D.C. His mind had been racing. How could he control the disaster? All he'd wanted to do was help save some lives, save some children. Now his own children would be taken from him. *The end of the world . . .*

Why had he even considered Cage's request for help?

A small TV sat on a table nearby. Parker turned on the news. It was just nine. The WPLT news team appeared on the screen.

Slade Phillips gazed at the camera with a grotesquely sincere expression.

> "Good evening. I'm Slade Phillips. Eleven people were killed and twenty-nine were wounded an hour ago in the third of the mass shootings that have terrorized Washington tonight. In

> addition, WPLT has learned that police and FBI agents were sent to a hotel where it was mistakenly believed that the killer would strike next. It's not known for certain who is responsible for this mix-up, but informed sources have reported . . ."

Phillips's voice faded, and he cocked his head, probably listening to someone through his earphone. A frown crossed his face. There was a brief pause, and his mouth registered defeat as he continued.

> "Informed sources have reported that Mayor Gerald D. Kennedy is currently being detained by federal authorities, possibly in connection with this unsuccessful stakeout. Now standing by at the site of the most recent shooting is Cheryl Vandover. Cheryl, could you tell us—"

Cage walked into the lab, wearing an overcoat. He turned the set off. Parker closed his eyes and exhaled in relief.

"Sorry, Parker," Cage said. "Things fall through the cracks sometimes, but we're keeping our end of the bargain. Oh, one thing—don't ever ask me how I did *this* one. You don't wanna know."

THE limo eased up to city hall like a yacht docking. Mayor Gerry Kennedy had just been at the Potomac riverside, comforting survivors and surveying the devastation. He and his wife, Claire, had been astonished at what the bullets had done. He leaned forward and turned the TV off.

"How could they?" Claire whispered, referring to the newscaster's suggestion that Kennedy had in some mysterious way been responsible for the deaths on the boat.

Wendell Jefferies leaned forward, resting his glossy head in his hands. "Phillips . . . I already paid him. I—"

Kennedy waved him silent. Apparently, the aide had forgotten about huge, bald Agent Ardell in the front seat. Bribing media was undoubtedly a federal offense of some kind.

"What do we do now?" Jefferies said.

"We wait. The Digger might still come forward and want the

money. I'm the only one who can authorize the payment. I still have a chance to meet him face to face."

Claire shook her head. "You couldn't trust him. He'd kill you."

Couldn't kill me any deader than the press has done tonight, Kennedy thought.

THE guns are finally loaded, the silencers packed and mounted. The Digger has lots and lots of ammunition.

He takes his suitcase down to the car. It's time to go. He packs his soup and dishes and takes them down, too.

The Digger returns to the room and looks at fragile Tye boy for a few minutes. Then he wraps the blanket around the boy and carries him, light as a puppy, down to the car and puts him in the back seat, tucks the blanket around his feet.

"I want you to sleep well," he says to the boy's still form.

He doesn't know where the words come from—some memory.

When I go to sleep at night,
I love you all the more.

He starts the car, then pulls out into the traffic.

THE third location . . . *place where I took you—the black* . . .

Parker Kincaid stood at the blackboard in the document division lab, staring at the puzzle in front of him.

"The black what?" Dr. Evans mused.

Cage shrugged. Lukas was on the phone with the PERT team on board *The Ritzy Lady.* She hung up and told the team there were few solid leads. Witnesses had reported a white man of indeterminate age in a dark coat.

Parker looked around. "Where's Hardy?"

Cage told him about the incident with the mayor at the Ritz.

"She fire him?" Parker asked, nodding toward Lukas.

"No. He's in the research library, trying to make amends."

Parker looked back at Geller. The young agent stared at the screen in front of him as the computer vainly tried to assemble more letters following the word "black." Parker felt the queasy sense of nearly but not quite figuring out a clue.

Lukas stood next to him. "Your boy all right?"

"He's fine. Just a little scared."

She nodded. A computer nearby announced, "You've got mail." She walked to it, read the message, and shook her head. "The prints on the shell casings are from one of the passengers on the boat picking up souvenirs. He checks out." She clicked the SAVE button.

Parker gazed at the screen. "E-mail's making me obsolete as a document examiner. Oh, people're writing more because of it—"

"But there's less handwriting?" she asked, continuing his thought.

"Right. And for me that's sad. Handwriting's a part of the person. It's one of the only things about people that really survives their death. It's about as close to immortality as we can get."

"Part of the person?" she asked. "But you said graphoanalysis was bogus."

"No. I mean that whatever somebody wrote is still a reflection of who they are. It doesn't matter what the words are. Just the fact that they thought of the words and their hands committed them to paper is what counts. It's almost a miracle to me."

She was staring at the floor, her head down.

Parker continued. "I've always thought of handwriting as a fingerprint of the heart and mind." He laughed self-consciously at this.

Margaret Lukas looked away quickly. With her head turned, he could see her reflection in the screen, and it seemed that her eyes were glistening with tears.

He was about to ask her if anything was wrong when Geller looked over from his computer. "The anagram thing isn't working. There isn't enough of the ash left to make any letters."

Parker paced, staring at the blackboard: " 'the black . . .' "

"Some African American organization?" Evans suggested.

"Possibly. But remember, the unsub was educated."

Cage frowned. "What do you mean?"

It was Lukas who answered. "The word 'black' is lowercase. If it were the name of a group, he'd probably capitalize it."

"Exactly," Parker said. "So I'd guess it's descriptive." He walked to the examination table, stared down at the extortion note, at the devil's teardrop dot above the letter *i*. What do you know? he asked the document silently. What secrets are you keeping?

"I've got something," a voice called from the doorway.

Detective Len Hardy trotted into the lab, a sheaf of papers under his arm. "I've found out about the name—the Digger." He put the papers down and asked Dr. Evans, "When you were checking out the name, what databases did you use?"

"The standard ones," Evans answered. He seemed defensive.

"Criminal?" Hardy asked. "VICAP, NYPD Violent Felons, John Jay?"

"Those, sure," the doctor said.

"That was fine, but I got to thinking why not try *noncriminal* resources? I finally found it. The database at the religious history department in Cambridge University." Hardy opened a notebook. "Now, this is interesting," he said excitedly. "There was a seventeenth-century communist group in England called the Diggers. They advocated abolishing private ownership of land. They were mostly economic and social, but they allied themselves with another group, which was sometimes militant. They were called the True Levelers. They objected to control of the people by the upper-class elite." He looked at Parker. "Dr. Evans thought that the unsub was intentionally going for upper-class targets."

"What does it mean for us?" Lukas asked.

Hardy said, "His motive. The unsub wanted to quote 'level' our capitalistic society."

"But *why?*" Lukas asked.

"Maybe he had a grudge," Parker said. "Somebody hurt him, and he wants to get even."

"But who? Who hurt him?" Hardy mused, staring at the note.

"He got fired?" Cage suggested. "Disgruntled worker."

"No," Evans said. "A psychotic might kill for that, but he wasn't psychotic. He was too smart and controlled."

Geller rasped, "Big business, big corporation, fat cats . . ."

"So what's his target here?" Hardy asked.

"Government," Parker answered. "That's about all we've got."

Looking over the team, Evans said, "Maybe the government was responsible for something that hurt him. Any thoughts on what?"

"Ideology?" Cage wondered aloud. "He's a Communist or with a right-wing militia cell."

Evans shook his head. "No. We'd have a manifesto by now. It's more personal."

Lukas and Hardy caught each other's eyes. It seemed to Parker that they came up with an identical thought at the same time. It was the detective who said, "The death of somebody he loved."

"Could be," the psychologist offered.

"Okay," Cage said. "What could the scenario have been? Who died?"

"Execution?" Hardy suggested. "Government car or truck involved in a crash, postal worker shooting spree . . ."

"Military," Evans suggested. "Somebody killed in action."

"Yes. Think about it," Hardy said. "The lower classes—the traditional victims of capitalism—tend to be frontline soldiers. That might explain why the Digger's targets were upper class."

"But," Lukas said, "there must be hundreds of fatalities every year in the armed forces. Was it an accident? Combat?"

"Desert Storm?" Cage suggested.

"How old was the unsub?" Parker asked.

Lukas grabbed the medical examiner's report. "Mid-forties."

Then Parker understood. He said, "The Black Wall!"

Lukas nodded. "The Vietnam Memorial."

"Someone he knew," Evans said, "was killed in Nam. Brother, sister. Maybe his wife was a soldier or a nurse."

Cage said, "But that was thirty years ago. Could something like this resurface now?"

"Sure," Evans said, "if his anger has been festering. And New Year's Eve's a time for resolutions and people taking action."

"Oh, Lord," Lukas said. "I just realized—the memorial's on the

Mall. There're going to be two hundred thousand people there for the fireworks. We've got to close off that part of the park."

"It's already packed," Parker said. "Baker'll have to handle it carefully. Otherwise there'll be a stampede."

"We need more manpower," Cage said. He called Artie, the building's night-entrance guard, who made an announcement over the PA that all available agents in the building were needed in the lobby for an emergency assignment.

Lukas called Jerry Baker and told him to get his tactical agents to the northwest portion of the Mall. She then paged the deputy director. He called back immediately, and she spoke to him for a moment, then hung up.

She looked at the team. "The dep director's on his way over. I'm going to brief him; then I'll meet you at the memorial."

Cage put his coat on. Geller stood and checked his weapon.

Lukas said, "Hold on, Tobe. You're going home."

"I can—"

"That's an order. You've already done enough."

He protested more. But in the end, Lukas won, though only after promising that she'd call him if she needed tech assistance.

Lukas walked over to Hardy. "Thanks, Detective. That was good police work. You still want a piece of the action?"

"Oh, you bet I do." The young detective grinned.

"Okay, but keep to the rear."

Parker, feeling the weight of the gun in the pocket, donned his jacket. Lukas glanced at him dubiously. "I'm going," he said.

She said, "You don't have to, Parker. You've done enough, too."

He smiled at her. "Just point and shoot, right?"

She hesitated, then said, "Just point and shoot."

HERE it comes; here it comes. . . . Oh man, look at them all! A dozen, two dozen agents running out of FBI headquarters.

As they ran toward their cars, then sped away, Henry Czisman took one last sip of Jim Beam and rested the bottle on the back seat of his rental car. He didn't follow them yet. He waited, patient as an adder. Then he saw the tall gray-haired agent, Cage, push through the front door. And yes! There he was: Parker Kincaid.

Czisman, a journalist for most of his life, could read people as perceptively as any street cop. And while *they* were undoubtedly running their retinal scans and voice-stress analysis on him, he was running his own tests. Less high-tech and more intuitive, his were nonetheless just as accurate as the Bureau's. One of the things he'd finally decided was that Jefferson was not Jefferson at all. Czisman had sent the man's license plate number to a private eye in Connecticut and had gotten his real identity: Parker Kincaid. A simple database search had revealed he was the former head of the Bureau's document division.

If the Bureau was using a former agent as a consultant, he must be good. Which meant he was the one worth following.

Kincaid climbed into an unmarked car with Cage and another young agent or officer. They turned on a red light on the dash and sped quickly west and south—toward the Mall.

Czisman easily slipped into the motorcade of cars. Soon, though, near Constitution Avenue, the crowds and traffic were so thick that the Bureau vehicles were forced to stop and the agents climbed out, ran to the Mall. Czisman was close behind.

Cage and Kincaid stood together, looking over the crowds. Kincaid pointed toward the west side of the Vietnam Memorial, and Cage nodded toward the east. They separated. The young officer trotted away from them both, toward Constitution.

Czisman was a heavy man and out of shape, but he managed to keep up with Parker Kincaid very easily, pausing only momentarily to take the pistol from the waistband of his slacks and slip it into his coat pocket.

THE Digger's coat is heavy.

Heavy from the weight of guns. And the weight of four clips, four hundred rounds of .22 . . . *click* . . . .22-caliber long-rifle ammunition and two nicely packed suppressors. The two machine guns are in the inside pockets of his nice dark blue or black overcoat, his Christmas present from Pamela. One of the pistols from the glove compartment of his Toyota is in the right outside pocket of his coat.

He's standing in shadows, and no one notices him. Tye is asleep in the back seat of the car a block away. What worries the Digger most is that if the police start shooting, Tye might wake up from the sound, and then he won't sleep well.

He's also worried that the boy will be cold. The temperature keeps falling, but the Digger remembers that he tripled the blanket over Tye. He'll be all right. He's sleeping.

He is standing by himself watching some of the people who are about to die. He calls one last time on his cell phone, and the lady says, "You have no new messages."

So it's okay to kill these people.

Then he'll get back into the car and check his messages, and if the man who tells him things still hasn't called, then he and Tye will drive until they find . . . *click* . . . they find California.

PARKER Kincaid was lost in a sea of people near the Vietnam Memorial. Looking for a man in a dark coat, wearing a crucifix.

Far too many people. Thousands of them. Ten thousand.

Cage was on the other side of the memorial. Len Hardy was on Constitution Avenue. Baker and the other tactical officers were making a sweep from the other side of the Mall.

Parker suddenly realized he'd been looking in the wrong places. He stepped out of the crowd and examined the grounds near the Vietnam Memorial. He thought of the unsub's mazes and realized that the man would have known that by the third attack the agents would have *some* description of the Digger. He would've told the Digger not to approach the memorial along one of the sidewalks, where he could be spotted more easily; he'd have told him he should come in through the trees.

Parker turned and disappeared into a thicket of maples.

HENRY Czisman was thirty feet behind Kincaid, walking past the Vietnam Memorial, when Kincaid turned suddenly and moved into a grove of trees. Czisman followed, looking around at the sea of people. What a target the Digger would have here! He could cut them down like grass.

Czisman's own pistol was in his hand, pointed at the ground. No one saw it. The crowd was wondering what was going on—with all the police and federal agents telling them to leave the Mall. And now Czisman saw a man in a dark overcoat step from behind a tree. It was a cautious, furtive movement and suggested that the man had been hiding. He moved deliberately, his head down, as if he were trying not to be noticed. Then he disappeared into the crowd not far from Kincaid. Czisman trotted after him.

Suddenly Kincaid turned. He glanced at Czisman, away, then back again with a frown, realizing that he'd seen the face before but couldn't place it. Czisman ducked away, looking again for the man in the dark overcoat.

There he was! He was unbuttoning the coat, looking with dull eyes at the crowds around him. And then Czisman saw the flash of gold on the man's neck. The agents in the bar had told him that the Digger wore a cross.

So here he is, Czisman thought. The Butcher, the Widow Maker, the Devil. The Digger.

"Hey!" a voice called. Czisman turned. It was Kincaid. After he'd spotted Czisman, he must have followed him through the crowd.

Now! Czisman lifted his revolver, aimed it toward his target.

"Wait!" Kincaid shouted, seeing the gun. "No."

But Czisman had no clear shot. There were too many people. He danced to the side and pushed through the crowd, losing Kincaid.

Twenty feet away, the Digger—oblivious to both men—looked over the crowds like a hunter gazing at a huge flock of geese. His coat fell open. In one of the inside pockets was a machine gun.

But nobody sees him! Czisman thought. It's as if he's invisible.

The Digger was squinting, looking for a good place to shoot from. He stepped onto a slight rise.

Kincaid emerged from the crowd.

Czisman pulled back the hammer of his pistol.

Chapter Eight

11:40 p.m.

THE limo had parked beside the Mall, near the box seats reserved for diplomats and members of Congress. Mayor Kennedy and his wife climbed out, accompanied by Agent C. P. Ardell.

Kennedy felt he was virtually under arrest, and he couldn't even avoid the humiliation of appearing in public in his own city without a baby-sitter.

Any doubt that his career was over was being tidily laid to rest by a few glances at the people who stood near the reviewing stand.

As he walked up, he waved to them and fielded their uneasy comments: "Where've you been hiding?" "How you doing, Gerry?" "What brings you out here?"

Well, what brought him out was Claire. He'd have been perfectly content to slink back home, but his wife had had a different idea. "Let's get drunk and go watch the damn fireworks," she'd said. "Go out with your head high."

And he'd decided it was the smartest thing he'd heard all night. She'd tracked down a bottle of Moët, and they'd drunk it on the way here.

As they wound through the crowd on the reviewing stand, Kennedy shook the hand of Congressman Lanier.

"Gerry," Lanier asked, "what's the latest on the shootings?"

"I'm still waiting to hear."

"We've got room for you right over there, Mayor," said a junior aide, pointing at a deserted bank of folding chairs.

"No, no," Kennedy said. "We'll just sit on the stairs." He dropped his jacket on the wood for Claire to sit on.

"Used to come here when I was a kid," C. P. Ardell said to the mayor and his wife as he sat down beside them.

"You live in the District, Agent Ardell?" Claire asked him.

"Wouldn't live anywhere else, ma'am."

Kennedy laughed faintly. At least if he had to be under informal arrest, he was glad his turnkey was a loyal citizen.

Feeling warm from the champagne, he moved closer to Claire and took her hand. They looked out over the Mall, gazed at the thousands of people milling about. Kennedy was pleased to see that there was no microphone on the reviewing stand. He didn't want to hear any speeches. All he wanted was to sit with his wife and watch the fireworks blossom over his city. And forget the agony of this day. The end of Project 2000. The end of all his hopes for the District.

But Kennedy noticed something odd. The spectators seemed to be moving east purposefully, as if they were being herded. Why? he wondered. The view was perfect from here. He turned to Claire, started to mention this, but suddenly she tensed.

"Gunshots," she said. "I hear gunshots."

Then they heard the screaming.

CZISMAN'S shots did what he'd intended.

When he'd realized that nobody had seen the Digger—and that he himself had no clean shot at the killer—he'd fired twice into the air to scatter the people and clear a line of fire.

The explosions sent the crowd into a panic. Screaming, everyone scattered, knocking the Digger to his knees. In seconds the area in front of the Vietnam Memorial was virtually empty.

Czisman saw Kincaid too, flinging himself to the ground and pulling a small automatic out of his pocket. The man hadn't seen the Digger—a thick stand of evergreens separated them.

That was fine with Czisman. *He* wanted the killer.

The Digger was rising slowly. One of the machine guns had fallen from his coat, and he looked around for it. As he did, he caught sight of Czisman and froze, gazing at him with the strangest eyes Czisman had ever seen. In those eyes was less feeling than in an animal's.

The Digger glanced at the gun in Czisman's hand. Then his eyes rose again, and he stared at the journalist's face.

Kincaid was shouting at Czisman, "Drop the weapon!"

Czisman lifted the gun toward the Digger. "You—"

But there was a soft explosion and a tuft of the Digger's overcoat popped outward. Czisman felt a hard fist in his chest, dropped to his knees. He fired, but the shot went wide.

The Digger removed his hand from his pocket, holding a small pistol. He aimed at Czisman's chest once more, fired twice.

Czisman flew backward under the impact of the rounds.

Kincaid was running from cover, looking around, confused. Czisman saw the Digger walk slowly toward his machine gun, pick it up, and fire a burst toward Kincaid, who dove behind a tree. The Digger trotted away, crouching, through the bushes, toward the fleeing crowd.

Czisman groped for his gun. "You . . . you . . ." But his hand fell to the ground like a rock, and there was only blackness.

A FEW people . . . *click* . . . people were huddled nearby. Frightened. The Digger could have easily shot them, but then the police would see him.

"The last time kill as many as you can," said the man who tells him things.

So he's hurrying after them, sort of running the way the crowd does, hunched over, looking around. *They* look scared. *He* tries to look scared. The way the man who tells him things told him to do.

The Digger has hidden the Uzi under his overcoat, the one that he loves because Pamela had given it to him. There are shouts nearby, but they don't seem to be directed at him, so he doesn't pay any attention. Nobody notices him. He's moving near the bushes and trees along that wide street—Constitution Avenue. There are buses and cars, thousands of people. If he can get to them, he can kill hundreds.

More shouting. People are running. Men and women and children. Police and agents. They have Uzis or Mac-10s or . . . *click* . . . pistols, like the pistol of the fat man who just tried to shoot him.

How far does he have to go to get to more people?

He's trotting toward them, but his path is taking him away from

Tye—from the parked car. He doesn't like that thought. He wants to get the shooting over with and get back to the boy.

When I travel on the road,
I love you all the more.

More people with guns are running over the grass. Suddenly, nearby he hears explosions—cracks and bangs and pops.

Are people shooting at him?

No, no. . . . Ah, look! Above him flowers are blossoming in the air. There's smoke and brilliant flowers, red and yellow. Also blue and white. Fireworks.

His watch beeps. It's midnight. Time to shoot.

But there aren't enough people. Not enough to make the man who tells him things happy.

Crack . . . A bullet streaks past him.

Now someone *is* shooting at him. Two men in FBI jackets in the middle of the field to the Digger's right have seen him. They're standing in front of a wooden platform, decorated with beautiful red-white-and-blue banners, like the ones the New Year's babies wear.

He turns toward them and fires the Uzi through his coat. He doesn't want to do this—to put holes in the beautiful dark coat Pamela had given him, but he has to. He can't let anyone see the gun.

The men clutch at their faces and necks and fall down.

The Digger turns and continues moving after the crowds.

WHEN the first bullets crashed into the wood around him, Mayor Kennedy shoved his wife off the platform and onto the ground. He jumped after her and lay on his side, shielding her.

"Honey?" he shouted.

"I'm all right." Her voice was edgy with panic. "What's going on?"

"Somebody's shooting. It must be him! The killer."

One person on the platform had been hit—a young aide, shot in the arm. But the killer had been aiming at the two agents in front of the viewing stand. Kennedy could see they were dead.

The mayor glanced up and saw C. P. Ardell holding his pistol, looking out over the field. He stood tall, wasn't even crouching.

"Agent Ardell!" Kennedy shouted. "There he is! Shoot!"

But the agent didn't shoot. Ardell started to turn, slowly revolving, a complete circle, and fell onto his back, staring up at the sky with glazed eyes.

"Oh, no!" Claire gave a gasp as a stream of the man's blood cascaded down the stairs.

Kennedy stood up. The Mall was dim, but in the headlights from the emergency vehicles Kennedy had a view of the chaos. He looked for the dark silhouette of the Digger.

"What are you doing in my city?" he shouted.

"Gerry, get down!" Claire pleaded.

But he stayed where he was, scanning the field. Where was the shooter?

Then he saw a man in the shadows, walking fast along a row of cherry trees not far from Constitution Avenue, making for the crowds farther east on the Mall.

Kennedy pried the pistol from the dead agent's hand.

"Oh, Gerry, no," Claire said. "No! Call on your phone."

"There's no time." He paused, turned to her, touched her cheek, kissed her forehead. Then he leaped over a huddling couple and sprinted over the grass. He thought, I'm going to have a heart attack. . . . But he didn't slow down. The familiar sights of the city were around him. The white Washington Monument, the stark cherry blossom trees, the gray neo-Gothic buildings of the museums, the tourist buses . . . He gasped and ran, gasped and ran.

The Digger was a hundred feet away. Then ninety, eighty . . .

Kennedy watched the killer move closer to the crowd and pull a black machine gun from under his coat.

There was a shot from the trees to Kennedy's left. A bullet snapped over his head. No! They were shooting at *him.* They'd seen a man with a gun and assumed he was the killer.

"No, no!" He crouched, pointed toward the Digger. "It's him!"

The killer was in the tree line, moving around to the side of the crowd. In just a minute he'd be close enough to kill hundreds.

Hell with it. Let's just hope the cops are bad shots. Kennedy began to sprint forward again. There was one more shot in his direction, but then someone must have identified him. Shouts over the bull-horn ordered the officers to cease fire.

"Get back!" Kennedy was shouting to the crowd. But there was nowhere for them to go. They were packed together like cattle. Ten thousand people. Some staring at the fireworks, some looking around, uneasy and confused.

His chest on fire, Kennedy sped toward the place where he'd last seen the Digger. What on earth am I doing? he thought. What kind of idiocy is this? The last time he'd fired a gun had been at summer camp with his son—thirty years ago. He'd fired three shots and missed the target completely, to the boy's shame.

Running closer to the tree line, closer to the Digger.

Agents had seen where he was headed. A dozen men and women in tactical police gear were jogging toward him.

The Digger stepped out of the bushes, pointing the machine gun toward the crowd. He nodded to himself.

Kennedy stopped running, lifted the pistol, and aimed. He wasn't even sure how the sights worked, whether he should aim high or low. But Kennedy held the gun very steady and squeezed the trigger.

The explosion was huge, and he wasn't prepared for the pistol to buck so high in the air. He lowered the gun. Squinted over the dim field. He laughed out loud. I did it! I hit him!

The Digger was on the ground, grimacing, clutching his left arm.

Kennedy fired again, missed, fired another round.

The Digger rolled to his feet. He started to aim at Kennedy, but the mayor fired again. This was a miss too, but it was close and the Digger stumbled backward. As he climbed to his feet, he fired a short burst toward Kennedy and then at the line of agents and cops moving toward him. One agent fell, and the others dropped into defensive postures. They aimed toward the Digger, but no one fired. Kennedy saw why—the crowds were directly behind the killer.

Only Kennedy had a clear shot. He stood and fired five more times, driving the Digger back, away from the crowds.

Then the gun clicked. It was empty. He squinted, looking past the silvery pistol.

The dark form of the Digger was gone.

PANTING now. Something within the Digger snaps, and he forgets everything the man told him. He forgets about killing as many people as he can. He wants to leave and get back to Tye.

The bullets that man was firing came so close. . . . He was nearly killed. And if he gets killed, what's going to happen to the boy?

He drops into a crouch and sprints toward a tour bus. The engine is idling, a cloud of exhaust rises from the tailpipe.

His arm hurts so badly. Oh, how it . . . *click* . . . how it hurts. He looks for the man who shot him. Why did he do that? The Digger doesn't understand. He's just doing what he's been told.

Fireworks blossom over the Mall.

A line of police and agents is moving closer. They start shooting. The Digger climbs up the stairs of the bus and turns, spraying bullets at the cluster of pursuing agents.

PARKER and Cage crouched behind a squad car. Bullets were flying everywhere. The Digger was firing through the shattered windows of the bus. Len Hardy was pinned down with several other District cops on the other side of Constitution Avenue.

Cage pressed his side and winced. He hadn't been hit, but bullets had ripped through the car they were using for cover, and he'd flung himself to the ground, landing hard on his side.

"You okay?" Parker asked.

"Rib," Cage moaned. "Feels broken."

Agents had cleared the area around the bus and were peppering it freely. Parker heard snippets of radio transmissions. "No target presenting. . . . Get a flash-bang inside. Who's got a grenade? . . . Snipers in position."

Then Cage glanced over the hood of the torn car. "What's the kid doing?" he gasped. Len Hardy, tiny gun in hand, was crawling from tree to tree toward the bus, firing a shot occasionally.

Parker said, "He's nuts. He doesn't even have body armor."

"Len!" Cage shouted, then winced at the pain.

Parker took over. "Len! Len Hardy! Get back." But Hardy sprinted toward the bus, emptying his weapon as he ran.

Cage wheezed, "It's like he's got some kind of death wish."

Parker saw the Digger move toward the back of the bus, where he'd have a good shot at Hardy. The detective huddled on the ground, reloading. "Len!" Parker cried. "Get under cover."

Hardy looked up and realized what was happening. He lifted the gun and fired three or four more times—all the shells he'd been able to reload—then stumbled backward, trying to get to cover.

Parker couldn't see exactly what happened next. He saw the Digger's silhouette near the emergency exit in the back of the bus. Then an agent rolled out from behind a car and fired a stream of bullets toward the Digger, who lurched sideways under the impact of the slugs. Then there was a *whoosh,* and fire erupted inside the bus.

Unhurt, Hardy struggled to his feet and ran for cover behind a District squad car.

There was a heartrending scream from inside the bus as the interior disappeared in a mass of orange flames.

Slowly the agents rose from cover. Fire trucks arrived and began pumping foam on the burning hulk of the vehicle. When the flames had died down, two agents in full body armor made their way to the door of the bus and looked inside.

A moment later Parker heard one of them on Cage's radio. "Vehicle is secure," the agent said. "Subject confirmed dead."

AS THEY walked back to the Vietnam Memorial, Parker told Cage about Czisman, how the shooting had started.

"He fired warning shots. If he hadn't done that, the Digger would've killed a hundred people right here. Maybe me, too."

In front of them a cop was covering Henry Czisman's body.

Cage bent down, grimacing in pain. He pulled aside the yellow rubberized sheet, went through the journalist's pockets, took out a book: leather bound with hand-stitched pages. The vellum paper was marbleized in red and gold. And inside, the calligraphic handwriting was as beautiful as an artist's. Parker couldn't help but admire it.

Cage flipped through several pages, read them, shaking his head. He handed it to Parker. "Check this out."

Parker frowned as he looked at the title written in gold ink on the cover: *A Chronicle of Sorrow.* He opened it, read out loud. " 'To the memory of my wife, Anne, the Butcher's first victim.' "

The book was divided into sections: Hartford, Boston, White Plains, Philadelphia. Parker turned the page and went on reading.

> "From the Hartford *News-Times.* 'Three Killed in Holdup. Hartford police are still searching for the man who walked into the offices of the *News-Times* on Saturday and opened fire with a shotgun, killing three employees in the classified advertising department.' "

He looked up. "One of the clerks killed at the paper was Anne Czisman. She was his wife."

"So he wanted the bastard as much as we did," Cage said.

"Let's call Lukas," Parker said. "Give her the news."

AT FBI headquarters Margaret Lukas was in the employees lobby, briefing the deputy director, a handsome man with a politician's trim graying hair. She'd heard the reports that the Digger was on the Mall and there had been shooting. Lukas was desperately eager to get to the Mall herself, but since she was primary on the case, protocol dictated that she keep the senior administrators in the Bureau informed.

Her phone buzzed. "Lukas here."

"Margaret," Cage said.

She knew immediately from his tone that they'd nailed the killer. "Collared or tagged?" Arrested or dead, she meant.

"Tagged," Cage responded. "And get this—the mayor winged him. Got off a few shots with his minder's weapon."

Lukas relayed this news to the deputy director.

"You okay?" she asked Cage.

"Fine," Cage responded. "Cracked a rib is all."

But her gut tightened. She heard something in his voice, a tone, a hollowness. "But?" she asked. "What is it, Cage? Kincaid?"

"No, Kincaid's okay," the agent said softly. "He got C.P., Margaret. He's dead."

She closed her eyes. Sighed. Fury steamed through her.

Cage continued. "The Digger fired toward where the mayor was sitting. C.P. just happened to be standing in the wrong place."

And it was the place that I'd sent him to. Oh, no . . .

Cage was adding, "He capped four other friendlies, and we've got three injured. Looks like six civies wounded. And that Czisman? Digger got him."

"What?"

"He wasn't a writer at all. I mean, he was, but that's not what he was doing here. The Digger'd killed his wife, and he was using us to get to him."

"What about Hardy?"

Cage told her a story that sounded as if the young detective had made a one-man assault on the bus the Digger'd holed up in. "I'll tell you, it looked like he was hell-bent on killing himself, but when it came right down to it, he backed off and went for cover. Guess he decided to stick around for a few years."

Lukas thought, Len Hardy, another changeling. Just like me.

"Is Evans there?" Cage asked.

Lukas looked around. Surprised that the doctor wasn't here. She'd thought he was coming down to the lobby to meet her. "I'm not sure where he is. Must be upstairs in the document lab."

"Find him and give him the good news. And tell him thanks."

"Will do. And I'll call Tobe, too."

"Parker and I are gonna do crime scene with PERT, then head back over there in forty-five minutes or so."

When she hung up, the dep director said, "I'm going down to the Mall. Who's in charge?"

She nearly said Parker Kincaid but caught herself. "Special Agent Cage. He's near the Vietnam Memorial with PERT."

"There'll have to be a press conference. I'll give the director a heads-up. He may want to make a statement, too."

IN THE document lab Dr. John Evans folded up his cell phone. He clicked the TV set off.

So they'd killed the Digger. From the news reports there'd been minimal fatalities—not like the Metro shooting and not like the yacht. Still, from the TV images Constitution Avenue looked like a war zone: smoke, a hundred emergency vehicles, people hiding behind cars, trees, and bushes.

Evans pulled on his parka. He slipped the heavy thermos into his knapsack, which he slung over his shoulder. Then he pushed through the double doors and started down the deserted corridor.

At the elevator he paused, looked at the building directory, trying to orient himself. His finger hovered over the DOWN button, but before he could push it, a voice called, "Hi." He turned. Saw somebody walking toward him from the second bank of elevators.

"Hi there, Doctor," the voice called. "You heard?"

It was Detective Hardy. His overcoat was no longer perfectly pressed. It was stained and sooty. There was a cut on his cheek.

Evans smiled, but he felt uncomfortable. He remembered the detective's comments in the lab an hour ago—about the Digger's name. He'd almost seemed to suggest that Evans had withheld information about the killer. He pushed the DOWN button. Twice.

"Just saw it on the news," Evans told him. He shrugged the backpack off his shoulder, began to unzip it.

Hardy glanced absently at the backpack. He said, "Man, I'll tell you, I spoke a little too fast there, volunteering to go after that guy. I went a little crazy. Some kind of battlefield hysteria."

"Uh-huh." Evans reached in the backpack and took out his thermos.

Hardy continued chatting. "He nearly nailed me. Shook me up some. I was about thirty feet from him. Saw his eyes, saw the muzzle of his gun. Man . . . I was suddenly real happy to be alive."

"That happens," Evans said. Where was the elevator?

Hardy glanced at the metal cylinder. "Say, you know where Agent Lukas is?" the detective asked, looking up the corridor.

"I think she's downstairs in the lobby," Evans said, unscrewing the lid to the thermos. "Didn't you just come that way?"

"I came in through the garage."

The doctor pulled the top off the thermos. He turned toward the detective. He looked down. He saw the black silenced pistol Hardy was pointing at his face.

"I'm sorry," Hardy said, though he didn't sound sorry at all.

Evans dropped the thermos. Coffee splashed onto the floor. He saw the flash of light from the muzzle. And that was all he saw.

Chapter Nine

12:30 a.m.

THE agent was young enough to still be thrilled at the idea of being an FBI employee. So he didn't mind one bit that he'd been assigned the midnight-to-eight shift New Year's Eve in the Bureau's security center on the third floor of headquarters.

There was also the fact that Louise, the clerk he was working with, wore a tight blue blouse and short black skirt and was flirting with him. Well, okay, she was talking about her cat, but the body language told him she was flirting.

The agent continued to gaze at the ten TV monitors that were his responsibility. Louise, on his left, had another ten. The scenes on the monitors changed every five seconds.

The intercom brayed. It couldn't have been Sam or Ralph—the two agents he and Louise had replaced twenty minutes ago; they had total-clearance entry cards and would've just walked inside.

The agent hit the intercom button. "Yes?"

"It's Detective Hardy, PD. I'm working with Margaret Lukas."

"Oh, the Metro shooter case?"

"Right."

The legendary Margaret Lukas. The agent pushed the ENTER button, spun around to face the door. "Can I help you?"

"I'm afraid I'm lost," Hardy said. "I'm trying to find the document lab."

"Documents? That's the seventh floor. Turn left. Can't miss it."

"Thanks."

"What's this?" Louise said suddenly. "Hey, what *is* this?"

The agent turned back as she pointed to one of the monitors. It showed a man lying on his back. Blood ran from his head.

"Oh, no." She reached for the phone. "It looks like Ralph."

From behind them came a soft *thunk*. Louise gave a sudden jerk as the front of her blouse disappeared in a mist of blood.

The young agent turned and lifted his hands, crying, "No, no."

In a calm voice Hardy said, "I just have a few questions."

"Don't kill me. Please—"

"I'll let you live if you tell me everything I ask. Now your computers are running Secure-Check software?"

"Yes." He started crying. "Secure-Check."

"So if you don't log in at regular intervals, a Code Forty-two goes out over the Inter-Gov System?"

"That's right." He glanced at Louise's body. "Oh, God . . ."

"When's the next time you have to log in?" Hardy asked.

The agent was crying hard now. "One oh seven."

Hardy glanced at the clock on the wall. He nodded with some satisfaction, then shot the agent twice in the head and pushed the button to release the door.

THE man who was not Detective Len Hardy, a fictional name, but was in reality Edward Fielding made his way to the elevator. As he walked through the deserted hallways, he reflected. No, Agent Lukas, Parker Kincaid, poor John Evans . . . No, my motive wasn't revenge or to expose social injustice. Nor was it greed. Twenty million? I could've asked for ten times that.

No, his motive was perfection. The perfect crime.

Perfection . . . It was intoxicating to him. Perfection was everything—the way he ironed his shirts and polished his shoes, the way he set up his crimes, the way they were executed.

If Fielding had had an aptitude for the law, he'd have been a lawyer and devoted his life to creating the perfect defenses for impossibly guilty clients. If he'd had a lust for the outdoors, he'd have made the perfect solo ascent to the summit of Everest.

But those activities didn't excite him. Crime did.

This was just a fluke, he supposed, to be born utterly amoral. Nature, he'd decided, not nurture. His parents were loving, and dullness was their only sin. Fielding's father had been an insurance executive in Hartford, his mother a homemaker. He experienced no deprivation, no abuse. From an early age, though, he simply believed that laws didn't apply to him.

So while he studied algebra and calculus and biology at St. Thomas High School, the young man also worked at his true calling.

And as in all disciplines, that education had ups and downs.

Fielding, in juvenile detention for setting fire to the boyfriend of a girl he had a crush on (should've parked his car nearby). Fielding, successfully extorting a major canned-food manufacturer by feeding their cattle an enzyme that mimicked a positive test for botulism (though he never picked up the money, because he couldn't figure out how to get away undetected). Live and learn . . .

College didn't interest him much. He enjoyed occasional felonious assaults on coeds. But Fielding's lust was for crime, not sex, and by his junior year he was focusing on what he called "clean crimes," like robbery. He buckled down to get his psych degree and dreamed about escaping into the real world, where he could practice his craft.

Over the next ten years Fielding, back in his native Connecticut, did just that: honed and practiced, robbery mostly.

He was twenty-seven when he killed for the first time. An impulse crime, very unlike him. He was in a coffee shop in a strip mall. He saw a woman come out of a jewelry store with an expensive-looking package. He got into his car and followed her. On a deserted stretch of road he pulled her over. Terrified, she thrust the bag at him and begged him to let her go. As he stood there, Fielding realized that he hadn't worn a mask or switched plates on his car. He reached into his glove compartment for a gun and shot her. And got away with it.

Still, he was arrested several times. In Florida he was collared for armed robbery, and the evidence against him was strong. But he had a good lawyer, who got him a reduced sentence on condition that Fielding seek treatment at a mental hospital. It turned out to be an astonishing two years. In the mental health facility Fielding could taste crime. He could smell it. Many, if not most, of the convicts were there because their lawyers were quick with the insanity defense. Dumb crooks are in prison; smart ones are in hospitals.

After two years and an exemplary appearance before the medical review panel, Fielding returned to Connecticut and got a job as an aide at a hospital for the criminally insane in Hartford. There he met David Hughes, a fascinating creature. Fielding decided he'd probably been a pretty decent fellow until he stabbed his wife to death in a jealous rage. What was so *interesting* was that before the wife died, she found a pistol and shot Hughes in the head.

Fielding didn't know what exactly had happened inside Hughes's cranium, neurologically speaking, but perhaps because Fielding was the first person Hughes saw when he awoke after surgery, some kind of odd bonding occurred between the two. Hughes would do whatever the hospital aide asked. Getting coffee, cleaning up for him, ironing shirts. It turned out that Hughes would do more than domestic chores, though. One evening, just after night-duty nurse Ruth Miller threatened to report Fielding for sexual assault, he had muttered to Hughes, "That Ruth Miller. Somebody ought to kill her."

And Hughes had said, "Hmm, okay."

"What?" Fielding had asked. "You'd kill her for me?"

"Uhm. I . . . Sure."

Fielding shushed him and took him for a walk on the grounds. They had a long talk. A day later Hughes showed up in Fielding's cubicle, covered with blood, carrying a piece of jagged glass and asking if he could have some soup.

Fielding cleaned him up, thinking he'd been a little careless about the murder and about getting away afterward. And so he told Hughes how to escape from the hospital and how to make his way to a nearby cottage that Fielding had rented.

It was that night that he decided how he could best put the man to use. Hartford, then Boston, then White Plains, then Phillie. Perfect crimes. And now Washington. Committing what was turning out to be the *most* perfect crime.

For the last six months he'd spent nearly eighteen hours a day planning the theft. Slowly breaching FBI security—masquerading as young Detective Hardy from the police department's research and statistics department. He first infiltrated the Bureau's District of Columbia field office, which had jurisdiction over major crimes in the District. He learned when the S.A.C. would be on vacation and which of his underlings would be "primary" on the Digger case. That would be, of course, Margaret Lukas, whose life he invaded as inexorably as he worked his way into the Bureau itself.

When sitting in conference rooms and copying crime statistics for his fictional reports, he would make trips to the vending machines and rest rooms, stealing glances at internal FBI memos and ID documentation and procedure manuals along the way. Meanwhile, at his home and at his safe house in Gravesend, he was spending time cruising the Internet about government facilities, police procedures, and security systems (and yes, Parker, foreign dialects).

Fielding made hundreds of calls to outside contractors who'd worked at FBI headquarters, to former clerks, security specialists, asking innocent questions. He usually managed to extract one vital fact—say, about the layout of headquarters, the staffing on holidays, the exits and entrances. He learned the general location of security cameras, the number and stations of the guards.

It was arduous work, but perfection requires patience. And when he thought he had enough information, then came the tricky part. He showed up at the Bureau doorstep that morning after the Metro shooting, looking indignant about being the third wheel on the investigation. Other agents would have double- or triple-checked his credentials, but not Margaret Lukas, the poor childless widow.

Because here was Len Hardy, soon to be childless widower, racked with the same sorrow she'd struggled through five years ago. Of course she accepted him into the fold without a thought.

He knew that the agents would be concentrating so hard on the extortion note, the linguistics, the handwriting, the trace evidence, and their computer programs that they'd never see the man himself standing—literally—three feet behind them.

He now came to the elevator. When it arrived, he didn't go to the document lab. He pushed 1B, and the car began to descend.

THE FBI's evidence room is the largest forensic storage facility in the country. It's operated around the clock, and usually there's a staff of two to help the agents log in evidence. Tonight, though, there were three agents on duty because of the value of a particular package of evidence sitting in the vault at the moment.

But because of the holiday, the two men and the woman were pretty casual. They were lounging around the log-in window, drinking coffee and talking. The two men had their backs to the window.

Fielding walked up to the window. "Hi," he said, and shot the woman in the head. The men died reaching for their weapons.

Fielding reached through the window, buzzed himself in. He lifted the keys from the dead woman's belt and opened the vault. It was a large room, about twenty by thirty, where agents stored drugs and cash taken from heists. He knew the agents would have brought the ransom money here. Mayor Kennedy, whom Fielding had psychologically profiled, would want to keep the cash available in case the Digger contacted him and demanded the ransom after all. And here it was, the money. *Perfect . . .*

A huge green canvas satchel. A red tag dangled from the strap: FEDERAL EVIDENCE. DO NOT REMOVE.

He looked at his watch. He estimated that he'd have twenty minutes before Cage, Kincaid, and the other agents returned from the Mall. Plenty of time, as long as he moved quickly.

Fielding unzipped the bag—it wasn't locked—and dumped the cash on the floor. The satchel was wired with several homing devices, as he'd known it would be. The money wrappers, too, he'd learned—a trick he hadn't anticipated. He pulled a silk backpack from under his shirt and began to pack the money into it.

He'd asked for twenty million because that was a credible amount for a scheme like this. Fielding, however, would only be able to carry four million—which would weigh seventy-two pounds. Generally unathletic, he'd worked out at a health club for six weeks so that he'd be strong enough to carry the cash.

The hundred-dollar bills were all traceable, but in Brazil, where Fielding would be in several days, the four million traceable cash would become three million two hundred thousand in gold and later *untraceable* U.S. and Euro dollars. Fielding had no regrets about leaving the rest of the money. Crime can't be about greed; it must be about craft.

He packed the cash and slung the heavy bag over his shoulder. Stepping into the corridor, he staggered to the elevator. He'd have to kill the guard at the front door, as well as anyone on the team who was still here. Lukas, he knew, was still in the building. She definitely would have to die. Under other circumstances, killing her wouldn't matter—he'd been very careful about hiding his identity and where he really lived. But the agents were much better than he'd anticipated. They'd actually found the safe house in Gravesend. He *never* thought they'd manage that. Fortunately, the man he'd hired to deliver the note—Gilbert Havel—had been to the safe house many times, so neighbors would see Havel's picture when the police were canvassing and assume he was the man who'd rented the place.

And nearly finding that *The Ritzy Lady* was the site of the second attack . . . He'd sat in the document lab in horror as the computer had assembled the fragments from the note at the safe house. He'd waited for just the right moment and blurted out, "Ritz. Maybe the Ritz-Carlton." And as soon as they'd heard that, the solution was set in stone.

That's how puzzle solving works, right, Parker?

And what *about* Parker?

Oh, he was far too smart, far too much of a risk to remain alive.

As Fielding walked slowly down the deserted corridors, he reflected that while he himself was the perfect criminal, Kincaid was the perfect detective.

What happens when perfect opposites meet?

But this was a rhetorical question, and he didn't waste time trying to answer it. He came to the elevator and pushed the UP button.

MARGARET Lukas swung open the door to the document lab.

She looked inside. "Hello? Dr. Evans?"

He didn't answer. Where was he? she wondered. Maybe waiting at the guard station. She walked to the elevator.

The hallways were deserted, and she was aware of the small noises of empty buildings at night. The place was dark and spooky. And it took a lot to spook Margaret Lukas. She sensed ghosts in these corridors. Ghosts of agents killed in the line of duty. Ghosts of victims of crimes that agents investigated here.

And her own personal ghosts? she thought. Oh, but they were with her all the time. Her husband and son. They never left.

She glanced down at the floor in front of the elevator. There was a dark stain on the floor. What was it? She smelled coffee. That must be it. The elevator door opened. Lukas got on the elevator and descended to the main floor.

At the employee-entrance guard station Artie looked up at her and nodded a pleasant greeting.

"Did that Dr. Evans sign out?" she asked him.

"Nope. Haven't seen him."

She'd wait for him here. Lukas exhaustedly sank into one of the comfortable lobby chairs—thinking about the report she'd have to write about the extortion incident, thinking about Parker Kincaid.

He wanted to ask her out. She knew he did. But she'd already decided to say no. He was handsome, energetic, filled with the love of children. How appealing that seemed. But she couldn't inflict herself on him, the sorrow that she believed she radiated like smoke from sour coal. Maybe Jackie Lukas might have had a chance with a man like Kincaid, but a changeling like Margaret never would.

Artie looked up from his paper. "Oh, forgot to say happy New Year, Agent Lukas."

"Happy New Year, Artie."

AS THE fire department spurted foam onto the burned-out bus, Parker and Cage stood together. *The Digger's gone. So long.* Manic verses from Dr. Seuss trooped through Parker's mind, no doubt the result of exhaustion and adrenaline.

He called the Whos and promised them he'd be home soon.

"Love you, Who," he told Stephanie.

"Love you too, Daddy," she said. "How's your friend?"

"He's going to be fine."

Cage was talking to an evidence tech from PERT as Parker jockeyed to get downwind of the pungent smoke from the bus. Parker was at the tail end of an evening like none other he'd ever had. Yet it's the mundane things in life that poke up like crocuses. He realized he didn't have enough cash to pay Mrs. Cavanaugh. He patted his pockets and dug out a small wad of bills. Twenty-two bucks. Not enough. He'd have to stop at an ATM on the way home.

He glanced at a piece of paper mixed in with the money. It was the transcription of the unsub's writing they'd found on the burned yellow pad. The references to the last two attack sites.

> . . . two miles south. The R . . .
> . . . place I showed you—the black . . .

"What's that?" Cage asked, kneading his wounded rib.

"Just a souvenir," Parker said, looking down at the words.

EDWARD Fielding paused at the end of the corridor, gasping under the weight of the money on his back.

He looked toward the reception area thirty feet away and saw Margaret Lukas facing away from him. Beyond her was the guard, reading the paper. The lights were out in the corridor, and even if they'd turned toward him, it would have been difficult to see him clearly.

Clutching the pistol in his right hand, he started down the hallway, his leather soles tapping faintly on the tile. *Tap, tap, tap . . .*

He closed the distance to his targets.

Perfect.

MARGARET Lukas, gazing at the Christmas tree in the lobby, stretched like a cat. She listened absently to footsteps coming up the hall behind her.

Tap, tap, tap . . .

She looked out the glass windows. Crowds, people returning from the Mall. She thought about the Digger. Wondered about the shoot-out, about who'd fired the shots that killed him. She'd been in two firefights in her career and remembered mostly confusion.

A buzzing phone startled her. In front of her Artie answered, "Front desk. . . . Oh, hello, Agent Cage."

Suddenly the guard was frowning. He glanced at Lukas, then focused past her. His eyes went wide. "Well," the guard said uneasily. "Detective Hardy? . . . He's *who?* What do you mean? . . . But he's right here, he's— Oh, God."

Artie was dropping the phone, fumbling for his weapon.

Tap, tap, taptaptaptap . . .

Instinctively Lukas knew that the footsteps, now running toward them, were an attacker's. She fell forward just as the rounds from the silenced pistol snapped through the back of the couch where she'd been sitting.

She looked behind her, twisting around, scrabbling for cover. It was . . . Wait, it couldn't be! It was Hardy.

Firing wildly, Artie shouted, "It's him! He's the killer. He . . . Oh, my. Oh, no . . ." The guard looked down at his chest. He'd been hit. He slumped to his knees, fell behind the desk.

Lukas curled for cover behind an anemic potted palm tree. She cringed as a bullet was loudly deflected by the chrome pot.

Lukas looked up quickly, searching for a target. But she had to duck fast as another bullet chopped through the thick green blades of leaf inches from her face. She rolled to her left, against the wall, rose, and fired three fast shots.

The slugs just missed Hardy and dug huge chunks out of the wall. He fired twice more, then vanished back down the corridor.

She ran to the wall beside the hallway, pressed her back against it. The tapping footsteps receded.

Another voice called from the corridor. "What's going on?"

Somewhere along the hallway a door slammed.

Lukas looked around the corner quickly, then went back to cover. She'd seen a man down at the end of the hall. She shouted, "I'm a federal agent! Identify yourself or I'll fire!"

"Ted Yan," the man called. "In software analysis."

Lukas knew him. He was a friend of Tobe Geller's. She thought, Great, I've got a computer nerd for backup. "You alone?"

"No. There're two of us. Susan Nance is here with me."

Nance, the document researcher, called, "Oh, Margaret, he got Louise in security. She's dead. And Phelps, too."

"Okay, quiet," Lukas barked. "Don't give away your position. Did anybody go past you?"

"No," Ted called. "I heard a door slam in the hallway here. He's somewhere between us."

"You armed?" Lukas called.

"Service," Ted said, meaning their service pistols. "Both of us."

"Cover me," Lukas called, and ran to the guard station. Artie was unconscious but wasn't bleeding badly. She picked up the phone, but Cage was no longer on the line. She hit 911, identified herself as a Justice Department agent, and called in a Code 42 at FBI headquarters. To her knowledge nobody'd ever done this in the entire history of the Bureau. It meant an assault on headquarters.

She studied the empty corridor. Eight doors in the hallway—five on the right, three on the left. He's behind one of them.

Here's a puzzle for you, Parker. Which door leads to our Judas?

Three hawks have been killing a farmer's chickens. . . .

Holding the gun out in front of her, she eased forward, saw the silhouettes of the other agents at the far end of the corridor. Using hand signals, she motioned them aside, back around the corner.

Which door? she wondered. Think . . . Come on! Think!

If Hardy had any sense of orientation, he'd know that the five offices on her right were exterior ones; he wouldn't have picked any on the left, because he'd risk getting trapped inside the building.

Okay, we'll narrow it down to those on the right.

She made her choice: the door nearest the lobby. It made sense. Hardy wouldn't have run thirty or forty feet down the corridor with an armed agent behind him before taking cover.

She tried the knob, but the door was locked. Were they always locked? she wondered. No, *he'd* locked it. He *had* to be in there. She ran to the guard station, got the keys from Artie's belt, returned, slipped the key in the hole, turned the latch.

It clicked. She pushed through the door fast, weapon up.

Nothing . . . He wasn't here. Wait . . . He could be behind the desk.

She stepped forward, pointing her weapon. Nothing.

Then, from the corner of her eye, faint motion. The door directly across the hallway from this one—a door marked MAINTENANCE—had opened slightly. The muzzle of a silenced gun was lowering toward her.

Lukas flung herself to the floor as Hardy fired twice.

But he wasn't aiming at her. The bullets were meant for the plate-glass window, which shattered into a thousand pieces.

Hardy, who ran awkwardly because of a large knapsack on his back, stumbled through the corridor and into the office, firing blindly in Lukas's direction. She rolled to the floor as he leaped out the window onto the deck overlooking Ninth Street. He jumped over the fence to street level and was gone.

Lukas climbed to her feet. She understood what had happened: Hardy had tried the door on the window side of the building and found it locked. He'd waited in a janitor's closet across the hall, out-guessing her. He'd used her to unlock the door.

She'd been dead wrong.

PARKER and Cage were in the document lab once more. Joined this time by the deputy director.

"Six dead," the director muttered. "Inside headquarters."

Dr. John Evans had been found in a seventh-floor closet. Artie the guard was badly wounded but would live.

"Who the hell *is* he?" the director demanded.

The man pretending to be Hardy had left some good fingerprints, and they were being run right now.

Lukas pushed through the door. Parker was alarmed to see a peppering of blood on her cheek.

"You all right?" he asked.

"Artie's," she said, noticing his eyes on the blood. "Not mine." She looked at Parker, then at Cage. "How did you know?"

Cage glanced toward Parker. "It was him figured it out."

"Tremble," Parker answered. He held out the sheet of paper that he'd found in his pocket, looking for baby-sitter money. "It's what happens when somebody tries to disguise their writing. I remembered it was Hardy who'd written down what I dictated, but why would he try to fake his writing? There was only one reason—because he'd written the extortion note. I checked the lowercase *i* in 'two miles,' and the dot was a devil's teardrop."

"What happened?" the deputy director asked.

"It was all a setup," Parker said, pacing. Somewhere in his mind the entire plot was falling into place. He asked Lukas, "How did Hardy get involved in the case?"

"He's been coming by the office for the past few months. Just flashed a badge and needed stats on felonies in the District. It's all public information, so nobody bothered to check. Today he showed up and said he's been assigned as liaison for the case. I guess he's been planning this for months."

"Planned every detail," Parker muttered. "Flawless."

Cage asked, "But the guy in the morgue. Who's he?"

Parker said, "A runner. Somebody hired to deliver the letter."

"But," Cage said, "he was killed in an accident."

"No, it wasn't an accident," Lukas said, stealing the very words from Parker's throat.

Nodding, he said, "Hardy ran him down in a stolen truck."

Lukas continued. "So we'd think the perp was dead and bring the money back to the evidence room."

"But he came up with the info about the Digger, didn't he?" the deputy director asked. "Because of him we stopped the shooter."

"Of *course,*" Parker responded. "That's why he *picked* the memorial. It's not far from here. He knew we'd virtually empty the building to get everybody out looking for the Digger."

"So he could just waltz into evidence and pick up the money," Lukas said bitterly.

A computer beeped. Cage leaned forward and read. "It's an AFIS report." He scrolled through the information. Hardy's picture came up on the screen. "His real name is Edward Fielding, last known address, Blakesly, Connecticut. Four arrests, one conviction. Treated repeatedly for antisocial behavior. Was an aide and orderly at Hartford State Hospital for the Criminally Insane. He left after a nurse he was accused of sexually harassing was found stabbed to death. The hospital administration thinks Fielding talked a patient, David Hughes, into killing her. Hughes had severe brain damage following a gunshot and was highly suggestible. Fielding helped Hughes escape in October of last year."

"Hughes is the Digger," Parker announced. "And the Hartford newspaper shooting—what got Czisman started on Fielding's trail—that was in November. That was their first crime. Didn't waste any time, did they?"

"But why so much death?" the dep director asked. "It can't just be for the money. He must've had some terrorist leanings."

"Nope," Parker said definitively. "Not terrorism at all. But you're absolutely right. It has nothing to do with the money. Oh, I recognize the type. He's like a document forger. Serious forgers see themselves as artists, not thieves. The point is to create a forgery that fools everyone. That's their goal: a perfect forgery."

Lukas nodded. "So the other crimes—in Hartford, Boston, White Plains, and Phillie—they were just exercises to perfect his technique."

"Exactly. And this was the culmination. This time he got a big chunk of money and was going to retire."

"Why do you think that?" Cage asked.

But Lukas knew the answer. "Because he sacrificed his errand boy so he could escape. He told us where the Digger was."

Parker added, "He may actually have been the one who shot the Digger. If we took him alive, he might have talked."

"But where is he?" the director asked.

Parker said, "Oh, he'll have his escape all planned out. He'll be out of the country by sunup and on a plastic surgeon's operating table in two days."

"It's two a.m. The airports are closed," said the dep director.

"He'll be driving to Louisville or Atlanta or New York," Lukas said. "But we'll put out a bulletin to the field offices. Get agents to all the airports, Amtrak stations, and bus terminals."

The dep director said, "I'll authorize ten-most-wanted status."

But Parker wasn't listening. He was staring at the extortion note. "Perfect forgery," he whispered to himself. He looked at his watch, then said, "I'm going to go see somebody."

"I'm going with you," Lukas said.

Parker hesitated. "Better if you didn't."

"No. I'm going."

Parker looked into her blue-gray eyes. He said, "Okay."

THEY drove through the streets of D.C., Parker at the wheel. He glanced to his right, caught Lukas's profile, her thin mouth, her rounded nose, her sweep of throat.

How much he wanted to take her hand, sit with her in a lounge or on his couch at home. And talk. Talk about anything. Perhaps about the secret of Margaret Lukas, whatever that might be. Or maybe they would share the war stories that cops—federal or state or crossing guards—loved to boast about.

The secret could wait. She'd have years to tell him.

Years . . . Suddenly he realized that he was considering a connection with her that might last for a long time. What did he have to base this fantasy on? Nothing really. It was pure illusion.

Or was it? He remembered the Whos in the Dr. Seuss book, a

race of creatures living on a dust mote, so small no one could see them. But they were there nonetheless. Why couldn't love be found in something that seemed invisible, too?

He looked at her again, and she at him. Spontaneously he reached his hand out and touched her knee. Her hand closed on his.

Then they were at the address he sought. He removed his hand, parked the car. Not a word said. Not a look between them. They climbed out. "This way," he said.

THE man was about five feet tall. He had a wiry beard and bushy hair. He wore a ratty bathrobe, and Parker had obviously wakened him when he banged fiercely on the rickety door.

He stared at Parker and Lukas for a moment, then without a word retreated quickly back into the apartment.

Lukas preceded Parker inside. The rooms were filled to overflowing with books and furniture and papers. On the walls hung a hundred signed letters and scraps of historical documents. An artist's drawing table was covered with bottles of ink and dozens of pens.

"How you doing, Jeremy?"

The man rubbed his eyes. He said, "My, Parker, it's late. Say, look at what I've got here. Do you like it?"

Parker took the acetate sheet Jeremy was holding up, picked up a hand glass, and examined the document inside. After a moment he said, "It's very good. The starts and lifts of the strokes are excellent, but you'd have to fake the aging of the ink with hydrogen peroxide. That's detectable."

"Maybe. Maybe not." Jeremy smiled. "Maybe I've got something new up my sleeve. Are you here to arrest me, Parker?"

"I'm not a cop anymore, Jeremy."

"No, but she is, isn't she?" Jeremy took the sheet back. "I haven't sold it." To Lukas he said, "It's just a hobby."

"What is it?" Lukas asked.

Parker said, "It's a letter from Robert E. Lee to one of his generals." He added, "I should say, *purporting* to be from Lee."

"But he forged it?" Lukas asked, glancing at Jeremy.

"That's right."

"I never admitted anything. I'm taking the Fifth."

Parker continued. "It's worth maybe fifteen thousand."

"*If* somebody were going to sell it. Which I never would. Parker arrested me once," Jeremy said to Lukas. "He was the only one in the world who caught me. You know how he did it?"

"How?" she asked. Parker noticed she seemed amused.

"The watermark on a letterhead," Jeremy said. "I got done in by a watermark. So Parker, what've I done now?"

"Oh, I think I know what you've done, Jeremy. I think I know."

"Oh, dear," Jeremy said.

"Oh, dear," echoed Parker.

FINALLY it was snowing. Large flakes parachuting to the ground. Two inches already, muting the night.

Edward Fielding, lugging the knapsack of money, waded through a belt of trees and brush in Bethesda, Maryland. He'd driven here from FBI headquarters, switching cars twice along the route. He'd stayed on major highways the whole way, keeping exactly to the speed limit. He parked on the other side of this grove of trees and walked the rest of the way, the bag of money slowing him down.

He eased through the side yard and paused by a fence separating his rented house from the one next door. On the street were no cars that he didn't recognize. Inside his house the lights were on just as he'd left them. No movement, no shadows.

He moved along the fence, checking out the ground. No footprints in the snow. He continued along the walk to his house. He'd rigged several security devices to let him know if there'd been any unwanted visitors: thread across the gate, the front-door latch lined up with a tiny fleck of dried paint on the storm door, the corner of the rattan mat resting against the door. He checked them carefully. Because that was what you did when you committed the perfect crime.

He unlocked the door, thinking of his next steps. He'd only be here for five or ten minutes—long enough to pack the money into boxes, collect his other suitcases, then drive, via three safe cars already planted along the route, to Ocean City, Maryland. There he'd get on the chartered boat and be in Miami in two days. Then a chartered plane to Costa Rica and on to Brazil. Then he'd—

He wasn't sure where she'd been hiding. Maybe behind the door. Before Fielding had time to feel shock, the pistol had been ripped from his hand and Margaret Lukas was screaming, "Freeze, freeze, federal agents!"

Fielding found himself tumbling forward and lying flat on his belly, under her strong grip, gun in his ear. The cash was pulled off him, and his hands were cuffed by two large agents. They pulled him to his feet and pushed him into an armchair. Cage and several other men and women walked through the front door.

He was completely mystified. "But the snow?" he asked Lukas. "There were no footprints. How'd you get in?"

"Oh, we borrowed a hook and ladder from the fire department and the SWAT team, and I climbed in through the upstairs window."

Just then Parker Kincaid walked through the front door. Lukas nodded toward him. "The fire truck was his idea," she explained.

Fielding didn't doubt that it was.

PARKER sat down in a chair opposite Fielding and crossed his arms. He remembered wishing earlier that the unsub were still alive so that he could see how the man's mind worked. But now he felt no professional curiosity, only revulsion.

Parker asked, "The Digger was a patient in your hospital, right? The hospital for the criminally insane? David Hughes?"

Fielding was impressed. "That's right. Funny guy, wasn't he? Sort of the boogeyman incarnate."

Then Parker suddenly understood something else and his heart froze. *Boogeyman . . .*

"In the command post—I was talking about my son, and not long after that Robby saw somebody in the garage. That was the Digger! You sent him to my house to scare my son!"

Fielding shrugged. "You were too good, Kincaid. I had to get you off the case for a while. When you went to raid my safe house, I left a message that my friend should peek into your little fella's window. I thought about killing them—well, and you too, of course—but I needed you to be at headquarters later. To make my deductions about the site of the last shooting more credible."

Trembling with rage, Parker lunged forward. Lukas caught his fist just before it crashed into Fielding's cringing face.

"I understand," she said, "but it won't do any good. My house was broken into a few months ago, too. It must have been him." She spoke directly to the killer. "You found out all about me. You found out about Tom. . . ."

Tom? Parker wondered. Another clue to Margaret Lukas.

"You cut your hair the same way as his; you read his letters to me." She closed her eyes. " 'Right as rain.' You stole his expression. And then you told me about having a wife in a coma. Why?"

"I needed to get inside your defenses."

"You stole my past, Fielding."

"What's the past for but to use?" he asked evenly.

"Who's the guy in the morgue?" Cage asked.

"His name is Gil Havel."

"Ah, the mysterious Gilbert Jones," Parker said. "He rented the helicopter, right?"

"I *had* to make you believe that I was really going to try to get away with the money from the drop on Gallows Road."

"Who was he? Havel."

"Just some loser. I promised him a hundred thousand dollars to deliver a note to city hall and help me with the helicopter and rent the safe house. I made him think he was my partner."

Parker said, "And you had him walk back to the Metro or bus stop along a particular route, where you were waiting with the van to run him down."

"You had to believe that the mastermind was dead, so you'd bring the money back to the evidence room."

"What about Kennedy? You sending him to the Ritz."

"The mayor?" Fielding asked. "That was a risk. I had to keep you focused on the Ritz-Carlton, not *The Ritzy Lady*. And then my penance for the betrayal was bringing you the bone about the Digger's name. You know, you really are something, Kincaid. How'd you figure it out?"

"That you were the unsub? Because of your handwriting. I had a sample—when I dictated to you from the sheets Tobe saved."

"I was worried about that," Fielding said. "But I couldn't very well balk just then, could I? You asking me to jot down something and everybody watching? But I tried to disguise my writing."

"The dot on your lowercase *i* gave you away."

"Oh, right. The devil's teardrop. It's always the little things."

"Not always, but usually."

Fielding looked around the room. "How'd you get *here?*"

"To this house?" Parker couldn't resist. "Perfection," he said, and watched the arrogant smile slide off the killer's face. "To escape after the perfect crime, you'd want the perfect passports. You'd find the best forger in the business. He happens to be a friend of mine. Well, let's just say we're close."

"But he didn't know my real name or address."

"No, but you called him," Parker countered.

"Not from here," Fielding said, argumentative, whiny.

Lukas nodded. "From the phone booth up the street. We ran the numbers." She held up a computer picture of Fielding. "We lifted it from the tape in the FBI headquarters security camera. Just showed it to a half-dozen people in the neighborhood tonight and got a beeline to your front door."

He swore, closed his eyes. "I knew you were the strong link, Parker. I should've had the Digger take care of you up front."

Cage said, "You didn't have a problem sacrificing your friend?"

"The Digger? He's hardly a friend. Anyway, this was going to be my last job. I don't need him anymore."

An agent started to lead him off. At the doorway Fielding turned back. "Admit it, Parker. I'm good. After all, I nearly did it."

Parker shook his head. "Either an answer to a puzzle's right or it's wrong. There's no nearly about it."

But when he was led out the door, Fielding was smiling.

Chapter Ten

2:20 a.m.

THE workmen were lashing the burned bus to a flatbed. The medical examiner had carted off the Digger's scorched body. Edward Fielding sat in federal detention, shackled and in slippers.

As Parker said good night to Cage, looking around for Margaret Lukas, he noticed Mayor Gerald Kennedy start toward them. He'd been here, with his wife and crew of journalists, surveying the damage. He walked up to them.

"Your Honor," Cage said.

"I have you to thank for that little news story, Agent Cage."

A shrug. "Investigation had priority, sir. Probably would've been better to keep politics out of it."

"You're probably right."

Kennedy turned to Parker. "And you're Agent—"

"Jefferson, Your Honor. First name's Tom."

"You're the one I've heard about. The document examiner?"

"That's right," Parker said. "I saw you do some pretty nifty shooting there."

"Not nifty enough." The mayor nodded at the smoking bus.

Then Lukas arrived. She nodded to the mayor.

Kennedy said, "I'm sorry about your friend, Agent Ardell."

Lukas said, "Tonight didn't turn out well for anybody, did it?"

"No, Agent Lukas," Kennedy said. "I suspect things like this never do." He took his wife's hand and walked to their limousine.

Margaret Lukas handed Cage some documents. Then, eyes on the scorched bus, she walked to her Ford Explorer. Parker wondered, Was she leaving without saying good-bye?

She opened the door, started the engine, and put the heater on—the temperature had dropped. The sky was thick with clouds, which were still shedding fat grains of snow. She left the truck's door open, leaned back into the seat.

Parker zipped up his jacket and walked toward her, noticing that she was looking at something in her hand. It seemed to be an old postcard. Just before Parker got to her vehicle, she put the card away, zipped up her purse. "What a night, hmm?" she said.

"What a night." He offered his hand.

She gripped it solidly. Then he enclosed her hand with his left.

"How're the kids?" she asked. "Have you talked to them?"

"They're fine." Reluctantly he released his grip. Was she reluctant, too? He couldn't tell. "You'll need a report, I assume?"

"We will," Lukas responded, "but there's no hurry."

"I'll do one on Monday. Oh, here." He handed her the pistol.

Lukas, in a skirt now, was no longer dressed for hiding backup weapons on her ankle. As she slipped the gun into her glove compartment, Parker's eyes strayed to the lovely curve of her legs. He knew she was looking at him, but he didn't mind getting caught.

"Hey, you doing anything tomorrow night?" he asked. "Want to have a ridiculously surburban dinner?"

She hesitated. Finally she smiled, but he saw at once that it was fake—a smile of stone, one that matched her eyes. "I'm sorry," she said formally. "I have plans. Maybe some other time."

Meaning never. "Sure," he said, disappointed. "Another time."

"Where's your car?" Lukas asked. "I'll give you a ride."

"No, that's okay. It's right over there."

He gripped her hand again, resisting the urge to pull her close.

"Night," she said.

He nodded, then walked to his car.

ON THE way home, driving through the quiet, snow-filled streets, Parker stopped and got cash from an ATM.

In his house he found Mrs. Cavanaugh asleep on the couch. He woke her, paid her twice what she asked for, then escorted her to the door and stood watching until she disappeared into her own house across the street.

The children had fallen asleep in his bed—his room sported a TV and VCR. The screen was a bright blue, circumstantial evidence that they'd watched a movie on video.

Parker was exhausted—beyond exhaustion, but sleep, he felt, was still an hour or so away. To work off his energy, he bundled up the trash and carted it out into the backyard, thinking, What a crazy life—to have been shot at an hour ago and now to be back in the middle of suburbia, lost in domestic chores.

As he raised the lid of the trash bin, Parker glanced into the backyard. He stopped, frowned. There were footprints in the snow. Only a few minutes old, he judged. The intruder had walked up to the guest-room window, then disappeared toward the front of the house.

Parker's heart began thudding. He set the garbage bag down and walked quietly back into the house.

He closed and locked the kitchen door behind him. Checked on the front door. It was locked.

Whose footprints? Just kids, maybe. Or Mr. Johnson looking for his dog. That's all it was. Sure . . .

But ten seconds later he was on the phone to the federal detention center in Washington, D.C. He identified himself. "I was working on that case tonight with Margaret Lukas."

"Sure. The Mall shooter."

"Right. The suspect—Fielding. He's not out on bail, is he?"

"Bail? No way. He won't be arraigned until Monday."

"He's locked down?"

"Yep. I can see him on the monitor. He's sitting on his bed. Talked to his lawyer on the phone about an hour ago, then went into his cell and has been there ever since. Why?"

"Just spooked, I guess. Thought I saw the boogeyman."

"Boogeyman. Ha. Hey, happy New Year."

Parker hung up, relieved. For about five seconds.

Talking to his lawyer? Parker didn't know any lawyer in the country who'd be up at this hour on a holiday, talking to a client who wouldn't be arraigned for two days.

Then he thought, Perfection. "Oh, God," he muttered.

Fielding—the man who had a plan for everything. He must have had a plan for escaping if he was caught.

He lifted the receiver and hit the first digit of 911.

The line went dead.

Motion outside the kitchen door. He looked up.

Standing on the back porch, gazing at him through the window in the door, was a man in a dark coat. There was blood on his left arm, burns on his face.

The man lifted his silenced machine gun and tapped the trigger as Parker dove to the floor. The doorknob and lock of the back door blew apart under the stream of bullets.

Leisurely the Digger pushed the door open and stepped inside.

THE Digger wants to get this over with and leave. He'd rather be outside. He likes the . . . *click* . . . the snow.

Oh, look, a nice Christmas tree in Parker Kincaid's house.

He fires again as Kincaid runs through the doorway.

Did he hit him? The Digger can't tell.

But no, guess not. He sees Kincaid crawling into another room, shutting out lights, rolling on the floor.

The Digger believes he's happy. The man who tells him things called again, an hour ago. Not a voice-mail message, but a real call on the Digger's cell phone.

"Listen to me," said the man. The Digger was supposed to kill three more people. Someone named Cage and someone named Lukas. And Parker Kincaid. "Kill him first. Okay?"

"Hmm, sure."

The Digger knows Kincaid. He came to this house earlier tonight. Kincaid has a little boy like Tye except the Digger doesn't like Kincaid's little boy, because Kincaid wants to take the Digger away from Tye.

"Then at four thirty a.m.," said the man who tells him things, "I want you to come to the federal detention center. I'll be in the clinic. It's on the first floor in the back. I'll be pretending I'm sick. Kill everyone you see and let me out."

Now walking into the dining room, the Digger sees Kincaid roll out from beneath the table and run into the hallway. He fires another stream of bullets as Kincaid disappears into another part of the house. But he won't leave, the Digger knows. The children are here. A father won't run out on his children.

The Digger knows this because he wouldn't leave Tye.

He steps into the living room, holding the gun in front of him.

PARKER rolled away from the Digger, rolled along the floor, elbows scraped, head throbbing from where he hit the edge of the kitchen table, diving away from the bullets.

The Whos! he thought in despair, scrabbling toward the stairs. He wouldn't let the Digger upstairs.

Another burst of shots. He turned from the stairs and dove into the living room. A weapon . . . What could he use? Why had he given back Lukas's gun?

Parker jumped behind the couch. Then he saw something—one of Robby's presents, an aluminum baseball bat. He snagged it, gripped the taped handle. Where is he? Where?

Then steps, faint. The crunch of the Digger walking over broken glass and pottery. *Crunch.* A pause. Another *crunch*.

Parker looked up. No! The Digger was at the foot of the stairs, about to climb them. Parker flung the bat into the dining room. It crashed into the china cabinet.

The Digger stopped, hearing the noise. He turned stiffly and walked toward it. When he was nearly to the arched doorway, Parker climbed out from behind the couch and charged him.

The Digger spun around just as Parker rammed into him, knocking him off-balance. He landed a fist on the man's jaw, but the Digger dodged away. Parker tried for the Digger's gun, but the man was too fast. Parker could do nothing but retreat again into the narrow space behind the couch. Nowhere else to go.

The Digger backed up, dim eyes squinting in the darkness.

Parker saw something glistening on the floor in front of him: a long shard of glass from the shattered breakfront. He grabbed it.

The killer located Parker. He stepped closer. Coming around the back of the couch.

Parker tucked his legs under him, got ready to leap.

The Digger walked around the couch and lifted the gun.

Parker tensed.

Then the stunning crack of the single, unsilenced gunshot.

The Digger shuddered. The machine gun fell from his hands. He fell forward, a bullet hole in the back of his skull.

What? Parker wondered frantically. What had happened?

Then he saw someone in the doorway. A young boy. Black. Holding a pistol. The boy walked forward slowly, staring at the corpse. Like a cop in a movie, he kept the large gun pointed at the Digger's back. He needed both hands to hold it.

"He kill mah daddy," the boy said to Parker. "I seen him do it."

"Give me the gun," Parker whispered.

The boy continued to stare at the Digger. Tears were running down his cheeks. "He kill mah daddy and brought me here."

"Let me have the gun. What's your name?"

"I been waiting t'cap him. Found this piece in his car."

"It's okay," Parker said. "What's your name?" He eased forward, but the boy pointed the gun toward him threateningly. Parker froze, backed off. "Just put that down. Would you do that? Please?"

The boy ignored him. His wary eyes scanned the room. They stopped momentarily on the Christmas tree.

Parker slowly rose, hands up. "Don't worry. I'm not going to hurt you. I'm just going over there." He nodded to the tree.

He skirted the boy and walked to the Christmas tree. He bent down and picked up something and returned, knelt. Parker held his empty right hand out, palm up. With his left he offered him Robby's *Star Wars* Millennium Falcon spaceship. "I'll trade you."

The boy studied the plastic toy. "Man," he said reverently. Then he handed Parker the pistol and took the spaceship toy.

Parker said, "Wait here. I'll be right back."

The boy didn't answer.

Parker picked up the machine gun and carried it and the pistol upstairs. He put the guns on the top shelf of the closet and locked the door.

Motion beside him. Robby had come down the corridor.

"Daddy? I had a dream. I heard a gun. I'm scared."

"Hey, Robby-O." Parked struggled to keep his voice from trembling. He put his arm around Robby and directed him back to the bedroom. "It was probably just fireworks."

He heard footsteps outside, slapping on the street in front of the house. Glanced outside. He saw the boy running across the front lawn, clutching the spaceship. He vanished up the street.

Headed for where? Parker wondered. He couldn't spare a moment's thought for the boy. His own son took all his attention.

Parker put Robby in bed, beside his sister. He needed to call 911 but wouldn't let go of Robby's hand.

Parker lay down next to the kids. He glanced at the clock. It was three thirty. Joan would be here at ten with her social worker. What a nightmare. Bullet holes in the walls. The breakfront shattered. And in the middle of the carpet was a bloody corpse.

"Daddy," Stephie mumbled sleepily, "I heard a firecracker. Petey Whelan's mom told him he couldn't have firecrackers, but he did."

"That's okay, honey. That's not our business."

Parker lay back, closed his eyes. Felt her slight weight on his chest. He imagined Joan's testimony in court. What could he do? What excuse could he come up with? What?

A moment later Parker Kincaid was breathing deeply. Content in the sleep of a parent whose children were close in his arms.

WHEN he opened his eyes, it was five minutes to ten. He had been awakened by a car door slamming and Joan's voice saying, "We're early, but I'm sure he won't mind."

Nauseated, head throbbing, Parker looked out the window.

Joan and Richard were walking toward the house, followed by a short woman who looked at the house appraisingly—the social worker. They came to the front door and rang the bell. Hopeless.

He stood in the upstairs hallway, toes curling on the carpet. Well, just don't let Joan in, he told himself. He'd stonewall. Make her get a court order. But that would only buy him a couple hours, and stalling would make Joan even more suspicious.

He took a deep breath and started down the stairs.

What could he possibly say about the bullet holes? The blood? Maybe he could— Parker stopped at the landing. Stunned.

A thin blond woman in a long black skirt and white blouse, her back to Parker, was opening the door.

Which was surprising enough. But what truly shocked him was the condition of the house: immaculate.

Not a piece of broken porcelain or glass anywhere. Not a bullet hole in any of the walls. They'd been plastered and primed; buckets of paint sat in the corner of the living room on white tarps. The chair that had been peppered with bullets last night had been replaced by a similar one. There was a new breakfront.

And the Digger's corpse—gone. On the spot where he'd died was a new Oriental carpet.

Joan, Richard, the social worker in the doorway, and the woman in the dark skirt turned. "Oh, Parker," said Margaret Lukas.

"Yes," he answered after a moment.

She smiled in a curious way. "How was your nap?" she asked. Then prompted, "Good?"

"Yes," he said, "it was good."

Lukas turned back to Joan. "You must be Parker's wife."

"Ex-wife," Joan said. The social worker—a pudgy brunette—entered next, followed by Richard.

Parker continued down the stairs and couldn't resist touching a wall where he *knew* he'd seen a cluster of bullets strike last night. The plasterboard was smooth as Stephie's cheek.

"Morning, Joan," he said. "Hello, Richard."

Joan didn't introduce Parker to the social worker, but the woman stepped forward. She shook his hand. She may or may not have given her name. Parker was too dumbfounded to notice.

Joan looked at Lukas. "I don't think we've met. You're . . ."

"Jackie Lukas. I'm a friend of Parker's."

Jackie? Parker lifted an eyebrow but said nothing.

Joan glanced at Lukas's trim figure with a neutral look. Then her eyes took in the living room. "Did you . . . What did you do? Redecorate or something? I didn't notice it yesterday."

"I had some free time. Thought I'd fix things up a little."

His ex studied Parker. "You look awful. Didn't you sleep well?"

Lukas laughed. "Parker invites me over for breakfast," she explained, "then he goes upstairs to wake up the children, and what's he do but fall back asleep."

Joan grunted, meaning *typical.*

Where was the blood? And all the shattered glass?

Lukas asked the guests, "You want some coffee? A sweet roll? Parker made them himself."

"I'll have coffee," the social worker said, "and half a roll."

"They're small," Lukas said. "Have a whole one." She disappeared into the kitchen and came back a moment later with a tray. She poured coffee for everyone and asked Parker, "What time did you get back from the hospital last night?"

"Uhm. I don't know what time. It was late."

"The hospital? Were the children sick?" Joan asked with overly dramatic concern, glancing at the social worker.

"Visiting a friend," Lukas responded.

"What friend?" Joan demanded.

"Harold Cage," Lukas said. "He'll be all right. Just a broken rib. Isn't that what they said?"

"Right. Broken rib," Parker recited. "He slipped and fell."

The social worker sipped her coffee and ate a second sweet roll. "Say, could I get the recipe for these?"

"Sure," Parker said.

"I'll get some more coffee," Lukas said.

"I'll help you," Parker said. In the kitchen he swung the door closed and turned to Lukas. "How? How on earth . . ."

She laughed. "You called detention last night. Said you were spooked. Night watch called me. I tried to call you. Bell Atlantic said your line'd been cut. Fairfax County SWAT got here around three thirty and found a body downstairs and you in bed. Who was the shooter? Who got the Digger? Wasn't you, right?"

"Some kid. He said the Digger killed his father. The Digger brought him here with him. Don't ask me why. He just took off. Now answer one for me. Who was the body on the bus?"

"The driver. We figure the Digger kept him alive and then made him run for the exit in the back. The Digger shot him, then shot the gas tank. When the fire started, he climbed out a window. Used the smoke for cover. Smarter than he seemed."

Parker shook his head. "No. It was Fielding. He told the Digger to do that. He wasn't going to sacrifice his boy at all. They probably had years of jobs ahead of them. But the house . . ." Parker waved his arms. "How—"

"That was Cage, the miracle worker. He made a few calls. We got you into this mess. It's the least we could do."

Parker wouldn't argue with that.

"Wait . . . What did you call yourself? Jackie?"

She hesitated. "Nickname," she said. "It's what my family calls me. I don't use it much."

There were footsteps on the stairs, soft thuds as the children came down to the living room. Parker and Lukas could hear the voices through the kitchen door, "Mommy! Hey!"

"Hello, both of you," Joan said.

Lukas said, "So that's your wife. You two don't seem much alike."

Parker laughed. What Lukas really meant was, How did you ever end up with her? A legitimate question and one he'd be happy to answer. But doing so would require a lot more time than they had right at the moment. And would also have to be part of a complicated ritual involving her sharing at least *some* of the answers to the puzzle of Margaret—or Jackie—Lukas.

And what a puzzle she was: Parker looked her over—the makeup, the jewelry, the softness of the white silk blouse. And she was wearing perfume today, not just fragrant soap.

She glanced at his perusing eyes.

Caught again. He didn't care.

"I'll stay until she leaves," Lukas said. "Thought a hint of a domestic life might help you out with the social worker."

"It's above and beyond the call," he said.

She gave a shrug worthy of Cage.

"Look," he said, "I know you said you had plans, but the Whos and I were going to do some yard work."

"In the snow?"

"Right. Cut down some bushes in the backyard. Then we were going sledding. I don't know if you'd be interested, but . . ."

"Is that an invitation?" Lukas asked.

"Uhm. Yes, it is."

"Those plans I had?" she said. "I was going to clean up my house and finish a blouse for a friend's daughter."

"Is that an acceptance?"

"I guess it is." Silence for a moment. She was facing the window, but her eyes moved once more toward the door. She was listening to the sound of the children. She turned back to Parker. "Oh, I've figured it out. The puzzle."

"Puzzle?"

"How many hawks were left on the roof? It's a trick question. There's more than one answer."

"That's good," Parker said. "You've realized that a legitimate answer is that there are several possible solutions. It's the first thing that puzzle masters learn."

"See," she continued, "you tend to think that all the facts you need are given in the puzzle, but there are some that aren't stated. And those facts have to do with the nature of hawks."

"Ah, and what does that have to do with the puzzle?"

"Because," she said, pointing a finger at him and revealing a sliver of girlishness he hadn't seen before, "hawks might be scared off by a gunshot. But they might not. Because, remember, they were far apart on the roof. That was a clue, right?"

"Right. Keep going."

"Okay, the farmer shoots one bird off the roof, but we don't know what the other two do. They both might stay. So then the answer'd be there're two left. Or one might fly off and that'd leave one. Or both might fly off, which'd leave none. So those're the three answers."

"Well, you were right to consider implied facts."

She frowned. "What does that mean? Am I right or not?"

"You're wrong."

"Well, I'm at least partly right, aren't I?"

"There's no such thing as partly right when it comes to puzzles. You want to know the answer?"

A hesitation. "No. I'm going to keep working on it."

It was a good moment to kiss her, and he did. Then as Lukas poured more coffee, Parker returned to the living room to hug his children and tell them good morning on the first day of the year.

Author's Note

IN TRYING to solve Parker's puzzle, Jackie Lukas's mistake was in making an assumption: that the hawk the farmer shot would fall off the roof. It might not have. The question didn't ask how many "living hawks" were left on the roof, just how many "hawks." So the answer is this: Three hawks would remain if the dead hawk didn't fall off and the other two don't fly away. Two hawks, if the dead hawk didn't fall off and one flies away or if the dead hawk does fall off and the other two stay. One hawk, if the dead hawk falls and one of the others flies away or if the dead hawk doesn't fall and the others fly away. No hawks, if the dead hawk falls off the roof and the others fly away.

JEFFERY DEAVER

BLAISE HAYWARD

"I'm the designer of verbal roller coasters," says Jeffery Deaver. "I want to give the reader the fastest thrill ride that I can." And as his many fans know, he has done just that in his fifteen thrillers.

Deaver's success didn't happen overnight. Born in Chicago, he attended journalism school and then worked for six years as a magazine writer before turning to law. Regarding his eight years at a Wall Street law firm, Deaver says, "I just wasn't temperamentally suited to law. I had a long commute, though, and wrote on the train every day."

Now, at age forty-nine, Deaver is well settled into his life as a novelist. He lives near Washington, D.C., the setting of his latest verbal roller coaster, *The Devil's Teardrop*.

A Walk to Remember

by Nicholas Sparks

My name is Landon Carter, and I'm seventeen years old. This is my story. I promise to leave nothing out.

First you will smile, and then you will cry. . . . Don't say you haven't been warned.

Here goes.

Prologue

When I was seventeen, my life changed forever.

I know that there are people who wonder about me when I say this. They look at me strangely, as if trying to fathom what could have happened back then, though I seldom bother to explain. Because I've lived here for most of my life, I don't feel that I have to explain, unless it's on my terms, and that would take more time than most people are willing to give me. My story can't be summed up in two or three sentences; it can't be packaged into something neat and simple that people would immediately understand. Despite the passage of forty years, the people still living here who knew me that year accept my lack of explanation without question. My story in some ways is their story because it was something that all of us lived through.

It was I, however, who was closest to it.

I'm fifty-seven years old, but even now I can remember everything from that year, down to the smallest details. I relive it often in my mind, bringing it back to life, and I realize that when I do, I always feel a strange combination of sadness and joy. There are moments when I wish I could roll back the clock and take all the sadness away, but I have the feeling that if I did, the joy would be gone as well. So I take the memories as they come, accepting them all, letting them guide me whenever I can.

It is April 12 in the last year before the millennium, and as I leave my house, I glance around. The sky is overcast and gray, but as I move down the street, I notice that the dogwoods and azaleas are blooming. I zip my jacket just a little. The temperature is cool, though I know it's only a matter of weeks before the gray skies will give way to the kind of days that make North Carolina one of the most beautiful places in the world.

With a sigh I feel it all coming back to me. I close my eyes, and the years begin to move in reverse, slowly ticking backward, like the hands of a clock rotating in the wrong direction. As if through someone else's eyes I watch myself grow younger. I see my hair changing from gray to brown; I feel the wrinkles around my eyes begin to smooth, my arms and legs grow sinewy. Lessons I've learned with age grow dimmer, and my innocence returns as that eventful year approaches.

Then, like me, the world begins to change. Suburban sprawl has been replaced with farmland; downtown streets teem with people. Men wear hats; women wear dresses. At the courthouse up the street, the bell tower rings. . . .

I open my eyes and pause. I am standing outside the Baptist church, and when I stare at the gable, I know exactly who I am.

My name is Landon Carter, and I'm seventeen years old.

Chapter One

In 1958, Beaufort, North Carolina, which is located on the coast near Morehead City, was a place like many other small southern towns. It was the kind of place where the humidity rose so high in the summer that walking out to get the mail made a person feel as if he needed a shower, and kids walked around barefoot from April through October beneath oak trees draped in Spanish moss. People waved from their cars whenever they saw someone on the street, whether they knew him or not, and the air smelled of pine, salt, and sea, a scent unique to the Carolinas. For many of the people there, fishing in the Pamlico Sound or crabbing in the Neuse River was a way of life, and boats were moored wherever you saw the Intracoastal Waterway. Only three channels came in on the television, though television was never important to those of us who grew up there. Instead, our lives were centered around the churches, of which there were eighteen within the town limits alone. They went by names like the Fellowship Hall Christian Church, the Church of the Forgiven People, the Church of Sunday Atonement. And then, of course, there were the Baptist churches. When I was growing up, it was far and away the most popular denomination around, and there were Baptist churches on practically every corner of town, though each considered itself superior to the others. There were Freewill Baptists, Southern Baptists, Congregational Baptists, Missionary Baptists, Independent Baptists—well, you get the picture.

Back then the big event of the year was sponsored by the Baptist church downtown—Southern, if you really want to know—in conjunction with the local high school. Every year at the Beaufort Playhouse they put on their Christmas pageant, which was actually a play that had been written by Hegbert Sullivan, a minister who'd been with the church since Moses parted the Red Sea. Okay, maybe he wasn't that old, but he was old enough that you could almost see through the guy's skin. It was sort of clammy and translucent, and his hair was as white as those bunnies you see in pet stores around Easter.

Anyway, he wrote this play called *The Christmas Angel* because he didn't want to keep on performing that old Charles Dickens classic, *A Christmas Carol.* In Hegbert Sullivan's mind Scrooge was a heathen who came to his redemption only because he saw ghosts, not angels—and who was to say whether they'd been sent by God anyway? And who was to say he wouldn't revert to his sinful ways if they hadn't been sent directly from heaven? The play didn't exactly tell you in the end—it sort of plays into faith and all—but Hegbert didn't trust ghosts if they weren't actually sent by God, and this was his big problem with Dickens's story.

So Hegbert decided to try his hand at writing his own play. He'd written his own sermons his whole life, and some of them, we had to admit, were actually interesting, especially when he talked about the "wrath of God coming down on the fornicators" and all that good stuff. That really got his blood boiling, I'll tell you, when he talked about the fornicators. That was his real hot spot. When we were younger, my friends and I would hide behind the trees and shout, "Hegbert is a fornicator," when we saw him walking down the street, and we'd giggle like idiots, like we were the wittiest creatures ever to inhabit the planet.

Old Hegbert, he'd stop dead in his tracks, and he'd turn this bright shade of red, like he'd just drunk gasoline. He'd peer from side to side, his eyes narrowing as he searched for us, and then just as suddenly he'd start to go pale again, back to that fishy skin. Boy, was it something to watch.

So we'd be hiding behind a tree, and Hegbert (what kind of parents name their kid Hegbert anyway?) would stand there waiting for us to give ourselves up, as if he thought we'd be that stupid. We'd put our hands over our mouths to keep from laughing out loud, but somehow he'd always zero in on us. He'd be turning from side to side, and then he'd stop, those beady eyes coming right at us, right through the tree. "I know who you are, Landon Carter," he'd say, "and the Lord knows too." He'd let that sink in for a minute or so, and then he'd finally head off again, and during the sermon that weekend he'd stare right at us and say something like, "God is merciful to children, but the children must be worthy as well." And we'd sort of lower ourselves in the seats, not from embarrassment, but to hide a new round of giggles. Hegbert didn't understand us at all, which was really sort of strange, being that he had a kid and all. But then again, she was a girl. More on that, though, later.

Anyway, like I said, Hegbert wrote *The Christmas Angel* one year and decided to put on that play instead. The play itself wasn't bad, which surprised everyone. It's the story of a man who lost his wife a few years back. This guy, Tom Thornton, used to be real religious, but he had a crisis of faith after his wife died during childbirth. He's raising this little girl all on his own, but he hasn't been the greatest father, and what the little girl really wants for Christmas is a special music box with an angel engraved on top, a picture of which she'd cut out from an old catalogue. The guy searches long and hard to find the gift but can't find it anywhere. So it's Christmas Eve, and he's still searching, and while he's out looking through the stores, he comes across a strange woman he's never seen before, and she promises to help him find the gift for his daughter. First, though, they help this homeless person (back then they were called bums, by the way); then they stop at an orphanage to see some kids, then visit a lonely old woman who just wanted some company on Christmas Eve. Eventually the mysterious woman asks Tom Thornton what he wants for Christmas, and he says that he wants his wife back. She brings him to the city fountain and tells him to look in the water and he'll find what he's looking for. When he looks in the water, he sees the face of his little girl, and he breaks down and cries right there. While he's sobbing, the mysterious lady runs off, and Tom Thornton searches but can't find her anywhere. So he heads home, the lessons from the evening playing in his mind. He walks into his little girl's room, and her sleeping figure makes him realize that she's all he has left of his wife, and he starts to cry again because he knows he hasn't been a good enough father to her. The next morning, magically, the music box is underneath the tree, and the angel that's engraved on it looks exactly like the woman he'd seen the night before.

So Hegbert's play wasn't that bad, really. If truth be told, people cried buckets whenever they saw it. The play sold out every year, and due to its popularity, Hegbert eventually had to move it from the church to the Beaufort Playhouse, which had a lot more seating. By the time I was a senior in high school, the performances ran twice to packed houses, which, considering who actually performed it, was a story in and of itself.

You see, Hegbert wanted young people to perform the play—seniors in high school, not the theater group. I reckon he thought it would be a good learning experience before the seniors headed off to college and came face to face with all the fornicators. He was that kind of guy, always wanting to save us from temptation. He wanted us to know that God is out there watching you, even when you're away from home, and that if you put your trust in God, you'll be all right. It was a lesson I would eventually learn, though it wasn't Hegbert who taught me.

AS I said before, Beaufort was fairly typical as far as southern towns went, though it did have an interesting history. Blackbeard the Pirate once owned a house there, and his ship, *Queen Anne's Revenge,* is supposedly buried somewhere in the sand just offshore. Beaufort's come a long way since the 1950s, but it's still not exactly a major metropolis or anything. Beaufort was and always will be on the smallish side, but when I was growing up, it barely warranted a place on the map. To put it into perspective, the congressional district that included Beaufort covered the entire eastern part of the state—some twenty thousand square miles—and there wasn't a single town with more than twenty-five thousand people. Even compared to those towns, Beaufort was on the small side. Everything east of Raleigh and north of Wilmington, all the way to the Virginia border, was the district my father represented.

I suppose you've heard of my father. He's sort of a legend even now. His name is Worth Carter, and he was a Congressman for almost thirty years. He was a bigwig, and everyone but everyone knew it, including old man Hegbert.

Now, Hegbert and my father didn't get along, not at all, despite the fact that my father went to church there whenever he was in town—which, to be frank, wasn't all that often. Hegbert, in addition to his belief that fornicators were destined to clean the urinals in hell, also believed that communism was "a sickness that doomed mankind to heathenhood." Even though heathenhood wasn't a word—I can't find it any dictionary—the congregation knew what he meant. They also knew that he was directing his words specifically to my father, who would sit with his eyes closed and pretend not to listen. My father was on one of the House committees that oversaw the "Red influence" supposedly infiltrating every aspect of the country, including national defense, higher education, and even tobacco farming. You have to remember that this was during the cold war. Tensions were running high, and we North Carolinians needed something to bring it down to a more personal level. My father had consistently looked for facts, which were irrelevant to people like Hegbert.

When my father would come home after the services, he'd say something like, "Reverend Sullivan was in rare form today. I hope you heard that part in the Scripture where Jesus was talking about the poor . . ."

Yeah, sure, Dad.

My father tried to defuse situations whenever possible. I think that's why he stayed in Congress for so long. The guy could kiss the ugliest babies known to mankind and still come up with something nice to say. "He's such a gentle child," he'd say when a baby had a giant head, or, "I'll bet she's the sweetest girl in the world," if she had a birthmark over her entire face. One time a lady showed up with a kid in a wheelchair. My father took one look at him and said, "I'll bet you ten to one that you're the smartest kid in your class." And he was! Yeah, my father was great at stuff like that. He could fling it with the best of 'em, that's for sure. And he wasn't such a bad guy, not really.

But he wasn't there for me growing up. I hate to say that, because nowadays people claim that sort of stuff and use it to excuse their behavior even if their parent *was* around. "My dad didn't love me. That's why I became a stripper." I'm not saying this to excuse the person I've become; I'm simply saying it as a fact. My father was gone nine months of the year, living three hundred miles away in a Washington, D.C., apartment. My mother didn't go with him, because both of them wanted me to grow up "the same way they had."

Of course, my father's father took him hunting and fishing, taught him to play ball, showed up for birthday parties, all that small stuff that adds up to quite a bit before adulthood. My father, on the other hand, was a stranger, someone I barely knew at all. For the first five years of my life I thought all fathers lived somewhere else. It wasn't until my best friend, Eric Hunter, asked me in kindergarten who that guy was who showed up at my house the night before that I realized something wasn't quite right about the situation.

"He's my father," I said proudly.

"Oh . . ." Eric said. "I didn't know you had a father."

Talk about something whacking you straight in the face.

So I grew up under the care of my mother. Now, she was a nice lady, sweet and gentle, the kind of mother most people dream about. But she wasn't, nor ever could be, a manly influence in my life, and that fact, coupled with my growing disillusionment with my father, made me become somewhat of a rebel even at a young age. Not a bad one, mind you. Me and my friends might sneak out late and soap up car windows now and then or eat boiled peanuts in the graveyard behind the church, but in the '50s that was the kind of thing that made other parents shake their heads and whisper to their children, "You don't want to be like that Carter boy. He's on the fast track to prison."

Anyway, my father and Hegbert didn't get along, but it wasn't only because of politics. No, it seems that they knew each other from way back when. Hegbert was about twenty years older than my father, and before he was a minister, he used to work for my father's father. My grandfather—even though he spent lots of time with my father—was a true bastard if there ever was one. He was the one who made the family fortune, but I don't want you to imagine him as the sort of man who slaved over his business, working diligently and watching it grow, prospering slowly over time. My grandfather was much shrewder than that. He started as a bootlegger, accumulating wealth throughout Prohibition by running rum up from Cuba. He then began buying land and hiring sharecroppers to work it. He took ninety percent of the money the sharecroppers made on their tobacco crop, then loaned them money whenever they needed it, at ridiculous interest rates. Of course, he never intended to collect the money. Instead, he would foreclose on any land or equipment they owned. Then, in what he called his "moment of inspiration," he started a bank called Carter Banking and Loan. The only other bank in a two-county radius had mysteriously burned down, and with the onset of the Depression it never reopened. Though everyone knew what had really happened, not a word was ever spoken, for fear of retribution. The bank wasn't the only building that had ever mysteriously burned down.

His interest rates were outrageous, and little by little he began amassing more land and property as people defaulted on their loans. When the Depression hit hardest, he foreclosed on dozens of businesses throughout the county while retaining the original owners on salary, paying them just enough to keep them where they were, because they had nowhere else to go. He told them that when the economy improved, he'd sell their businesses back to them, and people always believed him. Never once, however, did he keep his promise.

I'd like to tell you he eventually went to a terrible death, but he didn't. He died at the age of ninety-eight while sleeping with his mistress on his yacht off the Cayman Islands. Some end for a guy like that, huh? Life, I've learned, is never fair. If people teach anything in school, that should be it.

But back to the story. . . . Hegbert, once he realized what a bastard my grandfather really was, quit working for him and went into the ministry, then came back to Beaufort and started ministering in the same church we attended. He spent his first few years perfecting his fire-and-brimstone act with sermons on the evils of the greedy, and this left him scant time for anything else. He was forty-three before he married; he was fifty-five when his daughter, Jamie, was born. His wife, a wispy little thing twenty years younger than he, went through six miscarriages before Jamie was born. She died in childbirth, making Hegbert a widower who had to raise a daughter on his own.

Hence, of course, the story behind the Christmas play.

JAMIE Sullivan, Hegbert's daughter, was a senior in high school, just like me, and she'd already been chosen to play the angel in the play, not that anyone else even had a chance. This, of course, made the play extra special that year. It was going to be a big deal—maybe the biggest ever—at least in Miss Garber's mind. She was the drama teacher, and she was already glowing about the possibilities the first time I met her in class.

I hadn't really planned on taking drama that year, but it was either that or chemistry II. The thing was, I thought it would be a blow-off class. No papers, no tests, no tables where I'd have to memorize protons and neutrons. What could possibly be better for a senior? It seemed like a sure thing.

Miss Garber was big, at least six feet two, with flaming red hair and pale skin that showed her freckles well into her forties. She was also overweight—I'd say honestly she pushed two fifty—and she had a fondness for wearing flower-patterned muumuus. She had horn-rimmed glasses, and she greeted everyone with the word "Hel-loooooo," sort of singing the last syllable. Miss Garber was one of a kind, that's for sure, and she was single, which made it worse. A guy, no matter how old, couldn't help but feel sorry for a gal like her.

But I digress.

It wasn't until the first day of drama class that I noticed something unusual. Though Beaufort High School wasn't large, it was pretty much split fifty-fifty between males and females, which is why I was surprised when I saw that this class was at least ninety percent female. I counted only one other male, which in my frame of thinking was a good thing, and for a moment I felt flush with a "look out girls, here I come" kind of feeling.

Okay, so I wasn't the most forward-thinking guy on the block.

Miss Garber brought up the Christmas play and told everyone that Jamie Sullivan was going to be the angel that year. Miss Garber started clapping right away—she was a member of the church too, and there were a lot of people who thought she was gunning for Hegbert in a romantic sort of way. The first time I heard it, I remember thinking that it was a good thing they were too old to have children, if they ever did get together. Imagine—translucent with freckles? The very thought gave everyone shudders.

Miss Garber kept on clapping until all of us finally joined in, because it was obvious that was what she wanted. "Stand up, Jamie," she said. "Let the others see who you are." So Jamie stood up and turned around, and Miss Garber started clapping even faster, as if she were standing in the presence of a bona fide movie star.

Now, Jamie Sullivan was a nice girl. She really was. Beaufort was small enough that it had only one elementary school, so we'd been in the same classes our entire lives, and I'd be lying if I said I never talked to her. In second grade she'd sat in the seat right next to me for the whole year, and we'd even had a few conversations, but it didn't mean that I spent a lot of time hanging out with her in my spare time. Who I saw in school was one thing; who I saw *after* school was something completely different, and Jamie wasn't, nor ever had been, on my social calendar.

It's not that Jamie was unattractive—don't get me wrong. She wasn't hideous or anything like that. Fortunately, she'd taken after her mother, who, based on the pictures I'd seen, wasn't half bad. But Jamie wasn't exactly what I considered attractive either. Despite the fact that she was thin, with honey-blond hair and soft blue eyes, she looked sort of . . . plain, and that was when you noticed her at all. Jamie didn't care much about outward appearances, because she was always looking for things like "inner beauty," and I suppose that's part of the reason she looked the way she did. For as long as I'd known her, she'd worn her hair in a tight bun, almost like a spinster might, without a stitch of makeup on her face. Coupled with her usual brown cardigan and plaid skirt, she always looked as though she were on her way to interview for a job at the library. We used to think it was just a phase and that she'd eventually grow out of it, but she never had.

Still, it wasn't just the way that Jamie looked that made her different, it was also the way she acted. Jamie didn't spend any time hanging out at Cecil's Diner or going to slumber parties with other girls, and I knew for a fact that she'd never had a boyfriend her entire life. Old Hegbert would probably have had a heart attack if she did. But even if by some odd turn of events Hegbert would have allowed it, it still wouldn't have mattered. Jamie carried her Bible wherever she went, and if her looks and Hegbert didn't keep the boys away, the Bible sure did. Now, I liked the Bible as much as the next teenage boy, but Jamie seemed to enjoy it in a way that was completely foreign to me. Not only did she go to vacation Bible school every August but she would read the Bible during lunch break at school. In my mind that just wasn't normal, even if she was the minister's daughter. No matter how you sliced it, reading Paul's letters to the Ephesians wasn't nearly as much fun as flirting, if you know what I mean.

But Jamie didn't stop there. Because of all her Bible reading, or maybe because of Hegbert's influence, Jamie believed it was important to help others. She volunteered at the orphanage in Morehead City and was always in charge of one fund-raiser or another. She was the kind of girl who would pull weeds in someone's garden without being asked or stop traffic to help little kids cross the road. She'd even save her allowance to buy a new basketball for the orphans. She was, in other words, the kind of girl who made the rest of us look bad, and whenever she glanced my way, I couldn't help but feel guilty, even though I hadn't done anything wrong.

Nor did Jamie limit her good deeds to people. If she ever came across a wounded animal, she'd try to help it too. Dogs, cats, squirrels, frogs—it didn't matter to her. Dr. Rawlings, the vet, would shake his head whenever he saw her walking up to the door carrying a cardboard box with yet another critter inside. He'd take his eyeglasses off and wipe them with his handkerchief while Jamie explained what had happened to the poor creature. "He was hit by a car, Dr. Rawlings. I think it was in the Lord's plan to have me find him and try to save him. You'll help me, won't you?"

With Jamie everything was in the Lord's plan. That was another thing. She always mentioned the Lord's plan whenever you talked to her, no matter what the subject. The baseball game's rained out? Must be the Lord's plan to prevent something worse from happening. A surprise trigonometry quiz that everyone in class fails? Must be in the Lord's plan to give us challenges. Anyway, you get the picture.

Then, of course, there was the whole Hegbert situation. Being the minister's daughter couldn't have been easy, but she made it seem like it was the most natural thing in the world and like she was lucky to have been blessed in that way. That's how she used to say it too. "I've been so blessed to have a father like mine." Whenever she said it, all we could do was shake our heads and wonder what planet she actually came from.

Despite all these other strikes, though, the one thing that *really* drove me crazy about her was the fact that she was always so cheerful, no matter what was happening around her. I swear that girl never said a bad thing about anyone, even to those of us who weren't that nice to her. She would hum to herself as she walked down the street; she would wave to strangers driving by in their cars. Sometimes ladies would come running out of their house if they saw her walking by, offering her lemonade or, if they'd been baking, pumpkin bread. It seemed as if every adult in town adored her. "She's such a nice young lady," they'd say.

I was thinking about all this while Jamie stood in front of us on the first day of drama class, and I admit that I wasn't much interested in seeing her. But strangely, when Jamie turned to face us, I kind of got a shock. She wore a plaid skirt with a white blouse under the same brown cardigan I'd seen a million times, but there were two new bumps on her chest that I swore hadn't been there just three months earlier. She'd never worn makeup, and she still didn't, but she had a tan, probably from Bible school, and for the first time she looked—well, almost pretty. Of course, I dismissed that thought right away, but as she looked around the room, she stopped and smiled right at me, obviously glad to see that I was in the class. It wasn't until later that I would learn why.

AFTER HIGH SCHOOL I PLANNED to go to the University of North Carolina at Chapel Hill. My father wanted me to go to Harvard or Princeton like some of the sons of other Congressmen did, but with my grades it wasn't possible. Not that I was a bad student. I just didn't focus on my studies, and my grades weren't exactly up to snuff for the Ivy Leagues. By my senior year it was pretty much touch and go whether I'd even get accepted at U.N.C., and this was my father's alma mater, a place where he could pull some strings. During one of his few weekends home my father came up with the plan to put me over the top. I'd just finished my first week of school, and we were sitting down for dinner. He was home for three days on account of Labor Day weekend.

"I think you should run for student body president," he said. "You'll be graduating in June, and I think it would look good on your record. Your mother thinks so too, by the way."

My mother nodded as she chewed a mouthful of peas. Sometimes I think she liked to see me squirm, even though she was sweet.

"I don't have a chance at winning," I said. Though I was probably the richest kid in school, I was by no means the most popular. That honor belonged to Eric Hunter, my best friend. He'd led the football team to back-to-back state titles as the star quarterback. He was a stud. Even his name sounded cool.

"Of course you can win," my father said. "We Carters always win."

"But what if I don't want to?"

My father put his fork down and looked crossly at me. He was wearing a suit, though it was over eighty degrees in the house, and it made him even more intimidating. My father always wore a suit, by the way.

"I think," he said slowly, "that it would be a good idea."

I knew that when he talked that way, the issue was settled. That's the way it was in my family. My father's word was law. But the fact was, even after I agreed, I didn't want to do it. I didn't want to waste my afternoons meeting with teachers after school—after school!—every week for the rest of the year, dreaming up themes for school dances or trying to decide what colors the streamers should be. That's really all the class presidents did, at least back when I was in high school.

But then again, I knew my father had a point. If I wanted to go to U.N.C., I had to do something. I didn't play football or basketball. I didn't play an instrument. I didn't excel in the classroom. Hell, I didn't excel at much of anything. Growing despondent, I started listing the things I actually could do, but to be honest, there really wasn't that much. I could tie eight different types of sailing knots. I could walk barefoot across hot asphalt farther than anyone I knew. I could balance a pencil vertically on my finger for thirty seconds—but I didn't think that any of those things would really stand out on a college application. So there I was, lying in bed all night long, slowly coming to the sinking realization that I was a loser. Thanks, Dad.

The next morning I went to the principal's office and added my name to the list of candidates. There were two other people running—John Foreman and Maggie Brown. John was the kind of guy who'd pick lint off your clothes while he talked to you. He was a good student and raised his hand every time the teacher asked a question. If he was called to give the answer, he would almost always give the right one, and he'd turn his head from side to side with a smug look on his face, as if proving how superior his intellect was when compared to the other peons in the room. John didn't stand a chance. I knew that right off.

Maggie Brown was another matter. She was a good student as well. She'd been the junior class president the year before. The only real strike against her was the fact that she wasn't very attractive, and she'd put on another twenty pounds that summer. I knew that not a single guy would vote for her.

After seeing the competition, I figured that I might have a chance after all. My entire future was on the line here, so I formulated my strategy. Eric was the first to agree.

"Sure, I'll get all the guys on the team to vote for you."

"How about their girlfriends too?" I asked.

That was pretty much my entire campaign. Of course, I went to the debates, and I passed out those corny WHAT I'LL DO IF I'M ELECTED PRESIDENT flyers, but it was Eric Hunter who probably got me where I needed to be. Beaufort High had only about four hundred students, so getting the athletic vote was critical. In the end it worked out just the way I planned.

I was voted student body president by a fairly large majority. I had no idea what trouble it would eventually lead me to.

Chapter Two

When I was a junior, I went steady with a girl named Angela Clark. She was my first real girlfriend, though it lasted for only a few months. Just before school let out for the summer, she dumped me for a guy named Lew who was twenty years old and worked as a mechanic in his father's garage. His primary attribute, as far as I could tell, was that he had a really nice car. He always wore a white T-shirt with a pack of Camels folded into the sleeve, and he'd lean against the hood of his Thunderbird, looking back and forth, saying things like, "Hey, baby," whenever a woman walked by. He was a real winner, if you know what I mean.

Well anyway, the homecoming dance was coming up, and because of the whole Angela situation I still didn't have a date. Everyone on the student council had to attend—it was mandatory. I had to help decorate the gym and had to clean up the next day—and besides, it was usually a pretty good time. I called a couple of girls I knew, but they already had dates. By the final week the pickings were getting pretty slim. The pool was down to the kinds of girls who had thick glasses and talked with lisps, but then again, I had to find somebody. I didn't want to go to the dance without a date. What would that look like? I'd be the only student body president ever to attend the homecoming dance alone. I'd end up being the guy scooping punch all night or mopping up the barf in the bathroom. That's what people without dates usually did.

Growing panicky, I pulled out the yearbook from the year before and started flipping through the pages, looking for anyone who might not have a date. First I looked through the pages with the seniors. Though a lot of them were off at college, there were still a few around town. Even though I didn't think I had much of a chance with them, I called anyway, and sure enough, I was proved right. I couldn't find anyone who would go with me. I was getting pretty good at rejection, I'll tell you. My mom knew what I was going through, and she finally came into my room and sat down on the bed beside me.

"If you can't get a date, I'll go with you," she said.

"Thanks, Mom," I said dejectedly.

When she left the room, I felt even worse than I had before. Even my mom didn't think I could find somebody.

There was another guy in my boat, by the way. Carey Dennison had been elected treasurer, and he still didn't have a date either. Carey was the kind of guy no one wanted to spend time with, and the only reason he'd been elected was because he'd run unopposed. He played the tuba in the marching band, and his body looked all out of proportion, as if he'd stopped growing halfway through puberty. He had a great big stomach and gangly arms and legs. He also had a high-pitched way of talking, and he never stopped asking questions. Where did you go last weekend? Was it fun? Did you see any girls? He wouldn't even wait for an answer, and he'd move around constantly as he asked, so you had to keep turning your head to keep him in sight. I swear he was probably the most annoying person I'd ever met. If I didn't get a date, he'd stand off on one side all night long, firing questions like some deranged prosecutor.

So there I was, flipping through the pages in the junior class section of the yearbook, when I saw Jamie Sullivan's picture. I paused for just a second, then turned the page, cursing myself for even thinking about it. I spent the next hour searching for anyone halfway decent-looking, but there wasn't anyone left. I finally turned back to her picture. She isn't bad-looking, I told myself, and she's really sweet. She'd probably say yes.

I closed the yearbook. Jamie Sullivan? Hegbert's daughter? No way. Absolutely not. My friends would roast me alive. But compared with dating your mother or cleaning up puke?

I spent the rest of the evening debating the pros and cons of my dilemma, but in the end the choice was obvious even to me. I had to ask Jamie to the dance, and I paced around the room thinking of the best way to ask her.

It was then that I realized something terrible, something absolutely frightening. Carey Dennison was probably doing the exact same thing I was doing right now. He was probably looking through the yearbook too! He was weird, but he wasn't the kind of guy who liked cleaning up puke either. What if he asked Jamie first? Jamie wouldn't say no to him, and realistically, she was the only option he had. No one besides her would be caught dead with him. Jamie would probably listen to Carey's squeaky voice, see the goodness radiating from his heart, and accept right off the bat.

So there I was, sitting in my room, frantic with the possibility that Jamie might not go to the dance with me. I barely slept that night, I tell you. I'd planned to ask her first thing in the morning, while I still had my courage, but she wasn't in school. I assumed she was working with the orphans over in Morehead City, like she did every month. A few of us had tried to get out of school using that excuse too, but Jamie was the only one who ever got away with it. Even the principal knew she was reading to them or doing crafts with them. She wasn't sneaking out to the beach or hanging out at Cecil's Diner or anything.

"Got a date yet?" Eric asked me in between classes. He knew very well that I didn't, but even though he was my friend, he liked to stick it to me once in a while.

"Not yet," I said, "but I'm working on it."

Down the hall, Carey Dennison was reaching into his locker. I swear he shot me a beady glare when he thought I wasn't looking. That's the kind of day it was.

The minutes ticked by slowly during my final class. The way I figured it, if Carey and I got out at the same time, I'd be able to get to her house first. I started to psych myself up, and when the bell rang, I took off from school running at a full clip. I was flying for about a hundred yards or so, and then the cramp set in. Pretty soon all I could do was walk, but that cramp really started to get to me, and I had to bend over and hold my side while I kept moving. As I made my way through Beaufort, I looked like a wheezing version of the Hunchback of Notre Dame.

I thought I heard Carey's high-pitched laughter behind me. I turned around, digging my fingers into my gut to stifle the pain, but I couldn't see him. Maybe he was cutting through someone's backyard. He was sneaky, that guy. You couldn't trust him for a minute.

I started to stumble along even faster, and pretty soon I reached Jamie's street. I was sweating all over and wheezing something fierce. I reached her front door, took a second to catch my breath, and knocked. Despite my fevered rush to her house, my pessimistic side assumed that Carey would be the one who opened the door for me. I imagined him smiling at me with a victorious look in his eye.

But it wasn't Carey who answered, it was Jamie, and for the first time in my life I saw what she'd look like if she were an ordinary person. She was wearing jeans and a red blouse, and though her hair was still pulled up into a bun, she looked more casual than she usually did. I realized she could actually be cute if she gave herself the opportunity.

"Landon," she said as she held the door open, "this is a surprise! You look like you've been exercising."

"Not really," I lied. Luckily, the cramp was fading fast.

"You've sweat clean through your shirt."

"Oh, that?" I looked at my shirt. "That's nothing. I just sweat a lot sometimes."

"Maybe you should have it checked by a doctor."

"I'll be okay, I'm sure."

"I'll say a prayer for you anyway," she offered as she smiled. Jamie was always praying for someone.

"Thanks," I said.

She looked down and sort of shuffled her feet for a moment. "Well, I'd invite you in, but my father isn't home, and he doesn't allow boys in the house while he's not around."

"Oh," I said dejectedly. "That's okay. We can talk out here, I guess." If I'd had my way, I would have done this inside.

"Would you like some lemonade while we sit?" she asked.

"I'd love some," I said.

"I'll be right back." She walked into the house, but she left the door open, and I took a quick glance around. The house, I noticed, was small but tidy, with a piano that sat against one wall and a sofa against the other. A small fan sat oscillating in the corner. On the coffee table there were books with names like *Listening to Jesus,* and *Faith Is the Answer.*

A moment later Jamie returned with the lemonade, and we took a seat in two chairs near the corner of the porch. She and her father sat there in the evenings, I knew, from passing by their house now and then. As soon as we were seated, I saw Mrs. Hastings, her neighbor across the street, wave to us. Jamie waved back while I sort of scooted my chair so that Mrs. Hastings couldn't see my face. Even though I was going to ask Jamie to the dance, I didn't want anyone—even Mrs. Hastings—to see me there, on the off chance that Jamie had already accepted Carey's offer. It was one thing to actually go with Jamie; it was another thing to be rejected by her in favor of a guy like Carey.

"What are you doing?" Jamie asked me. "You're moving your chair into the sun."

"I like the sun," I said. Almost immediately I could feel the rays burning through my shirt and making me sweat again.

"If that's what you want," she said, smiling. "So what did you want to talk to me about?" She reached up and started to adjust her hair.

I took a deep breath, trying to gather myself, but I couldn't force myself to come out with it just yet. "So," I said instead, "you were at the orphanage today?"

Jamie looked at me curiously. "No. My father and I were at the doctor's office."

"Is he okay?"

She smiled. "Healthy as can be."

I nodded and glanced across the street. Mrs. Hastings had gone back inside, and I couldn't see anyone else in the vicinity. The coast was finally clear, but I still wasn't ready. "Sure is a beautiful day," I said, stalling.

"Yes, it is."

"Warm too."

"That's because you're in the sun."

I looked around, feeling the pressure building. "Why, I'll bet there's not a single cloud in the whole sky."

This time Jamie didn't respond, and we sat in silence a moment.

"Landon," she finally said, "you didn't come here to talk about the weather, did you?"

"Not really."

"Then why are you here?"

The moment of truth had arrived. "Well . . . I wanted to know if you were going to the homecoming dance."

"Oh," she said, her tone making it seem as if she were unaware that such a thing existed. "I really hadn't planned on going."

"But if someone asked you to go, you might?"

It took a moment for her to answer. "I'm not sure," she finally said. "I suppose I might go if I got the chance. I've never been to a homecoming dance before."

"They're fun," I said quickly. "Not *too* much fun, but fun."

She smiled at my turn of phrase. "I'd have to talk to my father, of course, but if he said it was okay, then I guess I could."

In the tree beside the porch a bird started to chirp noisily. I concentrated on the sound, trying to calm my nerves. Just two days ago I couldn't imagine myself even thinking about it, but suddenly there I was, listening to myself as I spoke the magic words.

"Well, would you like to go to the dance with me?"

I could tell Jamie was surprised by my question. Instead of

answering right away, though, she glanced away for a long moment. I got a sinking feeling in my stomach because I assumed she was going to say no. Visions of my mother, puke, and Carey Dennison flooded through my mind, and all of a sudden I regretted the way I'd behaved toward her all these years. I kept remembering the times I'd teased her or made fun of her behind her back. Just when I was feeling awful about the whole thing and imagining how I would ever be able to avoid Carey for five hours, she turned and faced me again.

She had a slight smile on her face. "I'd love to," she finally said, "on one condition."

I steadied myself, hoping it wasn't something *too* awful. "Yes?"

"You have to promise that you won't fall in love with me."

I knew she was kidding by the way she laughed, and I couldn't help but breathe a sigh of relief. Sometimes Jamie had a pretty good sense of humor. I smiled and gave her my word.

EVEN though Jamie hadn't been to a homecoming dance, she had been to church dances before. She wasn't a bad dancer—I'd gone to a few of those dances too and had seen her—but to be honest, it was fairly hard to judge how she'd do with someone like me. At the church dances she always danced with old people because no one her age would ask her, and she was real good at dances that were popular about thirty years ago. Frankly, I didn't know what to expect.

I admit that I also had some concerns about what she would wear. When Jamie went to the church dances, she usually wore an old sweater and one of the plaid skirts we saw in school every day, but the homecoming dance was supposed to be special. Most of the girls bought new dresses, and the boys wore suits. I knew Jamie wasn't going to buy a new dress, because she wasn't exactly well off. Ministering wasn't a profession where people made a lot of money, but of course ministers weren't in it for the monetary gain; they were in it for the long haul, if you know what I mean. But I didn't want her to wear the same thing she wore to school either. Not so much for me—I'm not that coldhearted—but because of what others might say. I didn't want people to make fun of her or anything.

The good news, if there was any, was that Eric didn't rib me too bad about the whole Jamie situation, because he was too busy thinking about his own date. He was taking Margaret Hays, the head cheerleader at our school. She wasn't the brightest bulb on the Christmas tree, but she was nice in her own way. By nice, of course, I'm talking about her legs. Eric offered to double-date, but I turned him down because I didn't want to take any chances with Eric teasing Jamie. He was a good guy, but he could be kind of heartless sometimes, especially when he had a few shots of bourbon in him.

The day of the dance was actually quite busy for me. I spent most of the afternoon helping to decorate the gym, and I had to get to Jamie's about a half hour early because her father wanted to talk to me. Jamie had sprung that one on me just the day before, and I can't say I was exactly thrilled by the prospect. I figured he was going to talk about temptation and the evil path it can lead us to. If he brought up fornication, though, I knew I would die right there on the spot. I said small prayers all day long in the hopes of avoiding this conversation, but I wasn't sure if God would put my prayers on the front burner, because of the way I'd behaved in the past.

After I showered, I put on my best suit, swung by the florist to pick up Jamie's corsage, then drove to her house. My mom had let me borrow the car. I parked it on the street in front of Jamie's house and strolled up the walkway to her door. I knocked and waited for a moment. I heard Hegbert say, "I'll be right there," but he wasn't exactly racing to the door. I must have stood there for two minutes, looking at the door, the moldings, the little cracks in the windowsills.

Finally the door creaked open. The light coming from the lamp inside shadowed Hegbert's face slightly. He was old, seventy-two by my reckoning. It was the first time I'd ever seen him up close, and I could see all the wrinkles on his face. His skin really was translucent, even more so than I imagined.

"Hello, Reverend," I said, swallowing my trepidation. "I'm here to take Jamie to the homecoming dance."

"Of course," he said. "But first I wanted to talk with you."

"Yes, sir. That's why I came early."

"C'mon in."

In church Hegbert was a fairly snappy dresser, but right now, dressed in overalls and a T-shirt, he looked like a farmer. He motioned for me to sit on the wooden chair he'd brought in from the kitchen. "I'm sorry it took a little while to open the door. I was working on tomorrow's sermon," he said.

I sat down. "That's okay, sir." I don't know why, but you just had to call him sir. He sort of projected that image.

"All right then, so tell me about yourself."

I thought it was a fairly ridiculous question, him having such a long history with my family and all. He was also the one who baptized me, by the way, and he'd seen me in church every Sunday since I'd been a baby.

"Well, sir," I began, "I'm the student body president. I don't know whether Jamie mentioned that to you."

He nodded. "She did. Go on."

"And . . . well, I hope to go to the University of North Carolina next fall. I've already received the application."

He nodded again. "Anything else?"

I had to admit I was running out of things after that. Part of me wanted to pick up the pencil off the end table and start balancing it, giving him the whole thirty seconds' worth, but he wasn't the kind of guy who would appreciate it.

"I guess not, sir."

"Do you mind if I ask you a question?"

"No, sir."

He sort of stared at me for a long time, as if thinking about it. "Why did you ask my daughter to the dance?" he finally said.

I was surprised, and I know that my expression showed it. "I don't know what you mean, sir."

"You're not planning to . . . embarrass her, are you?"

"No, sir," I said quickly, shocked by the accusation. "I needed someone to go with, and I asked her. It's as simple as that."

"You don't have any pranks planned?"

"No, sir. I wouldn't do that to her. . . ."

This went on for a couple more minutes—his grilling me about my true intentions, I mean—but luckily, Jamie stepped out of the back room, and both of us turned our heads at the same moment. Hegbert finally stopped talking, and I breathed a sigh of relief. She'd put on a nice blue skirt and a white blouse I'd never seen before. Thankfully, she'd left her sweater in the closet. What she was wearing wasn't too bad, I had to admit, though I knew she'd still be underdressed compared to others at the dance. As always, her hair was pulled up in a bun. Personally, I think it would have looked better if she'd kept it down, but that was the last thing I wanted to say. Jamie looked . . . well, exactly like she usually did, but at least she wasn't bringing her Bible. That would have just been too much to live down.

"You're not giving Landon a hard time, are you?" she said cheerfully to her father.

"We were just visiting," I said quickly, before he had a chance to respond.

"Well, we should probably go," Jamie said after a moment. I think she sensed the tension in the room. She walked over to her father and kissed him on the cheek. "Don't stay up too late working on the sermon, okay?"

"I won't," he said softly. I could tell he really loved her and wasn't afraid to show it, even with me in the room. It was how he felt about me that was the problem.

We said good-bye, and on our way to the car I handed Jamie her corsage and told her I'd show her how to put it on once we got in the car. I opened the door for her and walked around the other side, then got in as well. In that short period of time Jamie had already pinned on the flower.

"I'm not exactly a dimwit, you know," she said. "I do know how pin on a corsage."

I started the car, and we headed toward the high school, the conversation I'd just had with her father running through my mind.

"My father doesn't like you very much," she said, as if knowing what I was thinking.

I nodded without saying anything.

"He thinks you're irresponsible, and he doesn't like your father much either."

I nodded again.

"Or your family."

I get the picture.

"But do you know what I think?" she asked suddenly.

"Not really." By then I was pretty depressed.

"I think that all this was in the Lord's plan somehow. What do you think the message is?"

Here we go, I thought.

I DOUBT if the evening could have been much worse. Most of my friends kept their distance, and Jamie didn't have many friends to begin with, so we spent most of our time alone. Even worse, it turned out that my presence wasn't even required anymore. They'd changed the rule, owing to the fact that Carey couldn't get a date, and that left me feeling pretty miserable about the whole thing. But because of what her father had said to me, I couldn't exactly take Jamie home early, now could I? And more than that, she was really having a good time. She loved the decorations I'd helped put up; she loved the music; she loved everything about the dance. She asked me whether I might help her decorate the church someday for one of their dances. I mumbled that she should call me, and even though I said it without a trace of energy, Jamie thanked me for being so considerate. To be honest, I was depressed for at least the first hour, though she didn't seem to notice.

Jamie had to be home by eleven o'clock, an hour before the dance ended, which made it somewhat easier for me to handle. Once the music started, we hit the floor, and it turned out that she was a pretty good dancer—even better than some of the others—and that helped to pass the time. She followed my lead pretty well through about a dozen songs, and after that we headed to the tables and had what resembled an ordinary conversation. Sure, she threw in words like faith and joy and even salvation, and she talked about helping the orphans, but she was so darn happy it was hard to stay down for long.

So things weren't too terrible at first. It wasn't until Lew, Angela's boyfriend, showed up that everything really went sour.

He was wearing that stupid T-shirt again, Camels in his sleeve, and a gop of hair gel on his head. Angela was hanging all over him, and it didn't take a genius to realize she'd had a few drinks. Her dress was really flashy, and I noticed she'd picked up that ladylike habit called chewing gum. She really worked that gum, chewing it almost like a cow working her cud.

Well, good old Lew spiked the punch bowl, and a few more people started getting tipsy as well. By the time the teachers found out, most of the punch was already gone, and people were getting those glassy looks in their eyes, though you could tell that it would wear off in a while. With Angela, though, one more drink was all it would take, and when I saw her gobble up her second glass of punch, I knew I should keep my eye out for her.

Even though she'd dumped me, I didn't want anything bad to happen to her. She was the first girl I'd ever French-kissed, and I still had feelings for her.

So there I was, sitting with Jamie, barely listening as she described the wonders of Bible school, watching Angela out of the corner of my eye, when Lew spotted me looking at her. In one frenzied motion he grabbed Angela and dragged her over to the table, giving me one of those looks that means business. You know the one I'm talking about.

"Are you staring at my girl?" he asked, already tensing up.

"No."

"Yeah, he was," Angela said, kind of slurring out the words. "He's my old boyfriend, the one I told you about."

Lew's eyes turned into little slits. "So you're the one," he said.

Now, I'm not much of a fighter. Usually I didn't have much trouble staying away from things like this because of my passive nature, and besides, no one ever messed with me when Eric was around. But Eric was off with Margaret, probably behind the bleachers, and was nowhere to be seen.

"I wasn't staring," I said finally, "and I don't know what she told you, but I doubt if it was true."

Lew's eyes narrowed. "Are you calling Angela a liar?"

I think he would have hit me right there, but Jamie suddenly worked her way into the situation. "Don't I know you?" she said cheerfully, looking right at him. Sometimes Jamie seemed oblivious to situations that were happening right in front of her. "Wait—yes, I do. You work in the garage downtown. Your father's name is Joe, and your grandma lives out on Foster Road by the railroad crossing."

A look of confusion crossed Lew's face. "How do you know all that? What'd he do, tell you about me too?"

"No," Jamie said. "Don't be silly. I saw your picture in your grandma's house. I was walking by, and she needed some help bringing in the groceries. Your picture was on the mantel."

Lew was looking at Jamie like she had cornstalks growing out of her ears.

Meanwhile, Jamie was fanning herself with her hand. "Well, we were just sitting down to take a breather from all that dancing. It sure gets hot out there. Would you like to join us? I'd love to hear how your grandma is doing."

She sounded so happy about it that Lew didn't know what to do. Unlike those of us who were used to Jamie, he'd never come across someone like her before. He stood there for a moment or two, as if trying to decide whether to hit the guy who was with the girl who'd helped his grandma. He finally skulked off without responding, taking Angela with him.

Jamie and I watched him go, and when he was a safe distance away, I exhaled. I hadn't even realized I'd been holding my breath.

"Thanks," I mumbled sheepishly, realizing that Jamie—Jamie!—was the one who'd saved me from grave bodily harm.

Jamie looked at me strangely. "For what?" she asked, and when I didn't exactly spell it out for her, she went right back into her story about Bible school, as if nothing had happened at all. But this time I found myself actually listening to her, at least with one of my ears. It was the least I could do.

It turns out that it wasn't the last we saw of either Lew or Angela that evening. The two glasses of punch had really done Angela in, and she threw up all over the ladies' rest room. Lew, being the classy guy he was, left when he heard her retching, sort of slinking out the way he came in, and that was the last I saw of him. Jamie, as fate would have it, was the one who found Angela in the bathroom, and even to her it was obvious that Angela wasn't doing too well. The only option was to clean her up and take her home before the teachers found out about it. Getting drunk was a big deal back then, and Angela'd be looking at suspension, maybe even expulsion, if she got caught.

Jamie, bless her heart, didn't want that to happen any more than I did, and she took immediate charge of the situation. The two of us eventually located Eric behind the bleachers, and he agreed to stand guard at the bathroom door while Jamie and I went in to tidy it up. Angela had done a marvelous job, I tell you. The puke was everywhere—the walls, the floor, the sinks. So there I was, perched on all fours, cleaning up puke at the homecoming dance in my best blue suit, which was exactly what I had wanted to avoid in the first place. And Jamie, my date, was on all fours too, doing exactly the same thing.

I could practically hear Carey Dennison laughing a squeaky, maniacal laugh somewhere in the distance.

We ended up sneaking out the back door of the gym, keeping Angela stable by walking on either side of her. She kept asking where Lew was, but Jamie told her not to worry. She had a real soothing way of talking to Angela, though Angela was so far gone I doubt if she even knew who was speaking. We loaded Angela into the back seat of my car, where she passed out almost immediately. When we got to her house, her mother answered the door, took one look at her daughter, and brought her inside without so much as a word of thanks. I think she was embarrassed, and we really didn't have much to say to her. The situation pretty much spoke for itself.

By the time we dropped Angela off, it was ten forty-five, and we drove straight to Jamie's. I was really worried when we got there, because of the way she looked and smelled, and I said a silent prayer hoping that Hegbert wasn't awake. I didn't want to have to explain this to him. Oh, he'd probably listen to Jamie if she was the one who told him about it, but I had the sinking feeling that he'd find a way to blame me anyway.

So I walked her to the door, and we stood outside under the porch light. Jamie crossed her arms and smiled a little, looking just like she'd come in from an evening stroll.

"Please don't tell your father about this," I asked.

"I won't," she said. "I had a good time tonight. Thank you for taking me to the dance."

Here she was, covered in puke, thanking me for the evening. Jamie Sullivan could really drive a guy crazy sometimes.

Chapter Three

In the two weeks following the homecoming dance my life pretty much returned to normal. My father was back in Washington, D.C., which made things a lot more fun around my house, primarily because I could sneak out the window and head back to the graveyard for my late-night forays. I don't know what it was about the graveyard that attracted us so. Maybe it had something to do with the tombstones themselves, because as far as tombstones went, they were fairly comfortable to sit on.

We usually sat in a small plot where the Preston family had been buried about a hundred years ago. There were eight tombstones there, all arranged in a circle, making it easy to pass the boiled peanuts back and forth between us.

Well, Eric and I were out there one Saturday night with a couple of other friends, eating boiled peanuts and talking, when Eric asked me how my "date" with Jamie Sullivan went. He and I hadn't seen much of each other since the homecoming dance, because the football season was already in the play-offs and Eric had been out of town the past couple weekends.

"It was okay," I said, shrugging, doing my best to play it cool.

Eric playfully elbowed me in the ribs. "Did you kiss her?"

"No."

He took a long drink from his can of Budweiser as I answered. I don't know how he did it, but Eric never had trouble buying beer, which was strange, being that everyone in town knew how old he was.

He wiped his lips with the back of his hand, tossing me a sidelong glance. "I would have thought that after she helped you clean the bathroom, you would have at least kissed her good night."

"Well, I didn't."

"Why not?"

"She's not that kind of girl," I said, and even though we all knew it was true, it still sounded like I was defending her.

Eric latched on to that like a leech. "I think you like her," he said. "I think you're smitten."

I knew we were treading on dangerous ground. "I was just using her to impress Margaret," I said. "And with all the love notes she's been sending me lately, I reckon it must have worked."

Eric laughed aloud, slapping me on the back again. "You and Margaret—now *that's* funny."

I knew I'd just dodged a major bullet, and I breathed a sigh of relief as the conversation spun off in a new direction. I joined in now and then, but I wasn't really listening to what they were saying. Instead, I kept hearing this little voice inside me that made me wonder about what Eric had implied.

The thing was, Jamie was probably the best date I could have had that night, especially considering how the evening turned out. Not many dates would have done what she did. At the same time, her being a good date didn't mean I liked her. I hadn't talked to her since the dance, except when I saw her in drama class. If I liked her at all, I told myself, I would have wanted to talk to her. If I liked her, I would have offered to walk her home. If I liked her, I would have wanted to bring her to Cecil's Diner for a basket of hush puppies and some RC Cola. But I didn't want to do any of those things. I really didn't. In my mind I'd already served my penance.

THE next day, Sunday, I was in my room working on my application to U.N.C. They required five essays of the usual type: If you could meet one person in history, who would that person be and why? Name the most significant influence in your life and why you feel that way. What do you look for in a role model and why? The questions were fairly predictable—our English teacher had told us what to expect—and I'd worked on a couple of variations in class.

English was probably my best subject. I've never received anything lower than an A in it since I started school, and I was glad the emphasis for the application was on writing. If it had been on math, I might have been in trouble. It wasn't that I was bad in math—I usually pulled at least a C—but it didn't come naturally to me, if you know what I mean.

So I was writing one of my essays when the phone rang. The only phone we had was in the kitchen, and I had to run downstairs to grab the receiver. I was breathing so loud that I couldn't make out the voice too well, though it sounded like Angela. I smiled to myself. Even though she'd been sick all over the place and I'd had to clean it up, she was actually pretty fun to be around. I figured she was probably calling to thank me or even to get together for a barbecue sandwich or something.

"Landon?"

"Oh, hey," I said, playing it cool. "What's going on?"

There was a short pause on the other end. "How are you?"

It was then that I realized I wasn't speaking to Angela. Instead, it was Jamie, and I can't say that I was happy about hearing from her. I almost dropped the phone.

"Landon?"

"I'm fine," I finally blurted out, still in shock.

"Are you busy?" she asked.

"Sort of."

"Oh . . . I see. . . ." she said, trailing off. She paused again, and it took her a few seconds to get the words out. "I just wanted to know if you wouldn't mind coming by later this afternoon."

"Coming by?"

"Yes. To my house."

"Your house?" I didn't even try to disguise the growing surprise in my voice.

Jamie ignored it and went on. "There's something I want to talk to you about. I wouldn't ask if it wasn't important."

"Can't you just tell me over the phone?"

"I'd rather not."

"Well, I'm working on my essays all afternoon."

"Oh . . . well. Like I said, it's important, but I suppose I can talk to you Monday at school."

I suddenly realized that she wasn't going to let me off the hook and that we'd end up talking one way or the other. My brain clicked through the scenarios as I tried to figure out which one I should do—talk to her where my friends would see us or talk at her house. Though neither option was particularly good, there was something in the back of my mind reminding me that she'd helped me out when I'd needed it, and the least I could do was to listen to what she had to say. I may be irresponsible, but I'm a *nice* irresponsible, if I do say so myself. Of course, that didn't mean everyone else had to know about it.

"No," I said. "Today is fine."

We arranged to meet at five o'clock, and the rest of the afternoon ticked by slowly, like the drips from Chinese water torture. I left home twenty minutes early so I'd have time to get there. My house overlooked the Intracoastal Waterway and was located in the historic part of town, a few doors from where Blackbeard used to live. Jamie lived on the other side of town, across the railroad tracks.

It was November, and the temperature was finally cooling down. One thing I really liked about Beaufort was the fact that the springs and falls lasted practically forever. It might get hot in the summer or snow once every six years, but for the most part all you needed was a light jacket to make it through the winter. Today was one of those perfect days—mid-seventies, without a cloud in the sky.

I made it to Jamie's house right on time and knocked on her door. Jamie answered it, and a quick peek inside showed that Hegbert wasn't around. It wasn't quite warm enough for lemonade, and we sat on the porch again, without anything to drink. The sun was beginning to lower itself in the sky, and there wasn't anyone on the street. This time I didn't have to move my chair. It hadn't been moved since the last time I'd been there.

"Thank you for coming, Landon," she said. "I know you're busy, but I appreciate your taking the time to do this."

"So what's so important?" I said.

Jamie, for the first time since I'd known her, actually looked nervous as she sat with me. She kept bringing her hands together and pulling them apart. "I wanted to ask you a favor," she said seriously.

"A favor?"

She nodded.

At first I thought she was going to ask me to help her decorate the church, like she'd mentioned at homecoming, or maybe, since she didn't have her license yet, she needed me to use my mother's car to bring some stuff to the orphans.

She sighed. "I'd like to ask you if you wouldn't mind playing Tom Thornton in the school play."

Tom Thornton, like I said before, was the man in search of the music box for his daughter—the one who meets the angel. Except for the angel, it was far and away the most important role.

"Well—I don't know," I said, confused. "I thought Eddie Jones was going to be Tom. That's what Miss Garber told us."

Eddie Jones was a lot like Carey Dennison. He was really skinny, with pimples all over his face. He had a nervous tic, and he couldn't help but squinch his eyes whenever he got nervous, which was practically all the time. He'd probably end up spouting his lines like a psychotic blind man if you put him in front of a crowd. To make things worse, he had a stutter too. Miss Garber had given him the role because he'd been the only one who offered to do it.

"Miss Garber didn't say that exactly. What she said was that Eddie could have the role if no one else tried out for it."

"Can't someone else do it instead?"

But there wasn't really anyone else, and I knew it. Because of Hegbert's requirement that only seniors perform, the play was in a bind that year. There were about fifty senior boys at the high school, twenty-two of whom were on the football team, and with the team still in the running for the state title, none of them would have the time to go to the rehearsals. Of the thirty or so that were left, more than half were in the band, and they had after-school practice. A quick calculation showed that there were maybe a dozen other people who could possibly do it.

Now, I didn't want to do the play, and not only because I'd come to realize that drama was just about the most boring class ever invented. The thing was, I'd already taken Jamie to homecoming, and with her as the angel in the play I just couldn't bear the thought that I'd have to spend every afternoon with her for the next month or so. Being seen with her once was bad enough, but being seen with her every day? What would my friends say?

But I could tell this was really important to her. The simple fact that she'd asked made it clear. Jamie never asked anyone for a favor. I think she suspected that deep down no one would ever do her a favor, because of who she was. The very realization made me sad.

"What about Jeff Bangert? He might do it," I offered.

Jamie shook her head. "His father's sick, and he has to work in the store after school until his father gets back on his feet."

"What about Darren Woods?"

"He broke his arm last week. It's in a sling."

"Really? I didn't know that," I said, stalling.

"I've been praying about it, Landon," Jamie said simply, and sighed for the second time. "I'd really like the play to be special this year—not for me, but because of my father. I want it to be the best production ever. I know how much it would mean to him to see me be the angel, because this play reminds him of my mother." She paused, collecting her thoughts. "It would be terrible if the play was a failure this year, especially since I'm involved."

She stopped again before going on, her voice becoming more emotional. "I know Eddie would do the best he could. And I'm not embarrassed to do the play with him—he's a very nice person. But he told me that he's having second thoughts about doing it. Sometimes people at school can be so . . . so cruel, and I don't want Eddie to be hurt. But . . ." She took a deep breath. "But the real reason I'm asking is because of my father. He's such a good man, Landon. If people make fun of his memory of my mother while I'm playing the part . . . well, that would break my heart. And with Eddie and me, you know what people would say."

I nodded, knowing that I would have been one of those people she was talking about. In fact, I already was. Jamie and Eddie, the dynamic duo, we called them after Miss Garber had announced that they'd be the ones doing the roles. The very fact that it was I who had started it up made me feel almost sick to my stomach.

She straightened a little in her seat and looked at me sadly, as if she already knew I was going to say no. She went on. "I know that challenges are always part of the Lord's plan, but I don't want to believe that the Lord is cruel, especially to someone like my father. He devotes his life to God; he gives to the community. And he's already lost his wife and has had to raise me on his own. And I love him so much for it. . . ."

Jamie turned away, and I could see tears in her eyes. It was the first time I'd ever seen her cry, and part of me wanted to cry too.

"I'm not asking you to do it for me," she said softly. "I'm really not, and if you say no, I'll still pray for you. I promise. But if you'd like to do something kind for a wonderful man who means so much to me . . . Will you just think about it?"

Her eyes looked like those of a cocker spaniel that had just messed on the rug.

I looked down at my feet. "I don't have to think about it," I finally said. "I'll do it."

I really didn't have a choice, did I?

THE next day I talked to Miss Garber, went through the audition, and got the part. Eddie, by the way, wasn't upset at all. In fact, I could tell he was actually relieved about the whole thing.

Miss Garber gave him the role of the bum, and we knew he'd do fairly well in that role. The bum, you see, was completely mute, but the angel always knew what he was thinking. At one point in the play she has to tell the mute bum that God will always watch out for him because God especially cares for the poor and downtrodden. That was one of the tip-offs to the audience that she'd been sent from heaven. Like I said earlier, Hegbert wanted it to be real clear who offered redemption and salvation, and it certainly wasn't going to be a few rickety ghosts who just popped up out of nowhere.

Rehearsals started the next week, and we rehearsed in the classroom because the playhouse wouldn't open their doors for us until right before our first performance.

Fortunately, because of all his ministering duties, Hegbert wasn't involved with the actual production of the play. That role fell to Miss Garber, and the first thing she told us to do was to memorize our lines as quickly as possible. We didn't have as much time as was usually allotted for rehearsals, because Thanksgiving came close to the last day in November, and Hegbert didn't want the play to be performed too close to Christmas, so as not to interfere with its true meaning. That left us only three weeks to get the play just right, which was about a week shorter than usual.

The rehearsals began at three o'clock, and Jamie knew all her lines the first day, which wasn't really surprising. What was surprising was that she knew all my lines too, as well as everyone else's. We'd be going over a scene—she'd be doing it without the script—and I'd be looking down at a stack of pages, trying to figure out what my next line should be, and whenever I looked up, she had this real shiny look about her. The only lines I knew were the mute bum's, at least on that first day, and all of a sudden I was actually envious of Eddie, at least in that regard. This was going to be a lot of work—not exactly what I'd expected when I'd signed up for the class.

My noble feelings about doing the play had worn off by the second day of rehearsals. Even though I knew I was doing the right thing, my friends didn't understand it at all, and they'd been riding me. "You're doing what?" Eric said when he learned about it. "You're doing the play with Jamie Sullivan? Are you insane or just plain stupid?" I sort of mumbled that I had a good reason, but he wouldn't let it drop, and he told everyone that I had a crush on her. I denied it, of course, which just made them assume it was true, and they'd laugh all the louder and tell the next person they saw. The stories kept getting wilder too—by lunchtime I'd heard that I was thinking of getting engaged.

I guess that was when I started to resent Jamie again. I know it wasn't her fault, but I was the one who was taking the arrows for Hegbert, who hadn't exactly gone out of his way the night of homecoming to make me feel welcome. I began to stumble through my lines in class for the next few days, not really even attempting to learn them. After rehearsal was over, I'd head home to put the play out of my mind, and I wouldn't even bother to pick up the script. Instead, I'd joke with my friends about the weird things Jamie did and tell fibs about how it was Miss Garber who had forced me into the whole thing.

Jamie, though, wasn't going to let me off that easy. No. She got me right where it hurts, right smack in the old ego.

I was out with Eric on Saturday night, about a week after rehearsals had started. We were hanging out at the waterfront outside of Cecil's Diner, eating hush puppies and watching people cruising in their cars, when I saw Jamie walking down the street. She was a hundred yards away, wearing that old brown sweater again and carrying her Bible. It must have been nine o'clock or so, which was late for her to be out, and it was even stranger to see her in this part of town. I turned my back to her and pulled the collar up on my jacket, but even Margaret—who had banana pudding where her brain should have been—was smart enough to figure out who Jamie was looking for.

"Landon, your girlfriend is here."

"She's not my girlfriend," I said. "I don't have a girlfriend."

"Your fiancée, then."

"I'm not engaged," I said. "Now knock it off."

I glanced over my shoulder to see if Jamie had spotted me, and I guess she had. She was walking toward us. I pretended not to notice.

"Here she comes." Margaret giggled.

I glanced around again, and this time Jamie knew I'd seen her, and she smiled and waved at me. I turned away, and a moment later she was standing right beside me.

"Hello, Landon," she said to me, oblivious to my scorn. "Hello, Eric, Margaret . . ." She went around the group. Everyone sort of mumbled "hello" and tried not to stare at the Bible.

Eric was holding a beer, and he moved it behind his back so she wouldn't see it. Jamie could make even Eric feel guilty. They'd been neighbors at one time, and Eric had been on the receiving end of her talks before. Behind her back he called her the Salvation Lady, in obvious reference to the Salvation Army. But when she was standing right in front of him, it was another story. In his mind she had an in with God, and he didn't want to be in her bad graces.

"How are you doing, Eric? I haven't seen you around much recently." She said this like she still talked to him all the time.

He shifted from one foot to the other and looked at his shoes, playing that guilty look for all it was worth. "Well, I haven't been to church lately," he said.

Jamie smiled that glittery smile. "Well, that's okay, I suppose, as long as it doesn't become a habit or anything."

"It won't."

"You want a beer, Jamie?" Margaret asked. I think she was trying to be funny, but no one laughed.

Jamie put her hand to her hair, tugging gently at her bun. "Oh, no, not really. . . . Thank you, though."

She looked directly at me with a sweet glow, and right away I knew I was in trouble.

"Well, you did really well this week at rehearsals," she said to me. "I know you've got a lot of lines to learn, but I'm sure you'll get them all soon. And I just wanted to thank you for volunteering like you did. You're a real gentleman."

"Thanks," I said, a little pit forming in my stomach. I tried to be cool, but all my friends were looking right at me, suddenly wondering if I'd been telling them the truth about Miss Garber forcing it on me and everything. I hoped they missed it.

"Your friends should be proud of you," Jamie added, putting that thought to rest.

"Oh, we are," Eric said, pouncing. "Very proud. He's a good guy, that Landon, what with his volunteering and all."

Oh, no.

Jamie smiled at him, then turned back to me again, her old cheerful self. "I also wanted to tell you that if you need any help, you can come by anytime. We can sit on the porch like we did before and go over your lines if you need to."

I saw Eric mouth the words "like we did before" to Margaret. This really wasn't going well at all. By now the pit in my stomach was as big as Paul Bunyan's bowling ball.

"That's okay," I mumbled, wondering how I could squirm my way out of this. "I can learn them at home."

"Well, sometimes it helps if someone's there to read with you, Landon," Eric offered.

I told you he'd stick it to me, even though he was my friend.

"No, really," I said to him. "I'll learn the lines on my own."

"Maybe," Eric said, smiling, "you two should practice in front of the orphans once you've got it down a little better. Sort of a dress rehearsal, you know? I'm sure they'd love to see it."

You could practically see Jamie's mind start clicking at the mention of orphans. "Do you think so?" she asked.

Eric nodded. "I'm sure of it. Landon was the one who thought of it first, but I know that if I was an orphan, I'd love something like that, even if it wasn't exactly the real thing."

"Me too," Margaret piped in.

As they spoke, the only thing I could think about was that scene from *Julius Caesar* where Brutus stabs him in the back. *Et tu, Eric?*

"It was Landon's idea?" Jamie asked, furrowing her brow. She looked at me, and I could tell she was still mulling it over.

But Eric wasn't about to let me off the hook that easy. "You'd like to do that, wouldn't you, Landon?" he said. "Helping the orphans, I mean."

It wasn't exactly something you could answer no to, was it?

"I reckon so," I said, staring at my best friend.

"Good, then. It's all settled. That's if it's okay with you, Jamie." Eric's smile was so sweet it could have flavored half the RC Cola in the county.

"Well . . . Yes, I suppose. I'll have to talk to Miss Garber and the director of the orphanage, but if they say it's okay, I think it would be a fine idea." And the thing was, you could tell she was really happy about it.

The next day I spent fourteen hours memorizing my lines, cursing my friends, and wondering how my life had spun so out of control.

CHAPTER FOUR

The first thing we did was talk to Miss Garber about our plans for the orphans, and she thought it was a marvelous idea. That was her favorite word, by the way—marvelous. When she'd realized that I knew all my lines on Monday, she said, "Marvelous," and for the next two hours, whenever I'd finish up a scene, she'd say it again. By the end of the rehearsal on Monday I'd heard it about four zillion times.

Jamie, meanwhile, was getting really excited about performing for the orphans. During a break in rehearsals she pulled me aside and thanked me for thinking of them. "There's no way you would know," she said almost conspiratorially, "but I've been wondering what to do for the orphanage this year. I've been praying about it for months now because I want this Christmas to be the most special one of all."

"Why is this Christmas so important?" I asked her.

She smiled patiently, as if I'd asked a question that didn't really matter. "It just is," she said simply.

The next step was to talk it over with Mr. Jenkins, the director of the orphanage. Now, I'd never met Mr. Jenkins before, being that the orphanage was in Morehead City, which was across the bridge from Beaufort, and I'd never had any reason to go there. When Jamie surprised me with the news the following day that we'd be meeting him later that evening, I was sort of worried that I wasn't dressed nice enough. I know it was an orphanage, but a guy wants to make a good impression. Even though I wasn't as excited about it as Jamie was (no one was as excited as Jamie), I didn't want to be regarded as the Grinch who ruined Christmas for the orphans.

Before we went to the orphanage for our meeting, we had to walk to my house to pick up my mom's car, and while there I planned on changing into something a little nicer. The walk took about ten minutes, and Jamie didn't say much along the way, at least until we got to my neighborhood. The homes around mine were all large and well kept, and she asked who lived where and how old the houses were. I answered her questions without much thought, but when I opened the front door to my house, I suddenly realized how different this world was compared to her own. She had a shocked expression on her face as she looked around. No doubt it was the fanciest home she'd ever been in. A moment later I saw her eyes travel to the paintings that lined the walls. My ancestors. As with many southern families, my entire lineage could be traced in the dozen faces that lined the walls. She stared at them, looking for a resemblance, I think, then turned her attention to the furnishings. The furniture had been handmade, carved from mahogany and cherry and designed specifically for each room. It *was* nice, I had to admit, but it wasn't something I really thought about. To me it was just a house. My favorite part of it was the window in my room that led to the porch on the upper level. That was my escape hatch. I showed her around, though, giving her a tour of the sitting room, the library, the den, and the family room, Jamie's eyes growing wider with each new room. My mom was out on the sunporch, sipping a mint julep and reading, and she heard us poking around. She came back inside to say hello.

I think I told you that every adult in town adored Jamie, and this included my mom. Even though Hegbert was always giving sermons that had our family's name written all over them, my mom never held it against Jamie, because of how sweet she was. So they talked while I was upstairs riffling through my closet for a clean shirt and a tie. When I came back down the stairs, fully dressed, Jamie had already told my mom about the plan.

"It's a wonderful idea," Jamie said, beaming at me. "Landon's really got a special heart."

My mom—after making sure she'd heard Jamie correctly—faced me with her eyebrows raised. She stared at me like I was an alien. "So this was your idea?" she asked. Like everyone else in town, she knew Jamie didn't lie.

I cleared my throat, thinking of Eric and what I still wanted to do to him. It involved molasses and fire ants, by the way. "Kind of," I said.

"Amazing." It was the only word she could get out. She didn't know the details, but she knew I must have been boxed into a corner to do something like this. Mothers always know stuff like that, and I could see her peering closely at me and trying to figure it out. To escape her gaze, I checked my watch, feigned surprise, and casually mentioned to Jamie that we'd better be going.

As I walked Jamie to the car, I heard my mother's voice again.

"Come over anytime, Jamie!" she shouted. "You're always welcome."

Even mothers could stick it to you sometimes.

I was still shaking my head as I got in the car.

"Your mother's a wonderful lady," Jamie said.

I started the engine. "Yeah," I said. "I guess so."

"And your house is beautiful."

"Uh-huh."

"You should count your blessings."

"Oh," I said, "I do. I'm practically the luckiest guy alive."

Somehow she didn't catch the sarcastic tone of my voice.

WE GOT to the orphanage just about the time it was getting dark. We were a couple of minutes early, and the director was on the phone, so we made ourselves comfortable. We were waiting on a bench in the hallway outside his door, when Jamie turned to me. Her Bible was in her lap. I guess she wanted it for support, but then again, maybe it was just her habit.

"You did really well today," she said. "With your lines, I mean."

"Thanks," I said, feeling proud and dejected at exactly the same time.

Jamie smiled, and after a moment she changed the subject, sort of throwing me offtrack. "Do you ever think about the future, Landon?" she asked.

"Yeah, sure. I guess so," I answered cautiously.

"Well, what do you want to do with your life?"

I shrugged, a little wary of where she was going with this. "I don't know yet. I haven't figured that part out. I'm going to U.N.C. next fall, at least I hope so. I have to get accepted first."

"You will," she said.

"How do you know?"

"Because I've prayed for that too."

When she said it, I thought we were heading into a discussion about the power of prayer and faith, but Jamie tossed yet another curveball at me. "How about after college? What do you want to do then?"

"I don't know," I said, shrugging.

"I think you should become a minister," she said seriously. "You're good with people, and they'd respect what you have to say."

Though the concept was ridiculous, with her I just knew it came from the heart and she intended it as a compliment.

"Thanks," I said. "I don't know if I'll do that, but I'm sure I'll find something."

It took a moment for me to realize that the conversation had stalled and that it was my turn to ask a question. "How about you? What do you want to do in the future?"

Jamie turned away and got a far-off gaze in her eyes. "I want to get married," she said quietly. "And when I do, I want my father to walk me down the aisle, and I want everyone I know to be there. I want the church bursting with people."

"That's all?" Though I wasn't averse to the idea of marriage, it seemed kind of silly to hope for that as your life's goal.

"Yes," she said. "That's all I want."

The way she answered made me suspect that she thought she'd end up like Miss Garber.

I tried to make her feel better, even though it still seemed silly to me. "Well, you'll get married someday. You'll meet some guy, and the two of you will hit it off, and he'll ask you to marry him. And I'm sure that your father will be happy to walk you down the aisle."

I didn't mention the part about having a big crowd in the church. I guess it was the one thing that even I couldn't imagine.

Jamie thought carefully about my answer, really pondering it, though I didn't know why. "I hope so," she said finally.

I could tell she didn't want to talk about it anymore—don't ask me how—so I moved on to something new. "So how long have you been coming to the orphanage?" I asked conversationally.

"Seven years now. I was ten years old the first time I came."

"Do you enjoy it, or does it make you sad?"

"Both. Some of the children here came from really horrible situations. It's enough to break your heart when you hear about it. But when they see you come in with some books from the library or a new game to play, their smiles just take all the sadness away. It's the greatest feeling in the world."

She practically glowed when she spoke. Though she wasn't saying it to make me feel guilty, that was exactly the way I felt. It was one of the reasons it was so hard to put up with Jamie, but by then I was getting fairly used to it. She could twist you every way but normal, I'd come to learn.

At that moment Mr. Jenkins opened the door and invited us in. The office looked almost like a hospital room, with black-and-white-tiled floors, white walls, a metal cabinet against the wall, and a metal desk that was almost neurotically clean.

Jamie introduced me, and I shook Mr. Jenkins's hand. After we sat down, Jamie did most of the talking. They were old friends, and Mr. Jenkins had given her a big hug as soon as she'd entered. After smoothing out her skirt, Jamie explained our plan. Now, Mr. Jenkins had seen the play a few years back, and he knew exactly what she was talking about almost as soon as she started. But even though Mr. Jenkins liked Jamie a lot and knew she meant well, he said that he didn't think it was a good idea.

"Why not?" Jamie asked, her brow furrowed.

Mr. Jenkins sighed. "Even though it's a wonderful offer, and I know you'd like to do something special, the play is about a father who comes to realize how much he loves his daughter." He let that sink in for a moment. "Christmas is hard enough around here without reminding the kids of what they're missing. If the children see something like that . . ."

He didn't have to finish. Jamie put her hand to her mouth. "Oh, my," she said right away. "You're right. I hadn't thought about that."

Neither had I, to tell you the truth. But it was obvious right off the bat that Mr. Jenkins made sense.

He thanked us anyway and chatted for a while about what he planned to do instead. "We'll have a small tree and a few gifts—something that all of them can share. You're welcome to visit Christmas Eve."

After we said our good-byes, Jamie and I walked in silence. I could tell she was sad. The more I hung around Jamie, the more I realized she had lots of different emotions—she wasn't always cheerful and happy.

"I'm sorry it didn't work out," I said softly.

"I am too." She had that faraway look in her eyes again, and it was a moment before she went on. "I just wanted to do something different for them this year. Something special that they would remember forever. I thought for sure this was it."

She was quiet for a long time, and I looked at her. Seeing Jamie feeling bad was almost worse than feeling bad because of her. Unlike Jamie, I deserved to feel bad about myself—I knew what kind of person I was. But with her . . .

"While we're here, do you want to stop in to see the kids?" I asked into the silence. It was the only thing I could think to do that might make her feel better. "I could wait out here while you talk to them, or I could go to the car if you want."

"Would you visit them with me?" she asked suddenly.

To be honest, I wasn't sure I could handle it, but I knew she really wanted me there. And she was feeling so down that the words came out automatically. "Sure, I'll go."

"They'll be in the rec room now," she said.

We walked down the corridor to the end of the hall, where two doors opened into a good-sized room. Perched in the far corner was a small television, with about thirty metal folding chairs placed all around it. The kids were sitting in the chairs, crowded around the television, and you could tell that only the ones in the front row had a good view of the thing.

I glanced around. In the corner was an old Ping-Pong table. The surface was cracked and dusty, the net nowhere to be seen. Along the wall next to it were shelves with a few very old toys here and there—blocks and puzzles, a couple of games. Along the near walls were small individual desks piled with newspapers, scribbled on with crayons.

We stood in the doorway for just a second. We hadn't been noticed yet, and I asked what the newspapers were for.

"They don't have coloring books," she whispered, "so they use newspapers."

"Are these all the toys they have?" I asked.

She nodded. "Yes. Except for the stuffed animals. They're allowed to keep those in their rooms."

I guess she was used to it. To me, though, the sparseness of the room made the whole thing depressing. I couldn't imagine growing up in a place like this.

Jamie and I finally walked into the room, and one of the kids turned around at the sound of our steps. He was about eight or so, with red hair and freckles, his two front teeth missing.

"Jamie!" he shouted happily when he saw her, and all of a sudden the other heads turned. The kids ranged in age from about five to twelve, more boys than girls. After age twelve they had to be sent to live with foster parents, I later learned.

"Hey, Roger," Jamie said in response, "how are you?"

With that, Roger and some of the others began to crowd around us. One of the older kids asked if I was Jamie's boyfriend. By his tone, he seemed to have the same opinion of Jamie that most of the kids in our high school had.

"He's just a friend," she said. "But he's very nice."

Over the next hour we visited with the children. I got a lot of questions about where I lived and whether my house was big or what kind of car I owned, and when we finally had to leave, Jamie promised that she'd be back soon. I noticed that she didn't promise I would be with her.

While we were walking to the car, I said, "They're a nice bunch of kids. I'm glad you want to help them."

Jamie turned to me and smiled. She knew there wasn't much to add after that, but I could tell she was still wondering what she was going to do for them that Christmas.

BY EARLY December, just over two weeks into rehearsals, the sky was winter dark before Miss Garber would let us leave, and Jamie asked me if I wouldn't mind walking her home. I don't know why she wanted me to. Beaufort wasn't exactly a hotbed of criminal activity back then. But her house was on the way to mine, and I couldn't say no without hurting her feelings. It wasn't that I liked Jamie or anything, don't get the wrong idea, but when you've had to spend a few hours a day with someone and you're going to continue doing that for at least another week, you don't want to do anything that might make the next day miserable for either of you.

The play was going to be held that Friday and Saturday, and lots of people were already talking about it. Miss Garber had been so impressed by Jamie and me that she kept telling everyone it was going to be the best play the school had ever done. She had a real flair for promotion too, we found out. We had one radio station in town, and they interviewed her over the air, not once, but twice. "It's going to be marvelous," she pronounced. "Absolutely marvelous." She'd also called the newspaper, and they agreed to write an article about the play, primarily because of the Jamie–Hegbert connection, even though everyone in town already knew about it. But Miss Garber was relentless, and just that day she'd told us the playhouse was going to bring in extra seats to accommodate the extra-large expected crowd.

You might think I'd be getting excited about it too, but I really wasn't. My friends were still teasing me at school, and I hadn't had an afternoon off in what seemed like forever. The only thing that kept me going was the fact that I was doing the right thing. Occasionally I even felt sort of good about it too, though I never admitted it to anyone. I could practically imagine the angels in heaven staring wistfully down at me with little tears filling the corners of their eyes, talking about how wonderful I was for all my sacrifices.

So I was walking her home that first night, thinking about this stuff, when Jamie asked me a question. "Is it true you and your friends sometimes go to the graveyard at night?"

"Yeah," I said, shrugging. "Sometimes."

"What do you do there besides eat peanuts?"

"I don't know," I said. "Talk . . . joke around."

"Does it ever scare you?"

"No," I answered. "Why? Would it scare you?"

"I don't know," she said. "It might."

"Why?"

"Because I'd worry that I might do something wrong."

"We don't do anything bad there. I mean, we don't knock over the tombstones or leave our trash around," I said.

"Do you ever just sit around and listen to the sounds?" she asked. "Like the crickets chirping or the rustling of leaves when the wind blows? Or do you ever just lie on your backs and stare at the stars?"

Jamie didn't know the first thing about teenagers, even though she had been one for four years, and trying to understand teenage *boys* for her was like trying to decipher the theory of relativity.

"Not really," I said.

She nodded a little. "I think that's what I'd do if I were there. If I ever go, I mean. I'd just look around to really see the place, or sit quietly and listen."

This whole conversation struck me as strange, but I didn't press it, and we walked in silence for a few moments. And since she'd asked a little about me, I sort of felt obliged to ask her about herself. I mean, it was the least I could do.

"So what do you do?" I asked. "Besides working with the orphans or helping critters or reading the Bible, I mean."

She smiled at me. I think she was surprised by my question. "I do a lot of things. I study for my classes. I visit with my dad. We play gin rummy now and then. Things like that."

"Do you ever just go off with friends and goof around?"

"No," she said, and I could tell by the way she answered that even to her it was obvious no one wanted her around much.

"I'll bet you're excited about going off to college next year," I said, changing the subject.

It took her a moment to answer. "I don't think I'm going to go," she said matter-of-factly. Her answer caught me off guard. Jamie had some of the highest grades in our class, and depending on how the last semester went, she might even end up valedictorian.

We had a running pool going as to how many times she was going to mention the Lord's plan in her speech, by the way. My bet was fourteen.

"What about Mount Sermon? I thought that's where you were planning to go. You'd love a place like that," I offered.

She looked at me with a twinkle in her eye. "You mean I'd fit right in there, don't you?"

Those curveballs she sometimes threw could smack you right between the eyeballs.

"I didn't mean it that way," I said quickly. "I meant that I'd heard how excited you were to be going there next year."

She shrugged without really answering me, and to be honest, I didn't know what to make of it. By then we'd reached her house, and we stopped on the sidewalk out front.

"Thank you for walking me home, Landon," she said, and she glanced up at me for a moment before starting up the walk.

As I watched her go, I couldn't help but think that of all the times I'd ever talked to her, this was the strangest conversation we'd ever had. Despite the oddness of some of her answers, she seemed practically normal.

THE next night, as I was walking her home, she asked me about my father.

"He's all right, I reckon," I said. "But he's not around much."

"Do you miss that? Not growing up with him around?"

"Sometimes."

"I miss my mom too," she said. "Even though I never even knew her."

It was the first time I'd ever considered that Jamie and I might have something in common. I let that sink in for a while.

"It must be hard for you," I said sincerely. "Even though my father's a stranger to me, at least he's still around."

She looked up at me as we walked; then she faced forward again. She gently tugged at her hair. I was beginning to notice that she did this whenever she was nervous.

"It *is* hard sometimes. Don't get me wrong—I love my father with all my heart—but there are times when I wonder what it would have been like to have a mother around. I think she and I would have been able to talk about things in a way that my father and I can't."

I assumed she was talking about boys. It wasn't until later that I learned how wrong I was.

"What's it like living with your father? Is he like how he is in church?"

"No. He's actually got a pretty good sense of humor."

"Hegbert?" I blurted out. I couldn't even imagine it.

I think she was shocked to hear me call him by his first name, but she let me off the hook and didn't respond to my comment. Instead, she said, "Don't look so surprised. You'll like him once you get to know him."

"I doubt if I'll ever get to know him."

"You never know, Landon," she said, smiling, "what the Lord's plan is."

I hated when she said things like that. With her, you just knew she talked to the Lord every day. She might even have a direct ticket into heaven, if you know what I mean, being as how good a person she was.

"How would I get to know your father?" I asked.

She didn't answer, but she smiled to herself as if she knew some secret that she was keeping from me. Like I said, I hated it when she did that.

THE next night we talked about her Bible.

"Why do you always carry it with you?" I asked.

Now, I assumed she carried the Bible around simply because she was the minister's daughter. But the Bible she carried was old, and the cover was kind of ratty-looking, and I figured that she'd be the type of person who would buy a new one every year or so just to help out the Bible publishing industry or to show her renewed dedication to the Lord or something.

She walked a few steps before answering. "It was my mother's," she said simply.

"Oh. . . ." I said it like I'd stepped on someone's pet turtle, squashing it under my shoe.

She looked at me. "It's okay, Landon. How could you have known?"

"I'm sorry I asked."

"Don't be. You didn't mean anything by it." She paused. "My mother and father were given this Bible for their wedding, but my mom was the one who claimed it first. She read it all the time, especially whenever she was going through a hard time in her life."

I thought about all the miscarriages.

Jamie went on. "She loved to read it at night before she went to sleep, and she had it with her in the hospital when I was born. When my father found out that she had died, he carried the Bible and me out of the hospital at the same time."

"I'm sorry," I said again. Whenever someone tells you something sad, it's the only thing you can think to say.

"It just gives me a way to—to be a part of her. Can you understand that?" She wasn't saying it sadly, just more to let me know the answer to my question. Somehow that made it worse.

After she told me the story, I thought of her growing up with Hegbert, and I didn't really know what to say. As I was thinking about my answer, though, I heard a car blare its horn from behind us, and both Jamie and I stopped and turned around at the same time as we heard it pulling over to the side.

Eric and Margaret were in the car, Eric on the driver's side, Margaret on the side closest to us.

"Well, lookee who we have here," Eric said as he leaned over the steering wheel so that I could see his face. I hadn't told him I'd been walking Jamie home, and in the curious way that teenage minds work, this new development took priority over anything that I was feeling about Jamie's story.

"Hello, Eric. Hello, Margaret," Jamie said cheerfully.

"Walking her home, Landon?" I could see the little devil behind Eric's smile.

"Hey, Eric," I said, wishing he'd never seen me.

"It's a beautiful night for strolling, isn't it?" Eric said. There was no way he could let this opportunity pass without sticking it to me.

Jamie looked around and smiled. "Yes, it is."

Eric looked around too, with this wistful look in his eyes, before taking a deep breath. I could tell he was faking it. "Boy, it really is nice out there." He sighed and glanced toward us as he shrugged. "I'd offer you a ride, but it wouldn't be half as nice as actually walking under the stars, and I wouldn't want you two to miss it." He said this like he was doing us both a favor.

"Oh, we're almost to my house anyway," Jamie said. "I was going to offer Landon a cup of cider. Would you like to meet us there? We have plenty."

Cider? At her house? She hadn't mentioned that. I put my hands in my pockets, wondering if this could get any worse.

"Oh, no. That's all right. Margaret and I were just heading off to Cecil's Diner. We should probably be going. Enjoy your cider, you two."

"Thanks for stopping to say hello," Jamie said, waving.

Once they'd pulled out of sight, Jamie turned to me and smiled. "You have nice friends, Landon."

"Sure I do." Notice the careful way I phrased my answer.

After dropping Jamie off—no, I didn't stay for any cider—I started back to my house, grumbling the whole time. By then Jamie's story had left me completely, and I could practically hear my friends laughing about me all the way from Cecil's Diner.

See what happens when you're a nice guy?

BY THE next morning everyone at the school knew I was walking Jamie home, and this started up a new round of speculation about the two of us. This time it was even worse than before. It was so bad that I had to spend my lunch break in the library just to get away from it all.

That night the rehearsal was at the playhouse. It was the last one before the show opened, and we had a lot to do. Right after school the boys in drama class had to load all the props in the classroom into a rented truck to bring them to the playhouse. The only problem was that Eddie and I were the only two boys, and he's not exactly the most coordinated individual in history. We'd be walking through a doorway, carrying one of the heavier items, and his body would work against him. In every critical moment when I really needed his help to balance the load, he'd stumble over some dust or an insect on the floor, and the weight of the prop would come crashing down on my fingers, pinching them against the doorjamb in the most painful way possible. "S-s-sorry," he'd say. "D-d-did . . . th-th-that hurt?"

I'd stifle the curses rising in my throat and bite out, "Just don't do it again."

But Eddie couldn't stop himself from stumbling around any more than he could stop the rain from falling. Moving the props took three hours, and we didn't finish setting them up until a few minutes before everyone else arrived. And the worst thing was, I didn't even get a chance to eat before rehearsal started. Suffice it to say, I was in a pretty bad mood.

I ran through my lines without even thinking about them, and Miss Garber didn't say the word marvelous all night long. She had this concerned look in her eyes afterward, but Jamie simply smiled and told her not to worry, that everything was going to be all right. I knew Jamie was just trying to make things better for me, but when she asked me to walk her home, I told her no. The playhouse was in the middle of town, and to walk her home, I'd have to walk a good distance out of my way. Besides, I didn't want to be seen again doing it. But Miss Garber had overheard Jamie's request, and she said, very firmly, that I'd be glad to do it. "You two can talk about the play," she said. "Maybe you can work out the kinks." By kinks, of course, she meant me.

So once more I ended up walking Jamie home, but she could tell I wasn't in the mood to talk, because I walked a little bit in front of her, my hands in my pockets, without even turning back to see whether she was following.

"You're not in a very good mood, are you?" she finally asked.

"You don't miss a thing, do you?" I said sarcastically.

"Maybe I can help," she offered. She said it kind of happily, which made me even a little angrier.

"I doubt it," I snapped.

"Maybe if you told me what was wrong—"

I didn't let her finish. "Look," I said, stopping, turning to face her, "I've just spent all day hauling props, I haven't eaten since lunch, and now I have to trek a mile out of my way to make sure you get home."

It was the first time I'd ever raised my voice to her. To tell you the truth, it felt kind of good. It had been building up for a long time. Jamie was too surprised to respond, and I went on. "And the only reason I'm doing this is because of your father, who doesn't even like me. This whole thing is dumb, and I wish I had never agreed to do it."

"You're just saying this because you're nervous about the play—"

I cut her off with a shake of my head. Once I got on a roll, it was sometimes hard for me to stop. I could take her cheerfulness only so long, and today wasn't the day to push me too far.

"Don't you get it?" I said, exasperated. "I'm not nervous about the play; I just don't want to walk you home. I don't want my friends to keep talking about me, and I don't want to spend time with you. You keep acting like we're friends, but we're not. We're not anything. I just want the whole thing to be over so I can go back to my normal life."

She looked hurt by my outburst, and to be honest, I couldn't blame her. "I see," was all she said.

I waited for her to raise her voice at me, but she didn't. All she did was look toward the ground. I think part of her wanted to cry, but she didn't, and I finally stalked away. I started walking again, leaving her standing by herself. A moment later, though, I heard her start moving too. She was about five yards behind me the rest of the way to her house, and she didn't try to talk to me again until she started up the walkway. I was already moving down the sidewalk when I heard her voice.

"Thank you for walking me home, Landon," she called out.

I winced as soon as she said it. Even when I was mean to her face and said the most spiteful things, she could find some reason to thank me. She was just that kind of girl, and I think I actually hated her for it. Or rather, I think, I hated myself.

Chapter Five

The night of the play was cool and crisp, the sky absolutely clear without a hint of clouds. We had to arrive an hour early, and I'd been feeling pretty bad all day about the way I'd talked to Jamie the night before. She'd never been anything but nice to me, and I knew I'd been a jerk. I saw her in the hallways between classes, and I wanted to go up to apologize to her, but she'd sort of slip back into the crowd before I got the chance.

She was already at the playhouse by the time I arrived, and I saw her talking to Miss Garber and Hegbert off to one side, over by the curtains. Everyone was in motion, working off nervous energy, but she seemed strangely lethargic. She hadn't put on her costume yet—she was supposed to wear a white, flowing dress to give that angelic appearance—and she was still wearing the same sweater she'd worn at school.

Despite my trepidation at how she might react, I walked up to the three of them. "Hey, Jamie," I said. "Hello, Reverend . . . Miss Garber."

Jamie turned to me. "Hello, Landon," she said quietly. I could tell she'd been thinking about the night before too, because she didn't smile at me like she always did when she saw me. I asked if I could talk to her alone, and the two of us excused ourselves.

I glanced around the stage nervously. "I'm sorry about those things I said last night," I began. "I know they probably hurt your feelings, and I was wrong to have said them."

She looked at me as if wondering whether to believe me. "Did you mean those things you said?" she finally asked.

"I was just in a bad mood, that's all. I get sort of wound up sometimes." I knew I hadn't really answered her question.

"I see," she said. She said it like she had the night before, then turned toward the empty seats in the audience. Again she had that sad look in her eyes.

"Look," I said, reaching for her hand, "I promise to make it up to you." Don't ask me why I said it. It just seemed like the right thing to do at the moment.

For the first time that night she began to smile. "Thank you," she said, turning to face me.

"Jamie?"

Jamie turned. "Yes, Miss Garber?"

"I think we're about ready for you." Miss Garber was motioning with her hand.

"I've got to go," Jamie said to me.

"I know."

"Break a leg," she said.

I let go of her hand. "We both will. I promise."

After that we had to start getting ready, and we went to our separate dressing rooms.

IN THE play, Tom Thornton is amazed when he first sees the angel, which is why he goes around helping her as she shares Christmas with those less fortunate. The first words out of Tom's mouth are "You're beautiful," and I was supposed to say them as if I meant them from the bottom of my heart. This is the pivotal moment in the entire play, and it sets the tone for everything else that happens. The problem, however, was that I still hadn't nailed this line. Sure,

I said the words, but they didn't come off too convincingly, seeing as I probably said them like anyone would when looking at Jamie, with the exception of Hegbert. It was the only scene where Miss Garber had never said the word marvelous, so I was nervous about it.

Jamie was still in her dressing room when the curtains finally opened. I didn't see her beforehand, but that was okay. The first few scenes didn't include her anyway—they were mainly about Tom Thornton and his relationship with his daughter.

I didn't think I'd be too nervous when I stepped out onstage, being that I'd rehearsed so much, but it hits you right between the eyes when it actually happens. The playhouse was packed, and as Miss Garber had predicted, they'd even set up two extra rows of seats in the back. Normally, the place sat four hundred, but with those seats, there were at least another fifty people sitting down. In addition, people were standing against the walls, packed like sardines, but as soon as I stepped onstage, everyone was absolutely quiet. The crowd was mainly old ladies of the blue-haired type, the kind that play bingo and drink Bloody Marys at Sunday brunch, though I could see Eric sitting with all my friends near the back row. It was downright eerie, if you know what I mean, to be standing in front of them while everyone waited for me to say something.

So I did the best I could to put it out of my mind as I did the first few scenes in the play. Because she was sort of small for her age, a girl named Sally was playing my daughter, and we went through our scenes just as we'd rehearsed them. Neither of us blew our lines, though we weren't spectacular or anything, and when we closed the curtains for act two, we had to quickly reset the props. This time everyone pitched in, and my fingers escaped unscathed because I avoided Eddie at all costs.

I still hadn't seen Jamie. The next thing I knew, the curtains were opening again and I was back in Hegbert Sullivan's world, walking past storefronts and looking in windows for the music box my daughter wanted for Christmas. My back was turned away from where Jamie entered, but I heard the crowd collectively draw a breath as soon as she appeared onstage. I thought it was silent before, but now it went absolutely hush still. Just then, from the corner of my eye and off to the side of the stage, I saw Hegbert's jaw quivering as he stared at her. I readied myself to turn around, and when I did, I finally saw what it was all about.

For the first time since I'd known her, her honey-colored hair wasn't pulled into a tight bun. Instead, it was hanging loosely, longer than I imagined, reaching past her shoulder blades. There was a trace of glitter in her hair, and it caught the stage lights, sparkling like a crystal halo. Set against her flowing white dress that seemed to be tailored exactly for her, it was absolutely amazing to behold. She didn't look like the girl I'd grown up with or the girl I'd recently come to know. She wore a touch of makeup too—not a lot—just enough to bring out the softness of her features. She was smiling slightly, as if she were holding a secret close to her heart, just like the part called for her to do.

She looked exactly like an angel.

I know my jaw dropped a little, and I just stood there looking at her for what seemed like a long time, shocked into silence until I suddenly remembered that I had a line I had to deliver.

I took a deep breath, then slowly let it out. "You're beautiful," I finally said to her, and I think everyone in the whole auditorium—from the blue-haired ladies in front to my friends in the back row—knew that I actually meant it.

I'd nailed that line for the very first time.

TO SAY that the play was a smashing success was to put it mildly. The audience laughed, and the audience cried, which is pretty much what they were supposed to do. But because of Jamie's presence it really became something special, and I think everyone in the cast was as shocked as I was at how well the whole thing had come off. They all had that same look as I did when I first saw her, and it made the play that much more powerful when they were performing their parts. We finished the first performance without a hitch, and the next evening even more people showed up, if you can believe it. Even Eric came up to me afterward and congratulated me.

"The two of you did good," he said simply. "I'm proud of you, buddy."

While he said it, Miss Garber was crying out, "Marvelous!" to anyone who would listen to her.

I looked for Jamie after we'd pulled the curtains closed for the final time, and I spotted her off to the side, standing with her father. He had tears in his eyes, and Jamie went into his arms and they held each other for a long time. He was stroking her hair and whispering, "My angel," to her while her eyes were closed, and even I felt myself choking up over it.

The right thing, I realized, wasn't so bad after all.

After they finally let go of each other, Hegbert proudly motioned for her to visit with the rest of the cast, and she got a boatload of congratulations from everyone backstage. She was her normal cheerful self, but with her looking so pretty, it came across in a totally different way, at least to other people. I stood in the background, letting her have her moment, and I'll admit that there was part of me that felt like old Hegbert. I couldn't help but be happy for her and a little proud as well. When she finally saw me standing off to one side, she excused herself from the others and walked over, stopping when she was close.

Looking up at me, she smiled. "Thank you, Landon, for what you did. You made my father very happy."

"You're welcome," I said, meaning it.

The strange thing was, when she said it, I realized that Hegbert would be driving her home, and for once I wished that I would have had the opportunity to walk her there.

THE following Monday was our last week of school before Christmas break, and finals were scheduled in every class. I planned on hitting the books pretty hard that week. In addition I had to finish my application for U.N.C., which I'd been putting off because of all the rehearsals. Even so, I couldn't help but think about Jamie.

Jamie's transformation during the play had been startling, to say the least, and I assumed it had signaled a change in her. I don't know why I thought that way, but I did, and thus I was amazed when she showed up our first morning back dressed like her usual self—brown sweater, hair in a bun, plaid skirt, and all.

I couldn't help but feel sorry for her. She'd been regarded as normal—even special—over the weekend, but she'd somehow let it slip away. Oh, people were a little nicer to her, and the ones who hadn't talked to her yet told her what a good job she'd done, but I could tell that it wasn't going to last. Attitudes forged since childhood are hard to break, and part of me wondered if it might even get worse for her after this. Now that people actually knew she could look normal, they might even become more heartless.

I wanted to talk to her about my impressions, I really did, but I was planning to do so after the week was over. Not only did I have a lot to do but I wanted a little time to think of the best way to tell her. To be honest, I was still feeling a little guilty about the things I'd said to her on our last walk home, and it wasn't just because the play had turned out great. It had more to do with the fact that in all our time together Jamie had never once been anything but kind, and I knew that I'd been wrong.

I didn't think she wanted to talk to me either, to tell you the truth. I knew she could see me hanging out with my friends at lunch while she sat off in the corner reading her Bible, but she never made a move toward us. As I was leaving school that day, though, I heard her voice behind me asking me if I wouldn't mind walking her home. Even though I wasn't ready to tell her yet about my thoughts, I agreed. For old times' sake, you see.

A minute later Jamie got down to business. "Do you remember those things you said on our last walk home?" she asked.

I nodded, wishing she hadn't brought it up.

"You promised to make it up to me," she said.

For a moment I was confused. I thought I'd done that already with my performance in the play.

"Well, I've been thinking about what you could do," Jamie continued, without letting me get a word in edgewise, "and this is what I've come up with."

She asked if I wouldn't mind gathering the pickle jars and coffee cans she'd set out in businesses all over town earlier in the year. They sat on the counters, usually near the cash registers, so that people could drop their loose change in. The money was to go to the orphans.

I remembered seeing the containers in places like Cecil's Diner and the Crown Theater. My friends and I used to toss paper clips and slugs in there when the cashiers weren't looking, since they sounded sort of like a coin being dropped inside. Then we'd chuckle to ourselves about how we were putting something over on Jamie. We used to joke about how she'd open one of her cans, expecting something good because of the weight, and she'd dump it out and find nothing but slugs and paper clips. Sometimes, when you remember the things you used to do, it makes you wince, and that's exactly what I did.

Jamie saw the look on my face. "You don't have to do it," she said, obviously disappointed. "I was just thinking that since Christmas is coming up so quickly and I don't have a car, it'll simply take me too long to collect them all—"

"No," I said, cutting her off. "I'll do it."

SO THAT'S what I did, starting Wednesday, even though I had tests to study for and that application to finish. Jamie had given me a list of every place she'd put a can, and I borrowed my mom's car and started at the far end of town the following day. Jamie'd put out about sixty cans in all, and I figured it would take a day to collect them. It had taken her almost six weeks to put them out, because she'd had to find sixty empty jars and cans in the first place, and then she could put out only two or three a day, since she didn't have a car and could carry only so many at a time. Compared to putting them out, picking up the cans and jars would be a piece of cake.

I went from business to business collecting the containers, and by the end of the first day I realized it was going to take a little longer than I thought. I'd picked up only about twenty cans and jars, because I'd forgotten one fact of life in Beaufort. In a small town

like this, it was impossible to simply run inside and grab the can without chatting with the proprietor. So I'd sit there while some guy would be talking about the marlin he'd hooked last fall, or maybe he'd want my opinion on whether he should move the magazine rack over to the other side of the store. Jamie, I knew, would have been good at this, and I tried to act like I thought she would want me to. After all, it was her project.

To keep things moving, though, I didn't stop to check the take in between the businesses. I just dumped one jar or can into the next, combining them as I went along. By the end of the first day all the change was packed in two large jars, and I carried them up to my room. I saw a few bills through the glass—not too many—but I wasn't nervous until I emptied the contents onto my floor and saw that the change consisted primarily of pennies. Though there weren't nearly as many slugs as I thought there might be, I was still disheartened when I counted up the money. There was $20.32. Even in 1958 that wasn't a lot of money, especially when divided among thirty kids.

I didn't get discouraged, though. Thinking that it was a mistake, I went out the next day and chatted with another twenty proprietors while I collected cans and jars. The take: $23.89. The third day was even worse. I couldn't believe it. There was only $11.52.

Seeing how little had been collected in all—$55.73—made me feel awful. That night I was supposed to call Jamie to tell her the amount I'd collected, but I just couldn't do it. She'd told me how she'd wanted something extra special this year, and this wasn't going to do it—even I knew that. Instead, I lied to her and told her that I wasn't going to count the total until the two of us could do it together, because it was her project, not mine. I promised to bring the money over the following afternoon after school. Tomorrow was December 21. Christmas was only four days away.

"LANDON," she said after counting it up, "this is a miracle!"

"How much is there?" I asked. I knew exactly how much it was, by the way.

"There's almost two hundred and forty-seven dollars here!" She was absolutely joyous as she looked up at me. Since Hegbert was home, I was allowed to sit in the living room, and that's where Jamie had counted the money. It was stacked in neat little piles all over the floor, almost all quarters and dimes. Hegbert was in the kitchen, at the table, writing his sermon.

"Do you think that's enough?" I asked innocently.

Little tears were coming down her cheeks as she looked around the room, still not believing what she was seeing. Even after the play she hadn't been nearly this happy.

She looked right at me. "It's . . . wonderful," she said, smiling. There was more emotion than I'd ever heard in her voice before. "Last year I only collected seventy dollars."

"I'm glad it worked out better this year," I said through the lump that had formed in my throat. "If you hadn't placed those jars out so early in the year, you might not have collected nearly as much."

I know I was lying, but I didn't care. For once, it was the right thing to do.

I DIDN'T help Jamie pick out the toys—I figured she'd know better what the children would want—but she insisted that I go with her to the orphanage on Christmas Eve so that I could be there when the children opened their gifts.

Three days later, while my father and mother were at a party at the mayor's house, I dressed in a houndstooth jacket and my best tie and walked to my mom's car with Jamie's present beneath my arm. I'd spent my last few dollars on a nice sweater because that was all I could think to get her. She wasn't exactly the easiest person to shop for.

I was supposed to be at the orphanage at seven, but because the drawbridge was up near the Morehead City port, I had to wait until an outbound freighter slowly made its way down the channel. As a result, I arrived a few minutes late.

"Ah, you're here," Mr. Jenkins said happily when he opened the door. "We've been waiting for you. C'mon, I'll take you inside."

He led me down the hall to the rec room, the same place I'd been before. I paused for just a moment to exhale deeply before finally heading in. It was even better than I'd imagined.

In the center of the room I saw a giant tree decorated with tinsel and colored lights and a hundred different handmade ornaments. Beneath the tree, spread in all directions, were wrapped gifts of every size and shape. They were piled high, and the children were on the floor, sitting close together in a large semicircle. They were dressed in their best clothes. The boys wore navy-blue slacks and white collared shirts, while the girls had on navy skirts and long-sleeved blouses.

On the table beside the door, there was a bowl of punch, and platters of cookies shaped like Christmas trees. I could see some adults sitting with the children. A few of the smaller kids were sitting on the adults' laps, their faces rapt with attention as they listened to *'Twas the Night Before Christmas.*

I didn't see Jamie, though, at least not right off the bat. It was her voice that I recognized first. She was the one reading the story, and I finally located her. She was sitting on the floor in front of the tree, her legs bent beneath her.

To my surprise I saw that her hair hung loosely, just as it had the night of the play. Instead of the old brown cardigan, she was wearing a red V-necked sweater that somehow accentuated the color of her light blue eyes. Even without sparkles in her hair or a long, flowing white dress, the sight of her was arresting. Without even noticing it, I'd been holding my breath. I exhaled and smiled, trying to regain control.

Jamie paused only once to look up from the story. She noticed me standing in the doorway, then went back to reading to the children. It took her another minute or so to finish, and when she did, she stood up and smoothed her skirt, then walked around the children to make her way toward me.

"I'm sorry we started without you," she said when she finally reached me, "but the kids were just so excited."

"It's okay," I said, smiling, thinking how nice she looked.

"I'm so glad you could come."

"So am I."

Jamie smiled and reached for my hand to lead the way. "C'mon with me," she said. "Help me hand out the gifts."

We spent the next hour doing just that, and we watched as the children opened them one by one. Jamie had shopped all over town, picking up a few individual gifts for each child in the room. The gifts that Jamie bought weren't the only ones the children received, however—both the orphanage and the people who worked there bought some things as well. As paper was tossed around the room in excited frenzy, there were squeals of delight. To me, at least, it seemed that all of the children had received far more than they'd expected, and they kept thanking Jamie over and over.

By the time all the gifts were opened, the atmosphere began to calm down. The room was tidied up by Mr. Jenkins and a woman whom I'd never met, and some of the smaller children were beginning to fall asleep beneath the tree. Some of the older ones had already gone back to their rooms with their gifts, and they'd dimmed the overhead lights on their way out the door. The tree lights cast an ethereal glow as "Silent Night" played softly on a phonograph that had been set up in the corner. I was still sitting on the floor next to Jamie, who was holding a young girl who'd fallen asleep in her lap. Because of all the commotion we hadn't really had a chance to talk. We were both gazing up at the lights on the tree, and I wondered what Jamie was thinking. I thought—no, *I knew*—she was pleased with how the evening had gone, and deep down, so was I. It was the best Christmas Eve I'd ever spent.

I glanced at her. With the lights glowing on her face, she looked as pretty as anyone I'd ever seen.

"I brought you something," I finally said to her. "A gift, I mean." I spoke softly so I wouldn't wake the little girl.

Jamie turned from the tree to face me, smiling. "You didn't have to do that." She kept her voice low too, and it sounded almost musical.

"I know," I said. "But I wanted to." I'd kept the gift-wrapped package off to one side, and I reached for it, handing it to her.

"Could you open it for me?" she asked. "My hands are kind of full right now." She looked down at the little girl, then back to me.

I started unwrapping the gift. After removing the paper, I lifted the cover off the box and pulled the sweater out, holding it up to show her. It was brown, like the one she usually wore. But I figured she could use a new one. For some reason, I'm not sure why, I hoped she wasn't disappointed in it.

"It's beautiful, Landon," she said earnestly. "I'll wear it the next time I see you. Thank you."

We sat quietly for a moment, and once again I began to look at the lights.

"I brought you something too," Jamie finally whispered. She looked toward the tree, and my eyes followed her gaze. Her gift was still beneath the tree, partially hidden by the stand, and I reached for it. It was rectangular-shaped, flexible, and a little heavy. I brought it to my lap and held it there.

"Open it," she said, looking right at me.

"You can't give this to me," I said breathlessly. I already knew what was inside, and I couldn't believe what she had done. My hands began to tremble.

"Please," she said to me with the kindest voice I'd ever heard. "Open it. I want you to have it."

Reluctantly I slowly unwrapped the package. When it was finally free of the paper, I held it gently, afraid to damage it. I stared at it, mesmerized, brushing my fingers over the well-worn leather as tears filled my eyes. Jamie reached out and rested her hand on mine. It was warm and soft.

I glanced at her, not knowing what to say.

Jamie had given me her Bible.

"Thank you for doing what you did," she whispered to me. "It was the best Christmas I've ever had."

I turned away without responding and reached off to the side where I'd set my glass of punch. The chorus of "Silent Night" was still playing, and the music filled the room. I took a sip of the punch, trying to soothe the sudden dryness in my throat. As I drank, all the times I'd spent with Jamie came flooding into my mind. I thought about the homecoming dance. I thought about the play and how angelic she'd looked. I thought about the times I'd walked her home and how I'd helped collect jars and cans filled with pennies for the orphans.

As these images were going through my head, I looked at Jamie, doing my best to keep my composure. She smiled at me, and I smiled at her, and all I could do was wonder how I'd ever fallen in love with a girl like Jamie Sullivan.

I DROVE Jamie home from the orphanage later that night. I wasn't sure whether I should pull the old yawn move and put my arm around her shoulders, but to be honest, I didn't know exactly how she was feeling about me. Granted, she'd given me the most wonderful gift I'd ever received, and even though I'd probably never read it like she did, I knew it was like giving a piece of herself away. But Jamie was the type of person who would donate a kidney to a stranger she met walking down the street, if he really needed one. So I wasn't sure exactly what to make of it.

Jamie had once told me that she wasn't a dimwit, and I guess I finally came to the conclusion that she wasn't. She may have been—well, different—but she'd figured out what I'd done for the orphans, and looking back, I think she knew even as we were sitting on the floor of her living room. When she'd called it a miracle, I guess she was talking specifically about me.

Hegbert, I remembered, had come into the room as Jamie and I were talking about it, but he really hadn't had much to say. Old Hegbert hadn't been himself lately, at least as far as I could tell. Oh, his sermons were still on the money, but recently they were shorter than usual, and occasionally he'd pause right in the middle of one and have this strange look come over him, kind of like he was thinking of something else, something sad. I didn't know what to make of it, being that I really didn't know him that well.

So anyway, he'd come into the room while we counted the

money, and Jamie stood up with those tears in her eyes, and Hegbert didn't even seem to realize I was there. He told her that he was proud of her and that he loved her, but then he shuffled back to the kitchen to continue working on his sermon. He hadn't even said hello.

At the same time I was thinking about Hegbert, I glanced at Jamie sitting beside me. She was looking out the car window with a peaceful look on her face, kind of smiling but far away at the same time. I smiled. Maybe she was thinking about me. My hand started scooting across the seat closer to hers, but before I reached it, Jamie broke the silence.

"Landon," she asked as she turned toward me, "do you ever think about God?"

I pulled my hand back.

Now, when I thought about God, I usually pictured Him like those old paintings I'd seen in churches—a giant with long, flowing hair, hovering over the landscape, wearing a white robe—but I knew she wasn't talking about that. She was talking about the Lord's plan. It took a moment for me to answer.

"Sure," I said. "Sometimes, I reckon."

"Do you ever wonder why things have to turn out the way they do?"

I nodded uncertainly.

"I've been thinking about it a lot lately."

Even more than usual? I wanted to ask, but I didn't. I could tell she had more to say, and I stayed quiet.

"I know the Lord has a plan for us all, but sometimes I just don't understand what the message can be. Does that ever happen to you?"

She said this like it was something I thought about all the time.

"Well," I said, trying to bluff, "I don't think that we're meant to understand it all the time. I think that sometimes we just have to have faith."

It was a pretty good answer, I admit. I guess my feelings for Jamie were making my brain work a little faster than usual. I could tell she was thinking about my answer.

"Yes," she finally said, "you're right."

I smiled to myself and changed the subject, since talking about God wasn't the sort of thing that made a person feel romantic. "You know," I said casually, "it sure was nice tonight when we were sitting by the Christmas tree earlier."

"Yes, it was," she said. Her mind was still elsewhere.

"And you sure looked nice too."

"Thank you."

This wasn't working too well. "Can I ask you a question?" I finally said, in the hopes of bringing her back to me.

"Sure," she said.

I took a deep breath. "After church tomorrow, and well . . . After you've spent some time with your father . . . I mean . . ." I paused and looked at her. "Would you mind coming over to my house for Christmas dinner?"

Even though her face was still turned toward the window, I could see the faint outlines of a smile as soon as I'd said it.

"Yes, Landon, I would like that very much."

I sighed with relief, not believing I'd actually asked her and still wondering how all this had happened. I drove down streets where windows were decorated with Christmas lights, and through the Beaufort City Square. A couple of minutes later, when I reached across the seat, I finally took hold of her hand. To complete the perfect evening, she didn't draw it away.

When we pulled up in front of her house, the lights in the living room were still on, and I could see Hegbert behind the curtains. I suppose he was waiting up because he wanted to hear how it went this evening at the orphanage. Either that or he wanted to make sure I didn't kiss his daughter on the doorstep. I knew he'd frown on that sort of thing.

I was thinking about that—what to do when we finally said goodbye, I mean—when we got out of the car and started toward the door. Jamie was quiet and content at the same time, and I think she was happy because I'd asked her to come over the next day. Since she'd been smart enough to figure out what I'd done for the orphans, I figured that maybe she'd been smart enough to figure out the homecoming situation as well. I think she even realized that this was the first time I'd actually asked her to join me of my own volition.

Just as we got to her steps, I saw Hegbert peek out from behind the curtains and pull his face back. Now, I didn't know if Jamie would kiss me. In fact, I doubted that she would. But with her looking so pretty—with her hair down and all—and everything that had happened tonight, I didn't want to miss the opportunity if it came up. I could feel the little butterflies already starting to form in my stomach when Hegbert opened the door.

"I heard you pull up," he said quietly. His skin was that sallow color, as usual, but he looked tired.

"Hello, Reverend Sullivan," I said dejectedly.

"Hi, Daddy," Jamie said happily a second later. "I wish you could have come tonight. It was wonderful."

"I'm so glad for you." He seemed to gather himself then and cleared his throat. "I'll give you a bit to say good night. I'll leave the door open for you."

He turned around and went back into the living room. From where he sat down, I knew he could still see us. He pretended to be reading, though I couldn't see what was in his hands.

"I had a wonderful time tonight, Landon," Jamie said.

"So did I," I answered, feeling Hegbert's eyes on me.

"What time should I come over tomorrow?" she asked.

Hegbert's eyebrow raised just a little.

"I'll come over to get you. Is five o'clock okay?"

She looked over her shoulder. "Daddy, would you mind if I visited with Landon and his parents tomorrow?"

Hegbert sighed. "If it's important to you, you can," he said.

Not the most stirring vote of confidence I'd ever heard, but it was good enough for me.

We stood there for a moment without saying anything else, and I could tell Hegbert was growing a little impatient.

"I'll see you tomorrow," Jamie said finally.

"Okay," I said. "I'll pick you up at a quarter to five."

She glanced down at her feet for a moment, then back up at me. "Thank you for driving me home," she said.

With that, she turned and walked inside. I could barely see the slight smile playing gently across her lips as she peeked around the door just as it was about to close.

THE next day I picked her up right on schedule and was pleased to see that her hair was down once more. She was wearing the sweater I'd given her, just like she'd promised.

Both my mom and dad were a little surprised when I'd asked if it would be all right if Jamie came by for dinner. It wasn't a big deal—whenever my dad was around, my mom would have Helen, our cook, make enough food for a small army.

I guess I didn't mention that earlier—about the cook, I mean. We had a maid and a cook, not only because my family could afford them but because my mom wasn't the greatest homemaker in the world. She was all right at making sandwiches for my lunch now and then, but without Helen I would have grown up eating burned mashed potatoes and crunchy steak.

Our house was larger than most, but it wasn't a palace or anything. My father had bought it because of its historical value. Though it wasn't the house where Blackbeard had lived, which would have been more interesting to someone like me, it *had* been owned by Richard Dobbs Spaight, who'd signed the Constitution. This afforded my father some bragging rights in the halls of Congress, and whenever he walked around the garden, I could see him dreaming about the legacy he wanted to leave. In a way it made me sad, because no matter what he did, he'd never top old Richard Dobbs Spaight. Historical events like signing the Constitution only come along once every few hundred years, and no matter how you sliced it, debating farm subsidies for tobacco farmers was never going to cut it. Even someone like me knew that.

Our house was in the National Historic Register—still is, I suppose—and though Jamie had been there once before, she was still kind of awed when she walked inside. My mother and father were both dressed very nicely, as was I, and my mother kissed Jamie hello on the cheek. My mother—I couldn't help but think as I watched her do it—had scored before I did.

We had a nice dinner, fairly formal with four different courses, though it wasn't stuffy or anything like that. My parents and Jamie carried on the most marvelous conversation—think Miss Garber here—and though I tried to inject my own brand of humor, it didn't really go over too well, at least as far as my parents were concerned. Jamie, however, would laugh, and I took that as a good sign.

After dinner I invited Jamie to walk around the garden, even though it was winter and nothing was in bloom. She accepted, and after putting on our coats, we stepped outside into the chilled air. Our breath came out in little puffs.

"Your parents are wonderful people," she said to me. I guess she hadn't taken Hegbert's sermons to heart.

"They're nice," I responded, "in their own way. My mom's especially sweet."

Jamie stopped to look at the rosebushes. They looked like gnarled sticks, and I didn't see what her interest was in them. "Is it true about your grandfather?" she asked me. "The stories that people tell?"

"Yes," I said.

"That's sad. There's more to life than money."

"I know."

She looked at me. "Do you?"

I didn't meet her eyes as I answered. Don't ask me why. "I know that what my grandfather did was wrong."

"But you don't want to give it back, do you?"

"I've never really thought about it, to tell you the truth."

"Would you, though?"

I didn't answer right away, and Jamie turned from me. She was staring at the rosebushes again, and I suddenly realized that she'd wanted me to say yes. It's what she would have done without thinking twice about it.

"Why do you do things like that?" I blurted out before I could stop myself, blood rushing into my cheeks. "Making me feel guilty, I mean. I wasn't the one who did it. I just happened to be born into this family."

She reached out and touched a branch. "That doesn't mean you can't undo it," she said gently, "when you get the opportunity."

Her point was clear, and deep down, I knew she was right. But that decision, if it ever came, was a long way off. To my way of thinking, I had more important things on my mind.

I changed the subject back to something I could relate to better. "Does your father like me?" I asked. I wanted to know if Hegbert would allow me to see her again.

It took a moment for her to answer. "My father," she said slowly, "worries about me."

"Don't all parents?" I asked.

She looked toward her feet, then off to the side again before turning back to me. "I think that with him it's different than most. But my father does like you, and he knows that it makes me happy to see you. That's why he let me come over to your house for dinner tonight."

"I'm glad he did," I said, meaning it.

"So am I."

We looked at each other under the light of a waxing crescent moon, and I almost kissed her right then, but she turned away a moment too soon and said something that sort of threw me.

"My father worries about you too, Landon."

The way she said it—it was soft and sad at exactly the same time—let me know that it wasn't simply because he thought I was irresponsible, or because I used to hide behind the trees and call him names, or even because I was a member of the Carter family.

"Why?" I asked.

"For the same reason I do," she said. She didn't elaborate any further, and I knew right then that she was holding something back, something she couldn't tell me, something that made her sad as well. But it wasn't until later that I actually learned her secret.

BEING IN LOVE WITH A GIRL like Jamie Sullivan was without a doubt the strangest thing I'd ever been through. Not only was she a girl I'd never thought about before this year—even though we'd grown up together—but there was something different in the whole way my feelings for her had unfolded. Unlike Angela, whom I kissed the first time I was ever alone with her, I still hadn't kissed Jamie. I hadn't even taken her to Cecil's Diner or to a movie. I hadn't done any of the things that I normally did with girls, yet somehow I'd fallen in love.

The only problem was that I still didn't know how she felt about me. Oh, sure, there were some indications, and I hadn't missed them. The Bible was, of course, the biggie, but there was the way she looked at me when she'd closed the door on Christmas Eve, and she'd let me hold her hand on the ride home from the orphanage. To my way of thinking, there was definitely something there—I just wasn't exactly sure of how to take the next step.

When I'd finally taken her home after Christmas dinner, I'd asked if it would be okay if I came by from time to time, and she said it would be fine. That's exactly how she said it too—"That would be fine." I didn't take the lack of enthusiasm personally. Jamie had a tendency to talk like an adult, and I think that's why she got along with older people so well.

The following day I walked to her house, and the first thing I noticed was that Hegbert's car wasn't in the driveway. When she answered the door, I knew enough not to ask if I could come in.

"Hello, Landon," she said, as she always did. Again her hair was down, and I took this as a positive sign.

"Hey, Jamie," I said casually.

She motioned to the chairs. "My father's not home, but we can sit on the porch if you'd like—"

Don't even ask me how it happened, because I still can't explain it. One second I was standing there in front of her, expecting to walk to the side of the porch, and in the next second I wasn't. Instead of moving toward the chairs, I took a step closer to her and found myself reaching for her hand. I took it in mine and looked right at her, moving just a little closer. She didn't exactly step back, but her eyes widened, and for a tiny flickering moment I thought I'd done the wrong thing. I paused and smiled, sort of tilting my head to the side, and the next thing I saw was that she'd closed her eyes and was tilting her head too and that our faces were moving closer together.

It wasn't that long, and it certainly wasn't the kind of kiss you see in movies these days, but it was wonderful in its own way, and all I can remember about the moment is that when our lips first touched, I knew the memory would last forever.

Chapter Six

"You're the first boy I've ever kissed," she said to me.

It was a few days before the new year, and Jamie and I were standing at the Iron Steamer Pier in Pine Knoll Shores. To get there, we'd had to cross the bridge that spans the Intracoastal Waterway and drive a little way down the island. Nowadays the place has some of the most expensive beachfront property in the entire state, but back then it was mainly sand dunes nestled against the Maritime National Forest.

"I figured I might have been," I said.

"Why?" she asked innocently. "Did I do it wrong?"

"You're a great kisser," I said, giving her hand a squeeze.

She nodded and turned toward the ocean, her eyes getting that far-off look again. She'd been doing that a lot lately.

"Are you okay, Jamie?" I asked.

Instead of answering, she changed the subject. "Have you ever been in love?" she asked me.

I ran my hand through my hair and gave her one of those looks. "You mean before now?"

I said it like James Dean would have, the way Eric had told me to say it if a girl ever asked me that question. Eric was pretty slick with girls.

"I'm serious, Landon," she said, tossing me a sidelong glance.

I guess Jamie had seen those movies too. With Jamie, I'd come to realize, I always seemed to be going from high to low and back to high again in less time than it takes to swat a mosquito. I wasn't quite sure if I liked that part of our relationship yet, though to be honest, it kept me on my toes.

I was still feeling off-balance as I thought about her question. "Actually, I have," I said finally.

Her eyes were still fixed on the ocean. I think she thought I was talking about Angela, but looking back, I'd realized that what I'd felt for Angela was totally different from what I was feeling at that moment.

"How did you know it was love?" she asked me.

I watched the breeze gently moving her hair, and I knew it was no time to pretend I was something that I actually wasn't.

"Well," I said seriously, "you know it's love when all you want to do is spend time with the other person, and you sort of know that the other person feels the same way."

Jamie thought about my answer before smiling faintly. "I see," she said softly.

I waited for her to add something else, but she didn't, and I came to another sudden realization. Jamie may not have been all that experienced with boys, but to tell you the truth, she was playing me like a harp.

During the next two days, for instance, she wore her hair in a bun again.

ON NEW Year's Eve I took Jamie out to dinner. It was the very first real date she'd ever been on, and we went to a small waterfront restaurant in Morehead City called Flauvin's. Flauvin's was the kind of restaurant with tablecloths and candles and five different pieces of silverware per setting. The waiters wore black and white, like butlers, and when you looked out the giant windows that completely lined the wall, you could watch moonlight reflecting off the slowly moving water. There was a pianist and a singer too—not every night, but on holidays when they thought the place would be full.

It was actually my mom's idea to take Jamie out someplace special. A couple of days beforehand, on one of those days Jamie was wearing her hair in a bun, I talked to my mom about the things I was going through.

"She's all I think about, Mom," I confessed. "I mean, I know she likes me, but I don't know if she feels the same way I do."

"Well, what have you tried so far?" she asked.

"What do you mean?"

My mom smiled. "I mean that young girls, even Jamie, like to be made to feel special."

I thought about that for a moment, a little confused. Wasn't that what I was trying to do?

"Well, I've been going to her house every day to visit," I said.

My mom put her hand on my knee. Even though she wasn't a great homemaker and sometimes stuck it to me, like I said in the beginning, she really was a sweet lady.

"Going to her house is a nice thing to do. But it's not the most romantic thing there is. You should do something that will really let her know how you feel about her."

My mom suggested buying perfume, and though I knew Jamie would probably be happy to receive it, it didn't sound right to me. For one thing, since Hegbert didn't allow her to wear makeup—the single exception being the Christmas play—I was sure she couldn't wear perfume. I told my mom as much, and that was when she suggested taking her out to dinner.

"I don't have any money left," I said to her dejectedly. Though my family was wealthy and gave me an allowance, they never gave me more if I ran through it too quickly. "It builds responsibility," my father said, explaining it once.

"What happened to your money in the bank?"

I sighed, and my mom sat in silence while I explained what I had done. When I finished, a look of quiet satisfaction crossed her face, as if she knew I was finally growing up.

"Let me worry about that," she said softly. "You just find out if she'd like to go and if Reverend Sullivan will allow it. If she can, we'll find a way to make it happen. I promise."

THE following day I went to the church. I knew that Hegbert would be in his office. I hadn't asked Jamie yet, because I figured she would need his permission, and for some reason I wanted to be the one who asked. I guess it had to do with the fact that Hegbert hadn't exactly been welcoming me with open arms when I visited.

His door was partially open, and I saw him sitting behind his desk, spectacles propped on his nose. He was looking over some papers—they looked financial—and I figured he was trying to figure out the church budgets for the following year.

I knocked at the door, and he looked up with interest, then furrowed his brow when he saw that it was me.

"Hello, Reverend Sullivan," I said politely. "Do you have a moment?"

He took his glasses off and rubbed his eyes. He looked even more tired than usual. "Hello, Landon," he said wearily.

I'd dressed sharply for the occasion, by the way, with a jacket and tie. "May I come in?"

He nodded slightly, and I entered the office. He motioned for me to sit in the chair across from his desk.

"What can I do for you?" he asked.

I took a deep breath. "Well, sir, I wanted to ask if it would be all right with you if I took Jamie to dinner on New Year's Eve."

He sighed. "Is that all?" he said.

"Yes, sir. I'll bring her home anytime you'd need me to."

"Will your parents be joining you?" he asked.

"No, sir."

"Then I don't think that would be possible. But thank you for asking my permission first." He looked down at the papers, making it clear it was time for me to leave.

I stood from my chair and started toward the door. As I was about to go, I faced him again. "Reverend Sullivan?"

He looked up, surprised I was still there.

"I'm sorry for those things I used to do when I was younger, and I'm sorry that I didn't always treat Jamie the way she should have been treated. But from now on, things will change. I promise you that."

He seemed to look right through me. It wasn't enough.

"I love her," I said finally, and when I said it, his attention focused on me again.

"I know you do," he answered sadly, "but I don't want to see her hurt." Even though I must have been imagining it, I thought I saw his eyes begin to water.

"I wouldn't do that to her," I said.

He turned from me and looked out the window, watching as the winter sun tried to force its way through the clouds. It was a gray day, cold and bitter.

"Have her home by ten," he finally said, as though he knew he'd made the wrong decision.

I smiled and wanted to thank him, though I didn't. I could tell that he wanted to be alone. When I glanced over my shoulder on my way out the door, I was puzzled to see his face in his hands.

I ASKED Jamie about an hour later. She seemed surprised when I told her that I'd already spoken to her father, and I think it had an effect on how she viewed me after that. The one thing I hadn't told her was that it looked almost like Hegbert had been crying as I made my way out the door. Not only didn't I understand it completely, I didn't want her to worry.

I picked Jamie up right on schedule. Though I hadn't asked her to wear her hair down, she'd done it for me. Silently we drove over the bridge, down the waterfront to the restaurant.

It was crowded by the time we arrived, and all around us people were enjoying themselves. On New Year's people dressed fashionably, and we were the only two teenagers in the place. I didn't think we looked too out of place, though.

Jamie seemed nervously happy, and I knew right away that my mom had made the right suggestion.

"This is wonderful," she said to me. "Thank you for asking me to come."

"My pleasure," I said sincerely.

She looked out the window and stared at a boat that was passing by the restaurant, its lights blazing. For a moment she seemed lost in wonder. "It's beautiful here," she said.

"So are you," I answered.

Jamie blushed. "You don't mean that."

"Yes," I said quietly, "I do."

We held hands while we waited for dinner, and Jamie and I talked about some of the things that had happened in the past few months. She laughed when we talked about the homecoming dance, and I finally admitted the reason I'd asked her in the first place. She was a good sport about it—she sort of laughed it off cheerfully—and I knew that she'd already figured it out on her own.

"Would you want to take me again?" she teased.

"Absolutely."

Dinner was delicious—we both ordered the sea bass—and when the waiter finally removed our plates, the music started up. I offered Jamie my hand.

At first we were the only ones dancing, and everyone watched us as we glided around the floor. I think they all knew how we were feeling about each other, and it reminded them of when they were young. I could see them smiling wistfully at us. The lights were dim, and when the singer began a slow melody, I held Jamie close to me with my eyes closed, wondering if anything in my life had ever been this perfect and knowing at the same time that it hadn't.

I was in love, and the feeling was even more wonderful than I ever imagined it could be.

AFTER NEW YEAR'S WE SPENT the next week and a half together, doing the things that young couples did back then, though from time to time she seemed tired and listless. We spent time down by the Neuse River, tossing stones into the water, watching the ripples while we talked, or we went to the beach near Fort Macon. Even though it was winter, the ocean the color of iron, it was something that both of us enjoyed doing. After an hour or so Jamie would ask me to take her home, and we'd hold hands in the car. Sometimes, it seemed, she would almost nod off before we even got home.

Of course, spending time with Jamie also meant doing the things she enjoyed. Though I wouldn't go to her Bible-study class—I didn't want to look like an idiot in front of her—we did visit the orphanage twice more.

We kissed again too, though not every time we were together, and I didn't even think of trying to make it to second base. There wasn't any need to. There was something nice when I kissed her, something gentle and right, and that was enough for me. The more I did it, the more I realized that Jamie had been misunderstood her entire life, not only by me but by everyone.

Jamie wasn't simply the minister's daughter, someone who read the Bible and did her best to help others. Jamie was also a seventeen-year-old girl with the same hopes and doubts that I had. At least that's what I assumed, until she finally told me.

I'll never forget that day, because of how quiet she had been, and I had the funny feeling all day long that something important was on her mind.

I was walking her home from Cecil's Diner on the Saturday before school started up again. The day was blustery, with a fierce, biting wind, and while we walked, we'd had to stand close to each other to stay warm. Jamie had her arm looped through mine, and we were walking slowly, even more slowly than usual, and I could tell she wasn't feeling well again. She hadn't really wanted to go with me, because of the weather, but I'd asked her because of my friends. It was time, I remember thinking, that they finally knew about us. The only problem, as fate would have it, was that no one else was at Cecil's Diner. As in many coastal communities, things were quiet on the waterfront in the middle of winter.

She was silent as we walked, and I knew that she was thinking of a way to tell me something. I didn't expect her to start the conversation as she did.

"People think I'm strange, don't they?" she finally said.

"No, they don't," I lied. I kissed her cheek as I squeezed her arm a little tighter to me. She winced, and I could tell that I'd hurt her somehow. "Are you okay?" I asked, concerned.

"I'm fine," she said. "Will you do me a favor, though?"

"Anything," I said. I stopped walking and looked at her.

"Will you promise to tell me the truth from now on? Always?"

"Sure," I said, wondering where this was going. "I promise that from now on I'll always tell you the truth."

Somehow, when I said it, I knew that I'd come to regret it.

We started walking again. As we moved down the street, I glanced at her hand, which was looped through mine, and I saw a large bruise just below her ring finger. I had no idea where it had come from, since it hadn't been there the day before. For a second I thought it might have been caused by me, but then I realized that I hadn't even touched her there.

"People think I'm strange, don't they?" she asked again.

My breath was coming out in little puffs. "Yes," I finally answered. It hurt me to say it.

"Why?" She looked almost despondent.

I thought about it. "People have different reasons," I said vaguely, doing my best not to go any further.

"But why exactly? Is it because of my father? Or is it because I try to be nice to people?"

"I suppose," was all I could say. I felt a little queasy.

Jamie seemed disheartened. "Do you think I'm strange too?"

The way she said it made me ache more than I thought it would. We were almost at her house before I stopped her and held her close to me. I kissed her, and when we pulled apart, she looked toward the ground.

I put my finger beneath her chin, lifting her head up and making her look at me again. "You're a wonderful person, Jamie. You're beautiful, you're kind, you're gentle. . . . You're everything that I'd like to be. If people don't like you, or if they think you're strange, then that's their problem."

In the grayish glow of a cold winter day I could see her lower lip begin to tremble. Mine was doing the same thing, and I realized that my heart was speeding up as well.

I looked in her eyes, smiling with all the feeling I could muster, knowing that I couldn't keep the words inside any longer. "I love you, Jamie," I said to her. "You're the best thing that ever happened to me."

It was the first time I'd ever said the words to another person besides a member of my immediate family. When I'd imagined saying it to someone else, I'd somehow thought it was going to be hard, but it wasn't. I'd never been more sure of anything.

As soon as I said the words, though, Jamie bowed her head and started to cry. I wrapped my arms around her, wondering what was wrong. She was thin, and I realized for the first time that my arms went all the way around her. She'd lost weight, and I remembered that she'd barely touched her food earlier. She kept crying into my chest for what seemed like a long time. I wasn't sure what to think, or even if she felt the same way. Even so, I didn't regret the words. The truth is always the truth, and I'd just promised her that I would never lie again.

"Please don't say that," she said to me. "Please . . ."

"But I do," I said, thinking she didn't believe me.

She began to cry even harder. "I'm sorry," she whispered to me through her ragged sobs. "I'm so, so sorry."

My throat suddenly went dry. "Why're you sorry?" I asked, suddenly desperate to understand what was bothering her.

It took another long moment for her to stop crying, and in time she looked up at me. She kissed me gently, then ran her finger over my cheek. "You can't be in love with me, Landon," she said. "We can be friends, we can see each other, but you can't love me."

"Why not?" I shouted hoarsely, not understanding any of this.

"Because," she finally said softly, "I'm very sick, Landon."

The concept was so foreign that I couldn't comprehend what she was trying to say. "So what? You'll take a few days . . ."

A sad smile crossed her face, and I knew right then what she was trying to tell me. Her eyes never left mine as she finally said the words that numbed my soul. "I'm dying, Landon."

Chapter Seven

She had leukemia; she'd known it since last summer.

The moment she told me, the blood drained from my face and a sheaf of dizzying images fluttered through my mind. It was as though in that brief moment time had suddenly stopped, and I understood everything that had happened between us. I understood why she'd wanted me to do the play. I understood why, after we'd performed that first night, Hegbert had whispered to her with tears in his eyes, calling her his angel. I understood why he looked so tired all the time and why he fretted that I kept coming by the house. Everything became absolutely clear.

Why she wanted Christmas at the orphanage to be so special.

Why she didn't think she'd go to college.

Why she'd given me her Bible.

It all made perfect sense, and at the same time nothing seemed to make any sense at all.

Jamie Sullivan had leukemia.

Jamie, sweet Jamie, was dying. My Jamie . . .

"No, no," I whispered. "There has to be some mistake."

But there wasn't, and when she told me again, my world went blank. My head started to spin, and I clung to her tightly to keep from losing my balance. I closed my eyes, wanting the whole thing to go away.

"I'm so sorry, Landon," she kept saying over and over.

It was I who should have been saying it, however. I know that now, but my confusion kept me from saying anything.

Deep down I knew it wouldn't go away. I held her, not knowing what else to do, tears filling my eyes, trying and failing to be the rock I think she needed.

We cried together on the street for a long time, just a little way down the road from her house. We cried some more when Hegbert opened the door and saw our faces, knowing immediately that their secret was out. We cried when we told my mother later that afternoon, and my mother held us both to her bosom and sobbed loudly. On Sunday, Hegbert made the announcement to his congregation, his face a mask of anguish and fear, and he had to be helped back to his seat before he'd even finished.

Everyone in the congregation stared in silent disbelief at the words they'd just heard. Then, all at once, the wailing began.

WE SAT with Hegbert the day she told me, and Jamie patiently answered my questions. She didn't know how long she had left. No, there wasn't anything the doctors could do. It was a rare form of the disease, they'd said, one that didn't respond to available treatment. Yes, when the school year had started, she'd felt fine. It wasn't until the last few weeks that she'd begun to feel its effects.

"That's how it progresses," she said. "You feel fine, and then, when your body can't keep fighting, you don't."

Stifling my tears, I couldn't help but think about the play. "But those rehearsals, those long days . . . Maybe you shouldn't have—"

"Maybe," she said, reaching for my hand and cutting me off, "doing the play was the thing that kept me healthy for so long."

LATER she told me that seven months had passed since she'd been diagnosed. The doctors had given her a year, maybe less.

These days they could have treated her. These days Jamie would probably live. But this was happening forty years ago, and I knew what that meant. Only a miracle could save her.

WHY DIDN'T YOU TELL ME? This was the one question I hadn't asked her, the one I'd been thinking about. I hadn't slept that night, and my eyes were still swollen. I'd gone from shock to denial to sadness to anger and back again all night long, wishing it wasn't so.

We were in her living room the following day, the day that Hegbert had made the announcement to the congregation. It was January 11, 1959.

Jamie didn't look as depressed as I thought she would. But then again she'd been living with this for seven months. She and Hegbert had been the only ones to know, and neither of them had trusted even me. I was hurt by that and frightened at the same time.

"I'd made a decision," she explained to me, "that it would be better if I told no one, and I asked my father to do the same. You saw how people were after the services today. No one would even look me in the eye. If you had only a few months left to live, is that what you would have wanted?"

I knew she was right, but it didn't make it any easier. I was, for the first time in my life, completely and utterly at a loss. I'd never had anyone close to me die before, at least anyone that I could remember.

No one in my family or my circle of friends had ever had to confront something like this. Jamie was seventeen, a child on the verge of womanhood, dying and still very much alive at the same time. I was afraid, more afraid than I'd ever been, not only for her but for me as well. I lived in fear of doing something wrong, of doing something that would offend her. Was it okay to ever get angry in her presence? Was if okay to talk about the future anymore? My fear made talking to her difficult, though she was patient with me.

My fear, however, made me realize something else, something that made it all worse. I realized I'd never even known her when she'd been healthy. I had only started to spend time with her a few months earlier, and I'd been in love with her for only eighteen days. Those eighteen days seemed like my entire life, but now, when I looked at her, all I could do was wonder how many more days there would be.

On Monday she didn't show up for school, and I somehow knew that she'd never walk the hallways again. I'd never see her reading the Bible off by herself at lunch. I'd never see her brown cardigan moving through the crowd as she made her way to her next class. She was finished with school forever; she would never receive her diploma.

I couldn't concentrate on anything while I sat in class that first day back, listening as teacher after teacher told us what most of us had already heard. The responses were similar to those in church on Sunday. Girls cried; boys hung their heads; people told stories about her as if she were already gone.

I left school early and went to Jamie's. When I knocked at the door, she answered it the way she always did, cheerfully and without, it seemed, a care in the world.

"Hello, Landon," she said. "This is a surprise."

When she leaned in to kiss me, I kissed her back, though the whole thing made me want to cry.

"My father isn't home right now, but if you'd like to sit on the porch, we can."

"How can you do this?" I asked suddenly. "How can you pretend that nothing is wrong?"

"I'm not pretending that nothing is wrong, Landon. Let me get my coat, and we'll sit outside and talk, okay?"

She smiled at me, waiting for an answer, and I finally nodded.

She reached out and patted my arm. "I'll be right back."

I walked to the chair and sat down, Jamie emerging a moment later. She wore a heavy coat, gloves, and a hat to keep her warm.

"You weren't in school today," I said.

She looked down and nodded. "I know."

"Are you ever going to come back?"

"No," she said softly, "I'm not."

"Why? Are you that sick already?" I started to tear up, and she reached out and took my hand.

"No. Today I feel pretty good actually. It's just that I want to be home in the mornings, before my father has to go to the office. I want to spend as much time with him as I can."

Before I die, she meant to say, but didn't. I felt nauseated and couldn't respond.

"When the doctors first told us," she went on, "they said that I should try to lead as normal a life as possible for as long as I could. They said it would help me keep my strength up."

"There's nothing normal about this," I said bitterly.

"I know."

"Aren't you frightened?"

Somehow I expected her to say no or to explain to me that we can't presume to understand the Lord's plan.

She looked away. "Yes," she finally said, "I'm frightened all the time."

"Then why don't you act like it?"

"I do. I just do it in private."

"Because you don't trust me?"

"No," she said. "Because I know you're frightened too."

I BEGAN to pray for a miracle. They supposedly happen all the time, and I'd read about them in newspapers. People regaining use of their limbs after being told they'd never walk again, or somehow surviving a terrible accident when all hope was lost.

So that night I opened the Bible that Jamie had given me for Christmas and began to read. Now, I'd heard all about the Bible in Sunday school or at church, but to be frank, I just remembered the highlights—Jonah being swallowed by a whale, Jesus walking across the water or raising Lazarus from the dead. There were other biggies too. I knew that practically every chapter of the Bible has the Lord doing something spectacular, but I hadn't learned them all. As Christians, we leaned heavily on teachings of the New Testament, and I didn't know the first things about books like Joshua or Ruth or Joel. The first night, I read through Genesis; the second night I read through Exodus. Leviticus was next, followed by

Numbers and then Deuteronomy. The going got a little slow during certain parts, especially as all the laws were being explained, yet I couldn't put it down. It was a compulsion that I didn't fully understand.

It was late one night, and I was tired by the time I eventually reached Psalms, but somehow I knew this was what I was looking for. Everyone has heard the Twenty-third Psalm, which starts, *The Lord is my Shepherd, I shall not want,* but I wanted to read the others. After an hour I came across an underlined section that I assumed Jamie had noted because it meant something to her. This is what it said:

> *I cry to you, my Lord, my rock!*
>
> *Do not be deaf to me, for if you are silent, I shall go down to the pit like the rest. Hear my voice raised in petition as I cry to you for help, as I raise my hands, my Lord, toward your holy of holies.*

I closed the Bible with tears in my eyes, unable to finish the psalm. Somehow I knew she'd underlined it for me.

"I DON'T know what to do," I said numbly, staring into the dim light of my bedroom lamp. My mom and I were sitting on my bed. It was coming up on the end of January, the most difficult month of my life, and I knew that in February things would only get worse.

"I know this is hard for you," she murmured, "but there's nothing you can do."

"I don't mean about Jamie being sick—I know there's nothing I can do about that. I mean about Jamie and me."

My mother looked at me sympathetically. She was worried about Jamie, but she was also worried about me.

I went on. "It's hard for me to talk to her. All I can do when I look at her is think about the day when I won't be able to. So I spend all my time at school thinking about her, wishing I could see her right then, but when I get to her house, I don't know what to say."

"I don't know if there's anything you can say to make her feel better."

"Then what should I do?"

She looked at me sadly and put her arm around my shoulders. "You really love her, don't you?" she asked.

"With all my heart."

She looked as sad as I'd ever seen her. "What's your heart telling you to do?"

"I don't know."

"Maybe," she said gently, "you're trying too hard to hear it."

THE next day I was better with Jamie, though not much. Before I'd arrived, I'd told myself that I wouldn't say anything that might get her down—that I'd try to talk to her like I had before—and that's exactly how it went. I sat on her couch and told her what my friends were doing. I told her that I still hadn't heard from U.N.C., but I was hopeful I'd know within the next few weeks. I told her I was looking forward to graduation. I spoke as though she'd be back to school the following week, and I knew I sounded nervous the entire time. Jamie smiled and nodded at the appropriate times, asking questions every now and then. But I think we both knew by the time I finished talking that it was the last time I would do it. It didn't feel right to either of us.

My heart was telling me exactly the same thing.

I turned to the Bible again in the hope that it would guide me.

"HOW are you feeling?" I asked a couple of days later.

By now Jamie had lost more weight. Her skin was beginning to take on a slightly grayish tint, and the bones in her hands were starting to show through her skin. Again I saw bruises. We were inside her house in the living room; the cold was too much for her to bear. Despite all this, she still looked beautiful.

"I'm doing okay," she said, smiling valiantly. "The doctors have given me some pain medicine, and it helps a little."

"Can I get anything for you?"

"No, thank you. I'm doing fine."

I looked around the room, then back at her. "I've been reading the Bible," I finally said.

"You have?" Her face lit up, reminding me of the angel in the play. I couldn't believe that only six weeks had gone by.

"I read the Book of Job last night," I said, "where God stuck it to Job to test his faith."

She smiled and reached out to pat my arm, her hand soft on my skin. It felt nice. "You should read something else. That's not about God in one of his better moments."

"Do you ever feel like Job?"

She smiled, a little twinkle in her eyes. "Sometimes."

"But you haven't lost your faith?"

"No." I knew she hadn't, but I think I was losing mine.

"Is it because you think you might get better?"

"No," she said. "It's because it's the only thing I have left."

After that we started reading the Bible together. It somehow seemed like the right thing to do, but my heart was nonetheless telling me that there still might be something more.

At night I lay awake wondering about it.

READING the Bible gave us something to focus on, and all of a sudden everything started to get better between us, maybe because I wasn't as worried about doing something to offend her. What could be more right than reading the Bible? Though I didn't know nearly as much as she did about it, I think she appreciated the gesture, and occasionally when we read, she'd put her hand on my knee and simply listen to my voice.

Other times I'd be sitting beside her on the couch, looking at the Bible and watching Jamie out of the corner of my eye at the same time, and we'd come across a passage or a psalm, maybe even a proverb, and I'd ask her what she thought about it. She always had an answer, and I'd nod, thinking about it. Sometimes she asked me what I thought, and I did my best too.

One Friday night I brought her over for dinner at my house. My mom joined us for the main course, then left the table and sat in the den so that we could be alone.

It was nice there, sitting with Jamie, and I knew she felt the same way. She hadn't been leaving the house much, and this was a good change for her.

Since she'd told me about her illness, Jamie had stopped wearing her hair in a bun, and it was still as stunning as it had been the first time I saw her wear it down. She was looking at the china cabinet—my mom had one of those cabinets with lights inside—when I reached across the table and took her hand.

"Thank you for coming over tonight," I said.

"Thanks for inviting me."

I paused. "How's your father holding up?"

Jamie sighed. "Not too well. I worry about him a lot."

"He loves you dearly, you know."

"I know."

"So do I," I said, and when I did, she looked away. Hearing me say this seemed to frighten her again.

"Will you keep coming over to my house?" she asked. "Even later, you know, when . . ."

I squeezed her hand to let her know that I meant what I said. "As long as you want me to come, I'll be there."

She smiled. "You're a good friend, Landon. I don't know what I'd do without you."

She squeezed my hand, returning the favor. Sitting across from me, she looked radiant.

"I love you, Jamie," I said again, but this time she wasn't frightened. Instead, our eyes met across the table, and I watched as hers began to shine.

"I love you too," she finally whispered.

They were the words I'd been praying to hear.

I DON'T know if Jamie told Hegbert about her feelings for me, but I somehow doubted it, because his routine hadn't changed. It was his habit to leave the house whenever I came over after school, and this continued. I would knock at the door and listen as Hegbert explained to Jamie that he would be leaving and would be back in a couple of hours. "Okay, Daddy," I'd hear her say. Then I would wait for Hegbert to open the door. Once he let me in, he would open the hallway closet and silently pull out his coat and hat, buttoning the coat up all the way before he left the house. His coat was old-fashioned, black and long, the kind that was fashionable earlier this century.

Though he still didn't like me in the house if he wasn't there, he nonetheless allowed me to come in. I knew that part of the reason had to do with the fact that he didn't want Jamie to get chilled by sitting on the porch, and the only other alternative was to wait at the house while I was there. But I think Hegbert needed some time alone too, and that was the real reason for the change. He didn't talk to me about the rules of the house—I could see them in his eyes the first time he'd said I could stay. I was allowed to stay in the living room; that was all.

Jamie was still moving around fairly well, though the winter was miserable. A cold streak blew in during the last part of January and lasted nine days, followed by three straight days of drenching rain. Jamie had no interest in leaving the house in such weather, though after Hegbert had gone, she and I might stand on the porch for a couple of minutes to breathe the sea air. Whenever we did this, I found myself worrying about her.

People were always dropping by, some with food, others just to say hello. Even Eric and Margaret came over, and we sat in the living room and talked a little.

They were both nervous, and it took them a couple of minutes to finally get to the point. Eric had come to apologize, he said, and he said that he couldn't imagine why this had happened to her of all people. He also had something for her, and he set an envelope on the table, his hand shaking. His voice was choked up as he spoke, the words ringing with the most heartfelt emotion I'd ever heard him express.

"You've got the biggest heart of anyone I've ever met," he said to

Jamie, his voice cracking, "and even though I took it for granted and wasn't always nice to you, I wanted to let you know how I feel. I've never been more sorry about anything in my life." He paused and swiped at the corner of his eye. "You're the best person I'll probably ever know."

As he was fighting back his tears and sniffling, Margaret had already given in to hers and sat weeping on the couch, unable to speak. When Eric had finished, Jamie wiped her tears from her cheeks, stood slowly, and smiled, opening her arms in a gesture of forgiveness. Eric went to her willingly, finally beginning to cry openly as she gently caressed his hair, murmuring softly to him. The two of them held each other for a long time as Eric sobbed until he was too exhausted to cry anymore.

Then it was Margaret's turn, and she and Jamie did exactly the same thing.

When Eric and Margaret were finally ready to leave, they pulled on their jackets and looked at Jamie one more time, as if to remember her forever. I had no doubt that they wanted to think of her as she looked right then. In my mind she was beautiful, and I know they felt the same way.

"Hang in there," Eric said on his way out the door. "I'll be praying for you, and so will everybody else." Then he looked toward me, reached out, and patted me on the shoulder. "You too," he said, his eyes red. As I watched them leave, I knew I'd never been prouder of either of them.

Later, when we opened the envelope, we learned what Eric had done. Without telling us, he'd collected over four hundred dollars for the orphanage.

I WAITED for the miracle. It hadn't come.

In early February the pills Jamie was taking were increased to help offset the heightened pain she was feeling. The higher dosages made her dizzy, and twice she fell when walking to the bathroom. Afterward she insisted that the doctors cut back her medicine, and with reluctance they did. Though she was able to walk normally, the pain she was feeling intensified, and sometimes even raising her arm made her grimace.

Leukemia is a disease of the blood, but it weakened the rest of Jamie's body as well, preying on her muscles, making even simple things more difficult. In the first week of February she lost six pounds, and soon walking became difficult for her unless it was only for a short distance. That was, of course, if she could put up with the pain, which in time she couldn't. She went back to the pills again, accepting the dizziness in place of pain.

Still, we read the Bible.

Whenever I visited Jamie, I would find her on the couch with the Bible already opened, and I knew that eventually her father would have to carry her there if we wanted to continue. Though she never said anything to me about it, we both knew exactly what it meant.

I was running out of time, and my heart was still telling me that there was something more I could do.

ON FEBRUARY 14, Valentine's Day, Jamie picked out a passage from Corinthians that meant a lot to her. She told me that if she'd ever had the chance, it was the passage she'd wanted read at her wedding. This is what it said:

> *Love is always patient and kind. It is never jealous. Love is never boastful or conceited. It is never rude or selfish. It does not take offense and is not resentful. Love takes no pleasure in other people's sins, but delights in the truth. It is always ready to excuse, to trust, to hope, and to endure whatever comes.*

Jamie was the truest essence of that very description.

THREE days later, when the temperature slightly warmed, I showed her something wonderful, something I doubted she'd ever seen before, something I knew she would want to see.

Eastern North Carolina is a beautiful and special part of the country, blessed with temperate weather and, for the most part, wonderful geography. Nowhere is this more evident than Bogue Banks, an island right off the coast, near the place where we grew up. Twenty-four miles long and nearly a mile wide, this island is a fluke of nature, running from east to west, hugging the coastline a half-mile offshore. Those who live there can witness spectacular sunrises and sunsets every day of the year, both taking place over the expanse of the mighty Atlantic Ocean.

Jamie was bundled up heavily, standing beside me as this perfect southern evening descended. I pointed off into the distance and told her to wait. I had to support her as we stood there—she seemed lighter than the leaves of a tree that had fallen in autumn—but I knew it would be worth it.

In time the glowing, cratered moon began its seeming rise from the sea, casting a prism of light across the slowly darkening water, splitting itself into a thousand different parts, each more beautiful than the last. At exactly the same moment the sun was meeting the horizon in the opposite direction, turning the sky red and orange and yellow, as if heaven above had suddenly opened its gates and let all its beauty escape its holy confines. The ocean turned golden-silver as the shifting colors reflected off it, the water rippling and sparkling with the changing light, the vision glorious, almost like the beginning of time. The sun continued to lower itself, casting its glow as far as the eye could see, before finally, slowly, vanishing beneath the waves. The moon continued its slow drift upward, shimmering as it turned a thousand different shades of yellow, each paler than the last, before finally becoming the color of the stars.

Jamie watched in silence, my arm tight around her, her breathing shallow and weak. As the sky was turning to black and the first twinkling lights began to appear in the southern sky, I took her in my arms. I gently kissed both her cheeks and then, finally, her lips.

"That," I said, "is exactly how I feel about you."

A week later Jamie began regular trips to the hospital, although she insisted that she didn't want to stay there overnight. "I want to die at home," was all she said. Since the doctors couldn't do anything for her, they had no choice but to accept her wishes. At least for the time being.

"I'VE BEEN THINKING ABOUT the past few months," I said to her.

We were sitting in the living room holding hands as we read the Bible. Her face was growing thinner, her hair beginning to lose its luster. Yet her eyes, those soft blue eyes, were as lovely as ever. I don't think I'd ever seen someone as beautiful.

"I've been thinking about them too," she said.

"You knew, from the first day in Miss Garber's class, that I was going to do the play, didn't you? When you looked at me and smiled?"

She nodded. "Yes."

"And when I asked you to the homecoming dance, you made me promise that I wouldn't fall in love, but you knew that I was going to, didn't you?"

She had a mischievous gleam in her eye. "Yes."

"How did you know?"

She shrugged without answering, and we sat together for a few moments watching the rain as it blew against the windows.

"When I told you that I prayed for you," she finally said to me, "what did you think I was talking about?"

THE progression of her disease continued, speeding up as March approached. She was growing weak, and it looked like she'd have to go to the hospital to stay, despite her wishes.

It was my mother and father who changed all that.

My father had driven home from Washington, hurriedly leaving although Congress was still in session. Apparently my mother had called him and told him that if he didn't come home immediately, he might as well stay in Washington forever.

When my mother told him what was happening, my father said that Hegbert would never accept his help, that the wounds were too deep, that it was too late to do anything.

"This isn't about Reverend Sullivan or anything that happened in the past," my mom said, refusing to accept his answer. "This is about our son, who happens to be in love with a little girl who needs our help. And you're going to find a way to help her."

I don't know what my father said to Hegbert or how much the whole thing eventually cost. All I know is that Jamie was soon surrounded by expensive equipment and was watched by two full-time nurses while a doctor peeked in on her several times a day. She would be able to stay at home.

That night I cried on my father's shoulder for the first time in my life.

"DO YOU have any regrets?" I asked Jamie. She was in her bed under the covers, a tube in her arm feeding her the medication she needed. Her face was pale, her body featherlight.

"We all have regrets, Landon," she said, "but I've led a wonderful life."

"How can you say that?" I cried out, unable to hide my anguish. "With all that's happening to you?"

She squeezed my hand, her grip weak, smiling tenderly at me. "This," she admitted as she looked around her room, "could be better."

Despite my tears, I laughed, but then immediately felt guilty. I was supposed to be supporting *her,* not the other way around.

Jamie went on. "But other than that, I've been happy, Landon. I really have. I had a special father who taught me about God. I can look back and know that I couldn't have tried to help other people any more than I did." She paused and met my eyes. "I've even fallen in love and had someone love me back."

I kissed her hand, then held it against my cheek.

"It's not fair," I said.

She didn't answer.

"Are you still afraid?" I asked.

"Yes."

"I'm afraid too," I said.

"I know. And I'm sorry."

"What can I do?" I asked desperately. "I don't know what I'm supposed to do anymore."

"Will you read to me?"

I nodded, though I didn't know whether I'd be able to make it through the next page without breaking down.

Please, Lord, tell me what to do!

"MOM?" I asked my mother later that night.

"Yes?" We were sitting on the sofa in the den, the fire blazing before us. Earlier in the day Jamie had fallen asleep while I read to her, and knowing she needed her rest, I slipped out of her room. But before I did, I gently kissed her on the cheek. It was harmless, but Hegbert had walked in as I'd done so, and I could see the conflicting emotions in his eyes. He looked at me, knowing that I loved his daughter but also knowing that I'd broken one of the rules of his house, even an unspoken one. Had she been well, I know he would never have allowed me back inside. As it was, I showed myself to the door.

I couldn't blame him, not really. I found that spending time with Jamie sapped me of the energy to feel hurt by his demeanor. If Jamie had taught me anything over these last few months, she'd shown me that actions—not thoughts or intentions—were the way to judge others, and I knew that Hegbert would allow me in the following day. I was thinking about all this as I sat next to my mother on the sofa.

"Do you think we have a purpose in life?" I asked.

"I'm not sure I understand what you're asking," she said.

"I mean, how do you know what you're supposed to do?"

"Are you asking me about spending time with Jamie?"

I nodded, though I was still confused. "Sort of. I know I'm doing the right thing, but . . . something's missing. I spend time with her, and we talk and read the Bible, but . . ."

I paused, and my mother finished my thought for me. "You think you should be doing more?"

I nodded.

"I don't know that there's anything more you *can* do, sweetheart," she said gently.

"Then why do I feel the way I do?"

She moved a little closer on the sofa. "I think it's because you're frightened and you feel helpless. And the more you try, the more hopeless things seem."

"Is there any way to stop feeling this way?"

She put her arm around me and pulled me closer. "No," she said softly, "there isn't."

ANOTHER week went by, and Jamie grew steadily worse, her body weakening. Bedridden, she looked smaller, almost like a little girl again.

"Jamie," I pleaded, "what can I do for you?"

Jamie, my sweet Jamie, was sleeping for hours at a time now, even as I talked to her. She didn't move at the sound of my voice; her breaths were rapid and weak.

I sat beside the bed and watched her for a long time, thinking how much I loved her. I held her hand close to my heart, feeling the boniness of her fingers.

Why, I wondered, had all this happened to someone like Jamie? Was it all, as she would say, simply part of the Lord's plan? Did the Lord want me to fall in love with her, or was that something of my own volition? The longer Jamie slept, the more I felt her presence beside me, yet the answers to these questions were no clearer than they had been before.

On the nightstand by her bed I saw the collection of items that Jamie held close to her heart. There were photographs of her father—holding Jamie as a young child and standing outside of school on her first day of kindergarten; there was a stack of cards that children of the orphanage had sent. Sighing, I reached for them and opened the card on top.

Written in crayon, it said simply, "Please get better soon. I miss you."

It was signed by Lydia, the little girl who'd fallen asleep in Jamie's lap on Christmas Eve. The second card expressed the same sentiments, but what really caught my eye was the picture that the child, Roger, had drawn. He'd drawn a bird soaring above a rainbow.

Choking up, I closed the card. I couldn't bear to look any further, and as I put the stack back where it had been before, I noticed a newspaper clipping next to her water glass. I reached for the article and saw that it had been written about the play, published in the Sunday paper the day after we'd finished. In the photograph above the text I saw the only picture that had ever been taken of the two of us.

It seemed so long ago. I brought the article nearer to my face. As I stared, I remembered the way I felt when I had seen her that night. Peering closely at her image, I searched for any sign that she suspected what would come to pass. I knew she did, but her expression that night betrayed none of it. Instead, I saw only a radiant happiness. I sighed and set the clipping aside.

The Bible still lay open where I'd left off, and despite the fact that Jamie was sleeping, I felt the need to read some more. In time I came across another passage. This is what it said:

> *I am not commanding you, but I want to test the sincerity of your love by comparing it to the earnestness of others.*

The words made me choke up again, and just as I was about to cry, the meaning of it suddenly became clear. God had finally answered me, and I knew what I had to do.

I COULDN'T have made it to the church any faster even if I'd had a car. I took every shortcut I could, racing through people's backyards, jumping fences, and, in one case, cutting through someone's garage and out the side door. Everything I'd learned about the town when I was growing up came into play, and although I was never a particularly good athlete, on this day I was unstoppable.

I didn't care how I looked when I arrived, because I suspected Hegbert wouldn't care either. When I finally entered the church, I slowed to a walk, trying to catch my breath as I made my way to the back toward his office.

Hegbert looked up when he saw me, and I knew why he was here. At home he'd been dealing with Jamie's illness by cleaning the house almost obsessively. Here, though, papers were scattered across the desk; books were strewn about the room as if no one had straightened up for weeks. I knew that this was the place he thought about Jamie; this was the place where Hegbert came to cry.

"Reverend?" I said softly.

"I'd like to be alone," he croaked out.

He looked old and beaten. His face was drawn, and his hair had grown thinner since December. Even more than I, perhaps, he had to keep his spirits up around Jamie, and the stress of doing so was wearing him down.

I marched right up to his desk. "I'd like talk to you," I said firmly. "I wouldn't ask unless it was very important."

Hegbert sighed, and I sat down in the chair I had sat in before, when I'd asked him if he would let me take Jamie out for New Year's Eve. He listened as I told him what was on my mind.

When I was finished, Hegbert didn't say no. Instead, he wiped his eyes with his fingers and turned toward the window. Even he, I think, was too shocked to speak.

AGAIN I ran, again I didn't tire, my purpose giving me the strength I needed to go on. When I reached Jamie's house, I rushed in the door without knocking, and the nurse who'd been in her bedroom came out to see what had caused the racket.

"Is she awake?" I asked, euphoric and terrified at the same time.

"Yes," the nurse said cautiously. "When she woke up, she wondered where you were."

I apologized for my disheveled appearance and thanked her, then asked if she wouldn't mind leaving us alone. I walked into Jamie's room, partially closing the door behind me.

She was pale, so very pale, but her smile let me know she was still fighting. "Hello, Landon," she said, her voice faint. "Thank you for coming back."

I pulled up a chair and sat next to her, taking her hand in mine. Seeing her lying there made something tighten deep in my stomach, making me almost want to cry.

She lifted her hand slightly off the bed, and I kissed it, then leaned forward and kissed her cheek as well.

"Do you love me?" I asked her.

She smiled. "Yes."

"Do you want me to be happy?" As I asked her this, I felt my heart beginning to race.

"Of course I do."

"Will you do something for me, then?"

She looked away, sadness crossing her features. "I don't know if I can anymore," she said.

"But if you could, would you?"

I cannot adequately describe the intensity of what I was feeling. Love, anger, sadness, hope, and fear, whirling together, sharpened by nervousness. Jamie looked at me curiously, and I knew that I'd never felt as strongly for another person as I did at that moment. As I returned her gaze, this realization made me wish for the millionth time that I could make all this go away. Had it been possible, I would have traded my life for hers. I wanted to tell her my thoughts, but the sound of her voice silenced me.

"Yes," she finally said, her voice weak yet somehow still full of promise, "I would."

Finally getting control of myself, I kissed her again, then brought my hand to her face, gently running my fingers over her cheek. I marveled at the softness of her skin, the gentleness I saw in her eyes. Even now she was perfect. My throat began to tighten, but I knew what I had to do. Since it was not within my power to cure her, what I wanted was to give her something that she'd always wanted.

It was what my heart had been telling me to do all along.

Jamie, I understood then, had already given me the answer I'd been searching for, the one my heart had needed to find. She'd told me the answer as we'd sat outside Mr. Jenkins's office the night we asked him about doing the play.

I smiled softly, leaned closer, and took a deep breath. When I exhaled, these were the words that flowed with my breath: "Will you marry me?"

Chapter Eight

When I was seventeen, my life changed forever.

As I walk the streets of Beaufort forty years later, thinking back on that year of my life, I remember everything as clearly as if it were all still unfolding before my very eyes.

I remember Jamie saying yes to my breathless question and how we began to cry together. I remember talking to both Hegbert and my parents, explaining to them what I needed to do. They thought I was doing it only for Jamie, and all three of them tried to talk me out of it. What they didn't understand—and what I had to make clear to them—was that I needed to do it for me.

I was in love with her, so deeply in love that I didn't care if she was sick. I didn't care that we wouldn't have long together. All I cared about was doing something my heart told me was the right thing to do. In my mind it was the first time God had ever directly spoken to me, and I knew with certainty that I wasn't going to disobey.

I know that some of you may wonder if I was doing it out of pity. Some of the more cynical may even wonder if I did it because she'd be gone soon anyway and I wasn't committing much. The answer to both questions is no. I would have married Jamie Sullivan no matter what happened in the future. I would have married Jamie Sullivan if the miracle I was praying for had suddenly come true. I knew it at the moment I asked her, and I still know it today.

Jamie was more than just the woman I loved. In that year Jamie helped me become the man I am today. With her steady hand she showed me how important it was to help others; with her patience and kindness she showed me what life is really all about. Her cheerfulness and optimism, even in times of sickness, was the most amazing thing I have ever witnessed.

We were married by Hegbert in the Baptist church, my father standing beside me as the best man. That was another thing she did. In the South it's a tradition to have your father beside you, but for me it's a tradition that wouldn't have had much meaning before Jamie came into my life. Jamie had brought my father and me together again; somehow she'd also managed to heal some of the wounds between our two families. After learning what he'd done for me and for Jamie, I knew in the end that my father was someone that I could always count on, and our relationship grew steadily stronger as the years passed.

Jamie also taught me the value of forgiveness and the transforming power that it offers. I realized this the day that Eric and Margaret had come to her house. Jamie held no grudges. Jamie led her life the way the Bible taught.

Jamie was not only the angel who saved Tom Thornton, she was the angel who saved us all.

Just as she'd wanted, the church was bursting with people. There were over two hundred people inside, and more than that waited outside the doors as we were married on March 12, 1959. I saw everyone I knew—Miss Garber, Eric, Margaret, Eddie, Carey, Angela, and even Lew and his grandmother—and there wasn't a dry eye in the house when the entrance music began. Although Jamie hadn't moved from her bed in two weeks, she insisted on walking down the aisle so that her father could give her away. "It's very important to me, Landon," she'd said. "It's part of my dream, remember?" Though I assumed it would be impossible, I simply nodded. I couldn't help but wonder at her faith.

I knew she had planned on wearing the white dress she'd worn in the play, though it would hang more loosely than it had before. While I was wondering how she would look in the dress, my father laid his hand on my shoulder as we stood before the congregation.

"I'm proud of you, son."

I nodded. "I'm proud of you too, Dad." It was the first time I'd ever said those words to him.

My mom was in the front row, dabbing her eyes with her handkerchief when the wedding march began. The doors opened, and I saw Jamie, seated in her wheelchair, a nurse by her side. With all the strength she had left, Jamie stood shakily as her father supported her. Then Jamie and Hegbert slowly made their way down the aisle as everyone in the church sat silently in wonder. Halfway down the aisle Jamie suddenly seemed to tire, and they stopped while she caught her breath. Her eyes closed, and for a moment I didn't think she could go on. But finally she nodded slightly, and they started moving again. As they did so, I felt my heart surge with pride.

It was, I remember thinking, the most difficult walk anyone ever had to make. In every way a walk to remember.

The nurse had rolled the wheelchair up front as Jamie and her father made their way toward me. When she finally reached my side, there were gasps of joy, and everyone began to clap. The nurse rolled the wheelchair into position, and Jamie sat down again, spent. With a smile I lowered myself onto my knees so that I would be level with her. My father then did the same.

Hegbert, after kissing Jamie on the cheek, retrieved his Bible in order to begin the ceremony. All business now, he seemed to have abandoned his role as Jamie's father to something more distant, where he could keep his emotions in check. Yet I could see him struggling. He perched his glasses on his nose and opened the Bible, then looked at Jamie and me. From this position Hegbert towered over us, and I could tell that he hadn't anticipated our being so much lower. For a moment he stood before us, almost confused, then, surprisingly, decided to kneel as well. Jamie smiled and reached for his free hand, then reached for mine, linking us together.

Hegbert began the ceremony in the traditional way, then read the passage in the Bible that Jamie had once pointed out to me. Knowing how weak she was, I thought he would have us recite the vows right away, but once more Hegbert surprised me.

He cleared his throat, and his voice rose high enough so everyone could hear it. This is what he said: "As a father, I'm supposed to give away my daughter, but I'm not sure that I'm able to do this."

The congregation went silent, and Hegbert nodded at me,

willing me to be patient. Jamie squeezed my hand in support.

"I can no more give Jamie away than I can give away my heart. But what I can do is to let another share in the joy that she has always given me. May God's blessings be with you both."

It was then that he set the Bible aside. He reached out, offering his hand to mine, and I took it, completing the circle.

With that, he led us through our vows. My father handed me the ring my mother had helped me pick out, and Jamie gave me one as well. We slipped them on our fingers. Hegbert watched us as we did so, and when we were finally ready, he pronounced us husband and wife. I kissed Jamie softly as my mother began to cry. Then I held Jamie's hand in mine. In front of God and everyone else I promised my love and devotion, in sickness and in health, and I'd never felt so good about anything.

It was, I remember, the most wonderful moment of my life.

IT IS now forty years later, and I can still remember everything from that day. I may be older and wiser, I may have lived another life since then, but I know that when my time comes, the memories of that day will be the final images that float through my mind. I still love her, you see, and I've never removed my ring. In all these years I've never felt the desire to do so.

I breathe deeply, taking in the fresh spring air. Though Beaufort has changed and I have changed, the air itself has not. It's still the air of my childhood, the air of my seventeenth year, and when I finally exhale, I'm fifty-seven once more. But this is okay. I smile slightly, looking toward the sky, knowing there's one thing I still haven't told you: I now believe, by the way, that miracles can happen.

NICHOLAS SPARKS

BYRON HOLLAND

Does Nicholas Sparks believe in the kind of true love that evolves between the two young people in *A Walk to Remember?* You bet he does. Sparks not only grew up in a loving home—"my parents were in love and raised us with love"—but he and Cathy, his wife of ten years, have a strong marriage. He says, "I believe that if you're looking for love, you will find love."

Sparks often loosely bases his novels on people near and dear to him. Now that Nick and Cathy's family includes two sons—Miles and Ryan—readers can expect his next book to center around a young boy. Romance fans needn't worry, though. Sparks says, "It'll be my best love story yet!"

Born in Nebraska in 1965, Sparks spent most of his childhood in California. Running was his passion during high school, and he received a full track scholarship to Notre Dame. Sidelined by an injury during his freshman year, he spent that summer back home, icing his tendon and moping around the house. To keep him busy, his mother encouraged him to write a book. As Sparks says, "Eight weeks later I was the proud creator of my first novel." This book, a horror story, was never published and was laid to rest along with a second novel, a mystery. After college Sparks held a variety of jobs, including real estate appraiser, waiter, and pharmaceuticals salesman. Along the way he returned to writing, with phenomenal results. His first published book, *The Notebook,* became a nationwide best seller and was quickly followed by *Message in a Bottle.* He now pursues writing full-time. Sparks and his family live in North Carolina.

Thunderhead

by Douglas Preston and Lincoln Child

For a thousand years the ancient city of Quivira has slept undisturbed, its treasures hidden.

For a thousand years Quivira has been protected from the outside world.

And the outside world has been protected from Quivira.

Until now.

1 The freshly paved road left Santa Fe and arrowed west through piñon trees. An amber-colored sun was sinking into a scrim of dirty clouds behind the snowcapped Jemez Mountains, drawing a counterpane of shade across the landscape. Nora Kelly guided the rattletrap Ford pickup along the road, down chamiso-covered hills and across the beds of dry washes. It was the third time she had been out here in as many months.

She came up from Buckman's Wash into what had once been Jackrabbit Flats. A moment later her truck was speeding past manicured greens. Beyond stood the new Fox Run clubhouse, a massive structure of fake adobe. Nora looked away.

The truck rattled over a cattle guard, and suddenly the road was washboard dirt. She bounced past a cluster of ancient mailboxes and the crude, weather-beaten sign that read RANCHO DE LAS CABRILLAS. For a moment the memory of a summer day twenty years before passed through her mind: Once again she was holding a bucket, helping her father paint the sign. *Cabrillas,* he'd said, was the Spanish name for the constellation Pleiades. "To hell with the cattle," she remembered him saying. "I bought this place for its stars."

The road turned to ascend a rise, and she slowed. There in a grassy valley stood the old ranch house, windows boarded up, that was once the Kelly family home. No one had lived here in five years. It was no great loss, Nora told herself: The house was a mid-'50s prefab, already falling apart when she was growing up. Her father had spent all his money on the land. Maybe her brother was right and she should sell the place. She certainly couldn't afford to build her own house here—not on an assistant professor's salary.

She could see the lights coming on in the Gonzales ranch house, a quarter mile away. It was a real working ranch, not like her father's hobby ranchito. Teresa Gonzales, a girl she'd grown up with, now ran the place by herself. A big, smart, fearless woman, in recent years she'd taken it upon herself to look after the Kelly ranch, too. Teresa had left Nora a telephone message that for the past three or four nights she had seen dim lights in and around the empty house, and—she thought—large animals slinking about.

Nora waited a few minutes, looking for signs of life, but the ranch was quiet and empty. She eased the truck through the inner gate and down the last two hundred yards of road, parked around back, and killed the engine. Pulling a flashlight out of the glove compartment, she stepped lightly onto the dirt. The door of the house hung open, held precariously by a single hinge screw, its lock cut off long ago.

She flicked on the flashlight. The door moved aside at her push. The boarded windows made the interior difficult to make out. Beer bottles and broken glass lay strewn across the floor. The carpet had been ripped up and sofa cushions sliced in half and tossed about the room. Holes had been kicked in the drywall. It wasn't much worse than on her previous visit.

She turned into the kitchen. Drawers had recently been removed and strewn about the room. The linoleum was coming up in big curls, and someone had hastened the process, peeling off strips and even ripping up floorboards to expose the crawl space underneath. Vandalism is hard work, she thought.

She left the kitchen and began to climb the stairs, trying to bring a thought into focus. Somehow this fresh violence didn't seem quite as random as it had in the past. It was almost as if someone was looking for something. Halfway up the darkness of the stairwell, she stopped.

Was that the crunch of glass underfoot?

She waited, motionless in the dim light. There was no sound but the faint susurrus of wind. She continued up the stairs.

She turned right on the landing and shone the flashlight into her old bedroom. The pink wallpaper was hanging in strips; the mattress was one giant pack rat's nest; the floorboards were sprung. Across the hall her brother's room was also a wreck. But over the smell of ruin, she thought she detected the faintest scent of crushed flowers in the night air. Strange—the windows are all shuttered up here. She moved down the hall toward her parents' bedroom.

This time, there was no mistaking it: the faint tinkle of broken glass from below. She moved silently back to the top of the landing.

"Who is it?" she called out.

Only the wind answered.

She swung the flashlight beam into the empty stairwell.

"This is private property!" she yelled in her steadiest voice.

In the ensuing silence, there came a foot pad, close to the stairwell.

"Teresa?" Nora called, in a desperate hope.

And then she heard something else: a throaty, menacing sound that was almost a growl.

Dogs, she thought with a sudden flood of relief. "Yah!" she cried, waving the light. "Get out of here!"

Nora knew how to handle stray dogs. She stomped down the stairs, speaking loudly and firmly. Reaching the bottom, she swept the beam across the living room.

It was empty. The dogs must have run at the sound of her approach.

Nora took a deep breath. She heard a careful footstep, then another, excruciatingly slow and deliberate. That same scent of flowers wafted through the heavy air, this time stronger.

And then out of the corner of her eye she saw a huge pelted form racing along the wall. She turned to confront it as a stunning blow landed across her back.

She fell sprawling, feeling coarse fur at the nape of her neck.

There was a maniacal wet growling, like the slavered fighting of rabid hounds. She lashed into the figure with a vicious kick. It snarled but relaxed its grip slightly, giving Nora a moment to wrench free. Just as she jumped up, a second figure slammed into her and threw her to the ground, landing atop her. Nora twisted, feeling broken glass digging into her skin as the dark form pinned her to the ground. She glimpsed a naked belly covered with glowing spots; jaguar stripes; claws of horn and hair; a midriff—dank and matted—wearing a belt of silver conchas. Narrow eyes, terrifyingly red and bright, stared at her from grimy slits in a buckskin mask.

"Where is it?" a voice rasped in her face, washing her in the cloyingly sweet stench of rotten meat. "Where is the letter?" Viselike claws grasped her roughly around the neck and right arm. She began to choke in pain and terror.

Suddenly a flash of light and a deafening blast cut through the darkness. She felt the grip slacken, and in a frenzy she twisted free of the claws. She rolled over as a second blast ripped a hole in the ceiling overhead, showering her with plaster.

"Nora?" she heard. "That you, Nora?" Framed in the dim light of the front door was a plump figure, shotgun hanging forward.

"Teresa!" Nora sobbed. She scrambled to her feet and stumbled toward the light.

"You okay?" Teresa asked, grabbing Nora's arm, steadying her.

"I don't know."

"Let's get out of here."

Outside, Nora gulped the cool twilight air. "What happened?" she heard Teresa ask. "Those were some hellacious-looking wild dogs. Big as wolves, almost. But what kind of dogs could vanish so—"

"Teresa, one of them *spoke* to me."

Teresa stared at her, a skeptical look creeping into her eyes. "Must've been pretty terrifying," she said at last.

Nora knew the woman didn't believe her, but she didn't have the energy to argue.

"You need to either tear this place down, Nora, or sell it. It's becoming a problem, and not just for you."

"I know it's an eyesore. But I just hate to think of letting it go. I'm sorry it's caused trouble for you."

"I would've thought this might change your mind. Your arm looks bitten. You better get a rabies shot."

Nora watched as her neighbor turned onto the narrow trail that headed back up the hill. Then she eased into the driver's seat of her truck and locked all the doors with a shaking hand, wincing at a sudden stab of pain in her neck. She turned over the engine, unsuccessfully, and cursed. She needed a new vehicle, along with a new everything else in her life.

She tried it again, and after a sputtering protest the engine coughed into life. To one side a flash of silver winked briefly. She turned to see a huge shape, black and furred, bounding toward her against the last twilight in the western sky.

Nora slammed the old truck into gear, punched on the headlights, and went fishtailing out of the yard. As she careened through the inside gate, she saw with consummate horror that the thing was racing alongside her.

She jammed the accelerator to the floor, spraying mad patterns of dirt. And then the thing was gone. But she continued to accelerate down the road to the outer gate, wheels pounding the washboard. After an unbearably long moment her headlights finally picked up the outer cattle guard looming from the darkness ahead, the row of old mailboxes nailed to a long, horizontal board beside it. Too late, Nora jammed on the brakes; the truck struck the cattle guard and was airborne. It landed heavily and skidded in the sand, striking the old board. There was the crunch of splintering wood, and the boxes were flung to the ground.

She sat in the truck, breathing hard. In the glow of the headlights, she could see the damage. The row of mailboxes had been a rickety affair to begin with, recently supplanted by a shiny new set of post office boxes that stood nearby.

She jumped out and, glancing around for any sign of the figure, moved around to the front of the truck, picked up the rotten, abandoned mailboxes, and dragged them aside into the brush. An envelope lay in the dirt, and she grabbed it. As she turned to step back into the truck, the headlights caught the front of the envelope. Nora froze for a moment, gasping in surprise.

Then she shoved it into her shirt pocket, jumped into the truck, and peeled back onto the road, careering toward the distant, welcoming lights of town.

2

The Santa Fe Archaeological Institute stood on a low mesa between the Sangre de Cristo foothills and the town of Santa Fe itself. Wealthy, reserved, and much wedded to its traditions, it was looked on with both awe and envy by archaeologists across the country.

The institute's collections contained innumerable priceless artifacts, but nothing was as valuable as the contents of its map vault, housing the location of every known archaeological site in the Southwest.

Professor Nora Kelly dug into her bag, extracted her security card, and inserted it into a slot in the vault's metal door. When the red light above the door turned green, she heaved the door open and stepped inside. Before her, bathed in pitiless fluorescent light, lay two rows of metal safes. Nora approached one, punched in a code, and opened its door.

There were sixteen maps in the quadrants that interested her, covering eight hundred and eighty square miles. Lifting the maps by the edges of their metal rails, Nora gently spread them out on the scarred surface of a Formica table.

The sequence of 7.5-minute maps—the most detailed U.S. Geological Survey maps made—covered an exceedingly remote area of southern Utah, framed by Lake Powell to the south and west and Bryce Canyon to the east—slickrock sandstone country bisected by a diagonally trending maze of deep canyons.

It was into this desolate triangle, sixteen years before, that Nora's father had disappeared.

Nora slid two fingers into her jacket and removed the letter she had never allowed from her person since she found it just nightmarish hours before. The envelope was discolored and brittle, addressed faintly in pencil. And there, as she had in the glow of the headlights the previous night, she read the name of her mother, dead six months, and the address of the ranch. Slowly, almost unwillingly, she moved her gaze to the return address. "Padraic Kelly," it confirmed in the generous, loopy hand she remembered so well. "Somewhere west of the Kaiparowits."

A letter from her dead father to her dead mother, written and stamped sixteen years ago.

For perhaps the hundredth time since she first read the letter the night before, Nora found herself forced to squash a surge of hope. There was no way her father could still be alive. Obviously, somebody had found the letter and mailed it. The fresh postmark showed that it had been mailed from Escalante, Utah, only five weeks before.

But who? And why? And, more frighteningly, was this the letter the creatures in the abandoned ranch house were after?

She swallowed. It *had* to be; there was no other answer.

Carefully Nora removed the three sheets of yellowed paper from the envelope.

Thursday, August 2 (I think), 1983

Dearest Liz,

Although I'm a hundred miles from the nearest post office, I couldn't wait to write you any longer. I'll mail this first thing when I hit civilization. Better yet, maybe I'll hand-deliver it, and a lot more besides. I know you think I've been a bad husband, but now I can *promise* you that everything will change. We will be together again. Nora and Skip will have their father back. And we will be rich, dear heart. This time it's for real. I'm about to enter the lost city of Quivira.

Remember Nora's school report on Coronado and his search for the fabled city of gold? I got to thinking, What if all the stories Coronado heard were true? I found some documents that gave an unexpected hint. And I came out here.

> I didn't really expect to find anything. You know me, always dreaming. But, Liz, I *did* find it.
>
> Coming east from Old Paria, I hit Hardscrabble Wash past Ramey's Hole. I'm not sure which side canyon I took—on a whim, mostly. Maybe it was Muleshoe. There I found the ghostly trace of an ancient Anasazi road, and I followed it northeast. I crossed maybe three more canyons in the same way, following ancient trails.

Nora glanced at the maps. Locating Old Paria beside the Paria River, she began sweeping the nearby canyon country with her eyes. There were dozens of washes and small canyons, many unnamed. After a few minutes her heart leaped. There was Hardscrabble—and Ramey's Hole, a large circular depression cut by a bend in the wash. She traced an imaginary line northeast, then counted three canyons over. This brought her to an unnamed canyon, very narrow and deep.

> I traveled the next day up-canyon, veering northwest, sometimes losing the trail, sometimes finding it again. It was very tough going. The trail jumped to the next canyon through a kind of gap.

Breathing quickly, Nora traced the unnamed canyon. How far would he have gone that day? There was no way of knowing. And where was this gap? Frustration welled within her.

> The canyon split and split again, God knows how many times. But only when I reached what I call the Devil's Backbone, and the slot canyon beyond, was I sure.
>
> You see, I've found the city. I know it. There is a damn good reason why it remained unknown, when you see how fiendishly they hid it. The slot canyon led to a very deep, secret canyon beyond. There's a hand-and-toe trail leading up the rock face here to what must be a hidden alcove in the cliffs. If I can make it up without technical climbing gear, I'll reach the city tomorrow.

It is all yours if you want it. The divorce can be reversed and the clock turned back. I just want my family. My darling Liz, I love you so much. Kiss Nora and Skip a million times for me.

Pat

Nora gazed once again over the expanse of maps. If the ruin was really as important as he made out, it must also be unknown, because nothing remotely like it had been marked. The closest human habitation seemed to be an extremely remote Indian village, marked NANKOWEAP, that was at least several days' journey away.

She carefully slipped the letter back into its envelope.

It was clearly impossible to determine where he had gone by looking at the maps. If she wanted to find Quivira and perhaps solve the mystery of her father's disappearance, she would have to go into that country herself.

IF ANYTHING, the apartment was worse than Nora remembered. The dirty dishes in the sink tottered so precariously that no additional plates could be added. A tiny pyramid of cartons for pizza and Chinese food rose from the wastebasket and trailed onto the nearby floor like a bridal veil.

The apartment's inhabitant, her brother, Skip, slouched on a decomposing orange couch and looked over at her. He still had little bronze curls across his forehead and a smooth adolescent face. He'd be very handsome, Nora thought, if it weren't for the petulant, immature look to his face. It was hard—painful, really—to think of him as grown up, his physics degree from Stanford barely a year old, and doing absolutely nothing. Sometime after their mother's death six months ago, Skip had switched from beer to tequila; now he drained a fresh bottle into a Mason jar, a sullen look on his inflamed face.

"So what made you change your mind?" Skip asked. "I thought you were going to hold on to that ranch until hell froze over." He took a long sip from the Mason jar.

"Something happened there last night." Nora looked at him steadily. "I was attacked."

The sullen look vanished, and Skip sat up. "What? By who?"

"People dressed up as animals, I think. I'm not sure."

"Are you all right?" His face flushed with anger and concern.

"Teresa and her shotgun came along. Except for this scratch on my arm, I'm fine."

Skip slouched back, the energy gone as quickly as it had arrived. "What do you suppose they wanted?"

"They wanted a letter," she said. "I think it was this one." Carefully she pulled the yellowed envelope from her breast pocket and laid it on the table. Skip bent over it and then, with a sharp exhalation, picked it up. He read in silence. Nora could feel her heart pounding.

Skip laid the letter down. "Where did you find this?" he asked.

"It was near our old mailbox. Mailed five weeks ago."

"You think he's alive?" he said weakly, eyes filling with tears.

"No. Not a chance. He would never have abandoned us if he were alive. He *loved* us, Skip."

"But this letter—"

"Was written sixteen years ago. Skip, he's dead. We have to face that. But maybe now we can find out what happened to him."

Skip leaned back on the couch. "These guys who wanted the letter," he said, "how the hell did they find out about it?"

"Who knows? Dad had some pretty unsavory contacts—"

"So *Mom* said," Skip interrupted. "What are you planning to do?"

"I figured—" Nora paused. This was going to be the hard part. "I figured the way to find out what happened to him would be to find Quivira. And that will take money. Which is why I want to put Las Cabrillas on the market."

Skip shook his head and gave a wet laugh. "I get it. The institute won't fund anything, right? Can't say I'm surprised. I mean, Dad says here he never *saw* the city! He's all worked up over a trail. You know what Mom would say about this?"

"She'd say he was dreaming again. Are you saying it, too?"

Skip winced. "No. I'm not siding with Mom." The scornful tone had been stung from his voice. "I just don't want to lose a sister the way I lost a father."

"Come on, Skip. That's not going to happen."

Nora paused. Skip was right about one thing. Her supervisor at the institute, Dr. Murray Blakewood, had turned her down not an hour earlier.

She decided to try again. "Look, Skip, in the letter Dad says he was following an ancient road. If I can find that road, it would be the proof I need."

Suddenly Skip straightened up. "I've got an idea. A way that maybe you can find that road without going out there. I had a physics professor at Stanford, Leland Watkins. Now he works for JPL, the Jet Propulsion Laboratory at Caltech. It's a branch of NASA."

"How's that going to help us?"

"This guy's been working on the shuttle program. I read about this specialized radar they have that can see through thirty feet of sand. They were using it to map ancient trails in the Sahara."

Nora stared at her brother. "This radar can see old roads?"

"Right through the sand."

"And you took a class from this guy? You think he still remembers you?"

Skip's face suddenly became guarded. "Oh, yeah. He remembers me. He had this really cute girlfriend, a graduate student, and I . . ." Skip's face colored. "Sorry about that. If you want to talk to Watkins, I guess you're going to have to call him yourself."

NORA sat at a worktable in the institute's artifact analysis lab. With a sudden movement she turned toward the phone, dialing information.

"Pasadena," she said into the phone. "The Jet Propulsion Laboratory." It took one external and two internal operators to learn that Leland Watkins's extension was 2330.

"Yes?" came the voice at last, high-pitched and impatient.

"Hello. This is Nora Kelly, at the Santa Fe Archaeological Institute. We're working on a project in southeastern Utah, looking at ancient Anasazi roads. Would it be possible for you—"

"We don't have any radar coverage in that area," interrupted Watkins.

Nora took a deep breath. "Is there any way we might—"

"No, there is no way," said Watkins, his voice growing nasal in irritation. "I've got a list a mile long of people waiting for radar coverage: geologists, biologists, you name it."

"I see," said Nora, trying to keep her voice even.

"We're backed up two years with applications. And I'm too swamped to talk to you about it. Now will you excuse me? Write if you want an application."

"And the address—" Nora realized she was talking to a dial tone. "Arrogant jerk!" she shouted. "I'm *glad* my brother stole your girlfriend!" She slammed the phone into its cradle.

Then she paused, staring speculatively at the phone. Dr. Watkins's extension had been 2330.

Reaching again, she slowly and deliberately dialed a long-distance number. "Give me extension 2331, please."

PETER Holroyd had promised nothing except a meeting. A meeting far from JPL, of course—if Leland Watkins got even a whiff of extracurricular dealings, Holroyd would be in deep trouble. But these hints of a lost city had intrigued him more than he wanted to admit.

He glanced around and slid into his usual booth at Al's Pizza in his Monterey Park neighborhood. The traffic had made him late, but the place was still empty.

Al himself came over, a small, impossibly hirsute man. "Good evening, Professor!" he cried. "Nice night, eh?"

"Sure," said Holroyd. Over Al's shoulder he could see a small television tuned to CNN. There was an image of the shuttle *Republic,* showing an astronaut floating upside down. He felt a quick familiar longing and turned back to Al's cheerful face.

Al slapped the table with a floury hand. "What tonight? We've got good anchovy pizza coming out in five minutes."

"I love anchovies," he said. "Bring me two slices."

"Angelo! Two slices anchovy for the professor!" Al cried as he swept back behind the counter.

Holroyd heard the familiar squeal of the pizza parlor door and caught a glimpse of a young woman struggling through, lugging a large portfolio case. She had unusual bronze-colored hair that broke in waves over her shoulders. Her body was slim, and as she dragged the case through the door, he couldn't help but notice a shapely rear. She turned, and he looked up quickly, guiltily, only to be arrested by her face: smart, restless, impatient.

"Hi," she said. "Are you Peter Holroyd?"

He nodded. And experienced a moment of panic. This was not the frowsy scholar he'd expected: This woman was lovely.

"I'm Nora Kelly." She extended her hand, dumped her portfolio on the table, and slid into the far side of the booth.

Holroyd shook the proffered hand. The fingers were cool and unexpectedly strong.

"Thanks for meeting with me."

Holroyd tried a smile. "Well, your story was interesting, but a little vague. I'm interested in hearing more about this lost city."

"Well, I'm afraid it has to be vague for the time being. You can understand the need for secrecy."

"Then I'm not sure what I can do for you," Holroyd said. He hesitated. "What's your position at the institute?"

She leaned toward him. "Mr. Holroyd, I've got a confession to make. Right now I'm not working with the complete support of the institute. They won't even consider an expedition to find this city until I bring them proof. That's why I need your help."

Al appeared, bearing two huge slices of pizza, dense with anchovies. He slid them under Holroyd's nose. A salty aroma wafted upward.

"Not on the portfolio!" the woman cried. Taken aback by the sudden tone of command, Al scooped the slices onto a neighboring table, apologizing profusely as he backed away.

"And bring me an iced tea, please," she called after him, then turned back to Holroyd. "Look, Peter—can I call you Peter?—I didn't drive all the way here to waste your time on some dime-a-dozen dig site." She drew closer, and Holroyd caught a faint clean scent of shampoo. "Ever hear of Coronado, the Spanish explorer? He came into the Southwest in 1540, looking for the Seven Cities of

Gold. He found only mud pueblos, but the Indians told him about a city of priests, called Quivira, where they ate from plates of gold and drank from golden goblets."

The tea came, and she cracked the plastic seal from the cap and took a sip. "Coronado wasn't the only one to hear these stories. In 1776 two Spanish friars traveled westward from Santa Fe. I've got their report here somewhere." She dug into her portfolio, retrieved a creased sheet of paper, and began reading.

> "Our Paiute guides took us through difficult country, by what seemed to us a perverse route, northward instead of westward. When we remarked upon this, the response was that the Paiutes never traveled through the country to the west. Asked the reason, one spoke of a great city, destroyed because the priests there had enslaved the world and tried to usurp the power of the sun itself. Others hinted darkly of a slumbering evil which they dared not awaken."

She replaced the sheet of paper. "Today people assume these are all just myths. But I don't think so. I believe the reason nobody has ever found this city is because it is hidden in the most remote section of the lower forty-eight. Like other Anasazi cities, it was probably built high up on a cliff, in an alcove or under an overhang. And that's where you come in, Peter. You've got what I need: a radar system that can pinpoint the city."

Holroyd cleared his throat. "Excuse me for saying it, but this is rather a long shot. First of all, if the city is hidden under a ledge, no radar could see it."

"But I don't want you to find the city itself—just the road leading up to it. Here, look at this." She opened her portfolio again and pulled out a small map, overlaid with several thin, straight lines. "A thousand years ago the Anasazi built this mysterious road system. Your radar could surely see those roads from space. Right?"

"Maybe."

"I have an old report—a letter, actually—that states there is a similar road leading to the lost city of Quivira. If we could trace that road on a satellite image, we'd know where to look."

Holroyd spread his hands. "But it's not that simple. There's the waiting list. I'm sure Watkins must have told you about that. The imaging applications are prioritized by urgency and date of receipt. I take the pending jobs, and—"

"You." Nora nodded in satisfaction.

Holroyd fell silent.

"I'm sorry," Nora said suddenly. "Your dinner's getting cold." She replaced the map in her portfolio as Holroyd gathered up the congealing slices of pizza. "So it would be a simple matter to, say, push one of the applications to the top of the queue?"

"I suppose." Holroyd sank his teeth into the pizza.

"See? I fill out an application, you move it to the top of the pile, and we get our images."

Holroyd swallowed hard. "I can't," he said after a moment, in a very quiet voice. "I'd be risking my job."

Yet he found himself unaccountably drawn in by her passion and excitement. He had been to Mesa Verde as a child. The memory of those vast silent ruins still haunted him. He looked around, trying to collect his thoughts. Then his view moved back to the little image on the television screen of the *Republic* floating in space. It was always like that. The excitement of discovery that he had longed for growing up, the chance to explore a new planet or fly to the moon—all those dreams had withered in a cubicle at JPL while he watched someone else's adventure unfold on a dirty monitor.

He realized with a start that Nora was staring at him. "I bet you grew up wanting to be the first man on the moon," she said.

Holroyd blushed. "I was a little late for that. But I did have dreams of going to Mars."

"And now they're up there, orbiting the earth, and you're sitting here in a greasy pizza parlor."

It was as if she had read his mind. Holroyd felt a surge of resentment. "Look, I'm doing just fine. Those guys wouldn't be up there if it weren't for me and others like me."

Nora nodded. "But it's not quite the same thing, is it?" she said softly. "I'm offering you a chance to be part of what might be the greatest archaeological discovery since King Tut."

"Yeah," said Holroyd. "And my part would be to crunch some data and let you run with it. I'm sorry, but the answer is no."

The woman was silent, and it seemed to Holroyd that she was making some kind of private decision.

"Maybe I can offer you more than that," she said at last. "We'll need a remote sensing and computer specialist. Can you handle communications gear?"

Holroyd nodded. "I've got gear you've never even dreamed of."

"Could you take two, maybe three weeks off?"

"I've never taken a vacation," Holroyd heard himself say. "I could leave for six months and still get paid."

"Then that's it. You get me the data, and I get you on the expedition. I guarantee it, Peter, you won't be sorry. It's an adventure you'll remember for the rest of your life."

Holroyd put something together in his head. "The shuttle's devoting the next three days of the mission to radar sweeps, sixty-five orbits at varying latitudes. There's this mineral exploration company that's been wanting a sweep of some areas of Utah and Colorado. We've put them off for a while now. I could fit them into the lineup to get the areas you need."

"Now there's an idea," said Nora.

"We're going to have to beat up the data before we can see the road. Is there anything unusual about the Anasazi roads? Something that might differentiate them from animal trails and modern stuff?"

Nora thought for a moment. "The roads were exactly thirty feet wide, surfaced with adobe. When the Great North Road was finally abandoned around 1250, it seems to have been ritually closed. The Anasazi piled brush on the road and set it on fire."

Holroyd sat forward. "They burned brush on the road? How much?"

"A lot," said Nora. "We found large swaths of charcoal."

Holroyd sat back, his face shining with excitement. "Charcoal—carbon—has a very specific radar signature."

"So you think you can find my road to Quivira?" Nora asked.

"No. *Our* road to Quivira."

ONE WEEK LATER NORA, clutching tightly to the portfolio that now never left her side, stopped outside a closed oaken door labeled CHAIRMAN OF THE BOARD, SANTA FE ARCHAEOLOGICAL INSTITUTE. She had arrived a little after seven in the morning, her first day back from Pasadena, to find an unexpected message on her answering machine: a call from Ernest Goddard's office, requesting a meeting. Nora had never even spoken to the institute's chairman of the board, and she could think of no reason—no good reason, anyway—why he would want to see her. Had word of her deal with Holroyd somehow gotten out? No, that was impossible. But why else would Ernest Goddard want to see her?

Nora took a deep breath and grasped the doorknob firmly.

A small, nervous secretary ushered her through to the inner office. The space was as cool and spare as a church, with whitewashed adobe walls and a Mexican tile floor. Instead of the imposing power desk Nora had expected, there was a huge wooden worktable, badly scuffed and dented.

Behind the worktable stood Ernest Goddard, longish white hair haloing his gaunt face, a salt-and-pepper beard below lively blue eyes. A rumpled cotton handkerchief drooped from his jacket pocket. His body was thin and frail, and his gray suit hung loosely on his bony frame. Nora would have thought he was ill, except that his eyes were clear, bright, and full of fire.

"Dr. Kelly," he said, coming around the worktable to shake her hand. "So good to meet you at last."

"Please call me Nora," she replied guardedly. This cordial reception was the last thing she expected.

"I believe I will." Goddard paused to remove the handkerchief and cough into it with a delicate gesture. "Have a seat." He indicated a chair, then settled himself behind the worktable. "I had a visit from your supervisor yesterday, Nora. He mentioned this idea of yours, this search for the lost city of Quivira. Would you care to explain it to me?"

Nora moved in her chair, considering. "I have some radar images," she said finally, "that show an ancient Anasazi road leading to what I believe is Quivira."

"Do you indeed?" Goddard's face expressed astonishment. "And just where did these images come from?"

"I have a contact inside the Jet Propulsion Laboratory. He was able to manipulate radar images of the area. The course of this road matches the directions in a letter from my father."

Goddard nodded, his face curious and expectant. "This is extraordinary," he said.

Nora said nothing.

Goddard stood up and walked slowly around the room, looking away from her. "It happens that I, too, have long wondered about Quivira. There's never been a question in my mind that it existed. The question was always exactly *where.*"

He circled the table and came to rest on its corner. "I knew your father, Nora. If he said he found evidence for this lost city, I'd believe him."

Nora bit her lip against an unexpected well of emotion.

"I have the means to put the institute squarely behind your expedition. But I need to see the evidence first. The letter *and* the data. If what you say is true, we'll back you."

Nora placed a hand on her portfolio. She had seen too many young archaeologists lose credit to their older, more powerful colleagues. "I'd still like to keep it *my* project, if you don't mind."

"Well, perhaps I do mind. If I'm going to fund this expedition, I would like control, particularly over the personnel."

"Who did you envision leading the expedition?" she asked.

Goddard steadily met her gaze. "You would, of course. Aaron Black would go along as the geochronologist and Enrique Aragon as the medical doctor and physical anthropologist."

Nora sat back, surprised. Not only was he thinking ahead to the expedition, but he was already peopling it with the best scientists in their fields. "If you can get them," she said.

"Oh, I'm reasonably sure I can get them. The discovery of Quivira would be a watershed in southwestern archaeology. And since I can't go along myself"—he waved his handkerchief in explanation—"I'd want to send my daughter in my stead. She got her undergraduate degree from Smith and just took her Ph.D. at

Princeton in American archaeology. She's young, but she has one of the finest archaeological minds I've ever encountered. And she's highly skilled at field photography."

Nora frowned. Smith, she thought. "I'm not sure that's a good idea," she said. "It might muddy the chain of command. And this is going to be a difficult trip, particularly for a"—she paused—"a sorority girl."

"My daughter *must* go along," said Goddard quietly. "And she is no sorority girl, as you shall discover." An odd, mirthless smile flashed briefly across his lips before disappearing.

Nora realized the point was nonnegotiable.

"All right." She smiled. "But I've got a condition of my own. I need to take the JPL technician who assisted me along as a remote imaging specialist. He's young, but he's got experience."

"Very well."

"I also think we have to keep this confidential," she continued. "The expedition has to be assembled quickly and secretly."

Goddard looked at her speculatively. "May I ask why?"

"Because . . ." Nora stopped. Because I've been attacked by mysterious figures who will stop at nothing to find the location of Quivira. But she couldn't say that to Goddard; he'd think her crazy. "Because this information is very sensitive. Think what would happen if pothunters learned about it and tried to loot the site before we could reach it. And on a practical matter, we have to move fast. The flash flood season will be on us soon."

Goddard nodded slowly. "That makes sense," he said. "I'd like to include a journalist on the expedition. I have in mind a *New York Times* reporter with several books to his credit. You have no objection to ex post facto publicity, certainly?"

"No," Nora said, "I guess not."

She reached into her portfolio and removed a thirty- by sixty-minute U.S.G.S. topo. "The target area is this triangle just to the west of the Kaiparowits Plateau, here. As you can see, it contains dozens of canyon systems that all eventually drain into Lake Powell and the Grand Canyon." She handed Goddard a second U.S.G.S. map, onto which Holroyd had overprinted an image from his computer. "This was taken from last week's shuttle overflight and digitally enhanced. The faint, broken black line across it is the ancient Anasazi road."

Goddard took the sheet into his thin pale hands. "Extraordinary," he murmured.

"The dotted line shows a reconstruction of my father's route through this country, following what he thought to be that road. When we extrapolated the road from the shuttle radar image onto this map, it matched my father's route."

Goddard shook his head. "Amazing. There's more than enough evidence here to justify an expedition. Have you given any thought to how you might get in there? Helicopters, for example?"

"That was my first thought, but those canyons are too narrow and most are a thousand feet deep. We'll have to use horses. They're cheap and can pack a lot of gear."

Goddard grunted as he stared at the map. "Sounds good. But I'm not sure I see a route in, even on horseback. Lake Powell blocks access to the south"—he looked up—"unless you . . ."

"Exactly. We'll float the expedition up the lake. I've already called the Wahweap Marina in Page, and they have a seventy-foot barge that will do the job. If we started at Wahweap, floated the horses up to the head of Serpentine Canyon, and rode in from there, we could be at Quivira in three or four days."

Goddard broke into a smile. "Nora, this is inspired. Let's make it happen."

"There's one other thing," Nora said, replacing the maps in her portfolio without looking up. "My brother needs a job, and I know with the right supervision he'd be great covering my job here, sorting and cataloguing the Rio Puerco and Gallegos Divide material." And it will keep him in a safe place during the day, she thought.

"We have a rule against nepotism—" Goddard began, then stopped as Nora, despite herself, began to smile. "Nora, you're a damn good negotiator. Any other demands? You'd better present them now or forever hold your peace."

"No, that covers it."

Silently Goddard extended his hand.

3 The headlights of Nora's truck swung across the predawn dark, highlighting the wooden gates of the dude ranch. She came to a stop in a rutted parking area and killed the motor. Nearby she could see two dark-colored vehicles, a pickup and a van, each bearing the institute's seal. Two slant-load horse trailers had been backed up to nearby horse pens, and ranch hands were loading horses into them under electric lights.

Nora stepped out into the coolness of the early morning and lingered a moment. The air was filled with the sounds of her childhood: the slap of latigo, the whistles and shouts of the cowboys, and the boom of prancing hooves in the trailers. As the aroma of piñon smoke drifted near, a tight knot that had been growing within her began to relax. The expedition had come together with remarkable speed and smoothness.

A cowboy in a battered hat strode out of the corral, leading a horse in each hand. The man was barely five feet tall, skinny, barrel-chested and bandy-legged. He turned and shouted to some hands deeper in the dusty darkness. That must be Roscoe Swire, she thought, the wrangler Goddard had hired.

She pulled her saddle out of the back of her truck and stepped around. "Roscoe Swire?" she asked.

He turned and removed his hat in a gesture that managed to be both courtly and ironic. "At your service," he said in a surprisingly deep voice. He had a great overhanging mustache, large cow-sad eyes, and a certain scrappiness about his manner.

"I'm Nora Kelly," she said, shaking the small, rough hand.

"So you're the boss," said Swire with a grin. "Pleased." He glanced at the saddle. "What you got there?"

"It's my own. I figured you'd want to load it in the trailer."

Swire broke into another smile. "An archaeologist who can ride."

"I can pack a set of panniers and throw a pretty good diamond hitch, too," said Nora.

"Well now," Swire said, "you ain't shy about your accomplishments. Look, the others just went up to the circle. What can you tell me about them? Buncha New Yorkers on vacation, or what?"

Nora found herself liking Swire and his sardonic tone. "Most of them I haven't met. It's a mixed group, but I bet there'll be a couple of sore butts by the end of the first day."

"Good," said Swire. "If they ain't sore, they ain't having fun."

The fire circle lay north of the corrals, hidden in a stand of scrub juniper and piñon. Nora followed the trail, quickly spotting the flames through the trees. A fire circle before a long journey was an old Pueblo custom, Nora knew, and she wasn't particularly surprised Goddard had suggested it. It was an indication of his respect for Indian culture.

She stepped into the firelight. Several figures were seated on logs, murmuring quietly. They turned at her approach. She recognized Aaron Black, the imposing geochronologist from the University of Pennsylvania: six feet five inches tall, with a massive head and hands. He was the acknowledged master of archaeological dating. It was said that he had never been proved wrong, and his arrogant face looked it.

"Dr. Black," Nora said. "I'm Nora Kelly."

"Oh," Black said, standing up and shaking hands. "Pleased to meet you." He looked a little nonplussed. Probably doesn't like the idea of having a young woman for a boss, she thought. His brand-new desert outfit looked as if it had been lifted straight out of the pages of Abercrombie & Fitch.

Peter Holroyd came over and shook her hand. He had the luminous face of a Boy Scout setting out on his first camping trip.

"Dr. Kelly?" came a voice from the darkness. Another figure stepped into the light toward her—a small, dark man in his middle fifties who radiated an unsettling, even caustic intensity. He had a striking face: dark olive skin, black hair combed back, veiled eyes, a long, hooked nose. "I'm Enrique Aragon." He briefly took her hand; his fingers were long, sensitive, almost feminine. He spoke with a precise, dignified voice, in the faintest of Mexican accents. He was widely considered to be the country's finest physical anthropologist, winner of the Hrdlička Medal; but he was also a medical doctor—a highly convenient combination, which had undoubtedly figured in Goddard's choice.

"We've been making introductions," Aragon said with a brief smile. "This is Luigi Bonarotti, camp manager and cook." He indicated another figure, who had come up behind him to meet Nora.

A man with dark Sicilian eyes leaned over and took her hand and half bowed. He was impeccably dressed in pressed khakis, and Nora caught the faint whiff of an expensive aftershave.

"Where's the journalist who's going to be documenting all this for posterity?" Aaron Black asked. "Shouldn't he be here? I've been looking forward to meeting him."

"He's joining us at Wahweap Marina, along with Dr. Goddard's daughter," Nora said.

The others began to range themselves around the fire, and Nora settled down on a log, enjoying the warmth, inhaling the scent of cedar smoke, listening to the hiss and crackle taunt the surrounding darkness. There was a faint clicking noise and some yellow flashes. Then a lone figure stepped forward out of the shadow. Nora recognized the gaunt features of Ernest Goddard. He came silently toward the group, his white hair painted crimson by the fire. He moved something within his hand, and the flashes returned.

He stood for a long moment, holding each person in turn in his gaze, then slipped whatever was in his hand into a leather bag and tossed it over the flames to Nora. "Rub them together," he whispered. "Then pass them around."

Nora reached inside and felt two smooth, hard stones. She drew them out and held them to the firelight: beautiful specimens of quartz, carved with the ritual spiral design that signified the *sipapu,* the Anasazi entrance to the underworld. She rubbed them together, watching the miraculous internal sparks light up the hearts of the stones.

"Anasazi lightning stones," Goddard said in a quiet voice. "We used to believe the Anasazi used them in rain ceremonies to symbolize the generation of lightning. But nobody knows for sure." He coughed lightly. "And that's what I'm here to say to you. After three decades of mysterious and inexplicable discoveries, we realize that we know next to nothing about the Anasazi. We don't understand their culture; we don't understand their religion. We cannot read their petroglyphs and pictographs. We do not know why, in 1150, they suddenly abandoned Chaco Canyon, burned the roads, and retreated to the most inaccessible canyons in the Southwest, building mighty fortresses in the cliff faces. Some archaeologists believe we will *never* know."

Despite the warmth of the fire Nora couldn't help shivering.

"But I have a feeling." His voice was weaker, hoarser. "I have a *conviction* that Quivira will contain answers to these mysteries."

He glanced at each of them again, in turn. "All of you are about to embark on the adventure of a lifetime. You're headed for a site that may prove to be the biggest archaeological discovery of the decade, perhaps even the century. But let's not fool ourselves. Quivira will be a place of mystery as well as revelation. It may well pose as many questions as it answers. And it will challenge you, physically and mentally, in ways you cannot yet imagine."

He fixed Nora with his gaze. "Nora Kelly is in charge, and I have put my complete trust in her. When my daughter joins you, she will also report to Dr. Kelly; there can be no confusion of command." He took a step away from the fire, back toward the darkness. "There are some who do not believe Quivira exists. They think this expedition is foolhardy, that I'm throwing my money away." He paused. "But the city is there. You know it, and I know it. Now go and find it."

AT TWO o'clock that afternoon the horse trailers, followed by the pickup and the van, edged into a gigantic asphalt parking lot facing Lake Powell. Nora could see Wahweap Marina in all its glory. Styrofoam cups, beer cans, plastic bags, and floating pieces of newspaper bobbed in the brown shallows at the bottom of the boat ramp. Endless ranks of houseboats painted in garish colors lined the shore in either direction, and fleshy, beer-bellied throngs milled around the docks.

As Roscoe Swire went to help back the horse trailers around,

Nora noticed an incongruous sight: a black stretch limousine flying down the parking lot toward the docks. For a moment her heart sank. Not Sloane Goddard, she thought, not in a limo. She was relieved when the car came to a halt and a tall young man tumbled rather awkwardly out of the back.

Nora found herself staring at him. He was not particularly handsome, but there was something striking in the bemused, confident way he surveyed the scene before him.

Several teenagers on the dock instinctively moved toward him, and soon a crowd gathered. Nora could see the man was talking animatedly. She could barely hear his voice over the hubbub, making comments while he waved a paperback book in one hand. As she watched, he scribbled an autograph in it.

She walked to the edge of the crowd, intrigued. He was dressed in starchy new jeans, a red bandanna, and expensive alligator cowboy boots. As she was about to walk on, Nora heard the man say, quite distinctly, the words Nora Kelly. She stopped.

"It's a confidential project," the man was saying. "I can't talk about it, but you'll read about it soon enough."

"Hey!" Nora cried, pushing through the crowd. The young man looked down at her, surprise and consternation on his face. Then he broke into a smile. "You must be—"

She grabbed his hand and began pulling him through the crowd. "Just shut up," she retorted.

"Now hold on a minute—" the man began.

Nora continued to pull him across the tarmac toward the horse trailers, leaving the perplexed crowd behind to disperse.

"I'm Bill Smithback," the man said, trying to extend his hand as he skipped alongside her.

"I know who you are," Nora cried. She stopped at the horse trailers and faced him, breathing hard. "This expedition is supposed to be *confidential.*"

"But I didn't reveal anything," he protested. "I *am* here to write a book, after all, and—"

"One more stunt like that, and there won't be a book."

Smithback fell silent.

"Go tell your chauffeur to bring your stuff and put it with the rest. And keep a low profile, okay?"

"Okay! Okay. I understand." He went shambling off toward the limousine, head drooping in mock embarrassment.

It took a half hour to load the horse trailers onto their barge, and Sloane Goddard had still not shown up. They had to make the sixty-mile trip to the trailhead by nightfall: Off-loading the horses after dark would be too complicated and dangerous.

Nora jumped aboard and entered the tiny pilothouse. The barge's captain was fiddling with a sonar array. "We need to shake a leg," he said.

Nora looked up the ramp toward the parking lot, shimmering in the heat. "Get ready to shove off, then," she said.

The expedition was gathering forward of the pilothouse. Nora walked over and slipped the mooring lines from the dock. There was a roar from the diesels, and the boat began backing away from the ramp.

Peter Holroyd glanced around. "What about Dr. Goddard?"

"We can't wait around here any longer," Nora said.

The team looked at one another in surprise as the barge began a slow turn, the water boiling out from the stern.

"You've got to be kidding!" Aaron Black cried. "You aren't really leaving without her?"

Nora looked steadily back at the sweaty, incredulous face. "Oh, yes," she said, "I'm really leaving without her."

THREE hours later their barge had left the chaos of the marina fifty miles behind. The expedition had entered into a great mystical world of stone, and a cathedral silence closed around them. They were alone on the green expanse of lake, walled in by thousand-foot bluffs.

Luigi Bonarotti served a meal of cognac-braised, applewood-smoked quail with grapefruit and wilted arugula leaves. This remarkable accomplishment, achieved somehow on the barge's shabby gas grill, silenced even Black's undertone of complaints. They dined around an aluminum table, toasting the meal with a crisp Orvieto.

"Didn't you write that book on the museum murders in New York City?" Black was asking Smithback. "And that subway massacre a few years back?"

Smithback reached for an imaginary hat and doffed it with a grandiose flourish.

Black scratched his chin. "Don't get me wrong, but I've always understood that the institute was a low-profile entity."

"Well, I'm no longer Bill Smithback, terror of the tabloids," Smithback replied. "I work for the buttoned-down, respectable *New York Times* now." He turned and grinned at Nora. "You see, I'm a paragon of journalistic respectability that even a place as stuffy as your institute can't object to."

Nora caught herself as she was about to smile. There was nothing amusing in the journalist's braggadocio, even if it was tempered with a touch of self-deprecation.

She looked toward Holroyd, who was sitting on the metal floor of the barge, elbows on his knees, reading what to Nora's mind was a real book: a battered paperback copy of *Coronado and the City of Gold.* As she watched him, Holroyd looked up and smiled.

The boat moved past the Grand Bench. Nora could see the dark prow of the Kaiparowits Plateau rising far behind it, wild, inaccessible, tinged dusky rose by the setting sun. As if in response, the boat began to turn, heading for a narrow opening in the sandstone walls: the foot of Serpentine Canyon.

Once the boat was inside the narrow confines of the canyon, the water turned a deeper green. The sheer walls plunged straight down, so perfectly reflected it was hard to tell where stone stopped and water began.

Holroyd stretched. "I've been reading about Quivira," he said, indicating the book. "It's an amazing story. Listen to this:

> "The Cicuye Indians brought forward a slave they had captured in a distant land. The general questioned the slave through interpreters. The slave told him about a distant city, called Quivira. It is a holy city, he said, where the Rain Priests live, who guard the records of their history from the beginning

of time. He said it was a city of great wealth. Common table service was of the purest smoothed gold, and the pitchers, dishes, and bowls were also of gold, refined, polished, and decorated. He said they despised all other materials."

"Aaah," Smithback said, rubbing his hands with an exaggerated air. "I like that: 'They despised all other materials.' "

"There isn't a shred of evidence of any Anasazi having gold," Nora said. "The Indians were only telling Coronado what they knew he wanted to hear in order to keep him moving on."

"But listen," Holroyd said. "It goes on: 'The slave warned the general not to approach the city. The Rain and Sun Priests of Xochitl guard the city, he said, and call down the God of the Dust Devil on those who approach without their leave, and thereby destroy them.' "

The barge captain stepped out of the cabin. "Sonar's giving me shoaling water here," he said. "We'll probably be hitting the end of the lake round another bend or two."

"Then let's get ready to get this gear off-loaded," Nora said to the group. The expedition had begun in earnest.

TERESA Gonzales sat up suddenly, listening in the dark. Teddy Bear, her giant Rhodesian Ridgeback, was whining at the back door. Ridgebacks had been bred to hunt and kill lions in Africa. She had never heard him whine before.

She got out of bed and went through the dark house to the door. The dog came slinking in, whimpering.

"Teddy," she whispered. "What's wrong? You all right?"

The dog licked her hand and retreated across the kitchen, sliding his huge bulk under the kitchen table. Teresa looked out the kitchen door, down into the sea of darkness toward the old Las Cabrillas ranch house. There were no lights in the draw, and without a moon Teresa couldn't see the outlines of the abandoned house. Something out there had scared him half to death. She listened and thought she heard a faint sound of breaking glass and the distant howl of an animal.

Guess a wolf has wandered down from the mountains, she thought.

Teresa went back to her room, peeled off her nightgown, slid on her jeans, shirt, and boots, then walked across the room and opened the gun locker. She reached for her current favorite, a Winchester Defender, with its eighteen-and-one-half-inch barrel and extended magazine tube. This wasn't the first time since the attack on Nora that she'd heard sounds from the Kelly ranch.

She tucked the shotgun under her arm, shoved a flashlight into her back pocket, and crept out the kitchen door. Teresa was a large, heavy-boned woman, but she had the natural stealthy movements of a feline. She inhaled deeply, steadied the gun, then angled toward the trail in the inky blackness. She had descended this slope countless times to play with Nora when they were children, and her feet remembered the way.

Soon she was on the flat. The Kelly house stood across the draw, just on the side of the rise. A strange odor in the air reminded her of morning glories.

She snapped off the safety, gripped the flashlight tight, and moved toward the front of the house.

And then Teresa heard something, at the edge of audibility, that was not a wolf. It was a low, monotonous chanting drone—a hoarse, guttural cadence—dry and faint as parched leaves.

It came from inside the house.

Teresa licked her dry lips and took a deep breath. She stepped onto the front porch as quietly as she could. Then she took two more steps forward. The front door was open.

Inside, she switched on the flashlight. The house was as she remembered it from the previous week: a hurricane of ruin, dust, and old decay. The smell of flowers was stronger here, and the chanting was louder. It seemed to be coming from upstairs.

These were obviously not animals. Perhaps it would be better for her to creep quietly home and telephone the cops.

But no—by the time they arrived, these bastards would have slipped away. And Teresa would be left with the nagging worry that they might show up again. Perhaps they'd try her house next time. Or perhaps they'd catch her away from home, when she was unarmed. . . .

The time to act was now, while she could. With infinite caution she switched off the light and began to ascend the stairs. She moved instinctively, shifting her weight from foot to foot with extreme deliberation.

She paused at the top of the stairs. The sound was coming from Nora's old room.

She braced herself, gun in both hands, the flashlight firm against the barrel. Then with one smooth, swift motion she stepped forward, kicked the door fully open, swiveled the gun into position, and snapped on the flashlight.

Two figures, covered head to toe in heavy, dank pelts, crouched in the center of the room. Their red eyes turned toward the light, unblinking, feral. Between them rested a human skull, its top missing. Inside the skull was a small collection of objects—a doll's head, a girl's barrette. Nora's old things, Teresa realized, frozen with horror.

Suddenly one of the forms leaped up, moving faster than she thought possible. It passed out of the beam of her flashlight as she jerked the trigger. The shotgun bucked in her hands, and the deafening roar seemed to shake the house itself.

She blinked, straining to see through the dust and smoke. There was nothing but a ragged, smoking hole in the bedroom wall. Both figures had vanished.

She had to get downstairs. She pumped another round into the chamber. Then she switched off the light and darted forward.

A black shape lunged diagonally out from a far bedroom. With an involuntary cry Teresa turned and jerked the trigger. Eyes blinded by the muzzle flare, she stumbled backward and half rolled, half fell down the stairs, shotgun clattering away into the darkness. She scrambled to her knees at the bottom step, a sharp pain spiking through one ankle.

At the top of the stairs a large shape crouched, staring silently down at her. Teresa whirled, searching in the faint starlight for her weapon. But instead of the shotgun, her gaze fell upon the second shape, framed in the kitchen doorway, coming toward her with a slow confidence that was somehow terrible.

Teresa stared at the figure, paralyzed with terror. A low whimper escaped her throat.

NORA awakened to a marvelous smell. She stretched luxuriously; then, hearing the clatter of tins and the murmur of conversation, she opened her eyes and jumped out of her bedroll. It was six thirty, and the camp had already gathered around an open fire.

She quickly washed up at the edge of the lake, embarrassed at oversleeping on the first morning.

"Madam Chairman!" Bill Smithback called out good-humoredly. "Come on over and have a sip of this ebony nectar. I swear it's even better than the espresso at Café Reggio."

Nora joined the group and gratefully accepted a tin cup from Peter Holroyd. As she sipped, Aaron Black emerged from a tent, looking frowsy and bedraggled.

"It's cold," he muttered. "I barely slept a wink."

"Oh, you slept fine," Smithback said. "I've never heard such a cacophony of snores." Coffee in hand, Smithback settled on a fallen log, next to Black. "Aragon tells me that you're an expert on artifact dating. But what did he mean when he said you were a Dumpster diver?"

"Oh, he said that, did he?" Black gave the older man an angry glare.

"It's a technical term," Aragon said with a wry smile.

"I'm a stratigrapher," Black said. "Often midden heaps provide the best information at a site."

"Midden heaps?"

"Ancient trash piles," said Black, his lips compressing. "We work with anything to do with dating. Human hair, pollen, charcoal, bone, seeds, you name it."

Bonarotti announced breakfast was ready. Nora quickly fell in line behind the rest. Bonarotti slid a generous slice of omelette onto her plate. She took a seat and dug in hungrily. Perhaps it was the desert air, but she'd never tasted eggs half as delicious.

"Heaven," Smithback mumbled, mouth full.

"It has a slightly unusual flavor, almost musky," Holroyd said.

Smithback took another bite, then set his fork down with a clatter. "I know. Black truffles?"

Bonarotti's normally impassive eyes lit up at this. "Not quite," he replied. The cook turned to the curio box that he kept locked and under jealous guard. Opening one of its drawers, he pulled out a dusky-colored lump about the size of a tennis ball.

"*Tuber magantum pico,*" he said, placing it carefully back.

Smithback shook his head slowly. "You're looking at about a thousand dollars' worth of white truffle right there. If we don't find that huge stash of Indian gold, we can always raid the cabinet of Dr. Bonarotti."

"You are welcome to try, my friend," Bonarotti said impassively, pulling open his jacket and patting a monstrous revolver snugged into a holster around his waist.

There was a nervous laugh all around.

As Nora returned to her breakfast, she thought she heard a noise, distant but growing louder. She noticed the others heard it, too. The sound echoed around the stone walls, and she realized it was a plane. As she searched the empty blue sky, the noise increased dramatically and a float plane cleared the canyon rim.

"That guy's awfully low," said Holroyd, staring upward.

"He ain't just low," Swire said. "He's landing."

They watched as the plane touched down on the lake, sending up two fins of water in a flurry of spray. Nora nodded to Holroyd to take an inflatable raft out to meet them. Inside the cockpit she could see the pilot and copilot, checking gauges, making notes on a hanging clipboard. At last the pilot climbed out, waved, and swung down onto one of the pontoons.

The pilot was Sloane Goddard.

Holroyd had reached the side of the plane by now, and Goddard began swinging duffels into the raft from the cargo area behind the plane's seats. Then she slammed the hatch shut, slid down into the raft, and gave the copilot a sign. As Holroyd rowed back, the plane began to taxi down the canyon, where it revved its engines and began its takeoff. Nora's eyes moved from the vanishing plane back to the rapidly approaching figure.

Sloane Goddard sat in the rear of the raft, talking to Holroyd. She wore a long aviator's leather jacket, jeans, and narrow boots. Her black hair reminded Nora of a Fitzgerald-era flapper. Almond-shaped, brilliant amber eyes and a sensuous mouth lent an exotic touch to her features. Nora realized, quite consciously, that she was looking at one of the most beautiful women she had ever seen.

As the raft ground to a halt on the shore, Sloane leaped nimbly out and came walking briskly into camp. This wasn't the skinny sorority girl Nora had imagined. The woman approaching her had a voluptuous figure, yet her movements hinted at quick, lithe strength. Her skin glowed with health, and she brushed back her hair with a gesture that was both innocent and seductive.

She walked over to Nora and extended her hand. "Nora Kelly, I presume?"

"Yes," Nora exhaled. "And you must be Sloane Goddard. The belated Sloane Goddard."

The others had instinctively drawn round, and Nora wasn't surprised: Sloane radiated charisma and the easy self-confidence that came with money and good breeding.

She looked at Nora with a lazy smile. "Sorry about the dramatic entrance," she said. "I was delayed at Princeton by a failing student. I worked with him until it became too late to mess with commercial airlines."

"You had us worried back there at the marina."

"Well, you did the right thing, leaving without me."

Everyone on the team introduced themselves; then Swire brought the horses back from their grazing ground and Nora went over to help with the saddling. To Nora's surprise Sloane followed behind and joined in, deftly saddling two horses to Swire's three. They tied the horses to some brush and started on the pack animals.

When Nora stood back from the final horse and looked at her watch, it was just past eleven: still enough time for a decent ride, but short enough to help break in the greenhorns. She glanced at Swire. "Want to give them their first lesson?"

"Now's as good a time as any," he said, looking at the group. Nora thought she saw him grin beneath his droopy mustache.

He parceled out the horses according to ability and temperament, and soon everyone was holding a pair of horses by the halters and reins. Nora lofted herself into the saddle; Sloane and Aragon, both clearly experienced riders, followed her example.

Swire turned to the others. "Well," he said, "git on up!"

There was some grunting and nervous hopping, but soon everyone was sitting in the saddle.

"Lesson number one," said Swire. "Hold the reins in your left hand and the packhorse lead rope in your right. It's simple."

He walked over first to Holroyd, then Black, correcting their postures and grips. "Don't let the lead rope get wedged under your horse's tail," he said to Black. "Or you might find your horse with a sudden bellyful of bedsprings."

"Yes, yes, of course," Black said, hastily drawing in his slack.

"Nora plans to ride point," Swire said. "That's up front, for you dudes. I'll ride drag. And Dr. Goddard over there, she'll ride swing." He looked around. "Any questions?"

There were none.

"Well then, let's jingle our spurs."

Nora nudged her horse forward, and they headed into the sandstone wilderness.

THEY moved up Serpentine Canyon single file, crossing and recrossing the little creek that flowed in its bottom. Nora inhaled deeply. The gentle rocking motion of Fiddlehead, a twelve-year-old sorrel, felt familiar and comforting. While she was far from handsome, she was a strong and sensible animal. Except for Swire's own two mounts, Mestizo and Sweetgrass, the horses were similar to Nora's: not pretty, but solid ranch stock. She approved of Swire's judgment.

She looked back at the other riders, trailing behind her, packhorses in tow. While some of the riders, notably Black and Holroyd, looked lumpy and unbalanced, the rest looked competent. And Smithback was a surprise. His mount, Hurricane Deck, was clearly a more spirited horse, and there were a few tense moments at first. But Smithback knew enough to show the horse who was boss, and he was now riding confidently.

"Where'd you learn to ride?" she called back.

"I spent a couple of years at a prep school in Arizona," the writer answered. "My parents thought it would make a man of me." He shook his head at the memory, chuckling.

Suddenly the smile on his face was replaced with a look of shock. "What the hell?" He spun around. Following his gaze, Nora saw Smithback's packhorse, Beetlebum, dart back. A rope of saliva was dripping off Smithback's leg.

"That horse just tried to bite me!" Smithback roared. The packhorse looked back, his face a picture of innocence.

"That old Beetlebum," said Swire, shaking his head affectionately. "He's sure got a sense of humor."

Smithback wiped his leg. "So I see."

After another half hour of uneventful riding, Nora brought the group to a halt.

"Time for a GPS reading," she said. She knew that six miles up Serpentine Canyon they had to branch off into a smaller canyon, marked HARD TWIST on the map.

Holroyd dug into his saddlebag and pulled out the Global Positioning System unit, a laptop into which he had downloaded all the navigation and way-point data. While Nora waited, he booted the computer, then began to tap at the keyboard. After a few minutes he grimaced, then shook his head.

"I was afraid of that," he said. "It has to locate at least three geostationary satellites simultaneously to get a reading. With these high canyon walls, it can't even pick up one."

"Want me to climb up and take the reading?" Sloane asked.

Nora looked at her curiously.

"I brought some gear," Sloane said, lifting the top of a saddlebag and displaying a sling loaded with carabiners, chocks, nuts, and pitons. "Doesn't look too bad. I could probably free climb my way up."

"Let's save that for when we really need it," Nora said. "Until then we'll do things the old-fashioned way. Dead reckoning." She spread Holroyd's map across her saddle horn and stared at it closely, estimating their speed and travel time. She marked a dot at their probable position, the date and time beside it.

"Done a lot of this before?" Holroyd asked at her side.

Nora nodded. "All archaeologists have to be good at reading maps. What makes it harder is this." She pointed to a note in the corner of the map that read WARNING: DATA NOT FIELD-CHECKED. "Most of these maps are created from stereogrammatic images taken from the air. Sometimes what you see from a plane is a lot different from what you see on foot."

"Reassuring," she heard Black mutter.

Replacing the map, Nora nudged her horse forward, and they continued up the canyon. Each time they passed a narrow side canyon, Nora would stop and mark it on the map. Just after four she noted a broad sandy beach where they could camp, high enough to be beyond the reach of any unexpected flash flood. So far the trip had been an easy ride, but she knew that could not last.

THE next morning they veered left into the dry streambed of Hard Twist Canyon. True to its name, Hard Twist was choked with rocks, hot and close, with none of the charm of the previous day's ride.

The brush grew thicker, and Nora and Sloane dismounted to hack a path. It was hot, miserable work. Making things worse, they found only a few stagnant potholes of water, which did not keep up with the horses' thirst. The riders seemed to bear up well enough, except for Black's sarcastic protest when told they would have to ration water for a while. His personality was beginning to seem a high price to pay for his expertise.

At last they came across a large muddy pool, hidden on the far side of a rockslide.

"Maybe this is a good time to stop for lunch," Nora said.

After a quick meal, with the horses watered and the canteens full of purified water, they set out again.

Around three o'clock they stopped to rest the horses. Taking refuge under an overhang, they sat eating handfuls of dried fruits and nuts. Sloane retrieved her binoculars and began scanning a series of alcoves in a canyon opposite them.

After a minute she turned to Nora. "There's a small cliff dwelling up there. First one I've seen since we started out."

Taking the binoculars, Nora peered at the small ruin, perched high on the cliff face. It was set into a shallow alcove, oriented to the south in the Anasazi way, ensuring shade in the summer and warmth in the winter.

"Let me see," Holroyd said. He gazed at the ruin, motionless. "Incredible," he breathed at last. "How did they live?"

"They probably farmed the canyon bottom—corn, squash, and beans. I'd guess it housed a single extended family."

Sloane had been scanning the cliffs with a shaded hand. Now she took the binoculars from Holroyd and examined the rock more carefully. "I think there's a hand-and-toe trail which goes all the way to the ledge. Do we have time to try it?"

Nora glanced at her watch. They were already hopelessly behind schedule—one more hour wouldn't matter. "All right," she said, reaching for her camera. "It doesn't look technical."

"I'd like to go, too," said Holroyd excitedly.

Nora looked at the group. "Anybody else want to come?"

"No thanks," Black said. "I value my life."

Aragon glanced up from a notebook he was writing in and shook his head. Bonarotti had gone off to gather mushrooms. Smithback stretched luxuriously. "Guess I'd better tag along with you, Madam Chairman," he said. "It wouldn't do to have you find an Anasazi Rosetta stone while I was loafing around down here."

They crossed the dry streambed, scrambled over boulders and up a talus slope, loose rocks clattering behind them. The sandstone ahead sloped upward at a forty-five-degree angle, notched with a series of eroded dimples set into the rock.

"That's the hand-and-toe trail." Nora pointed. "The Anasazi pounded them out with quartzite hammerstones."

"I'll go first," said Sloane. She shot nimbly upward, limbs tawny in the sunlight, hands and feet finding the holds with the instinctive assurance of a veteran rock climber. "Come on up!" she said a minute later, kneeling on the ledge above their heads. Holroyd followed, then Nora and Smithback.

After a short distance the ledge broadened out, curved around a corner, and the ruin came into view. Nora made a quick visual inspection. A low masonry retaining wall had been built at the lip of the alcove and filled with rubble, leveling the surface. Behind were small roomblocks of flat stones mortared with mud—one with a keyhole door, the rest with tiny windows. The builders had used the natural sandstone roof of the alcove as their ceiling.

Nora turned to Holroyd and Smithback. "Sloane and I should make an initial survey. Mind waiting for a few minutes?"

"Only if you promise not to find anything," Smithback replied.

Nora shone a penlight inside the first roomblock and found the interior relatively well preserved. The plastered walls still showed traces of painted decorations. In one corner she could see a metate—a grinding stone—protruding from the dirt. The room beyond was exceptionally dusty and—very unusually—seemed at one time to have been painted with thick, heavy black paint. Or perhaps it was from cooking. Moving through a low doorway, she advanced into a third room. It, too, was empty, save for a hearth with several firedogs still propping up a comal, or polished cooking stone.

Sloane continued exploring, while Nora, moving back through the rooms, leaned out into the sudden warmth of the sun and beckoned the waiting Holroyd and Smithback. They followed her into the roomblock, stooping through the low doorways.

"This is incredible," Holroyd said in a reverential whisper.

"There's nothing like the feeling of one of these ancient ruins," Nora replied. "Even an unremarkable one like this."

"Unremarkable to you, maybe," Holroyd said.

Sloane came from the back of the ruin, shouldering her rucksack.

"Find anything?" Nora asked.

Sloane nodded. "A dozen or so pictographs, including three reversed spirals."

Nora looked up in surprise to meet the woman's glance.

Holroyd caught the look. "What?" he asked.

"In Anasazi iconography," Nora said, "the counterclockwise direction is usually associated with negative supernatural forces. Clockwise, or sunwise, was considered to be the direction of travel of the sun across the sky. Counterclockwise was therefore considered a perversion of nature, a reversal of the normal balance."

"And I found this," Sloane said, lifting one hand. In it she held a small, broken human skull. "It was next to the granary."

"And you just picked it up?" Nora asked sharply.

"Why not?" Sloane asked, her eyes narrowing.

"For one thing," Nora snapped, "we don't disturb human remains unless it's absolutely critical for our research. And you've touched it, which means we can't do bone collagen DNA on it."

"All I did was pick it up," Sloane said, her voice suddenly low.

Nora took a breath. Don't lose your cool. "Now that it's been disturbed," she said in a quiet voice, "we'll bring it back for Aragon to analyze. Being a ZST type, he may object, but the deed's been done. Sloane, I don't want you ever doing any invasive procedures without my express permission. Is that understood?"

"Understood," said Sloane, looking suddenly contrite as she handed the skull to Nora. "I wasn't thinking. The excitement of the moment, I guess."

Nora slipped the skull into a sample bag and tucked it in her pack. It seemed to her there had been something challenging in the way Sloane had come forward holding the skull, and Nora wondered if it had been a deliberate provocation. After all, it was clear that Sloane was well versed in the protocol of fieldwork.

"What's a ZST?" Smithback asked.

"It stands for Zero Site Trauma," Nora said. "The idea that an archaeological site should never be physically disturbed. People like Aragon believe any intrusion, no matter how careful or subtle, destroys it for future archaeologists who might come along with more sophisticated tools. They tend to work with artifacts that have already been excavated by others."

"If Aragon feels that way, why did he come along?" Holroyd asked.

"I suppose that on a project as important as this, he's willing to put his personal feelings aside to some extent." Nora looked around. "What do you make of these walls?" she asked Sloane. "I've never seen an Anasazi room painted black before."

"Beats me," Sloane replied. She removed a small glass tube and a dentist's pick from her pack. Then she glanced with a quick smile at Nora. "May I take a sample?" She paused.

Nora nodded wordlessly, watching as Sloane expertly flaked a few pieces into the glass test tube and stoppered it.

The sun was now low in the sky. "Let's get back," Nora said. As they turned to walk out on the ledge, Nora glanced back at the reversed spirals on the wall behind the ruin. She shivered briefly in spite of the heat.

THE following day the group toiled up through a warren of fractured canyons, moving deeper into a surreal, waterless world that seemed more a landscape of dream than anything of the earth. The mute stone halls spoke of eons of fury: uplift and erosion, floods, earthquakes, and the endless scouring of the wind.

At every turn Nora realized her dead reckoning grew more difficult and prone to error. The GPS laptop was still not functioning, and Holroyd's map was of little help: At this point of the journey the underlying topographical elevations on the map were ludicrously off.

By evening they were so exhausted that dinner was a cold, silent, impromptu affair. The lack of water had compelled Nora to institute severe rationing. Bonarotti, forced to cook with no water, grew sullen.

After dinner the group gravitated apathetically toward the campfire. Swire sat down beside Nora and spit. "Come morning, these horses won't have had decent water for thirty-six hours. Don't know how much longer they can last."

"I couldn't care less about the horses," Black said from across the fire. "I'm wondering when *we're* going to die of thirst."

Swire turned to him. "Maybe you don't realize it, but if the horses die, we die. It ain't any more complicated than that."

Nora glanced in Black's direction. In the firelight his face was haggard, a look of incipient panic in his eyes. "You said we were going to reach Quivira tomorrow," he said huskily. "I've been watching you all afternoon, struggling with those maps and trying to get that useless GPS unit to work. I think we're lost."

"No," Nora replied. "I don't believe we're lost."

His voice grew loud. "Is that supposed to be encouraging?"

In the flickering light Nora looked around at the rest of the group. Everyone was filthy from the lack of water and badly scratched from heavy brush. Only Sloane, sifting sand thoughtfully through her fingers, and Aragon, wearing his usual distant expression, appeared unconcerned.

"I'm doing the best I can," Nora said slowly. "If any of you have any constructive ideas, I'd like to hear them."

"The answer is to keep going," said Aragon with a quiet vehemence. "Twentieth-century humans are unused to any real physical challenge. The people who lived in these canyons dealt with this kind of thirst and heat every day, without complaint."

"Oh, *now* I feel better," said Black. "And here I thought I was suffering from thirst."

Aragon turned his dark eyes on Black. "You are suffering more from a personality disorder than from thirst, Dr. Black."

Black turned to look at him, speechless with rage. Then he stood up on trembling limbs and made his way toward his tent.

The group began to break up, leaving Nora and Aragon gazing thoughtfully into the fire. Nora felt movement nearby; then Sloane sat down beside her. All three fell silent, staring into the dying flames.

"So?" Sloane prompted at last.

"So what?"

"Are we lost?" she asked gently.

Nora sighed. "I don't know. Guess we'll find out tomorrow."

Aragon grunted. "If this is indeed an Anasazi road, it's unlike any other I've encountered. It's as if the Anasazi wanted to eradicate any trace of its existence." He shook his head. "I sense a darkness, a malignancy, about this road."

Nora looked at him. "Why do you say that?"

Silently the Mexican reached into the pack and removed the test tube containing the flakes of black paint, cradling it in his palm. "I performed a PBT with luminol on one of these samples," he said quietly. "It came up positive."

"I've never heard of that test," Nora said.

"It's a simple test used to identify the presence of human blood. That wasn't paint you saw. It was human blood. Layers upon layers upon layers of crusted, dried blood."

"My God," Nora said. A passage from the Coronado report came back to her unbidden: "*Quivira* in their language means The House of the Bloody Cliff." Perhaps "bloody cliff" was not merely symbolic after all. . . .

Aragon removed a small padded bag and carefully pulled out the small skull they had found at the ruin. He handed it to Nora. "After I discovered that, I decided to take a closer look at this skull. It belongs to a young girl, maybe nine or ten years old. Definitely Anasazi: You can see how the back of the skull was flattened by a hard cradleboard when the child was a baby." He turned it over carefully in his hands. "At first I thought she had died an accidental death. But when I looked more closely, I noticed these." He pointed to a series of grooves on the back of the skull. "These were made with a flint knife."

"No," Sloane whispered.

"Oh, yes. This little girl was scalped."

4 Skip Kelly sauntered down a shaded walkway of the institute's manicured campus, rubbing bleary eyes. It was a breathtaking summer morning, warm and dry and full of promise.

Ahead of him lay a long, low Pueblo Revival structure. A small wooden sign set into the ground before it read ARTIFACTUAL ASSEMBLAGES. Skip opened the door and walked inside.

The door closed behind him with a squeal of metal, and he winced. What a headache. His mouth was parched and tasted of mildew and old socks, and he dug a piece of chewing gum out of his pocket. Oh, man. Better switch to beer. It was the same thing he thought every morning.

Before she left, Nora had put Skip to work on a huge bag of assorted potsherds donated by an unskilled amateur archaeologist. At first Skip found the work both boring and confusing. But then, almost imperceptibly, he grew more sure in his identifications: Kayenta black-on-white, Cibola ware, St. John's Polychrome, Mogollon Brownware. It was instinctive almost. The shape, condition, even composition of the sherds could speak as loudly as the design itself.

On this morning the lab was empty. As Skip worked, memories of long afternoons spent with his father, pacing over some ruin in the middle of nowhere, came back with a bittersweet tang. He started when a voice rang out on the far side of the room. "Skip Kelly?"

He glanced up. A large man in a blue uniform walked toward him. "You Skip Kelly?" he asked in a low, calm baritone.

"Yes," said Skip, going cold, his mind racing.

The man flipped open an ID wallet. "I'm Lieutenant Detective Al Martinez, Santa Fe Police Department, Mr. Kelly," he said in a voice that managed to be both friendly and neutral at the same time. "Are you the owner of an abandoned ranch house beyond Fox Run, address Rural Route Sixteen, Box Twelve, Santa Fe, New Mexico?"

"Yes. My sister and I own it together."

"And your sister is Nora Waterford Kelly?"

"That's right. She's on an archaeological expedition to Utah."

Martinez nodded. "Do you know a Teresa Gonzales?"

Skip licked his lips. "Yeah. I know Teresa. She's our neighbor out at the ranch."

"When did you last see Teresa?"

"I don't know. Ten months ago, maybe eleven."

"Mr. Kelly, Teresa Gonzales was found dead last night at your ranch house."

Suddenly Skip's body felt strangely heavy. "Teresa? Oh, my God." He shook his head. "I can't believe it."

"When she was reported missing, we went out there. We found no sign of her on the property, so we decided to visit the neighboring ranches. Your place was our first stop." The lieutenant took a slow breath. "We saw movement inside. Turned out to be dogs, fighting over something." He stopped, pursed his lips.

"Was she killed by dogs?"

"We thought so at first. But the coroner's initial examination found definitive evidence that it was a homicide."

Skip looked at him. "What kind of evidence?"

"An unusual kind of mutilation to the fingers and toes, among other things. We'll know a lot more when the autopsy is completed this afternoon. Meantime, please don't go near the farmhouse. And most important of all, stay where we can find you."

THE expedition proceeded northwest, up a harsh, brutal canyon destitute of vegetation. Even at the early morning hour, heat was rising from the split rocks, making them look airy and insubstantial. The unwatered horses were irritable and difficult to control.

As they continued, the canyon system grew increasingly complex, branching and rebranching into a twisted maze. It continued to be impossible to get a GPS reading, and Nora found she was spending as much time consulting the map as traveling. Several times they were forced to backtrack out of a blind canyon; other times the expedition had to wait while Nora and Sloane scouted ahead to find a route.

Nora struggled with doubts. Had her father really gone this far? Had they taken a wrong turn somewhere? What if her father had been delirious when he wrote the letter?

By midmorning the canyon had ended in a sudden puzzle of hoodoo rocks. They squeezed through an opening and topped out in a broken valley peppered with scrub junipers. As she went over the rise, Nora glanced to the right. She could see the Kaiparowits Plateau as a high dark line against the horizon.

Then she faced forward, and the vista she saw both horrified and elated her.

On the far side of the valley, raked by the morning sun, rose what could only be the Devil's Backbone: the ridge she had been anticipating and dreading since they first set out. It was a giant, irregular fin of sandstone at least a thousand feet high and many miles long, pocked with windblown holes and riven with vertical fractures. The top was notched like a dinosaur's back.

Nora led the group over to the shade of a large rock, where they dismounted. She stepped aside with Swire.

"Let's see if we can scout a trail up it first," Nora said. "It looks pretty tough."

For a moment Swire didn't answer. "From here I wouldn't exactly call it tough," he said. "I'd call it impossible."

"My father made it over with his two horses."

"So you said. But I want to see the trail with my own eyes before I take any horses up it."

"Fair enough," Nora replied.

The two hiked north along the base of the ridge, looking for a notch or break in the smooth rock that might signal the beginnings of a trail. It was a weird landscape, unfinished, as if God had simply given up trying to impose order on the unruly rocks.

Suddenly Nora parted some salt cedars and stopped dead. Swire came up, breathing hard.

"Look at this," she breathed. "Petroglyphs."

Nora knelt, examining the drawings more closely. They were complex and beautiful: a mountain lion, a curious pattern of dots with a small foot, a star inside the moon inside the sun, and a detailed image of Kokopelli, the humpbacked flute player, believed to be the god of fertility. The panel ended with another complicated grid of dots overlaid by a huge reversed spiral, like the ones Sloane had seen at the ruin.

They pushed a little farther through the cedars and stumbled on a crevasse filled with loose rock that slanted diagonally across the sandstone monolith. It was steep and narrow, and it rose up the dizzying face and disappeared. The trail had a raised lip of rock along its outer edge that had the uncanny effect of causing most of it to disappear into the smooth sandstone from only several paces off.

"I've never seen anything so well hidden," Nora said. "This has to be our trail."

"It sure wasn't built for horses," Swire said.

"The Anasazi didn't have horses."

"We do," came the curt reply.

They moved carefully forward. In places the cut path had peeled away from the sloping cliff face, forcing them to take a harrowing step across vacant space. At one of these places Nora saw a tumble of rocks more than five hundred feet beneath her. She felt a surge of vertigo and hastily stepped across.

The grade gradually lessened, and in twenty minutes they were at the top. The ridge itself was narrow, perhaps twenty feet across, and in another moment Nora had walked to the far edge.

She looked down the other side into a deep, lush riddle of canyons and washes that merged into a green valley. At the far end of the valley a stream passed through a canebreak, then disappeared into a narrow canyon, perhaps ten feet wide at the entrance. That, Nora thought with a rising feeling of excitement, must be the slot canyon my father mentioned.

Swire had settled his back against the rock. "I ain't bringing my horses up that trail," he said.

Nora's elation fell away. "Roscoe, this isn't impossible. We'll unload and carry everything up by hand. Then we'll guide the horses, unroped, giving them their heads."

Swire shook his head. "We'll kill horses on that trail, no matter what we do." A truculent note had crept into his voice.

Nora felt her face flush. "When you signed on to this trip, you knew the danger. You *can't* back out now. It can be done, and we're going to do it, with you or without you."

"Nope," he said.

Nora slumped against the rock, resting her forehead in her hands. She didn't know what to do in the face of Swire's flat refusal. They couldn't go on without him, and the horses were technically his. And then she realized something.

"The last water I remember was a two-day ride back."

Swire's face showed a sudden, curious blankness. Then he swore softly, as he realized the water the horses so desperately needed was in the green valley that lay ahead, far below their feet. He shook his head slowly and spit. "Looks like you get your wish," he said.

By the time they returned to camp, it was noon. A palpable air of anxiety hung over the group, and the thirsty horses, tied in the shade, were prancing and slinging their heads.

"You didn't happen to pass a Starbucks, did you?" Smithback asked with forced joviality. "I could really use an iced *latte.*"

"We've got a tough stretch of trail ahead," Nora said. She looked around at the dirty faces. "The good news is, there's water on the far side of the ridge. The bad news is that we're going to have to carry the gear up by hand. Then Roscoe and I will bring the horses."

Aaron Black groaned. Nora could see naked fear on his face.

"Take no more than thirty pounds at a time," Nora went on. "Don't try to rush things. It's a rough trail, even on foot. We're going to have to make a couple of trips each."

Sloane stood abruptly, walked over to the line of gear, and hefted a pannier onto her shoulder. Holroyd followed, then Aragon and Smithback. At last Black raised himself from the rocks and followed them.

ALMOST three hours later Nora stood at the top of the Devil's Backbone with the others, breathing heavily and sharing the last of the water. The gear had been brought up over the course of three arduous trips and was now neatly lined up to one side. Black was a wreck—sitting on a rock, soaked with sweat, his hands shaking. The rest were almost as exhausted.

Nora turned to look back down the hogback ridge up which they had come. The hard part, bringing the horses up, was still before her. My God, she thought. Sixteen of them . . . A small sickness began to grow in the pit of her stomach.

"Let me help with the horses," Sloane said.

Nora opened her mouth to answer, but Swire interrupted. "No!" he barked. "The fewer there are of us on that ridge, the fewer are gonna get hurt."

Leaving Sloane in charge, Nora hiked back down the trail. Swire, his face dark, brought the animals around. Only the horse that would lead, one of his own, had a rope clipped to its halter.

"We're gonna drive them up the trail, single file," he said harshly. "I'll guide Mestizo. You bring up the rear with Fiddlehead. Keep your head up. If a horse falls, get out of the way."

Nora nodded.

"Once we get on the trail, you can't stop. Not for anything. Give a horse time to think on that ridge, and he'll panic and try to turn around. So keep them moving, *no matter what.* Got that?"

"Loud and clear," she said.

They started up the trail. At one point the animals hesitated, as if by general consensus, but with some prodding, Swire got Mestizo moving again, and the rest instinctively followed. As they began to gain altitude, the horses grew more fearful; they lathered up and started blowing hard, showing the whites of their eyes.

Nora craned her neck upward. The worst part of the journey stretched ahead, just a cut in the sloping sandstone, eroded by time into the merest whisper of a path. In the places where it had peeled away, the horses would have to step over blue space.

Speaking in low tones and flicking the end of his lasso well behind the horse, Swire kept Mestizo moving. The others followed, working their way upward at a painful pace, the only sounds now the thump and scrape of ironshod toes digging into canted slickrock and the occasional blow of fear.

They arrived at the first switchback. Sweetgrass skidded on the slickrock and scrabbled at the edge. For a moment Nora thought the horse would go over. Then she recovered, eyes wide, flanks trembling.

After agonizing minutes they arrived at the second switchback, a wickedly sharp turn over a narrow section of trail. Reaching the far side, Mestizo suddenly balked. The second horse, Beetlebum, stopped as well, then began to back up. Watching from below, Nora saw the animal place one hind foot over the edge of the trail and out into space.

She froze. The horse's hindquarters dropped, and the foot kicked out twice, looking for a purchase that wasn't there. As she watched, the horse's balance shifted inexorably backward. The animal dropped over the edge, rolled once, and then hurtled down toward her, letting out a strange, high-pitched scream. Nora watched, paralyzed. Time seemed to slow as the horse tumbled, limbs kicking in a terrifying ballet. She felt its shadow cross her face, and then it struck Fiddlehead, directly in front of her, with a massive smack. Both animals hurtled off the edge of the ridge into the void.

"Close up and keep moving!" came Swire's harsh, strained command from above. Forcing herself into action, Nora urged the new rearward horse forward—Smithback's horse, Hurricane Deck. But he wouldn't move. A clonus of horror trembled along the animal's flanks. Then, in a galvanic instant, he reared up, whirling around toward her. Nora instinctively grabbed his halter. With a frenzied clawing of steel on rock, Hurricane scrabbled at the edge of the trail, wide eyes staring at her. Realizing her mistake, she released the halter, but already the falling horse had pulled her off balance. She had a brief glimpse of yawning blue space. Then she landed on her side, her legs rolling over the edge of the cliff, hands scrabbling to grip the smooth sandstone. She heard, as if from a great distance, Swire shouting and then, from below, the soggy, bursting sound of a wet bag as Hurricane Deck hit bottom.

She clawed at the rock, fingernails fighting for purchase as she dangled in the abyss. She could feel the updrafts of wind tickling her legs. In desperation she clutched the stone tighter, her nails tearing and splitting as she continued to slide backward down the tipped surface of stone. Then her right hand brushed against a projecting rill, no more than a quarter inch high, but enough to get a handhold. Now or never, she thought, and she gave a great heave, swinging herself up sideways. It was just enough to get one foot back onto the trail. With a second heave she managed to roll her body up and over. She lay on her back, heart hammering a frantic cadence.

"Get the hell up! Keep moving!" she heard faintly from above. She rose shakily to her feet and started forward, as if in a dream.

She did not remember the rest of the journey. The next clear memory was of lying facedown, hugging the warm, dusty rock of the ridge summit; then a pair of hands were gently turning her over, and Aragon's calm, steady face stared down into her own. Beside him were Smithback and Holroyd.

"The horses—" Nora began.

"There was no other way," Aragon interrupted quietly, taking her hands. "You're hurt."

Nora looked down. Her hands were covered with blood from her ruined fingernails. Aragon opened his medical kit. He dabbed at the fingertips, removing a few pieces of grit and fingernail with tweezers. He worked swiftly, expertly, smearing on topical antibiotic and placing butterfly bandages over the ends of her fingertips. "Wear your gloves for a few days," he said. "You'll be uncomfortable for a while, but the injuries are superficial."

Nora glanced at the group. They were looking back at her, shocked into silence. "Where's Swire?" she managed to ask.

"Back down the trail," Sloane replied.

Nora dropped her head into her hands. And then, as if in answer, three well-spaced gunshots sounded below, echoing crazily among the canyons before dying away into distant thunder.

Ten minutes later Swire appeared, breathing heavily. He passed Nora and went toward the horses, redividing and repacking the loads in silence. Holroyd came over to her and gently took her hand. "I got a decent GPS reading," he whispered.

Nora glanced up at him, hardly caring.

"We're right smack on the trail," he said, smiling.

Nora could only shake her head.

COMPARED to the nightmarish ascent, the trail down into the valley offered few difficulties. The horses, smelling water, charged ahead. Tired as they were, the group began to jog, and Nora found the events of the last hours temporarily receding in her devouring thirst. They splashed into the water upstream from the horses, and Nora fell to her stomach, burying her face in the water. It was the most exquisite sensation she had ever felt.

After a rest the group remounted and traveled down the valley, which narrowed as it approached the broad sandstone plateau rising in front of them, now less than a mile away. The stream made a bend, at last disappearing into the narrow slot canyon carved into the plateau's side. According to the radar map, this canyon should open, about a mile farther along, into the small valley that—she hoped—contained Quivira. But the slot canyon itself was clearly too narrow for horses.

As they rode up to the massive sandstone wall, Nora noticed a large rock beside the stream with some markings on its flanks. As she dismounted and came nearer, she could see a small panel of petroglyphs: a series of dots and a small foot, along with another star and a sun. She couldn't help but notice that there was a large reversed spiral carved on top of the other images.

The rest came up beside her. She noticed Aragon gazing at the glyphs, an intent expression on his face.

"What do you think?" she asked.

"The footlike glyph indicates walking," he said at last, "and the dots indicate distance. Based on other sites I've seen, each dot represents a walking distance of about sixteen minutes. The sun is the symbol for the supreme deity and the star a symbol of truth. I take the whole thing to be an indicator that an oracle, a kind of Anasazi Delphi, lies ahead."

"You mean Quivira?" Nora asked.

Aragon nodded.

"And what does this spiral mean?" asked Holroyd.

Aragon hesitated a moment. "In the context of the other things we've seen, I'd call it a warning, or omen. A notice to travelers not to proceed, an indication of evil."

There was a sudden silence.

"Lions and tigers and bears, oh my," murmured Smithback.

As they moved away, Holroyd gave a shout. He had walked around to the side of the rock nearest the entrance to the slot canyon. Now he pointed to a much fresher inscription. Scraped into the rock with a penknife were a series of narrow grooves that spelled out P.K. 1983.

Nora touched her father's initials on the rock. A knot of tension, tightened over the harrowing days, loosened abruptly, and she felt an intense, overwhelming flood of relief. Her father *had* been here. They *had* been following his trail. She realized dimly that the group was crowding around, congratulating her.

Slowly she rose to her feet. She gathered the expedition under a small grove of gambel oaks, near the point where the stream plunged into the slot canyon.

"We're almost there," she said. She turned toward Sloane. In the woman's eyes she immediately saw the same eagerness that was kindling within her.

"Sloane and I are going through the canyon to reconnoiter," she said. "It may turn out to be an overnight trip. Any objections?"

There were none. While the camp settled down to its routine, Nora loaded a sleeping bag into a backpack. Sloane did the same, adding a length of rope and some climbing equipment to hers. Bonarotti wordlessly pressed small, heavy packets of food into each of their hands.

Shouldering their packs, they waved good-bye and hiked down the creek into the slot canyon, splashing in the shallow water. Deerflies and no-see-ums danced and droned in the thick air. Nora waved them away with an impatient hand.

The narrow walls quickly pressed in around them, leaving the uncomfortable feeling that they were walking along the bottom of a long, slender container. There were only occasional glimpses of sky, and as the canyon descended, the light grew dimmer. At one point a huge cottonwood trunk, horribly scarred and mauled, had somehow become jammed in the canyon walls about twenty feet above their heads. Nearby there was a narrow hollow in the rock face, above a small stepped ledge.

"Must've been some storm that put that tree up there," Sloane murmured, glancing upward at the trunk. "I'd sure hate to be caught in a flash flood in one of these canyons."

"I've heard the first thing you feel is a rising wind," Nora replied. "Then you hear a sound, almost like distant voices or applause. At that point you get your butt out as fast as possible. If you're still in the canyon by the time you hear the roar of water, it's too late. You're dead meat."

As they walked on, the canyon narrowed still further and sloped downward in a series of pools, each filled with chocolate-colored water. Sometimes the water was only an inch deep, other times it was over their heads. Each pool was connected to the next by a pitched slot so narrow they had to squeeze through it sideways, holding their packs.

After half an hour's struggle they came to an especially long, narrow pool. Taking the lead, Nora eased down in and swam across toward a small boulder wedged between the walls about six feet above the ground. A thick curtain of weeds and roots trailed from it, through which came a sheen of sunlight. Nora paused at the shaggy curtain.

"It's like the entrance to something magical," Sloane said as she approached. "But what?"

Nora glanced at her for a moment. Then, placing her arms together, she pushed through the dense tangle.

As her eyes adjusted, Nora could see a small valley open up below them: only about four hundred yards long by two hundred yards wide, a jeweled pocket in the red sandstone. The mellow sunlight fell upon a riot of color: blooming Apache plumes, Indian paintbrush, scarlet gilia.

After the long dark crawl through the slot canyon, arriving at this beautiful valley was like stumbling upon a lost world. Everything about it—its intimate size, its high surrounding walls, its incredible remoteness—filled Nora with the sensation of discovering a hidden paradise.

Light as a cat, Sloane moved silently down to the valley floor. Nora followed her to a sandy benchland, where a small grove of cottonwoods provided shade.

"How's this for a campsite?" Sloane asked, dropping her pack.

"Couldn't be more perfect," Nora replied. She unshouldered her pack, pulled out her soggy sleeping bag, shook it out, and draped it over a bush.

Then her eyes turned ineluctably back toward the towering cliffs that surrounded them on four sides. Pulling the waterproof binoculars from her pack, she began scanning the rock faces, searching for the telltale signs of a trail. Her father had seen a clear hand-and-toe trail. She saw nothing.

Nora glanced around for Sloane. The woman was already walking along the base of the cliffs, peering intently at the ground. Looking for potsherds or flint chips, Nora thought approvingly, always a good way to locate a hidden ruin above.

"Any luck?" Nora asked her.

Sloane shook her head. "I'm having trouble believing there was a city here. I haven't found *anything.*"

The sun had now dipped low enough to bring creeping shadows across the valley floor. "Look, Sloane," Nora said, "we haven't even begun to examine this valley. Tomorrow morning we'll make a careful survey. And if we still don't find anything, we'll bring the proton magnetometer in and scan for structures beneath the sand."

Sloane gave a slow smile. "Maybe you're right," she said. "Let's get a fire going and see if we can dry out these bags."

After she had scooped out a shallow firepit and built a ring of stones, Nora changed the damp bandages on her fingers. The sleeping bags began to steam slightly in the heat.

Sloane retrieved a pot from her daypack, boiled some water, then grabbed the small packet Bonarotti had thrust into her hand. "Couscous with savory herbs," she whispered. "Isn't Bonarotti a prince?"

She added the mixture to the water and ten minutes later pulled it from the fire. From the couscous they moved on to Nora's dish—lentils with sun-dried vegetables in a curried beef broth—then cleared away the dishes. Nora shook her bag out and laid it in the soft sand, close to the fire. Then, stripping off most of her wet clothes, she climbed in and lay back, breathing the clean air of the canyon, gazing at the dome of stars overhead.

"So what'll we find tomorrow, Nora?" Sloane's husky voice, surprisingly close in the near darkness, echoed her own thoughts.

"I don't know," Nora replied. "What do you think we'll find?"

"Quivira," came the reply, almost whispered.

"You didn't seem so sure an hour ago."

Sloane shrugged. "Oh, it'll be here," she said.

Within moments Nora could hear her breathing, regular and serene. But Nora lay still, eyes open to the stars, for a long time.

NORA awoke with a start. She had slept so deeply, so heavily, that for a moment she did not know where she was. Dawn light was just bloodying the rimrock above her head. A throbbing at the ends of her bandaged fingers brought back memories of the previous day: the terrible struggle on the ridge, the discovery of the slot canyon and this hidden valley beyond. She looked around. The sleeping bag beside her was empty.

She rose, sore muscles protesting, and stirred up the fire. Rummaging in her pack, she filled a tiny, two-cup espresso pot with grounds and water, put it on the fire, then went down to the creek to wash. When she returned, the pot was hissing. She poured herself a cup just as Sloane walked up.

"There's nothing here, Nora," Sloane said. "I just spent the last hour going over this place inch by inch."

Nora set down her coffee. "I don't believe it."

"Take a look for yourself."

Nora walked to the base of the cliffs and began making a clockwise circuit of the valley, systematically searching the cliffs, setbacks, and rimrock above her. The morning invasion of light into the valley continued, each minute creating fresh angles and shadows on the rock. Every twenty steps she stopped and searched again, forcing her eyes across the same rock faces from different angles, straining to recognize something—a toehold, a shaped building block, a faded petroglyph, anything that indicated human occupation. After completing the circuit, she crossed the valley from north to south and from east to west, heedlessly wading through the stream again and again, peering up at the walls, trying to get every possible view of the towering cliffs above.

Ninety minutes later she came back into camp, wet and tired. She sat down beside Sloane, saying nothing. Sloane, her head bowed, was staring into the sand, idly tracing a circle with a stick. "I can't tell you how sorry I am, Nora."

Nora said nothing. They remained beside the dying fire wordlessly for perhaps ten minutes, perhaps twenty, as the full weight of the colossal defeat settled upon them.

"I just can't believe it," Nora said at last. "I can't believe I dragged you all out here, wasted your father's money, risked lives, killed horses, for nothing."

Sloane took one of Nora's hands and gave it a reassuring squeeze. Then she stood up.

"Come on," she said. "The others are waiting for us."

Nora stowed the cooking gear and her sleeping bag into her pack, then shouldered it wearily. She looked up yet again at the rock, picking out the same landmarks she had seen earlier. The morning light was coming in at a different angle, raking along the lower cliffs. Her eyes instinctively scoured the rock face, but it remained clear and barren. She raised her eyes higher.

And then she saw something: a single, shallow notch in the rock, forty feet above the ground. It probably was natural, but she found herself digging into her pack anyway for her binoculars. She focused and looked again. Magnified, it looked a little less natural. But where was the rest of the trail?

Angling her binoculars down, she saw the answer: A section of the cliff face had recently peeled off. At the base of the cliffs was the proof—a small heap of broken rubble.

She turned and found Sloane staring at her curiously. She handed over the binoculars. "Look at that."

Sloane examined the indicated spot. Her body tensed.

"It's a Moki step," she said breathlessly. "The top of a trail."

"That little landslide must have happened since my father saw the trail," Nora said. But Sloane was already digging into her pack, pulling out a rope.

"You're going up there?" Nora asked.

"Damn right I'm going up there." She worked frantically, pulling out her equipment.

"What about me?" Nora asked.

"You? What about your hands?"

"They're fine," Nora said. "I'll wear my gloves."

"Then let's do it," said Sloane with a sudden radiant grin.

In a moment they were at the base of the cliff. As Nora watched, Sloane moved up the rock with care and precision. At one point she called out, "Rock!" and Nora dodged a shower of chips. Another minute and Sloane had reached the single toehold, then gained the ledge above it.

There was a brief silence. Then she cried out again. "I can see a route!" The sound echoed crazily around the valley. "Nora, the city must be recessed in an alcove just above!"

"I'm coming up!" Nora shouted.

She began working her way up the cliff face, the muscles of her arms and calves twitching from the strain of clinging to the thin holds. Despite the gloves, the ends of her fingers were exquisitely painful.

Sloane half pulled her the last few feet onto the ledge. Nora climbed shakily to her feet, massaging her fingers. From this vantage point she could see that the canyon wall sloped back at a terrifying angle. But Sloane was right: Though invisible from the ground, from up here the hand-and-toe trail was unmistakable.

"You okay?" Sloane asked. Nora nodded, and her companion began a second pitch up the rock. With the trail still in place, it was the work of a minute to climb the last remaining stretch.

They stood motionless on the benchland, staring ahead. There was nothing: no city, no alcove, just the naked shelf of rock.

And then Nora glanced across the canyon for the first time.

There, on the opposite cliff face, a huge alcove arched across the length of the canyon, poised halfway between ground and sky. Tucked inside was a ruined city. Four great towers rose from its corners, and between them lay a complicated arrangement of circular kivas and roomblocks dotted with black windows and doorways. The morning sun gilded the walls and towers into a dream city: insubstantial, airy, ready to evaporate into the desert air.

Nora closed her eyes, squeezed them shut, then opened them again. The city was still there. She gazed slowly across the vista, drinking it in. Wedged into the middle of the city, she could make out the circular outline of a great kiva—the largest she had ever seen—still roofed. An intact great kiva, the equivalent of a cathedral in a medieval city . . . nothing like it had ever been found.

Suddenly her knees grew weak and she dropped slowly to the ground. Seated, she continued to stare across the valley. There was a rustling sound, and Sloane knelt down beside her.

"Nora," came the voice, the slightest trace of irony leavening the reverence, "I think we've found Quivira."

5

Twelve hours later the city of Quivira lay in shadow, the late afternoon sun blazing its last on the valley cliffs opposite the ruin. Quivira had a gracefulness, a sense of balance, that belied its massive stone construction. It was as if the city had been planned and built as a unit, rather than growing by accretion, as most other large Anasazi cliff dwellings had. There were still traces of gypsum whitewash on the outer walls, and the great kiva showed traces of what had once been a blue disk painted on its side.

The four towers were paired, two on each side of the alcove, with the main city lying between and the circular great kiva at the very center. Each tower rose about fifty feet. The front two were freestanding; the rear two were actually mortared to the natural stone roof of the alcove.

The ruin was in beautiful condition, but on closer view it was far from perfect. There were several ugly fractures snaking up the sides of the four towers. In one place the masonry had peeled off part of an upper story, revealing a dark interior. In the terraced city between the towers, several of the third-story rooms had collapsed. Others appeared to have burned. But overall the city was remarkably well preserved, its huge walls built of stone courses mortared with adobe. Wooden ladders stood against some of the walls. Hundreds of rooms were still intact and roofed—a complicated arrangement of roomblocks and smaller circular kivas. The great kiva that dominated the center seemed almost untouched. It was a city made to last forever.

The rooms were not empty. There were extraordinary pots, smooth, polished, painted with fantastic geometric designs. There were prayer sticks, carved, feathered, and painted, gleaming with color even in the dull light; fetishes of different animals, fashioned from semiprecious stones; bowls filled with perfect, tiny bird points, all flaked out of the blackest obsidian; cradleboards and exquisite woven bags; painted artifacts and carved crystals; delicately woven baskets.

Nora rested on an ancient retaining wall, feeling as drained as she had ever felt in her life. She could hear the excited voices of the rest of the expedition ringing out of the city, distorted and magnified by the vast pregnant hollow of rock in which Quivira stood.

Nora glanced down at the rope ladder and pulley system, rigged by Sloane to provide quick access to the ruin. Far below, in a grove of cottonwood trees where they had made their camp, she could see the smoke of Bonarotti's campfire. The cook had promised them—amazingly—two bottles of Château Pétrus in celebration. It had been, she thought, the longest—and greatest—day of her life: "that day of days," as Howard Carter had described it when he first entered King Tutankhamen's tomb.

Aragon, Holroyd, and Black emerged from the ruin, Sloane and Smithback bringing up the rear. "This is the discovery of the century," Black boomed. "There's more in one room than the greatest museums have in their entire collections."

Nora turned to Aragon. He smiled widely and genuinely. "It's fantastic," he said as he took her hand and pressed it. "Nora, you have the congratulations of all of us."

Nora felt a sudden flush of pleasure as she listened to the chorus of clapping. Then Smithback was hoisting a canteen. "And I'd like to propose a toast to Padraic Kelly. If it weren't for him, we'd never be here."

This sudden reference to her father, coming from a source as unexpected as Smithback, brought a sudden welling of emotion. Her father had never been far from her thoughts all day.

"Thank you," she said.

The group fell silent. Light was draining fast from the valley, and

it was time they made their way down the rope ladder to supper. And yet everyone seemed reluctant to leave the magical place.
"What I can't figure out is why they left all that stuff behind," Smithback said. "It's like walking away from Fort Knox."
"The sheer wealth of this city and the many ceremonial artifacts make me think it must have been a religious center that overshadowed even Chaco," said Aragon. "A city of priests."
"A city of priests?" Black repeated skeptically. "Why would a city of priests be located way out here, at the very edge of the Anasazi realm? What I found more interesting was the amazingly defensive nature of the place—it's nearly impregnable."
"Then why did they abandon the city?" Holroyd asked.
"They probably overfarmed the valley below," Black replied with a shrug. "Simple soil exhaustion."
Nora shook her head. "There's no way, given its size, that the farmland in the valley could support the city to begin with. There must be a hundred granaries back there. They *had* to have been importing tons of food from someplace else. But all this begs the question: Why put such a huge city here in the first place—at the end of a circuitous road, at the end of a narrow slot canyon? During the rainy season that canyon would have been impassable half the time."
"What really intrigues me," Smithback said, "is the idea of gold and silver."
There he goes again, Nora thought. "Like I told you on the barge," she said, "the Anasazi had no precious metals."
"What about the Coronado reports? Quivira wasn't made up by the Indians. So why should the gold be?"
Black suddenly spoke up. "Anasazi graves have been found containing parrot and macaw feathers imported from the Aztec empires and their Toltec predecessors. The Anasazi traded extensively with the Toltecs and Aztecs—slaves, obsidian, agate, salt, and pottery. It's not entirely unreasonable to think the Anasazi obtained gold."
Nora was surprised at hearing this from Black. "If they did have gold," Nora began, trying to keep patient, "then, in the tens of thousands of Anasazi sites excavated over the last hundred and fifty

years, we'd have found some. The bottom line is, if the Anasazi had gold, then where is it all?"

"Maybe right here," said Smithback quietly.

Nora stared at him. Then she began to laugh. "Bill, if we do find gold in Quivira, I'll eat that hat of yours. Okay? Now let's get down and see what miracle Chef Bonarotti has prepared for dinner."

THE work at Quivira went exceptionally well. The core members of the expedition set to their tasks with a professionalism that both impressed and heartened Nora. With the help of a hoisting system and a rope ladder installed by Sloane, Holroyd set up a weather receiver and communications gear atop the rim of the canyon, far above Quivira. He then assembled a wireless paging network, designed around a central transmitter, to allow the members of the group to communicate with each other from anywhere within the site.

In the shadows of the ancient adobe walls, at the far end of the ruin's front plaza, Black and Smithback were working in the city's great midden heap, a dusty, oversized mound of dirt, broken animal bones, charcoal, and potsherds. As Nora approached, she could see Smithback's head pop up from a cut at the far end, face dirty, cowlick bobbing with displeasure. She smiled despite herself at the sight.

Black came around the mound in high spirits, carrying a trowel in one hand and a whisk broom in the other. "Nora," he said with a smile. "I don't believe there's been a clearer cultural sequence since Kidder excavated the mound at Pecos. And that's just from the control pit."

He guided her to a small, precise cut in the side of the midden. Dozens of thin layers of brown, gray, and black soil were exposed, revealing how the trash mound had grown over time.

The layers had each been labeled with tiny numbered flags, and even smaller flags marked spots where artifacts had been removed. On the ground beside the cut were dozens of Baggies and glass tubes, carefully aligned, each with its own artifact, seed, bone, or lump of charcoal.

Nearby, Nora could see that Black had set up a portable water flotation lab and stereozoom microscope for separating pollen, small seeds, and human hair from the detritus. It was a highly professional job, executed with remarkable assurance and speed.

"The sequence begins abruptly at about A.D. 950," said Black. "Below this layer"—he squatted beside the soil profile and pointed to a layer of light brown dirt—"is sterile soil."

"Meaning the city was built all at once," Nora said.

"Exactly. What's more, the trash mound was segregated."

Nora stared at him curiously. "Segregated?"

"Yes. In the back part there are fragments of beautiful painted pottery and the bones of animals used for food: turkeys, deer, elk, bear. There are a lot of beads, whole arrowheads, even chipped pots. But in the front we find only the crudest, ugliest corrugated pottery. And the food we found in the front of the mound was clearly different."

"What kinds of foods?"

"Mostly rats," said Black. "Squirrels, snakes, a coyote or two, a lot of crushed insect carapaces."

"They were eating insects?" Nora asked incredulously.

"Without a doubt. In other sites this kind of thing points directly to slavery. The masters and slaves ate different things and dumped their trash in different places."

"There isn't a shred of evidence that the Anasazi had slaves."

Black looked at her. "There is now. Either slavery, or we're looking at a deeply stratified society."

Nora glanced around the city. The discovery seemed to violate all that they knew about the Anasazi. "Let's keep an open mind until all the evidence is in," she said at last.

"Naturally."

"By the way," Nora continued, "did you know that most of those granaries in the rear of the city are still bulging with corn and beans?"

Black straightened up. "No, I didn't."

"Sloane told me earlier this morning. That suggests the site was abandoned in the fall, at harvesttime. And very quickly."

"Sloane," Black repeated casually. "Where is she now?"

"Somewhere in the central roomblocks, I think. I'll be checking in with her later. But now I'm off to see what Aragon is up to." She raised her radio to her lips. "Enrique, this is Nora. Where are you?"

"In a crawl space behind the granaries."

"What are you doing back there?"

There was a short silence. "Better see for yourself. Come in from the west side."

Nora walked around the back of the midden heap and past the first great tower. She picked up a small passageway that ran behind the granaries toward the back of the cave. It was dark and cool here behind the ruin, and the air smelled of sandstone and smoke. As she moved forward, the ceiling of the passageway became so low that she had to drop to her hands and knees. There was a long moment of close, oppressive darkness; then ahead she could see the glow from Aragon's lantern.

She rose to her feet inside a cramped space. Before her sat Aragon. Nora drew in her breath—beyond him lay a sea of human bones. The place was silent except for the hiss of the lantern.

"What is all this?" Nora asked. "Some kind of catacomb?"

Aragon looked up, his face an unreadable mask. "It's the largest ossuary I've ever encountered," he said. "I've heard of such things in old-world megalithic sites, but never in North America. And never on this kind of scale."

Nora glanced from him to the bones. There were many complete skeletons lying on the top of the pile, but beneath them appeared to be a thick scattering of disarticulated bones, most of them broken, including countless crushed skulls.

"These skeletons on top," Aragon said, "the complete ones, seem to have been dragged in here and hastily thrown on top of a deep layer of preexisting bones."

Nora looked around, feeling an unpleasant gnawing in the pit of her stomach. "What could it mean?" she asked.

"A large number of simultaneous burials usually means a single cause. Famine, disease, war"—he paused—"or sacrifice."

At that moment her radio crackled. "Nora, this is Sloane."

Nora pulled out her radio. "I'm with Aragon. What is it?"

"There's something you need to see. Both of you." Through the microphone the quiver of suppressed excitement in her voice was clear. "Meet me at the central plaza."

A few minutes later Sloane was leading Nora and Aragon through a complicated series of second-story roomblocks at the far end of the ruin. "We were doing a routine survey," she was saying, "and then Peter found a large cavity in one of the floors with the proton magnetometer." They stepped beneath a doorway and entered a large room, only dimly lit by the portable lantern.

Nora was gazing into the center of the room, where a section of floor had been removed, exposing a slab-lined cist.

"Who opened this grave?" she heard Aragon ask sharply.

Nora stepped forward, anger at this breach of authority flooding through her. Then she looked down and stopped short.

This was no ordinary Anasazi burial. Two completely disarticulated skeletons lay in the center of the grave, the broken bones of each arranged in a circular pattern in its own large painted bowl, surmounted by their broken skulls. The scalps of both individuals had been laid in the grave on top of their skulls. One had long white hair, beautifully braided and decorated with incised turquoise ornaments. The other had brown hair, also braided, with two huge dishes of polished abalone fixed to the ends of each braid. In both skulls the front teeth had been drilled and inlaid with red carnelian.

Nora stared in astonishment. The bodies were surrounded by an unheard-of wealth of grave goods: turquoise, crystals, fetishes, pots filled with ground pigments. There were also two bowls of carved quartz, filled to the brim with fine reddish powder. The entire burial was covered with a layer of yellow dust.

"I examined that dust under the stereozoom," said Sloane. "It's pollen from at least fifteen species of flowers. The entire cist was once filled with hundreds of pounds of flowers."

Nora shook her head in disbelief. "The Anasazi never buried their dead like that."

Aragon was kneeling by the grave, shining a flashlight over the remains. "I would like permission to temporarily remove several bones for examination," he said, his voice coldly formal. "And I'd like to take a sample of that reddish powder."

More than anything else, this request, coming from Aragon, capped Nora's mystification. "After we photograph and document everything, of course," she heard herself say.

He departed wordlessly, but Nora continued to stand at the edge of the cist, staring down into the dark hole in the floor. There was something odd, even wrong, about this: the bones broken and burned, the thick flower dust, the grave goods ranged so carefully.

I don't think this is a burial at all, Nora thought. I think it's an offering.

AS THEY stepped out onto the first-floor roof, its farthest edges tipped in noontime sun, Nora gently laid a hand on Sloane's arm. "I thought we had an agreement," she said.

Sloane turned to look at her. "What are you talking about?"

"You shouldn't have opened that grave without consulting me first. That isn't how a professional archaeologist should work, simply digging up what interests her."

Sloane moved closer, so close that Nora could feel the heat and anger radiating from her. "You, Nora Kelly, are a control freak. I did nothing wrong. The magnetometer showed a cavity, and all I did was lift the stone. I touched *nothing.*"

Nora struggled to maintain her composure. "If you can't abide by the rules," she said as evenly as she could, "I'll place you under Aragon, where you can learn respect for the integrity of an archaeological site . . . and obedience to the expedition director."

"Director?" Sloane sneered. "By all rights, *I* should be the expedition director. Don't forget who's paying for all this."

Sloane pivoted on her heel. Nora watched her descend the ladder and walk deliberately away, erect and proud, her dark hair burned violet by the sun.

A ROUGH preliminary survey of Quivira had been completed, and Holroyd had downloaded the location coordinates and field elevations into a geographic information systems database. It was time to enter the great kiva, the central religious structure of the city. The group assembled at the base of the structure with ill-disguised anticipation.

An unusually subdued Bill Smithback was fumbling with a cassette recorder. Beside him stood Aragon, face gray and thoughtful. Black was resting on a rock, drumming his fingers and chatting with Peter Holroyd. The only person missing was Sloane.

Holroyd stood and approached Nora, shaking a plant he was holding. "Have a look at this," he said.

It was an oversized, bushy explosion of green stalks, with a tapered root at one end and a creamy flower at the other.

"What is it?" she asked.

"I have a side interest in botanical poisons," he explained. "This one's datura. The root's loaded with a highly potent hallucinogen."

"Hallucinogen?"

"The alkaloid is concentrated in the upper sections of the root," Aragon interjected. "Among Yaqui shamans fortitude is measured by just how far up the root you can ingest." He glanced at Holroyd. "But certainly you've noticed that's not the only illegal plant in this valley."

Holroyd nodded. "Not only datura, but psilocybin, mescal cactus. . . . The place is a veritable smorgasbord of psychedelics."

"The curious thing," Aragon said, "is that those three plants you mention—which seem to run riot here—are sometimes taken by shamans and medicine men. In combination they can induce a wild frenzy, like an overdose of PCP."

"The flower's pretty, at least," Nora said.

"Looks like a morning glory, doesn't it?" Holroyd asked. "That's another funny thing. There's an enzyme in the datura root that the body can't metabolize. Instead, it gets exuded in the sweat. And I've heard that's exactly what people who take it smell like: morning glories."

Unconsciously Nora leaned forward, bringing the flower to her nose. She inhaled the delicate scent deeply.

Then she froze, fingers turning cold. In a moment her mind was back in the upstairs hallway of her parents' abandoned ranch house, hearing the crunch of glass underfoot, smelling the scent of crushed flowers on the still night air. . . .

She heard a clatter and turned to see Sloane approaching, burdened by a portable acetylene lantern and her 4x5 camera. The woman put down the equipment and came over. She slid a graceful arm around Nora's waist.

"Sorry," she whispered in Nora's ear. "You were right. It won't happen again."

"Thank you," Nora said, dropping the plant.

Then she turned to the group, doing her best to push thoughts of Holroyd's plant out of her mind. "Okay, here's the protocol. Sloane and I will enter the kiva first to make an initial analysis and do the photography. The rest of you will follow."

One at a time they ascended a ladder to the roof of the structure. As with all kivas, the great kiva was entered from a hole in its roof. Protruding from the opening were the two ends of an Anasazi ladder, still in perfect condition, leading down into the interior. As she stared at the ladder, Nora felt her mouth go dry.

"Let's light the lantern," she said.

There was the hiss of gas, and with a pop of ignition the lantern sprang to life. Sloane directed the brilliant white light down into the gloom. But from their vantage point nothing but bare floor was visible.

The ladder descended about fifteen feet, ending in an anchor groove cut into the sandstone floor. Sloane rapidly climbed down to the bottom, and after a deep breath Nora followed.

The circular wall of the kiva was covered with a brilliantly colored mural. Ranged around the top were four huge thunderbirds, their outstretched wings almost covering the entire upper part of the kiva wall. Jagged lightning shot from the birds' eyes and beaks. Below, clouds drifted across a field of brilliant turquoise, dropping dotted curtains of white rain.

Nora dropped her eyes. Below the mural, ranging around the circumference of the kiva, was a stone *banco*. On the *banco* lay a huge number of gleaming objects, appearing and disappearing as the lantern beam moved slowly over them. As she stared, Nora realized, with a kind of remote surprise, that they were all skulls. There were dozens, if not hundreds of them: human, bear, buffalo, wolf, deer, mountain lion, jaguar—each completely covered with an inlay of polished turquoise. But it was the eyes that struck Nora most of all. In each eye socket lay a carved globe of rose quartz crystal, inlaid with carnelian, that refracted, magnified, and threw back the beam of the lamp, causing the eyes to gleam hideously pink in the murk. It was a grinning crowd of the dead.

Nora glanced at Sloane, who was arranging her camera's flash units. "I'm going to invite the others in," said Nora.

Sloane nodded curtly.

The others filed down the ladder in silent astonishment and gathered at the bottom. Nora found herself drawn to a curious design of two large circles at the northern end of the mural. One circle enclosed an incised disk of blue and white, showing miniature clouds and rain. The second circle was painted yellow and white, and it enclosed an incised disk of the sun, surrounded by rays of light. As the beam of the lantern moved across it, the image glittered like gold.

"This is obviously a moiety," said Black, approaching. He pointed at the two circles, his large, craggy face backlighted by the lamp.

"A moiety?"

"Yes. Many Anasazi societies were organized into moieties. They were divided into halves—summer and winter societies, male and female, earth and sky." He pointed to the two circles. "This blue disk matches the one outside this kiva. That would imply that this city was divided into rain and sun societies. The first circle represents the Rain Kiva, and the second the Sun Kiva."

"Interesting," said Nora, surprised. "So we must be standing in the Rain Kiva itself."

"So?" said Smithback, who had been listening. "If this is the Rain Kiva, then where's the Sun Kiva?"

Black cleared his throat. "That's a very good question."

"It must be at some other site, if it exists at all," Nora said.

"No doubt you're right," Aragon murmured. "Still, the longer I am here, I have this feeling of something . . . something that, for whatever reason, we're not seeing."

Nora turned to him. "I don't understand."

The older man returned the glance. "Don't you get the sense that there's a piece of the puzzle still missing? All the riches, all the bones, all this massive construction . . . there has to be some reason for it." He shook his head. "I thought the answer would be in this kiva. But now I am not so sure. I dislike making value judgments, but I feel there was an overarching purpose to all this. A *sinister* purpose."

THAT night Nora slept poorly and awoke early, the memory of ugly dreams receding quickly into forgetfulness. She sat up, immediately wide-awake, and heard the distant plash of water in the creek. She glanced around. Swire was already up and gone on his wearisome daily slog through the slot canyon to check on the horses. The rest of the camp slumbered in the predawn darkness.

Dressing quickly in the shivery cold, she walked over to the kitchen area, unbanked the coals, and tossed some twigs on to start the fire. She filled the blue-flecked enamel coffeepot with water and placed it on the grill.

As she did so, she saw a form emerge from the darkness of a distant grove of cottonwoods: Sloane. Nora momentarily wondered why she had not slept in her tent. Probably likes to sleep under the stars, like me, she thought.

"Sleep well?" Sloane asked, tossing her bedroll into her tent and taking a seat beside Nora.

"Not especially," Nora said, gazing into the fire. "You?"

"I did all right." She seemed in high spirits, a stark contrast to Nora's own subdued mood.

The coffeepot began to stir and shake on the grill as the water boiled. Heaving herself to her feet, Nora removed it from the fire, threw in a fistful of grounds, and stirred the pot with her knife.

"Bonarotti would die if he saw you making that cowboy coffee," Sloane said. "He'd brain you with his espresso pot."

"Waiting for him to get up and make coffee in the morning is like waiting for Godot," Nora said. She put the pot back on the fire and stirred the grounds down.

Smithback and Black came over and joined them, and Nora poured them each a cup. They all sat around the fire, nursing their coffee and speaking little.

Nora heard the whisper of footfalls on sand and looked up to see Aragon, bundled against the chill. He sat down and wordlessly poured himself a cup of coffee, hands unsteady.

"I noticed you were burning the midnight oil last night, Enrique," Nora said.

He turned his dark eyes to Nora. "Yes, I was up quite late."

"Still working on those bones, I suppose?" asked Black.

"Yes." Something in Aragon's tone silenced the company. He set his cup down.

"As I told Nora when I first discovered it, the placement of the bones in the crawl space is exceedingly odd." He removed from his coat a small plastic container. He placed it on the ground and gently unbuckled the lid. Inside were three fragmentary bones and a portion of a cranium.

"Lying sprawled on top are perhaps fifty or sixty articulated skeletons," he continued. "Some still have the remains of clothing, rich jewelry. They were well-fed, healthy individuals, most in the prime of their lives. They all seemed to have died at the same time, yet there is no sign of violence on the bones."

"So what's the explanation?" Nora asked.

"It seems to me that whatever happened, it happened so suddenly that there wasn't time to give the bodies a proper burial." His expression changed. "The bones underneath tell a very different story. They are the broken, disarticulated remains of thousands of individuals, accumulated over years. Unlike the skeletons on top, these bones come from individuals who clearly died of violence. Extreme violence."

Nora felt her unease grow.

Aragon pointed with a pair of rubber-tipped forceps at a broken bone in the container. "Many of the bones have been broken in a special way, the same way the Anasazi broke deer and elk bones in order to extract the marrow."

"Wait," said Smithback. "To extract the marrow for—"

"Let me finish. There are also marks on the bones consistent with the marks made by stone tools when a carcass is dismembered. Butchered and defleshed, if you will. I found dozens of fractured skulls, mostly of children, with cut marks on the calvaria that are made only by scalping, just like the skull we found earlier. I also found that many of the skulls had been drilled and a circular piece of bone removed."

From the corner of her eye Nora saw that Smithback was furiously taking notes.

"And there's more." Aragon picked up a smaller bone with the forceps. "Take a look at the broken ends with this loupe."

Nora examined it under magnification. "I can't see anything unusual, except maybe for this faint sheen on the broken ends."

"That sheen has been called pot polish."

"Pot polish?"

"It only occurs to bones that have been boiled and stirred in a rough ceramic pot for a long time, turned around and around." And then he added unnecessarily, "It's how you make soup."

"Are you saying they were cooking and *eating* people?" Smithback asked.

"Of course that's what he's saying," Black snapped. "Enrique, you're the last person I would have suspected of jumping to sensational conclusions. There are dozens of ways bones could be scratched and polished other than cannibalism."

"I am merely reporting what I've seen," Aragon said.

"This is irresponsible," Black bellowed. "The Anasazi were a peaceful, agrarian people."

"Unlike the Aztecs," Aragon said. "Dr. Black, you said Anasazi cannibalism is impossible. But not Aztec cannibalism. Cannibalism not for food, but as a tool of social control and terror."

"What's your point?" Black said. "This is America, not Mexico. We're digging an Anasazi site."

"An Anasazi site with a ruling class? An Anasazi site that features royal burial chambers filled with flowers? An Anasazi site that may or may not display signs of ritual cannibalism?" Aragon shook his head. "Forensic tests on the skulls point to the two groups of skeletons being from *entirely* different populations—Anasazi slaves beneath, Aztec rulers above. *All* the evidence I've found at Quivira demonstrates one thing: A group of Aztecs, or rather their Toltec predecessors, invaded the Anasazi civilization around A.D. 950 and established themselves here as a priestly nobility."

"I've never heard anything so ridiculous," Black said. "It goes against a hundred years of scholarship."

"Let's not be too hasty," Nora said. "That theory would explain a lot. The city's strange location, for one thing."

"And the concentration of wealth," Sloane added in a low, thoughtful voice. "Maybe *trade* with the Aztecs has been the wrong word all along. These were foreign invaders, establishing an oligarchy, maintaining power through religious ritual and sacrificial cannibalism."

As Smithback began to ask a question, Nora heard a distant shout. In unison the group turned toward the sound. Roscoe Swire was running down the canyon, bashing and stomping crazily through the brush as he approached camp.

He came to a frantic stop before them, still dripping wet from the slot canyon, breathing raggedly. Bloody water dripped from his hair, and his shirt was stained pink.

"Our horses," he said, gasping for air. "They've been gutted."

Nora raised her hands to silence the explosion of talk. "Roscoe," she said, "I want you to tell us exactly what happened."

Swire sat down near the fire, still heaving from his scramble through the slot canyon, oblivious to a nasty gash on his arm. "When I reached the horses, they were all lathered up." He stopped a moment. "A couple were missing. Then I saw them . . . what was left of them, anyway. Hoosegow and Crow Bait, gutted and . . ." His face darkened. "They unwound their guts and laid them out in a spiral. There were sticks with feathers shoved into the eyes"—he paused—"other stuff, too."

At the mention of the spirals Nora went cold.

"I just came back here to tell you I'm going after them," Swire said. He stood up abruptly and went into his tent.

Nora could hear the sound of bullets being pushed into chambers. A moment later he reemerged, rifle slung behind his back, revolver buckled around his waist.

"Wait a minute, Roscoe," Nora said. "You can't just run off without a plan and go kill someone."

"I've got a plan," came the answer. "I'm gonna find the bastard that—"

"Agreed," Nora said, cutting off Swire's words. "But you're not the person to do it."

"What?" Swire's expression turned to one of scornful disbelief. "And just who else is going to do it for me?"

"I am."

Swire opened his mouth to speak.

"Think for a minute," Nora went on quickly. "He or they or whatever killed two horses. Not for food, not for sport, but to send a message. You're the only person who knows enough to keep the rest of the horses safe until this is resolved. If somebody has to go, I'm the only choice."

Black turned to Nora. "This is insane. You can't go, you're the expedition director."

"That's why I can't ask anybody else to do this." Nora looked around. "I'll only be gone a day, overnight at the most. Meantime, you, Sloane, and Aragon can make decisions by majority consent."

There was a brief pause. Then Smithback spoke up, surprisingly quiet and firm. "I'll go with her."

Nora looked at him, then nodded. "All I'm going to do," she continued, "is try to find out who did this and why. We can let the law take care of it when we get back to civilization."

Wordlessly the cook turned on his heel and entered his tent. A moment later, he emerged with his weapon, a box of bullets, and a leather holster. He handed them to Nora. Strapping the holster around her waist, Nora opened the heavy gun, spun the cylinder, and closed it again.

"We'll take care of it," she said evenly.

6

Skip stopped at the top of the rise, the sudden dust cloud rolling over the car and drifting off into the hot afternoon sky. It was a parched June day, the kind that only occurred before the onset of the summer rains.

For a moment he decided the best thing would be to simply turn around and go back into town. He'd sat up in bed the night before with a sudden inspiration. He'd take Teresa's dog, Teddy Bear, under his wing. After all, Teresa had been killed in their home. In some formless way Skip felt responsible. And who better to take care of her dog than her old neighbor?

But what seemed like such a good idea last night didn't seem so great now. Detective Martinez had made it clear that he wasn't to go near the house. Skip knew he could get in a lot of trouble just for being here.

He put the car into gear and drove down the hill, past their old ranch house and up the rise to Teresa's place. It was dark and silent, the livestock all taken away. This was stupid, Skip thought. Whoever took the animals probably took Teddy Bear as well. Still, he'd come all this way.

Leaving the car running and the door open, he walked up to the house. "Teddy Bear!" he called out.

Silence.

Maybe the dog had wandered down toward their old house. He started for the path, then stopped. His hand slid down to his belt and rested briefly on the handle of his father's old .357. It was big and clumsy, it fired like a cannon, but it stopped whatever it hit. Reassured, he continued down the dirt path, then circled around to the back of the ranch house. "Yo, Teddy, you old mutt!" he called in a softer voice.

He stepped up to the portal, through the open door, and into the house. The smell assailed him first, followed almost instantly by the roar of flies. He took an instinctive step backward, gagging. Then, with a deep breath, he moved cautiously up to the yellow band of crime-scene tape and peered into the living room.

A huge pool of blood had congealed in the center of the room. It seemed to spread in twisted, eccentric rivulets almost to the far walls.

Skip swayed slightly and reached for the doorframe to steady himself. The flies, disturbed, rose in an angry curtain.

"Teresa, I'm so sorry," he murmured. He turned and walked on wooden legs out to the kitchen. "Teddy Bear!" he called one last time.

He knew he should leave. Some cop could come by at any time. But he remained another minute, staring at the dinner table of his childhood.

Vaguely, very vaguely, he remembered his father sitting at this table, telling him a story. For some reason, Skip couldn't remember the story. But he remembered his mother frowning, telling Skip's dad to talk about something else.

Something else . . . there was something else that dovetailed with all this in a strange and awful way.

With a sigh he stepped outside and walked back up the hill toward his car. There, sitting in the driver's seat, was Teddy Bear.

"Teddy Bear, you old rascal!" cried Skip.

The dog whined, slobbering over his hand.

"Move over. I'm the one with a driver's license." He shoved Teddy into the passenger seat and got behind the wheel.

Placing the gun in the glove compartment, Skip put the car in gear and maneuvered his way toward the main road.

When he finally reached the apartment, dragging Teddy Bear behind him, Skip made a beeline to the bookshelf of cinder block and plywood that leaned precariously against a far wall. Kneeling in front of the lowest row, his fingers traced across the old spines of the books that had been his father's.

Then his fingers stopped on a thin, battered gray book. *"Skinwalkers, Witches, and Curanderas: Witchcraft and Sorcery Practices of the Southwest,"* Skip softly breathed the title aloud.

There was terrible and hideous knowledge in this book, he recalled. More than anything, Skip did not want to have that knowledge confirm the fear that was now growing inside him.

He knelt there by the old books for what seemed a long time. Then at last he gripped the volume in both hands, carried it to the orange couch, opened it carefully, and began to read.

NORA and Smithback rode away from the stream, angling across the valley toward the heavy bulk of the ridge ahead. Over the thin murmur of the stream and the call of the canyon wrens, Nora could now hear a different sound: a low, steady drone, like the hum of a magneto. Then they topped a small rise, and two low forms came into view: the remains of Hoosegow and Crow Bait. A black cloud of flies hung over them.

"I'm going to take a minute to look more closely," Nora said.

Dismounting and giving her reins to Smithback, Nora walked over. As Swire had said, the entrails had been arranged in a spiral pattern. Brightly colored macaw feathers, shockingly out of place in the arid landscape, protruded from the eye sockets.

As she was about to turn away, she noticed something else. A circular patch of skin had been cut from the foreheads of both horses. Similar patches had been removed symmetrically from a spot on either side of the horses' chests and from two more spots on either side of their lower bellies.

She shook her head and retreated from the killing ground. "Who could do such a thing?" Smithback asked as she remounted.

Who indeed? It was the question Nora had been asking herself for the last hour. The answer that seemed most likely was too frightening to contemplate.

Within twenty minutes they had reached the base of the ridge. In another twenty, following the gentle trail up, they crested the top of the Devil's Backbone. Directly ahead were the narrow vicious switchbacks that led down the face of the hogback ridge.

"Tell me we're not going down that again," Smithback said.

Nora remained silent. The terrifying memory of how she'd scrabbled at the cliff face, feet kicking in dead space, returned with redoubled force. She dismounted and took a few steps from the horses, scouring the patches of sand that lay among the rocks. There was nothing but old hoofprints. She shivered; she knew very well there was no other way into the valley. And yet, somehow, the mysterious horse killers had left no sign of their passing.

Tearing her eyes away, she looked back around to the steep trail ahead of them. She took a deep breath, then another. And then she began carefully down the ridge, leading her new horse, Arbuckles. The horse balked at the lip of the trail, and after some firm coaxing Nora got him to take one step and then another. Smithback followed silently, leading Compañero, the horse Swire had given him to replace Hurricane Deck.

Just before the second switchback Nora heard Arbuckles's hooves skid, and in a panic she dropped the lead rope, but after a brief scrabble the horse stopped, shaking.

After twenty more heart-stopping minutes Nora found herself at the bottom of the trail. Turning, she saw Smithback make the last pitch to the bottom. She was so relieved she almost felt like hugging him.

The three dead horses were lying perhaps fifty yards away, draped over some broken boulders. Whoever had come this way would no doubt have inspected those horses.

She walked in the direction of the horses, fighting rising feelings of horror and guilt. And there were the tracks she was seeking: the tracks of an unshod horse. To her surprise she saw the tracks had not come up from the south, as their expedition had, but led instead from the north: in the direction of the tiny Indian village of Nankoweap, many days' ride away.

"There's a trail going north," she said to Smithback.

"I'm impressed," the writer replied. "Was it a pinto or a palomino?"

Nora shot him an irritated glance and walked on in the direction of the footprints in the sand.

There was a long moment of silence. Then Smithback spoke again. "Nora," he asked quietly, "what is it, exactly, you don't like about me?"

Nora turned toward him in surprise. The writer wore a serious expression, one of the few she remembered seeing on his face. "I didn't mean to snap at you just now," she said. "And I don't dislike you. You almost screwed up everything, that's all."

"How exactly did I do that?"

"What do you know about how I discovered Quivira?" she asked.

"Dr. Goddard told me your father was the one who originally discovered it. I'd been meaning to ask you more about that, only . . ." Smithback's voice fell away.

Only you knew I'd snap your head off, Nora thought with a twinge of guilt. "About two weeks ago," she began, "I was attacked in my family's old ranch house by a couple of men. At least, I think they were men, dressed up as animals. They demanded I give them a letter. My neighbor chased them away with her shotgun. Then I came upon this letter my father had written to my mother years and years ago. Somebody mailed it just recently. Who, or why, I don't know, and I can't get that out of my head. Anyway, in the letter my father said that he'd discovered Quivira. He gave directions—vague, but with Peter's help, enough to get us here. I think those stalkers also wanted to learn the location of Quivira so they could loot it. That's why I tried to keep the expedition a secret. And then you showed up at the marina, notebook in one hand and megaphone in the other."

"Oh." She could hear the sheepish note in the writer's voice. "Sorry." He paused. "I didn't give anything away, you know."

Nora sighed. "Let's forget it, okay? I overreacted. I was a little tense myself—for obvious reasons."

They mounted up and rode quietly for a while. "So what do you think of my story?" Nora asked at last.

"Do you suppose these guys are really still after you?"

"Why do you think I insisted on taking this little field trip myself? I'm pretty sure that the people who killed our horses and the ones who attacked me might be the same."

Abruptly the trail topped out on a narrow, fingerlike mesa. Breathtaking views surrounded them on all sides, canyons layered against canyons, disappearing into the purple depths.

"I didn't realize we were gaining so much altitude," said Smithback, stopping his horse and gazing around.

Just then Nora caught a faint whiff of cedar smoke. She signaled Smithback to dismount quietly.

"Smell that?" she whispered. "We're not far from a campfire."

Tying their mounts to sagebrush, they began walking through the sand. "Wouldn't it be nice if there were a bathtub full of ice and *cervezas* on the other side?" Smithback said under his breath as they approached a jumble of rocks hiding the landscape beyond from view. Nora dropped to her knees and peered through a gap in the rocks. Smithback did the same, creeping up beside her.

Under a dead, corkscrewed juniper was a small fire, smoking faintly. What appeared to be a jackrabbit, skinned and spitted, was propped above it between two forked sticks. An old army bedroll lay unrolled in the lee of the rock.

"Looks like nobody's home," whispered Nora.

"Yeah, but they couldn't be far."

They returned to their horses, moved them well off the trail, and brushed out their tracks. Then they climbed up behind the camp and waited in a small nook between two large boulders. As they settled in, Nora heard an ominous, rattling buzz. About fifty yards away, in the shadow of a rock, a rattlesnake had reared up in an S-coil, its anvil-shaped head swaying slightly.

"Now you can show me your marksmanship," said Smithback.

"Do you really want to alert whoever's out there?"

Smithback suddenly stiffened. "I think it's too late for that," he said.

There, on one of the flanking ridges behind them, Nora saw a lone man silhouetted against the sky, his face in shadow. A gun hung off his right hip. How long had he been watching them?

Nora waited in indecision. If this was one of the men who had attacked her, killed the horses . . .

The man stepped down from the ridge and began walking toward them, a curious walk on stiff, long legs. And then, in a instant of terrifying speed, Nora saw him stop short, draw his gun, and fire.

The rattler's head blew apart in a spray of blood and venom.

Nora glanced from the snake to Smithback. The writer's face was ashen.

The man walked toward them with slow deliberate steps. "Jumpy, ain't you?" he said, holstering his gun.

He was an extraordinary-looking man. His hair was long and white, and plaited in two long braids in the traditional Native American fashion. His shirt of tanned buckskin was decorated with strips of fine beadwork, and a turquoise necklace circled his neck. But it was the face above the necklace that most arrested Nora. There was a gravity and dignity there that seemed at variance with the glittering, amused liveliness of his black eyes.

"You look a long way from home," the man said in a thin, reedy voice. "Did you find what you needed in my camp?"

Nora looked into the mercurial eyes. "We didn't disturb your camp," she said. "We're searching for the person that murdered our horses."

The man's good humor seemed to vanish. For a moment Nora wondered if he would raise his gun again.

Then the tension seemed to ease, and the man took a step forward. "It's a hard thing to lose horses," he said. "I've got some cool water down there in camp and some roasted jackrabbit and chilies. Why don't you come along?" He paused.

"We'd be happy to," said Nora. They followed him down the rock pile and into camp. He gestured for them to find a seat on the nearby rocks; then he squatted by the fire and turned the jackrabbit. He poked a stick into the ashes and pulled out several tinfoil-wrapped chilies, piling them at the edge of the fire to keep warm. "I heard you folks coming, so I decided to head on up there and check you out from above. Don't get a lot of visitors out here, you know. Pays to be careful."

"Were we that obvious?" Smithback asked.

The man looked at him with cool black eyes.

"Really," said Smithback. "That obvious, huh?"

The man pulled a canteen out of the sand in the shadow of a rock and passed it to Nora. She accepted the water silently, realizing how thirsty she was. The man freshened the fire with a few pieces of juniper, then sat down across from them. "My name is John Beiyoodzin," he said.

"I'm Nora Kelly, and this is Bill Smithback. I'm an archaeologist, and Bill is a journalist."

Beiyoodzin digested this in silence. Then the glittering eyes softened, a smile appeared on his face, and he shook his head. "Jackrabbit's done," he said. He expertly carved off two haunches. He placed each on a flat, thin piece of sandstone and handed them to Nora and Smithback. Then he unwrapped the chilies, carefully saving the tinfoil. He quickly slipped off the roasted skin of each chili and handed them over. "We're a little short on amenities," he said, skewering his own piece of rabbit with a knife.

The chili was almost indescribably hot, and Nora's eyes watered as she ate, but she felt famished. Beside her, Smithback was attacking his own meal avidly.

Beiyoodzin passed the canteen around afterward, and there was an awkward pause.

"Nice view," said Smithback. "What's the rent on this joint?"

Beiyoodzin laughed, tilting his head back. "The rent is in the getting here. Forty miles on horseback over waterless country from my village." Then he looked around, the wind stirring his hair. "I come out here every summer to camp for a week or two."

"Why?"

"In Nankoweap, my village, I herd sheep most of the time, and I do ceremonies. Healing ceremonies."

"You're a medicine man?" Smithback asked.

"I prefer to be called a traditional healer," he said. "I come out here to pray and fast for a while, for spiritual healing. And to remind myself that we don't need much to be happy. That's all."

They watched as the sun sank below the horizon and darkness came rolling over the landscape. Beiyoodzin rolled a cigarette, lit it, and began puffing furiously, holding it awkwardly between thumb and index finger, as if it were the first time he had smoked.

"I'm sorry to bring this up," Nora said, "but if you know anything about who might have killed our horses, I'd like to hear it. It's possible our activities might have offended someone."

"Your activities"—the man blew a cloud of smoke into the still twilight—"you still haven't told me about those."

"We're excavating an Anasazi cliff dwelling," Nora said slowly.

"We never go into Chilbah Valley," Beiyoodzin said slowly.

"Why not?"

He looked at Nora through veiled eyes. "How were your horses killed?" he asked.

"They were sliced open," she replied. "Their guts pulled out and arranged in spirals. Feathers were shoved into their eyes. And pieces of skin had been cut off."

Beiyoodzin became agitated, dropping the cigarette into the fire and smoothing a hand across his forehead. "Skin cut off? Where?"

"In two places on the breast and lower belly, and on the forehead."

Nora could see that the old man's hand was shaking, and it frightened her. "You shouldn't be in there," he said in a low, urgent voice. "What happened to your horses is a kind of witchcraft. It's a terrible evil. What you're doing, digging in that city, is going to kill you if you don't get out, right now. Especially now that they've found you."

"They?" Smithback asked. "Who's they?"

Beiyoodzin's voice dropped. "The spotted-clay witches. The skinwalkers. The wolfskin runners."

In the darkness Nora's blood went cold.

"I'm sorry," Smithback spoke up. "You said *witches?*"

The Indian gazed at the writer, his face indistinct in the growing darkness. "I don't know what you call your evil people, but we call ours skinwalkers, wolfskin runners. And they are drawn to that city. It was a place of sorcery, cruelty, witchcraft, sickness, and death."

Nora barely heard this. Wolfskin runners. Her mind fled back to the shadow-knitted ranch house, the dark matted form that had towered over her, the furred thing that had kept pace with her truck along the rutted dirt road.

"I don't doubt what you say," Smithback replied. "But where do these skinwalkers come from?"

Beiyoodzin rolled another cigarette, then turned his gaze toward the ground. "To become a witch, you have to kill someone you love. Someone close, brother or sister, mother or father. You kill them to get the power. When that person is buried, you secretly dig the body up." He lit the cigarette. "Then you turn the life force of that person to evil."

"How?" Smithback whispered.

"When life is created, wind, *liehei,* the life force, enters the body. Where the wind enters, it leaves a little eddy, like a ripple in water. It leaves these marks on the tips of the fingers, toes, the back of the head. The witch cuts these off the corpse. They dry them, grind them up, make a kind of powder. And they drill out the skull behind and make a disk for throwing spells."

"Good God," Smithback groaned.

"You go to a remote spot at night. You strip off your clothes. You cover your body with spots of white clay and wear the jewelry buried with the dead, the silver and turquoise. You place wolfskins on either side of you. Then you say certain lines of the 'Night Wind Chant' backward. One of those skins will leap off the ground and stick to you. And then you have the power."

"What is this power?" Nora asked. The repeated hoot of an owl echoed mournfully through the endless canyons.

"Our people believe you get the power to move at night, like the wind but without sound. You can become invisible. And with the corpse powder, you can kill. Oh, can you *kill.*"

After a moment Beiyoodzin looked up. Even in the dark Nora could feel the intensity of his gaze.

"You said your horses were cut in five places—on the forehead and two places on each side of breast and belly," he said. "Those are the five places where the fur of a horse forms a whorl."

The light had completely vanished from the sky, and a huge dome of stars was cast over their heads. Somewhere in the distance, out on the plain, a coyote began yipping and wailing.

"I shouldn't have told you any of this," Beiyoodzin said. "No good can come to me. But maybe now you know why you must leave this place at once."

Nora took a deep breath. "Mr. Beiyoodzin, thank you for your help. I'd be lying if I told you I wasn't frightened by what you've said. It scares me to death. But I'm running the excavation of a ruin that my father gave up his life to find."

This seemed to astonish Beiyoodzin. "Your father died out here?" he asked.

"Yes. But we never found his body." Something about the way he spoke put her on guard. "Do you know something about it?"

"I know nothing." Then the man was abruptly on his feet. His agitation seemed to have increased. "Now I think I'll turn in. I've got to get up early. Tomorrow help yourself to breakfast if you like. I won't be around."

"That won't be necessary—" Nora began. But the old man turned away and began to busy himself with the bedroll.

"I think we've been given the brush-off," murmured Smithback. They went back to their horses, unsaddled them, and made a small camp of their own on the far side of the pile of rocks.

"WHAT a character," Smithback muttered a little later as he unrolled his bag. "First he spooks us with all that talk about skinwalkers. Then he suddenly announces it's bedtime."

"Yes," Nora replied. "Just when the talk got around to my father." She shook out her own bedroll.

"That witchcraft stuff was pretty vile. Do you believe it?"

"I believe in the power of evil," Nora said after a moment.

They both fell silent, and the cool night air moved over them.

"Which way is downwind?" Smithback asked suddenly.

Nora looked at him.

"I want to know where to put my boots," he explained. In the dark Nora thought she could see a crooked smile on the journalist's face.

"Put them at the foot of your bedroll and point them east," she said. "Maybe they'll keep the rattlers away."

She pulled off her own boots with a sigh, lay down, and pulled the bag up around her dusty clothes. A few yards away she could hear Smithback grunting as he flounced around, making preparations for sleep.

"Why did you come on this trip?" she asked him.

Smithback turned in his sleeping bag. "Well, if you get right down to it, newspaper work can be boring. *This* is what it's all about, really: discovering lost cities, listening to tales of murder, lying under the stars with a lovely—" He cleared his voice. "Well, you know what I mean."

"No, I don't," Nora said, surprised at the sudden excitement that flooded through her.

"Lying under the stars with someone like you," he finished. "Sounds kind of lame, doesn't it?"

"As come-ons go, yes, it does. But thanks just the same." She glanced at the lanky form of Smithback, faintly outlined in starlight. "So?" she said after a moment.

"So what?"

"Are you glad you came along?"

His eyes turned toward her, luminous in the starlight. "Yes," he said simply.

Holding his gaze in her own, she reached toward him in the darkness. Finding his hand, she squeezed it briefly.

"I'm glad, too," she replied.

BY MIDNIGHT a half-moon had risen in the dark sky, and the gnarled badlands of southern Utah were bathed in pale light. Two forms moved slowly up a secret trail, a fissure in the rock, fiendishly hidden, now worn away to the faintest lines after centuries of erosion and disuse. It was the Priest's Trail: the back door to Quivira.

Emerging out of the inky blackness of the rocks, the figures topped out on the sandstone plateau in which the city was hidden. Far below, in the long valley behind them, a horse nickered and stamped in agitation. But this evening they had left the horses unharmed, just as they had slipped past the cowboy who guarded them without running a knife across his throat. His time would come soon enough.

Now, with animal stealth, they scuttled along the wide mesa far above the valley floor. Though the moon laid a dappled byway across the sandstone, the figures avoided the faint light, keeping to the shadows. The heavy animal pelts on their backs dragged along the rough rock beneath them. Occasional sounds drifted up from below: the call of an owl, the babble of water, the rustle of leaves in a night breeze. Once, a belt of silver conchas clinked around the midriff of one of the figures; otherwise, they made no noise in the time it took to reach the top of the rope ladder.

Here the figures paused, examining the communications equipment. One of them glided to the edge of the cliff face and gazed down the thin ladder. A low, guttural sound rose out from deep within his frame, at last dying away into a groan that resolved itself into a faint, monotonous chant. Then he turned back toward the equipment.

In ten minutes their work there was done.

Slinking further along the rimrock, they made their way back to the secret trail that wormed down through a cut, descending toward the narrow canyon at the far side of the Quivira valley.

In time the figures reached the sandy bottom. They moved stealthily past a rockfall, then along the base of the canyon wall, keeping in the deeper darkness of moon shadow. They stopped when they neared the first member of the expedition: a figure beyond the edge of the camp, sleeping beneath the stars, pale face looking deathlike in gray half-light.

Reaching into the matted pelt that lay across his back, one of the figures pulled out a small pouch. Loosening the leather thong around it, the figure reached inside and, with extreme caution, drew out a disk of bone and an ancient tube of willow wood incised with a long, reversed spiral. Placing one end of the tube to his lips, he leaned toward the face of the sleeping figure. There was a sudden breath of wind, and a brief cloud of dust flowered in the moonlight. Then, with the tread of ghosts, the two figures retreated back toward the cliff face, disappearing once again into the woven shadows.

COUGHING, Peter Holroyd woke abruptly out of dark dreams.

Gripping the edges of his bedroll, he looked around. The half-moon threw zebra stripes of silvery blue light across the camp. He glanced from tent to tent and at the black lumps of bedrolls. Everything was still.

Holroyd stared up at the night sky. There was a funny taste in his mouth, and his jaw ached. The beginning of a headache was forming around his temples. He sighed, closing his eyes against the pressure in his head.

7

With a tug on the guide rope, Nora brought Arbuckles to a halt. She stood beside Smithback and looked down from the crest of the Devil's Backbone into the valley. She felt drained, sickened, by the climb back to the top, and Arbuckles was shaking and lathered with stress. But they had made it once again.

The wind was blowing hard across the fin of rock, and ragged afternoon thunderheads were coalescing over the distant mountains to the north, but the valley itself remained a vast bowl of sunlight.

They mounted their horses and moved forward. Better get through the slot canyon before the system moves in, Nora thought. When they reached the opening, they unsaddled their horses, wrapped and stowed the saddles, then turned the animals loose to find the rest of the herd.

It was the work of a long, wet, weary hour to toil through the slot canyon, the gear deadweight on their backs. At last Nora parted the hanging weeds and began walking down toward the camp. Smithback fell in step beside her.

Suddenly Nora stopped short. Something was wrong. The camp was deserted, the fire untended and smoking. Instinctively she looked up toward Quivira. Although the city itself was hidden, she could hear the faint sounds of loud, hurried conversation.

Despite her weariness, she shrugged the pack from her back, jogged toward the base of the rope ladder, and climbed to the city. As she clambered onto the bench, she saw Sloane and Black near the city's central plaza, talking animatedly. On the far side of the plaza sat Bonarotti, legs crossed, watching them.

Sloane saw her approaching and broke away from Black. "Nora," she said. "Our communications equipment—it's been smashed to pieces."

Exhausted, Nora sank onto the retaining wall. "Tell me about it," she said.

"It must have happened during the night," Sloane went on. "The transmitter, the paging network—everything but the weather receiver. Guess they didn't think to look up in the juniper tree where Peter installed it."

Nora sighed deeply. "Where is Peter now?"

"I don't know," Sloane said. "He went down the ladder from the summit before I did. I figured he'd gone back to his tent to lie down. He was pretty upset and . . . well, frankly, he wasn't making much sense. He was sobbing."

Nora stood up and walked to the rope ladder. "Bill!" she shouted down into the valley. "See if you can find Holroyd."

She waited, scanning the tops of the canyon walls. "Nobody home," Smithback called up a few minutes later.

Nora returned to the retaining wall. "Then he must be in the ruin somewhere," she said.

"That's possible," Sloane replied. "He said something yesterday about calibrating the magnetometer."

"What about the horse killers?" Black interrupted.

Nora hesitated a moment. She decided there was no point in alarming everybody with Beiyoodzin and his story of witches. "There was only one set of prints, and they led to the camp of an old Indian. He clearly wasn't the killer. Since our equipment was smashed last night, that probably means the horse killers are still around here somewhere."

Black licked his lips. "That's great," he said.

Nora looked at her watch. "Let's find Peter."

"I'll check the roomblock where he stashed the magnetometer." Sloane walked away, Black following in her wake.

There was a scuffling noise, then Smithback's shaggy head appeared at the top of the rope ladder. "What's up?" he said, coming over to the retaining wall.

"Somebody snuck into the valley last night," Nora replied. "Our communications gear was smashed." She was interrupted by an urgent shout from within the city. Sloane had emerged from one of the roomblocks, waving an arm.

"It's Peter!" Her voice echoed across the ghostly city. "Something's wrong! He's sick."

Immediately Nora was on her feet. "Find Aragon," she said to Bonarotti. "Have him bring his emergency medical kit." Then she was running across the plaza, Smithback at her side.

They ducked inside a roomblock near the site of the burial cist. As Nora's eyes grew accustomed to the dim light, she could see Sloane on her knees beside Holroyd's prone form. Black was standing well back, a look of horror on his face.

Holroyd's mouth was wide open. His tongue, black and swollen, protruded from puffy, glaucous lips. His eyes were bulging, and a foul graveyard stench washed up from each shallow breath.

There was movement in the doorway; then Aragon was beside Nora. "Hold my light, please," he said calmly, laying two canvas duffels on the floor, opening one of them, and removing a light. "And the rest of you, please step outside."

Nora knelt down and trained the light on Holroyd. His eyes were glassy, pupils narrowed to pinpoints. "Peter, Enrique's here to help you," she murmured, taking his hand in hers. "Everything's going to be fine."

Aragon pressed his hands beneath Holroyd's jaw, probed his chest and abdomen, then pulled a stethoscope and blood pressure cuff from one of the duffels and began to check his vital signs. As the doctor opened Holroyd's shirt and pressed the stethoscope to his chest, Nora saw to her horror a scattering of dark lesions across the pale skin.

"What is it?" Nora said.

Aragon shook his head. He peered intently into Holroyd's face, then examined the man's fingertips. "He's cyanotic," he murmured. "I'm going to have to tube him."

Holroyd gave a strangled cough. His eyes bulged wider still, ringed red with panic, searching aimlessly. His lips trembled, as if he was trying to force speech from a paralyzed jaw. "I let you down, Nora," came a strangled whisper.

"Peter, that's not true. If it weren't for you, none of us would have found Quivira. You're the whole reason we're here."

Holroyd began to struggle with more words, but Nora gently touched his lips. "Save your strength," she whispered.

Aragon fished in one of his duffels and pulled out an endotrachial tube attached to a black rubber bag. He gently laid Holroyd's head back and began snaking the clear plastic into his lungs. He pressed the Ambu bag into Nora's hands. "Squeeze this every five seconds," he said, dropping his ear to Holroyd's chest. A tremor passed through Holroyd's body, and his eyes rolled up. Aragon straightened up and, with violent heaves, began emergency heart massage.

As if in a dream, Nora sat beside Holroyd, filling his lungs, willing him to breathe. There were no sounds except for the cracking thumps of Aragon's fists and the sigh of the Ambu bag.

Then it was over. Aragon sat back, agonized face drenched with sweat. He looked up briefly, unseeing, and let his face sink into his hands. Holroyd was dead.

AN HOUR later the expedition had gathered around the campfire in silence. The afternoon sky was smeared with metal-colored clouds, and the air carried the mingled scents of ozone and humidity.

Nora glanced at each haggard face in turn. Their expressions betrayed the same emotions she felt: numbness, shock, disbelief. Her own feelings were augmented by an overpowering sense of guilt. She'd approached Holroyd. She'd convinced him to come along. Oh, Peter, she thought. Please forgive me.

"Enrique," she began, careful to keep her voice even. "What can you tell us?"

Aragon looked up, his black eyes unreadable. "Not nearly as much as I would like. I've cultured him up—blood, sputum, urine. But so far the results are inconclusive."

"What I want to know," Black said, "was whether this is infectious. Whether others might have been exposed."

Aragon sighed and stared at the ground. "It's hard to say. The evidence doesn't point in that direction. It looks more like acute poisoning than disease, but I really hate to speculate. . . . I suppose we have to assume it might be infectious."

Silence fell in the canyon. There was a roll of distant thunder from over the Kaiparowits Plateau.

"What are we going to do?" Black asked.

Nora looked at him. "Isn't it obvious? We have to leave here as quickly as possible."

"No!" Sloane burst out. "We can't leave Quivira, just like that. It's too important a site."

"A man has just *died,*" Nora said. "Possibly of an infectious disease, possibly even by poison. Either way, we have no choice. We've lost all contact with the outside world. The lives of the expedition members are my first responsibility."

"This is the greatest find in modern archaeology," Sloane said, her husky voice now low and urgent. "Are we going to just roll things up and leave? That would cheapen Peter's sacrifice."

Black, who paled a bit during this speech, still managed to nod his support.

Nora fought to keep her tone even. "Look, we won't just leave willy-nilly. We'll take the rest of the day to finish up the most pressing work, shut down the dig, and take a series of documentary photographs. We'll pack a small selection of representative artifacts. Then we'll leave first thing tomorrow."

"The rest of the day?" Black said. "To close this site properly will take a hell of a lot longer than that."

"I'm sorry. We'll do the best we can."

Nobody spoke. Her face an unreadable mask of emotions, Sloane stared at Nora.

"Let's get going," Nora said, turning away wearily. "We've got a lot to do before sunset."

THE dirty sky of the afternoon had lifted, and the air above the canyon of Quivira was suffused with the last golden light of sunset. Already the gloom of night was gathering in the bottom of the canyon, in strange juxtaposition to the brilliant narrow strip of sky above. A brief rain had released the scents of the desert—wet sand, the sweet smell of cottonwoods—which mingled with the fragrant cedarwood from Bonarotti's fire. Nora noticed none of the beauty, smelled none of the scents. To her, still numbed by the events of the day, the valley was anything but benign.

A few minutes before, Swire and Smithback had returned from the grisly errand of moving Peter Holroyd's body. They had carried it, sealed in a dry sack, about a quarter of the way through the slot canyon and laid it above the high-water mark, in a small rock shelter that Nora had remembered. There it could be retrieved at a later time. They now rested by the fire, exhausted, faces blank.

A harsh, ragged shout from the direction of the rope ladder intruded on Nora's thoughts. She looked up to see Aaron Black come striding through the gloaming, his face gray with dirt, his clothing streaked, hair wild. For a terrifying moment she was certain he had caught whatever it was that killed Holroyd. But this fear was quickly dispelled by the look of triumph on his face.

"I found it," he shouted.

"Found what?"

"The Sun Kiva."

Nora straightened up. "You found *what?*"

"There was a blocked opening behind the city. Nobody noticed it before. But *I* did. I found it." Black's chest was heaving, and he could barely get out the words. "Behind the crawl space at the back of the city is a narrow passageway that leads into another cavern. And, Nora, there's a whole city hidden back there. Right in front is a sealed kiva. It's like nothing we've seen before."

Nora felt sudden anger course through her. "My God, Aaron, all you've done is open up a new area to be looted. Have you forgotten we're about to leave?"

Black stood rooted in place, anger and disbelief growing in his face. "You haven't heard what I said. *I found the Sun Kiva.* We can't leave now. The gold will be stolen."

Nora looked at him more intently. "Gold?" she repeated.

"What else do you think is in there, Nora? Corn? The evidence is overwhelming. I just found the Anasazi Fort Knox."

As Nora stared at him in growing consternation and disbelief, she saw Sloane come up through the twilight.

"Sloane!" Black called out. "I found it!" She looked from him to Nora with a quizzical expression.

"What's this?" Sloane asked.

"Black found a sealed cave behind the city," Nora replied. "He says the Sun Kiva is inside it."

"It's there, Sloane," Black said. "A great kiva, sixty feet in diameter, with a sun disk painted on its side."

A powerful play of emotions ran quickly across Sloane's face. "What kind of disk?"

"A great sun in yellow pigment mixed with mica. It looks just like gold. It's exactly the kind of symbolic representation you'd find on the outside if they were storing—"

"Take me to it," Sloane said urgently. Black grabbed her hand, and they turned away.

"Hold on!" Nora barked.

The two turned to look at her, and with dismay Nora read the passion in their faces. "Just a minute," she continued. "Aaron, you should never have broken through that wall. I'm sorry, but we can't have any more disturbance."

Sloane looked at her, saying nothing, but Black's face grew dark. "And *I'm* sorry," he said loudly, "but we're going up there."

Nora looked into Black's eyes and saw there was no point in arguing with him. If she were to keep the group together, she had no choice but to bend just a little. The harm had been done.

"All right," she said. "We'll make a short visit and then decide how best to reseal the cave. No more violations of any sort. Am I understood?" She turned to Sloane. "Bring the four-by-five camera. And Aaron, you get the fluorescent lamp."

TEN minutes later a small group stood huddled together in the confines of the inner cave. Nora gazed in awe, overwhelmed despite herself by the richness of the site, by the perfect little gem of an Anasazi city hidden behind the mysterious kiva. It was a small pueblo, no more than thirty rooms—no doubt some kind of sanctum sanctorum for the priests. It would be very interesting to study.

The Sun Kiva itself was unadorned except for the great polished disk glinting in the harsh light. Thick, ribbed dust lay in drifts against its base and along its walls. The structure had been carefully plastered with adobe, and the opening in its side was blocked with rocks. Even the roof opening was totally sealed shut.

The group stood silently while Sloane moved about the cavern, shooting the kiva and its associated roomblocks from a variety of angles. Soon she rejoined them, folded up her tripod, and put the camera body back in its case.

"Done?" Nora asked. Sloane nodded.

"Before we leave tomorrow morning," Nora went on, "we'll re-block the hole as best we can."

"Before we leave?" Black repeated.

Nora looked at him and nodded.

"By God, not until we open this kiva," said Black.

"If we don't do it now," Sloane said, her voice loud, "nothing will be left when we return."

Nora took measured breaths, thinking about what she was going to say and how she was going to say it.

"Sloane," she began quietly. "Aaron. This expedition is facing a crisis. One person has died. There are people out there who killed our horses and who may try to kill us. It's my choice to make. And we're leaving tomorrow."

"If we do," Sloane said, "you'll have thrown away perhaps the greatest discovery in American archaeology." She was shaking in anger. "Run if you want. Just leave me a horse and some supplies."

"Is that your final word?" Nora asked quietly.

Sloane merely stared in return.

"Then you leave me no choice but to relieve you of your position on the archaeological team."

Sloane's eyes widened. Then her gaze swiveled to Black.

"Nora," Black said, a pleading note entering his voice. "Just on the other side of that adobe wall is a king's ransom in Aztec gold. I just don't think we can leave it for . . ."

His voice trailed off. Ignoring Black, Nora looked hard at Sloane.

But Sloane had turned away, her eyes fixed on the kiva. Then she gave Nora one last, hateful look and walked to the low passageway. In a moment she was gone. Black stood his ground a little longer. Then, swallowing heavily, he tore himself away and wordlessly followed Sloane out.

SKIP Kelly was doing his best to keep his car from bottoming out on the dirt road. Tano Road North was terrible, all washboard and ruts: the kind of road that was a much-coveted asset in many of Santa Fe's priciest neighborhoods. Every quarter mile or so he passed another enormous set of wrought-iron gates flanked by adobe pillars, portals to unseen estates.

He elbowed Teddy Bear's huge muzzle out of his face and once again checked the number scribbled onto a folded sheet of paper, dim in the evening light. Not far now.

To the left a great rock of granite rose out of the earth. Its face had been polished flat, and ESG had been engraved on it in simple, sans-serif letters. Beyond the rock was an old ranch gate.

Leaving the engine running, he got out of the car, pushed the single red button beneath an intercom speaker, and waited.

"Yes?" came a voice. "Who is it?"

With mild surprise Skip realized that the voice wasn't that of a housekeeper or butler. It was Ernest Goddard himself.

He leaned toward the intercom. "It's Skip Kelly," he said. "I'm Nora Kelly's brother."

There was a brief movement in the vegetation beside the gate, and Skip turned to see a hidden camera swivel toward him.

"What is it?" The voice did not sound particularly friendly.

Skip swallowed. "I need to talk to you, sir. It's important."

He waited, painfully conscious of the camera regarding him. The intercom remained silent. Instead, there was the heavy clank of a lock being released, and the old gate began to swing open.

Skip returned to the car, put it in gear, and eased past the fence. Then he drove slowly up the remainder of the driveway, parking his car next to a Mercedes Gelaendewagen. He got out and closed the door behind him. "Stay," he told Teddy Bear.

The entrance to the house was a huge set of eighteenth-century zaguan doors. Pulled from some hacienda in Mexico, I'll bet, Skip thought as he approached. Clutching a book under one arm, he searched for a doorbell, found nothing, and knocked.

Almost immediately the door opened, revealing a long hallway, grandly appointed but dimly lit. Beyond it he could see a garden with a stone fountain. In front of him stood Ernest Goddard. The long white hair and closely trimmed beard framed a pair of lively but rather displeased blue eyes. He turned without a word, and Skip followed his gaunt frame as it retreated down the hall.

Passing several doors, Goddard at last ushered Skip into a large, two-story library, its tall rows of books clad in dark mahogany shelves. Goddard pointed Skip toward an old leather chair beside a limestone fireplace. Taking a seat opposite, he crossed his legs, coughed lightly, and looked inquiringly at Skip.

Skip fidgeted with unaccustomed nervousness. Then, remembering the book beneath his arm, he brought it forward. "Have you heard of this book, *Skinwalkers, Witches, and Curanderas?*" he asked.

"Heard of it?" murmured Goddard, a trace of irritation in his voice. "Who hasn't? It's a classic anthropological study."

Skip paused. Sitting here, in the quiet library, what he thought he had discovered began to seem faintly ridiculous. He realized the best thing would be to simply relate what had happened.

"A few weeks ago," he said, "my sister was attacked at our old farmhouse out past Buckman Road. . . ."

THAT night a soft but steady rain drummed on the tents of the Quivira expedition, but when morning came, the sky was a clear, clean, washed blue, without a cloud in sight. The birds filled the trees with their calls, and the leaves dripped with water that caught and fractured the bright rays of the rising sun.

Uncharacteristically, Bonarotti was up early, tending the fire, the espresso pot just signaling its completion with a brief roar. He looked up as Nora came over. *"Caffè?"* he asked.

Nora nodded her thanks as he handed her a steaming cup.

"Is there really gold in that kiva?" Bonarotti asked in a quiet voice.

She eased herself down on the log and drank. Then she shook her head. "No, there isn't. The Anasazi didn't have any gold."

"But what about Black? What he said?"

Nora shook her head again. "Black is wrong."

The cook turned back to his fire, silent and dissatisfied. As Nora sipped her coffee, the rest of the camp began to stir. It was clear that the tension of the previous day had not gone away. If anything, it had increased. Black took a seat by the fire and hunched over his coffee, his face dark and inflamed. Smithback gave Nora a tired smile, then retreated to a rock to scratch quietly in his notebook. Sloane refused to meet Nora's eyes. If I don't get them out of here today, Nora thought, I'm never going to get them out.

She finished her cup, swallowed, cleared her throat. "This is how it's going to work," she said. "Enrique, please secure the medical gear we'll need. Luigi will pack up the last of the food. Aaron, I want you to climb to the top of the rim and get a weather report."

"But the sky is blue," protested Black.

"Right here it's blue," said Nora. "But this valley drains off the Kaiparowits. If it's raining there, we could get a flash flood just as sure as if it were raining directly on top of us. Nobody goes through the slot canyon until we get the weather report. If it's clear, we'll leave here in two hours." She looked around. "Is everyone clear on their duties?"

Everyone nodded but Sloane, who sat with a dark, unresponsive look on her face. Nora wondered what would happen if, at the last minute, she refused to go. We'll cross that bridge when we come to it, Nora thought.

Just as she was rising, a flash of color caught her eye: Swire, emerging from the mouth of the slot canyon and coming down the valley. Something about the way he was moving toward them filled her with dread. Not more dead horses, please.

Swire sprinted across the creek and into camp. "Someone got Holroyd's body," he said, fighting to catch his breath.

"Someone?" Aragon asked. "Are you sure it wasn't animals?"

"Unless an animal can scalp a man, cut off his toes and fingers, and drill out a piece of his skull. He's lying up there in the creek, not far from where we buried him."

The group looked at one another in horror. Nora glanced at Smithback and could tell from his expression that he, too, remembered what Beiyoodzin had said.

"Did you go on to check the horses?" Nora heard herself ask.

"Horses are fine," said Swire.

"Then we have no more time to waste," Nora continued, standing up. "I'll take our first load out through the slot canyon and pick up Peter's body on the way. We'll have to pack it out on one of the horses. I'll need someone to give me a hand."

"I'll help," said Smithback quickly.

Nora nodded her thanks.

"I will go, too," said Aragon. "I would like to examine the corpse."

Nora glanced at him. "We could use a third hand with the body. And listen, all of you: Stay in pairs. I don't want anyone going anywhere alone. Sloane, you'd better go with Aaron."

Nobody moved. The tension that had drawn her nerves tight—the fear and revulsion she felt at the thought of Peter's body, violated in death—suddenly coalesced into exasperation.

"Damn it!" she cried out. "What the hell are you waiting for? Let's move!"

SILENTLY Aaron Black followed Sloane toward the rope ladder. At the last minute she would refuse to leave; Black felt certain she would. He himself was torn: There was danger here, he knew. And yet, leaving the valley without seeing the inside of the Sun Kiva seemed almost unimaginable to him.

"Sloane, talk to me," he called as she climbed the ladder. "Are you going to leave the kiva behind, just like that?"

Sloane didn't answer.

He heaved up the ladder, sweating and grunting. Above, he saw Sloane preparing to make the final climb around the terrifying brow of rock just below the summit. Taking a deep breath, he followed her. He struggled up over the rim and threw himself into the sand, exhausted, angry, utterly despondent. He sucked the air deep into his lungs, trying to catch his breath.

"All this way," he said. "All this work. Just to be cheated out of the greatest discovery at the last minute."

Sloane didn't answer. He was aware of her presence, standing to one side, silent and unmoving. With a muttered curse he stood up and glanced at her.

Sloane's expression was so unfamiliar, so unexpectedly dramatic, that he simply stared. In a strange trick of the light he saw her amber eyes deepen to mahogany, as if a sudden shadow had been cast upon them. At last he slowly turned to follow her gaze.

Above the lofty prow of the Kaiparowits Plateau rose a thunderhead the likes of which Black had never seen. It looked, he thought, more like an atomic explosion than a storm. Its moiled foot ran at least thirty miles along the spine of the plateau, turning the ridge into a zone of dead black; from this base rose the body of the storm, surging and billowing upward to perhaps forty thousand feet. It flattened itself against the tropopause and sheared off into an anvil-shaped head at least fifty miles across. A heavy, tenebrous curtain of rain dropped from its base, as opaque as steel. Inside the thunderhead was a monstrous play of lightning, vast flickerings and dartings, ominously silent in the distance.

Black remained motionless, transfixed by the awful sight, as Sloane moved slowly, like a sleepwalker, toward the stunted tree that held the weather receiver. There was a snap of a switch, then a low wash of static. As the unit locked on to the preset wavelength, the static gave way to the monotonous, nasal voice of a weather announcer in Page, Arizona, giving a litany of details, statistics, and numbers. Then Black heard, with superhuman clarity, the forecast: "Clear skies and warmer temperatures for the rest of the day, with less than five percent chance of precipitation."

He stared at Sloane. Her whole being was tense with an internal epiphany. She snapped off the instrument.

"What—" Black began to ask, but the look on Sloane's face silenced him.

"You heard Nora's orders. Let's get this disassembled and down into camp." Sloane's voice was brisk, businesslike, neutral. She swung up into the juniper and in a moment had unwound the antenna, taken down the receiver, and packed it in a net bag. She glanced at Black.

"Let's go," she said. She swung the bag over her shoulder and walked to the ladder. In a moment she had disappeared down into blue space.

Confused, Black took hold of the rope ladder and began to follow her down.

TEN minutes later he stepped off the rope ladder. Overhead, the sky was an immaculate azure from rim to rim. There was no hint of the cataclysm taking place twenty miles away.

"What's the report?" he heard Nora ask Sloane.

"Clear skies and warmer temperatures for the rest of the day," Sloane said. "Less than a five percent chance of precipitation."

A strange, utterly foreign sensation began to creep up Black's spine. With a growing sense of unreality, he came up beside Sloane and watched as Nora gave a shout and a wave to Smithback. They were quickly joined by Aragon. Then the three walked toward the rows of supplies, shouldered their dry sacks, and started for the mouth of the slot canyon.

After a moment Black tore himself away and turned toward Sloane. "What are you doing?" he asked, his voice cracking.

Sloane met his gaze. "I'm not doing anything, Aaron."

"But we saw—" Black began, then faltered.

"What did we see?" Sloane hissed suddenly, rounding on him. "All I did was get the weather report and give it to Nora. Just as she demanded. If *you* saw something, say so now. If not, then shut your mouth about it forever."

Black stared into her eyes: Her whole frame was trembling, her lips white with emotion. He glanced up-canyon, in time to see the group of three disappear into the dark, terrible slit of rock.

Then he looked back at Sloane. As she read his eyes, the tension in her frame ebbed away.

8 John Beiyoodzin halted his horse at the top of the hogback ridge and looked down into the valley. The horse had taken the trail well, but he was still trembling, damp with perspiration. Beiyoodzin patted him soothingly on the neck. He closed his eyes a moment, calming himself, trying to reconcile his mind to the confrontation that lay ahead.

But calm would not come. He felt a sudden surge of anger at himself: He should have told the woman everything when he had the chance. It had been unkind and selfish to lie. And now, as a result of his weakness, he found himself on a journey that he would have given almost anything to avoid.

Sixteen years before, a small imbalance, a minor ugliness—*ni zshinitso*—had been injected into the small world of his people. It was because of this old imbalance, this absence of truth, that these people were now down there digging. He shuddered. And it was because of this imbalance that the *eskizzi,* the wolfskin runners, had become active again.

He reluctantly turned around and gazed toward the storm, amazed to see the thunderhead still growing and swelling, like some vast malignant beast. Here, as if he needed it, was a physical manifestation of the imbalance. It was a tremendous rain, a five-hundred-year rain. Beiyoodzin had never seen its equal.

He would not, of course, attempt to ride into the second valley, the valley of Quivira, through the slot canyon. The flood would be coming through within minutes. That meant he would have to take the secret Priest's Trail over the top. It would be very difficult for an old man. Maybe, after all these years, it would be impossible. But he had no choice; the imbalance had to be corrected.

NORA parted the curtain of weeds and eased into the water. She breaststroked across the first pool, Smithback following, Aragon bringing up the rear.

They traveled in silence for a while, going from pool to pool, wading along the shallows, the quiet sounds of their passage whispering off the confined spaces of the slot canyon. Then in the distance ahead Nora could make out the narrow ledge that led to the space where Holroyd's body had been laid.

Her eyes fell from the ledge to the jumble of rocks below and to the narrow pool that stretched the eight or ten feet across the canyon's bottom. Her gaze came to rest at a smear of yellow, floating at the near end. Holroyd's body bag. Reluctantly she forced herself forward.

Holroyd's decomposing body was lying on its back half out of the water. It was swollen inside its clothes, a grotesque parody of obesity. The fingers were now just pink-edged stubs, and his feet were missing their toes. At the back of the head a large circular whorl of hair been scalped off, and the disk of skull directly beneath drilled out.

Aragon pulled the body onto a narrow stone shelf beside the pool. Working swiftly, he donned a pair of plastic gloves, removed a scalpel from his kit, positioned it just below the last rib, and with a short movement opened the body. Reaching inside with a long narrow set of forceps, he twisted his hand sharply, then retracted it. On the end of the forceps was a small bit of pink flesh that looked to Nora like lung tissue. Aragon dropped it inside a test tube already half filled with a clear liquid. Adding two drops from a separate vial, he stoppered the tube and swirled it around in his hands. Nora watched as the color of the solution turned a light blue.

Aragon nodded to himself, carefully placed the tube inside a Styrofoam case, and repacked his instruments. Then, still kneeling, he turned toward Nora.

"Do you know what killed him?" Nora asked.

"I believe the abandonment of Quivira is intimately connected with Holroyd's death." He wiped his face with the sleeve of his shirt. "No doubt you've noticed the cracks in the towers, the collapsed third-story rooms of the city."

Nora nodded.

"Black told me that the damage was done by a mild earthquake that struck around the same time the city was abandoned."

"An earthquake killed all those people?" Nora asked.

"No, no. But it was enough to raise a large cloud of dust in the valley."

"But what does a seven-century-old dust cloud have to do with Holroyd's death?" Smithback asked.

Aragon gave a wan smile. "A great deal, as it turns out. Because the dust within Quivira is riddled with *Coccidioides immitis.* It's a microscopic fungal spore that lives in soil. It's usually associated with very dry, often remote, desert areas. It's the cause of a deadly disease known as coccidioidomycosis—or, as you might know it, valley fever."

Nora frowned. "Valley fever?"

Aragon nodded. "There was an earthquake in the desert near San Joaquin many years ago. That quake triggered a small landslide that raised a cloud of dust, which rolled over the town. Hundreds became ill, and twenty died, infected with coccidioidomycosis." He wiped his face again. "At first Holroyd's symptoms were baffling to me. And then I remembered those two pots full of rust-colored powder from the royal burial. That dust turned out to be dried, ground-up human flesh and bone. It is a substance known to certain southwestern Indian tribes as corpse powder."

Nora glanced at Smithback and saw her own horror reflected in his eyes.

"When I examined this powder under the microscope, I found it absolutely packed with *Coccidioides immitis.* It is, quite literally, corpse powder that *really* kills."

"And you think Holroyd was murdered with it?"

"Given the huge dose he must have received to die so quickly, I would say yes. Although his illness was surely made worse by constant exposure to dust. He did quite a lot of digging in the rear of the ruin in the days before his death."

"I did my share of digging," Smithback said, his voice a little shaky. "How much longer before we get sick, too?"

"I don't know. But it's vital that we get out of here and get treatment as soon as possible."

"So there's a cure?" Smithback asked.

"Yes. Ketoconazole or, in advanced cases where the fungus has invaded the central nervous system, amphotericin B." He paused. "I told you my theory that this city was not really Anasazi after all, that it was Aztecan in origin. Well, when I first analyzed that burial cist Sloane uncovered, I felt it to be a result of cannibalism. The marks on the bones seemed to point to that. But I now believe those marks tell an even more terrible tale."

He looked at Nora with haunted eyes. "I believe the Aztec priests of the city were infecting prisoners or slaves with the disease, waiting for them to die, and then processing their bodies to make corpse powder. With the powder, they could maintain their rule through ritual and terror. But in the end the fungus turned on them. The mild earthquake that damaged the towers raised a fungal cloud in the valley here, just like in San Joaquin. All those skeletons thrown atop the broken bodies in the back of the cave were its priestly Aztec victims."

Aragon stopped speaking and looked away from Nora. His face, she thought, had never looked so drawn, so exhausted.

"Now it's time for me to tell you something," Nora replied slowly. "Modern-day witches may be the ones trying to drive us out of the valley." She briefly told Aragon about the attack in the ranch house and the conversation with Beiyoodzin. "They followed us out here," she concluded. "And now they're trying to drive us away so they can loot the site for themselves."

Aragon shook his head. "No, I don't think they're here to loot the city. I think they were actually trying to *protect* it. How else could they have traced us here so quickly? And if indeed they killed Holroyd with corpse powder, where else could they have gotten it except from this place?"

"So they weren't after the letter to learn Quivira's location," Nora murmured. "They wanted to destroy the letter to keep us from coming here."

"Nothing else makes sense to me," Aragon replied.

They sat a moment longer, three figures ranged around the still form of Holroyd. Then a sudden breeze, chill with moisture, stirred the hair on Nora's forehead.

She looked up, scanning the canyon ahead. Then she froze. There was another breath of wind on her cheek, stronger this time. Along with it came the sudden, strangely pleasant scent of crushed vegetation.

Fear sent blood surging in her ears. The wind was accelerating with an almost machinelike precision.

"Flash flood," she said.

"Yeah?" The sky overhead was calm and blue; Smithback's tone was curious, not worried. "How can you tell?"

But Nora didn't hear him. Her mind was calculating furiously. They were at least a quarter mile into the slot canyon. There was no way to get out in time. Their only chance was to climb.

Quickly she pointed up toward the cavity in the rock where Holroyd's corpse had been stored. "Let's go!"

Smithback began to protest. "We can't just—"

"Come on, hurry! *Hurry!*" she cried.

She floundered across the pool, breath coming in sobs. The wind grew and grew, and then there was a painful pop in her ears: a drastic change in air pressure. She looked back at Smithback and Aragon, and tried to scream at them to hurry. Her voice was drowned by a vast, distorted roar that washed through the slot canyon, popping her ears a second time.

In its wake came an intense silence. The wind had suddenly dropped.

From what seemed to be a vast distance, she could make out clatterings and crunchings, the sound of boulders and logs ricocheting off the narrow canyon walls on their way toward them. As she ran, a fresh wind rose to a screaming pitch. The flood, she knew, would first turn the slot canyon into a wind tunnel.

She thrashed forward toward the spot where the ledge angled upward to the small cave. The sound in the canyon grew to a terrible howl, and the ever rising hurricane of wind tore at their backs. We're not going to make it, Nora thought. Gasping and coughing, she reached the ledge and grasped it with both hands. She hugged the rock face in an effort to keep the wind from plucking her off.

A tongue of twisting water came racing past below them, almost sucking them from the canyon wall. Nora glanced back and saw that Aragon had fallen behind. Pausing in his climb, Smithback reached down, grabbed Aragon's shirt, and hauled him upward. As Nora watched from above, powerless to help, another surge grabbed at Aragon's leg. Over the cry of the flood she thought she heard the man scream: a strange, hollow, despairing sound.

There was a silent parting of fabric, and Smithback fell back against the cliff, a tattered remnant of Aragon's collar in his hand. A furious gust of wind buoyed Aragon above the dancing rocks, whirling him downstream. Caught by another packet of water, his body was slammed into the canyon wall and vanished into the boiling spume.

Choking back a sob, Nora turned and grabbed the next handhold, hoisted herself up, then reached for the next. Higher, she thought, higher, closer and closer to the cavity in the rock. Behind her Smithback was coming up fast.

And then, at last, the main body of the flood came: a huge shadow, looming far above them, a wedge of darkness shutting out the last of the light; a foaming spasm of air, water, mud, rock, and brutalized wood, pushing before it a wind of tornado-like intensity. Nora felt Smithback's arm wrap itself around her as he pulled her up the narrow ledge. As he jammed her into the cavity, forcing himself in after her, there was a sudden fusillade of sound as countless small rocks scoured the walls of the canyon. She felt Smithback go rigid, heard the wet hollow thumps as the rocks glanced off his back.

Then the beast descended, wrapping them inside an endless, black, suffocating roar. The noise went on and on and on, the roar and vibration so loud that Nora felt she was losing her sanity. Rolled into a protective ball, she squeezed her arms tighter around herself and prayed for the shaking to stop. Jets of water forced their way into the cavity around her, battering her shoulders, pulling at her limbs as if trying to suck her out of the refuge.

In a remote corner of her mind it seemed strange that it was taking so long to die. She tried to breathe, but the oxygen seemed to have been sucked out of the air. She felt the iron grip of Smithback's arms relax with a horrifying twitch—and then the world folded in on itself and she lost consciousness.

RICKY Briggs listened to the distant sound with irritation. That rhythmic swat meant only one thing: a helicopter, heading this way by the sound of it. The marina manager shook his head. Helicopters were supposed to keep out of Wahweap's airspace. They annoyed the boaters.

Idly he leaned forward to glance out the window. What he saw caused him to jump from his seat.

Two massive helicopters were hovering just beyond the marina's no-wake zone. They sported amphibious hulls, and coast guard logos were emblazoned on their sides. A large pontoon boat dangled from one of them.

Briggs grabbed his cellular and ran outside, punching up the number for the Page air-control tower as he went.

Out in the baking heat an additional surprise awaited him: a huge horse trailer parked at the ramp, same as before, SANTA FE ARCHAEOLOGICAL INSTITUTE stenciled on one side. As he watched, two National Guard trucks pulled in behind it. The pontoon boat dropped from the helicopter with an enormous splash.

His phone chirruped, and a voice sounded through the tiny speaker. "Page," it said.

"This is Wahweap!" Briggs screamed into the telephone. "What the hell is going on at our marina?"

"Calm yourself, Mr. Briggs," came the unruffled voice of the air-traffic supervisor. "There's a big search and rescue being organized. It's in the back country, west of Kaiparowits."

Must be those dumb-ass archaeologists, Briggs thought. Another approaching engine added to the din, and he turned to see a semi backing a large, sleek-looking motorboat toward the water.

"Why the helicopters?" Briggs complained into the phone. "There's such a maze of canyons back there you'd never find anything. Besides, you couldn't land anywhere."

"I understand they're just ferrying equipment to the far end of the lake. I told you, this is *big*."

The boat had been set in the water with remarkable speed. It rumbled to life, turned, and nudged the dock, waiting just long enough for two men to board: one a young man wearing a Jose Cuervo T-shirt, the other a thin, white-haired man in khakis. A monstrous-looking brown dog leaped in behind them. Immediately the boat took off, roaring through the no-wake zone at full speed. The helicopters dug their noses in the air and turned to follow.

Briggs watched with disbelief as the horse trailer came sliding down the ramp toward the waiting pontoon boat.

"This can't be happening," he murmured.

BLACK sank down beside the dead fire, exhausted and soaked through. The rain beat its regular cadence upon his shoulders, not as furiously as it had an hour before, but steadily, with large, fat drops. He paid it no heed.

For a while Black had thought that the flood would actually surmount the steep banks on either side of the plain and take away their camp. But instead, it worried, chewed, and ate away at the stone edges of the benchland, its fury contained but made all the more violent. Now, although the initial surge of the flood had abated, the water continued to roar down the center of the valley, its brown, moiling surface like the muscled back of some monstrous beast. For almost two hours they had hovered at the water's edge. Sloane had made a valiant rescue effort: roving the banks, spanning the flood with rescue ropes, scanning the water ceaselessly for survivors. Black had never seen such a believable piece of acting.

Eventually they had gravitated away from the water's edge to the camp. Bonarotti silently began to unpack his kitchen gear. This, more than anything else, seemed to be a mute statement that hope had been lost.

"I think we have to accept the fact that nobody survived the flood." Sloane's voice was low and a little unsteady. "We've done everything we can. Our first duty now is to mourn their loss. Let's take a minute to remember them in our prayers."

She lowered her head. A silence fell, broken only by the sound of water. Black swallowed. His throat was painfully dry.

After a few minutes Sloane looked up again. "What happened today was a tragedy," she said. "But it's within our power to ensure that Nora, Peter, Enrique, and Bill are remembered not for their deaths but for their discoveries." She paused. "We must document the Sun Kiva. It's what Nora would have wanted."

"Is that right?" Swire spoke up suddenly. "What Nora would have wanted, you say? Tell me, was this before or after she fired you from the expedition?"

Sloane turned to him. "Do you have an objection, Roscoe?"

"I have a question," Swire replied. "A question about that weather report of yours."

Black felt his gut seize up in fear. But Sloane simply returned the cowboy's cool gaze. "What about it?" she asked.

"That flash flood came down twenty minutes after you reported clear weather."

"You of all people know how unpredictable the weather is out here," Sloane said, more coldly now. "The storm could have come from anywhere."

Swire seemed to digest this for a moment. Then he said, "You can see a whole lot of anywhere from the top of that canyon."

Sloane leaned toward him. "Are you calling me a liar?"

There was something so subtly menacing in her silky tone that Black saw Swire draw back. "I ain't calling you nothing. But last I heard, Nora said we wasn't to open up that kiva."

"Last *I* heard, you were the horse wrangler," Sloane said icily. "This is a decision that does not concern you."

Swire looked at her, his jaw working. Then he stood up abruptly and walked out of camp.

BLACK pulled himself up the last rung of the rope ladder with a grunt and stepped onto the rocky floor of Quivira, slinging the small bag of equipment beside him. He turned around once again to survey the valley. It was hard to believe that, barely four hours before, he had stood at this same spot and witnessed the flash flood. Now, afternoon light, fresh and innocent, glowed off the walls of the canyon. The air was cool and perfumed with moisture from the rain. Birds were chirping. The only sign of the catastrophe was the torrent of rushing water that divided the small valley like a brown scar.

He turned away and approached Sloane, who had arrayed her gear along the retaining wall. He noticed that she had snugged the camp's spare pistol into her belt.

"What's that for?" he asked, pointing at the weapon.

"Remember what happened to Holroyd?" Sloane replied. "I don't want any nasty surprises while we're documenting that kiva."

Bonarotti came into view at the top of the ladder, the oversized .44 hanging from his side, digging tools slung over his shoulder. "Do you really think there's gold in that kiva?" he asked.

"Yes, I do," Black replied. "All the evidence points to it."

Together they followed Sloane across the central plaza toward the rear of the dead city. They made their way through the narrow passageway, then ducked into the inner sanctum.

"I don't need to emphasize the importance of what we're about to do," Sloane said. "This kiva is the archaeological find of several lifetimes, and we're going to proceed by the book. Luigi, you dig the sand and dust away from the doorway. Aaron, you can remove the rubble and stabilize the doorway."

Almost imperceptibly Sloane had taken over the role of leader. As he worked, Black realized that perhaps he should be annoyed by this; he had more experience and seniority by far. But he was now too caught up in the excitement to care, and—

His thoughts were cut short by a racking cough. He stepped back from the doorway for a moment, wiping his face with his sleeve. The dust had risen to a miasmic thickness, and in the center of it all was Bonarotti, toiling with his shovel.

Taking a few more deep breaths, Black waded back in. The upper tier of rocks had been removed, and behind the rocks he could now make out a patch of reddish brown.

"Sloane!" he called. "There's a mud seal behind these rocks."

In a moment she was beside him. "Clear the rocks away, please," she said. "Be careful not to damage the seal."

Within minutes the seal was fully exposed: a large square of clay stamped against what seemed to be a layer of plaster. A reversed spiral had been molded into the seal.

"This is odd," Sloane said. "The seal looks fresh."

Black examined it more carefully. It was definitely fresh—*too fresh,* he thought, to be seven hundred years old. His breath coming in short, excited gasps, Black redoubled his efforts at clearing the wall of rocks.

ROSCOE Swire, sitting atop a broken boulder, was profoundly agitated. He thought of all the horses he had lost on this trip, each one with its own personality. The quirks, the peculiar habits, the trails they had ridden . . . it was almost more than he could bear.

And then his thoughts turned to Nora. More than once she had made him very angry. But he had been forced to admire her bravery, the occasional recklessness of her determination.

His eyes swiveled up in the direction of the hidden city. To think those three were up there now, opening the kiva as if nothing had happened. They would get the glory. He spit disgustedly.

Then he stopped and looked around again at the darkened valley. The place seemed suspended between night and day, caught in that mysterious stasis that occurred only in the deepest canyons of Utah. Everything was quiet.

But instinct told him he was being watched.

His right hand dropped to his holster and rested easily there. With a flash he realized who it must be. They were the ones who had killed his horses. The bastards who had gutted his animals.

And now they were coming for him.

A surge of anger pushed away his rising apprehension. Lightly he hopped off the rock and strolled out into the open, glancing around, looking for a place from which to defend himself.

His eyes moved toward a small grove of gambel oaks near the far end of the valley. Twelve hours before, the trees had been fifty feet from the water. Now they were at its edge. He nodded slowly to himself. The oaks would hide him, and he would have a view out across the benchland. It would give him time for several clear shots.

He began strolling down toward the river, quickening his pace as he neared the copse. Once, he almost turned around, heart beating fast, but he checked himself in time: He must not show that he knew they were there.

A few more steps brought him into the stand of oaks. It was dark beneath the hanging limbs, and water dripped onto his head and back. He was at the very edge of the flood now, and the water gurgled through the tree trunks, curling and tugging around his boots. He slipped his gun out of the holster, waiting.

It was too dark to see anything, and the sound of the water was like a heavy cloak, depriving him of his most valuable sense. All he had left, in fact, was smell. And even that wasn't working properly: By some trick of his overcharged brain, he felt surrounded by the beautiful, delicate scent of morning glories.

Just then, to his left, he saw a terrible movement of shadow: a violent wrenching of black upon black. Too late he realized the things had been in the grove all the time, watching and waiting, while he came to *them.* He raised the gun with a cry, but the shot went wild and the weapon tumbled into the flood. As the muzzle flare died away, Swire saw the blade of a knife, impossibly black and cold, slicing down through the night.

IN THE depths of the hidden cavern Black carefully edged a penknife beneath the uppermost clay seal, his arms shaking with exhaustion and excitement. He coughed into his hand, then again, more violently, finding flecks of mud in the phlegm. He shook it away in disgust and reached down for a pick. He hefted it in his bruised hands, then swung it toward the wall.

A piece of plaster fell away. Black swung the pick again, then again, enlarging the hole considerably: a dark, ragged rectangle in the glare of the lights. Excitedly he dropped the pick.

Instantly Sloane was at his side. Taking a flashlight from her pocket, she thrust it deep into the hole, pressing her face against the plaster. Black saw her body tense. Then she withdrew, her face alive with excitement. Black grabbed the light from her and crowded forward.

The feeble yellow gleam of the small flashlight could barely penetrate the murk within. But as he played it about, Black felt his heart swell. A yellow glimmer filled the kiva, winking and flashing everywhere: the rich mellow shine of a thousand curvilinear golden surfaces.

"It's stuffed with gold!" he cried.

He seized the pick and resumed working along the top of the doorway. Grabbing a second pick, Bonarotti stood beside him, driving it furiously into the adobe in time with Black's own blows. Soon the hole was large enough to admit a person.

Black picked up one of Sloane's lanterns and moved forward. "Get out of my way," he said, peremptorily shoving Bonarotti aside. Sloane followed quickly.

Everywhere, from all sides, the gleam of gold sprang out of the murk. Almost snorting with excitement, Black bent forward and seized the closest object—a dish, filled with some kind of powder.

Instantly he knew something was wrong. The dish in his hand was light, the material warm to the touch: not like gold at all. Tossing the powder from the bowl, he brought it closer to his face.

Then he straightened up, flinging the object away with a sob.

"What are you doing?" Sloane cried.

But Black did not hear her. He looked around the Sun Kiva with a sudden, wild desperation, grabbing things, dropping them again. It was all wrong. He staggered, fell, then rose with an effort. The disappointment was more than he could comprehend.

Then Black slowly turned his eyes toward Sloane. Her face, instead of despair, reflected shining, complete vindication.

9

It was impossible to know how much time had passed before—at long, long last—Nora felt a cool gush of air stir the damp hair on her forehead. Slowly the memory of where she was and what had happened returned.

There was a deadweight pushing against her back. She struggled, and the weight moved slightly, allowing a dim light to filter into the cavity. The roar in the canyon had now abated to a deep-throated, thunderous vibration that rattled her gut.

Uncramping her legs and turning painfully around inside the cavity, she saw that the deadweight was Smithback. He was lying on his side, motionless. His shirt lay across his chest in torn ribbons. His back was lacerated. Smithback had shielded her—and taken the brunt of the water's force—with his own back.

Nora gently laid her head on his chest. The heartbeat was faint, but at least it was there. Hardly knowing what she was doing, she kissed his face. His eyelids struggled open, the eyes beneath glassy and dull. After a moment the eyes focused.

"Can you sit up?" she asked.

Smithback struggled, wincing and breathing hard. Nora helped him into a sitting position.

"You saved my life," she said, squeezing his hand.

"It's not saved yet," he gasped, shivering.

Carefully she peered out from their shelter; there was no way to climb farther up. She looked down and was surprised to see that the water seemed to be rising, not falling. It must be raining hard again in the upper watershed. They had to get out of the cavity. If the water rose farther—or if another flood surge came through—they could not hope to survive. But there was no way out.

No way, except to launch themselves into the current, which was now fast but smooth. If they could make it out into the middle, they might be able to ride it through the slot and into the valley without being battered against the canyon walls along the way.

"Can you swim?" she asked Smithback.

He shrugged.

"I'm going to bind us together," she said.

"No," he protested. "I'll only drag you down."

"You saved my life. Now you're stuck with me." Carefully she peeled off the tattered remnant of his shirt. She tied one end to her left wrist and the other end to Smithback's right.

"This is a crazy—" Smithback began.

"Save your breath for the ride. We're only going to get one chance at this. The most dangerous moment will be when the flood drops us into the valley. Once we're there, we'd better head for the shore near our campground damn quick. If we get swept through into the far canyon, we're done for."

Smithback nodded, eyes narrow, lips white. Their eyes locked as she took tight hold of his hand. There was a moment's hesitation. And then, together, they slid out into the flood.

The current was shockingly strong. As they tore along, Nora realized there was no chance of controlling their descent: All she could do was struggle to keep from colliding with the murderous walls, sometimes mere inches away.

The surface of the water boiled hysterically around them. Deeper, a chaos of gravel and sand churning in the turbulence battered her legs. Smithback struggled beside her, crying out once when the gnarled root of a tree collided with his shoulder.

A harrowing minute passed. Suddenly they were soaring out of the canyon, riding a huge hump of water that collapsed into a boiling pool. There was an angry roar, and Nora felt herself tumbled under the waves. Jerking on the improvised cord, she frantically propelled them upward, breaking the surface. Looking around and spitting water, she was horrified to see they had already traveled halfway through the valley.

She thrashed, dragging Smithback along, his head barely above water. Suddenly her feet touched bottom, wonderfully solid after the flood. Slowly she pulled herself up on the muddy bank, toward the copse of cottonwoods, Smithback staggering behind her. They sat down heavily amid a whirlwind of splintered branches, Smithback collapsing in pain. Nora undid the twisted rag that bound them, then rolled onto her back, sides heaving, coughing up water.

There was a ragged flash of lightning, followed by the sharp crackle of thunder. It began to rain. Nora looked up the ruined bank toward camp. It had been set up again, the struck tents repitched. Yet the camp was deserted.

She helped Smithback to his feet; he staggered a little, took a few steps, then staggered against her again. She half dragged him to the high ground of the camp, hauling him into the medical tent. She rummaged through the supplies, picking out a painkiller, antibiotic ointment, and gauze bandages. She handed Smithback a couple of pills, passed him a canteen, then began dressing the horrible lacerations on his back. He stiffened but did not complain.

"How come you're not protesting?" she asked.

"Don't know," came the slurred response. "Guess I'm numb."

He's going into shock, she thought. The rain outside was increasing steadily, and the wind was buffeting the sides of the tent.

"Keep that sleeping bag bundled close," she said, stroking his cheek. "I'm going to see if I can't get some hot liquid into you." Hunching her shoulders against the rain, she moved across the camp, heading for the supply cache.

SLOANE Goddard stood in the murk of the kiva, gazing on the rows of gleaming pots. For a long time she saw nothing else. As she stared, she forgot everything—Holroyd's death, the flash flood, Nora and the others, the creeping presence of the horse killers.

Only a few small sherds of black-on-yellow micaceous pottery had ever been found. To see them whole was a revelation. They were transcendentally beautiful, each piece perfectly shaped and formed. The clay they had been made from was fired to an intense yellow, but the color had been immeasurably enhanced by the addition of crushed mica to the clay. The resulting pottery shimmered with an internal light that Sloane felt was more beautiful than gold. Each piece had been decorated with geometric and zoomorphic designs of superlative artistry and skill: the entire pictographical history of the Anasazi people, laid out before her. Sloane was now the leader of the expedition, and hers would be the name forever linked with the discovery of the fabulous pottery.

Slowly she came back to the present. From the corner of her eye she saw Bonarotti, cloaked in silent disappointment, shambling on stiff legs toward the hole he had helped cut. In another moment he had vanished out into the cavern, ignoring one of the richest troves in all North American history.

Excitedly she turned toward Black. What she saw of him, in the murk of the kiva, shocked her. He looks terrible, she thought. The man's flesh seemed to have shrunk on his frame. Two red, wet eyes stared hollowly out of a face caked in pale dust.

"Pottery," he said woodenly. She watched him try to step forward, teetering in place.

"Aaron," she said urgently. "Don't you see? This is worth *more* than gold. Much more. These pots tell—"

She broke off abruptly. Black's face was screwed up, his hands pressed to his temples. As she watched, his legs began to tremble and he sank against the inner kiva wall.

"Aaron, you're sick," she said, a sense of panic displacing her feelings of triumph. "I'm going down to the medical tent. I'll be back as soon as I can."

She climbed quickly out of the kiva. Then, shaking the dust from her legs, she half walked, half ran into the silent city.

KNEELING beside Smithback, Nora stuffed a flashlight retrieved from the dry sacks into her pocket and helped the journalist swallow a small cup of steaming bouillon. She had replaced his soaked shirt and pants with dry ones, and his shock seemed to be passing. She glanced at the field wristwatch that had been strapped around the head tent pole. It was after nine o'clock. And yet, inexplicably, nobody had returned to camp.

Smithback looked up at her with a weak smile.

"Thanks," he said.

"You get some sleep," she replied. "I'm going up to the ruin."

He nodded, but his eyes were already closing. Grasping the flashlight, she slipped out of the tent into the darkness. Switching it on, she followed the cylinder of light toward the base of the rope ladder. Her bruised body ached, and she half dreaded what she might find in the ruined city. But as expedition leader, she had no choice but to learn for herself exactly what was going on.

The raindrops flashed through the yellow beam like fitful streaks of light. As she approached the rock face, she saw a dark figure climb down the ladder and leap lightly to the sand. Sloane's silhouette, her graceful movement, were unmistakable.

"Is that you, Roscoe?" Sloane's voice called out.

"No," Nora replied. "It's me." She stepped forward and looked into Sloane's face, illuminated in the glare of the flashlight. She saw not relief but shock and confusion.

"*You,*" breathed Sloane. She seemed stunned.

She looks as if she's seen a ghost, Nora thought.

And then, in an instant, she realized that was precisely it.

"You didn't expect to see me alive, did you?" she asked. Her voice was steady, but she could feel herself trembling from head to foot. "You gave me a false weather report."

Sloane shook her head vigorously. "The weather report is a matter of public record. You can check it when we get back. . . ."

Nora shook her head. "No," she said. "I think I'll check the satellite images instead. And I know what I'll find: a gigantic thunderhead centered directly over the Kaiparowits Plateau."

At this, Sloane's face went dead white. "Nora, listen. It's possible I never looked in that direction. You've got to believe me, and—"

"Aragon is dead," Nora interrupted, speaking in a barely controlled fury. "Sloane, you were going to break into that kiva no matter what the cost. And that cost was *murder.*"

The ugly word hung in the heavy air.

"You're going to jail, Sloane," Nora said. "I'm going to make sure of that personally."

There was a flash of jagged lightning, followed almost instantly by a great peal of thunder. In that instant Nora saw the dull glint of the gunmetal tucked into Sloane's belt. The woman seemed to straighten up, draw a sudden breath. Her jaw set. Nora thought she saw a resolution begin to form.

"No," Nora murmured, backing up into the darkness.

Sloane's hand dropped toward the gun.

In a sudden, desperate movement Nora snapped off her light and wheeled away, sprinting into the darkness.

SOMETHING terrible was happening to Aaron Black. He lay in the kiva, confused and horribly frightened. His limbs seemed unwilling or unable to respond to his commands.

"I can't move!" he cried. And then, with a sudden terror, he realized he hadn't been able to articulate the words. Air had come out of his mouth, yes—an ugly splutter—but no words came. In a spasm of panic he struggled unsuccessfully to rise. Weird shapes and writhing figures began crowding the darkness beyond his eyes; he turned to look away, but his neck refused to move.

The lantern flickered and went black.

He tried to scream, but nothing happened. Sloane was supposed to be bringing medicine. Where was she? Was he dying in the horrible darkness of this kiva?

Then he saw another light, very faint, almost indivisible from the darkness. It was accompanied by a rustling sound. His heart surged with fresh hope. Sloane was returning at last.

The light grew stronger. And then he saw it, through the film of his sickness: fire, strangely disembodied, moving through the darkness of the kiva. And carrying this burning brand was a hideous apparition, half man, half animal.

Black smelled the ripe, sweet scent of morning glories; he saw in the flickering light the glittering black of an obsidian blade. Distantly he wondered where such an image could have come from. Some grotesque recess of his mind, no doubt; some dreadful ceremony that perhaps he'd read about in graduate school. Only a person who was as gravely ill as he was, he knew, could hallucinate something so . . .

And then he felt the unyielding knife blade trace a hard cold line across his neck, felt the gush of hot blood filling his windpipe, and he realized, with transcendent astonishment, that it was not a hallucination after all.

THERE was a break in the storm, and the rain had slowed to an occasional patter. Sloane, every muscle tensed, listened with rapt concentration. Someone was sneaking up toward the camp—someone exercising exceptional care.

Sloane waited, barrel leveled steadily. The steps were so quiet and spaced so far apart she could not tell if they were approaching or receding. And then at last a shadow interposed itself between her and the tents.

Sloane breathed out slowly. The shadow was too tall to be Swire, too short for Black or Bonarotti. It could only be Nora.

Carefully Sloane aimed the gun, centering on the shadow. She suspended her breathing and squeezed the trigger.

The .38 jerked back violently in her hands as the shot reverberated down the canyon. There was a gasp, the sound of spasmodic kicking, a brief, retreating scrabble. When her eyes cleared, the silhouette had disappeared and all was silent.

It was done. Snapping on her light, keeping the gun drawn, she came forward.

Instead of Nora's body lying before the tent, broken and bleeding, there was nothing.

Sloane looked down at the sand, horrified. How could she have missed? It was practically a point-blank shot. She swiveled her light around, looking for something, anything.

And then, in the sand at the far edge of the tent, the cone of light caught something. It was a thick gout of blood. And, beside it, a partial bloody footprint in the damp earth. The print did not belong to Nora—or, it seemed, to any other human being. It looked, in fact, like a clawed forepaw.

Sloane drew back and glanced around, swinging her flashlight as she did so. As she slowly circled the camp with her light, something resolved itself against the farthest row of tents. She staggered in disbelief.

The cold light had fallen across a terrifying apparition. It stood, humped and ragged, staring silently back at her. Red eyes bored like dots of fire through holes cut into a buckskin mask. Wild painted designs of white along the legs and arms were spattered crimson with blood. Its pelt steamed in the humid air.

Sloane took a step backward. This was what she had shot. She could see the great wound in its midriff. And yet it remained standing. More than that: Its chest heaved slowly, and then, with terrifying, deliberate malevolence, the creature took a step toward her.

Instantly panic took over. Dropping the flashlight, Sloane wheeled and ran. For a moment the kiva, the flood, everything was forgotten in her desire to escape. *This* was the thing that massacred the horses, desecrated Holroyd's body. . . . Then suddenly her legs were churning even faster, the night air tearing in and out of her lungs.

She caught sight of Nora, climbing toward the city. Desperately Sloane veered to follow, keeping her eyes locked on the ladder, running with reckless abandon, trying with all the power of her will to ignore the awful, low, flapping sounds of the pelted thing as it came racing up the darkness behind her.

NORA heaved herself over the rim, scrambled to her feet, and sprinted away from the edge of the cliff. Vaulting over the retaining wall, she dashed across the central plaza into the deeper darkness beneath the shadow of the roomblocks. A single, fleeting image was burned into her mind: Sloane standing in the camp after the sound of that terrible shot. She had found Bill and killed him.

"Nora!" she heard Sloane call out wildly. "Nora, for God's sake, wait!"

Nora wheeled, diving away from the plaza, back toward the curved rear wall of the city. Keeping to the darkest shadows, moving as swiftly as she dared, she moved along the edge of the city, approaching the dark bulk of the first tower.

The sound of running footsteps rang out against stone. Nora shrank quickly behind a pole ladder propped against the tower, trying to make herself as inconspicuous as possible. And there, coming around from the front side of the tower, was Sloane, pistol in hand.

Nora glanced around in fresh desperation: There was nowhere left to run. Slowly she turned back toward Sloane, steeling herself for the roar of the gun, the sudden lance of pain.

But Sloane was crouched at the base of the tower, peering cautiously around its front edge. Her gun hand was pointed not at Nora but out into the darkness of the plaza.

"Nora, listen," Sloane gasped over her shoulder. "There's something after us. Something *horrible.* The only chance we have is to stick together."

Nora stared out into the darkness, toward the granaries and the hidden maw of the crawl space. The woman, she knew, had brought tragedy to the expedition. But right now she could think only of the dreadful apparition that, at any moment, could come scuttling toward her out of the black.

The city was full of recesses in which they could hide. But hiding in the dark was not the answer. It would be just a matter of time until the skinwalker tracked them down. What they needed was some defensible place where they could hold out for a while.

There was nowhere to go except up.

"The tower," she said.

Sloane turned quickly to her. The question in her eyes disappeared as she followed Nora's gaze toward the structure that reared above them.

Grasping the pole ladder, Nora scrambled up to the small second-story rooftop. Sloane followed, kicking the ladder away behind her. They dashed through the low, crumbling doorway and into the enfolding darkness of the great tower.

Nora paused within, digging out her flashlight and shining it into the rectangle of darkness above them. The sight was terrifying: a series of rickety pole ladders, balanced on ledges of projecting stone, rising into the darkness. To climb, she would have to place one foot on a series of projecting stones that ascended the inside wall and the other foot on the notches of the poles. There were three series of ladders, one above the other, separated by narrow stone shelves that ran around the inner walls of the tower. It had been deliberately designed to be the most precarious climb possible.

"Go on!" Sloane whispered urgently.

Nora checked her flashlight. Its beam was growing feeble. But she had no choice: They could not make the climb in total darkness. Sliding the lit flashlight into her shirt pocket, she reached for the first pole, testing its sturdiness. Taking a deep breath, she hoisted herself up, climbing as fast as she dared, trying not to think of the pole swaying under her weight, creaking with dry rot. Sloane followed behind her.

Reaching the first platform, Nora stopped to catch her breath. As she crouched, gasping, she heard a faint clatter from outside the tower: the sound of a pole ladder being thrust up against adobe walls. Instantly she leaped for the second pole. She scrambled upward and threw herself onto the second shelf.

Just then she heard the patter of footsteps below. Beside her, Sloane cursed under her breath. A dark form momentarily blotted out the dim light at the entrance to the tower. The choking terror of the encounter in the abandoned ranch house returned to Nora in full force. Then she was shocked back to the present by the deafening blast of a pistol shot. Heart in her mouth, Nora took out her flashlight and angled it downward. The figure was swarming up the first ladder, swift and sure. Sloane raised her weapon again.

"Save your bullets for the top!" Nora cried. She urged Sloane onto the third and final ladder. It was time to take a desperate chance.

Taking a firm hold on the stone shelf, Nora drew her leg back and kicked at the bracing of the second pole as hard as she could. She felt it shudder with the impact. She kicked at it a second time, then a third. Below, she could hear a desperate scrabbling as the figure rode the shaking structure. Summoning all her strength, Nora kicked at the pole once again. With a shriek of rending wood, the pole lurched outward about six inches, whipsawing itself into a notch of rock. Nora heard a muffled roar from below. Chancing another look down, she saw the skinwalker lose its grip and begin to fall away toward the base of the tower. Then, catlike, it lashed out, grasping a set of supports. It clung there for a moment. Then, with careful deliberation, it began climbing toward her again.

Nora leaped for the third pole and climbed toward the third shelf and the hole leading to the redoubt at the top of the tower. Moments later she was onto the ledge. From the small room beyond, Sloane reached out a hand to help her in.

Crouching beneath the low ceiling, Nora swept her flashlight around the room. It was tiny, perhaps four by six feet. Above her head a small ragged hole led up onto the roof of the tower. Her heart sank as she saw there were no stones, no weapons—nothing they could use to defend themselves.

But they still had the gun.

Shielding the flashlight, Nora leaned back out into the cool dark shaft of the tower. Two bobbing red eyes reflected the feeble beam: It was on the second ladder again and coming inexorably closer.

She shrank back into the redoubt. "How many bullets?" she whispered, shining the veiled light toward Sloane.

Mutely Sloane held up three fingers.

"Listen," Nora went on, hearing distinctly the quaver in her own voice. "I'll turn off the light, and we'll wait here in the opening. When it's close, I'll aim the beam and you fire. Okay?"

Sloane suppressed a cough, nodded urgently.

Nora snapped off her light, and together they moved toward the opening of the redoubt. The sound of scrabbling claws on wood grew closer, ever closer.

"Get ready," she whispered.

She waited a moment, then another, hearing the hammering thud of her heart. Then she snapped on the light.

And there it was below her, terrifyingly close. With an involuntary cry, she took in the petrifying image: musky wolfskin, feral eyes, tortured, howling mask.

"Now!" she cried. The roar of the gun drowned out her voice.

In the faint beam she saw the skinwalker jerk to one side.

"Again!" she shouted, fighting to keep the dwindling pinpoint of light on the twisting figure. There was another blast. As the light guttered out, Nora saw the figure crumple in on itself and fall away, swallowed by the well of darkness. She dropped the useless flashlight into the gulf.

"Come on!" Sloane said, pulling Nora toward the hole in the ceiling. Grasping the adobe framework, Nora pulled herself up onto the roof. She backed away from the opening as Sloane came up behind, gasping and coughing.

Here, far above the ruins of Quivira, Nora stood motionless, emotionally and physically exhausted. There was no parapet on the tower; the roof ended in open space. Beyond it the city lay stretched out below her feet.

No sound or movement came from the darkness below. "It's over," Sloane said. She snugged the gun into her belt. "So what now?" she asked huskily.

Nora looked up at her, slowly, uncomprehending.

"I just saved your life. Isn't that going to count for something?"

Nora could not bring herself to speak.

"It's true," Sloane said. "I saw that storm. So did Black. But the *true* wrong was yours: walking away, ready to deprive the world of the most glorious pottery ever made by man."

"Pottery," Nora repeated.

"Yes." Sloane leaned forward. "The Sun Kiva was full—is full—of black-on-yellow micaceous pottery. No intact examples have ever been found. That's because *they're all here,* Nora."

For a moment Nora forgot the horror and danger as she thought of the magnitude of such a discovery. If this is true, she thought, then it makes all of our other discoveries seem like . . .

And then Sloane coughed, drawing the back of her hand across her mouth. She seemed pale, her breathing rapid. The sickness is coming on her, Nora thought.

"We could give this great gift to the world together, Nora." Sloane drew a ragged breath. "If I'm willing to share this with you, then surely you can forget what's happened here today."

"Sloane—" Nora began, then stopped. "You don't get it, do you? It's not about archaeology anymore."

Sloane stared at her for a moment. Then she placed her hand on the butt of her gun. "You leave me no choice."

"You always have a choice."

Sloane drew the gun quickly, pointing it at her. "Right," she said. "Endless fame or a lifetime in disgrace."

There was a brief silence as the two women stood, facing each other. Sloane coughed once again—a sharp, ragged sound.

"Turn around, Nora. Walk to the edge of the roof." Sloane's voice had grown very quiet. "There's only one bullet left in the chamber. But that's all I'll need if it comes down to that. So turn around, Nora. Please."

A form suddenly emerged from the hole in the roof: a dark, matted shape, wolf pelt twisting around naked painted skin. A crimson patch of fur stained the figure's midriff.

Sloane pivoted quickly as the thing rushed at her with a great howl of vengeance. There was a flash of moonlight on the gun, the arc of a knife, and both figures went down, rolling frantically in the loose dirt of the tower roof. Nora dropped to her knees and crawled crablike away from the edge, eyes riveted to the struggle. In the pitiless moonlight she could see the figure burying the horrible black knife again and again into Sloane's chest and stomach. Sloane cried out, and with a supreme effort she tried to pull herself away. She half rose, gun hand swiveling around desperately, only to be pulled down again. There was a terrible thrashing, and the gun fired at last, blowing the knife into hundreds of glittering slivers of obsidian. With a howl the dark shape flung itself upon her. And then both figures were gone.

Nora rushed quickly to the edge, peering down in horror as the bodies, locked together, bounced off the retaining wall, flew apart, then rolled off the edge of the city into the valley below. The moon winked briefly off Sloane's pistol as it spun lazily, end over end, into the unfathomable night.

Trembling, Nora pulled herself back, sprawled across the roof, breathing hard. They had not killed the skinwalker after all. Using consummate stealth, it had hidden itself somewhere within the blackness of the tower, waiting for the right moment in which to strike. But it was not the sudden, terrible encounter on the roof that filled her with absolute terror. *Two* figures in wolfskins had assaulted her in the ranch house. And that meant only one thing.

There was another skinwalker, loose somewhere in the valley of Quivira.

WITH extreme caution Nora descended through the complex labyrinth of ancient wood to the base of the tower.

The city seemed silent and asleep. The moon, alternately emerging from and disappearing behind the racing clouds, painted uncertain fingers of light across the roomblocks. And yet a sense of imminent danger washed over her, instincts ringing five alarm. She realized what it was: Borne on the fitful midnight wind came the faint scent of morning glories.

Galvanized into action, she found herself running with a desperate, reckless speed, heedless of obstacles. She dashed into an alley alongside the granaries. Halfway down the alley's gentle curve she stopped at a notched pole ladder leaning against the rearward set of roomblocks and climbed as quietly as she could to the second-floor setback. Stepping onto the roof, she pulled the ladder up behind her. At least that would slow the skinwalker down, buy her a few more seconds of time.

A sudden footfall invaded the darkness. Dropping to her stomach, Nora crawled to the side of the roof and cautiously peered over the edge into the pool of darkness. Empty.

She rose to her feet, the smell of flowers stronger now: overripe, sickly sweet. Her heart was hammering an overwhelming cadence in her chest. There was only one possibility, remote though it was. Somehow she had to even the playing field, to minimize the risk. And that meant finding a weapon. Quickly she ducked into the nearest room.

Nora glanced quickly around. A pile of war-god masks stood in one corner. She crept through the next doorway into another room, letting her memory of the place guide her steps.

Cautiously she felt her way into the third room. A shaft of pale light came through a crack in the roof, and there they were: a stack of fire-hardened wooden spears, ending in razor-sharp obsidian tips. She hefted a few, selected the lightest, and moved out of the room into a narrow passageway. As quickly as she could, she ducked into the darkest corner of the next room in the block and waited, listening. The spear on her shoulder felt puny, insubstantial, in her sweaty fist.

She tensed at the faint sound of a footfall in the room beyond. The reek of flowers grew overpowering. Struggling to keep her wits about her, Nora raised the spear. A ragged shadow, black upon black, seemed to fill the doorway. With an involuntary shout she heaved the spear with all the strength she could muster. Immediately she jumped away, running through the far door and onto the flat roof along the front of the structure.

There was a sudden scrabbling sound behind her; then a heavy weight fell across her back, forcing her violently to the ground. Crying out in pain and surprise, she tried to struggle away. A heavy pelt of fur fell across her face. She looked up to see the masked head rear back over her, spear bobbing crazily from one shoulder. An arm raised up, obsidian knife flashing.

With a tremendous effort she pulled herself to one side. There was a searing pain in her calf as the knife struck a glancing blow. Without pausing, she tumbled headfirst off the roof of the roomblock. Landing in a pile of sand, she scrambled to her feet and ran. She was aware that she whimpered as she moved. Her leg throbbed, and she could feel the wet gush of blood running down around her ankle.

From behind came a heavy thump, as of a large body leaping to the ground. She ducked into the doorway of the nearest room, then half ran, half limped through a series of galleries to a small dark chamber. She knew that beyond this chamber lay the central plaza.

A ghostly aura crept across the walls of the room as moonlight slanted into the city. Nora swiveled to face the doorway leading out of the room.

And froze.

In the far corner, illuminated by the sepulchral moonlight, lay Luigi Bonarotti. His glazed eyes were wide open in a sightless stare. Nora took in the outrageous, horrifying details: fingers cut off, unbooted feet torn away, head partially scalped. She fell to her knees and covered her mouth, gagging.

As if from a great distance, she heard the skinwalker moving in the alley behind the roomblocks.

Her gaze returned to Bonarotti. There, still holstered around his waist, was the monstrous gun.

Without thinking, she leaped for it, fumbled with the catch, and pulled it from the holster. A .44-magnum Super Blackhawk, deadly as hell. Another footstep sounded, closer.

Suddenly, with terrible speed, the skinwalker appeared in the doorway, thick pelt fluttering. Then, with a low growl, it sprang forward.

In the confines of the small adobe room, the blast of the .44 was deafening. There was a frenzied howl. Squeezing her eyes shut, Nora fired a second time at the sound. Ears ringing, she scrambled in the direction of the doorway, then tripped and fell sprawling out into the central plaza. Quickly she rolled onto her back and pointed the gun toward the doorway. Incredibly, the skinwalker was framed within it, crouching, arms gripping its midriff. It straightened, saw her, and leaped with a snarl of rage and hatred. She fired a third time directly into the mask, and the force of the massive bullet stopped the figure in midair. Raising herself to one knee, Nora fired again and again and again.

And then, after a long time, came silence. Slowly, painfully, she raised herself to her feet. She took two steps toward the retaining wall, faltered, stepped forward again. Then she sank back to the ground, laying the gun aside. It was over.

AFTER several minutes Nora rose to her feet. The valley of Quivira lay bathed in a faint silver light. Hesitantly, like a sleep-walker, she made her way to the rope ladder. She climbed painfully down, one rung at a time, mechanically, still in shock.

She went a few paces, then stopped. There, a few feet away from the cliff base, was Sloane's body, lying broken and crumpled in the sand. Nora shuddered, then glanced away, looking automatically for the body of the skinwalker.

It was nowhere to be seen.

A sharp current of fear brought her fully alert once more. She looked around more carefully. There, in the sand half a dozen feet from Sloane, was a large depression, smeared with blood. But there was no skinwalker body. She took an instinctive step back, eyes searching the landscape. But there was nothing.

Turning, she sprinted toward the medical tent, her torn calf protesting at every step. It was worse than she could have ever feared: The inside of the tent had been torn to ribbons, equipment and supplies strewn about, the sleeping bag shredded. There were spatters of blood everywhere. Smithback was gone.

Nora backed away, staggering. And then she felt a thin, but incredibly strong, arm slide its way over her shoulders and clamp down across her mouth and neck. For a moment she struggled frantically. Then she went limp, unable to struggle further.

"Hush," whispered the quiet, gentle voice into her ear.

The grip loosened, and Nora turned, her eyes widening in wonder. It was John Beiyoodzin. "You!" she gasped.

In the moonlight the old man's braids seemed to be painted with quicksilver. He touched a finger to his lips. "I have your friend hidden at the far end of the valley."

"Bill Smithback? He's alive?"

Beiyoodzin nodded.

Relief and unexpected joy flooded through her, and she gripped Beiyoodzin's hands with newfound strength. "Look, there's somebody else still missing. Roscoe Swire, our wrangler—"

Something in Beiyoodzin's expression stopped her from continuing. "The man who watched your horses," he said. "He is dead. The skinwalkers got him. Now we must go."

He freed himself and began to turn away, gesturing for her to follow. But she put a restraining hand on his arm.

"I killed one of them up in the city," she said, forcing away the bitter tears, willing herself to be strong. "But there's another one. He's wounded, but I think he's still alive."

Beiyoodzin nodded. "I know," he said simply. "That is why we must leave at once."

"But how?"

"I know a secret trail. The one the skinwalkers themselves use to get in and out of the valley. It is extremely difficult. But we must get you and your friend away from this place."

Beiyoodzin began moving rapidly and noiselessly through the dappled shadows, out of camp and back toward the overhanging cliff face. Using the darkness of the rock wall for cover, they made their way to the far end of the canyon, where the swollen river disappeared in a violent waterfall. The sound of water was much louder here, and the entire mouth of the canyon was covered in a pall of mist. Without pausing, Beiyoodzin stepped through the curtain of spray and disappeared. Hesitating just a moment, Nora followed.

She found herself on a small, sloping ledge of rock. Billows of cold mist rose from the tumbling water, encircling her like a cloak.

Here the constant presence of moisture had created a bizarre microclimate of mosses, hanging flowers, and dense greenery. Moving to one side, Beiyoodzin parted a veil of lush ferns, and in the gloom beyond, Nora could just make out Smithback, sitting, arms clasped around himself, waiting.

"Bill!" she cried as he rose in astonishment.

"Oh, my God," he said. "Nora, I thought you were dead." Embracing her weakly, he kissed her, then kissed her again.

"We must keep moving," Beiyoodzin said urgently.

He pointed ahead, and Nora followed his gesture. She could make out the dim, narrow trail leading upward along the canyon face, zigzagging through the clefts and pinnacles of rock.

"I'll go first," he whispered. "Then Bill. And then you."

He turned and began to climb, keeping his weight toward the wall of the canyon, moving up the slope with surprising nimbleness for one so old. Smithback grasped a handhold and, trembling, pulled himself up behind. Nora followed.

They made their way slowly and painfully up the precipitous trail, careful to avoid the slippery moss and algae that clung to the ledges underfoot. Nora could see that Smithback was barely able to pull himself up; each step required all his strength.

Terrifying minutes later they were out of the microclimate. The slot canyon was narrowing, and the resulting loss of moonlight made progress even more difficult. Some distance ahead, at the limit of vision, Nora could see the trail make a sharp switchback and disappear around a corner. At the bend a small parapet of rock led out over the roaring cataract below.

"How are you doing?" she asked Smithback.

He gasped, coughed, and gave a thumbs-up.

Suddenly Beiyoodzin stopped short, raising a warning hand over his shoulder. Nora caught the sweet scent of morning glories.

"He's following us up the trail," Beiyoodzin said. The years suddenly seemed to show on his lined, drawn face. Without another word he resumed his climb.

They followed him as quickly as they could up the precipitous cliff face. "Faster," Beiyoodzin urged.

"He can't go any—" Nora began. Then she stopped short.

Ahead of them, at the sharp bend in the trail, a shape had appeared: a clot of black against the dimly shining rock face. The heavy pelt steamed, and the fringe of fur along its bottom edge was caked in blood. It took a shambling step toward them, then stopped. Sick with fear and horror, Nora could hear the rasping breath being sucked in through the blood-soaked mask.

Unexpectedly Beiyoodzin moved forward. Reaching the outcropping of rock before the switchback, he stepped out onto it carefully. The skinwalker watched him, motionless. Digging into his clothing, Beiyoodzin drew out his medicine bag, tugged it open, and sprinkled a small, almost invisible line of pollen and cornmeal onto the narrow ledge between them, chanting softly.

As Nora watched in silent dread, the skinwalker took a step forward, toward the line of pollen. Beiyoodzin spoke a word: *"Kishlinchi."*

The skinwalker stopped, listening.

"Please, no more," Beiyoodzin said. "Let it end here."

With a growl of anger the skinwalker unsheathed an obsidian knife. It took a step forward, breaking the line of pollen, and raised the knife within striking distance of Beiyoodzin's heart.

"If you will not come back with me, then I beg you to stay here, in this place," Beiyoodzin said quickly, his voice cracking. "If evil is your choice, then stay with evil. Take the city if you must. Take these outsiders if nothing else will satisfy your bloodlust. But leave the people, leave the village alone."

"What are you saying?" Smithback cried in outraged surprise. But neither the skinwalker nor Beiyoodzin seemed to hear. Now the old man pulled out another bag, much older, its edges trimmed in silver and turquoise.

"You know what this is," Beiyoodzin said. "This bag holds the Mirage Stone of the Fathers. The most treasured artifact of the Nankoweap people. Once, *you* treasured it, too. I offer it to you as earnest of my promise. Stay here; trouble our village no more."

Slowly, reverently, he opened the bag, then held it forward, his outstretched hands trembling. The skinwalker hesitated.

"Take it," Beiyoodzin whispered. The matted figure moved forward and reached for it, leaning outward.

Suddenly, with lightning speed, Beiyoodzin thrust the open bag toward the skinwalker.

A heavy cloud of dust erupted from within, flying up into the figure's mask, spraying in long gray lines across the bloody pelt. The skinwalker roared in surprise and outrage, twisting around, tugging violently at the mask, growing more and more off-balance. With the agility of a cat Beiyoodzin leaped from the outcropping of rock back onto the trail. The skinwalker kicked frantically as it struggled, teetering a moment at the edge of the precipice. Then it went over with a howl of fury. Nora watched the plunge into the violet, moon-drenched shadows: matted pelt flapping crazily, limbs scrabbling at the air, mask pulling free as the bloodcurdling cry meshed with the roar of the flood beneath. And then, suddenly, it was gone.

Beiyoodzin looked at Nora and Smithback, and nodded grimly. "I'm sorry to have scared you like that," he said, "but sometimes the only defense left us is to play the coyote, the trickster."

Nora saw kindness and compassion, as well as an infinite sadness, in his eyes. For a moment there was silence between them. Then Beiyoodzin reached out and took Nora's hand in his.

"When you are ready," he said in a small, clear voice, "let me take you to your father."

Epilogue

Moving at a steady, easy pace, the four riders made their way up the canyon known as Raingod Gulch. John Beiyoodzin, atop a magnificent buckskin, led the way. Nora Kelly followed, riding abreast of her brother, Skip. The massive form of Teddy Bear padded alongside. Bill Smithback brought up the rear, his unruly hair imprisoned beneath a suede cowboy hat. The exhausting course of antibiotic treatment he and Nora had undergone had ended two weeks before, but beneath the hat brim the writer's skin was still struggling to regain a healthy color.

Nora realized how lucky she was to have him here, how lucky she was to be here herself. Briefly her thoughts returned to their struggle out of the wilderness a month earlier: Smithback weak, Nora herself growing steadily weaker as the fungal infection took hold. If Skip and Ernest Goddard had not met them halfway down the trail with fresh horses—and if there had not been a powerboat waiting at the trailhead or helicopters idling at Page—they would probably have died. And yet, for a time, Nora almost thought it would have been easier to die than to tell Goddard the news: how their incredible discovery had turned into such a terrible personal tragedy for him.

Here, thirty-odd miles northwest of the ruin of Quivira, the countryside seemed built on a smaller scale: friendly, verdant, well-watered. John Beiyoodzin had paused in his long story frequently during the ride, giving his narrative time to sink in.

As they rode on through the sunlit silence, Nora allowed her thoughts to move gradually from Goddard to her own father and to what she had so far been able to piece together of his own last trip up this canyon. He had taken very little from Quivira. In fact, he had carefully refilled what excavations he had made in a way that would have pleased even Aragon. But in doing so, he had exposed himself to the fungal dust and grown sick. Riding north in hopes of finding help, his sickness had worsened to the point where he could hardly sit his horse. Eventually he had dismounted, turned his horses free, and waited to die.

"It was my cousin who found the body," Beiyoodzin said, resuming his story. "It was lying in a cave at the top of a small rise. The coyotes couldn't reach it, so it hadn't been disturbed. Next to the body was the notebook—the one Nora has now. Sticking out of the front shirt pocket was a letter, stamped and addressed. And beside him was a satchel holding the skull of a mountain lion, inlaid in turquoise. So my cousin went back to Nankoweap, and he was a talker, and soon the entire village knew of the dead white man in the canyon to the south. And because of the turquoise skull, they also knew this white man had found the city."

His voice trailed away for a moment before returning. "This was not a city of our ancestors. It was a city of death, of oppression and slavery, of witchcraft and evil. There are stories in our past of a people who came out of the south, who enslaved the Anasazi and forced them to build these great cities and roads. But they were destroyed by the very god who gave them power. Most who went to the city came back with ghost sickness and soon died. That was many, many years ago. None of my people have returned to the city since. Until recently."

Beiyoodzin deftly rolled a cigarette with one hand. "The discovery of the body caused a problem for the tribe, because to reveal the presence of the body would be to betray the secret of the city. So for sixteen years the body lay there. Unburied. The simplest thing to do was to do nothing."

Beiyoodzin stopped his horse abruptly and turned toward Nora. "But doing nothing caused an imbalance. Because we all knew that the body in the cave had a family. That somebody loved him, wondered where he had gone and whether he was still alive. And this imbalance grew until it ended in all these terrible killings."

Nora reined in her own horse beside Beiyoodzin's. "Who mailed the letter?" she asked quietly.

"There were three brothers. They lived in a trailer outside our village with their alcoholic father. The mother had run off with someone years before. These were smart boys, though, and they all got scholarships and went down to Arizona for college. They were hurt by this contact with the outside world, but hurt in very different ways. Two of the boys dropped out and came back early. They had grown restless, angry, eager for the kind of wealth and power that you can't come by in a village such as ours. They began searching out forbidden knowledge, learning forbidden practices. In time they turned to the greatest taboo of all—the ancient ruins—and eagerly picked up what dark hints of its history still remained among our village.

"The third brother graduated and came back home. Unlike his other brothers, he had converted to the Anglo religion. He knew of the body in the cave, and he felt that to leave it there was a sin. So he searched out the body, carefully arranged the man's possessions, covered the body with sand, planted a cross. And he mailed the letter. Perhaps he did the right thing. I don't know. But what he did caused a terrible break with the other two brothers. They accused him of betraying the secret of the city to the outside world. And the two brothers killed the third."

Beiyoodzin turned his horse's head, and they resumed their slow journey up the canyon.

"In all but name those two had already been transformed into *eskizzi*—witches. And with the killing of their brother, the transformation was complete. In our belief the final requirement in becoming a skinwalker is to murder someone you love."

As they rounded a bend, the canyon gave way to a small grove of cottonwoods. Beiyoodzin halted and motioned for them all to dismount. Turned loose, the horses wandered off to graze the rich carpet of grass along a nearby stream. Skip walked over to Nora and placed his arm around her shoulders.

"How are you doing?" he asked, giving her a squeeze.

"I'm okay," she said. "You?"

Skip took a deep breath. "A little nervous. But actually, pretty good. To be honest, I don't remember feeling better."

"I'll thank you to take your paws off my date," said Smithback, ambling over and joining them. Together they watched as Beiyoodzin untied his medicine kit from the saddle strings, examined it briefly, then nodded toward a gentle path that led up the side of the hill to a small rounded shoulder of rock. Above, Nora could see the rock shelter where their father's skeleton lay.

"What a beautiful place," Skip murmured.

Beiyoodzin led the way up the path and over the last little hump of slickrock. Nora paused at the top and let her gaze fall over the canyon. The rains had brought up a carpet of flowers—Indian paintbrush, sego lilies, datura, scarlet gilia, desert lupines. After much discussion the two children of Padraic Kelly had decided to leave the body where it lay. It was in the red-rock country he loved so well, overlooking one of the most beautiful and isolated canyons of the Escalante.

She felt Skip's arm around her shoulder again, and she turned at last to face the shelter.

In the dim light of the interior she could make out her father's saddle and saddlebags carefully lined up along the back wall of the rock shelter, the leather cracked and faded with age. Beside them was the turquoise skull, beautiful yet vaguely sinister even here, far from the evil pall of the Rain Kiva. Beneath a thin layer of sand lay her father's bones; she could see that he had died looking down into the valley below.

For a long time nobody spoke. Then, slowly, Nora reached into her pocket. Her fingers closed over a small notebook: her father's journal. She felt Smithback's hand come forward to grasp her own, and she returned the pressure gratefully.

In time, she knew, they would return to Quivira. A handpicked team from the institute, armed with respirators and environmental suits, would make careful video documentaries of the site. Sloane's discovery—the micaceous pottery of transcendent beauty and value—would be carefully studied and documented. And perhaps Smithback would even write an account of the expedition—or, at least, the part of the expedition that would not bring unendurable pain to Goddard.

Nora watched as Beiyoodzin untied the little buckskin bag and bowed his head. Pinching out some yellow cornmeal and pollen, he sprinkled it on the body and began a soft, rhythmic chant, beautiful in its simple monotony. The others bowed their heads.

When the chant was done, Beiyoodzin looked at Nora. His eyes were shining. "I thank you," he said, "for letting me put this to rest. I thank you for myself and for my people."

Nora took a deep breath, steadied her hands. Then she turned to the final entry in her father's journal and began to read.

> "To my dearest and most wonderful children, Nora and Skip,
>
> "By the time you read this, I will be gone. I have been stricken with a disease, which I fear I contracted in the city I discovered: the city of Quivira. Although I cannot be sure this will ever reach you, I want to speak to you through this journal one last time.
>
> "If it is within your power, let the great ruins of Quivira lie

undisturbed. Some knowledge is better left alone, to die and return to the earth just as we do.

"I have just one request to make each of you. Skip, please don't drink. It runs in the family, and, I promise you, you won't be able to handle it. I could not. And, Nora, please forgive your mother. I know that in my absence, she may blame me for what has happened. In a way she's right to blame me. And she has always loved you deeply.

"This is a beautiful place to die, children. The night sky is filled with stars; the stream splashes below. I came here for riches, but Quivira changed my mind. In fact, I left no mark of my passage there. I have taken one thing only from it, and that was meant for you, Nora, as proof your father really found the fabled city. For it was there that I learned, for the first time, that I had left my real, my true successes—the two of you—far behind in Santa Fe.

"I know I have not been a great father or even a good father, but let me tell you this: I love you both. And I will love you from eternity to eternity. My love for you burns brighter than all the thousands of stars that carpet the sky above my head. I may die, but my love for you never will.

"Dad"

Nora fell silent and closed her eyes. For a moment the entire canyon seemed to drop into reverential silence. Then she looked up, shut the notebook, and carefully placed it on the ground beside her father. She turned and gave Smithback a tearful smile.

Then the four of them made their way down the faint path, to the waiting horses and home.